THE
COMPLETE
FUZZY

THE
COMPLETE
FUZZY

H. BEAM PIPER

ACE BOOKS, NEW YORK

THE COMPLETE FUZZY

An Ace Science Fiction Book

PRINTING HISTORY
Ace trade paperback edition / December 1998

THE
COMPLETE
FUZZY

LITTLE
FUZZY

JACK HOLLOWAY FOUND himself squinting, the orange sun full in his eyes. He raised a hand to push his hat forward, then lowered it to the controls to alter the pulse rate of the contragravity-field generators and lift the manipulator another hundred feet. For a moment he sat, puffing on the short pipe that had yellowed the corners of his white mustache, and looked down at the red rag tied to a bush against the rock face of the gorge five hundred yards away. He was smiling in anticipation.

"This'll be a good one," he told himself aloud, in the manner of men who have long been their own and only company. "I want to see this one go up."

He always did. He could remember at least a thousand blast-shots he had fired back along the years and on more planets than he could name at the moment, including a few thermonuclears, but they were all different and they were always something to watch, even a little one like this. Flipping the switch, his thumb found the discharger button and sent out a radio impulse; the red rag vanished in an upsurge of smoke and dust that mounted out of the gorge and turned to copper when the sunlight touched it. The big manipulator, weightless on contragravity, rocked gently; falling debris pelted the trees and splashed in the little stream.

He waited till the machine stabilized, then glided it down to where he had ripped a gash in the cliff with the charge of cataclysmite. Good shot: brought down a lot of sandstone, cracked the vein of flint and hadn't thrown it around too much. A lot of big slabs were loose. Extending the forward claw-arms, he pulled and tugged, and then used the underside grapples to pick up a chunk and drop it on the flat ground between the cliff and the stream. He dropped another chunk on it, breaking both of them, and then another and another, until he had all he could work over for the rest of the day. Then he set down, got the toolbox and the long-handled contragravity lifter, and climbed to the ground where he opened the box, put on gloves and an eyescreen and got out a microray scanner and a vibrohammer.

The first chunk he cracked off had nothing in it; the scanner gave the uninterrupted pattern of homogenous structure. Picking it up with the lifter, he swung it and threw it into the stream. On the fifteenth chunk, he got an interruption pattern that told him that a sunstone—or something, probably something—was inside.

Some fifty million years ago, when the planet that had been called Zarathustra (for the last twenty-five million) was young, there had existed a marine life form, something like a jellyfish. As these died, they had sunk into the sea-bottom ooze; sand had covered the ooze and pressed it tighter and tighter, until it had become glassy flint, and the entombed jellyfish little beans of dense stone. Some of them, by some ancient biochemical quirk, were intensely thermofluorescent; worn as gems, they glowed from the wearer's body heat.

On Terra or Baldur or Freya or Ishtar, a single cut of polished sunstone was worth a small fortune. Even here, they brought respectable prices from the Zarathustra Company's gem buyers. Keeping his point of expectation safely low, he got a smaller vibrohammer from the toolbox and began chipping cautiously around the foreign object, until the flint split open and revealed a smooth yellow ellipsoid, half an inch long.

"Worth a thousand sols—if it's worth anything," he commented. A deft tap here, another there, and the yellow bean became loose from the flint. Picking it up, he rubbed it between gloved palms. "I don't think it is." He rubbed harder, then held it against the hot bowl of his pipe. It still didn't respond. He dropped it. "Another jellyfish that didn't live right."

Behind him, something moved in the brush with a dry rustling. He dropped the loose glove from his right hand and turned, reaching toward his hip. Then he saw what had made the noise—a hard-shelled thing a foot in length, with twelve legs, long antennae and two pairs of clawed mandibles. He stooped and picked up a shard of flint, throwing it with an oath. Another damned infernal land-prawn.

He detested land-prawns. They were horrible things, which, of course, wasn't their fault. More to the point, they were destructive. They got into things at camp; they would try to eat anything. They crawled into machinery, possibly finding the lubrication tasty, and caused jams. They cut into electric insulation. And they got into his bedding, and bit, or rather pinched, painfully. Nobody loved a land-prawn, not even another land-prawn.

This one dodged the thrown flint, scuttled off a few feet and turned, waving its antennae in what looked like derision. Jack reached for his hip again, then checked the motion. Pistol cartridges cost like crazy; they weren't to be wasted in fits of childish pique. Then he reflected that no cartridge fired at a target is really wasted, and that he hadn't done any shooting recently. Stooping again, he picked up another stone and tossed it a foot short and to the left of the prawn. As soon as it was out of his fingers, his hand went for the butt of the long automatic. It was out and the safety off before the flint landed; as the prawn fled, he fired from the hip. The quasi-crustacean disintegrated. He nodded pleasantly.

"Ol' man Holloway's still hitting things he shoots at."

Was a time, not so long ago, when he took his abilities for granted. Now he was getting old enough to have to verify them. He thumbed on the safety and holstered the pistol, then picked up the glove and put it on again.

Never saw so blasted many land-prawns as this summer. They'd been bad last year, but nothing like this. Even the oldtimers who'd been on Zarathustra since the first colonization said so. There'd be some simple explanation, of course; something that would amaze him at his own obtuseness for not having seen it at once. Maybe the abnormally dry weather had something to do with it. Or increase of something they ate, or decrease of natural enemies.

He'd heard that land-prawns had no natural enemies; he questioned that. Something killed them. He'd seen crushed prawn shells, some of them close to his camp. Maybe stamped on by something with hoofs, and then picked clean by insects. He'd ask Ben Rainsford; Ben ought to know.

Half an hour later, the scanner gave him another interruption pattern. He laid it aside and took up the small vibrohammer. This time it was a large bean, light pink in color. He separated it from its matrix of flint and rubbed it, and instantly it began glowing.

"Ahhh! This is something like it, now!"

He rubbed harder; warmed further on his pipe bowl, it fairly blazed. Better than a thousand sols, he told himself. Good color, too. Getting his gloves off, he drew out the little leather bag from under his shirt, loosening the drawstrings by which it hung around his neck. There were a dozen and a half stones inside, all bright as live coals. He looked at them for moment, and dropped the new sunstone in among them, chuckling happily.

VICTOR GREGO, LISTENING to his own recorded voice, rubbed the sunstone on his left finger with the heel of his right palm and watched it brighten. There was, he noticed, a boastful ring to his voice—not the suave, unemphatic tone considered proper on a message-tape. Well, if anybody wondered why, when they played that tape off six months from now in Johannesburg on Terra, they could look in the cargo holds of the ship that had brought it across five hundred light-years of space. Ingots of gold and platinum and gadolinium. Furs and biochemicals and brandy. Perfumes that defied synthetic imitation; hardwoods no plastic could copy. Spices. And the steel coffer full of sunstones. Almost all luxury goods, the only really dependable commodities in interstellar trade.

And he had spoken of other things. Veldbeest meat, up seven percent from last month, twenty percent from the last year, still in demand on a dozen planets unable to produce Terran-type foodstuffs. Grain, leather, lumber. And he had added a dozen more items to the lengthening list of what Zarathustra could now produce in adequate quantities and no longer needed to import. Not fishhooks and boot buckles, either—blasting explosives and propellants, contragravity-field generator parts, power tools, pharmaceuticals, synthetic textiles. The Company didn't need to carry Zarathustra any more; Zarathustra could carry the Company, and itself.

Fifteen years ago, when the Zarathustra Company had sent him here, there had been a cluster of log and prefab huts beside an improvised landing field, almost exactly where this skyscraper now stood. Today, Mallorysport was a city of seventy thousand; in all, the planet had a population of nearly a million, and it was still growing. There were steel mills and chemical plants and reaction plants and machine works. They produced all their fissionables, and recently begun to export a little refined plutonium; they had even started producing collapsium shielding.

The recorded voice stopped. He ran back the spool, set for sixty-speed, and transmitted it to the radio office. In twenty minutes, a copy would be aboard the ship that would hyper out for Terra that night. While he was finishing, his communication screen buzzed.

"Dr. Kellogg's screening you, Mr. Grego," the girl in the outside office told him.

He nodded. Her hands moved, and she vanished in a polychromatic explosion; when it cleared, the chief of the Division of Scientific Study and Research was looking out of the screen instead. Looking slightly upward at the showback over his own screen, Victor was getting his warm, sympathetic, sincere and slightly too toothy smile on straight.

"Hello, Leonard. Everything going all right?"

It either was and Leonard Kellogg wanted more credit than he deserved or it wasn't and he was trying to get somebody else blamed for it before anybody could blame him.

"Good afternoon, Victor." Just the right shade of deference about using the first name—big wheel to bigger wheel. "Has Nick Emmert been talking to you about the Big Blackwater project today?"

Nick was the Federation's resident-general; on Zarathustra he was, to all intents and purposes, the Terran Federation Government. He was also a large stockholder in the chartered Zarathustra Company.

"No. Is he likely to?"

"Well, I wondered, Victor. He was on my screen just now. He says there's some adverse talk about the effect on the rainfall in the Piedmont area of Beta Continent. He was worried about it."

"Well, it would affect the rainfall. After all, we drained half a million square miles of swamp, and the prevailing winds are from the west. There'd be less atmospheric moisture to the east of it. Who's talking adversely about it, and what worries Nick?"

"Well, Nick's afraid of the effect on public opinion on Terra. You know how strong conversation sentiment is; everybody's very much opposed to any sort of destructive exploitation."

"Good Lord! The man doesn't call the creation of five hundred thousand square miles of new farmland destructive exploitation, does he?"

"Well, no, Nick doesn't call it that; of course not. But he's concerned about some garbled story getting to Terra about our upsetting the ecological balance and causing droughts. Fact is, I'm rather concerned myself."

He knew what was worrying both of them. Emmert was afraid the Federation Colonial Office would blame him for drawing fire on them from the conservationists. Kellogg was afraid he'd be blamed for not predicting the effects before his division endorsed the project. As a division chief, he had advanced as far as he would in the Company hierarchy; now he was on a Red Queen's racetrack, running like hell to stay in the same place.

"The rainfall's dropped ten percent from last year, and fifteen percent from the year before that," Kellogg was saying. "And some non-Company people have gotten hold of it, and so had Interworld News. Why, even some of my people are talking about ecological side-effects. You know what will happen when a story like that gets back to Terra. The conservation fanatics will get hold of it, and the Company'll be criticized."

That would hurt Leonard. He identified himself with the Company. It was something bigger and more powerful than he was, like God.

Victor Grego identified the Company with himself. It was something big and powerful, like a vehicle, and he was at the controls.

"Leonard, a little criticism won't hurt the Company," he said. "Not where it matters, on the dividends. I'm afraid you're too sensitive to criticism. Where did Emmert get this story anyhow? From your people?"

"No, absolutely not, Victor. That's what worries him. It was this man Rainsford who started it."

"Rainsford?"

Dr. Bennett Rainsford, the naturalist. Institute of Zeno-Sciences. I never trusted any of those people; they always poke their noses into things, and the Institute always reports their findings to the Colonial Office."

"I know who you mean now; little fellow with red whiskers, always looks as though he'd been sleeping in his clothes. Why, of course the Zeno-Sciences people poke their noses into things, and of course they report their findings to the government." He was beginning to lose patience. "I don't see what all this is about, Leonard. This man Rainsford just made a routine observation of meteorological effects. I suggest you have your meteorologists check it, and if it's correct pass it on to the news services along with your other scientific findings."

"Nick Emmert thinks Rainsford is a Federation undercover agent."

That made him laugh. Of course there were undercover agents on Zarathustra, hundreds of them. The Company had people here checking on him; he knew and accepted that. So did the big stockholders, like Interstellar Explorations and the Banking Cartel and Terra-Baldur-Marduk Spacelines. Nick Emmert had his corps of spies and stool pigeons, and the Terran Federation had people here watching both him and Emmert. Rainsford could be a Federation agent—a roving naturalist would have a wonderful cover occupation. But this Big Blackwater business was so utterly silly. Nick Emmert had too much graft on his conscience; it was too bad that overloaded consciences couldn't blow fuses.

"Suppose he is, Leonard. What could he report on us? We are a chartered company, and we have an excellent legal department, which keeps us safely inside our charter. It is a very liberal charter, too. This is a Class-III uninhabited planet; the Company owns the whole thing outright. We can do anything we want as long as we don't violate colonial law or the Federation Constitution. As long as we don't do that, Nick Emmert hasn't anything to worry about. Now forget this whole damned business, Leonard!" He was beginning to speak sharply, and Kellogg was looking hurt. "I know you were concerned about injurious reports getting back to Terra, and that was quite commendable, but . . ."

By the time he got through, Kellogg was happy again. Victor blanked the screen, leaned back in his chair and began laughing. In a moment, the screen buzzed again. When he snapped it on, his screen-girl said:

"Mr. Henry Stenson's on, Mr. Grego."

"Well, put him on." He caught himself just before adding that it would be a welcome change to talk to somebody with sense.

The face that appeared was elderly and thin; the mouth was tight, and there were squint-wrinkles at the corners of the eyes.

"Well, Mr. Stenson. Good of you to call. How are you?"

"Very well, thank you. And you?" When he also admitted to good health, the caller continued: "How is the globe running? Still in synchronization?"

Victor looked across the office at his most prized possession, the big globe of Zarathustra that Henry Stenson had built for him, supported six feet from the floor on its own contragravity unit, spotlighted in orange to represent the KO sun, its two satellites circling about it as it revolved slowly.

"The globe itself is keeping perfect time, and Darius is all right. Xerxes is a few seconds on longitude ahead of true position."

"That's dreadful, Mr. Gergo!" Stenson was deeply shocked. "I must adjust that the first thing tomorrow. I should have called to check on it long ago, but you know how it is. So many things to do, and so little time."

"I find the same trouble myself, Mr. Stenson."

They chatted for a while, and then Stenson apologized for taking up so much of Mr. Grego's valuable time. What he meant was that his own time, just as valuable to him, was wasting. After the screen blanked, Grego sat looking at it for a moment, wishing he had a hundred men like Henry Stenson in his own organization. Just men with Stenson's brains and character; wishing for a hundred instrument makers with Stenson's skills would have been unreasonable, even for wishing. There was only one Henry Stenson, just as there had been only one Antonio Stradivari. Why a man like that worked in a little shop on a frontier planet like Zarathustra . . .

Then he looked, pridefully, at the globe. Alpha Continent had moved slowly to the right, with the little speck that represented Mallorysport twinkling in the orange light. Darius, the inner moon, where the Terra-Baldur-Marduk Space-lines had their leased terminal, was almost directly over it, and the outer moon, Xerxes, was edging into sight. Xerxes was the one thing about Zarathustra that the Company didn't own; the Terran Federation had retained that as a naval base. It was the one reminder that there was something bigger and more powerful than the Company.

GERD VAN RIEBEEK saw Ruth Ortheris leave the escalator, step aside and stand looking around the cocktail lounge. He set his glass, with its inch of tepid highball, on the bar; when her eyes shifted in his direction, he waved to her, saw her brighten and wave back and then went to meet her. She gave him a quick kiss on the cheek, dodged when he reached for her and took his arm.

"Drink before we eat?" he asked.

"Oh, Lord, yes! I've just about had it for today."

He guided her toward one of the bartending machines, inserted his credit key, and put a four-portion jug under the spout, dialing the cocktail they always had when they drank together. As he did, he noticed what she was wearing: short black jacket, lavender neckerchief, light gray skirt. Not her usual vacation get-up.

"School department drag you back?" he asked as the jug filled.

"Juvenile court." She got a couple of glasses from the shelf under the machine as he picked up the jug. "A fifteen-year-old burglar."

They found a table at the rear of the room, out of the worst of the cocktail-hour uproar. As soon as he filled her glass, she drank half of it, then lit a cigarette.

"Junktown?" he asked.

She nodded. "Only twenty-five years since this planet was discovered, and we have slums already. I was over there most of the afternoon, with a pair of city police." She didn't seem to want to talk about it. "What were you doing today?"

"Ruth, you ought to ask Doc Mallin to drop in on Leonard Kellogg sometime, and give him an unobstrusive going over."

"You haven't been having trouble with him again?" she asked anxiously.

He made a face, and then tasted his drink. "It's trouble just being around that character. Ruth, to use one of those expressions your profession deplores, Len Kellogg is just plain nuts!" He drank some more of his cocktail and helped himself to one of her cigarettes. "Here," he continued, after lighting it. "A couple of days ago, he told me he'd been getting inquiries about this plague of land-prawns they're having over on Beta. He wanted me to set up a research project to find out why and what to do about it."

"Well?"

"I did. I made two screens calls, and then I wrote a report and sent it up to him. That was where I jerked my trigger; I ought to have taken a couple of weeks and made a real production out of it."

"What did you tell him?"

"The facts. The limiting factor on land-prawn increase is the weather. The eggs hatch underground and the immature prawns dig their way out in the spring. If there's been a lot of rain, most of them drown in their holes or as soon as they emerge. According to growth rings on trees, last spring was the driest in the Beta Piedmont in centuries, so most of them survived, and as they're parthenogenetic females, they all laid eggs. This spring, it was even drier, so now they have land-prawns all over central Beta. And I don't know that anything can be done about them."

"Well, did he think you were just guessing?"

He shook his head in exasperation. "I don't know what he thinks. You're the psychologist, you try to figure it. I sent him that report yesterday morning. He seemed quite satisfied with it at the time. Today, just after noon, he sent for me and told me it wouldn't do at all. Tried to insist that the rainfall on Beta had been normal. That was silly; I referred him to his meteorologists and climatologists, where I'd gotten my information. He complained that the news services were after him for an explanation. I told him I'd given him the only explanation there was. He said he simply couldn't use it. There had to be some other explanation."

"If you don't like the facts, you ignore them, and if you need facts, dream up some you do like," she said. "That's typical rejection of reality. Not psychotic, not even psychoneurotic. But certainly not sane." She had finished her first drink and was sipping slowly at her second. "You know, this is interesting. Does he have some theory that would disqualify yours?"

"Not that I know of. I got the impression that he just didn't want the subject of rainfall on Beta discussed at all."

"That is odd. Has anything else peculiar been happening over on Beta lately?"

"No. Not that I know of," he repeated. "Of course, that swamp-drainage project over there was what caused the dry weather, last year and this year, but I don't see . . ." His own glass was empty, and when he tilted the jug over it, a few drops trickled out. He looked at his watch. "Think we could have another cocktail before dinner?" he asked.

2

JACK HOLLOWAY LANDED the manipulator in front of the cluster of prefab huts. For a moment he sat still, realizing that he was tired, and then he climbed down from the control cabin and crossed the open grass to the door of the main living hut, opening it and reaching in to turn on the lights. Then he hesitated, looking up at Darius.

There was a wide ring around it, and he remembered noticing the wisps of cirrus clouds gathering overhead through the afternoon. Maybe it would rain tonight. This dry weather couldn't last forever. He'd been letting the manipulator stand out overnight lately. He decided to put it in the hangar. He went and opened the door of the vehicle shed, got back onto the machine and floated it inside. When he came back to the living hut, he saw that he had left the door wide open.

"Damn fool!" he rebuked himself. "Place could be crawling with prawns by now."

He looked quickly around the living room—under the big combination desk and library table, under the gunrack, under the chairs, back of the communication screen and the viewscreen, beyond the metal cabinet of the microfilm library—and saw nothing. Then he hung up his hat, took off his pistol and laid it on the table, and went back to the bathroom to wash his hands.

As soon as he put on the light, something inside the shower stall said, "*Yeeeek!*" in a startled voice.

He turned quickly, to see two wide eyes staring up at him out of a ball of golden fur. Whatever it was, it had a round head and big ears and a vaguely humanoid face with a little snub nose. It was sitting on its haunches, and in that position it was about a foot high. It had two tiny hands with opposing thumbs. He squatted to have a better look at it.

"Hello there, little fellow," he greeted it. "I never saw anything like you before. What are you anyhow?"

The small creature looked at him seriously and said, "Yeek," in a timid voice.

"Why, sure; you're a Little Fuzzy, that's what you are."

He moved closer, careful to make no alarmingly sudden movements, and kept on talking to it.

"Bet you slipped in while I left the door open. Well, if a Little Fuzzy finds a door open, I'd like to know why he shouldn't come in and look around."

He touched it gently. It started to draw back, then reached out a little hand and felt the material of his shirtsleeve. He stroked it, and told it that it had the softest, silkiest fur ever. Then he took it on his lap. It yeeked in pleasure, and stretched an arm up around his neck.

"Why, sure; we're going to be good friends, aren't we? Would you like something to eat? Well, suppose you and I go see what we can find."

He put one hand under it, to support it like a baby—at least, he seemed to recall having seen babies supported in that way; babies were things he didn't fool with if the could help it—and straightened. It weighed between fifteen and twenty pounds. At first, it struggled in panic, and then quieted and seemed to enjoy being carried. In the living room he sat down in his favorite armchair, under a standing lamp, and examined his new acquaintance.

It was a mammal—there was a fairly large mammalian class on Zarathustra—but beyond that he was stumped. It wasn't a primate, in the Terran sense. It wasn't like anything Terran, or anything else on Zarathustra. Being a biped put it in a class by itself for this planet. It was just a Little Fuzzy, and that was the best he could do.

That sort of nomenclature was the best anybody could do on a Class-III planet. On a Class-IV planet, say Loki, or Shesha, or Thor, naming animals was a cinch. You pointed to something and asked a native, and he'd gargle a mouthful of syllables at you, which might only mean, "Whaddaya wanna know for?" and you took it down in phonetic alphabet and the whatzit had a name. But on Zarathustra there were no natives to ask. So this was a Little Fuzzy.

"What would you like to eat, Little Fuzzy?" he asked. "Open your mouth, and let Pappy Jack see what you have to chew with."

Little Fuzzy's dental equipment, allowing for the the fact that his jaw was rounder, was very much like his own.

"You're probably omnivorous. How would you like some nice Terran

Federation Space Forces Emergency Ration, Extraterrestrial, Type Three?" he asked.

Little Fuzzy made what sounded like an expression of willingness to try it. It would be safe enough; Extee Three had been fed to a number a Zarathustran mammals without ill effects. He carried Little Fuzzy out into the kitchen and put him on the floor, then got out a tin of the field ration and opened it, breaking off a small piece and handing it down. Little Fuzzy took the piece of golden-brown cake, sniffed at it, gave it a delighted yeek and crammed the whole piece in his mouth.

"You never had to live on that stuff and nothing else for a month, that's for sure!"

He broke the cake in half and broke one half into manageable pieces and put it down on a saucer. Maybe Little Fuzzy would want a drink, too. He started to fill a pan with water, as he would for a dog, then looked at his visitor sitting on his haunches eating with both hands and changed his mind. He rinsed a plastic cup cap from an empty whisky bottle and put it down beside a deep bowl of water. Little Fuzzy was thirsty, and he didn't have to be shown what the cup was for.

It was too late to get himself anything elaborate; he found some leftovers in the refrigerator and combined them into a stew. While it was heating, he sat down at the kitchen table and lit his pipe. The spurt of flame from the lighter opened Little Fuzzy's eyes, but what really awed him was Pappy Jack blowing smoke. He sat watching this phenomenon, until, a few minutes later, the stew was hot and the pipe was laid aside; then Little Fuzzy went back to nibbling Extee Three.

Suddenly he gave a yeek of petulance and scampered into the living room. In a moment, he was back with something elongated and metallic which he laid on the floor beside him.

"What have you got there, Little Fuzzy? Let Pappy Jack see?"

Then he recognized it as his own one-inch wood chisel. He remembered leaving it in the outside shed after doing some work about a week ago, and not being able to find it when he had gone to look for it. That had worried him; people who got absent-minded about equipment didn't last long in the wilderness. After he finished eating and took the dishes to the sink, he went over and squatted beside his new friend.

"Let Pappy Jack look at it, Little Fuzzy," he said. "Oh, I'm not going to take it away from you. I just want to see it."

The edge was dulled and nicked; it had been used for a lot of things wood chisel oughtn't to be used for. Digging, and prying, and most likely, it had been used as a weapon. It was a handy-sized, all-purpose tool for a Little Fuzzy. He laid it on the floor where he had gotten it and started washing the dishes.

Little Fuzzy watched him with interest for a while, and then he began investigating the kitchen. Some of the things he wanted to investigate had to be taken away from him; at first that angered him, but he soon learned that there were things he wasn't suppose to have. Eventually, the dishes got washed.

There were more things to investigate in the living room. One of them was the wastebasket. He found that it could be dumped, and promptly dumped it, pulling out everything that hadn't fallen out. He bit a corner off a sheet of paper, chewed on it and spat it out in disgust. Then he found that crumpled paper could be flattened out and so he flatted a few sheets, and then discovered that it could also be folded. Then he got himself gleefully tangled in a snarl of wornout recording tape. Finally he lost interest and started away. Jack caught him and brought him back.

"No, Little Fuzzy," he said. "You do not dump wastebaskets and then walk away from them. You put things back in." He touched the container and said, slowly and distinctly, "Waste . . . basket." Then he righted it, doing it as Little Fuzzy would have to, and picked up a piece of paper, tossing it in from Little Fuzzy's shoulder height. Then he handed Little Fuzzy a wad of paper and repeated, "Waste . . . basket."

Little Fuzzy looked at him and said something that sounded as though it might be: "What's the matter with you, Pappy; you crazy or something?" After a couple more tries, however, he got it, and began throwing things in. In a few minutes, he had everything back in except a brightly colored plastic cartridge box and a wide-mouthed bottle with a screw cap. He held these up and said, "Yeek?"

"Yes, you can have them. Here; let Pappy Jack show you something."

He showed Little Fuzzy how the box could be opened and shut. Then, holding it where Little Fuzzy could watch, he unscrewed the cap and then screwed it on again.

"There, now. You try it."

Little Fuzzy looked up inquiringly, then took the bottle, sitting down and holding it between his knees. Unfortunately, he tried twisting it the wrong way and only screwed the cap on tighter. He yeeked plaintively.

"No, go ahead. You can do it."

Little Fuzzy look at the bottle again. Then he tried twisting the cap the other way, and it loosened. He gave a yeek that couldn't possibly be anything but "Eureka!" and promptly took it off, holding it up. After being commended, he examined both the bottle and the cap, feeling the threads, and then screwed the cap back on again.

"You know, you're a smart Little Fuzzy." It took a few seconds to realize just how smart. Little Fuzzy had wondered why you twist the cap one way to take it off and the other way to put it on, and he had found out. For pure reasoning ability, that topped anything in the way of animal intelligence he'd ever seen. "I'm going to tell Ben Rainsford about you."

Going to the communication screen, he punched out the wave-length combination of the naturalist's camp, seventy miles down Snake River from the mouth of Cold Creek. Rainsford's screen must have been on automatic; it lit as soon as he was through punching. There was a card set up in front of it, lettered: AWAY ON TRIP, BACK THE FIFTEENTH. RECORDER ON.

"Ben, Jack Holloway," he said. "I just ran into something interesting." He explained briefly what it was. "I hope he stays around till you get back. He's totally unlike anything I've ever seen on this planet."

Little Fuzzy was disappointed when Jack turned off the screen; that had been interesting. He picked him up and carried him over to the armchair, taking him on his lap.

"Now," he said, reaching for the control panel of the viewscreen. "Watch this; we're going to see something nice."

When he put on the screen, at random, he got a view, from close up, of the great fires that were raging where the Company people were burning off the dead forests on what used to be Big Blackwater Swamp. Little Fuzzy cried out in alarm, flung his arms around Pappy Jack's neck and buried his face in the bosom of his shirt. Well, forest fires started from lightning sometimes, and they'd be bad things for a Little Fuzzy. He worked the selector and got another pickup, this time on the top of Company House in Mallorysport, three time zones west, with the city spread out below and the sunset blazing in the west. Little Fuzzy stared at it in wonder. It was pretty impressive for a little fellow who'd spent all his life in the big woods.

So was the spaceport, and a lot of other things he saw, though a view of the planet as a whole from Darius puzzled him considerably. Then, in the middle of a symphony orchestra concert from Mallorysport Opera House, he wriggled loose, dropped to the floor and caught up his wood chisel, swinging it back over his shoulder like a two-handed sword.

"What the devil? Oh-oh!"

A land-prawn, which must have gotten in while the door was open, was crossing the living room. Little Fuzzy ran after and past it, pivoted and brought the corner of the chisel edge down on the prawn's neck, neatly beheading it. He looked at his victim for a moment, then slid the chisel under it and flopped it over on its back, slapping it twice with the flat and cracking the undershell. Then he began pulling the dead prawn apart, tearing pieces of meat and eating them delicately. After disposing of the larger chunks, he used the chisel to chop off one of the prawn's mandibles to use as a pick to get the less accessible morsels. When he had finished, he licked his fingers clean and started back to the armchair.

"No." Jack pointed at the prawn shell. "Wastebasket."

"Yeek?"

"Wastebasket."

Little Fuzzy gathered up the bits of shell, putting them where they belonged. Then he came back and climbed up on Pappy Jack's lap, and looked at things in the screen until he fell asleep.

Jack lifted him carefully and put him down on the warm chair seat without wakening him, then went to the kitchen, poured himself a drink and brought it in to the big table, where he lit his pipe and began writing up his diary for the day. After a while, Little Fuzzy woke, found that the lap he had gone to sleep on had vanished, and yeeked disconsolately.

A folded blanket in one corner of the bedroom made a satisfactory bed, once Little Fuzzy had assured himself that there were no bugs in it. He brought in his bottle and his plastic box and put them on the floor beside it. Then he ran to the front door in the living room and yeeked to be let out. Going about twenty feet from the house, he used the chisel to dig a small hole, and after it had served its purpose he filled it in carefully and came running back.

Well, maybe Fuzzies were naturally gregarious, and were homemakers— den-holes, or nest, or something like that. Nobody wants messes made in the house, and when the young ones did it, their parents would bang them around to teach them better manners. This was Little Fuzzy's home now; he knew how he ought to behave in it.

THE NEXT MORNING at daylight, he was up on the bed, trying to dig Pappy Jack out from under the blankets. Besides being a most efficient land-prawn eradicator, he made a first-rate alarm clock. But best of all, he was Pappy Jack's Little Fuzzy. He wanted out; this time Jack took his movie camera and got the whole operation on film. One thing, there'd have to be a little door, with a spring to hold it shut, that Little Fuzzy could operate himself. That was designed during breakfast. It only took a couple of hours to make and install it; Little Fuzzy got the whole idea as soon as he saw it, and figured out how to work it for himself.

Jack went back to the workshop, built a fire on the hand forge and forged a pointed and rather broad blade, four inches long, on the end of a foot of quarter-inch round tool-steel. It was too point-heavy when finished, so he welded a knob on the other end to balance it. Little Fuzzy knew what that was for right away; running outside, he dug a couple of practice holes with it, and then began casting about in the grass for land-prawns.

Jack followed him with the camera and got movies of a couple of prawn killings, accomplished with smooth, by-the-numbers precision. Little Fuzzy hadn't learned that chop-slap-slap routine in the week since he had found the wood chisel.

Going into the shed, he hunted for something without more than a general idea of what it would look like, and found it where Little Fuzzy had discarded it when he found the chisel. It was a stock of hardwood a foot long, rubbed down and polished smooth, apparently with sandstone. There was a paddle at one end, with enough of an edge to behead a prawn, and the other end had been worked into a point. He took it into the living hut and sat down at the desk to examine it with a magnify glass. Bits of soil embedded in the sharp end—that had been used as a pick. The paddle end had been used as a shovel, beheader and shell-cracker. Little Fuzzy had known exactly what he wanted when he'd started making that thing, he'd kept on until it was as perfect as possible, and he had stopped short of spoiling it by overrefinement.

Finally, Jack put it away in the top drawer of the desk. He was thinking about what to get for lunch when Little Fuzzy burst into the living room, clutching his new weapon and yeeking excitedly.

"What's the matter, kid? You got troubles?" He rose and went to the gunrack, picking down a rifle and checking the chamber. "Show Pappy Jack what it is."

Little Fuzzy followed him to the big door for human-type people, ready to bolt back inside if necessary. The trouble was a harpy—a thing about the size and general design of a Terran Jurassic pterodactyl, big enough to take a Little Fuzzy at one mouthful. It must have made one swoop at him already, and was circling back for another. It ran into a 6-mm rifle bullet, went into a backward loop and dropped like a stone.

Little Fuzzy made a very surprised remark, looked at the dead harpy for a moment and then spotted the ejected empty cartridge. He grabbed it and held it up, asking if he could have it. When told that he could, he ran back to the bedroom with it. When he returned, Pappy Jack picked him up and carried him to the hangar and up into the control cabin of the manipulator.

The throbbing of the contragravity-field generator and the sense of rising worried him at first, but after they had picked up the harpy with the grapples and risen to five hundred feet he began to enjoy the ride. They dropped the harpy a couple of miles up what the latest maps were designating as Holloway's Run, and then made a wide circle back over the mountains. Little Fuzzy thought it was fun.

After lunch, Little Fuzzy had a nap on Pappy Jack's bed. Jack took the manipulator up to the diggings, put off a couple more shots, uncovered more flint and found another sunstone. It wasn't often that he found stones on two successive days. When he returned to the camp, Little Fuzzy was picking another land-prawn apart in front of the living hut.

After dinner—Little Fuzzy like cooked food, too, if it wasn't too hot—they went into the living room. He remembered having seen a bolt and nut in the desk drawer when he had been putting the wooden prawn-killer away, and he got it out, showing it to Little Fuzzy. Little Fuzzy studied it for a moment, then ran into the bedroom and came back with his screw-top bottle. He took the top off, put it on again and then screwed the nut off the bolt, holding it up.

"See, Pappy?" Or yeeks to that effect. "Nothing to it."

Then he unscrewed the bottle top, dropped the bolt inside after replacing the nut and screwed the cap on again.

"Yeek," he said, with considerable self-satisfaction.

He had a right to be satisfied with himself. What he'd been doing had been generalizing. Bottle tops and nuts belonged to the general class of things-that-screwed-onto-things. To take them off, you turned left; to put them on again, you turned right, after making sure that the threads engaged. And since he could conceive of right- and left-handedness, that might mean that he could think of properties apart from objects, and that was forming abstract ideas. Maybe that was going a little far, but . . .

"You know, Pappy Jack's got himself a mighty smart Little Fuzzy. Are you a grown-up Little Fuzzy, or are you just a baby Little Fuzzy? Shucks, I'll bet you're Professor Doctor Fuzzy."

He wondered what to give the professor, if that was what he was, to work on next, and he doubted the wisdom of teaching him too much about taking things apart, just at present. Sometime he might come home and find something important taken apart, or, worse, taken apart and put together incorrectly. Finally, he went to a closet, rummaging in it until he found a tin cannister. By the time he returned, Little Fuzzy had gotten up on a chair, found his pipe in the ashtray and was puffing on it and coughing.

"Hey, I don't think that's good for you!"

He recovered the pipe, wiped the stem on his shirtsleeve and put it in his mouth, then placed the cannister on the floor, and put Little Fuzzy on the floor beside it. There were about ten pounds of stones in it. When he had first settled here, he had made a collection of the local minerals, and, after learning what he'd wanted to, he had thrown them out, all twenty or thirty of the prettiest specimens. He was glad, now, that he had kept these.

Little Fuzzy looked the can over, decided that the lid was a member of the class of things-that-screwed-onto-things and got it off. The inside of the lid was mirror-shiny, and it took him a little thought to discover that what he saw in it was only himself. He yeeked about that, and looked into the can. This, he decided, belonged to the class of things-that-can-be-dumped, like wastebaskets, so he dumped it on the floor. Then he began examining the stones and sorting them by color.

Except for an interest in colorful views on the screen, this was the first real evidence that Fuzzies possessed color perception. He proceeded to give further and more impressive proof, laying out the stones by shade, in correct spectral order, from a lump of amethystlike quartz to a dark red stone. Well, maybe he'd seen rainbows. Maybe he'd lived near a big misty waterfall, where there was always a rainbow when the sun was shining. Or maybe that was just his natural way of seeing colors.

Then, when he saw what he had to work with, he began making arrangements with them, laying them out in odd circular and spiral patterns. Each time he finished a pattern, he would yeek happily to call attention to it, sit and look at it for a while, and then take it apart and start a new one. Little Fuzzy was capable of artistic gratification too. He made useless things, just for the pleasure of making and looking at them.

Finally, he put the stones back into the tin, put the lid on and rolled it into the bedroom, righting it beside his bed along with his other treasures. The new weapon he laid on the blanket beside him when he went to bed.

THE NEXT MORNING, Jack broke up a whole cake of Extee Three and put it down, filled the bowl with water, and, after making sure he had left nothing lying around that Little Fuzzy could damage or on which he might hurt himself, took the manipulator up to the diggings. He worked all morning, cracking nearly a ton and a half of flint, and found nothing. Then he set off a string of shots, brought down an avalanche of sandstone and exposed more flint, and sat down under a pool-ball tree to eat his lunch.

Half an hour after he went back to work, he found the fossil of some jellyfish that hadn't eaten the right things in the right combinations, but a little later, he found four nodules, one after another, and two of them were sunstones; four or five chunks later, he found a third. Why, this must be the Dying Place of the Jellyfish! By late afternoon, when he had cleaned up all his loose flint, he had nine, including one deep red monster an inch in diameter. There must have been some connection current in the ancient ocean that had swirled them all into this one place. He considered setting off some more shots, decided that it was too late and returned to camp.

"Little Fuzzy!" he called, opening the living-room door. "Where are you, Little Fuzzy? Pappy Jack's rich; we're going to celebrate!"

Silence. He called again; still no reply or scamper of feet. Probably cleaned up all the prawns around the camp and went hunting farther into the woods, thought Jack. Unbuckling his gun and dropping it onto the table, he went out to the kitchen. Most of the Extee Three was gone. In the bedroom, he found that Little Fuzzy had dumped the stones out of the biscuit tin and made an arrangement, and laid the wood chisel in a neat diagonal across the blanket.

After getting dinner assembled and in the oven, he went out and called for a while, then mixed a highball and took it into the living room, sitting down with it to go over his day's findings. Rather incredulously, he realized that he had cracked out at least seventy-five thousand sols' worth of stones today. He put them into the bag and sat sipping the highball and thinking pleasant thoughts until the bell on the stove warned him that dinner was ready.

He ate alone—after all the years he had been doing that contentedly, it had suddenly become intolerable—and in the evening he dialed through his microfilm library, finding only books he had read and reread a dozen times, or books he kept for reference. Several times he thought he heard the little door open, but each time he was mistaken. Finally he went to bed.

As soon as he woke, he looked across at the folded blanket, but the wood chisel was still lying athwart it. He put down more Extee Three and changed the water in the bowl before leaving for the diggings. That day he found three more sunstones, and put them in the bag mechanically and without pleasure. He quit work early and spent over an hour spiraling around the camp, but saw nothing. The Extee Three in the kitchen was untouched.

Maybe the little fellow ran into something too big for him, even with his fine new weapon—a hobthrush, or a bush-goblin, or another harpy. Or maybe he'd just gotten tired staying in one place, and had moved on.

No; he'd liked it here. He'd had fun, and been happy. He shook his head sadly. Once he, too, had lived in a pleasant place, where he'd had fun, and could have been happy if he hadn't thought there was something he'd had to do. So he had gone away, leaving grieved people behind him. Maybe that was how it was with Little Fuzzy. Maybe he didn't realize how much of a place he had made for himself here, or how empty he was leaving it.

He started for the kitchen to get a drink, and checked himself. Take a drink because you pity yourself, and then the drink pities you and has a drink, and then two good drinks get together and that calls for drinks all around. No; he'd have one drink, maybe a little bigger than usual, before he went to bed.

3

HE STARTED AWAKE, rubbed his eyes and looked at the clock. Past twenty-two hundred; now it really was time for a drink, and then to bed. He rose stiffly and went out to the kitchen, pouring the whisky and bringing it in to the table desk, where he sat down and got out his diary. He was almost finished with the day's entry when the little door behind him opened and a small voice said, "Yeeek." He turned quickly.

"Little Fuzzy?"

The small sound was repeated, impatiently. Little Fuzzy was holding the door open, and there was an answer from outside. Then another Fuzzy came in, and another; four of them, one carrying a tiny, squirming ball of white fur in her arms. They all had prawn-killers like the one in the drawer, and they stopped just inside the room and gaped about them in bewilderment. Then, laying down his weapon, Little Fuzzy ran to him; stooping from the chair, he caught him and then sat down on the floor with him.

"So that's why you ran off and worried Pappy Jack? You wanted your family here, too!"

The others piled the things they were carrying with Little Fuzzy's steel weapon and approached hesitantly. He talked to them, and so did Little Fuzzy—at least it sounded like that—and finally one came over and fingered his shirt, and then reached up and pulled his mustache. Soon all of them were climbing onto him, even the female with the baby. It was small enough to sit on his palm, but in a minute it had climbed to his shoulder, and then it was sitting on his head.

"You people want dinner?" he asked.

Little Fuzzy yeeked emphatically; that was a word he recognized. He took them all into the kitchen and tried them on cold roast veldbeest and yummiyams and fried pool-ball fruit; while they were eating from a couple of big pans, he went back to the living room to examine the things they had brought with them. Two of the prawn-killers were wood, like the one Little Fuzzy had discarded in the shed. A third was of horn, beautifully polished, and the fourth looked as though it had been made from the shoulder bone of something like a zebralope. Then there was a small *coup de poing* ax, rather low paleolithic, and a chipped implement of flint the shape of a slice of orange and about five inches along the straight edge. For a hand the size of his own, he would have called it a scraper. He puzzled over it for a while, noticed that the edge was serrated, and decided that it was a saw. And there were three very good flake knives, and some shells, evidently drinking vessels.

Mamma Fuzzy came in while he was finishing the examination. She seemed suspicious, until she saw that none of the family property had been taken or damaged. Baby Fuzzy was clinging to her fur with one hand and holding a slice of pool-ball fruit, on which he was munching, with the other. He crammed what was left of the fruit into his mouth, climbed up on Jack and sat down on his head again. Have to do something to break him of that. One of these days, he'd be getting too big for it.

In a few minutes, the rest of the family came in, chasing and pummeling each other and yeeking happily. Mama jumped off his lap and joined the free-for-all, and then Baby took off from his head and landed on Mama's back. And he thought he'd lost his Little Fuzzy, and, gosh, here he had five Fuzzies and a Baby Fuzzy. When they were tired of romping, he made beds for them in the living room, and brought out Little Fuzzy's bedding and his treasures. One Little Fuzzy in the bedroom was just fine; five and a Baby Fuzzy were a little too much of a good thing.

They were swarming over the bed, Baby and all, to waken him the next morning.

THE NEXT MORNING he made a steel chopper-digger for each of them, and half a dozen extras for replacements in case more Fuzzies showed up. He also made a miniature ax with a hardwood handle, a handsaw out of a piece of broken power-saw blade and half a dozen little knives forged in one piece from quarter-inch coil-spring material. He had less trouble trading the Fuzzies' own things away from them than he had expected. They had a very keen property sense, but they knew a good deal when one was offered. He put the wooden and horn and bone and stone artifacts away in the desk drawer. Start of the Holloway

Collection of Zarathustran Fuzzy Weapons and Implements. Maybe he'd will it to the Federation Institute of Zeno-Sciences.

Of course, the family had to try out the new chopper-diggers on land-prawns, and he followed them around with the movie camera. They killed a dozen and a half that morning, and there was very little interest in lunch, though they did sit around nibbling, just to be doing what he was doing. As soon as they finished, they all went in for a nap on his bed. He spent the afternoon pottering about camp doing odd jobs that he had been postponing for months. The Fuzzies all emerged in the late afternoon for a romp in the grass outside.

He was in the kitchen, getting dinner, when they all came pelting in through the little door into the living room, making an excited outcry. Little Fuzzy and one of the other males came into the kitchen. Little Fuzzy squatted, put one hand on his lower jaw, with thumb and little finger extended, and the other on his forehead, first finger upright. Then he thrust out his right arm stiffly and made a barking noise of a sort he had never made before. He had to do it a second time before Jack got it.

There was a large and unpleasant carnivore, called a damnthing—another example of zoological nomenclature on uninhabited planets—which had a single horn on its forehead and one on either side of the lower jaw. It was something for Fuzzies, and even for human-type people, to get excited about. He laid down the paring knife and the yummiyam he had been peeling, wiped his hands and went into the living room, taking a quick nose count and satisfying himself that none of the family was missing as he crossed to the gunrack.

This time, instead of the 6-mm he had used on the harpy, he lifted down the big 12.7 double express, making sure that it was loaded and pocketing a few spare rounds. Little Fuzzy followed him outside, pointing around the living hut to the left. The rest of the family stayed indoors.

Stepping out about twenty feet, he started around counter-clockwise. There was no damnthing on the north side, and he was about to go around to the east side when Little Fuzzy came dashing past him, pointing to the rear. He whirled, to see the damnthing charging him from behind, head down, and middle horn lowered. He should have thought of that; damnthings would double and hunt their hunters.

He lined the sights instinctively and squeezed. The big rifle roared and banged his shoulder, and the bullet caught the damnthing and hurled all half-ton of it backward. The second shot caught it just below one of the fungoid-looking ears, and the beast gave a spasmotic all-over twitch and was still. He reloaded mechanically, but there was no need for a third shot. The damnthing was as dead as he would have been except for Little Fuzzy's warning.

He mentioned that to Little Fuzzy, who was calmly retrieving the empty cartridges. Then, rubbing his shoulder where the big rifle had pounded him, he went in and returned the weapon to the rack. He used the manipulator to carry the damnthing away from the camp and drop it into a treetop, where it would furnish a welcome, if puzzling, treat for the harpies.

THERE WAS ANOTHER alarm in the evening after dinner. The family had come in from their sunset romp and were gathered in the living room, where Little Fuzzy was demonstrating the principle of things-that-screwed-onto-things with the wide-mouthed bottle and the bolt and nut, when something huge began hooting directly overhead. They all froze, looking up at the ceiling, and then ran over and got under the gunrack. This must be something far more serious than a damnthing, and what Pappy Jack would do about it would be nothing short of catastrophic. They were startled to see Pappy Jack merely go to the door, open it and step outside. After all, none of them had ever heard a Constabulary aircar klaxon before.

The car settled onto the grass in front of the camp, gave a slight lurch and went off contragravity. Two men in uniform got out, and in the moonlight he recognized both of them: Lieutenant George Lunt and his driver, Ahmed Khadra. He called a greeting to them.

"Anything wrong?" he asked.

"No; just thought we'd drop in and see how you were making out," Lunt told him. "We don't get up this way often. Haven't had any trouble lately, have you?"

"Not since the last time." The last time had been a couple of woods tramps, out-of-work veldbeest herders from the south, who had heard about the little bag he carried around his neck. All the Constabulary had needed to do was remove the bodies and write up a report. "Come on in and hang up your guns awhile. I have something I want to show you."

Little Fuzzy had come out and was pulling at his trouser leg; he stooped and picked him up, setting him on his shoulder. The rest of the family, deciding that it must be safe, had come to the door and were looking out.

"Hey! What the devil are those things?" Lunt asked, stopping short halfway from the car.

"Fuzzies. Mean to tell me you've never seen Fuzzies before?"

"No, I haven't. What are they?"

The two Constabulary men came closer, and Jack stepped back into the house, shooing the Fuzzies out of the way. Lunt and Khadra stopped inside the door.

"I just told you. They're Fuzzies. That's all the name I know for them."

A couple of Fuzzies came over and looked up at Lieutenant Lunt; one of them said, "Yeek?"

"They want to know what you are, so that makes it mutual."

Lunt hesitated for a moment, then took off his belt and holster and hung it on one of the pegs inside the door, putting his beret over it. Khadra followed his example promptly. That meant that they considered themselves temporarily off duty and would accept a drink if one were offered. A Fuzzy was pulling at Ahmed Khadra's trouser leg and asking to be noticed, and Mamma Fuzzy was holding Baby up to show to Lunt. Khadra, rather hesitantly, picked up the Fuzzy who was trying to attract his attention.

"Never saw anything like them before, Jack," he said. "Where did they come from?"

"Ahmed; you don't know anything about those things," Lunt reproved.

"They won't hurt me, Lieutenant; they haven't hurt Jack, have they?" He sat down on he floor, and a couple more came to him. "Why don't you get acquainted with them? They're cute."

George Lunt wouldn't let one of his men do anything he was afraid to do; he sat down on the floor, too, and Mamma brought her baby to him. Immediately, the baby jumped onto his shoulder and tried to get onto his head.

"Relax, George," Jack told him. "They're just Fuzzies; they want to make friends with you."

"I'm always worried about strange life forms," Lunt said. "You've been around enough to know some of the things that have happened—"

"They are not a strange life form; they are Zarathustran mammals. The same life form you've had for dinner every day since you came here. Their biochemistry's identical with ours. Think they'll give you the Polka-Dot Plague, or something?" He put Little Fuzzy down on the floor with the others. "We've been exploring this planet for twenty-five years, and nobody's found anything like that here."

"You said it yourself, Lieutenant," Khadra put in. "Jack's been around enough to know."

"Well . . . They are cute little fellows." Lunt lifted Baby down off his head and gave him back to Mamma. Little Fuzzy had gotten hold of the chain of his whistle and was trying to find out what was on the other end. "Bet they're a lot of company for you."

"You just get acquainted with them. Make yourselves at home; I'll go rustle up some refreshments."

While he was in the kitchen, filling a soda siphon and getting ice out of the refrigerator, a police whistle began shrilling in the living room. He was opening a bottle of whisky when Little Fuzzy came dashing out, blowing on it, a couple more of the family pursuing him and trying to get it away from him. He opened a tin of Extee Three for the Fuzzies; as he did, another whistle in the living room began blowing.

"We have a whole shoebox full of them at the post," Lunt yelled to him above the din. "We'll just write these two off as expended in service."

"Well, that's real nice of you, George. I want to tell you that the Fuzzies appreciate that. Ahmed, suppose you do the bartending while I give the kids their candy."

By the time Khadra had the drinks mixed and he had distributed the Extee Three to the Fuzzies, Lunt had gotten into the easy chair, and the Fuzzies were sitting on the floor in front of him, still looking him over curiously. At least the Extee Three had taken their minds off the whistles for a while.

"What I want to know, Jack, is where they came from," Lunt said, taking his drink. "I've been up here for five years, and I never saw anything like them before."

"I've been here five years longer, and I never saw them before, either. I think they came down from the north, from the country between the Cordilleras and the West Coast Range. Outside of an air survey at ten thousand feet and a few spot landings here and there, none of that country has been explored. For all anybody knows, it could be full of Fuzzies."

He began with his first encounter with Little Fuzzy, and by the time he had gotten as far as the wood chisel and the killing of the land-prawn, Lunt and Khadra were looking at each other in amazement.

"That's it!" Khadra said. "I've found prawn-shells cracked open and the meat picked out, just the way you describe it. I always wondered what did that. But they don't all have wood chisels. What do you suppose they used ordinarily?"

"Ah!" He pulled the drawer open and began getting things out. "Here's the one Little Fuzzy discarded when he found my chisel. The rest of this stuff the others brought in when they came."

Lunt and Khadra rose and came over to look at the things. Lunt tried to argue that the Fuzzies couldn't have made that stuff. He wasn't even able to convince himself. Having finished their Extee Three, the Fuzzies were looking expectantly at the viewscreen, and it occurred to him that none of them except Little Fuzzy had ever seen it on. Then Little Fuzzy jumped up on the chair Lunt had vacated, reached over to the control-panel and switched it on. What he got was an empty stretch of moonlit plain to the south, from a pickup on one of the steel towers the veldbeest herders used. That wasn't very interesting; he twiddled the selector and finally got a night soccer game at Mallorysport. That was just fine; he jumped down and joined the others in front of the screen.

"I've seen Terran monkeys and Freyan Kholphs that liked to watch screens and could turn them on and work the selector," Lunt said. It sounded like the token last salvo before the surrender.

"Kholphs are smart," Khadra agreed. "They use tools."

"Do they make tooks? Or tools to make tools with, like that saw?" There was no argument on that. "No. Nobody does that except people like us and the Fuzzies."

It was the first time he had come right out and said that; the first time he had even consciously thought it. He realized that he had been convinced of it all along, though. It startled the constabulary lieutenant and trooper.

"You mean you think—?" Lunt began.

"They don't talk, and they don't build fires," Ahmed Khadra said, as though that settled it.

"Ahmed, you know better than that. That talk-and-build-a-fire rule isn't any scientific test at all."

"It's a legal test." Lunt supported his subordinate.

"It's a rule-of-thumb that was set up so that settlers on new planets couldn't get away with murdering and enslaving the natives by claiming they thought they were only hunting and domesticating wild animals," he said. "Anything that talks and builds a fire is a sapient being, yes. That's the law. But that doesn't mean that anything that doesn't isn't. I haven't seen any of this gang building fires, and as I don't want to come home sometime and find myself burned out, I'm not going to teach them. But I'm sure they have some means of communication among themselves."

"Has Ben Rainsford seen them yet?" Lunt asked.

"Ben's off on a trip somewhere. I called him as soon as Little Fuzzy, over there, showed up here. He won't be back till Friday."

"Yes, that's right; I did know that." Lunt was still looking dubiously at the Fuzzies. "I'd like to hear what he thinks about them."

If Ben said they were safe, Lunt would accept that. Ben was an expert, and Lunt respected expert testimony. Until then, he wasn't sure. He'd probably order a medical check-up for himself and Khadra the first thing tomorrow, to make sure they hadn't picked up some kind of bug.

4

THE FUZZIES TOOK the manipulator quite calmly the next morning. That wasn't any horrible monster, that was just something Pappy Jack took rides in. He found one rather indifferent sunstone in the morning and two good ones in the afternoon. He came home early and found the family in the living room; they had dumped the wastebasket and were putting things back into it. Another land-prawn seemed to have gotten into the house; its picked shell was with the other rubbish in the basket. They had dinner early, and he loaded the lot of them into the airjeep and took them for a long ride to the south and west.

The following day, he located the flint vein on the other side of the gorge and spent most of the morning blasting away the sandstone above it. The next time he went into Mallorysport, he decided, he was going to shop around for a good power-shovel. He had to blast a channel to keep the little stream from damming up on him. He didn't get any flint cracked at all that day. There was another harpy circling around the camp when he got back; he chased it with the manipulator and shot it down with his pistol. Harpies probably found Fuzzies as tasty as Fuzzies found land-prawns. The family was all sitting under the gunrack when he entered the living room.

The next day he cracked flint, and found three more stones. It really looked as though he had found the Dying Place of the Jellyfish at that. He knocked off early that afternoon, and when he came in sight of the camp, he saw an airjeep grounded on the lawn and a small man with a red beard in a faded Khaki bush-jacket sitting on the bench by the kitchen door, surrounded by Fuzzies. There was a camera and some other equipment laid up where the Fuzzies couldn't get at it. Baby Fuzzy, of course, was sitting on his head. He looked up and waved, and then handed Baby to his mother and rose to his feet.

"Well, what do you think of them, Ben?" Jack called down, as he grounded the manipulator.

"My God, don't start me on that now!" Ben Rainsford replied, and then laughed. "I stopped at the constabulary post on the way home. I thought George Lunt had turned into the biggest liar in the known galaxy. Then I went home, and found your call on the recorder, so I came over here."

"Been waiting long?"

The Fuzzies had all abandoned Rainsford and come trooping over as soon as the manipulator was off contragravity. He climbed down among them, and they followed him across the grass, catching at his trouser legs and yeeking happily.

"Not so long." Rainsford looked at his watch. "Good Lord, three and a half hours is all. Well, the time passed quickly. You know, your little fellows have good ears. They heard you coming a long time before I did."

"Did you see them killing any prawns?"

"I should say! I got a lot of movies of it." He shook his head slowly. "Jack, this is almost incredible."

"You're staying for dinner, of course."

"You try and chase me away. I want to hear all about this. Want you to make a tape about them, if you're willing."

"Glad to. We'll do that after we eat." He sat down on the bench, and the Fuzzies began climbing upon and beside him. "This is the original, Little Fuzzy. He brought the rest in a couple of days later. Mamma Fuzzy, and Baby Fuzzy. And these are Mike and Mitzi. I call this one Ko-Ko, because of the ceremonious way he beheads land-prawns."

"George says you call them all Fuzzies. Want that for the official designation?"

"Sure. That's what they are, isn't it?"

"Well, let's call the order Hollowayans," Rainsford said. "Family, Fuzzies; genus, Fuzzy. Species, Holloway's Fuzzy—*Fuzzy fuzzy holloway*. How'll that be?"

That would be all right, he supposed. At least, they didn't try to Latinize things in extraterrestrial zoology anymore.

"I suppose our bumper crop of land-prawns is what brought them into this section?"

"Yes, of course. George was telling me you thought they'd come down from the north; about the only place they could have come from. This is probably just the advance guard; we'll be having Fuzzies all over the place before long. I wonder how fast they breed."

"Not very fast. Three males and two females in this crowd, and only one young one." He set Mike and Mitzi off his lap and got to his feet. "I'll go start dinner now. While I'm doing that, you can look at the stuff they brought in with them."

When he had placed the dinner in the oven and taken a couple of highballs into the living room, Rainsford was still sitting at the desk, looking at the artifacts. He accepted his drink and sipped it absently, then raised his head.

"Jack, this stuff is absolutely amazing," he said.

"It's better than that. It's unique. Only collection of native weapons and implements on Zarathustra."

Ben Rainsford looked up sharply. "You mean what I think you mean?" he asked. "Yes; you do." He drank some of his highball, set down the glass and picked up the polished-horn prawn-killer. "Anything—pardon, anybody—who does this kind of work is good enough native for me." He hesitated briefly. "Why, Jack this tape you said you'd make. Can I transmit a copy to Juan Jimenez? He's chief mammalogist with the Company science division; we exchange information. And there's another Company man I'd like to have hear it. Gerd van Riebeek. He's a general xeno-naturalist, like me, but he's especially interested in animal evolution."

"Why not? The Fuzzies are a scientific discovery. Discoveries ought to be reported."

Little Fuzzy, Mike and Mitzi strolled in from the kitchen. Little Fuzzy jumped up on the armchair and switched on the viewscreen. Fiddling with the selector, he got the Big Blackwater woods-burning. Mike and Mitzi shrieked delightedly, like a couple of kids watching a horror show. They knew, by now, that nothing in the screen could get out and hurt them.

"Would you mind if they came out here and saw the Fuzzies?"

"Why, the Fuzzies would love that. They like company."

Mamma and Baby and Ko-Ko came in, seemed to approve what was on the screen and sat down to watch it. When the bell on the stove rang, they all got up, and Ko-Ko jumped onto the chair and snapped the screen off. Ben Rainsford looked at him for a moment.

"You know, I have married friends with children who have a hell of a time teaching eight-year-olds to turn off screens when they're through watching them," he commented.

IT TOOK AN hour, after dinner, to get the whole story, from the first little yeek in the shower stall, on tape. When he had finished, Ben Rainsford made a few remarks and shut off the recorder, then looked at his watch.

"Twenty hundred; it'll be seventeen hundred in Mallorysport," he said. "It could catch Jimenez at Science Center if I called now. He usually works a little late."

"Go ahead. Want to show him some Fuzzies?" He moved his pistol and some other impedimenta off the table and set Little Fuzzy and Mamma Fuzzy and Baby upon it, then drew up a chair beside it, in range of the communication screen, and sat down with Mike and Mitzi and Ko-Ko. Rainsford punched out a wave-length combination. Then he picked up Baby Fuzzy and set him on his head.

In a moment, the screen flickered and cleared, and a young man looked out of it, with the momentary upward glance of one who wants to make sure his public face is on straight. It was a bland, tranquilized, life-adjusted, group-integrated sort of face—the face turned out in thousands of copies every year by the educational production lines on Terra.

"Why, Bennett, this is a pleasant surprise," he began. "I never expec—" Then he choked; at least, he emitted a sound of surprise. "What in the name of Dai-Butsu are those things on the table in front of you?" he demanded. "I never saw anything—*And what is that on your head?*"

"Family group of Fuzzies," Rainsford said. "Mature male, mature female, immature male." He lifted Baby Fuzzy down and put him in Mamma's arms. Species *Fuzzy fuzzy holloway zarathustra*. The gentleman on my left is Jack Holloway, the sunstone operator, who is the original discoverer. Jack, Juan Jimenez."

They shook their own hands at one another in the ancient Terran-Chinese gesture that was used on communication screens, and assured each other— Jimenez rather absently—that it was a pleasure. He couldn't take his eyes off the Fuzzies.

"Where did they come from?" he wanted to know. "Are you sure they're indigenous?"

"They're not quite up to spaceships, yet, Dr. Jimenez. Fairly early Paleolithic, I'd say."

Jimenez thought he was joking, and laughed. The sort of a laugh that could be turned on and off, like a light. Rainsford assured him that the Fuzzies were really indigenous.

"We have everything that's known about them on tape," he said. "About an hour of it. Can you take sixty-speed?" He was making adjustments on the recorder as he spoke. "All right, set and we'll transmit to you. And can you get hold of Gerd van Riebeek? I'd like him to hear it too; it's as much up his alley as anybody's."

When Jimenez was ready, Rainsford pressed the play-off button, and for a minute the recorder gave a high, wavering squeak. The Fuzzies all looked startled. Then it ended.

"I think, when you hear this, that you and Gerd will both want to come out and see these little people. If you can, bring somebody who's a qualified psychologist, somebody capable of evaluating the Fuzzies' mentation. Jack wasn't kidding about early Paleolithic. If they're not sapient, they only miss it by about one atomic diameter."

Jimenez looked almost as startled as the Fuzzies had. "You surely don't mean that?" He looked from Rainsford to Jack Holloway and back. "Well, I'll call you back, when we've both heard the tape. You're three time zones west of us, aren't you? Then we'll try to make it before your midnight—that'll be twenty-one hundred."

He called back half an hour short of that. This time, it was from the living room of an apartment instead of an office. There was a portable record player in the foreground and a low table with snacks and drinks, and two other people were with him. One was a man of about Jimenez's age with a good-humored, non-life-adjusted, non-group-integrated and slightly weather-beaten face. The other was a woman with glossy black hair and a Mona Lisa-ish smile. The Fuzzies had gotten sleepy, and had been bribed with Extee Three to stay up a little longer. Immediately, they registered interest. This was more fun than the viewscreen.

Jimenez introduced his companions as Gerd van Riebeek and Ruth Ortheris. "Ruth is with Dr. Mallin's section; she's been working with the school department and the juvenile court. She can probably do as well with your Fuzzies as a regular xeno-psychologist."

"Well, I have worked with extraterrestrials," the woman said. "I've been on Loki and Thor and Shesha."

Jack nodded. "Been on the same planets myself. Are you people coming out here?"

"Oh, yes," van Riebeek said. "We'll be out by noon tomorrow. We may stay a couple of days, but that won't put you to any trouble; I have a boat that's big enough for the three of us to camp on. Now, how do we get to your place?"

Jack told him, and gave map coordinates. Van Riebeek noted them down.

"There's one thing, though, I'm going to have to get firm about. I don't want to have to speak about it again. These little people are to be treated with consideration, and not as laboratory animals. You will not hurt them, or annoy them, or force them to do anything they don't want to do."

"We understand that. We won't do anything with the Fuzzies without your approval. Is there anything you'd want us to bring out?"

"Yes. A few things for the camp that I'm short of; I'll pay you for them when you get here. And about three cases of Extee Three. And some toys. Dr. Ortheris, you heard the tape, didn't you? Well, just think what you'd like to have if you were a Fuzzy, and bring it."

5

VICTOR GREGO CRUSHED out his cigarette slowly and deliberately.

"Yes, Leonard," he said patiently. "It's very interesting, and doubtless an important discovery, but I can't see why you're making such a production of it. Are you afraid I'll blame you for letting non-Company people beat you to it? Or do you merely suspect that anything Bennett Rainsford's mixed up in is necessarily a diabolical plot against the Company and, by consequence, human civilization?"

Leonard Kellogg looked pained. "What I was about to say, Victor, is that both Rainsford and this man Holloway seemed convinced that these things they call Fuzzies aren't animals at all. They believe them to be sapient beings."

"Well, that's—" He bit that off short as the significance of what Kellogg had just said hit him. "Good God, Leonard! I beg your pardon abjectly; I don't blame you for taking it seriously. Why, that would make Zarathustra a Class-IV inhabited planet."

"For which the Company holds a Class-III charter," Kellogg added. "For an uninhabited planet."

Automatically void if any race of sapient beings were discovered on Zarathustra.

"You know what will happen if this is true?"

"Well, I should imagine the charter would have to be renegotiated, and now that the Colonial Office knows what sort of a planet this is, they'll be anything but generous with the Company. . . ."

"They won't renegotiate anything, Leonard. The Federation government will simply take the position that the Company has already made an adequate return on the original investments, and they'll award us what we can show as in our actual possession—I hope—and throw the rest into the public domain."

The vast plains on Beta and Delta continents, with their herds of veldbeest—all open range, and every 'beest that didn't carry a Company brand a maverick. And all the untapped mineral wealth, and the untilled arable land; it would take years of litigation even to make the Company's claim to Big Blackwater stick. And Terra-Baldur-Marduk Spacelines would lose their monopolistic franchise and get sticky about it in the courts, and in any case, the Company's import-export monopoly would go out the airlock. And the squatters rushing in and swamping everything—

"Why, we won't be any better off than the Yggdrasil Company, squatting on a guano heap on one continent!" he burst out. "Five years from now, they'll be making more money out of bat dung than we'll be making out of this whole world!"

And the Company's good friend and substantial stockholder, Nick Emmert, would be out, too, and a Colonial Governor General would move in, with regular army troops and a complicated bureaucracy. Elections, and a representative parliament, and every Tom, Dick and Harry with a grudge against the Company would be trying to get laws passed—And, of course, a Native Affairs Commission, with its nose in everything.

"But they couldn't just leave us without any kind of a charter," Kellogg insisted. Who was he trying to kid—besides himself? "It wouldn't be fair!" As though that clinched it. "It isn't our fault!"

He forced more patience into his voice. "Leonard, please try to realize that the Terran Federation government doesn't give one shrill soprano hoot on Nifflheim whether it's fair or not, or whose fault what is. The Federation government's been repenting that charter they gave the Company ever since they found out what they'd chartered away. Why, this planet is a better world than Terra ever was, even before the Atomic Wars. Now, if they have a chance to get it back, with improvements, you think they won't take it? And what will stop them? If those creatures over on Beta Continent are sapient beings, our charter isn't worth the parchment it's engrossed on, and that's the end of it." He was silent for a moment. "You heard that tape Rainsford transmitted to Jimenez. Did either he or Holloway actually claim, in so many words, that these things really are sapient beings?"

"Well, no; not in so many words. Holloway consistently alluded to them as people, but he's just an ignorant old prospector. Rainsford wouldn't come out and commit himself one way or another, but he left the door wide open for anybody else to."

"Accepting their account, could these Fuzzies be sapient?"

"Accepting the account, yes," Kellogg said, in distress. "They could be."

They probably were, if Leonard Kellogg couldn't wish the evidence out of existence.

"Then they'll look sapient to these people of yours who went over to Beta this morning, and they'll treat it purely as a scientific question and never consider the legal aspects. Leonard, you'll have to take charge of the investigation, before they make any reports everybody'll be sorry for."

Kellogg didn't seem to like that. It would mean having to exercise authority and getting tough with people, and he hated anything like that. He nodded very reluctantly.

"Yes. I suppose I will. Let me think about it for a moment, Victor."

One thing about Leonard; you handed him something he couldn't delegate or dodge and he'd go to work on it. Maybe not cheerfully, but conscientiously.

"I'll take Ernst Mallin along," he said at length. "This man Rainsford has no grounding whatever in any of the psychosciences. He may be able to impose on Ruth Ortheris, but not on Ernst Mallin. Not after I've talked to Mallin first." He thought some more. "We'll have to get these Fuzzies away from this man Holloway. Then we'll issue a report of discovery, being careful to give full credit to both Rainsford and Holloway—we'll even accept the designation they've coined for them—but we'll make it very clear that while highly intelligent, the Fuzzies are not a race of sapient beings. If Rainsford persists in making any such claim, we will brand it as a deliberate hoax."

"Do you think he's gotten any report off to the Institute of Xeno-Sciences yet?"

Kellogg shook his head. "I think he wants to trick some of our people into supporting his sapience claims; at least, corroborating his and Holloway's alleged observations. That's why I'll have to get over to Beta as soon as possible."

By now, Kellogg had managed to convince himself that going over to Beta had been his idea all along. Probably also convincing himself that Rainsford's report was nothing but a pack of lies. Well, if he could work better that way, that was his business.

"He will, before long, if he isn't stopped. And a year from now, there'll be a small army of investigators here from Terra. By that time, you should have both Rainsford and Holloway thoroughly discredited. Leonard, you get those Fuzzies away from Holloway and I'll personally guarantee they won't be available for investigation by then. Fuzzies," he said reflectively. "Fur-bearing animals, I take it?"

"Holloway spoke, on the tape, of their soft and silky fur."

"Good. Emphasize that in your report. As soon as it's published, the

Company will offer two thousand sols apiece for Fuzzy pelts. By the time Rainsford's report brings anybody here from Terra, we may have them all trapped out."

Kellogg began to look worried.

"But, Victor, that's genocide!"

"Nonsense! Genocide is defined as the extermination of a race of sapient beings. These are fur-bearing animals. It's up to you and Ernst Mallin to prove that."

THE FUZZIES, PLAYING on the lawn in front of the camp, froze into immobility, their faces turned to the west. Then they all ran to the bench by the kitchen door and scrambled up onto it.

"Now what?" Jack Holloway wondered.

"They hear the airboat," Rainsford told him. "That's the way they acted yesterday when you were coming in with your machine." He looked at the picnic table they had been spreading under the featherleaf trees. "Everything ready?"

"Everything but lunch; that won't be cooked for an hour yet. I see them now."

"You have better eyes than I do, Jack. Oh, I see it. I hope the kids put on a good show for them," he said anxiously.

He'd been jittery ever since he arrived, shortly after breakfast. It wasn't that these people from Mallorysport were so important themselves; Ben had a bigger name in scientific circles than any of this Company crowd. He was just excited about the Fuzzies.

The airboat grew from a barely visible speck, and came spiraling down to land in the clearing. When it was grounded and off contragravity, they started across the grass toward it, and the Fuzzies all jumped down from the bench and ran along with them.

The three visitors climbed down. Ruth Ortheris wore slacks and a sweater, but the slacks were bloused over a pair of ankle boots. Gerd van Riebeek had evidently done a lot of field work: his boots were stout, and he wore old, faded khakis and a serviceable-looking sidearm that showed he knew what to expect up here in the Piedmont. Juan Jimenez was in the same sports-casuals in which he had appeared on screen last evening. All of them carried photographic equipment. They shook hands all around and exchanged greetings, and then the Fuzzies began clamoring to be noticed. Finally all of them, Fuzzies and other people, drifted over to the table under the trees.

Ruth Ortheris sat down on the grass with Mamma and Baby. Immediately

Baby became interested in a silver charm which she wore on a chain around her neck which tinkled fascinatingly. Then he tried to sit on her head. She spent some time gently but firmly discouraging this. Juan Jimenez was squatting between Mike and Mitzi, examining them alternately and talking into a miniature recorder phone on his breast, mostly in Latin. Gerd van Riebeek dropped himself into a folding chair and took Little Fuzzy on his lap.

"You know, this is kind of surprising," he said. "Not only finding something like this, after twenty-five years, but finding something as unique as this. Look, he doesn't have the least vestige of a tail, and there isn't another tailless mammal on the planet. Fact, there isn't another mammal on this planet that has the slightest kinship to him. Take ourselves; we belong to a pretty big family, about fifty-odd genera of primates. But this little fellow hasn't any relatives at all."

"Yeek?"

"And he couldn't care less, could he?" Van Riebeek pummeled Little Fuzzy gently. "One thing, you have the smallest humanoid known; that's one record you can claim. Oh-oh, what goes on?"

Ko-Ko, who had climbed upon Rainsford's lap, jumped suddenly to the ground, grabbed the chopper-digger he had left beside the chair and started across the grass. Everybody got to their feet, the visitors getting cameras out. The Fuzzies seemed perplexed by all the excitement. It was only another land-prawn, wasn't it?

Ko-Ko got in front of it, poked it on the nose to stop it and then struck a dramatic pose, flourishing his weapon and bringing it down on the prawn's neck. Then, after flopping it over, he looked at it almost in sorrow and hit it a couple of whacks with the flat. He began pulling it apart and eating it.

"I see why you call him Ko-Ko," Ruth said, aiming her camera. "Don't the others do it that way?"

"Well, little Fuzzy runs along beside them and pivots and gives them a quick chop. Mike and Mitzi flop theirs over first and behead them on their backs. And Mamma takes a swipe at their legs first. But beheading and breaking the undershell, they all do that."

"Uh-huh; that's basic," she said. "Instinctive. The technique is either self-learned or copied. When Baby begins killing his own prawns, see if he doesn't do it the way Mamma does!"

"Hey, look!" Jimenez cried. "He's making a lobster pick for himself!"

Through lunch, they talked exclusively about Fuzzies. The subjects of the discussion nibbled things that were given to them, and yeeked among themselves. Gerd van Riebeek suggested that they were discussing the odd habits of human-type people. Juan Jimenez looked at him, slightly disturbed, as though wondering just how seriously he meant it.

"You know, what impressed me most in the taped account was the incident of the damnthing," said Ruth Ortheris. "Any animal associating with man will try to attract attention if something's wrong, but I never heard of one, not even a Freyan kholph or a Terran chimpanzee, that would use descriptive pantomime. Little Fuzzy was actually making a symbolic representation, by abstracting the distinguishing characteristic of the damnthing."

"Think that stiff-arm gesture and bark might have been intended to represent a rifle?" Gerd van Riebeek asked. "He'd seen you shooting before, hadn't he?"

"I don't think it was anything else. He was telling me, 'Big nasty damnthing outside; shoot it like you did the harpy.' And if he hadn't run past me and pointed back, that damnthing would have killed me."

Jimenez, hesitantly, said, "I know I'm speaking from ignorance. You're the Fuzzy expert. But isn't it possible that you're overanthropomorphizing? Endowing them with your own characteristics and mental traits?"

"Juan, I'm not going to answer that right now. I don't think I'll answer at all. You wait till you've been around these Fuzzies a little longer, and then ask it again, only ask yourself."

"So YOU SEE, Ernst, that's the problem."

Leonard Kellogg laid the words like a paperweight on the other words he had been saying, and waited. Ernst Mallin sat motionless, his elbows on the desk and his chin in his hands. A little pair of wrinkles, like parentheses, appeared at the corners of his mouth.

"Yes. I'm not a lawyer, of course, but . . ."

"It's not a legal question. It's a question for a psychologist."

That left it back with Ernst Mallin, and he knew it.

"I'd have to see them myself before I could express an opinion. You have that tape of Holloway's with you?" When Kellogg nodded, Mallin continued: "Did either of them make any actual, overt claim of sapience?"

He answered it as he had when Victor Grego had asked the same question, adding:

"The account consists almost entirely of Holloway's uncorroborated statements concerning things to which he claims to have been the sole witness."

"Ah." Mallin permitted himself a tight little smile. "And he's not a qualified observer. Neither, for that matter, is Rainsford. Regardless of his position as a xeno-naturalist, he is complete layman in the psychosciences. He's just taken this other man's statements uncritically. As for what he claims to have observed for himself, how do we know he isn't including a lot of erroneous inferences with his descriptive statements?"

"How do we know he's not perpetrating a deliberate hoax?"

"But, Leonard, that's a pretty serious accusation."

"It's happened before. That fellow who carved a Late Upland Martian inscription in that cave in Kenya, for instance. Or Hellermann's claim to have cross-bred Terran mice with Thoran tilbras. Or the Piltdown Man, back in the first century Pre-Atomic?"

Mallin nodded. "None of us likes to think of a thing like that, but, as you say, it's happened. You know, this man Rainsford is just the type to do something like that, too. Fundamentally an individualistic egoist; badly adjusted personality type. Say he wants to make some sensational discovery which will assure him the position in the scientific world to which he believes himself entitled. He finds this lonely old prospector, into whose isolated camp some little animals have strayed. The old man has made pets of them, taught them a few tricks, finally so projected his own personality onto them that he has convinced himself that they are people like himself. This is Rainsford's great opportunity; he will present himself as the discoverer of a new sapient race and bring the whole learned world to his feet." Mallin smiled again. "Yes, Leonard, it is altogether possible."

"Then it's our plain duty to stop this thing before it develops into another major scientific scandal like Hellermann's hybrids."

"First we must go over this tape recording and see what we have on our hands. Then we must make a thorough, unbiased study of these animals, and show Rainsford and his accomplice that they cannot hope to foist these ridiculous claims on the scientific world with impunity. If we can't convince them privately, there'll be nothing to do but expose them publicly."

"I've heard the tape already, but let's play it off now. We want to analyze these tricks this man Holloway has taught these animals, and see what they show."

"Yes, of course. We must do that at once," Mallin said. "Then we'll have to consider what sort of statement we must issue, and what sort of evidence we will need to support it."

AFTER DINNER WAS romptime for Fuzzies on the lawn, but when the dusk came creeping into the ravine, they all went inside and were given one of their new toys from Mallorysport—a big box of many-colored balls and short sticks of transparent plastic. They didn't know that it was a molecule-model kit, but they soon found that the sticks would go into holes in the balls, and that they could be built into three-dimensional designs.

This was much more fun than the colored stones. They made a few experimental shapes, then dismantled them and began on a single large design. Several times they tore it down, entirely or in part, and began over again, usually with considerable yeeking and gesticulation.

"They have artistic sense," van Riebeek said. "I've seen lots of abstract sculpture that wasn't half as good as that job they're doing."

"Good engineering, too," Jack said. "They understand balance and center-of-gravity. They're bracing it well, and not making it top-heavy."

"Jack, I've been thinking about that question I was supposed to ask myself," Jimenez said. "You know, I came out here loaded with suspicion. Not that I doubted your honesty; I just thought you'd let your obvious affection for the Fuzzies lead you into giving them credit for more intelligence than they possess. Now I think you've consistently understated it. Short of actual sapience, I've never seen anything like them."

"Why short of it?" van Riebeek asked. "Ruth, you've been pretty quiet this evening. What do you think?"

Ruth Ortheris looked uncomfortable. "Gerd, it's too early to form opinions like that. I know the way they're working together looks like cooperation on an agreed-upon purpose, but I simply can't make speech out of that yeek-yeek-yeek."

"Let's keep the talk-and-build-a-fire rule out of it," van Riebeek said. "If they're working together on a common project, they must be communicating somehow."

"It isn't communication, it's symbolization. You simply can't think sapiently except in verbal symbols. Try it. Not something like changing the spools on a recorder or fieldstripping a pistol; they're just learned tricks. I mean ideas."

"How about Helen Keller?" Rainsford asked. "Mean to say she only started thinking sapiently after Anna Sullivan taught her what words were?"

"No, of course not. She thought sapiently—And she only thought in sense-imagery limited to feeling." She looked at Rainsford reproachfully; he'd knocked a breach in one of her fundamental postulates. "Of course, she had inherited the cerebroneural equipment for sapient thinking." She let that trail off, before somebody asked her how she knew that the Fuzzies hadn't.

"I'll suggest, just to keep the argument going, that speech couldn't have been invented without preexisting sapience," Jack said.

Ruth laughed. "Now you're taking me back to college. That used to be one of the burning questions in first-year psych students' bull sessions. By the time we got to be sophomores, we'd realized that it was only an egg-and-chicken argument and dropped it."

"That's a pity," Ben Rainsford said. "It's a good question."

"It would be if it could be answered."

"Maybe it can be," Gerd said. "There's a clue to it, right there. I'll say that those fellows are on the edge of sapience, and it's an even-money bet which side."

"I'll bet every sunstone in my bag they're over."

"Well, maybe they're just slightly sapient," Jimenez suggested.

Ruth Ortheris hooted at that. "That's like talking about being just slightly dead or just slightly pregnant," she said. "You either are or you aren't."

Gerd van Riebeek was talking at the same time. "This sapience question is just as important in my field as yours, Ruth. Sapience is the result of evolution by natural selection, just as much as a physical characteristic, and it's the most important step in the evolution of any species, our own included."

"Wait a minute, Gerd," Rainsford said. "Ruth, what do you mean by that? Aren't there degrees of sapience?"

"No. There are degrees of mentation—intelligence, if you prefer—just as there are degrees of temperature. When psychology becomes an exact science like physics, we'll be able to calibrate mentation like temperature. But sapience is qualitatively different from nonsapience. It's more than just a higher degree of mental temperature. You might call it a sort of mental boiling point."

"I think that's a damn good analogy," Rainsford said. "But what happens when the boiling point is reached?"

"That's what we have to find out," van Riebeek told him. "That's what I was talking about a moment ago. We don't know any more about how sapience appeared today than we did in the year zero, or in the year 654 Pre-Atomic for that matter."

"Wait a minute," Jack interrupted. "Before we go any deeper, let's agree on a definition of sapience."

Van Riebeek laughed. "Ever try to get a definition of life from a biologist?" he asked. "Or a definition of number from a mathematician?"

"That's about it." Ruth looked at the Fuzzies, who were looking at their colored-ball construction as though wondering if they could add anything more without spoiling the design. "I'd say: a level of mentation qualitatively different from nonsapience in that it includes ability to symbolize ideas and store and transmit them, ability to generalize and ability to form abstract ideas. There; I didn't say a word about talk-and-build-a-fire, did I?"

"Little Fuzzy symbolizes and generalizes," Jack said. "He symbolizes a damnthing by three horns, and he symbolizes a rifle by a long thing that points and makes noises. Rifles kill animals. Harpies and damnthings are both animals. If a rifle will kill a harpy, it'll kill a damnthing too."

Juan Jimenez had been frowning in thought; he looked up and asked, "What's the lowest known sapient race?"

"Yggdrasil Khooghras," Gerd van Riebeek said promptly. "Any of you ever been on Yggdrasil?"

"I saw a man shot once on Mimir, for calling another man a son of a Khooghra," Jack said. "The man who shot him had been on Yggdrasil and knew what he was being called."

"I spent a couple of years among them," Gerd said. "They do build fires; I'll give them that. They char points on sticks to make spears. And they talk. I learned their language, all eighty-two words of it. I taught a few of the intelligentsia how to use machetes without maiming themselves, and there was one mental giant I could trust to carry some of my equipment, if I kept an eye on him, but I never let him touch my rifle or my camera."

"Can they generalize?" Ruth asked.

"Honey, they can't do nothin' else but! Every word in their language is a high-order generalization. *Hroosha*, live-thing. *Noosha*, bad-thing. *Dhishta*, thing-to-eat. Want me to go on? There are only seventy-nine more of them."

Before anybody could stop him, the communication screen got itself into an uproar. The Fuzzies all ran over in front of it, and Jack switched it on. The caller was a man in gray semiformals; he had wavy gray hair and a face that looked like Juan Jimenez's twenty years from now.

"Good evening; Holloway here."

"Oh, Mr. Holloway, good evening." The caller shook hands with himself, turning on a dazzling smile. "I'm Leonard Kellogg, chief of the Company's science division. I just heard the tape you made about the——the Fuzzies?" He looked down at the floor. "Are these some of the animals?"

"These are the Fuzzies." He hoped it sounded like the correction it was intended to be. "Dr. Bennett Rainsford's here with me now, and so are Dr. Jimenez, Dr. van Riebeek and Dr. Ortheris." Out of the corner of his eye he could see Jimenez squirming as though afflicted with ants, van Riebeek getting his poker face battened down and Ben Rainsford suppressing a grin. "Some of us are out of screen range, and I'm sure you'll want to ask a lot of questions. Pardon us a moment, while we close in."

He ignored Kellogg's genial protest that that wouldn't be necessary until the chairs were placed facing the screen. As an afterthought, he handed Fuzzies around, giving Little Fuzzy to Ben, Ko-Ko to Gerd, Mitzi to Ruth, Mike to Jimenez and taking Mamma and Baby on his own lap.

Baby immediately started to climb up onto his head, as expected. It seemed to disconcert Kellogg, also as expected. He decided to teach Baby to thumb his nose when given some unobtrusive signal.

"Now, about that tape I recorded last evening," he began.

"Yes, Mr. Holloway." Kellogg's smile was getting more mechanical every minute. He was having trouble keeping his eyes off Baby. "I must say, I was simply astounded at the high order of intelligence claimed for these creatures."

"And you wanted to see how big a liar I was. I don't blame you; I had trouble believing it myself at first."

Kellogg gave a musically blithe laugh, showing even more dental equipment.

"Oh, no, Mr. Holloway; please don't misunderstand me. I never thought anything like that."

"I hope not," Ben Rainsford said, not too pleasantly. "I vouched for Mr. Holloway's statements, if you'll recall."

"Of course, Bennett; that goes without saying. Permit me to congratulate you upon a most remarkable scientific discovery. An entirely new order of mammals—"

"Which may be the ninth extrasolar sapient race," Rainsford added.

"Good heavens, Bennett!" Kellogg jettisoned his smile and slid on a look of shocked surprise. "You surely can't be serious?" He looked again at the Fuzzies, pulled the smile back on and gave a light laugh.

"I thought you'd heard that tape," Rainsford said.

"Of course, and the things reported were most remarkable. But sapience! Just because they've been taught a few tricks, and use sticks and stones for weapons—" He got rid of the smile again, and quick-changed to seriousness. "Such an extreme claim must only be made after careful study."

"Well, I won't claim they're sapient," Ruth Ortheris told him. "Not till day after tomorrow, at the earliest. But they very easily could be. They have learning and reasoning capacity equal to that of any eight-year-old Terran Human child, and well above that of the adults of some recognizedly sapient races. And they have not been taught tricks; they have learned by observation and reasoning."

"Well, Dr. Kellogg, mentation levels isn't my subject," Jimenez took it up, "but they do have all the physical characteristics shared by other sapient races—lower limbs specialized for locomotion and upper limbs for manipulation, erect posture, stereoscopic vision, color perception, erect posture, hand with opposing thumb—all the characteristics we consider as prerequisite to the development of sapience."

"I think they're sapient, myself," Gerd van Riebeek said, "but that's not as important as the fact that they're on the very threshold of sapience. This is the first race of this mental level anybody's ever seen. I believe that study of the

Fuzzies will help us solve the problem of how sapience developed in any race."

Kellogg had been laboring to pump up a head of enthusiasm; now he was ready to valve it off.

"But this is amazing! This will make scientific history! Now, of course, you all realize how pricelessly valuable these Fuzzies are. They must be brought at once to Mallorysport, where they can be studied under laboratory conditions by qualified psychologists, and—"

"No."

Jack lifted Baby Fuzzy off his head and handed him to Mamma, and set Mamma on the floor. That was reflex; the thinking part of his brain knew he didn't need to clear for action when arguing with the electronic image of a man twenty-five hundred miles away.

"Just forget that part of it and start over," he advised.

Kellogg ignored him. "Gerd, you have your airboat; fix up some nice comfortable cages—"

"Kellogg!"

The man in the screen stopped talking and stared in amazed indignation. It was the first time in years he had been addressed by his naked patronymic, and possibly the first time in his life he had been shouted at.

"Didn't you hear me the first time, Kellogg? Then stop gibbering about cages. These Fuzzies aren't being taken anywhere."

"But Mr. Holloway! Don't you realize that these little beings must be carefully studied? Don't you want them given their rightful place in the hierarchy of nature?"

"If you want to study them, come out here and do it. That's so long as you don't annoy them, or me. As far as study's concerned, they're being studied now. Dr. Rainsford's studying them, and so are three of your people, and when it comes to that, I'm studying them myself."

"And I'd like you to clarify that remark about qualified psychologists," Ruth Ortheris added, in a voice approaching zero-Kelvin. "You wouldn't be challenging my professional qualifications, would you?"

"Oh, Ruth, you know I didn't mean anything like that. Please don't misunderstand me," Kellogg begged. "But this is highly specialized work—"

"Yes; how many Fuzzy specialists have you at Science Center, Leonard?" Rainsford wanted to know. "The only one I can think of is Jack Holloway, here."

"Well, I'd thought of Dr. Mallin, the Company's head psychologist."

"He can come too, just as long as he understands that he'll have to have my permission for anything he wants to do with the Fuzzies," Jack said. "When can we expect you?"

Kellogg thought some time late the next afternoon. He didn't have to ask how to get to the camp. He made a few efforts to restore the conversation to its original note of cordiality, gave that up as a bad job and blanked out. There was a brief silence in the living room. Then Jimenez said reproachfully:

"You certainly weren't very gracious to Dr. Kellogg, Jack. Maybe you don't realize it, but he is a very important man."

"He isn't important to me, and I wasn't gracious to him at all. It doesn't pay to be gracious to people like that. If you are, they always try to take advantage of it."

"Why, I didn't know you knew Len," van Riebeek said.

"I never saw the individual before. The species is very common and widely distributed." He turned to Rainsford. "You think he and this Mallin will be out tomorrow?"

"Of course they will. This is a little too big for underlings and non-Company people to be allowed to monkey with. You know, we'll have to watch out or in a year we'll be hearing from Terra about the discovery of a sapient race on Zarathustra; *Fuzzy fuzzy Kellogg*. As Juan says, Dr. Kellogg is a very important man. That's how he got important."

6

THE RECORDED VOICE ceased; for a moment the record player hummed voicelessly. Loud in the silence, a photocell acted with a double click, opening one segment of the sun shielding and closing another at the opposite side of the dome. Space Commodore Alex Napier glanced up from his desk and out at the harshly angular landscape of Xerxes and the blackness of airless space beyond the disquieting close horizon. Then he picked up his pipe and knocked the heel out into the ashtray. Nobody said anything. He began packing tobacco into the bowl.

"Well, gentlemen?" He invited comment.

"Pancho?" Captain Conrad Greibenfeld, the Exec., turned to Lieutenant Ybarra, the chief psychologist.

"How reliable is this stuff?" Ybarra asked.

"Well, I knew Jack Holloway thirty years ago, on Fenris, when I was just an ensign. He must be past seventy now," he parenthesized. "If he says he saw anything, I'll believe it. And Bennett Rainsford's absolutely reliable, of course."

"How about the agent?" Ybarra insisted.

He and Stephen Aelborg, the Intelligence officer, exchanged glances. He nodded, and Aelborg said:

"One of the best. One of our own, lieutenant j.g., Naval Reserve. You don't need to worry about credibility, Pancho."

"They sound sapient to me," Ybarra said. "You know, this is something I've always been half hoping and half afraid would happen."

"You mean an excuse to intervene in that mess down there?" Greibenfeld asked.

Ybarra looked blankly at him for a moment. "No. No, I meant a case of borderline sapience; something our sacred talk-and-build-a-fire rule won't cover. Just how did this come to our attention, Stephen?"

"Well, it was transmitted to us from Contact Center in Mallorysport late Friday night. There seem to be a number of copies of this tape around; our agent got hold of one of them and transmitted it to Contact Center, and it was relayed on to us, with the agent's comments," Aelborg said. "Contact Center ordered a routine surveillance inside Company House and, to play safe, at the Residency. At the time, there seemed no reason to give the thing any beat-to-quarters-and-man-guns treatment, but we got a report on Saturday afternoon — Mallorysport time, that is — that Leonard Kellogg had played off the copy of the tape that Juan Jimenez had made for file, and had alerted Victor Grego immediately.

"Of course, Grego saw the implications at once. He sent Kellogg and the chief Company psychologist, Ernst Mallin, out to Beta Continent with orders to brand Rainsford's and Holloway's claims as a deliberate hoax. Then the Company intends to encourage the trapping of Fuzzies for their fur, in hopes that the whole species will be exterminated before anybody can get out from Terra to check on Rainsford's story."

"I hadn't heard that last detail before."

"Well, we can prove it," Aelborg assured him.

It sounded like a Victor Grego idea. He lit his pipe slowly. Damnit, he didn't want to have to intervene. No Space Navy C.O. did. Justifying intervention on a Colonial planet was too much bother — always a board of inquiry, often a court-martial. And supersession of civil authority was completely against Service Doctrine. Of course, there were other and more important tenets of Service Doctrine. The sovereignty of the Terran Federation for one, and the inviolability of the Federation Constitution. And the rights of extraterrestrials, too. Conrad Greibenfeld, too, seemed to have been thinking about that.

"If those Fuzzies are sapient beings, that whole setup down there is illegal, Company, Colonial administration and all," he said. "Zarathustra's a Class-IV planet, and that's all you can make out of it."

"We won't intervene unless we're forced to. Pancho, I think the decision will be largely up to you."

Pancho Ybarra was horrified.

"Good God, Alex! You can't mean that. Who am I? A nobody. All I have is an ordinary M.D., and a Psych. D. Why, the best psychological brains in the Federation—"

"Aren't on Zarathustra, Pancho. They're on Terra, five hundred light-years away, six months' ship voyage each way. Intervention, of course, is my responsibility, but the sapience question is yours. I don't envy you, but I can't relieve you of it."

• • •

Gerd van Riebeek's suggestion that all three of the visitors sleep aboard the airboat hadn't been treated seriously at all. Gerd himself was accommodated in the spare room of the living hut. Juan Jimenez went with Ben Rainsford to his camp for the night. Ruth Ortheris had the cabin of the boat to herself. Rainsford was on the screen next morning, while Jack and Gerd and Ruth and the Fuzzies were having breakfast; he and Jimenez had decided to take his airjeep and work down from the head of Cold Creek in the belief that there must be more Fuzzies around in the woods.

Both Gerd and Ruth decided to spend the morning at the camp and get acquainted with the Fuzzies on hand. The family had had enough breakfast to leave them neutral on the subject of land-prawns, and they were given another of the new toys, a big colored ball. They rolled it around in the grass for a while, decided to save it for their evening romp and took it into the house. Then they began playing aimlessly among some junk in the shed outside the workshop. Once in a while one of them would drift away to look for a prawn, more for sport than food.

Ruth and Gerd and Jack were sitting at the breakfast table on the grass, talking idly and trying to think of excuses for not washing the dishes. Mamma Fuzzy and Baby were poking about in the tall grass. Suddenly Mamma gave a shrill cry and started back for the shed, chasing Baby ahead of her and slapping him on the bottom with the flat of her chopper-digger to hurry him along.

Jack started for the house at a run. Gerd grabbed his camera and jumped up on the table. It was Ruth who saw the cause of the disturbance.

"Jack! Look, over there!" She pointed to the edge of the clearing. "Two strange Fuzzies!"

He kept on running, but instead of the rifle he had been going for, he collected his movie camera, two of the spare chopper-diggers and some Extee Three. When he emerged again, the two Fuzzies had come into the clearing and stood side by side, looking around. Both were females, and they both carried wooden prawn-killers.

"You have plenty of film?" he asked Gerd. "Here, Ruth; take this." He handed her his own camera. "Keep far enough away from me to get what I'm doing and what they're doing. I'm going to try to trade with them."

He went forward, the steel weapons in his hip pocket and the Extee Three in his hand, talking softly and soothingly to the newcomers. When he was as close to them as he could get without stampeding them, he stopped.

"Our gang's coming up behind you," Gerd told him. "Regular skirmish line; choppers at high port. Now they've stopped, about thirty feet behind you."

He broke off a piece of Extee Three, put it in his mouth and ate it. Then he broke off two more pieces and held them out. The two Fuzzies were tempted, but not to the point of rashness. He threw both pieces within a few feet of them. One darted forward, threw a piece to her companion and then snatched the other piece and ran back with it. They stood together, nibbling and making soft delighted noises.

His own family seemed to disapprove strenuously of this lavishing of delicacies upon outsiders. However, the two strangers decided that it would be safe to come closer, and soon he had them taking bits of field ration from his hand. Then he took the two steel chopper-diggers out of his pocket, and managed to convey the idea that he wanted to trade. The two strange Fuzzies were incredulously delighted. This was too much for his own tribe; they came up yeeking angrily.

The two strange females retreated a few steps, their new weapon ready. Everybody seemed to expect a fight, and nobody wanted one. From what he could remember of Old Terran history, this was a situation which could develop into serious trouble. Then Ko-Ko advanced, dragging his chopper-digger in an obviously pacific manner, and approached the two females, yeeking softly and touching the first one and then the other. Then he laid his weapon down and put his foot on it. The two females began stroking and caressing him.

Immediately the crisis evaporated. The others of the family came forward, stuck their weapons in the ground and began fondling the strangers. Then they all sat in circle, swaying their bodies rhythmically and making soft noises. Finally Ko-Ko and the two females rose, picked up their weapons and started for the woods.

"Jack, stop them," Ruth called out. "They're going away."

"If they want to go, I have no right to stop them."

When they were almost at the edge of the woods, Ko-Ko stopped, drove the point of his weapon into the ground and came running back to Pappy Jack, throwing his arms around the human knees and yeeking. Jack stooped and stroked him, but didn't try to pick him up. One of the two females pulled his chopper-digger out, and they both came back slowly. At the same time, Little Fuzzy, Mamma Fuzzy, Mike and Mitzi came running back. For a while, all the Fuzzies embraced one another, yeeking happily. Then they all trooped across the grass and went into the house.

"Get that all, Gerd?" he asked.

"On film, yes. That's the only way I did, though. What happened?"

"You have just made the first film of intertribal social and mating customs, Zarathustran Fuzzy. This is the family's home; they don't want any strange Fuzzies hanging around. They were going to run the girls off. Then Ko-Ko decided he liked their looks, and he decided he'd team up with them. That made everything different; the family sat down with them to tell them what a fine husband they were getting and to tell Ko-Ko good-bye. Then Ko-Ko remembered that he hadn't told me good-bye, and he came back. The family decided that two more Fuzzies wouldn't be in excess of the carrying capacity of this habitat, seeing what a good provider Pappy Jack is, so now I should imagine they're showing the girls the family treasures. You know, they married into a mighty well-to-do family."

The girls were named Goldilocks and Cinderella. When lunch was ready, they were all in the living room, with the viewscreen on; after lunch, the whole gang went into the bedroom for a nap on Pappy Jack's bed. He spent the afternoon developing movie film, while Gerd and Ruth wrote up the notes they had made the day before and collaborated on an account of the adoption. By late afternoon, when they were finished, the Fuzzies came out for a frolic and prawn hunt.

They all heard the aircar before any of the human people did, and they all ran over and climbed up on the bench beside the kitchen door. It was a constabulary cruise car; it landed, and a couple of troopers got out, saying that they'd stopped to see the Fuzzies. They wanted to know where the extras had come from, and when Jack told them, they looked at one another.

"Next gang that comes along, call us and keep them entertained till we can get here," one of them said. "We want some at the post, for prawns if nothing else."

"What's George's attitude?" he asked. "The other night, when he was here, he seemed half-scared of them."

"Aah, he's got over that," one of the troopers said. "He called Ben Rainsford; Ben said they were perfectly safe. Hey, Ben says they're not animals; they're people."

He started to tell them about some of the things the Fuzzies did. He was talking when the Fuzzies heard another aircar and called attention to it. This time, it was Ben Rainsford and Juan Jimenez. They piled out as soon as they were off contragravity, dragging cameras after them.

"Jack, there were Fuzzies all over the place up there," Rainsford began, while he was getting out. "All headed down this way; regular *Volkerwanderung*. We saw over fifty of them—four families, and individuals and pairs. I'm sure we missed ten for every one we saw."

"We better get up there with a car tomorrow," one of the troopers said. "Ben, just where were you?"

"I'll show you on the map." Then he saw Goldilocks and Cinderella. "Hey! Where'd you two girls come from? I never saw you around here before."

There was another clearing across the stream, with a log footbridge and path to the camp. Jack guided the big airboat down onto it, and put his airjeep alongside with the canopy up. There were two men on the forward deck of the boat, Kellogg and another man who would be Ernst Mallin. A third man came out of the control cabin after the boat was off contragravity. Jack didn't like Mallin. He had a tight, secretive face, with arrogance and bigotry showing underneath. The third man was younger. His face didn't show anything much, but his coat showed a bulge under the left arm. After being introduced by Kellogg, Mallin introduced him as Kurt Borch, his assistant.

Mallin had to introduce Borch again at the camp, not only to Ben Rainsford but also to van Riebeek, to Jimenez and even to Ruth Ortheris, which seemed a little odd. Ruth seemed to think so, too, and Mallin hastened to tell her that Borch was with Personnel, giving some kind of tests. That appeared to puzzle her even more. None of the three seemed happy about the presence of the constabulary troopers, either; they were all relieved when the cruise car lifted out.

Kellogg became interested in the Fuzzies immediately, squatting to examine them. He said something to Mallin, who compressed his lips and shook his head, saying:

"We simply cannot assume sapience until we find something in their behavior which cannot be explained under any other hypothesis. We would be much safer to assume nonsapience and proceed to test that assumption."

That seemed to establish the keynote. Kellogg straightened, and he and Mallin started one of those "of course I agree, doctor, but don't you find, on the other hand, that you must agree" sort of arguments, about the difference between scientific evidence and scientific proof. Jimenez got into it to the extent of agreeing with everything Kellogg said, and differing politely with everything Mallin said that he thought Kellogg would differ with. Borch said nothing; he just stood and looked at the Fuzzies with ill-concealed hostility. Gerd and Ruth decided to help getting dinner.

They ate outside on the picnic table, with the Fuzzies watching them interestedly. Kellogg and Mallin carefully avoided discussing them. It wasn't until after dusk, when the Fuzzies brought their ball inside and everybody was in the living room, that Kellogg, adopting a presiding-officer manner, got the conversation onto the subject. For some time, without giving anyone else an opportunity to say anything, he gushed about what an important discovery the Fuzzies were. The Fuzzies themselves ignored him and began dismantling the stick-and-ball construction. For a while Goldilocks and Cinderella watched interestedly, and then they began assisting.

"Unfortunately," Kellogg continued, so much of our data is in the form of uncorroborated statements by Mr. Holloway. Now, please don't misunderstand me. I don't, myself, doubt for a moment anything Mr. Holloway said on that tape, but you must realize that professional scientists are most reluctant to accept the unsubstantiated reports of what, if you'll pardon me, they think of as nonqualified observers."

"Oh, rubbish, Leonard!" Rainsford broke in impatiently. "I'm a professional scientist, of a good many more years' standing than you, and I accept Jack Holloway's statements. A frontiersman like Jack is a very careful and exact observer. People who aren't don't live long on frontier planets."

"Now, please don't misunderstand me," Kellogg reiterated. " I don't doubt Mr. Holloway's statements. I was just thinking of how they would be received on Terra."

"I shouldn't worry about that, Leonard. The Institute accepts my reports, and I'm vouching for Jack's reliability. I can substantiate most of what he told me from personal observation."

"Yes, and there's more than just verbal statements," Gerd van Riebeek chimed in. "A camera is not a nonqualified observer. We have quite a bit of film of the Fuzzies."

"Oh, yes; there was some mention of movies," Mallin said. "You don't have any of them developed yet, do you?"

"Quite a lot. Everything except what was taken out in the woods this afternoon. We can run them off right now."

He pulled down the screen in front of the gunrack, got the film and loaded his projector. The Fuzzies, who had begun on a new stick-and-ball construction, were irritated when the lights went out, then wildly excited when Little Fuzzy, digging a toilet pit with the wood chisel, appeared. Little Fuzzy in particular was excited about that; if he didn't recognize himself, he recognized the chisel. Then there were pictures of Little Fuzzy killing and eating land-prawns, Little Fuzzy taking the nut off the bolt and putting it on again, and pictures of the others, after they had come in, hunting and at play. Finally, there was the film of the adoption of Goldilocks and Cinderella.

"What Juan and I got this afternoon, up in the woods, isn't so good, I'm afraid," Rainsford said when the show was over and the lights were on again. "Mostly it's rear views disappearing into the brush. It was very hard to get close to them in the jeep. Their hearing is remarkably acute. But I'm sure the pictures we took this afternoon will show the things they were carrying—wooden prawn-killers like the two that were traded from the new ones in that last film."

Mallin and Kellogg looked at one another in what seemed oddly like consternation.

"You didn't tell us there were more of them around," Mallin said, as though it were an accusation of duplicity. He turned to Kellogg. "This alters the situation."

"Yes, indeed, Ernst," Kellogg burbled delightedly. "This is a wonderful opportunity. Mr. Holloway, I understand that all this country up here is your property, by land-grant purchase. That's right, isn't it? Well, would you allow us to camp on that clearing across the run, where our boat is now? We'll get prefab huts—Red Hill's the nearest town, isn't it?—and have a Company construction gang set them up for us, and we won't be any bother at all to you. We had only intended staying tonight on our boat, and returning to Mallorysport in the morning, but with all these Fuzzies swarming around in the woods, we can't think of leaving now. You don't have any objection, do you?"

He had lots of objections. The whole business was rapidly developing into an acute pain in the neck for him. But if he didn't let Kellogg camp across the run, the three of them could move seventy to eighty miles in any direction and be off his land. He knew what they'd do then. They'd live-trap or sleep-gas Fuzzies; they'd put them in cages, and torment them with maze and electric-shock experiments, and kill a few for dissection, or maybe not bother killing them first. On his own land, if they did anything like that, he could do something about it.

"Not at all. I'll have to remind you again, though, that you're to treat these little people with consideration."

"Oh, we won't do anything to your Fuzzies," Mallin said.

"You won't hurt any Fuzzies. Not more than once, anyhow."

THE NEXT MORNING, during breakfast, Kellogg and Kurt Borch put in an appearance, Borch wearing old clothes and field boots and carrying his pistol on his belt. They had a list of thing they thought they would need for their camp. Neither of them seemed to have more than the foggiest notion of camp requirements. Jack made some suggestions which they accepted. There was a lot of scientific equipment on the list, including an X-ray machine. He promptly ran a pencil line through that.

"We don't know what these Fuzzies' level of radiation tolerance is. We're not going to find out by overdosing one of my Fuzzies."

Somewhat to his surprise, neither of them gave him any argument. Gerd and Ruth and Kellogg borrowed his airjeep and started north; he and Borch went across the run to make measurements after Rainsford and Jimenez arrived and picked up Mallin. Borch took off soon after with the boat for Red Hill. Left alone, he loafed around the camp, and developed the rest of the movie film, making three copies of everything. Toward noon, Borch brought the boat back, followed by a couple of scowlike farmboats. In a few hours, the Company construction men from Red Hill had the new camp set up. Among other things, they brought two more airjeeps.

The two jeeps returned late in the afternoon, everybody excited. Between them, the parties had seen almost a hundred Fuzzies, and had found three camps, two among rocks and one in a hollow pool-ball tree. All three had been spotted by belts of filled-in toilet pits around them; two had been abandoned and the third was still occupied. Kellogg insisted on playing host to Jack and Rainsford for dinner at the camp across the run. The meal, because everything had been brought ready-cooked and only needed warming, was excellent.

Returning to his own camp with Rainsford, Jack found the Fuzzies finished with their evening meal and in the living room, starting a new construction—he could think of no other name for it—with the molecule-model balls and sticks. Goldilocks left the others and came over to him with a couple of balls fastened together, holding them up with one hand while she pulled his trouser leg with the other.

"Yes, I see, It's very beautiful," he told her.

She tugged harder and pointed at the thing the others were making. Finally, he understood.

"She wants me to work on it, too," he said. "Ben, you know where the coffee is; fix us a pot. I'm going to be busy here."

He sat down on the floor, and was putting sticks and balls together when Ben brought in the coffee. This was more fun than he'd had in a couple of days. He said so while Ben was distributing Extee Three to the Fuzzies.

"Yes, I ought to let you kick me all around the camp for getting this started," Rainsford said, pouring the coffee. "I could make some excuses, but they'd all sound like 'I didn't know it was loaded.'"

"Hell, I didn't know it was loaded, either." He rose and took his coffee cup, blowing on it to cool it. "What do you think Kellogg's up to, anyhow? That whole act he's been putting on since he came here is phony as a nine-sol bill."

"What I told you, evening before last," Rainsford said. "He doesn't want non-Company people making discoveries on Zarathustra. You notice how hard he and Mallin are straining to talk me out of sending a report back to Terra before he can investigate the Fuzzies? He wants to get his own report in first. Well, the hell with him! You know what I'm going to do? I'm going home, and I'm going to sit up all night getting a report into shape. Tomorrow morning I'm going to give it to George Lunt and let him send it to Mallorysport in the constabulary mail pouch. It'll be on a ship for Terra before any of this gang knows it's been sent. Do you have any copies of those movies you can spare?"

"About a mile and a half. I made copies of everything, even the stuff the others took."

"Good. We'll send that, too. Let Kellogg read about it in the papers a year from now." He thought for a moment, then said: "Gerd and Ruth and Juan are bunking at the other camp now; suppose I move in here with you tomorrow. I assume you don't want to leave the Fuzzies alone while that gang's here. I can help you keep an eye on them."

"But, Ben you don't want to drop whatever else you're doing—"

"What I'm doing, now, is learning to be a Fuzzyologist, and this is the only place I can do it. I'll see you tomorrow, after I stop at the constabulary post."

THE PEOPLE ACROSS the run—Kellogg, Mallin and Borch, and van Riebeek, Jimenez and Ruth Ortheris—were still up when Rainsford went out to his airjeep. After watching him lift out, Jack went back into the house, played with his family in the living room for a while and went to bed. The next morning he watched Kellogg, Ruth and Jimenez leave in one jeep and, shortly after, Mallin and van Riebeek in the other. Kellogg didn't seem to be willing to let the three who had come to the camp first wander around unchaperoned. He wondered about that.

Ben Rainsford's airjeep came over the mountains from the south in the late morning and settled onto the grass. Jack helped him inside with his luggage, and then they sat down under the big featherleaf trees to smoke their pipes and watch the Fuzzies playing in the grass. Occasionally they saw Kurt Borch pottering around outside the other camp.

"I sent the report off," Rainsford said, then looked at his watch. "It ought to be on the mail boat for Mallorysport by now; this time tomorrow it'll be in hyperspace for Terra. We won't say anything about it; just sit back and watch Len Kellogg and Ernst Mallin working up a sweat trying to talk us out of sending it." He chuckled. "I made a definite claim of sapience; by the time I got the report in shape to tape off, I couldn't see any other alternative."

"Damned if I can. You hear that, kids?" he asked Mike and Mitzi, who had come over in hope that there might be goodies for them. "Uncle Ben says you're sapient."

"Yeek?"

"They want to know if it's good to eat. What'll happen now?"

"Nothing, for about a year. Six months from now, when the ship gets in, the Institute will release it to the press, and then they'll send an investigation team here. So will any of the other universities or scientific institutes that may be

interested. I suppose the government'll send somebody, too. After all, subcivi-
lized natives on colonized planets are wards of the Terran Federation."

He didn't know that he liked that. The less he had to do with the government
the better, and his Fuzzies were wards of Pappy Jack Holloway. He said as
much.

Rainsford picked up Mitzi and stroked her. "Nice fur," he said. "Fur like that
would bring good prices. It will, if we don't get these people recognized as
sapient beings."

He looked across the run at the new camp and wondered. Maybe Leonard
Kellogg saw that, too, and saw profits for the Company in Fuzzy fur.

The airjeeps returned in the middle of the afternoon, first Mallin's, and then
Kellogg's. Everybody went inside. An hour later, a constabulary car landed in
front of the Kellogg camp. George Lunt and Ahmed Khadra got out. Kellogg
came outside, spoke with them and then took them into the main living hut. Half
an hour later, the lieutenant and the trooper emerged, lifted their car across the
run and set it down on the lawn. The Fuzzies ran to meet them, possibly
expecting more whistles, and followed them into the living room. Lunt and
Khadra took off their berets, but made no move to unbuckle their gun belts.

"We got your package off all right, Ben," Lunt said. He sat down and took
Goldilocks on his lap; immediately Cinderella jumped up, also. "Jack, what the
hell's that gang over there up to anyhow?"

"You got that, too?"

"You can smell it on them for a mile, against the wind. In the first place, that
Borch. I wish I could get his prints; I'll bet we have them on file. And the whole
gang's trying to hide something, and what they're trying to hide is something
they're scared of, like a body in a closet. When we were over there, Kellogg did
all the talking; anybody else who tried to say anything got shut up fast. Kellogg
doesn't like you, Jack, and he doesn't like Ben, and he doesn't like the Fuzzies.
Most of all he doesn't like the Fuzzies."

"Well, I told you what I thought this morning," Rainsford said. "They don't
want outsiders discovering things on this planet. It wouldn't make them look
good to the home office on Terra. Remember, it was some non-Company people
who discovered the first sunstones, back in 'Forty-eight."

George Lunt looked thoughtful. On him, it was a scowl.

"I don't think that's it, Ben. When we were talking to him, he admitted very
freely that you and Jack discovered the Fuzzies. The way he talked, he didn't
seem to think they were worth discovering at all. And he asked a lot of funny
questions about you, Jack. The kind of questions I'd ask if I was checking up on
somebody's mental competence." The scowl became one of anger now. "By
God, I wish I had an excuse to question him—with a veridicator!"

Kellogg didn't want the Fuzzies to be sapient beings. If they weren't they'd be . . . fur-bearing animals. Jack thought of some overfed society dowager on Terra or Baldur, wearing the skins of Little Fuzzy and Mamma Fuzzy and Mike and Mitzi and Ko-Ko and Cinderella and Goldilocks wrapped around her adipose carcass. It made him feel sick.

7

TUESDAY DAWNED HOT and windless, a scarlet sun coming up in a hard, brassy sky. The Fuzzies, who were in to wake Pappy Jack with their whistles, didn't like it; they were edgy and restless. Maybe it would rain today after all. They had breakfast outside on the picnic table, and then Ben decided he'd go back to his camp and pick up a few things he hadn't brought and now decided he needed.

"My hunting rifle's one," he said, "and I think I'll circle down to the edge of the brush country and see if I can pick off a zebralope. We ought to have some more fresh meat."

So, after eating, Rainsford got into his jeep and lifted away. Across the run, Kellogg and Mallin were walking back and forth in front of the camp, talking earnestly. When Ruth Ortheris and Gerd van Riebeek came out, they stopped, broke off their conversation and spoke briefly with them. Then Gerd and Ruth crossed the footbridge and came up the path together.

The Fuzzies had scattered, by this time, to hunt prawns. Little Fuzzy and Ko-Ko and Goldilocks ran to meet them; Ruth picked Goldilocks up and carried her, and Ko-Ko and Little Fuzzy ran on ahead. They greeted Jack, declining coffee; Ruth sat down in a chair with Goldilocks, Little Fuzzy jumped up on the table and began looking for goodies, and when Gerd stretched out on his back on the grass Ko-Ko sat down on his chest.

"Goldilocks is my favorite Fuzzy," Ruth was saying. "She is the sweetest thing. Of course, they're all pretty nice. I can't get over how affectionate and trusting they are; the ones we saw out in the woods were so timid."

"Well, the ones out in the woods don't have any Pappy Jack to look after them," Gerd said. "I'd imagine they're very affectionate among themselves, but they have so many things to be afraid of. You know, there's another prerequisite for sapience. It develops in some small, relatively defenseless, animal surrounded by large and dangerous enemies he can't outrun or outfight. So, to survive, he has to learn to outthink them. Like our own remote ancestors, or like Little Fuzzy; he had his choice of getting sapient or getting exterminated."

Ruth seemed troubled. "Gerd, Dr. Mallin has found absolutely nothing about them that indicates true sapience."

"Oh, Mallin be bloodied; he doesn't know what sapience is any more than I do. And a good deal less than you do, I'd say. I think he's trying to prove that the Fuzzies aren't sapient."

Ruth looked startled. "What makes you say that?"

"It's been sticking out all over him ever since he came here. You're a psychologist; don't tell me you haven't seen it. Maybe if the Fuzzies were proven sapient it would invalidate some theory he's gotten out of a book, and he'd have to do some thinking for himself. He wouldn't like that. But you have to admit he's been fighting the idea, intellectually and emotionally, right from the start. Why, they could sit down with pencils and slide rules and start working differential calculus and it wouldn't convince him."

"Dr. Mallin's trying to—" she began angrily. Then she broke it off. "Jack, excuse us. We didn't really come over here to have a fight. We came to meet some Fuzzies. Didn't we, Goldilocks?"

Goldilocks was playing with the silver charm on the chain around her neck, holding it to her ear and shaking it to make it tinkle, making small delighted sounds. Finally she held it up and said, "Yeek?"

"Yes, sweetie-pie, you can have it." Ruth took the chain from around her neck and put it over Goldilocks' head; she had to loop it three times before it would fit. "There now; that's your very own."

"Oh, you mustn't give her things like that."

"Why not. It's just cheap trade-junk. You've been on Loki, Jack, you know what it is." He did; he'd traded stuff like that to the natives himself. "Some of the girls at the hospital there gave it to me for a joke. I only wear it because I have it. Goldilocks likes it a lot better than I do."

An airjeep rose from the other side and floated across. Juan Jimenez was piloting it; Ernst Mallin stuck his head out the window on the right, asked her if she were ready and told Gerd that Kellogg would pick him up in a few minutes. After she had gotten into the jeep and it had lifted out, Gerd put Ko-Ko off his chest and sat up, getting cigarettes from his shirt pocket.

"I don't know what the devil's gotten into her," he said, watching the jeep vanish. "Oh, yes, I do. She's gotten the Word from On High. Kellogg hath spoken. Fuzzies are just silly little animals," he said bitterly.

"You work for Kellogg, too, don't you?"

"Yes. He doesn't dictate my professional opinion, though. You know, I thought, in the evil hour when I took this job—" He rose to his feet, hitching his belt to balance the weight of the pistol on the right against the camera-binoculars on the left, and changed the subject abruptly. "Jack, has Ben Rainsford sent a report on the Fuzzies to the Institute yet?" he asked.

"Why?"

"If he hasn't, tell him to hurry up and get one in."

There wasn't time to go into that further. Kellogg's jeep was rising from the camp across the run and approaching.

He decided to let the breakfast dishes go till after lunch. Kurt Borch had stayed behind at the Kellogg camp, so he kept an eye on the Fuzzies and brought them back when they started to stray toward the footbridge. Ben Rainsford hadn't returned by lunchtime, but zebralope hunting took a little time, even from the air. While he was eating, outside, one of the rented airjeeps returned from the northeast in a hurry, disgorging Ernst Mallin, Juan Jimenez and Ruth Ortheris. Kurt Borch came hurrying out; they talked for a few minutes, and then they all went inside. A little later, the second jeep came in, even faster, and landed; Kellogg and van Riebeek hastened into the living hut. There wasn't anything more to see. He carried the dishes into the kitchen and washed them, and the Fuzzies went into the bedroom for their nap.

He was sitting at the table in the living room when Gerd van Riebeek knocked on the open door.

"Jack, can I talk to you for a minute?" he asked.

"Sure. Come in."

Van Riebeek entered, unbuckling his gun belt. He shifted a chair so that he could see the door from it, and laid the belt on the floor at his feet when he sat down. Then he began to curse Leonard Kellogg in four or five languages.

"Well, I agree, in principle; why in particular, though?"

"You know what that son of a Kooghra's doing?" Gerd asked. "He and that—" He used a couple of Sheshan words, viler than anything in Lingua Terra. "—that quack headshrinker, Mallin, are preparing a report, accusing you and Ben Rainsford of perpetrating a deliberate scientific hoax. You taught the Fuzzies some tricks; you and Rainsford, between you, made those artifacts yourselves and the two of you are conspiring to foist the Fuzzies off as sapient beings. Jack, if it weren't so goddamn stinking contemptible, it would be the biggest joke of the century!"

"I take it they wanted you to sign this report, too?"

"Yes, and I told Kellogg he could—" What Kellogg could do, it seemed, was both appalling and physiologically impossible. He cursed again, and then lit a cigarette and got hold of himself. "Here's what happened. Kellogg and I went up that stream, about twenty miles down Cold Creek, the one you've been working on, and up onto the high flat to a spring and a stream that flows down in the opposite direction. Know where I mean? Well, we found where some Fuzzies had been camping, among a lot of fallen timber. And we found a little grave, where the Fuzzies had buried one of their people."

He should have expected something like that, and yet it startled him. "You mean, they bury their dead? What was the grave like?"

"A little stone cairn, about a foot and a half by three, a foot high. Kellogg said it was just a big toilet pit, but I was sure of what it was. I opened it. Stones under the cairn, and then filled-in earth, and then a dead Fuzzy wrapped in grass. A female; she'd been mangled by something, maybe a bush-goblin. And get this Jack; they'd buried her prawn-stick with her."

"They bury their dead! What was Kellogg doing, while you were opening the grave?"

"Dithering around having ants. I'd been taking snaps of the grave, and I was burbling away like an ass about how important this was and how it was positive proof of sapience, and he was insisting that we get back to camp at once. He called the other jeep and told Mallin to get to camp immediately, and Mallin and Ruth and Juan were there when we got in. As soon as Kellogg told them what we'd found, Mallin turned fish-belly white and wanted to know how we were going to suppress it. I asked him if he was nuts, and then Kellogg came out with it. They don't dare let the Fuzzies be proven sapient."

"Because the Company wants to sell Fuzzy furs?"

Van Riebeek looked at him in surprise. "I never thought of that. I doubt if they did, either. No. Because if the Fuzzies are sapient beings, the Company's charter is automatically void."

This time Jack cursed, not Kellogg but himself.

"I am a senile old dotard! Good Lord, I know colonial law; I've been skating on the edge of it on more planets than you're years old. And I never thought of that; why, of course it would. Where are you now, with the Company, by the way?"

"Out, but I couldn't care less. I have enough in the bank for the trip back to Terra, not counting what I can raise on my boat and some other things. Xeno-naturalists don't need to worry about finding jobs. There's Ben's outfit, for instance. And, brother, when I get back to Terra, what I'll spill about this deal!"

"If you get back. If you don't have an accident before you get on the ship." He thought for a moment. "Know anything about geology?"

"Why, some; I have to work with fossils. I'm as much a paleonotologist as a zoologist. Why?"

"How'd you like to stay here with me and hunt fossil jellyfish for a while? We won't make twice as much, together, as I'm making now, but you can look one way while I'm looking the other, and we may both stay alive longer that way."

"You mean that, Jack?"

"I said it, didn't I?"

Van Riebeek rose and held out his hand; Jack came around the table and shook it. Then he reached back and picked up his belt, putting it on.

"Better put yours on, too, partner. Borch is probably the only one we'll need a gun for, but—"

Van Riebeek buckled on his belt, then drew his pistol and worked the slide to load the chamber. "What are we going to do?" he asked.

"Well, we're going to try to handle it legally. Fact is, I'm even going to call the cops."

He punched out a combination on the communication screen. It lighted and opened a window into the constabulary post. The sergeant who looked out of it recognized him and grinned.

"Hi, Jack. How's the family?" he asked. "I'm coming up, one of these evenings, to see them."

"You can see some now." Ko-Ko and Goldilocks and Cinderella were coming out of the hall from the bedroom; he gathered them up and put them on the table. The sergeant was fascinated. Then he must have noticed that both Jack and Gerd were wearing their guns in the house. His eyes narrowed slightly.

"You got problems, Jack?" he asked.

"Little ones; they may grow, though. I have some guests here who have outstayed their welcome. For the record, better make it that I have squatters I want evicted. If there were a couple of blue uniforms around, maybe it might save me the price of a few cartridges."

"I read you. George was mentioning that you might regret inviting that gang to camp on you." He picked up a handphone. "Calderon to Car Three," he said. "Do you read me, Three? Well, Jack Holloway's got a little squatter trouble. Yeah; that's it. He's ordering them off his grant, and he thinks they might try to give him an argument. Yeah, sure, Peace Lovin' Jack Holloway, that's him. Well, go chase his squatters for him, and if they give you anything about being Company big wheels, we don't care what kind of wheels they are, just so's they start rolling." He replaced the phone. "Look for them in about an hour, Jack."

"Why, thanks, Phil. Drop in some evening when you can hang up your gun and stay awhile."

He blanked the screen and began punching again. This time he got a girl, and then the Company construction boss at Red Hill.

"Oh, hello, Jack; is Dr. Kellogg comfortable?"

"Not very. He's moving out this afternoon. I wish you'd have your gang come up with those scows and get that stuff out of my backyard."

"Well, he told us he was staying for a couple of weeks."

"He got his mind changed for him. He's to be off my land by sunset."

The Company man looked troubled. "Jack, you haven't been having trouble with Dr. Kellogg, have you?" he asked. "He's a big man with the Company."

"That's what he tells me. You'll still have to come and get that stuff, though."

He blanked the screen. "You know," he said, "I think it would be no more than fair to let Kellogg in on this. What's his screen combination?"

Gerd supplied it, and he punched it out. One of those tricky special Company combinations. Kurt Borch appeared in the screen immediately.

"I want to talk to Kellogg."

"*Doctor* Kellogg is very busy, at present."

"He's going to be a damned sight busier; this is moving day. The whole gang of you have till eighteen hundred to get off my grant."

Borch was shoved aside, and Kellogg appeared. "What's this nonsense?" he demanded angrily.

"You're ordered to move. You want to know why? I can let Gerd van Riebeek talk to you; I think there are a few things he's forgotten to call you."

"You can't order us out like this. Why, you gave us permission—"

"Permission cancelled. I've called Mike Hennen in Red Hill; he's sending his scows back for the stuff he brought here. Lieutenant Lunt will have a couple of troopers here, too. I'll expect you to have your personal things aboard your airboat when they arrive."

He blanked the screen while Kellogg was trying to tell him that it was all a misunderstanding.

"I think that's everything. It's quite a while till sundown," he added, "but I move for suspension of rules while we pour a small libation to sprinkle our new partnership. Then we can go outside and observe the enemy."

There was no observable enemy action when they went out and sat down on the bench by the kitchen door. Kellogg would be screening Mike Hennen and the constabulary post for verification, and there would be a lot of gathering up and packing to do. Finally, Kurt Borch emerged with a contragravity lifter piled with boxes and luggage, and Jimenez walking beside to steady the load. Jimenez climbed up onto the airboat and Borch floated the load up to him and then went back into the huts. This was repeated several times. In the meantime, Kellogg and Mallin seemed to be having some sort of exchange of recriminations in front. Ruth Ortheris came out, carrying a briefcase, and sat down on the edge of a table under the awning.

Neither of them had been watching the Fuzzies, until they saw one of them start down the path toward the footbridge, a glint of silver at the throat identifying Goldilocks.

"Look at that fool kid; you stay put, Gerd, and I'll bring her back."

He started down the path; by the time he had reached the bridge, Goldilocks was across and had vanished behind one of the airjeeps parked in front of the Kellogg camp. When he was across and within twenty feet of the vehicle, he heard a sound he had never heard before—a shrill, thin shriek, like a file on saw teeth. At the same time, Ruth's voice screamed.

"Don't! Leonard, stop that!"

As he ran around the jeep, the shrieking broke off suddenly. Goldilocks was on the ground, her fur reddened. Kellogg stood over her, one foot raised. He was wearing white shoes, and they were both spotted with blood. He stamped the foot down on the little bleeding body, and then Jack was within reach of him, and something crunched under the fist he drove into Kellogg's face. Kellogg staggered and tried to raise his hands; he made a strangled noise, and for an instant the idiotic thought crossed Jack's mind that he was trying to say, "Now, please don't misunderstand me." He caught Kellogg's shirt front in his left hand, and punched him again in the face, and again, and again. He didn't know how many times he punched Kellogg before he heard Ruth Ortheris' voice:

"Jack! Watch out! Behind you!"

He let go of Kellogg's shirt and jumped aside, turning and reaching for his gun. Kurt Borch, twenty feet away, had a pistol drawn and pointed at him.

His first shot went off as soon as the pistol was clear of the holster. He fired the second while it was still recoiling; there was a spot of red on Borch's shirt that gave him an aiming point for the third. Borch dropped the pistol he hadn't been able to fire, and started folding at the knees and then at the waist. He went down in a heap on his face.

Behind him, Gerd van Riebeek's voice was saying, "Hold it, all of you; get your hands up. You, too, Kellogg."

Kellogg, who had fallen, pushed himself erect. Blood was gushing from his nose, and he tried to stanch it on the sleeve of his jacket. As he stumbled toward his companions, he blundered into Ruth Ortheris, who pushed him angrily away from her. Then she went to the little crushed body, dropping to her knees beside it and touching it. The silver charm bell on the neck chain jingled faintly. Ruth began to cry.

Juan Jimenez had climbed down from the airboat; he was looking at the body of Kurt Borch in horror.

"You killed him!" he accused. A moment later, he changed that to "murdered." Then he started to run toward the living hut.

Gerd van Riebeek fired a bullet into the ground ahead of him, bringing him up short.

"You'll stop the next one, Juan," he said. "Go help Dr. Kellogg; he got himself hurt."

"Call the constabulary," Mallin was saying. "Ruth, you go; they won't shoot at you."

"Don't bother. I called them. Remember?"

Jimenez had gotten a wad of handkerchief tissue out of his pocket and was trying to stop his superior's nosebleed. Through it, Kellogg was trying to tell Mallin that he hadn't been able to help it.

"The little beast attacked me; it cut me with that spear it was carrying."

Ruth Ortheris looked up. The other Fuzzies were with her by the body of Goldilocks; they must have come as soon as they had heard the screaming.

"She came up to him and pulled at his trouser leg, the way they all do when they want to attract your attention," she said. "She wanted him to look at her new jingle." Her voice broke, and it was a moment before she could recover it. "And he kicked her, and then stamped her to death."

"Ruth, keep your mouth shut!" Mallin ordered. "The thing attacked Leonard; it might have given him a serious wound."

"It did!" Still holding the wad of tissue to his nose with one hand, Kellogg pulled up his trouser leg with the other and showed a scar on his shin. It looked like a briar scratch. "You saw it yourself."

"Yes, I saw it. I saw you kick her and jump on her. And all she wanted was to show you her new jingle."

Jack was beginning to regret that he hadn't shot Kellogg as soon as he saw what was going on. The other Fuzzies had been trying to get Goldilocks onto her feet. When they realized that it was no use, they let the body down again and crouched in a circle around it, making soft, lamenting sounds.

"Well, when the constabulary get here, you keep quiet," Mallin was saying. "Let me do the talking."

"Intimidating witnesses, Mallin?" Gerd inquired. "Don't you know everybody'll have to testify at the constabulary post under veridication? And you're drawing pay for being a psychologist, too." Then he saw some of the Fuzzies raise their heads and look toward the southeastern horizon. "Here come the cops, now."

However, it was Ben Rainsford's airjeep, with a zebralope carcass lashed along one side. It circled the Kellogg camp and then let down quickly; Rainsford jumped out as soon as it was grounded, his pistol drawn.

"What happened, Jack?" he asked, then glanced around, from Goldilocks to Kellogg to Borch to the pistol beside Borch's body. "I get it. Last time anybody pulled a gun on you, they called it suicide."

"That's what this was, more or less. You have a movie camera in your jeep? Well, get some shots of Borch, and some of Goldilocks. Then stand by, and if the Fuzzies start doing anything different, get it all. I don't think you'll be disappointed."

Rainsford looked puzzled, but he holstered his pistol and went back to his jeep, returning with a camera. Mallin began insisting that, as a licensed M.D., he had a right to treat Kellogg's injuries. Gerd van Riebeek followed him into the living hut for a first-aid kit. They were just emerging, van Riebeek's automatic in the small of Mallin's back, when a constabulary car grounded beside Rainsford's airjeep. It wasn't Car Three. George Lunt jumped out, unsnapping the flap of his holster, while Ahmed Khadra was talking into the radio.

"What's happened, Jack? Why didn't you wait till we got here?"

"This maniac assaulted me and murdered that man over there!" Kellogg began vociferating.

"Is your name Jack, too?" Lunt demanded.

"My name's Leonard Kellogg, and I'm a chief of division with the Company—"

"Then keep quiet till I ask you something. Ahmed, call the post; get Knabber and Yorimitsu, with investigative equipment, and find out what's tying up Car Three."

Mallin had opened the first-aid kit by now; Gerd, on seeing the constabulary, had holstered his pistol. Kellogg, still holding the sodden tissues to his nose, was wanting to know what there was to investigate.

"There's the murderer; you have him red-handed. Why don't you arrest him?"

"Jack, let's get over where we can watch these people without having to listen to them," Lunt said. He glanced toward the body of Goldilocks. "That happen first?"

"Watch out, Lieutenant! He still has his pistol!" Mallin shouted warningly.

They went over and sat down on the contragravity-field generator housing one of the rented airjeeps. Jack started with Gerd van Riebeek's visit immediately after noon.

"Yes, I thought of that angle myself," Lunt said disgustedly. "I didn't think of it till this morning, though, and I didn't think things would blow up as fast as this. Hell, I just didn't think! Well, go on."

He interrupted a little later to ask: "Kellogg was stamping on the Fuzzy when you hit him. You were trying to stop him?"

"That's right. You can veridicate me on that if you want to."

"I will; I'll veridicate this whole damn gang. And this guy Borch had his heater out when you turned around? Nothing to it, Jack. We'll have to have some kind of a hearing, but it's just plain self-defense. Think any of this gang will tell the truth here, without taking them in and putting them under veridication?"

"Ruth Ortheris will, I think."

"Send her over here, will you."

She was still with the Fuzzies, and Ben Rainsford was standing beside her, his camera ready. The Fuzzies were still swaying and yeeking plaintively. She nodded and rose without speaking, going over to where Lunt waited.

"Just what did happen, Jack?" Rainsford wanted to know. "And whose side is he on?" He nodded toward van Riebeek, standing guard over Kellogg and Mallin, his thumbs in his pistol belt.

"Ours. He's quit the Company."

Just as he was finishing, Car Three put in an appearance; he had to tell the same story over again. The area in front of the Kellogg camp was getting congested; he hoped Mike Hennen's labor gang would stay away for a while. Lunt talked to van Riebeek when he had finished with Ruth, and then with Jimenez and Mallin and Kellogg. Then he and one of the men from Car Three came over to where Jack and Rainsford were standing. Gerd van Riebeek joined them just as Lunt was saying:

"Jack, Kellogg's made a murder complaint against you. I told him it was self-defense, but he wouldn't listen. So, according to the book, I have to arrest you."

"All right." He unbuckled his gun and handed it over. "Now, George, I herewith make complaint and accusation against Leonard Kellogg, charging him with the unlawful and unjustified killing of a sapient being, to wit, an aboriginal native of the planet of Zarathustra commonly known as Goldilocks."

Lunt looked at the small battered body and the six mourners around it.

"But, Jack, they aren't legally sapient beings."

"There is no such thing. A sapient being is a being on the mental level of sapience, not a being that has been declared sapient."

"Fuzzies are sapient beings," Rainsford said. "That's the opinion of a qualified xeno-naturalist."

"Two of them," Gerd van Riebeek said. "That is the body of a sapient being. There's the man who killed her. Go ahead, Lieutenant, make your pinch."

"Hey! Wait a minute!"

The Fuzzies were rising, sliding their chopper-diggers under the body of Goldilocks and lifting it on the steel shafts. Ben Rainsford was aiming his camera as Cinderella picked up her sister's weapon and followed, carrying it; the others carried the body toward the far corner of the clearing, away from the camp. Rainsford kept just behind them, pausing to photograph and then hurrying to keep up with them.

They set the body down. Mike and Mitzi and Cinderella began digging; the others scattered to hunt for stones. Coming up behind them, George Lunt took off his beret and stood holding it in both hands; he bowed his head as the grass-wrapped body was placed in the little grave and covered.

Then, when the cairn was finished, he replaced it, drew his pistol and checked the chamber.

"That does it, Jack," he said. "I am now going to arrest Leonard Kellogg for the murder of a sapient being."

8

JACK HOLLOWAY HAD been out on bail before, but never for quite so much. It was almost worth it, though, to see Leslie Coombes's eyes widen and Mohammed Ali O'Brien's jaw drop when he dumped the bag of sunstones, blazing with the heat of the day and of his body, on George Lunt's magisterial bench and invited George to pick out twenty-five thousand sols' worth. Especially after the production Coombes had made of posting Kellogg's bail with one of those precertified Company checks.

He looked at the whisky bottle in his hand, and then reached into the cupboard for another one. One for Gus Brannhard, and one for the rest of them. There was a widespread belief that that was why Gustavus Adolphus Brannhard was practicing sporadic law out here in the boon docks of a boon-dock planet, defending gun fighters and veldbeest rustlers. It wasn't. Nobody on Zarathustra knew the reason, but it wasn't whisky. Whisky was only the weapon with which Gus Brannhard fought off the memory of the reason.

He was in the biggest chair in the living room, which was none too ample for him; a mountain of a man with tousled gray-brown hair, his broad face masked in a tangle of gray-brown beard. He wore a faded and grimy bush jacket with clips of rifle cartridges on the breast, no shirt and a torn undershirt over a shag of gray-brown chest hair. Between the bottoms of his shorts and the tops of his ragged hose and muddy boots, his legs were covered with hair. Baby Fuzzy was sitting on his head, and Mamma Fuzzy was on his lap. Mike and Mitzi sat one on either knee. The Fuzzies had taken instantly to Gus. Bet they thought he was a Big Fuzzy.

"Aaaah!" he rumbled, as the bottle and glass were placed beside him. "Been staying alive for hours hoping for this."

"Well, don't let any of the kids get at it. Little Fuzzy trying to smoke pipes is bad enough; I don't want any dipsos in the family, too."

Gus filled the glass. To be on the safe side, he promptly emptied it into himself.

"You got a nice family, Jack. Make a wonderful impression in court—as long as Baby doesn't try to sit on the judge's head. Any jury that sees them and hears that Ortheris girl's story will acquit you from the box, with a vote of censure for not shooting Kellogg, too."

"I'm not worried about that. What I want is Kellogg convicted."

"You better worry, Jack," Rainsford said. "You saw the combination against us at the hearing."

Leslie Coombes, the Company's top attorney, had come out from Mallorysport in a yacht rated at Mach 6, and he must have crowded it to the limit all the way. With him, almost on a leash, had come Mohammed Ali O'Brien, the Colonial Attorney General, who doubled as Chief Prosecutor. They had both tried to get the whole thing dismissed—self-defense for Holloway, and killing an unprotected wild animal for Kellogg. When that had failed, they had teamed in flagrant collusion to fight the inclusion of any evidence about the Fuzzies. After all it was only a complaint court; Lieutenant Lunt, as a police magistrate, had only the most limited powers.

"You saw how far they got, didn't you?"

"I hope we don't wish they'd succeeded," Rainsford said gloomily.

"What do you mean, Ben?" Brannhard asked. "What do you think they'll do?"

"I don't know. That's what worries me. We're threatening the Zarathustra Company, and the Company's too big to be threatened safely," Rainsford replied. "They'll try to frame something on Jack."

"With veridication? That's ridiculous, Ben."

"Don't you think we can prove sapience?" Gerd van Riebeek demanded.

"Who's going to define sapience? And how?" Rainsford asked. "Why, between them, Coombes and O'Brien can even agree to accept the talk-and-build-a-fire rule."

"Huh-uh!" Brannhard was positive. "Court ruling on that, about forty years ago, on Vishnu. Infanticide case, woman charged with murder in the death of her infant child. Her lawyer moved for dismissal on the grounds that murder is defined as the killing of a sapient being, a sapient being is defined as one that can talk and build a fire, and a newborn infant can do neither. Motion denied; the court ruled that while ability to speak and produce fire is positive proof of sapience, inability to do either or both does not constitute legal proof of nonsapience. If O'Brien doesn't know that, and I doubt if he does, Coombes will." Brannhard poured another drink and gulped it before the sapient beings around him could get at it. "You know what? I will make a small wager, and I will even give odds, that the first thing Ham O'Brien does when he gets back to Mallorysport will be to enter *nolle prosequi* on both charges. What I'd like would be for him to *nol. pros.* Kellogg and let the charge against Jack go to court. He would be dumb enough to do that himself, but Leslie Coombes wouldn't let him."

"But if he throws out the Kellogg case, that's it," Gerd van Riebeek said. "When Jack comes to trial, nobody'll say a mumblin' word about sapience."

"I will, and I will not mumble it. You all know colonial law on homicide. In the case of any person killed while in commission of a felony, no prosecution may be brought in any degree, against anybody. I'm going to contend that Leonard Kellogg was murdering a sapient being, that Jack Holloway acted lawfully in attempting to stop it and that when Kurt Borch attempted to come to Kellogg's assistance he, himself, was guilty of felony, and consequently any prosecution against Jack Holloway is illegal. And to make that contention stick, I shall have to say a great many words, and produce a great deal of testimony, about the sapience of Fuzzies."

"It'll have to be expert testimony," Rainsford said. "The testimony of psychologists. I suppose you know that the only psychologists on this planet are employed by the chartered Zarathustra Company." He drank what was left of his highball, looked at the bits of ice in the bottom of his glass and then rose to mix another one. "I'd have done the same as you did, Jack, but I still wish this hadn't happened."

"*Huh!*" Mamma Fuzzy looked up, startled by the exclamation. "What do you think Victor Grego's wishing, right now?"

VICTOR GREGO REPLACED the hand-phone. "Leslie, on the yacht," he said. "They're coming in now. They'll stop at the hospital to drop Kellogg, and then they're coming here."

Nick Emmert nibbled a canape. He had reddish hair, pale eyes and a wide, bovine face.

"Holloway must have done him up pretty badly," he said.

"I wish Holloway'd killed him!" He blurted it angrily, and saw the Resident General's shocked expression.

"You don't really mean that, Victor?"

"The devil I don't! He gestured at the recorder-player, which had just finished the tape of the hearing, transmitted from the yacht at sixty-speed. "That's only a teaser to what'll come out at the trial. You know what the Company's epitaph will be? *Kicked to death, along with a Fuzzy, by Leonard Kellogg.*"

Everything would have worked out perfectly if Kellogg had only kept his head and avoided collision with Holloway. Why, even the killing of the Fuzzy and the shooting of Borch, inexcusable as that had been, wouldn't have been so bad if it hadn't been for that asinine murder complaint. That was what had provoked Holloway's countercomplaint, which was what had done the damage.

And, now that he thought of it, it had been one of Kellogg's people, van Riebeek, who had touched off the explosion in the first place. He didn't know van Riebeek himself, but Kellogg should have, and he had handled him the wrong way. He should have known what van Riebeek would go along with and what he wouldn't.

"But, Victor, they won't convict Leonard of murder," Emmert was saying. "Not for killing one of those little things."

"'Murder shall consist of the deliberate and unjustified killing of any sapient being, of any race,'" he quoted. "That's the law. If they can prove in court that the Fuzzies are sapient beings . . ."

Then, some morning, a couple of deputy marshals would take Leonard Kellogg out in the jail yard and put a bullet through the back of his head, which, in itself, would be no loss. The trouble was, they would also be shooting an irreparable hole in the Zarathustra Company's charter. Maybe Kellogg could be kept out of that court, at that. There wasn't a ship blasted off from Darius without a couple of drunken spacemen being hustled aboard at the last moment; with the job Holloway must have done, Kellogg should look just right as a drunken spaceman. The twenty-five thousand sols' bond could be written off; that was pennies to the Company. No, that would still leave them stuck with the Holloway trial.

"You want me out of here when the others come, Victor?" Emmert asked, popping another canape into his mouth.

"No, no; sit still. This will be the last chance we'll have to get everybody together; after this, we'll have to avoid anything that'll look like collusion."

"Well, anything I can do to help; you know that, Victor," Emmert said.

Yes, he knew that. If worst came to utter worst and the Company charter were invalidated, he could still hang on here, doing what he could to salvage something out of the wreckage—if not for the Company, then for Victor Grego. But if Zarathustra were reclassified, Nick would be finished. His title, his social position, his sinecure, his grafts and perquisites, his alias-shrouded Company expense account—all out the airlock. Nick would be counted upon to do anything he could—however much that would be.

He looked across the room at the levitated globe, revolving imperceptibly in the orange spotlight. It was full dark on Beta Continent now, where Leonard Kellogg had killed a Fuzzy named Goldilocks and Jack Holloway had killed a gunman named Kurt Borch. That angered him, too; hell of a gunman! Clear shot at the broad of a man's back, and still got himself killed. Borch hadn't been any better choice than Kellogg himself. What was the matter with him; couldn't he pick men for jobs anymore? And Ham O'Brien! No, he didn't have to blame himself for O'Brien. O'Brien was one of Nick Emmert's boys. And he hadn't picked Nick, either.

The squawk-box on the desk made a premonitory noise, and a feminine voice advised him that Mr. Coombes and his party had arrived.

"All right; show them in."

Coombes entered first, tall, suavely elegant, with a calm, untroubled face. Leslie Coombes would wear the same serene expression in the midst of a bombardment or an earthquake. He had chosen Coombes for chief attorney, and thinking of that made him feel better. Mohammed Ali O'Brien was neither tall, elegant nor calm. His skin was almost black—he'd been born on Agni, under a hot B3 sun. His bald head glistened, and a big nose peeped over the ambuscade of a bushy white mustache. What was it they said about him? Only man on Zarathustra who could strut sitting down. And behind them, the remnant of the expedition to Beta Continent—Ernst Mallin, Juan Jimenez and Ruth Ortheris. Mallin was saying that it was a pity Dr. Kellogg wasn't with them.

"I question that. Well, please be seated. We have a great deal to discuss, I'm afraid."

MR. CHIEF JUSTICE Frederic Pendarvis moved the ashtray a few inches to the right and the slender vase with the spray of starflowers a few inches to the left. He set the framed photograph of the gentle-faced, white-haired woman directly in front of him. Then he took a thin cigar from the silver box, carefully punctured the end and lit it. Then, unable to think of further delaying tactics, he drew the two bulky loose-leaf books toward him and opened the red one, the criminal-case docket.

Something would have to be done about this; he always told himself so at this hour. Shoveling all this stuff onto Central Courts had been all right when Mallorysport had a population of less than five thousand and nothing else on the planet had had more than five hundred, but that time was ten years past. The Chief Justice of a planetary colony shouldn't have to wade through all this to see

who had been accused of blotting the brand on a veldbeest calf or who'd taken
a shot at whom in a barroom. Well, at least he'd managed to get a few
misdemeanor and small-claims courts established; that was something.

The first case, of course, was homicide. It usually was. From Beta,
Constabulary Fifteen, Lieutenant George Lunt. Jack Holloway—so old Jack
had cut another notch on his gun—Cold Creek Valley, Federation citizen,
race Terran human; willful killing of a sapient being, to wit Kurt Borch,
Mallorysport, Federation citizen, race Terran human. Complainant, Leonard
Kellogg, the same. Attorney of record for the defendant, Gustavus Adolphus
Brannhard. The last time Jack Holloway had killed anybody, it had been a
couple of thugs who'd tried to steal his sunstones; it hadn't even gotten into
complaint court. This time he might be in trouble. Kellogg was a Company
executive. He decided he'd better try the case himself. The Company might try
to exert pressure.

The next charge was also homicide, from Constabulary, Beta Fifteen. He
read it and blinked. Leonard Kellogg, willful killing of a sapient being, to wit,
Jane Doe alias Goldilocks, aborigine, race Zarathustran Fuzzy; complainant,
Jack Holloway, defendant's attorney of record, Leslie Coombes. In spite of the
outrageous frivolity of the charge, he began to laugh. It was obviously an
attempt to ridicule Kellogg's own complaint out of court. Every judicial
jurisdiction ought to have at least one Gus Brannhard to liven things up a little.
Race Zarathustra Fuzzy!

Then he stopped laughing suddenly and became deadly serious, like an
engineer who finds a cataclysmite cartridge lying around primed and connected
to a discharger. He reached out to the screen panel and began punching a
combination. A spectacled young man appeared and greeted him deferentially.

"Good morning, Mr. Wilkins," he replied. "A couple of homicides at the
head of this morning's docket—Holloway and Kellogg, both from Beta Fifteen.
What is known about them?"

The young man began to laugh. "Oh, your Honor, they're both a lot of
nonsense. Dr. Kellogg killed some pet belonging to old Jack Holloway, the
sunstone digger, and in the ensuing unpleasantness—Holloway can be very
unpleasant, if he feels he has to—this man Borch, who seems to have been
Kellogg's bodyguard, made the suicidal error of trying to draw a gun on
Holloway. I'm surprised at Lieuenant Lunt for letting either of those charges get
past hearing court. Mr. O'Brien has entered *nolle prosequi* on both of them, so
the whole thing can be disregarded."

Mohammed O'Brien knew a charge of cataclysmite when he saw one, too.
His impulse had been to pull the detonator. Well, maybe this charge ought to be
shot, just to see what it would bring down.

"I haven't approved the *nolle prosequi* yet, Mr. Wilkins," he mentioned gently. "Would you please transmit to me the hearing tapes on these cases, at sixty-speed? I'll take them on the recorder of this screen. Thank you."

He reached out and made the necessary adjustments. Wilkins, the Clerk of the Courts, left the screen, and returned. There was a wavering scream for a minute and a half. Going to take more time than he had expected. Well . . .

THERE WASN'T ENOUGH ice in the glass, and Leonard Kellogg put more in. Then there was too much, and he added more brandy. He shouldn't have started drinking this early, be drunk by dinnertime if he kept it up, but what else was there to do? He couldn't go out, not with his face like this. In any case, he wasn't sure he wanted to.

They were all down on him. Ernst Mallin, and Ruth Ortheris, and even Juan Jimenez. At the constabulary post, Coombes and O'Brien had treated him like an idiot child who had to be hushed in front of company and coming back to Mallorysport they had ignored him completely. He drank quickly, and then there was too much ice in the glass again. Victor Grego had told him he'd better take a vacation till the trial was over, and put Mallin in charge of the division. Said he oughtn't to be in charge while the division was working on defense evidence. Well, maybe; it looked like the first step toward shoving him completely out of the Company.

He dropped into a chair and lit a cigarette. It tasted badly, and after a few puffs he crushed it out. Well, what else could he have done? After they'd found that little grave, he had to make Gerd understand what it would mean to the Company. Juan and Ruth had been all right, but Gerd—The things Gerd had called him; the things he'd said about the Company. And then that call from Holloway, and the humiliation of being ordered out like a tramp.

And then that disgusting little beast had come pulling at his clothes, and he had pushed it away—well, kicked it maybe—and it had struck at him with the little spear it was carrying. Nobody but a lunatic would give a thing like that to an animal anyhow. And he had kicked it again, and it had screamed. . . .

The communication screen in the next room was buzzing. Maybe that was Victor. He gulped the brandy left in the glass and hurried to it.

It was Leslie Coombes, his face remotely expressionless.

"Oh, hello, Leslie."

"Good afternoon, Dr. Kellogg." The formality of address was studiously rebuking. "The Chief Prosecutor just called me; Judge Pendarvis has denied the *nolle prosequi* he entered in your case and in Mr. Holloway's, and ordered both cases to trial."

"You mean they're actually taking this seriously?"

"It is serious. If you're convicted, the Company's charter will be almost automatically voided. And, although this is important only to you personally, you might, very probably, be sentenced to be shot." He shrugged that off, and continued: "Now, I'll want to talk to you about your defense, for which I am responsible. Say ten-thirty tomorrow, at my office. I should, by that time, know what sort of evidence is going to be used against you. I will be expecting you, Dr. Kellogg."

He must have said more than that, but that was all that registered. Leonard wasn't really conscious of going back to the other room, until he realized that he was sitting in his relaxer chair, filling the glass with brandy. There was only a little ice in it, but he didn't care.

They were going to try him for murder for killing that little animal, and Ham O'Brien had said they wouldn't, he'd promised he'd keep the case from trial and he hadn't, they were going to try him anyhow and if they convicted him they would take him out and shoot him for just killing a silly little animal he had killed it he kicked it and jumped on it he could still hear it screaming and feel the horrible soft crunching under his feet. . . .

He gulped what was left in the glass and poured and gulped more. Then he staggered to his feet and stumbled over to the couch and threw himself onto it, face down, among the cushions.

Leslie Coombes found Nick Emmert with Victor Grego in the latter's office when he entered. They both rose to greet him, and Grego said "You've heard?"

"Yes. O'Brien called me immediately. I called my client—my client of record, that is—and told him. I'm afraid it was rather a shock to him."

"It wasn't any shock to me," Grego said as they sat down. "When Ham O'Brien's as positive about anything as he was about that, I always expect the worst."

"Pendarvis is going to try the case himself," Emmert said. "I always thought he was a reasonable man, but what's he trying to do now? Cut the Company's throat?"

"He isn't anti-Company. He isn't pro-Company either. He's just pro-law. The law says that a planet with native sapient inhabitants is a Class-IV planet, and has to have a Class-IV colonial government. If Zarathustra is a Class-IV planet, he wants it established, and the proper laws applied. If it's a Class-IV planet, the Zarathustra Company is illegally chartered. It's his job to put a stop to illegality. Frederic Pendarvis' religion is the law, and he is its priest. You never get anywhere by arguing religion with a priest."

They were both silent for a while after he had finished. Grego was looking at the globe, and he realized, now, that while he was proud of it, his pride was the pride in a paste jewel that stands for a real one in a blank vault. Now he was afraid that the real jewel was going to be stolen from him. Nick Emmert was just afraid.

"You were right yesterday, Victor. I wish Holloway'd killed that son of a Khooghra. Maybe it's not too late—"

"Yes, it is, Nick. It's too late to do anything like that. It's too late to do anything but win the case in court." He turned to Grego. "What are your people doing?"

Grego took his eyes from the globe. "Ernst Mallin's studying all the filmed evidence we have and all the descriptions of Fuzzy behavior, and trying to prove that none of it is the result of sapient mentation. Ruth Ortheris is doing the same, only she's working on the line of instinct and conditioned reflexes and nonsapient, single-stage reasoning. She has a lot of rats, and some dogs and monkeys, and a lot of apparatus, and some technician from Henry Stenson's instrument shop helping her. Juan Jimenez is studying mentation for Terran dogs, cats and primates, and Freyan kholphs and Mimir black slinkers."

"He hasn't turned up any simian or canine parallels to that funeral, has he?"

Grego said nothing, merely shook his head. Emmert muttered something inaudible and probably indecent.

"I didn't think he had. I only hope those Fuzzies don't get up in court, build a bonfire and start making speeches in Lingua Terra."

Nick Emmert cried out in panic. "You believe they're sapient yourself!"

"Of course. Don't you?"

Grego laughed sourly. "Nick thinks you have to believe a thing to prove it. It helps, but it isn't necessary. Say we're a debating team; we've been handed the negative of the question. *Resolved: that Fuzzies are Sapient Beings.* Personally, I think we have the short end of it, but that only means we'll have to work harder on it."

"You know, I was on a debating team at college," Emmert said brightly. When that was disregarded, he added: "If I remember, the first thing was definition of terms."

Grego looked up quickly. "Leslie, I think Nick has something. What is the legal definition of a sapient being?"

"As far as I know, there isn't any. Sapience is something that's just taken for granted."

"How about talk-and-build-a-fire?"

He shook his head. *"People of the Colony of Vishnu* versus Emily Morrosh, 612 A.E." He told them about the infanticide case. "I was looking up rulings on sapience; I passed the word on to Ham O'Brien. You know, what your people will have to do will be to produce a definition of sapience, acceptable to the court, that will include all known sapient races and at the same time exclude the Fuzzies. I don't envy them."

"We need some Fuzzies of our own to study," Grego said.

"Too bad we can't get hold of Holloway's," Emmert said. "Maybe we could, if he leaves them alone at his camp."

"No. We can't risk that." He thought for a moment. "Wait a moment. I think we might be able to do it at that. Legally."

9

JACK HOLLOWAY SAW Little Fuzzy eying the pipe he had laid in the ashtray, and picked it up, putting it in his mouth. Little Fuzzy looked reproachfully at him and started to get down onto the floor. Pappy Jack was mean; didn't he think a Fuzzy might want to smoke a pipe, too? Well, maybe it wouldn't hurt him. He picked Little Fuzzy up and set him back on his lap, offering the pipestem. Little Fuzzy took a puff. He didn't cough over it; evidently he had learned how to avoid inhaling.

"They scheduled the Kellogg trial first," Gus Brannhard was saying, "and there wasn't any way I could stop that. You see what the idea is? They'll try him first, with Leslie Coombes running both the prosecution and the defense, and if they can get him acquitted, it'll prejudice the sapience evidence we introduce in your trial."

Mamma Fuzzy made another try at intercepting the drink he was hoisting, but he frustrated that. Baby had stopped trying to sit on his head, and was playing peek-a-boo from behind his whiskers.

"First," he continued, "they'll exclude every bit of evidence about the Fuzzies that they can. That won't be much, but there'll be a fight to get any of it in. What they can't exclude, they'll attack. They'll attack credibility. Of course, with veridication, they can't claim anybody's lying, but they can claim self-deception. You make a statement you believe, true or false, and the veridicator'll back you up on it. They'll attack qualifications on expert testimony. They'll quibble about statements of fact and statements of opinion. And what they can't exclude or attack, they'll accept, and then deny that it's proof of sapience.

"What the hell do they want for proof of sapience?" Gerd demanded. "Nuclear energy and contragravity and hyperdrive?"

"They will have a nice, neat, pedantic definition of sapience, tailored especially to exclude the Fuzzies, and they will present it in court and try to get it accepted, and it's up to us to guess in advance what that will be, and have a refutation of it ready, and also a definition of our own."

"Their definition will have to include Khooghras. Gerd, do the Khooghras bury their dead?"

"Hell, no; they eat them. But you have to give them this, they cook them first."

"Look, we won't get anywhere arguing about what Fuzzies do and Khooghras don't do," Rainsford said. "We'll have to get a definition of sapience. Remember what Ruth said Saturday night?"

Gerd van Riebeek looked as though he didn't want to remember what Ruth had said, or even remember Ruth herself. Jack nodded, and repeated it. "I got the impression of nonsapient intelligence shading up to a sharp line, and then sapience shading up from there, maybe a different color, wavy lines instead of straight ones."

"That's a good graphic representation," Gerd said. "You know, that line's so sharp I'd be tempted to think of sapience as a result of mutation, except that I can't quite buy the same mutation happening in the same way on so many different planets."

Ben Rainsford started to say something, then stopped short when a constabulary siren hooted over the camp. The Fuzzies looked up interestedly. They knew what that was. Pappy Jack's friends in the blue clothes. Jack went to the door and opened it, putting the outside light on.

The car was landing; George Lunt, two of his men and two men in civilian clothes were getting out. Both the latter were armed, and one of them carried a bundle under his arm.

"Hello, George; come on in."

"We want to talk to you, Jack." Lunt's voice was strained, empty of warmth or friendliness. "At least, these men do."

"Why, yes. Sure."

He backed into the room to permit them to enter. Something was wrong; something bad had come up. Khadra came in first, placing himself beside and a little behind him. Lunt followed, glancing quickly around and placing himself between Jack and the gunrack and also the holstered pistols on the table. The third trooper let the two strangers in ahead of him, and then closed the door and put his back against it. He wondered if the court might have cancelled his bond and ordered him into custody. The two strangers—a beefy man with a scrubby black mustache and a smaller one with a thin, saturnine face—were looking expectantly at Lunt. Rainsford and van Riebeek were on their feet. Gus Brannhard leaned over to refill his glass, but did not rise.

"Let me have the papers," Lunt said to the beefy stranger.

The other took a folded document and handed it over.

"Jack, this isn't my idea," Lunt said. "I don't want to do it, but I have to. I wouldn't want to shoot you, either, but you make any resistance and I will. I'm no Kurt Borch; I know you, and I won't take any chances."

"If you're going to serve that paper, serve it," the bigger of the two strangers said. "Don't stand yakking all night."

"Jack," Lunt said uncomfortably, "this is a court order to impound your Fuzzies as evidence in the Kellogg case. These men are deputy marshals from Central Courts; they've been ordered to bring the Fuzzies into Mallorysport."

"Let me see the order, Jack," Brannhard said, still remaining seated.

Lunt handed it to Jack, and he handed it across to Brannhard. Gus had been drinking steadily all evening; maybe he was afraid he'd show it if he stood up. He looked at it briefly and nodded.

"Court order, all right, signed by the Chief Justice." He handed it back. "They have to take the Fuzzies, and that's all there is to it. Keep that order, though, and make them give you a signed and thumbprinted receipt. Type it up for them now, Jack."

Gus wanted to busy him with something, so he wouldn't have to watch what was going on. The smaller of the two deputies had dropped the bundle from under his arm. It was a number of canvas sacks. He sat down at the typewriter, closing his ears to the noises in the room, and wrote the receipt, naming the Fuzzies and describing them, and specifying that they were in good health and uninjured. One of them tried to climb to his lap, yeeking frantically; it clutched his shirt, but it was snatched away. He was finished with his work before the invaders were with theirs. They had three Fuzzies already in sacks. Khadra was catching Cinderella. Ko-Ko and Little Fuzzy had run for the little door in the outside wall, but Lunt was standing with his heels against it, holding it shut; when they saw that, both of them began burrowing in the bedding. The third trooper and the smaller of the two deputies dragged them out and stuffed them into sacks.

He got to his feet, still stunned and only half comprehending, and took the receipt out of the typewriter. There was an argument about it; Lunt told the deputies to sign it or get the hell out without the Fuzzies. They signed, inked their thumbs and printed after their signatures. Jack gave the paper to Gus, trying not to look at the six bulging, writhing sacks, or hear the frightened little sounds.

"George, you'll let them have some of their things, won't you?" he asked.

"Sure, what kind of things?"

"Their bedding. Some of their toys."

"You mean this junk?" The smaller of the two deputies kicked the ball-and-stick construction. "All we got orders to take is the Fuzzies."

"You heard the gentleman." Lunt made the word sound worse than son of a Khooghra. He turned to the two deputies. "Well, you have them; what are you waiting for?"

Jack watched from the door as they put the sacks into the aircar, climbed in after them and lifted out. Then he came back and sat down at the table.

"They don't know anything about court orders," he said. "They don't know why I didn't stop it. They think Pappy Jack let them down."

"Have they gone, Jack?" Brannhard asked. "Sure?" Then he rose, reaching behind him, and took up a little ball of white fur. Baby Fuzzy caught his beard with both tiny hands, yeeking happily.

"Baby! They didn't get him!"

Brannhard disengaged the little hands from his beard and handed him over.

"No, and they signed for him, too." Brannhard downed what was left of his drink, got a cigar out of his pocket and lit it. "Now, we're going to go to Mallorysport and get the rest of them back."

"But . . . But the Chief Justice signed that order. He won't give them back just because we ask him to."

Brannhard made an impolite noise. "I'll bet everything I own Pendarvis never saw that order. They have stacks of those things, signed in blank, in the Chief of the Court's office. If they had to wait to get one of the judges to sign an order every time they wanted to subpoena a witness or impound physical evidence, they'd never get anything done. If Ham O'Brien didn't think this up for himself, Leslie Coombes thought it up for him."

"We'll use my airboat," Gerd said. "You coming along, Ben? Let's get started."

HE COULDN'T UNDERSTAND. The Big Ones in the blue clothes had been friends; they had given the whistles, and shown sorrow when the killed one was put in the ground. And why had Pappy Jack not gotten the big gun and stopped them? It couldn't be that he was afraid; Pappy Jack was afraid of nothing.

The others were near, in bags like the one in which he had been put; he could hear them, and called to them. Then he felt the edge of the little knife Pappy Jack had made. He could cut his way out of this bag now and free the others, but that would be no use. They were in one of the things the Big Ones went up into the sky in, and if he got out now, there would be nowhere to go and they would be caught at once. Better to wait.

The one thing that really worried him was that he would not know where they were being taken. When they did get away, how would they ever find Pappy Jack again?

Gus BRANNHARD WAS nervous, showing it by being over-talkative, and that worried Jack. He'd stopped twice at mirrors along the hallway to make sure that his gold-threaded gray neckcloth was properly knotted and that his black jacket was zipped up far enough and not too far. Now, in front of the door marked THE CHIEF JUSTICE, he paused before pushing the button to fluff his newly shampooed beard.

There were two men in the Chief Justice's private chambers. Pendarvis he had seen once or twice, but their paths had never crossed. He had a good face, thin and ascetic, the face of a man at peace with himself. With him was Mohammed Ali O'Brien, who seemed surprised to see them enter, and then apprehensive. Nobody shook hands; the Chief Justice bowed slightly and invited them to be seated.

"Now," he continued, when they found chairs, "Miss Ugatori tells me that you are making complaint against an action by Mr. O'Brien here."

"We are indeed, your Honor." Brannhard opened his briefcase and produced two papers—the writ, and the receipt for the Fuzzies, handing them across the desk. "My client and I wish to know upon what basis of legality your Honor sanctioned this act, and by what right Mr. O'Brien sent his officers to Mr. Holloway's camp to snatch these little people from their friend and protector, Mr. Holloway."

The judge looked at the two papers. "As you know, Miss Ugatori took prints of them when you called to make this appointment. I've seen them. But believe me, Mr. Brannhard, this is the first time I have seen the original of this writ. You know how these things are signed in blank. It's a practice that has saved considerable time and effort, and until now they have only been used when there was no question that I or any other judge would approve. Such a question should certainly have existed in this case, because had I seen this writ I would never have signed it." He turned to the now fidgeting Chief Prosecutor. "Mr. O'Brien," he said, "one simply does not impound sapient beings as evidence, as, say, one impounds a veldbeest calf in a brand-alteration case. The fact that the sapience of these Fuzzies is still *sub judice* includes the presumption of its possibility. Now you know perfectly well that the courts may take no action in the face of the possibility that some innocent person may suffer wrong."

"And, your Honor," Brannhard leaped into the breach, "it cannot be denied that these Fuzzies have suffered a most outrageous wrong! Picture them—no, picture innocent and artless children, for that is what these Fuzzies are, happy, trusting little children, who, until then, had known only kindness and affection—rudely kidnaped, stuffed into sacks by brutal and callous men—"

"Your Honor!" O'Brien's face turned even blacker than the hot sun of Agni had made it. "I cannot hear officers of the court so characterized without raising my voice in protest!"

"Mr. O'Brien seems to forget that he is speaking in the presence of two eye witnesses to this brutal abduction."

"If the officers of the court need defense, Mr. O'Brien, the court will defend them. I believe that you should presently consider a defense of your own actions."

"Your Honor, I insist that I only acted as I felt to be my duty," O'Brien said. "These Fuzzies are a key exhibit in the case of *People* versus *Kellogg,* since only by demonstration of their sapience can any prosecution against the defendant be maintained."

"Then why," Brannhard demanded, "did you endanger them in this criminally reckless manner?"

"Endanger them?" O'Brien was horrified. "Your Honor, I acted only to insure their safety and appearance in court."

"So you took them away from the only man on this planet who knows anything about their proper care, a man who loves them as he would his own human children, and you subjected them to abuse which, for all you knew, might have been fatal to them."

Judge Pendarvis nodded. "I don't believe, Mr. Brannhard, that you have overstated the case. Mr. O'Brien, I take a very unfavorable view of your action in this matter. You had no right to have what are at least putatively sapient beings treated in this way, and even viewing them as mere physical evidence I must agree with Mr. Brannhard's characterization of your conduct as criminally reckless. Now, speaking judicially, I order you to produce those Fuzzies immediately and return them to the custody of Mr. Holloway."

"Well, of course, your Honor." O'Brien had been growing progressively distraught, and his face now had the gray-over-brown hue of a walnut gunstock that has been out in the rain all day. "It'll take an hour or so to send for them and have them brought here."

"You mean they're not in this building?" Pendarvis asked.

"Oh, no, your Honor, there are no facilities here. I had them taken to Science Center—"

"*What?*"

Jack had determined to keep his mouth shut and let Gus do the talking. The exclamation was literally forced out of him. Nobody noticed; it had also been forced out of both Gus Brannhard and Judge Pendarvis. Pendarvis leaned forward and spoke with dangerous mildness:

"Do you refer, Mr. O'Brien, to the establishment of the Division of Scientific Study and Research of the chartered Zarathustra Company?"

"Why, yes; they have facilities for keeping all kinds of live animals, and they do all the scientific work for—"

Pendarvis cursed blasphemously. Brannhard looked as startled as though his own briefcase had jumped at his throat and tried to bite him. He didn't look half as startled as Ham O'Brien did.

"So you think," Pendarvis said, recovering his composure with visible effort, "that the logical custodian of prosecution evidence in a murder trial is the defendant? Mr. O'Brien, you simply enlarge my view of the possible!"

"The Zarathustra Company isn't the defendant," O'Brien argued sullenly.

"Not of record, no," Brannhard agreed. "But isn't the Zarathustra Company's scientific division headed by one Leonard Kellogg?"

"Dr. Kellogg's been relieved of his duties, pending the outcome of the trial. The division is now headed by Dr. Ernst Mallin."

"Chief scientific witness for the defense; I fail to see any practical difference."

"Well, Mr. Emmert said it would be all right," O'Brien mumbled.

"Jack, did you hear that?" Brannhard asked. "Treasure it in your memory. You may have to testify to it in court sometime." He turned to the Chief Justice. "Your Honor, may I suggest the recovery of these Fuzzies be entrusted to Colonial Marshal Fane, and may I further suggest that Mr. O'Brien be kept away from any communication equipment until they are recovered."

"That sounds like a prudent suggestion, Mr. Brannhard. Now, I'll give you an order for the surrender of the Fuzzies, and a search warrant, just to be on the safe side. And, I think, an Orphans' Court from naming Mr. Holloway as guardian of these putatively sapient beings. What are their names? Oh, I have them here on this receipt." He smiled pleasantly. "See, Mr. O'Brien, we're saving you a lot of trouble."

O'Brien had little enough wit to protest. "But these are the defendant and his attorney in another murder case I'm prosecuting," he began.

Pendarvis stopped smiling. "Mr. O'Brien, I doubt if you'll be allowed to prosecute anything or anybody around here anymore, and I am specifically relieving you of any connection with either the Kellogg or the Holloway trial, and if I hear any argument out of you about it, I will issue a bench warrant for your arrest on charges of malfeasance in office."

10

Colonial Marshal Max Fane was as heavy as Gus Brannhard and considerably shorter. Wedged between them on the back seat of the marshal's car, Jack Holloway contemplated the backs of the two uniformed deputies on the front seat and felt a happy smile spread through him. Going to get his Fuzzies back. Little Fuzzy, and Ko-Ko, and Mike, and Mamma Fuzzy, and Mitzi, and Cinderella; he named them over and imagined them crowding around him, happy to be back with Pappy Jack.

The car settled onto the top landing stage of the Company's Science Center, and immediately a Company cop came running up. Gus opened the door, and Jack climbed out after him.

"Hey, you can't land here!" the cop was shouting. "This is for Company executives only!"

Max Fane emerged behind them and stepped forward; the two deputies piled out from in front.

"The hell you say, now," Fane said. "A court order lands anywhere. Bring him along, boys; we wouldn't want him to go and bump himself on a communication screen anywhere."

The Company cop started to protest, then subsided and fell in between the deputies. Maybe it was beginning to dawn on him that the Federation courts were bigger than the chartered Zarathustra Company after all. Or maybe he just thought there'd been a revolution.

Leonard Kellogg's—temporarily Ernst Mallin's—office was on the first floor of the penthouse, counting down from the top landing stage. When they stepped from the escalator, the hall was crowded with office people, gabbling excitedly in groups; they all stopped talking as soon as they saw what was coming. In the division chief's outer office three or four girls jumped to their feet; one of them jumped into the bulk of Marshal Fane, which had interposed itself between her and the communication screen. They were all shooed out into the hall, and one of the deputies was dropped there with the prisoner. The middle office was empty. Fane took his badgeholder in his left hand as he pushed through the door to the inner office.

Kellogg's—temporarily Mallin's—secretary seemed to have preceded them by a few seconds; she was standing in front of the desk sputtering incoherently. Mallin, starting to rise from his chair, froze, hunched forward over the desk. Juan Jimenez, standing in the middle of the room, seemed to have seen them first; he was looking about wildly as though for some way of escape.

Fane pushed past the secretary and went up to the desk, showing Mallin his badge and then serving the papers. Mallin looked at him in bewilderment.

"But we're keeping those Fuzzies for Mr. O'Brien, the Chief Prosecutor," he said. "We can't turn them over without his authorization."

"This," Max Fane said gently, "is an order of the court, issued by Chief Justice Pendarvis. As for Mr. O'Brien, I doubt if he's Chief Prosecutor anymore. In fact, I suspect that he's in jail. *And that,*" he shouted, leaning forward as far as his waistline would permit and banging on the desk with his fist, *"is where I'm going to stuff you, if you don't get those Fuzzies in here and turn them over immediately!"*

If Fane had suddenly metamorphosed himself into a damnthing, it couldn't have shaken Mallin more. Involuntarily he cringed from the marshal, and that finished him.

"But I can't," he protested. "We don't know exactly where they are at the moment."

"You don't know." Fane's voice sank almost to a whisper. "You admit you're holding them here, but you . . . don't . . . know . . . where. *Now start over again; tell the truth this time!"*

At that moment, the communication screen began making a fuss. Ruth Ortheris, in a light blue tailored costume, appeared in it.

"Dr. Mallin, what *is* going on here?" she wanted to know. "I just came in from lunch, and a gang of men are tearing my office up. Haven't you found the Fuzzies yet?"

"What's that?" Jack yelled. At the same time, Mallin was almost screaming: "Ruth! Shut up! Blank out and get out of the building!"

With surprising speed for a man of his girth, Fane whirled and was in front of the screen, holding his badge out.

"I'm Colonel Marshal Fane. Now, young woman; I want you up here right away. Don't make me send anybody after you, because I won't like that and neither will you."

"Right away, Marshal." She blanked the screen.

Fane turned to Mallin. "Now." He wasn't bothering with vocal tricks anymore. "Are you going to tell me the truth, or am I going to run you in and put a veridicator on you? Where are those Fuzzies?"

"But I don't know!" Mallin wailed. "Juan, you tell him; you took charge of them. I haven't even seen them since they were brought here."

Jack managed to fight down the fright that was clutching at him and got control of his voice.

"If anything's happened to those Fuzzies, you two are going to envy Kurt Borch before I'm through with you," he said.

"All right, how about it?" Fane asked Jimenez. "Start with when you and Ham O'Brien picked up the Fuzzies at Central Courts Building last night."

"Well, we brought them here. I'd gotten some cages fixed up for them, and—"

Ruth Ortheris came in. She didn't try to avoid Jack's eyes, nor did she try to brazen it out with him. She merely nodded distantly, as though they'd met on a ship sometime, and sat down.

"What happened, Marshal?" she asked. "Why are you here with these gentlemen?"

"The court's ordered the Fuzzies returned to Mr. Holloway." Mallin was in a dither. "He has some kind of writ or something, and we don't know where they are."

"Oh, *no!*" Ruth's face, for an instant, was dismay itself. "Not when—" Then she froze shut.

"I came in about o-seven-hundred," Jimenez was saying, "to give them food and water, and they'd broken out of their cages. The netting was broken loose on one cage and the Fuzzy that had been in it had gotten out and let the others out. They got into my office—they made a perfect shambles of it—and got out the door into the hall, and now we don't know where they are. And I don't know how they did any of it."

Cages built for something with no hands and almost no brains. Ever since Kellogg and Mallin had come to the camp, Mallin had been hypnotizing himself into the just-silly-little-animals doctrine. He must have succeeded; last night he'd acted accordingly.

"We want to see the cages," Jack said.

"Yeah." Fane went to the outer door. "Miguel."

The deputy came in, herding the Company cop ahead of him.

"You heard what happened?" Fane asked.

"Yeah. Big Fuzzy jailbreak. What did they do, make little wooden pistols and bluff their way out?"

"By God, I wouldn't put it past them. Come along. Bring Chummy along with you; he knows the inside of this place better than we do. Piet, call in. We want six more men. Tell Chang to borrow from the constabulary if he has to."

"Wait a minute," Jack said. He turned to Ruth. "What do you know about this?"

"Well, not much. I was with Dr. Mallin here when Mr. Grego—I mean, Mr. O'Brien—called to tell us that the Fuzzies were going to be kept here till the trial. We were going to fix up a room for them, but till that could be done, Juan got some cages to put them in. That was all I knew about it till o-nine-thirty, when I came in and found everything in an uproar and was told that the Fuzzies had gotten loose during the night. I knew they couldn't get out of the building, so I went to my office and lab to start overhauling some equipment we were going to need with the Fuzzies. About ten-hundred, I found that I couldn't do anything with it, and my assistant and I loaded it on a pickup truck and took it to Henry Stenson's instrument shop. By the time I was through there, I had lunch and then came back here."

He wondered briefly how a polyencephalographic veridicator would react to some of those statements; might be a good idea if Max Fane found out.

"I'll stay here," Gus Brannhard was saying, "and see if I can get some more truth out of these people."

"Why don't you screen the hotel and tell Gerd and Ben what's happened?" he asked. "Gerd used to work here; maybe he could help us hunt."

"Good idea. Piet, tell our reenforcements to stop at the Mallory on the way and pick him up." Fane turned to Jimenez. "Come along; show us where you had these Fuzzies and how they got away."

"You say one of them broke out of his cage and then released the others," Jack said to Jimenez as they were going down on the escalator. "Do you know which one it was?"

Jimenez shook his head. "We just took them out of the bags and put them into the cages."

That would be Little Fuzzy; he'd always been the brains of the family. With his leadership, they might have a chance. The trouble was that this place was full of dangers Fuzzies knew nothing about—radiation and poisons and electric wiring and things like that. If they really had escaped. That was a possibility that began worrying Jack.

On each floor they passed going down, he could glimpse parties of

Company employees in the halls, armed with nets and blankets and other catching equipment. When they got off Jimenez led them through a big room of glass cases—mounted specimens and articulated skeletons of Zarathustran mammals. More people were there, looking around and behind and even into the cases. He began to think that the escape was genuine, and not just a cover-up for the murder of the Fuzzies.

Jimenez took them down a narrow hall beyond to an open door at the end. Inside, the permanent night light made a blue-white glow; a swivel chair stood just inside the door. Jimenez pointed to it.

"They must have gotten up on that to work the latch and open the door," he said.

It was like the doors at the camp, spring latch, with a handle instead of a knob. They'd have learned how to work it from watching him. Fane was trying the latch.

"Not too stiff," he said. "Your little fellows strong enough to work it?"

He tried it and agreed. "Sure. And they'd be smart enough to do it, too. Even Baby Fuzzy, the one your men didn't get, would be able to figure that out."

"And look what they did to my office," Jimenez said, putting on the lights.

They'd made quite a mess of it. They hadn't delayed long to do it, just thrown things around. Everything was thrown off the top of the desk. They had dumped the wastebasket, and left it dumped. He saw that and chuckled. The escape had been genuine all right.

"Probably hunting for things they could use as weapons, and doing as much damage as they could in the process." There was evidently a pretty wide streak of vindictiveness in Fuzzy character. "I don't think they like you, Juan."

"Wouldn't blame them," Fane said. "Let's see what kind of Houdini they did on these cages now."

The cages were in a room—file room, storeroom, junk room—behind Jimenez's office. It had a spring lock, too, and the Fuzzies had dragged one of the cages over and stood on it to open the door. The cages themselves were about three feet wide and five feet long, with plywood bottoms, wooden frames and quarter-inch netting on the sides and tops. The tops were hinged, and fastened with hasps, and bolts slipped through the staples with nuts screwed on them. The nuts had been unscrewed from five and the bolts slipped out; the sixth cage had been broken open from the inside, the netting cut away from the frame at one corner and bent back in a triangle big enough for a Fuzzy to crawl through.

"I can't understand that," Jimenez was saying. "Why that wire looks as though it had been cut."

"It was cut. Marshal, I'd pull somebody's belt about this, if I were you. Your men aren't very careful about searching prisoners. One of the Fuzzies hid a knife out on them." He remembered how Little Fuzzy and Ko-Ko had burrowed into the bedding in apparently unreasoning panic, and explained about the little spring-steel knives he had made. "I suppose he palmed it and hugged himself into a ball, as though he was scared witless, when they put him in the bag."

"Waited till he was sure he wouldn't get caught before he used it, too," the marshal said. "That wire's soft enough to cut easily." He turned to Jimenez. "You people ought to be glad I'm ineligible for jury duty. Why don't you just throw it in and let Kellogg cop a plea?"

Gerd van Riebeek stopped for a moment in the doorway and looked into what had been Leonard Kellogg's office. The last time he'd been here, Kellogg had had him on the carpet about that land-prawn business. Now Ernst Mallin was sitting in Kellogg's chair, trying to look unconcerned and not making a very good job of it. Gus Brannhard sprawled in an armchair, smoking a cigar and looking at Mallin as he would look at a river pig when he doubted whether it was worth shooting it or not. A uniformed deputy turned quickly, then went back to studying an elaborate wall chart showing the interrelation of Zarathustran mammals—he'd made the original of that chart himself. And Ruth Ortheris sat apart from the desk and the three men, smoking. She looked up and then, when she saw that he was looking past and away from her, she lowered her eyes.

"You haven't found them?" he asked Brannhard.

The fluffy-bearded lawyer shook his head. "Jack has a gang down in the cellar, working up. Max is in the psychology lab, putting the Company cops who were on duty last night under veridication. They all claim, and the veridicator backs them up, that it was impossible for the Fuzzies to get out of the building."

"They don't know what's impossible, for a Fuzzy."

"That's what I told him. He didn't give me any argument, either. He's pretty impressed with how they got out of those cages."

Ruth spoke. "Gerd, we didn't hurt them. We weren't going to hurt them at all. Juan put them in cages because we didn't have any other place for them, but we were going to fix up a nice room, where they could play together. . . ." Then she must have seen that he wasn't listening, and stopped, crushing out her cigarette and rising. "Dr. Mallin, if these people haven't any more questions to ask me, I have a lot of work to do."

"You want to ask her anything, Gerd?" Brannhard inquired.

Once he had had something very important he had wanted to ask her. He was glad, now, that he hadn't gotten around to it. Hell, she was so married to the Company it'd be bigamy if she married him too.

"No. I don't want to talk to her at all."

She started for the door, then hesitated. "Gerd, I . . ." she began. Then she went out. Gus Brannhard looked after her, and dropped the ash of his cigar on Leonard Kellogg's—now Ernst Mallin's—floor.

GERD DETESTED HER, and she wouldn't have had any respect for him if he didn't. She ought to have known that something like this would happen. It always did, in the business. A smart girl, in the business, never got involved with any one man; she always got herself four or five boyfriends, on all possible sides, and played them off one against another.

She'd have to get out of the Science Center right away. Marshal Fane was questioning people under veridication; she didn't dare let him get around to her. She didn't dare go to her office; the veridicator was in the lab across the hall, and that's where he was working. And she didn't dare—

Yes, she could do that, by screen. She went into an office down the hall; a dozen people recognized her at once and began bombarding her with questions about the Fuzzies. She brushed them off and went to a screen, punching a combination. After a slight delay, an elderly man with a thin-lipped, bloodless face appeared. When he recognized her, there was a brief look of annoyance on the thin face.

"Mr. Stenson," she began, before he could say anything. "That apparatus I brought to your shop this morning—the sensory-response detector—we've made a simply frightful mistake. There's nothing wrong with it whatever, and if anything's done with it, it may cause serious damage."

"I don't think I understand, Dr. Ortheris."

"Well, it was a perfectly natural mistake. You see, we're all at our wits' end here. Mr. Holloway and his lawyer and the Colonial Marshal are here with an order from Judge Pendarvis for the return of those Fuzzies. None of us knows what we're doing at all. Why the whole trouble with the apparatus was the fault of the operator. We'll have to have it back immediately, all of it."

"I see, Dr. Ortheris." The old instrument maker looked worried. "But I'm afraid the apparatus has already gone to the workroom. Mr. Stephenson has it now, and I can't get in touch with him at present. If the mistake can be corrected, what do you want done?"

"Just hold it; I'll call or send for it."

She blanked the screen. Old Johnson, the chief data synthesist, tried to detain her with some question.

"I'm sorry, Mr. Johnson. I can't stop now. I have to go over to Company House right away."

•　　•　　•

THE SUITE AT the Hotel Mallory was crowded when Jack Holloway returned with Gerd van Riebeek; it was noisy with voices, and the ventilators were laboring to get rid of the tobacco smoke. Gus Brannhard, Ben Rainsford and Baby Fuzzy were meeting the press.

"Oh, Mr. Holloway!" somebody shouted as he entered. "Have you found them yet?"

"No; we've been all over Science Center from top to bottom. We know they went down a few floors from where they'd been caged, but that's all. I don't think they could have gotten outside; the only exit on the ground level's through a vestibule where a Company policeman was on duty, and there's no way for them to have climbed down from any of the terraces or landing stages."

"Well, Mr. Holloway, I hate to suggest this," somebody else said, "but have you eliminated the possibility that they must have hidden in a trash bin and been dumped into the mass-energy converter?"

"We thought of that. The converter's underground, in a vault that can be entered only by one door, and that was locked. No trash was disposed of between the time they were brought there and the time the search started, and everything that's been sent to the converter since has been checked piece by piece."

"Well, I'm glad to hear that, Mr. Holloway, and I know that everybody hearing this will be glad, too. I take it you've not given up looking for them?"

"Are we on the air now? No, I have not; I'm staying here in Mallorysport until I either find them or am convinced that they aren't in the city. And I am offering a reward of two thousand sols apiece for their return to me. If you'll wait a moment, I'll have descriptions ready for you. . . ."

Victor Grego unstoppered the refrigerated cocktail jug. "More?" he asked Leslie Coombes.

"Yes, thank you." Coombes held his glass until it was filled. "As you say, Victor, you made the decision, but you made it on my advice, and the advice was bad."

He couldn't disagree, even politely, with that. He hoped it hadn't been ruinously bad. One thing, Leslie wasn't trying to pass the buck, and considering how Ham O'Brien had mishandled his end of it, he could have done so quite plausibly.

"I used bad judgment," Coombes said dispassionately, as though discussing some mistake Hitler had made, or Napoleon. "I thought O'Brien wouldn't try to use one of those presigned writs, and I didn't think Pendarvis would admit, publicly, that he signed court orders in blank. He's been severely criticized by the press about that."

He hadn't thought Brannhard and Holloway would try to fight a court order either. That was one of the consequences of being too long in a seemingly irresistible position; you didn't expect resistance. Kellogg hadn't expected Jack Holloway to order him off his land grant. Kurt Borch had thought all he needed to do with a gun was pull it and wave it around. And Jimenez had expected the Fuzzies to just sit in their cages.

"I wonder where they got to," Coombes was saying. "I understand they couldn't be found at all in the building."

"Ruth Ortheris has an idea. She got away from Science Center before Fane could get hold of her and veridicate her. It seems she and an assistant took some apparatus out, about ten o'clock, in a truck. She thinks the Fuzzies hitched a ride with her. I know that sounds rather improbable, but hell, everything else sounds impossible. I'll have it followed up. Maybe we can find them before Holloway does. They're not inside Science Center, that's sure." His own glass was empty; he debated a refill and voted against it. "O'Brien's definitely out, I take it?"

"Completely. Pendarvis gave him his choice of resigning or facing malfeasance charges."

"They couldn't really convict him of malfeasance for that, could they? Malfeasance, maybe, but—"

"They could charge him. And then they could interrogate him under veridication about his whole conduct in office, and you know what they would bring out," Coombes said. "He almost broke an arm signing his resignation. He's still Attorney General of the Colony, of course; Nick issued a statement supporting him. That hasn't done Nick as much harm as O'Brien could do spilling what he knows about Residency affairs.

"Now Brannhard is talking about bringing suit against the Company, and he's furnishing copies of all the Fuzzy films Holloway has to the news services. Interworld News is going hog-wild with it, and even the services we control can't play it down too much. I don't know who's going to be prosecuting these cases, but whoever it is, he won't dare pull any punches. And the whole thing's made Pendarvis hostile to us. I know, the law and the evidence and nothing but the law and the evidence, but the evidence is going to filter into his conscious mind through this hostility. He's called a conference with Brannhard and myself for tomorrow afternoon; I don't know what that's going to be like."

11

THE **TWO** **LAWYERS** had risen hastily when Chief Justice Pendarvis entered; he responded to their greetings and seated himself at his desk, reaching for the silver cigar box and taking out a panatella. Gustavus Adolphus Brannhard picked up the cigar he had laid aside and began puffing on it; Leslie Coombes took a cigarette from his case. They both looked at him, waiting like two drawn weapons—a battle ax and a rapier.

"Well, gentlemen, as you know, we have a couple of homicide cases and nobody to prosecute them," he began.

"Why bother, your Honor?" Coombes asked. "Both charges are completely frivolous. One man killed a wild animal, and the other killed a man who was trying to kill him."

"Well, your Honor, I don't believe my client is guilty of anything, legally or morally," Brannhard said. "I want that established by an acquittal." He looked at Coombes. "I should think Mr. Coombes would be just as anxious to have his client cleared of any stigma of murder, too."

"I am quite agreed. People who have been charged with crimes ought to have public vindication if they are innocent. Now, in the first place, I planned to hold the Kellogg trial first, and then the Holloway trial. Are you both satisfied with that arrangement?"

"Absolutely not, your Honor," Brannhard said promptly. "The whole basis of the Holloway defense is that this man Borch was killed in commission of a felony. We're prepared to prove that, but we don't want our case prejudiced by an earlier trial."

Coombes laughed. "Mr. Brannhard wants to clear his client by preconvicting mine. We can't agree to anything like that."

"Yes, and he is making the same objection to trying your client first. Well, I'm going to remove both objections. I'm going to order the two cases combined, and both defendants tried together."

A momentary glow of unholy glee on Gus Brannhard's face; Coombes didn't like the idea at all.

"Your Honor, I trust that that suggestion was only made facetiously," he said.

"It wasn't, Mr. Coombes."

"Then if your Honor will not hold me in contempt for saying so, it is the most shockingly irregular—I won't go so far as to say improper—trial procedure I've ever heard of. This is not a case of accomplices charged with the same crime; this is a case of two men charged with different criminal acts, and the conviction of either would mean the almost automatic acquittal of the other. I don't know who's going to be named to take Mohammed Ali O'Brien's place, but I pity him from the bottom of my heart. Why, Mr. Brannhard and I could go off somewhere and play poker while the prosecutor would smash the case to pieces."

"Well, we won't have just one prosecutor, Mr. Coombes, we will have two. I'll swear you and Mr. Brannhard in as special prosecutors, and you can prosecute Mr. Brannhard's client, and he yours. I think that would remove any further objections."

It was all he could do to keep his face judicially grave and unmirthful. Brannhard was almost purring, like a big tiger that had just gotten the better of a young goat; Leslie Coombes's suavity was beginning to crumble slightly at the edges.

"Your Honor, that is a most excellent suggestion," Brannhard declared. "I will prosecute Mr. Coombes's client with the greatest pleasure in the universe."

"Well, all I can say, your Honor, is that if the first proposal was the most irregular I had ever heard, the record didn't last long!"

"Why, Mr. Coombes, I went over the law and the rules of jurisprudence very carefully, and I couldn't find a word that could be construed as disallowing such a procedure."

"I'll bet you didn't find any precedent for it either!"

Leslie Coombes should have known better than that; in colonial law, you can find a precedent for almost anything.

"How much do you bet, Leslie?" Brannhard asked, a larcenous gleam in his eye.

"Don't let him take your money away from you. I found, inside an hour, sixteen precedents, from twelve different planetary jurisdictions."

"All right, your Honor," Coombes capitulated. "But I hope you know what you're doing. You're turning a couple of cases of the People of the Colony into a common civil lawsuit."

Gus Brannhard laughed. "What else is it?" he demanded. *"Friends of Little Fuzzy* versus *The chartered Zarathustra Company;* I'm bringing action as friend of incompetent aborigines for recognition of sapience, and Mr. Coombes, on behalf of the Zarathustra Company, is contesting to preserve the Company's charter, and that's all there is or ever was to this case."

That was impolite of Gus. Leslie Coombes had wanted to go on to the end pretending that the Company charter had absolutely nothing to do with it.

THERE WAS AN unending stream of reports of Fuzzies seen here and there, often simultaneously in impossibly distant parts of the city. Some were from publicity seekers and pathological liars and crackpots; some were the result of honest mistakes or overimaginativeness. There was some reason to suspect that not a few had originated with the Company, to confuse the search. One thing did come to light which heartened Jack Holloway. An intensive if concealed search was being made by the Company police, and by the Mallorysport police department, which the company controlled.

Max Fane was giving every available moment to the hunt. This wasn't because of ill will for the Company, though that was present, nor because the Chief Justice was riding him. The Colonial Marshal was pro-Fuzzy. So were the Colonial Constabulary, over whom Nick Emmert's administration seemed to have little if any authority. Colonel Ian Ferguson, the commandant, had his appointment direct from the Colonial Office on Terra. He had called by screen to offer his help, and George Lunt, over on Beta, screened daily to learn what progress was being made.

Living at the Hotel Mallory was expensive, and Jack had to sell some sunstones. The Company gem buyers were barely civil to him; he didn't try to be civil at all. There was also a noticeable coolness toward him at the bank. On the other hand, on several occasions, Space Navy officers and ratings down from Xerxes Base went out of their way to accost him, introduce themselves, shake hands with him and give him their best wishes.

Once, in one of the weather-domed business centers, an elderly man with white hair showing under his black beret greeted him.

"Mr. Holloway, I want to tell you how grieved I am to learn about the disappearance of those little people of yours," he said. "I'm afraid there's nothing I can do to help you, but I hope they turn up safely."

"Why, thank you, Mr. Stenson." He shook hands with the old master instrument maker. "If you could make me a pocket veridicator, to use on some of these people who claim they saw them, it would be a big help."

"Well, I do make rather small portable veridicators for the constabulary, but I think what you need is an instrument for detection of psychopaths, and that's slightly beyond science at present. But if you're still prospecting for sunstones, I have an improved microray scanner I just developed, and . . ."

He walked with Stenson to his shop, had a cup of tea and looked at the scanner. From Stenson's screen, he called Max Fane. Six more people had claimed to have seen the Fuzzies.

Within a week, the films taken at the camp had been shown so frequently on telecast as to wear out their interest value. Baby, however, was still available for new pictures, and in a few days a girl had to be hired to take care of his fan mail. Once, entering a bar, Jack thought he saw Baby sitting on a woman's head. A second look showed that it was only a life-sized doll, held on with an elastic band. Within a week, he was seeing Baby Fuzzy hats all over town, and shop windows were full of life-sized Fuzzy dolls.

In the late afternoon, two weeks after the Fuzzies had vanished, Marshal Fane dropped him at the hotel. They sat in the car for a moment, and Fane said:

"I think this is the end of it. We're all out of cranks and exhibitionists now."

He nodded. "That woman we were talking to. She's crazy as a bedbug."

"Yeah. In the past ten years she's confessed to every unsolved crime on the planet. It shows you how hard up we are that I waste your time and mine listening to her."

"Max, nobody's seen them. You think they just aren't, any more, don't you?"

The fat man looked troubled. "Well, Jack, it isn't so much that nobody's seen them. Nobody's seen any trace of them. There are land-prawns all around, but nobody's found a cracked shell. And six active, playful, inquisitive Fuzzies ought to be getting into things. They ought to be raiding food markets, and fruit stands, getting into places and ransacking. But there hasn't been a thing. The Company police have stopped looking for them now."

"Well, I won't. They must be around somewhere." He shook Fane's hand, and got out of the car. "You've been awfully helpful, Max. I want you to know how much I thank you."

He watched the car lift away, and then looked out over the city—a vista of treetop green, with roofs and the domes of shopping centers and business centers and amusement centers showing through, and the angular buttes of tall buildings rising above. The streetless contragravity city of a new planet that had never known ground traffic. The Fuzzies could be hiding anywhere among those trees—or they could all be dead in some manmade trap. He thought of all the deadly places into which they could have wandered. Machinery, dormant and quiet, until somebody threw a switch. Conduits, which could be flooded without warning, or filled with scalding steam or choking gas. Poor little Fuzzies, they'd think a city was as safe as the woods of home, where there was nothing worse than harpies and damnthings.

Gus Brannhard was out when he went down to the suite; Ben Rainsford was at a reading screen, studying a psychology text, and Gerd was working at a desk that had been brought in. Baby was playing on the floor with the bright new toys they had gotten for him. When Pappy Jack came in, he dropped them and ran to be picked up and held.

"George called," Gerd said. "They have a family of Fuzzies at the post now."

"Well, that's great." He tried to make it sound enthusiastic. "How many?"

"Five, three males and two females. They call them Dr. Crippen, Dillinger, Ned Kelly, Lizzie Borden, and Calamity Jane."

Wouldn't it be just like a bunch of cops to hang names like that on innocent Fuzzies?

"Why don't you call the post and say hello to them?" Ben asked.

"Baby likes them; he'd think it was fun to talk to them again."

He let himself be urged into it, and punched out the combination. They were nice Fuzzies; almost, but of course not quite, as nice as his own.

"If your family doesn't turn up in time for the trial, have Gus subpoena ours," Lunt told him. "You ought to have some to produce in court. Two weeks from now, this mob of ours will be doing all kinds of things. You ought to see them now, and we only got them yesterday afternoon."

He said he hoped he'd have his own by then; he realized that he was saying it without much conviction.

They had a drink when Gus came in. He was delighted with the offer from Lunt. Another one who didn't expect to see Pappy Jack's Fuzzies alive again.

"I'm not doing a damn thing here," Rainsford said. "I'm going back to Beta till the trial. Maybe I can pick up some ideas from George Lunt's Fuzzies. I'm damned if I'm getting any from this crap!" He gestured at the reading screen. "All I have is a vocabulary, and I don't know what half the words mean." He snapped it off. "I'm beginning to wonder if maybe Jimenez mightn't have been right and Ruth Ortheris is wrong. Maybe you can be just a little bit sapient."

"Maybe it's possible to be sapient and not know it," Gus said. "Like the character in the old French play who didn't know he was talking prose."

"What do you mean, Gus?" Gerd asked.

"I'm not sure I know. It's just an idea that occurred to me today. Kick it around and see if you can get anything out of it."

"I BELIEVE THE difference lies in the area of consciousness," Ernst Mallin was saying. "You all know, of course, the axiom that only one-tenth, never more than one-eighth, of our mental activity occurs above the level of consciousness. Now let us imagine a hypothetical race whose entire mentation is conscious."

"I hope they stay hypothetical," Victor Grego, in his office across the city, said out of the screen. "They wouldn't recognize us as sapient at all."

"We wouldn't be sapient, as they'd define the term," Leslie Coombes, in the same screen with Grego, said. "They'd have some equivalent of the talk-and-build-a-fire rule, based on abilities of which we can't even conceive."

Maybe, Ruth thought, they might recognize us as one-tenth to as much as one-eighth sapient. No, then we'd have to recognize, say, a chimpanzee as being one-one-hundredth sapient, and a flatworm as being sapient to the order of one-billionth.

"Wait a minute," she said. "If I understand, you mean that nonsapient beings think, but only subconsciously?"

"That's correct, Ruth. When confronted by some entirely novel situation, a nonsapient animal will think, but never consciously. Of course, familiar situations are dealt with by pure habit and memory-response."

"You know, I've just thought of something," Grego said. "I think we can explain that funeral that's been bothering all of us in nonsapient terms." He lit a cigarette, while they all looked at him expectantly. "Fuzzies," he continued, "bury their ordure: they do this to avoid an unpleasant sense-stimulus, a bad smell. Dead bodies quickly putrefy and smell badly; they are thus equated, subconsciously, with ordure and must be buried. All Fuzzies carry weapons. A Fuzzy's weapon is—still subconsciously—regarded as a part of the Fuzzy, hence it must also be buried."

Mallin frowned portentiously. The idea seemed to appeal to him, but of course he simply couldn't agree too promptly with a mere layman, even the boss.

"Well, so far you're on fairly safe ground, Mr. Grego," he admitted. "Association of otherwise dissimilar things because of some apparent similarity is a recognized element of nonsapient animal behavior." He frowned again. "That *could* be an explanation. I'll have to think of it."

About this time tomorrow, it would be his own idea, with grudging recognition of a suggestion by Victor Grego. In time, that would be forgotten; it would be the Mallin Theory. Grego was apparently agreeable, as long as the job got done.

"Well, if you can make anything out of it, pass it on to Mr. Coombes as soon as possible, to be worked up for use in court," he said.

12

BEN RAINSFORD WENT back to Beta Continent, and Gerd van Riebeek remained in Mallorysport. The constabulary at Post Fifteen had made steel chopper-diggers for their Fuzzies, and reported a gratifying abatement of the land-prawn nuisance. They also made a set of scaled-down carpenter tools, and their Fuzzies were building themselves a house out of scrap crates and boxes. A pair of Fuzzies showed up at Ben Rainsford's camp, and he adopted them, naming them Flora and Fauna.

Everybody had Fuzzies now, and Pappy Jack only had Baby. He was lying on the floor of the parlor, teaching Baby to tie knots in a piece of string. Gus Brannhard, who spent most of the day in the office in the Central Courts building which had been furnished to him as special prosecutor, was lolling in an armchair in red-and-blue pajamas, smoking a cigar, drinking coffee—his whisky consumption was down to a couple of drinks a day—and studying texts on two reading screens at once, making an occasional remark into a stenomemophone. Gerd was at the desk, spoiling notepaper in an effort to work something out by symbolic logic. Suddenly he crumpled a sheet and threw it across the room, cursing. Brannhard looked away from his screens.

"Trouble, Gerd?"

Gerd cursed again. "How the devil can I tell whether Fuzzies generalize?" he demanded. "How can I tell whether they form abstract ideas? How can I prove, even, that they have ideas at all? Hell's blazes, how can I even prove, to your satisfaction, that I think consciously?"

"Working on that idea I mentioned?" Brannhard asked.

"I was. It seemed like a good idea but . . ."

"Suppose we go back to specific instances of Fuzzy behavior, and present them as evidence of sapience?" Brannhard asked. "That funeral, for instance."

"They'll still insist that we define sapience."

The communication screen began buzzing. Baby Fuzzy looked up disinterestedly, and then went back to trying to untie a figure-eight knot he had tied. Jack shoved himself to his feet and put the screen on. It was Max Fane, and for the first time that he could remember, the Colonial Marshal was excited.

"Jack, have you had any news on the screen lately?"

"No. Something turn up?"

"God, yes! The cops are all over the city hunting the Fuzzies; they have orders to shoot on sight. Nick Emmert was just on the air with a reward offer—five hundred sols apiece, dead or alive."

It took a few seconds for that to register. Then he became frightened. Gus and Gerd were both on their feet and crowding to the screen behind him.

"They have some bum from that squatters' camp over on the East Side who claims the Fuzzies beat up his ten-year-old daughter," Fane was saying. "They have both of them at police headquarters, and they've handed the story out to Zarathustra News, and Planetwide Coverage. Of course, they're Company-controlled; they're playing it for all it's worth."

"Have they been veridicated?" Brannhard demanded.

"No, and the city cops are keeping them under cover. The girl says she was playing outdoors and these Fuzzies jumped her and began beating her with sticks. Her injuries are listed as multiple bruises, fractured wrist and general shock."

"I don't believe it! They wouldn't attack a child."

"I want to talk to that girl and her father," Brannhard was saying. "And I'm going to demand that they make their statements under veridication. This thing's a frameup, Max; I'd bet my ears on it. Timing's just right; only a week till the trial."

Maybe the Fuzzies had wanted the child to play with them, and she'd gotten frightened and hurt one of them. A ten-year-old human child would look dangerously large to a fuzzy, and if they thought they were menaced they would fight back savagely.

They were still alive and in the city. That was one thing. But they were in worse danger than they had ever been; that was another. Fane was asking Brannhard how soon he could be dressed.

"Five minutes? Good, I'll be along to pick you up," he said. "Be seeing you."

Jack hurried into the bedroom he and Brannhard shared; he kicked off his moccasins and began pulling on his boots. Brannhard, pulling his trousers up over his pajama pants, wanted to know where he thought he was going.

"With you. I've got to find them before some dumb son of a Khooghra shoots them."

"You stay here," Gus ordered. "Stay by the communication screen, and keep the viewscreen on for the news. But don't stop putting your boots on; you may have to get out of here fast if I call you and tell you they've been located. I'll call you as soon as I get anything definite."

Gerd had the screen on for news, and was getting Planetwide, openly owned and operated by the Company. The newscaster was wrought up about the brutal attack on the innocent child, but he was having trouble focusing the blame. After all, who'd let the Fuzzies escape in the first place? And even a skilled semanticist had trouble making anything called a Fuzzy sound menacing. At least he gave particulars, true or not.

The child, Lolita Lurkin, had been playing outside her home at about twenty-one hundred when she had suddenly been set upon by six Fuzzies, armed with clubs. Without provocation, they had dragged her down and beaten her severely. Her screams had brought her father, and he had driven the Fuzzies away. Police had brought both the girl and her father, Oscar Lurkin, to headquarters, where they had told their story. City police, Company police and constabulary troopers and parties of armed citizens were combing the eastern side of the city; Resident General Emmert had acted at once to offer a reward of five thousand sols apiece. . . .

"The kid's lying, and if they ever get a veridicator on her, they'll prove it," he said. "Emmert, or Grego, or the two of them together, bribed those people to tell that story."

"Oh, I take that for granted," Gerd said. "I know that place. Junktown. Ruth does a lot of work there for juvenile court." He stopped briefly, pain in his eyes, and then continued: "You can hire anybody to do anything over there for a hundred sols, especially if the cops are fixed in advance."

He shifted to the Interworld News frequency; they were covering the Fuzzy hunt from an aircar. The shanties and parked airjalopies of Junktown were floodlighted from above; lines of men were beating the brush and poking among them. Once a car passed directly below the pickup, a man staring at the ground from it over a machine gun.

"Wooo! Am I glad I'm not in that mess!" Gerd exclaimed. "Anybody sees something he thinks is a Fuzzy and half that gang'll massacre each other in ten seconds."

"I hope they do!"

Interworld News was pro-Fuzzy; the commentator in the car was being extremely saracastic about the whole thing. Into the middle of one view of a rifle-bristling line of beaters somebody in the studio cut a view of the Fuzzies, taken at the camp, looking up appealing while waiting for breakfast. "These," a voice said, "are the terrible monsters against whom all these brave men are protecting us."

A few moments later, a rife flash and a bang, and then a fusillade brought Jack's heart into his throat. The pickup car jetted toward it; by the time it reached the spot, the shooting had stopped, and a crowd was gathering around something white on the ground. He had to force himself to look, then gave a shuddering breath of relief. It was a zaragoat, a three-horned domesticated ungulate.

"Oh-Oh! Some squatter's milk supply finished." The commentator laughed. "Not the first one tonight either. Attorney General—former Chief Prosecutor— O'Brien's going to have quite a few suits against the administration to defend as a result of this business."

"He's going to have a goddamn thundering big one from Jack Holloway!"

The communication screen buzzed; Gerd snapped it on.

"I just talked to Judge Pendarvis," Gus Brannhard reported out of it. "He's issuing an order restraining Emmert from paying any reward except for Fuzzies turned over alive and uninjured to Marshal Fane. And he's issuing a warning that until the status of the Fuzzies is determined, anybody killing one will face charges of murder."

"That's fine, Gus! Have you seen the girl or her father yet?"

Brannhard snarled angrily. "The girl's in the the Company hospital, in a private room. The doctors won't let anybody see her. I think Emmert's hiding the father in the Residency. And I haven't seen the two cops who brought them in, or the desk sergeant who booked the complaint, or the detective lieutenant who was on duty here. They've all lammed out. Max has a couple of men over in Junktown, trying to find out who called the cops in the first place. We may get something out of that."

The Chief Justice's action was announced a few minutes later; it got to the hunters a few minutes after that and the Fuzzy hunt began falling apart. The City and Company police dropped out immediately. Most of the civilians, hoping to grab five thousand sols' worth of live Fuzzy, stayed on for twenty minutes, and so, apparently to control them, did the constabulary. Then the reward was canceled, the airborne floodlights went off and the whole thing broke up.

Gus Brannhard came in shortly afterward, starting to undress as soon as he heeled the door shut after him. When he had his jacket and neckcloth off, he dropped into a chair, filled a water tumbler with whisky, gulped half of it and then began pulling off his boots.

"If that drink has a kid sister, I'll take it," Gerd muttered. "What happened, Gus?"

Brannhard began to curse. "The whole thing's a fake; it stinks from here to Nifflheim. It would stink *on* Nifflheim." He picked up a cigar butt he had laid aside when Fane's call had come in and relighted it. "We found the woman who called the police. Neighbor; she says she saw Lurkin come home drunk, and a little later she heard the girl screaming. She says he beats her up every time he gets drunk, which is about five times a week, and she'd made up her mind to stop it the next chance she got. She denied having seen anything that even looked like a Fuzzy anywhere around."

The excitement of the night before had incubated a new brood of Fuzzy reports; Jack went to the marshal's office to interview the people making them. The first dozen were of a piece with the ones that had come in originally. Then he talked to a young man who had something of different quality.

"I saw them as plain as I'm seeing you, not more than fifty feet away," he said. "I had an autocarbine, and I pulled up on them, but, gosh, I couldn't shoot them. They were just like little people, Mr. Holloway, and they looked so scared and helpless. So I held over their heads and let off a two-second burst to scare them away before anybody else saw them and shot them."

"Well, son, I'd like to shake your hand for that. You know, you thought you were throwing away a lot of money there. How many did you see?"

"Well, only four. I'd heard that there were six, but the other two could have been back in the brush where I didn't see them."

He pointed out on the map where it had happened. There were three other people who had actually seen Fuzzies; none was sure how many, but they were all positive about locations and times. Plotting the reports on the map, it was apparent that the Fuzzies were moving north and west across the outskirts of the city.

Brannhard showed up for lunch at the hotel, still swearing, but half amusedly.

"They've exhumed Ham O'Brien, and they've put him to work harassing us," he said. "Whole flock of civil suits and dangerous-nuisance complaints and that sort of thing; idea's to keep me amused with them while Leslie Coombes is working up his case for the trial. Even tried to get the manager here to evict Baby; I threatened him with a racial-discrimination suit, and that stopped that. And I just filed suit against the Company for seven million sols on behalf of the Fuzzies—million apiece for them and a million for their lawyer."

"This evening," Jack said, "I'm going out in a car with a couple of Max's deputies. We're going to take Baby, and we'll have a loud-speaker on the car." He unfolded the city map. "They seem to be traveling this way; they ought to be about here, and with Baby at the speaker, we ought to attract their attention."

They didn't see anything, though they kept at it till dusk. Baby had a wonderful time with the loud-speaker; when he yeeked into it, he produced an ear-splitting noise, until the three humans in the car flinched every time he opened his mouth. It affected dogs too; as the car moved back and forth, it was followed by a chorus of howling and baying on the ground.

The next day, there were some scattered reports, mostly of small thefts. A blanket spread on the grass behind a house had vanished. A couple of cushions had been taken from a porch couch. A frenzied mother reported having found her six-year-old son playing with some Fuzzies; when she had rushed to rescue him, the Fuzzies had scampered away and the child had begun weeping. Jack and Gerd rushed to the scene. The child's story, jumbled and imagination-colored, was definite on one point—the Fuzzies had been nice to him and hadn't hurt him. They got a recording of that on the air at once.

When they got back to the hotel, Gus Brannhard was there, bubbling with glee.

"The Chief Justice gave me another job of special prosecuting," he said. "I'm to conduct an investigation into the possibility that this thing, the other night, was a frame-up, and I'm to prepare complaints against anybody who's done anything prosecutable. I have authority to hold hearings, and subpoena witnesses, and interrogate them under veridication. Max Fane has specific orders to cooperate. We're going to start, tomorrow, with Chief of Police Dumont and work down. And maybe we can work up, too, as far as Nick Emmert and Victor Grego." He gave a rumbling laugh. "Maybe that'll give Leslie Coombes something to worry about."

GERD BROUGHT THE car down beside the rectangular excavation. It was fifty feet square and twenty feet deep, and still going deeper, with a power shovel in it and a couple of dump scows beside. Five or six men in coveralls and ankle boots advanced to meet them as they got out.

"Good morning, Mr. Holloway," one of them said. "It's right down over the edge of the hill. We haven't disturbed anything."

"Mind running over what you saw again? My partner here wasn't in when you called."

The foreman turned to Gerd. "We put off a couple of shots about an hour ago. Some of the men, who'd gone down over the edge of the hill, saw these Fuzzies run out from under that rock ledge down there, and up the hollow, that way." He pointed. "They called me, and I went down for a look, and saw where they'd been camping. The rock's pretty hard here, and we used pretty heavy charges. Shock waves in the ground was what scared them."

They started down a path through the flower-dappled tall grass toward the edge of the hill, and down past the gray outcropping of limestone that formed a miniature bluff twenty feet high and a hundred in length. Under an overhanging ledge, they found two cushions, a red-and-gray blanket, and some odds and ends of old garments that looked as though they had once been used for polishing rags. There was a broken kitchen spoon, and a cold chisel, and some other metal articles.

"That's it, all right. I talked to the people who lost the blanket and the cushions. They must have made camp last night, after your gang stopped work; the blasting chased them out. You say you saw them go up that way?" he asked, pointing up the little stream that came down from the mountains to the north.

The stream was deep and rapid, too much so for easy fording by Fuzzies; they'd follow it back into the foothills. He took everybody's names and thanked them. If he found the Fuzzies himself and had to pay off on an information-received basis, it would take a mathematical genius to decide how much reward to pay whom.

"Gerd, if you were a Fuzzy, where would you go up there?" he asked.

Gerd looked up the stream that came rushing down from among the wooded foothills.

"There are a couple more houses farther up," he said. "I'd get above them. Then I'd go up one of those side ravines, and get up among the rocks, where the damnthings couldn't get me. Of course, there are no damnthings this close to town, but they wouldn't know that."

"We'll need a few more cars. I'll call Colonel Ferguson and see what he can do for me. Max is going to have his hands full with this investigation Gus started."

PIET DUMONT, THE Mallorysport chief of police, might have been a good cop once, but for as long as Gus Brannhard had known him, he had been what he was now—an empty shell of unsupported arrogance, with a sagging waistline and a puffy face that tried to look tough and only succeeded in looking unpleasant. He was sitting in a seat that looked like an old-fashioned electric chair, or like one of those instruments of torture to which beauty-shop customers submit themselves. There was a bright conical helmet on his head, and electrodes had been clamped to various portions of his anatomy. On the wall behind him was a circular screen which ought to have been a calm turquoise blue, but which was flickering from dark blue through violet to mauve. That was simple nervous tension and guilt and anger at the humiliation of being subjected to veridicated interrogation. Now and then there would be a stabbing flicker of bright red as he toyed mentally with some deliberate misstatement of fact.

"You know, yourself, that the Fuzzies didn't hurt that girl," Brannhard told him.

"I don't know anything of the kind," the police chief retorted. "All I know's what was reported to me."

That had started out a bright red; gradually it faded into purple. Evidently Piet Dumont was adopting a rules-of-evidence definition of truth.

"Who told you about it?"

"Luther Woller. Detective lieutenant on duty at the time."

The veridicator agreed that that was the truth and not much of anything but the truth.

"But you know that what really happened was that Lurkin beat the girl himself, and Woller persuaded them both to say the Fuzzies did it," Max Fane said.

"I don't know anything of the kind!" Dumont almost yelled. The screen blazed red. "All I know's what they told me; nobody said anything else." Red and blue, juggling in a typical quibbling pattern. "As far as I know, it was the Fuzzies done it."

"Now, Piet," Fane told him patiently. "You've used the same veridicator here often enough to know you can't get away with lying on it. Woller's making you the patsy for this, and you know that, too. Isn't it true, now, that to the best of your knowledge and belief those Fuzzies never touched that girl, and it wasn't till Woller talked to Lurkin and his daughter at headquarters that anybody even mentioned Fuzzies?"

The screen darkened to midnight blue, and then, slowly, it lightened.

"Yeah, that's true," Dumont admitted. He avoided their eyes, and his voice was surly. "I thought that was how it was, and I asked Woller. He just laughed at me and told me to forget it." The screen seethed momentarily with anger. "That son of a Khooghra thinks he's chief, not me. One word from me and he does just what he damn pleases!"

"Now your being smart, Piet," Fane said. "Let's start all over. . . ."

A CONSTABULARY CORPORAL was at the controls of the car Jack had rented from the hotel: Gerd had taken his place in one of the two constabulary cars. The third car shuttled between them, and all three talked back and forth by radio.

"Mr. Holloway." It was the trooper in the car Gerd had been piloting. "Your partner's down on the ground; he just called me with his portable. He's found a cracked prawn-shell."

"Keep talking; give me direction," the corporal at the control said, lifting up.

In a moment, they sighted the other car, hovering over a narrow ravine on the left bank of the stream. The third car was coming in from the north. Gerd was still squatting on the ground when they let down beside him. He looked up as they jumped out.

"This is it, Jack," he said. "Regular Fuzzy job."

So it was. Whatever they had used, it hadn't been anything sharp; the head was smashed instead of being cleanly severed. The shell, however, had been broken from underneath in the standard manner, and all four mandibles had been broken off for picks. They must have all eaten at the prawn, share alike. It had been done quite recently.

They sent the car up, and while all three of them circled about, they went up the ravine on foot, calling: "Little Fuzzy! Little Fuzzy!" They found a footprint, and then another, where seepage water had moistened the ground. Gerd was talking excitedly into the portable radio he carried slung on his chest.

"One of you, go ahead a quarter of a mile, and then circle back. They're in here somewhere."

"I see them! I see them!" a voice whooped out of the radio. "They're going up the slope on you right, among the rocks!"

"Keep them in sight; somebody come and pick us up, and we'll get above them and head them off."

The rental car dropped quickly, the corporal getting the door open. He didn't bother going off contragravity; as soon as they were in and had pulled the door shut behind them, he was lifting again. For a moment, the hill sung giddily as the car turned, and then Jack saw them, climbing the steep slope among the rocks. Only four of them, and one was helping another. He wondered which ones they were, what had happened to the other two and if the one that needed help had been badly hurt.

The car landed on the top, among the rocks, settling at an awkward angle. He, Gerd and the pilot piled out and started climbing and sliding down the declivity. Then he found himself in reach of a Fuzzy and grabbed. Two more dashed past him, up the steep hill. The one he snatched at had something in his hand, and aimed a vicious blow at his face with it; he had barely time to block it with his forearm. Then he was clutching the Fuzzy and disarming him; the weapon was a quarter-pound ball-peen hammer. He put it in his hip pocket and then picked up the struggling Fuzzy with both hands.

"You hit Pappy Jack!" he said reproachfully. "Don't you know Pappy any more? Poor scared little thing!"

The Fuzzy in his arms yeeked angrily. Then he looked, and it was no Fuzzy he had ever seen before—not Little Fuzzy, nor funny, pompous Ko-Ko, not mischievous Mike. It was a stranger Fuzzy.

"Well, no wonder; of course you didn't know Pappy Jack. You aren't one of Pappy Jack's Fuzzies at all!"

At the top, the constabulary corporal was sitting on a rock, clutching two Fuzzies, one under each arm. They stopped struggling and peeked piteously when they saw their companion also a captive.

"Your partner's down below, chasing the other one," the corporal said. "You'd better take these too; you know them and I don't."

"Hang onto them; they don't know me any better than they do you."

With one hand, he got a bit of Extee Three out of his coat and offered it; the Fuzzy gave a cry of surprised pleasure, snatched it and gobbled it. He must have eaten it before. When he gave some to the corporal, the other two, a male and a female, also seemed familiar with it. From below, Gerd was calling:

"I got one. It's a girl Fuzzy; I don't know if it's Mitzi or Cinderella. And, my God, wait till you see what she was carrying."

Gerd came into sight, the fourth Fuzzy struggling under one arm and a little kitten, black with a white face, peeping over the crook of his other elbow. He was too stunned with disappointment to look at it with more than vague curiosity.

"They aren't our Fuzzies, Gerd. I never saw any of them before."

"Jack, are you sure?"

"Of course I'm sure!" He was indignant. "Don't you think I know my own Fuzzies? Don't you think they'd know me?"

"Where'd the pussy come from?" the corporal wanted to know.

"God knows. They must have picked it up somewhere. She was carrying it in her arms, like a baby."

"They're somebody's Fuzzies. They've been fed Extee Three. We'll take them to the hotel. Whoever it is, I'll bet he misses them as much as I do mine."

His own Fuzzies, whom he would never see again. The full realization didn't hit him until he and Gerd were in the car again. There had been no trace of his Fuzzies from the time they had broken out of their cages at Science Center. This quartet had appeared the night the city police had manufactured the story of the attack on the Lurkin girl, and from the moment they had been seen by the youth who couldn't bring himself to fire on them, they had left a trail that he had been able to pick up at once and follow. Why hadn't his own Fuzzies attracted as much notice in the three weeks since they had vanished?

Because his own Fuzzies didn't exist anymore? They had never gotten out of the Science Center alive. Somebody Max Fane hadn't been able to question under veridication had murdered them. There was no use, anymore, trying to convince himself differently.

"We'll stop at their camp and pick up the blanket and the cushions and the rest of the things. I'll send the people who lost them checks," he said. "The Fuzzies ought to have those things."

13

THE MANAGEMENT OF the Hotel Mallory appeared to have undergone a change of heart, or of policy, toward Fuzzies. It might have been Gus Brannhard's threats of action for racial discrimination and the possibility that the Fuzzies might turn out to be a race instead of an animal species after all. The manager might have been shamed by the way the Lurkin story had crumbled into discredit, and influenced by the revived public sympathy for the Fuzzies. Or maybe he just decided that the chartered Zarathustra Company wasn't as omnipotent as he'd believed. At any rate, a large room, usually used for banquets, was made available for the Fuzzies George Lunt and Ben Rainsford were bringing in for the trial, and the four strangers and their black-and-white kitten were installed there. There were a lot of toys of different sorts, courtesy of the management, and a big viewscreen. The four strange Fuzzies dashed for this immediately and turned it on, yeeking in delight as they watched landing craft coming down and lifting out at the municipal spaceport. They found it very interesting. It only bored the kitten.

With some misgivings, Jack brought Baby down and introduced him. They were delighted with Baby, and Baby thought the kitten was the most wonderful thing he had ever seen. When it was time to feed them, Jack had his own dinner brought in, and ate with them. Gus and Gerd came down and joined him later.

"We got the Lurkin kid and her father," Gus said, and then falsettoed: " 'Naw, Pop gimme a beaten', and the cops told me to say it was the Fuzzies.' "

"She say that?"

"Under veridication, with the screen blue as a sapphire, in front of half a dozen witnesses and with audiovisuals on. Interworld's putting it on the air this evening. Her father admitted it, too; named Woller and the desk sergeant. We're still looking for them; till we get them, we aren't any closer to Emmert or Grego. We did pick up the two car cops, but they don't know anything on anybody but Woller."

That was good enough, as far as it went, Brannhard thought, but it didn't go far enough. There were those four strange Fuzzies showing up out of nowhere, right in the middle of Nick Emmert's drive-hunt. They'd been kept somewhere by somebody—that was how they'd learned to eat Extee Three and found out about viewscreens. Their appearance was too well synchronized to be accidental. The whole thing smelled to him of a booby trap.

One good thing had happened. Judge Pendarvis had decided that it would be next to impossible, in view of the widespread public interest in the case and the influence of the Zarathustra Company, to get an impartial jury, and had proposed a judicial trial by a panel of three judges, himself one of them. Even Leslie Coombes had felt forced to agree to that.

He told Jack about the decision. Jack listened with apparent attentiveness, and then said:

"You know, Gus, I'll always be glad I let Little Fuzzy smoke my pipe when he wanted to, that night out at camp."

The way he was feeling, he wouldn't have cared less if the case was going to be tried by a panel of three zaragoats.

Ben Rainsford, his two Fuzzies, and George Lunt, Ahmed Khadra and the other constabulary witnesses and their family, arrived shortly before noon on Saturday. The Fuzzies were quartered in the stripped-out banquet room, and quickly made friends with the four already there, and with Baby. Each family bedded down apart, but they ate together and played with each other's toys and sat in a clump to watch the viewscreen. At first, the Ferny Creek family showed jealousy when too much attention was paid to their kitten, until they decided that nobody was trying to steal it.

It would have been a lot of fun, eleven Fuzzies and a Baby Fuzzy and a black-and-white kitten, if Jack hadn't kept seeing his own family, six quiet little ghosts watching but unable to join the frolicking.

MAX FANE BRIGHTENED when he saw who was on his screen.

"Well, Colonel Ferguson, glad to see you."

"Marshal," Ferguson was smiling broadly. "You'll be even gladder in a minute. A couple of my men, from Post Eight, picked up Woller and that desk sergeant, Fuentes."

"Ha!" He started feeling warm inside, as though he had just downed a slug of Baldur honey-rum. "How?"

"Well, you know Nick Emmert has a hunting lodge down there. Post Eight keeps an eye on it for him. This afternoon, one of Lieutenant Obefemi's cars was passing over it, and they picked up some radiation and infrared on their detectors, as though the power was on inside. When they went down to investigate, they found Woller and Fuentes making themselves at home. They brought them in, and both of them admitted under veridication that Emmert had given them the keys and sent them down there to hide out till after the trial.

"They denied that Emmert had originated the frameup. That had been one of Woller's own flashes of genius, but Emmert knew what the score was and went right along with it. They're being brought up here the first thing tomorrow morning."

"Well, that's swell, Colonel! Has it gotten out to the news services yet?"

"No. We would like to have them both questioned here in Mallorysport, and their confessions recorded, before we let the story out. Otherwise, somebody might try to take steps to shut them up for good."

That had been what he had been thinking of. He said so, and Ferguson nodded. Then he hesitated for a moment, and said:

"Max, do you like the situation here in Mallorysport? Be damned if I do."

"What do you mean?"

"There are too many strangers in town," Ian Ferguson said. "All the same kind of strangers—husky-looking young men, twenty to thirty, going around in pairs and small groups. I've been noticing it since day before last, and there seem to be more of them every time I look around."

"Well, Ian, it's a young man's planet, and we can expect a big crowd in town for the trial. . . ."

He didn't really believe that. He just wanted Ian Ferguson to put a name on it first. Ferguson shook his head.

"No, Max. This isn't a trial-day crowd. We both know what they're like; remember when they tried the Gawn brothers? No whooping it up in bars, no excitement, no big crap games; this crowd's just walking around, keeping quiet, as though they expected a word from somebody."

"Infiltration." Goddamit, he'd said it first, himself after all! "Victor Grego's worried about this."

"I know it, Max. And Victor Grego's like a veldbeest bull; he isn't dangerous till he's scared, and then watch out. And against the gang that's moving in here, the men you and I have together would last about as long as a pint of trade-gin at a Sheshan funeral."

"You thinking of pushing the panic-button?"

The constabulary commander frowned. "I don't want to. A dim view would be taken back on Terra if I did it without needing to. Dimmer view would be taken of needing to without doing it, though. I'll make another check, first."

GERD VAN RIEBEEK sorted the papers on the desk into piles, lit a cigarette and then started to mix himself a highball.

"Fuzzies are members of a sapient race," he declared. "They reason logically, both deductively and inductively. They learn by experiment, analysis and association. They formulate general principles, and apply them to specific instances. They plan their activities in advance. They make designed artifacts, and artifacts to make artifacts. They are able to symbolize, and convey ideas in symbolic form, and form symbols by abstracting from objects.

"They have aesthetic sense and creativity," he continued. "They become bored in idleness, and they enjoy solving problems for the pleasure of solving them. They bury their dead ceremoniously, and bury artifacts with them."

He blew a smoke ring, and then tasted his drink. "They do all these things, and they also do carpenter work, blow police whistles, make eating tools to eat land-prawns with and put molecule-model balls together. Obviously they are sapient beings. But don't, *please* don't ask me to define sapience, because God damn it to Nifflheim, I still can't!"

"I think you just did." Jack said.

"No, that won't do. I need a definition."

"Don't worry, Gerd," Gus Brannhard told him. "Leslie Coombes will bring a nice shiny new definition into court. We'll just use that."

14

THEY WALKED TOGETHER, Frederic and Claudette Pendarvis, down through the roof garden toward the landing stage, and, as she always did, Claudette stopped and cut a flower and fastened it in his lapel.

"Will the Fuzzies be in court?" she asked.

"Oh, they'll have to be. I don't know about this morning; it'll be mostly formalities." He made a grimace that was half a frown and half a smile. "I really don't know whether to consider them as witnesses or as exhibits, and I hope I'm not called on to rule on that, at least at the start. Either way, Coombes or Brannhard would accuse me of showing prejudice."

"I want to see them. I've seen them on screen, but I want to see them for real."

"You haven't been in one of my courts for a long time, Claudette. If I find that they'll be brought in today, I'll call you. I'll even abuse my position to the extent of arranging for you to see them outside the courtroom. Would you like that?"

She'd love it. Claudette had a limitless capacity for delight in things like that. They kissed good-bye, and he went to where his driver was holding open the door of the aircar and got in. At a thousand feet he looked back; she was still standing at the edge of the roof garden, looking up.

He'd have to find out whether it would be safe for her to come in. Max Fane was worried about the possibility of trouble, and so was Ian Ferguson, and neither was given to timorous imaginings. As the car began to descend toward the Central Courts buildings, he saw that there were guards on the roof, and they weren't just carrying pistols—he caught the glint of rifle barrels, and the twinkle of steel helmets. Then, as he came in, he saw that their uniforms were a lighter shade of blue that the constabulary wore. Ankle boots and red-striped trousers; Space Marines in dress blues. So Ian Ferguson had pushed the button. It occurred to him that Claudette might be safer here than at home.

A sergeant and a couple of men came up as he got out; the sergeant touched the beak of his helmet in the nearest thing to a salute a Marine ever gave anybody in civilian clothes.

"Judge Pendarvis? Good morning, sir."

"Good morning, sergeant. Just why are Federation Marines guarding the court building?"

"Standing by, sir. Orders of Commodore Napier. You'll find that Marshal Fane's people are in charge below-decks, but Marine Captain Casagra and Navy Captain Greibenfeld are waiting to see you in your office."

As he started toward the elevators, a big Zarathustra Company car was coming in. The sergeant turned quickly, beckoned a couple of his men and went toward it on the double. He wondered what Leslie Coombes would think about those Marines.

The two officers in his private chambers were both wearing sidearms. So, also, was Marshal Fane, who was with them. They all rose to greet him, sitting down when he was at his desk. He asked the same question he had of the sergeant above.

"Well, Constabulary Colonel Ferguson called Commodore Napier last evening and requested armed assistance, your Honor," the officer in Space Navy black said. "He suspected, he said, that the city had been infiltrated. In that, your Honor, he was perfectly correct; beginning Wednesday afternoon, Marine Captain Casagra, here, on Commodore Napier's orders, began landing a Marine infiltration force, preparatory to taking over the Residency. That's been accomplished now; Commodore Napier is there, and both Resident General Emmert and Attorney General O'Brien are under arrest, on a variety of malfeasance and corrupt-practice charges, but that won't come into your Honor's court. They'll be sent back to Terra for trial."

"Then Commodore Napier's taken over the civil government?"

"Well, say he's assumed control of it, pending the outcome of this trial. We want to know whether the present administration's legal or not."

"Then you won't interfere with the trial itself?"

"That depends, your Honor. We are certainly going to participate." He looked at this watch. "You won't convene court for another hour? Then perhaps I'll have time to explain."

•   •   •

MAX FANE MET them at the courtroom door with a pleasant greeting. Then he
saw Baby Fuzzy on Jack's shoulder and looked dubious.

"I don't know about him, Jack. I don't think he'll be allowed in the
courtroom."

"Nonsense!" Gus Brannhard told him. "I admit, he is both a minor child and
an incompetent aborigine, but he is the only surviving member of the family of
the decedent Jane Doe alias Goldilocks, and as such has an indisputable right to
be present."

"Well, just as long as you keep him from sitting on people's heads. Gus, you
and Jack sit over there; Ben, you and Gerd find seats in the witness section."

It would be half an hour till court would convene, but already the spectators'
seats were full, and so was the balcony. The jury box, on the left of the bench,
was occupied by a number of officers in Navy black and Marine blue. Since
there would be no jury, they had apparently appropriated it for themselves. The
press box was jammed and bristling with equipment.

Baby was looking up interestedly at the big screen behind the judges' seats;
while transmitting the court scene to the public, it also showed, like a
nonreversing mirror, the same view to the spectators. Baby wasn't long in
identifying himself in it, and waved his arms excitedly. At that moment, there
was a bustle at the door by which they had entered, and Leslie Coombes came
in, followed by Ernst Mallin and a couple of his assistants, Ruth Ortheris, Juan
Jimenez—and Leonard Kellogg. The last time he had seen Kellogg had been at
George Lunt's complaint court, his face bandaged and his feet in a pair of
borrowed moccasins because his shoes, stained with the blood of Goldilocks,
had been impounded as evidence.

Coombes glanced toward the table where he and Brannhard were sitting,
caught sight of Baby waving to himself in the big screen and turned to Fane with
an indignant protest. Fane shook his head. Coombes protested again, and drew
another headshake. Finally he shrugged and led Kellogg to the table reserved for
them, where they sat down.

Once Pendarvis and his two associates—a short, round-faced man on his
right, a tall, slender man with white hair and a black mustache on his left—were
seated, the trial got underway briskly. The charges were read, and then
Brannhard, as the Kellogg prosecutor, addressed the court—"being known as
Goldilocks . . . sapient member of a sapient race . . . willful and deliberate
act of the said Leonard Kellogg . . . brutal and unprovoked murder." He
backed away, sat on the edge of the table and picked up Baby Fuzzy, fondling

him while Leslie Coombes accused Jack Holloway of brutally assaulting the said Leonard Kellogg and ruthlessly shooting down Kurt Borch.

"Well, gentlemen, I believe we can now begin hearing the witnesses," the Chief Justice said. "Who will start prosecuting whom?"

Gus handed Baby to Jack and went forward; Coombes stepped up beside him.

"Your Honor, this entire trial hinges upon the question of whether a member of the species *Fuzzy fuzzy holloway zarathustra* is or is not a sapient being," Gus said. "However, before any attempt is made to determine this question, we should first establish, by testimony, just what happened at Holloway's Camp, in Cold Creek Valley, on the afternoon of June 19, Atomic Era Six Fifty-Four, and once this is established, we can then proceed to the question of whether or not the said Goldilocks was truly a sapient being."

"I agree," Coombes said equably. "Most of these witnesses will have to be recalled to the stand later, but in general I think Mr. Brannhard's suggestion will be economical of the court's time."

"Will Mr. Coombes agree to stipulate that any evidence tending to prove or disprove the sapience of Fuzzies in general be accepted as proving or disproving the sapience of the being referred to as Goldilocks?"

Coombes looked that over carefully, decided that it wasn't booby-trapped and agreed. A deputy marshal went over to the witness stand, made some adjustments and snapped on a switch at the back of the chair. Immediately the two-foot globe in a standard behind it lit, a clear blue. George Lunt's name was called; the lieutenant took his seat and the bright helmet was let down over his head and the electrodes attached.

The globe stayed a calm, untroubled blue while he stated his name and rank. Then he waited while Coombes and Brannhard conferred. Finally Brannhard took a silver half-sol piece from his pocket, shook it between cupped palms and slapped it onto his wrist. Coombes said, "Heads," and Brannhard uncovered it, bowed slightly and stepped back.

"Now, Lieutenant Lunt," Coombes began, "when you arrived at the temporary camp across the run from Holloway's camp, what did you find there?"

"Two dead people," Lunt said. "A Terran human, who had been shot three times through the chest, and a Fuzzy, who had been kicked or trampled to death."

"Your Honors!" Coombes expostulated, "I must ask that the witness be requested to rephrase his answer, and that the answer he has just made be stricken from the record. The witness, under the circumstances, has no right to refer to the Fuzzies as 'people.'"

"Your Honors," Brannhard caught it up, "Mr. Coombes's objection is no less prejudicial. He has no right, under the circumstances, to deny that the Fuzzies be referred to as 'people.' This is tantamount to insisting that the witness speak of them as nonsapient animals."

It went on like that for five minutes. Jack began doodling on a notepad. Baby picked up a pencil with both hands and began making doodles too. They looked rather like the knots he had been learning to tie. Finally, the court intervened and told Lunt to tell, in his own words, why he went to Holloway's camp, what he found there, what he was told and what he did. There was some argument between Coombes and Brannhard, at one point, about the difference between hearsay and *res gestae*. When he was through, Coombes said, "No questions."

"Lieutenant, you placed Leonard Kellogg under arrest on a complaint of homicide by Jack Holloway. I take it that you considered this complaint a valid one?"

"Yes, sir. I believed that Leonard Kellogg had killed a sapient being. Only sapient beings bury their dead."

Ahmed Khadra testified. The two troopers who had come in the other car, and the men who had brought the investigative equipment and done the photographing at the scene testified. Brannhard called Ruth Ortheris to the stand, and, after some futile objections by Coombes, she was allowed to tell her own story of the killing of Goldilocks, the beating of Kellogg and the shooting of Borch. When she had finished, the Chief Justice rapped with his gavel.

"I believe that this testimony is sufficient to establish the fact that the being referred to as Jane Doe alias Goldilocks was in fact kicked and trampled to death by the defendant Leonard Kellogg, and that the Terran human known as Kurt Borch was in fact shot to death by Jack Holloway. This being the case, we may now consider whether or not either or both of these killings constitute murder within the meaning of the law. It is now eleven forty. We will adjourn for lunch, and court will reconvene at fourteen hundred. There are a number of things, including some alterations to the courtroom, which must be done before the afternoon session . . . Yes, Mr. Brannhard?"

"Your Honors, there is only one member of the species *Fuzzy fuzzy holloway zarathustra* at present in court, an immature and hence nonrepresentative individual." He picked up Baby and exhibited him. "If we are to take up the question of the sapience of this species, or race, would it not be well to send for the Fuzzies now saying at the Hotel Mallory and have them on hand?"

"Well, Mr. Brannhard," Pendarvis said, "we will certainly want Fuzzies in court, but let me suggest that we wait until after court reconvenes before sending

for them. It may be that they will not be needed this afternoon. Anything else?"
He tapped with his gavel. "Then court is adjourned until fourteen hundred."

SOME ALTERATIONS IN the courtroom had been a conservative way of putting it.
Four rows of spectators' seats had been abolished, and the dividing rail moved
back. The witness chair, originally at the side of the bench, had been moved to
the dividing rail and now faced the bench, and a large number of tables had been
brought in and arranged in an arc with the witness chair in the middle of it.
Everybody at the tables could face the judges, and also see everybody else by
looking into the big screen. A witness on the chair could also see the veridicator
in the same way.

Gus Brannhard looked around, when he entered with Jack, and swore softly.
"No wonder they gave us two hours for lunch. I wonder what the idea is."
Then he gave a short laugh. "Look at Coombes; he doesn't like it a bit."

A deputy with a seating diagram came up to them.

"Mr. Brannhard, you and Mr. Holloway over here, at this table." He pointed
to one a little apart from the others, at the extreme right facing the bench. "And
Dr. van Riebeek, and Dr. Rainsford over here, please."

The court crier's loud-speaker, overhead, gave two sharp whistles and
began:

"Now hear this! Now hear this! Court will convene in five minutes—"

Brannhard's head jerked around instantly, and Jack's eyes followed his. The
court crier was a Space Navy petty officer.

"What the devil is this?" Brannhard demanded. "A Navy court-martial?"

"That's what I've been wondering, Mr. Brannhard," the deputy said.
"They've taken over the whole planet, you know."

"Maybe we're in luck, Gus. I've always heard that if you're innocent you're
better off before a court-martial and if you're guilty you're better off in a civil
court."

He saw Leslie Coombes and Leonard Kellogg being seated at a similar table
at the opposite side of the bench. Apparently Coombes had also heard that. The
seating arrangements at the other tables seemed a little odd too. Gerd van
Riebeek was next to Ruth Ortheris, and Ernst Mallin was next to Ben Rainsford,
with Juan Jimenez on his other side. Gus was looking up at the balcony.

"I'll bet every lawyer on the planet's taking this in," he said. "Oh-oh! See
the white-haired lady in the blue dress, Jack? That's the Chief Justice's wife.
This is the first time she's been in court for years."

"Hear ye! Hear ye! Hear ye! Rise for the Honorable Court!"

Somebody must have given the petty officer a quick briefing on courtroom phraseology. He stood up, holding Baby Fuzzy, while the three judges filed in and took their seats. As soon as they sat down, the Chief Justice rapped briskly with his gavel.

"In order to forestall a spate of objections, I want to say that these present arrangements are temporary, and so will be the procedures which will be followed. We are not, at the moment, trying Jack Holloway or Leonard Kellogg. For the rest of this day, and, I fear, for a good many days to come, we will be concerned exclusively with determining the level of mentation of *Fuzzy fuzzy holloway zarathustra.*

"For this purpose, we are temporarily abandoning some of the traditional trial procedures. We will call witnesses; statements of purported fact will be made under veridication as usual. We will also have a general discussion, in which all of you at these tables will be free to participate. I and my associates will preside; as we can't have everybody shouting disputations at once, anyone wishing to speak will have to be recognized. At least, I hope we will be able to conduct the discussion in this manner.

"You will all have noticed the presence of a number of officers from Xerxes Naval Base, and I suppose you have all heard that Commodore Napier has assumed control of the civil government. Captain Greibenfeld, will you please rise and be seen? He is here participating as *amicus curiae,* and I have given him the right to question witnesses and to delegate that right to any of his officers he may deem proper. Mr. Coombes and Mr. Brannhard may also delegate that right as they see fit."

Coombes was on his feet at once. "Your Honors, if we are now to discuss the sapience question, I would suggest that the first item on our order of business be the presentation of some acceptable definition of sapience. I should, for my part, very much like to know what it is that the Kellogg prosecution and the Holloway defense mean when they use that term."

That's it. They want us to define it. Gerd van Riebeek was looking chagrined; Ernst Mallin was smirking. Gus Brannhard, however, was pleased.

"Jack, they haven't any more damn definition than we do," he whispered.

Captain Greibenfeld, who had seated himself after rising at the request of the court, was on his feet again.

"Your Honors, during the past month we at Xerxes Naval Base have been working on exactly that problem. We have a very considerable interest in having the classification of this planet established, and we also feel that this may not be the last time a question of disputable sapience may arise. I believe, your Honors, that we have approached such a definition. However, before we begin discussing it, I would like the court's permission to present a demonstration which may be of help in understanding the problems involved."

"Captain Greibenfeld has already discussed this demonstration with me, and it has my approval. Will you please proceed, Captain," the Chief Justice said.

Greibenfeld nodded, and a deputy marshal opened the door on the right of the bench. Two spacemen came in, carrying cartons. One went up to the bench; the other started around in front of the tables, distributing small battery-powered hearing aids.

"Please put them in your ears and turn them on," he said. "Thank you."

Baby Fuzzy tried to get Jack's. He put the plug in his ear and switched on the power. Instantly he began hearing a number of small sounds he had never heard before, and Baby was saying to him: *"He-inta sa-wa'aka; igga sa geeda?"*

"Muhgawd, Gus, he's talking!"

"Yes, I hear him; what do you suppose—?"

"Ultrasonic; God, why didn't we think of that long ago?"

He snapped off the hearing aid. Baby Fuzzy was saying, "Yeeek." When he turned it on again, Baby was saying, *"Kukk-ina za zeeva."*

"No, Baby, Pappy Jack doesn't understand. We'll have to be awfully patient, and learn each other's language."

"Pa-pee Jaaak!" Baby cried. *"Ba-bee za-hinga; Pa-pee Jaak za zag ga he-izza!"*

"That yeeking is just the audible edge of their speech; bet we have a lot of transsonic tones in our voices, too."

"Well, he can hear what we say; he's picked up his name and yours."

"Mr. Brannhard, Mr. Holloway," Judge Pendarvis was saying, "may we please have your attention? Now, have you all your earplugs in and turned on? Very well; carry on, Captain."

This time, an ensign went out and came back with a crowd of enlisted men, who had six Fuzzies with them. They set them down in the open space between the bench and the arc of tables and backed away. The Fuzzies drew together into a clump and stared around them, and he stared, unbelievingly, at them. They couldn't be; they didn't exist any more. But they were—Little Fuzzy and Mamma Fuzzy and Mike and Mitzi and Ko-Ko and Cinderella. Baby whooped something and leaped from the table, and Mamma came stumbling to meet him, clasping him in her arms. Then they all saw him and began clamoring: *"Pa-pee Jaaak! Pa-pee Jaaak!"*

He wasn't aware of rising and leaving the table; the next thing he realized, he was sitting on the floor, his family mobbing him and hugging him, gabbling with joy. Dimly he heard the gavel hammering, and the voice of Chief Justice Pendarvis: "Court is recessed for ten minutes!" By that time, Gus was with him; gathering the family up, they carried them over to their table.

They stumbled and staggered when they moved, and that frightened him for a moment. Then he realized that they weren't sick or drugged. They'd just been in low-G for a while and hadn't become reaccustomed to normal weight. Now he knew why he hadn't been able to find any trace of them. He noticed that each of them was wearing a little shoulder bag—a Marine Corps first-aid pouch—slung from a webbing strap. Why the devil hadn't he thought of making them something like that? He touched one and commented, trying to pitch his voice as nearly like theirs as he could. They all babbled in reply and began opening the little bags and showing him what they had in them—little knives and miniature tools and bits of bright or colored junk they had picked up. Little Fuzzy produced a tiny pipe with a hardwood bowl, and little pouch of tobacco from which he filled it. Finally, he got out a small lighter.

"Your Honors!" Gus shouted, "I know court is recessed, but please observe what Little Fuzzy is doing."

While they watched, Little Fuzzy snapped the lighter and held the flame to the pipe bowl, puffing.

Across on the other side, Leslie Coombes swallowed once or twice and closed his eyes.

When Pendarvis rapped for attention and declared court reconvened, he said:

"Ladies and gentlemen, you have all seen and heard this demostration of Captain Greibenfeld's. You have heard these Fuzzies uttering what certainly sounds like meaningful speech, and you have seen one of them light a pipe and smoke. Incidentally, while smoking in court is discountenanced, we are going to make an exception, during this trial, in favor of Fuzzies. Other people will please not feel themselves discriminated against."

That brought Coombes to his feet with a rush. He started around the table and then remembered that under the new rules he didn't have to.

"Your Honors, I objected strongly to the use of that term by a witness this morning; I must object even more emphatically to its employment from the bench. I have indeed heard these Fuzzies make sounds which might be mistaken for words, but I must deny that this is true speech. As to this trick of using a lighter, I will undertake, in not more than thirty days, to teach it to any Terran primate or Freyan kholph."

Greibenfeld rose immediately. "Your Honors, in the past thirty days, while these Fuzzies were at Xerxes Naval Base, we have compiled a vocabulary of a hundred-odd Fuzzy words, for all of which definite meanings have been established, and a great many more for which we have not as yet learned the meanings. We even have the beginning of a Fuzzy grammar. As for this so-called trick of using a lighter, Little Fuzzy—we didn't know his name then and referred to him as M2—learned that for himself, by observation. We didn't teach him to smoke a pipe either; he knew that before we had anything to do with him."

Jack rose while Greibenfeld was still speaking. As soon as the Space Navy captain had finished, he said:

"Captain Greibenfeld, I want to thank you and your people for taking care of the Fuzzies, and I'm very glad you learned how to hear what they're saying, and thank you for all the nice things you gave them, but why couldn't you have let me know they were safe? I haven't been very happy the last month, you know."

"I know that, Mr. Holloway, and if it's any comfort to you, we were all very sorry for you, but we could not take the risk of compromising our secret intelligence agent in the Company's Science Center, the one who smuggled the Fuzzies out the morning after their escape." He looked quickly across in front of the bench to the table at the other end of the arc. Kellogg was sitting with his face in his hands, oblivious to everything that was going on, but Leslie Coombes's well-disciplined face had broken, briefly, into a look of consternation. "By the time you and Mr. Brannhard and Marshal Fane arrived with an order of the court for the Fuzzies' recovery, they had already been taken from Science Center and were on a Navy landing craft for Xerxes. We couldn't do anything without exposing our agent. That, I am glad to say, is no longer a consideration."

"Well, Captain Greibenfeld," the Chief Justice said, "I assume you mean to introduce further testimony about the observations and studies made by your people on Xerxes. For the record, we'd like to have it established that they were actually taken there, and when, and how."

"Yes, your Honor. If you will call the fourth name on the list I gave you, and allow me to do the questioning, we can establish that."

The Chief Justice picked up a paper. "Lieutenant j.g. Ruth Ortheris, TFN Reserve," he called out.

This time, Jack Holloway looked up into the big screen, in which he could see everybody. Gerd van Riebeek, who had been trying to ignore the existence of the woman beside him, had turned to stare at her in amazement. Coombes's face was ghastly for an instant, then froze into corpselike immobility: Ernst Mallin was dithering in incredulous anger; beside him Ben Rainsford was grinning in just as incredulous delight. As Ruth came around in front of the bench, the Fuzzies gave her an ovation; they remembered and liked her. Gus Brannhard was gripping his arm and saying: "Oh, brother! This is it, Jack; it's all over but shooting the cripples!"

Lieutenant j.g. Ortheris, under a calmly blue globe, testified to coming to

Zarathustra as a Federation Naval Reserve officer recalled to duty with Intelligence, and taking a position with the Company.

"As a regularly qualified doctor of psychology, I worked under Dr. Mallin in the scientific division, and also with the school department and the juvenile court. At the same time I was regularly transmitting reports to Commander Aelborg, the chief of Intelligence on Xerxes. The object of this surveillance was to make sure that the Zarathustra Company was not violating the provisions of their charter or Federation law. Until the middle of last month, I had nothing to report beyond some rather irregular financial transactions involving Resident General Emmert. Then, on the evening of June fifteen—"

That was when Ben had transmitted the tape to Juan Jimenez; she described how it had come to her attention.

"As soon as possible, I transmitted a copy of this tape to Commander Aelborg. The next night, I called Xerxes from the screen on Dr. van Riebeek's boat and reported what I'd learned about the Fuzzies. I was then informed that Leonard Kellogg had gotten hold of copy of the Holloway-Rainsford tape and had alerted Victor Grego; that Kellogg and Ernst Mallin were being sent to Beta Continent with instructions to prevent publication of any report claiming sapience for the Fuzzies and to fabricate evidence to support an accusation that Dr. Rainsford and Mr. Holloway were perpetrating a deliberate scientific hoax."

"Here, I'll have to object to this, your Honor," Coombes said, rising. "This is nothing but hearsay."

"This is part of a Navy Intelligence situation estimate given to Lieutenant Ortheris, based on reports we had received from other agents," Captain Greibenfeld said. "She isn't the only one we have on Zarathustra, you know. Mr. Coombes, if I hear another word of objection to this officer's testimony from you, I am going to ask Mr. Brannhard to subpoena Victor Grego and question him under veridication about it."

"Mr. Brannhard will be more than happy to oblige, Commander," Gus said loudly and distinctly.

Coombes sat down hastily.

"Well, Lieutenant Ortheris, this is most interesting, but at the moment, what we're trying to establish is how these Fuzzies got to Xerxes Naval Base," the chubby associate justice, Ruiz, put in.

"I'll try to get them there as quickly as possible, your Honor," she said. "On the night of Friday the twenty-second, the Fuzzies were taken from Mr. Holloway and brought into Mallorysport; they were turned over by Mohammed Ali O'Brien to Juan Jimenez, who took them to Science Center and put them in cages in a room back of his office. They immediately escaped. I found them, the next morning, and was able to get them out of the building, and to turn them over to Commander Aelborg, who had come down from Xerxes to take personal charge of the Fuzzy operation. I will not testify as to how I was able to do this. I am at present and was then an officer of the Terran Federation Armed Forces; the courts have no power to compel a Federation officer to give testimony involving breach of military security. I was informed, through my contact in Mallorysport, from time to time, of the progress of the work of measuring the Fuzzies' mental level there; I was able to pass on suggestions occasionally. Any time any of these suggestions was based on ideas originating with Dr. Mallin, I was careful to give him full credit."

Mallin looked singularly unappreciative.

Brannhard got up. "Before this witness is excused, I'd like to ask if she knows anything about four other Fuzzies, the ones found by Jack Holloway up Ferny Creek on Friday."

"Why, yes; they're my Fuzzies, and I was worried about them. Their names are Complex, Syndrome, Id and Superego."

"Your Fuzzies, Lieutenant?"

"Well, I took care of them and worked with them; Juan Jimenez and some Company hunters caught them over on Beta Continent. They were kept at a farm center about five hundred miles north of here, which had been vacated for the purpose. I spent all my time with them, and Dr. Mallin was with them most of the time. Then, on Monday night, Mr. Coombes came and got them."

"Mr. Coombes, did you say?" Gus Brannhard asked.

"Mr. Leslie Coombes, the Company attorney. He said they were needed in Mallorysport. It wasn't till the next day that I found out what they were needed for. They'd been turned loose in front of that Fuzzy hunt, in the hope that they would be killed."

She looked across at Coombes; if looks were bullets, he'd have been deader than Kurt Borch.

"Why would they sacrifice four Fuzzies merely to support a story that was bound to come apart anyhow?" Brannhard asked.

"That was no sacrifice. They had to get rid of those Fuzzies, and they were afraid to kill them themselves for fear they'd be charged with murder along with Leonard Kellogg. Everybody, from Ernst Mallin down, who had anything to do with them was convinced of their sapience. For one thing, we'd been using those hearing aids ourselves; I suggested it, after getting the idea from Xerxes. Ask Dr. Mallin about it, under verdication. Ask him about the multiordinal polyencephalograph experiments, too."

"Well, we have the Holloway Fuzzies placed on Xerxes," the Chief Justice said. "We can hear the testimony of the people who worked with them there at any time. Now, I want to hear from Dr. Ernst Mallin."

Coombes was on his feet again. "Your Honors, before any further testimony is heard, I would like to confer with my client privately."

"I fail to see any reason why we should interrupt proceedings for that purpose, Mr. Coombes. You can confer as much as you wish with your client after this session, and I can assure you that you will be called upon to do nothing on his behalf until then." He gave a light tap with his gavel and then said: "Dr. Ernst Mallin will please take the stand."

15

ERNST MALLIN SHRANK, as though trying to pull himself into himself, when he heard his name. He didn't want to testify. He had been dreading this moment for days. Now he would have to sit in that chair, and they would ask him questions, and he couldn't answer them truthfully and the globe over his head—

When the deputy marshal touched his shoulder and spoke to him, he didn't think, at first, that his legs would support him. It seemed miles, with all the staring faces on either side of him. Somehow, he reached the chair and sat down, and they fitted the helmet over his head and attached the electrodes. They used to make a witness take some kind of oath to tell the truth. They didn't any more. They didn't need to.

As soon as the veridicator was on, he looked up at the big screen behind the four judges; the globe above his head was a glaring red. There was a titter of laughter. Nobody in the courtroom knew better than he what was happening. He had screens in his laboratory that broke it all down into individual patterns—the steady pulsing waves from the cortex, the alpha and beta waves; beta-aleph and beta-beth and beta-gimel and beta-daleth. The thalamic waves. He thought of all of them, and of the electromagnetic events which accompanied brain activity. As he did, the red faded and the globe became blue. He was no longer suppressing statements and substituting other statements he knew to be false. If he could keep it that way. But, sooner or later, he knew, he wouldn't be able to.

The globe stayed blue while he named himself and stated his professional background. There was a brief flicker of red while he was listing his publication—that paper, entirely the work of one of his students, which he had published under his own name. He had forgotten about that, but his conscience hadn't.

"Dr. Mallin," the oldest of the three judges, who sat in the middle, began, "what, in your professional opinion, is the difference between sapient and nonsapient mentation?"

"The ability to think consciously," he stated. The globe stayed blue.

"Do you mean that nonsapient animals aren't conscious, or do you mean they don't think?"

"Well, neither. Any life form with a central nervous system has some consciousness—awareness of existence and of its surroundings. And anything having a brain thinks, to use the term at its loosest. What I meant was that only the sapient mind thinks and knows that it is thinking."

He was perfectly safe so far. He talked about sensory stimuli and responses, and about conditioned reflexes. He went back to the first century Pre-Atomic, and Pavlov and Korzybski and Freud. The globe never flickered.

"The nonsapient animal is conscious only of what is immediately present to the senses and responds automatically. It will perceive something and make a single statement about it—this is good to eat, this sensation is unpleasant, this is a sex-gratification object, this is dangerous. The sapient mind, on the other hand, is conscious of thinking about these sense stimuli, and makes descriptive statements about them, and then makes statements about those statements, in a connected chain. I have a structural differential at my seat; if somebody will bring it to me—"

"Well, never mind now, Dr. Mallin. When you're off the stand and the discussion begins you can show what you mean. We just want your opinion in general terms, now."

"Well, the sapient mind can generalize. To the nonsapient animal, every experience is either totally novel or identical with some remembered experience. A rabbit will flee from one dog because to the rabbit mind it is identical with another dog that has chased it. A bird will be attracted to an apple, and each apple will be a unique red thing to peck at. The sapient being will say, 'These red objects are apples; as a class, they are edible and flavorsome.' He sets up a class under the general label of apples. This, in turn, leads to the formation of abstract ideas—redness, flavor, et cetera—conceived of apart from any specific physical object, and to the ordering of abstractions—'fruit' as distinguished from apples, 'food' as distinguished from fruit."

The globe was still placidly blue. The three judges waited, and he continued:

"Having formed these abstract ideas, it becomes necessary to symbolize them, in order to deal with them apart from the actual object. The sapient being is a symbolizer, and a symbol communicator; he is able to convey to other sapient beings his ideas in symbolic form."

"Like *'Pa-pee Jaak'?*" the judge on his right, with the black mustache, asked.

The globe flashed red at once.

"Your Honors, I cannot consider words picked up at random and learned by rote speech. The Fuzzies have merely learned to associate that sound with a specific human, and use it as a signal, not as a symbol."

The globe was still red. The Chief Justice, in the middle, rapped with his gavel.

"Dr. Mallin! Of all the people on this planet, you at least should know the impossibility of lying under veridication. Other people just know it can't be done; you know why. Now I'm going to rephrase Judge Janiver's question, and I'll expect you to answer truthfully. If you don't I'm going to hold you in contempt. When those Fuzzies cried out, 'Pappy Jack!' do you or do you not believe that they were using a verbal expression which stood, in their minds, for Mr. Holloway?"

He couldn't say it. This sapience was all a big fake; he had to believe that. The Fuzzies were only little mindless animals.

But he didn't believe it. He knew better. He gulped for a moment.

"Yes, your Honor. The term 'Pappy Jack' is, in their minds, a symbol standing for Mr. Jack Holloway."

He looked at the globe. The red had turned to mauve, the mauve was becoming violet, and then clear blue. He felt better than he had felt since the afternoon Leonard Kellogg had told him about the Fuzzies.

"Then Fuzzies do think consciously, Dr. Mallin?" That was Pendarvis.

"Oh, yes. The fact that they use verbal symbols indicates that, even without other evidence. And the instrumental evidence was most impressive. The mentation pictures we got by encephalography compare very favorably with those of any human child of ten or twelve years old, and so does their learning and puzzle-solving ability. On puzzles, they always think the problem out first, and, then do the mechanical work with about the same mental effort, say, as a man washing his hands or tying his neckcloth."

The globe was perfectly blue. Mallin had given up trying to lie; he was simply gushing out everything he thought.

LEONARD KELLOGG SLUMPED forward, his head buried in his elbows on the table, and misery washed over him in tides.

I am a murderer; I killed a person. Only a funny little person with fur, but she was a person, and I knew it when I killed her, I knew it when I saw that little

grave out in the woods, and they'll put me in the chair and make me admit it to
everybody, and then they'll take me out in the jail yard and somebody will shoot
me through the head with a pistol, and —

And all the poor little thing wanted was to show me her new jingle!

"DOES ANYBODY WANT to ask the witness any questions?" the Chief Justice
was asking.

"I don't," Captain Greibenfeld said. "Do you, Lieutenant?"

"No, I don't think so," Lieutenant Ybarra said. "Dr. Mallin's given us a very
lucid statement of his opinions."

He had, at that, after he'd decided he couldn't beat the veridicator. Jack
found himself sympathizing with Mallin. He'd disliked the man from the first,
but he looked different now—sort of cleaned and washed out inside. Maybe
everybody ought to be veridicated, now and then, to teach them that honesty
begins with honesty to self.

"Mr. Coombes?" Mr. Coombes looked as though he never wanted to ask
another witness another question as long as he lived. "Mr. Brannhard?"

Gus, got up, holding a sapient member of a sapient race who was hanging
onto his beard, and thanked Ernst Mallin fulsomely.

"In that case we'll adjourn until o-nine-hundred tomorrow. Mr. Coombes, I
have here a check on the chartered Zarathustra Company for twenty-five
thousand sols. I am returning it to you and I am canceling Dr. Kellogg's bail,"
Judge Pendarvis said, as a couple of attendants began getting Mallin loose from
the veridicator.

"Are you also canceling Jack Holloway's?"

"No, and I would advise you not to make an issue of it, Mr. Coombes. The
only reason I haven't dismissed the charge against Mr. Holloway is that I don't
want to handicap you by cutting off your foothold in the prosecution. I do not
consider Mr. Holloway a bail risk. I do so consider your client, Dr. Kellogg."

"Frankly, your Honor, so do I," Coombes admitted. "My protest was merely
an example of what Dr. Mallin would call conditioned reflex."

Then a crowd began pushing up around the table; Ben Rainsford, George
Lunt and his troopers, Gerd and Ruth, shoving in among them, their arms around
each other.

"We'll be at the hotel after a while, Jack," Gerd was saying. "Ruth and I
are going out for a drink and something to eat; we'll be around later to pick up
her Fuzzies."

Now his partner had his girl back, and his partner's girl had a Fuzzy family
of her own. This was going to be real fun. What were their names now?
Syndrome, Complex, Id and Superego. The things some people named Fuzzies!

16

Т HEY STOPPED WHISPERING at the door, turned right, and ascended to the bench, bearing themselves like images in a procession, Ruiz first, then himself and then Janiver. They turned to the screen so that the public whom they served might see the faces of the judges, and then sat down. The court crier began his chant. They could almost feel the tension in the courtroom. Yves Janiver whispered to them:

"They all know about it."

As soon as the crier had stopped, Max Fane approached the bench, his face blankly expressionless.

"Your Honors, I am ashamed to have reported that the defendant, Leonard Kellogg, cannot be produced in court. He is dead; he committed suicide in his cell last night. While in my custody," he added bitterly.

The stir that went through the courtroom was not shocked surprise, it was a sigh of fulfilled expectation. They all knew about it.

"How did this happen, Marshal?" he asked, almost conversationally.

"The prisoner was put in a cell by himself; there was a pickup eye, and one of the deputies was keeping him under observation by screen." Fane spoke in a toneless, almost robotlike voice. At twenty-two thirty, the prisoner went to bed, still wearing his shirt. He pulled the blankets up over his head. The deputy observing him thought nothing of that; many prisoner do that, on account of the light. He tossed about for a while, and then appeared to fall asleep.

"When a guard went in to rouse him this morning, the cot, under the blanket, was found saturated with blood. Kellogg had cut his throat, by sawing the zipper track of his shirt back and forth till he severed his jugular vein. He was dead."

"Good heavens, Marshal!" He was shocked. The way he'd heard it, Kellogg had hidden a penknife, and he was prepared to be severe with Fane about it. But a thing like this! He found himself fingering the toothed track of this own jacket zipper. "I don't believe you can be at all censured for not anticipating a thing like that. It isn't a thing anybody would expect."

Janiver and Ruiz spoke briefly in agreement. Marshal Fane bowed slightly and went off to one side.

Leslie Coombes, who seemed to be making a very considerable effort to look grieved and shocked, rose.

"Your Honors, I find myself here without a client," he said. " In fact, I find myself here without any business at all; the case against Mr. Holloway is absolutely insupportable. He shot a man who was trying to kill him, and that's all there is to it. I therefore pray your Honors to dismiss the case against him and discharge him from custody."

Captain Greibenfeld bounded to his feet.

"Your Honors, I fully realized that the defendant is now beyond the jurisdiction of this court, but let me point out that I and my associates are here participating in this case in the hope that the classification of this planet may be determined, and some adequate definition of sapience established. These are most serious questions, your Honors."

"But, your Honors," Coombes protested, "we can't go through the farce of trying a dead man."

"*People of the Colony of Baphomet* versus *Jamshar Singh, Deceased,* charge of arson and sabotage, A.E. 604," the Honorable Gustavus Adolphus Brannhard interrupted.

Yes, you could find a precedent in colonial law for almost anything.

Jack Holloway was on his feet, a Fuzzy cradled in the crook of his left arm, his white mustache bristling truculently.

"I am not a dead man, your Honors, and I am on trial here. The reason I'm not dead is why I am on trial. My defense is that I shot Kurt Borch while he was aiding and abetting in the killing of a Fuzzy. I want it established in this court that it is murder to kill a Fuzzy."

The judge nodded slowly. "I will not dismiss the charges against Mr. Holloway," he said. "Mr. Holloway had been arraigned on a charge of murder; if he is not guilty, he is entitled to the vindication of an acquittal. I am afraid, Mr. Coombes, that you will have to go on prosecuting him."

Another brief stir, like a breath of wind over a grain field, ran through the courtroom. The show was going on after all.

• • •

ALL THE FUZZIES were in court this morning: Jack's six, and the five from the constabulary post, and Ben's Flora and Fauna, and the four Ruth Ortheris claimed. There was too much discussion going on for anybody to keep an eye on them. Finally one the constabulary Fuzzies, either Dillinger or Dr. Crippen, and Ben Rainsford's Flora and Fauna, came sauntering out into the open space between the tables and the bench dragging the hose of a vacuum-duster. Ahmed Khadra ducked under a table and tried to get it away from them. This was wonderful; screaming in delight, they all laid hold of the other end, and Mike and Mitzi and Superego and Complex ran to help them. The seven of them dragged Khadra about ten feet before he gave up and let go. At the same time, an incipient fight broke out on either side of the arc of tables between the head of the language department of Mallorysport Academy and a spinsterish amateur phoneticist. At this point, Judge Pendarvis, deciding that if you can't prevent it, relax and enjoy it, rapped a few times with his gavel, and announced that court was recessed.

"You will all please remain here; this is not an adjournment, and if any of the various groups who seem to be discussing different aspects of the problem reach any conclusion they feel should be presented in evidence, will they please notify the bench so that court can be reconvened. In any case, we will reconvene at eleven thirty."

Somebody wanted to know if smoking would be permitted during the recess. The Chief Justice said that it would. He got out a cigar and lit it. Mamma Fuzzy wanted a puff: she didn't like it. Out of the corner of his eye, he saw Mike and Mitzi, Flora and Fauna scampering around and up the steps behind the bench. When he looked again, they were all up on it, and Mitzi was showing the court what she had in her shoulder bag.

He got up, with Mamma and Baby, and crossed to where Leslie Coombes was sitting. By this time, somebody was bringing in a coffee urn from the cafeteria. Fuzzies ought to happen oftener in court.

THE GAVEL TAPPED slowly. Little Fuzzy scrambled up onto Jack Holloway's lap. After five days in court, they had all learned that the gavel meant for Fuzzies and other people to be quiet. It might be a good idea, Jack thought, to make a little gavel, when he got home, and keep it on the table in the living room for when the family got too boisterous. Baby, who wasn't gavel-trained yet, started out onto the floor; Mamma dashed after him and brought him back under the table.

The place looked like a courtroom again. The tables were ranged in a neat row facing the bench, and the witness chair and the jury box were back where they belonged. The ashtrays and the coffee urn and the ice tubs for beer and soft drinks had vanished. It looked like the party was over. He was almost regretful; it had been fun. Especially for seventeen Fuzzies and a Baby Fuzzy and a little black-and-white kitten.

There was one unusual feature; there was now a fourth man on the bench, in gold-braided Navy black; sitting a little apart from the judges, trying to look as though he weren't there at all—Space Commodore Alex Napier.

Judge Pendarvis laid down his gavel. "Ladies and gentlemen are you ready to present the opinions you have reached?" he asked.

Lieutenant Ybarra, the Navy psychologist, rose. There was a reading screen in front of him; he snapped it on.

"Your Honors," he began, "there still exists considerable difference of opinion on matters of detail but we are in agreement on all major points. This is quite a lengthy report, and it has already been incorporated into the permanent record. Have I the court's permission to summarize it?"

The court told him he had. Ybarra glanced down at the screen in front of him and continued:

"It is our opinion," he said, "that sapience may be defined as differing from nonsapience in that it is characterized by conscious thought, by ability to think in logical sequence and by ability to think in terms other than mere sense data. We—meaning every member of every sapient race—think consciously, and we know what we are thinking. This is not to say that all our mental activity is conscious. The science of psychology is based, to a large extent, upon our realization that only a small portion of our mental activity occurs above the level of consciousness, and for centuries we have been diagraming the mind as an iceberg, one-tenth exposed and nine-tenths submerged. The art of psychiatry consists largely in bringing into consciousness some of the content of this submerged nine-tenths, and as a practitioner I can testify to its difficulty and uncertainty.

"We are so habituated to conscious thought that when we reach some conclusion by any nonconscious process, we speak of it as a 'hunch,' or an 'intuition,' and question its validity. We are so habituated to acting upon consciously formed decisions that we must laboriously acquire, by systematic drill, those automatic responses upon which we depend for survival in combat or other emergencies. And we are by nature so unaware of this vast submerged mental area that it was not until the first century Pre-Atomic that its existence was more than vaguely suspected, and its nature is still the subject of acrimonious professional disputes."

There had been a few of those, off and on, during the past four days, too.

"If we depict sapient mentation as an iceberg, we might depict nonsapient mentation as the sunlight reflected from its surface. This is a considerably less exact analogy; while the nonsapient mind deals, consciously, with nothing but present sense data, there is a considerable absorption and reemission of subconscious memories. Also, there are occasional flashes of what must be conscious mental activity, in dealing with some novel situation. Dr. van Riebeek, who is especially interested in the evolutionary aspect of the question, suggests that the introduction of novelty because of drastic environmental changes may have force nonsapient beings into more or less sustained conscious thinking and so initiated mental habits, in time, gave rise to true sapience.

"The sapient mind not only thinks consciously by habit, but it thinks in connected sequence. It associates one thing with another. It reasons logically, and forms conclusions, and uses those conclusions as premises from which to arrive at further conclusions. It groups associations together, and generalizes. Here we pass completely beyond any comparison with nonsapience. This is not merely more consciousness, or more thinking; it is thinking of a radically different kind. The nonsapient mind deals exclusively with crude sensory material. The sapient mind translates sense impressions into ideas, and then forms ideas *of* ideas, in ascending orders of abstraction, almost without limit.

"This, finally, brings us to one of the recognized overt manifestations of sapience. The sapient being is a symbol user. The nonsapient being cannot symbolize, because the nonsapient mind is incapable of concepts beyond mere sense images."

Ybarra drank some water, and twisted the dial of his reading screen with the other hand.

"The sapient being," he continued, "can do one other thing. It is a combination of the three abilities already enumerated, but combining them creates something much greater than the mere sum of the parts. The sapient being can imagine. He can conceive of something which has no existence whatever in the sense-available world of reality, and then he can work and plan toward making it part of reality. He can not only imagine, but he can also create."

He paused for a moment. "This is our definition of sapience. When we encounter any being whose mentation includes these characteristics, we may know him for a sapient brother. It is the considered opinion of all of us that the beings called Fuzzies are such beings."

Jack hugged the small sapient one on his lap, and Little Fuzzy looked up and murmured, *"He-inta?"*

"You're in, kid," he whispered. "You just joined the people."

Ybarra was saying, "They think consciously and continuously. We know that by instrumental analysis of their electroencephalographic patterns, which compare closely to those of an intelligent human child of ten. They think in connected sequence; I invite consideration of all the different logical steps involved in the invention, designing and making of their prawn-killing weapons, and in the development of tools with which to make them. We have abundant evidence of their ability to think beyond present sense data, to associate, to generalize, to abstract and to symbolize.

"And above all, they can imagine, not only a new implement, but a new way of life. We see this in the first human contact with the race which, I submit, should be designated as *Fuzzy sapiens*. Little Fuzzy found a strange and wonderful place in the forest, a place unlike anything he had ever seen, in which lived a powerful being. He imagined himself living in this place, enjoying the friendship and protection of this mysterious being. So he slipped inside, made friends with Jack Holloway and lived with him. And then he imagined his family sharing this precious comfort and companionship with him, and he went and found them and brought them back with him. Like so many other sapient beings, Little Fuzzy had a beautiful dream; like a fortunate few, he made it real."

The Chief Justice allowed the applause to run on for a few minutes before using his gavel to silence it. There was a brief colloquy among the three judges, and then the Chief Justice rapped again. Little Fuzzy looked perplexed. Everybody had been quiet after he did it the first time, hadn't they?

"It is the unanimous decision of the court to accept the report already entered into the record and just summarized by Lieutenant Ybarra, TFN, and to thank him and all who have been associated with him.

"It is now the ruling of this court that the species known as *Fuzzy fuzzy holloway zarathustra* is in fact a race of sapient beings, entitled to the respect of all other sapient beings and to the full protection of the law of the Terran Federation." He rapped again, slowly, pounding the decision into the legal framework.

Space Commodore Napier leaned over and whispered; all three of the judges nodded emphatically. The naval officer rose.

"Lieutenant Ybarra, on behalf of the Service and of the Federation, I thank you and those associated with you for a lucid and excellent report, the culmination of work which reflects credit upon all who participated in it. I also wish to state that a suggestion made to me by Lieutenant Ybarra regarding possible instrumental detection of sapient mentation is being credited to him in my own report, with the recommendation that it be given important priority by the Bureau of Research and Development. Perhaps the next time we find people who speak beyond the range of human audition, who have fur and live in a mild climate, and who like their food raw, we'll know what they are from the beginning."

Bet Ybarra gets another stripe, and a good job out of this. Jack hoped so. Then Pendarvis was pounding again.

"I had almost forgotten; this is a criminal trial," he confessed. "It is the verdict of this court that the defendant, Jack Holloway, is not guilty as here charged. He is herewith discharged from custody. If he or his attorney will step up here, the bail bond will be refunded." He puzzled Little Fuzzy by hammering again with his gavel to adjourn court.

This time, instead of keeping quiet, everybody made all the noise they could, and Uncle Gus was holding him high over his head and shouting:

"The *winnah!* By unanimous decision!"

17

RUTH ORTHERIS SIPPED at the tart, cold cocktail. It was good; oh, it was good, all good! The music was soft, the lights were dim, the tables were far apart; just she and Gerd, and nobody was paying any attention to them. And she was clear out of the business, too. An agent who testified in court always was expended in service like a fired round. They'd want her back, a year from now, to testify when the board of inquiry came out from Terra, but she wouldn't be Lieutenant j.g. Ortheris then, she'd be Mrs. Gerd van Riebeek. She set down the glass and rubbed the sunstone on her finger. It was a lovely sunstone, and it meant such a lovely thing.

And we're getting married with a ready-made family, too. Four Fuzzies and a black-and-white kitten.

"You're sure you really want to go to Beta?" Gerd asked. "When Napier gets this new government organized, it'll be taking over Science Center. We could both get our old jobs back. Maybe something better."

"You don't want to go back?" He shook his head. "Neither do I. I want to go to Beta and be a sunstone digger's wife."

"And a Fuzzyologist."

"And a Fuzzyologist. I couldn't drop that now. Gerd, we're only beginning with them. We know next to nothing about their psychology."

He nodded seriously. "You know, they may turn out to be even wiser than we are."

She laughed. "Oh, Gerd! Let's don't get too excited about them. Why, they're just like little children. All they think about is having fun."

"That's right. I said they were wiser than we are. They stick to important things." He smoked silently for a moment. "It's not just their psychology; we don't know anything much about their psychology, or biology either." He picked up his glass and drank. "Here; we had eighteen of them in all. Seventeen adults and one little one. Now what kind of ration is that? And the ones we saw in the woods ran about the same. In all, we sighted about a hundred and fifty adults and only ten children."

"Maybe last year's crop have grown up," she began.

"You know any other sapient races with a one-year maturation period?" he asked. "I'll bet they take ten or fifteen years to mature. Jack's Baby Fuzzy hasn't gained a pound in the last month. And another puzzle; this craving for Extee Three. That's not a natural food; except for the cereal bulk matter, it's purely synthetic. I was talking to Ybarra; he was wondering if there mightn't be something in it that caused an addiction."

"Maybe it satisfies some kind of dietary deficiency."

"Well, we'll find out." He inverted the jug over his glass. "Think we could stand another cocktail before dinner?"

SPACE COMMODORE NAPIER sat at the desk that had been Nick Emmert's and looked at the little man with the red whiskers and the rumpled suit, who was looking back at him in consternation.

"Good Lord, Commodore; you can't be serious?"

"But I am. Quite serious, Dr. Rainsford."

"Then you're nuts!" Rainsford exploded. "I'm no more qualified to be Governor General than I'd be to command Xerxes Base. Why, I never held an administrative position in my life."

"That might be a recommendation. You're replacing a veteran administrator."

"And I have a job. The Institute of Zeno-Sciences—"

"I think they'll be glad to give you leave, under the circumstances. Doctor, you're the logical man for this job. You're an ecologist; you know how disastrous the effects of upsetting the balance of nature can be. The Zarathustra Company took care of this planet, when it was their property, but now nine-tenths of it is public domain, and people will be coming in from all over the Federation, scrambling to get rich overnight. You'll know how to control things."

"Yes, as Commissioner of Conservation, or something I'm qualified for."

"As Governor General. Your job will be to make policy. You can appoint the adminstrators."

"Well, who, for instance?"

"Well, you're going to need an Attorney General right away. Who will you appoint for that position?"

"Gus Brannhard," Rainsford said instantly.

"Good. And who—this question is purely rhetorical—will you appoint as Commissioner of Native Affairs?"

JACK HOLLOWAY WAS going back to Beta Continent on the constabulary airboat. Official passenger: Mr. Commissioner Jack Holloway. And his staff: Little Fuzzy, Mamma Fuzzy, Baby Fuzzy, Mike, Mitzi, Ko-Ko and Cinderella. Bet they didn't know they had official positions!

Somehow he wished he didn't have one himself.

"Want a good job, George?" he asked Lunt.

"I have a good job."

"This'll be a better one. Rank of major, eighteen thousand a year. Commandant, Native Protection Force. And you won't lose seniority in the constabulary; Colonel Ferguson'll give you indefinite leave."

"Well, cripes, Jack, I'd like to, but I don't want to leave the kids. And I can't take them away from the rest of the gang."

"Bring the rest of the gang along. I'm authorized to borrow twenty men from the constabulary as a training cadre, and you only have sixteen. Your sergeants'll get commissions, and all your men will be sergeants. I'm going to have a force of a hundred and fifty for a start."

"You must think the Fuzzies are going to need a lot of protection."

"They will. The whole country between the Cordilleras and the West Coast Range will be Fuzzy Reservation and that'll have to be policed. Then the Fuzzies outside that will have to be protected. You know what's going to happen. Everybody wants Fuzzies; why, even Judge Pendarvis approached me about getting a pair for his wife. There'll be gangs hunting them to sell, using stun-bombs and sleep-gas and everything. I'm going to have to set up an adoption bureau; Ruth will be in charge of that. And that'll mean a lot of investigators—"

Oh, it was going to be one hell of a job! Fifty thousand a year would be chicken feed to what he'd lose by not working his diggings. But somebody would have to do it, and the Fuzzies were his responsibility.

Hadn't he gone to law to prove their sapience?

THEY WERE GOING home, home to the Wonderful Place. They had seen many wonderful places, since the night they had been put in the bags: the place where everything had been light and they had been able to jump so high and land so gently, and the place where they had met all the others of their people and had so much fun. But now they were going back to the old Wonderful Place in the woods, where it had all started.

And they had met so many Big Ones, too. Some Big Ones were bad, but only a few; most Big Ones were good. Even the one who had done the killing had felt sorry for what he had done; they were all sure of that. And the other Big Ones had taken him away, and they had never seen him again.

He had talked about that with the others—with Flora and Fauna, and Dr. Crippen, and Complex, and Superego, and Dillinger and Lizzie Borden. Now that they were all going to live with the Big Ones, they would have to use those funny names. Someday they would find out what they meant, and that would be fun, too. And they could; now the Big Ones could put things in their ears and hear what they were saying, and Pappy Jack was learning some of their words, and teaching them some of his.

And soon all the people would find Big Ones to live with, who would take care of them and have fun with them and love them, and give them the Wonderful Food. And with the Big Ones taking care of them, maybe more of their babies would live and not die so soon. And they would pay the Big Ones back. First they would give their love and make them happy. Later, when they learned how, they would give their help, too.

FUZZY
SAPIENS

1

VICTOR GREGO FINISHED the chilled fruit juice and pushed the glass aside, then lit a cigarette and poured hot coffee into the half-filled cup that had been cooling. This was going to be another Nifflheim of a day, and the night's sleep had barely rested him from the last one and the ones before that. He sipped the coffee, and began to feel himself rejoining the human race.

Staff conferences, all day, of course, with everybody bickering and recriminating. He hoped, not too optimistically, that this would be the end of it. By this evening all the division chiefs ought to know what had to be done. If only they wouldn't come running back to him for decisions they ought to make themselves, or bother him with a lot of nit-picking details. Great God, wasn't a staff supposed to handle staff work?

The trouble was that for the last fifteen years, twelve at least, all the decisions had been made in advance, and the staff work had all been routine, but that had been when Zarathustra had been a Class-III planet and the Company had owned it outright. In the Chartered Zarathustra Company, emergencies had simply not been permitted to arise. Not, that was, until old Jack Holloway had met a small person whom he had named Little Fuzzy.

Then everybody had lost their heads. He'd lost his own a few times, and done some things he now wished he hadn't done. Most of his subordinates hadn't recovered theirs, yet, and the Charterless Zarathustra Company was operating, if that was the word for it, in a state of total and permanent emergency.

The cup was half empty, again; he filled it to the top and lit a fresh cigarette from the old one before crushing it out. Might as well get it started. He reached to the switch and flicked on the communication screen across the breakfast table.

In a moment, Myra Fallada appeared in it. She had elaborately curled white hair, faintly yellowish, a round face, protuberant blue eyes, and a lower lip of the sort associated with the ancient Hapsburg family. She had been his secretary ever since he had come to Zarathustra, and she thought that what had happened a week ago in Judge Pendarvis's court had been the end of the world.

"Good morning, Mr. Grego." She was eyeing his dressing gown and counting the cigarette butts in the ashtray, trying to estimate how soon he'd be down at his desk. "An awful lot of business has come in this morning."

"Good morning, Myra. What kind of business?"

"Well, things are getting much worse in the cattle country. The veldbeest herders are all quitting their jobs; just flying off and leaving the herds. . . ."

"Are they flying off in company aircars? If they are, have Harry Steefer put out wants for them on stolen-vehicle charges."

"And the *City of Malverton;* she's spacing out from Darius today." She went on to tell him about that.

"I know. That was all decided yesterday. Just tell them to carry on with it. Now, is there anything I really have to attend to personally? If there is, bundle it up and send it to the staff conference room; I'll handle it there with the people concerned. Rubber-stamp the rest and send it back where it belongs, which is not on my desk. I won't be in; I'm going straight to the conference room. That will be in half an hour. Tell the houseboy he can come in to clean up then, and tell the chef I won't be eating here at all. I'll have lunch off a tray somewhere, and dinner with Mr. Coombes in the Executive Room."

Then he waited, mentally counting to a hundred. As he had expected, before he reached fifty Myra was getting into a flutter.

"Mr. Grego, I almost forgot!" She usually did. "Mr. Evins wants inside the gem-reserve vault; he's down there now."

"Yes, I told him to make inventory and appraisal today. I'd forgotten about that myself. Well, we can't keep him waiting. I'll go down directly."

He blanked the screen, gulped what was left of the coffee and rose, leaving the kitchenette-breakfast room and crossing the short hall to his bedroom, taking off his dressing gown as he went. That he should not have forgotten: the problem represented by the contents of the gem-reserve vault was of greater importance, though of less immediacy, than what was going on in the cattle country.

Up to a week ago, when Chief Justice Pendarvis had smashed the company's charter with a few taps of his gavel, sunstones had been a company monopoly. It had been illegal for anybody but the company to buy sunstones, or for anybody to sell one except to a company gem buyer, but that had been company law, and the Pendarvis decisions had wiped out the company's law-making powers. Sunstone deposits were always too scattered for profitable large-scale mining. They were found by free-lance prospectors, who sold them to the company at the company's prices. Jack Holloway, who had started the whole trouble, had been one of the most successful of prospectors.

Now sunstones were in the open competitive market on Zarathustra, and something would have to be done about establishing a new gem-buying policy. Before he could do that, he wanted to know just how many of them the company had in reserve.

So he had to go down and open the vault, before Conrad Evins, the chief gem buyer, could get in to find out. He knew the combination. So—in case anything happened to him—did Leslie Coombes, the head of the legal division, and, against the possibility that both he and Coombes were killed or incapaci- tated, there was a copy of it neatly typed on a slip of paper in a special-security box at the Bank of Mallorysport, which could only be gotten out by the Colonial Marshal with a court order. It was a bother, but too many people couldn't be trusted with that combination.

The gem rooms were on the fifteenth level down; they were surrounded by the company police headquarters, and there was only one way in, through a door barred by a heavy steel portcullis. The guard who controlled this sat in a small cubicle fronted by two inches of armor glass; several other guards, with submachine guns, sat or stood behind a low counter in front of it. Harry Steefer, the chief of company police, was there, and so was Conrad Evins, the gem buyer, a small man with graying hair and a bulging brow and narrow chin. With them were two gray-smocked assistants.

"Sorry to keep you gentlemen waiting," he greeted them. "Ready, Mr. Evins?"

Evins was. Steefer nodded to the men inside the armor-glass cubicle; the portcullis rose silently. They entered a bare hallway, covered by viewscreen pickups at either end and with sleep-gas release nozzles on the ceiling. The door at the other end opened, and in the small anteroom beyond they all showed their identity cards to a guard: Evins and his two assistants, the sergeant and the two guards accompanying them, Grego, even Chief Steefer. The guard spoke into a phone; somebody completely out of sight and reach pressed a button or flipped a switch and the door beyond opened. Grego went through alone, and down a short flight of steps to another door, brightly iridescent with a plating of collapsium, like a spaceship's hull or a nuclear reactor.

There was a keyboard, like the keyboard of a linotype machine. He went to it, punching out the letters of a short sentence, then waited ten seconds. The huge door receded slowly, then slid aside.

"All right, gentlemen," he called out. "The vault's open."

Then he walked through, into a circular room beyond. In the middle of it was a round table, its top covered with black velvet, with a wide circular light-shade above it. The wall was lined by a steel cabinet with many shallow drawers. The Chief, a sergeant with a submachine gun, Evins, and his two assistants followed him in. He lit a cigarette, watching the smoke draw up around the light-shade and vanish out the ventilator above. Evins's two assistants began getting out paraphernalia and putting things on the table; the gem buyer felt the black velvet and nodded. Grego put his hand on it, too. It was warm, almost hot.

One of the assistants brought a drawer from the cabinet and emptied it on the table—several hundred smooth, translucent pebbles. For a moment they looked like so much gravel. Then, slowly, they began to glow, until they were blazing like burning coals.

Some fifty million years ago, when Zarathustra had been almost completely covered by seas, there had been a marine life-form, not unlike a big jellyfish, and for a million or so years the seas had abounded with them, and as they died they had sunk into the ooze and been covered by sand. Ages of pressure had reduced them to hard little beans of stone, and the ooze to gray flint. Most of them were just pebbles, but by some ancient biochemical quirk, a few were intensely thermofluorescent. Worn as gems, they would glow from the body heat of the wearer, as they were glowing now on the electrically heated tabletop. They were found nowhere in the galaxy but on Zarathustra, and even a modest one was worth a small fortune.

"Just for a quick estimate, in round figures, how much money have we in this room?" he asked Evins.

Evins looked pained. He had the sort of mind which detested expressions like "quick estimate," and "round figures."

"Well, of course, the Terra market quotation, as of six months ago, was eleven hundred and twenty-five sols a carat, but that's just the average price. There are premium-value stones . . ."

He saw one of those, and picked it up; an almost perfect sphere, an inch in diameter, deep blood-red. It lay burning in his palm; it was beautiful. He wished he owned it himself, but none of this belonged to him. It belonged to an abstraction called the Chartered—no, Charterless—Zarathustra Company, which represented thousands of stockholders, including a number of other abstractions called Terra-Baldur-Marduk Spacelines, and Interstellar Explorations, Ltd., and the Banking Cartel. He wondered how Conrad Evins felt, working with these beautiful things, knowing how much each of them was worth, and not owning any of them.

"But I can tell you how little they are worth," Evins was saying, at the end of a lecture on the Terra gem market. "The stones in this vault are worth not one millisol less than one hundred million sols."

That sounded like a lot of money, if you said it quickly and didn't think. The Chartered, even the Charterless, Zarathustra Company was a lot of company, too, and all its operations were fantastically expensive. That wouldn't be six months' gross business for the company. They couldn't let the sunstone business live on its reserve.

"This is new, isn't it?" he asked, laying the red globe of light back on the heated tabletop.

"Yes, Mr. Grego. We bought that less than two months ago. Shortly before the Trial." He captitalized the word; the day Pendarvis beat the company down with his gavel would be First Day, Year Zero, on Zarathustra from now on. "It was bought," he added, "from Jack Holloway."

2

SNAPPING OFF THE shiny new stenomemophone, Jack Holloway relit his pipe and pushed back his chair, looking around what had been the living room of his camp before it had become the office of the Commissioner of Native Affairs for the Class-IV Colonial Planet of Zarathustra. It had been a pleasant room, a place where a man could spread out by himself, or entertain the infrequent visitors who came this far into the wilderness. The hardwood floor was scattered with rugs made from the skins of animals he had shot; the deep armchairs and the couch were covered with smaller pelts. Like the big table at which he worked, he had built them himself. There was a reading screen, a metal-cased library of microbooks; the gunrack reflected soft gleams from polished stocks and barrels. And now look at the damn place!

Two extra viewscreens, another communication screen, a vocowriter, a teleprint machine, all jammed together. An improvised table on trestles at right angles to the one at which he sat, its top littered with plans and blueprints and things; mostly things. And this red-upholstered swivel chair; he hated that worst of all. Forty years ago, he'd left Terra to get the seat of his pants off the seat of a chair like that, and here he was in the evening of life—well, late afternoon, call it around second cocktail time—trapped in one.

It wasn't just this room, either. Through the open door he could hear what was happening outside. The thud of axes, and the howl of chain-saws; he was going to miss all those big feathered trees from around the house. The machine-gun banging of power-hammers, the clanking and grunting of bulldoz-ers. A sudden warning cry, followed by a falling crash and a multivoiced burst of blasphemy. He hoped none of the Fuzzies had been close enough to whatever had happened to get hurt.

Something tugged gently at his trouser-leg, and a small voice said, "Yeek?" His hands went to his throat, snapping on the ultrasonic hearing-aid and inserting the earplug. Immediately, he began to hear a number of small sounds that had been previously inaudible, and the voice was saying, "Pappy Jack?"

He looked down at the Zarathustran native whose affairs he had been commissioned to administer. He was an erect biped, two feet tall, with a wide-eyed humanoid face, his body covered with soft golden fur. He wore a green canvas pouch lettered TFMC, and a two-inch silver disc on a chain about his neck, and nothing else. The disc was lettered LITTLE FUZZY, and *Jack Holloway, Cold Creek Valley, Beta Continent,* and the numeral *I.* He was the first Zarathustra aborigine he or any other Terran human had ever seen.

He reached down and stroked his small friend's head.

"Hello, Little Fuzzy. You want to visit with Pappy Jack for a while?"

Little Fuzzy pointed to the open door. Five other Fuzzies were peeping bashfully into the room, making comments among themselves.

"Fuzzee no shu do-bizzo do-mitto zat-hakko," Little Fuzzy informed him. *"Heeva so si do-mitto."*

Some Fuzzies who hadn't been here before had just come; they wanted to stay. At least, that was what he thought Little Fuzzy was saying; it had only been ten days since he had known that Fuzzies could talk at all. He pressed a button to start the audiovisual recorder; it was adjusted to transform their ultrasonic voices to audible frequencies.

"Make talk." He picked his way through his hundred-word Fuzzy vocabulary. "Pappy Jack friend. Not hurt, be good to them. Give good things."

"Josso shoddabag?" Little Fuzzy asked. *"Josso shoppo-diggo? Josso t'heet? Esteefee?"*

"Yes, Give shoulder-bags and chopper-diggers and treats," he said. "Give Extee-Three."

Friendly natives; distribution of presents to. Function of the Commissioner of Native Affairs. Little Fuzzy began a speech. This was Pappy Jack, the greatest and wisest of all the Big Ones, the Hagga, the friend of all the People, the Gashta, only the Big Ones called the Gashta Fuzzies. He would give wonderful things. *Shoddabag,* in which things could be carried, leaving the hands free. He displayed his own. And weapons so hard that they never wore out. He ran to the jumbled pile of bedding under the gunrack and came back with a six-inch leaf-shaped blade on a twelve-inch shaft. And Pappy Jack would give the *Hoksu-Fusso,* the Wonderful Food, *esteefee.*

Rising, he went out to what had been his kitchen before it had been crammed with supplies. There were plenty of chopper-diggers; he'd had a couple of hundred made up before he left Mallorysport. Shoulder-bags were in shorter supply. They were all either Navy black or Marine Corps green, first-aid pouches and tool-kit pouches and belt pouches for submachine gun and auto-rifle magazines, all fitted with shoulder straps. He hung five of them over his arm, then unlocked a cupboard and got out two rectangular tins with blue labels marked EMERGENCY FIELD RATION, EXTRATERRESTRIAL SERVICE TYPE THREE. All Fuzzies were crazy about Extee-Three, which demonstrated that, while sapient beings, they were definitely not human. Only a completely starving human would eat the damn stuff.

When he returned, the five newcomers were squatting in a circle inside the door with Little Fuzzy, examining his steel weapon and comparing it with the paddle-shaped hardwood sticks they had made for themselves. The word *zatku* was being frequently used.

It was an important word to Fuzzies, their name for a big pseudocrustacean Terrans called a land-prawn. Fuzzies hunted *zatku* avidly, and, until they had tasted Extee-Three, preferred them to any other food. If it hadn't been for the *zatku*, the Fuzzies would have stayed in the unexplored country of northern Beta Continent, and it would have been years before any Terran would have seen one.

Quite a few Terrans, especially Victor Grego, the Zarathustra Company manager-in-chief, were wishing the Fuzzies had stayed permanently undiscovered. Zarathustra had been listed as a Class-III planet, inhabitable by Terran humans but uninhabited by any native race of sapient beings, and on that misunderstanding the Zarathustra Company had been chartered to colonize and exploit it and had been granted outright ownership of the planet and one of the two moons, Darius. The other moon, Xerxes, had been retained as a Federation Navy base, which had been fortunate, because suddenly Zarathustra had turned into a Class-IV planet, with a native population.

The members of the native population here present looked up expectantly as he opened one of the tins and cut the gingerbread-colored cake into six equal portions. The five newcomers sniffed at theirs and waited until Little Fuzzy began to eat. Then, after a tentative nibble, they gobbled avidly, with full-mouthed sounds of delight.

From the first, he had suspected that they weren't just cute little animals, but people—sapient beings, like himself and like the eight other sapient races discovered since Terrans had gone out to the stars. When Bennett Rainsford, then a field naturalist for the Institute of Xeno-Sciences, had seen them, he had agreed, and had named the species *Fuzzy fuzzy holloway*. They had both been excited, and very proud of the discovery, and neither of them had thought, until it was brought forcibly to their attention, of the effect on the Zarathustra Company's charter.

Victor Grego had thought of that at once; he had fought desperately, viciously, and with all the resources of the company, to prevent the recognition of the Fuzzies as sapient beings and the invalidation of the company's charter. The battle had ended in court, with Jack Holloway charged with murder for shooting a company gunman and a company executive name Leonard Kellogg similarly charged for kicking to death a Fuzzy named Goldilocks. The two cases, tried as one, had hinged on the question of the sapience of the Fuzzies. On the docket, it had been *People of the Colony of Zarathustra* versus *Holloway and Kellogg*. His lawyer, Gus Brannhard, had insisted on referring to it as *Friends of Little Fuzzy* versus *The Chartered Zarathustra Company*.

Little Fuzzy and his friends had won, and with their sapience recognized, the company's charter was out the airlock, and so was the old Class-III Colonial Government, and Space Commodore Napier, the commandant of Xerxes Base, had been compelled, since Zarathustra was without legal government, to proclaim martial rule and supervise the establishment of a new Class-IV Government. He had appointed Bennett Rainsford Governor.

And just who do you suppose Ben Rainsford appointed as Commissioner of Native Affairs?

Well, somebody had to take it, and who'd started all this Fuzzy business, anyhow?

The five newcomers had finished their Extee-Three, and been given their shoulder-bags and their steel chopper-diggers, and were trying the balance of the latter and beheading imaginary land-prawns with them. He opened the other tin of Extee-Three and divided it. This time, they nibbled slowly, with appreciative comments. Little Fuzzy gathered up the two empty tins and put them in the wastebasket.

"How you come this place?" he asked, when Little Fuzzy had rejoined the circle.

They all began talking at once; with Little Fuzzy's help, he got the general sense of it. They had heard strange noises and had come to the edge of the woods, and seen frightening things. But Fuzzies were people; they investigated, even if they were frightened. Then they had seen other people. *Hagga-gashta,* big people, and *shi-mosh-gashta,* people like us.

Little Fuzzy instantly corrected the speaker. *Hagga-gashta* were just Hagga, Big Ones, and *shi-mosh-gashta* were Fuzzies. Why were the Gashta called Fuzzies? Because Pappy Jack said so, that was why. That seemed to settle it.

"But why come this place? You come from another place, far away. Why come here?"

More argument. Little Fuzzy was explaining what he meant, and the newcomers were answering.

"Tell them here are many-many *zatku*. They come, many lights and darks. Many-many."

Fuzzies could count up to five, the fingers of one hand. The other·hand had to be used to count with. They could count in multiples of five to a hand of hands, and after that it was many, and then many-many. Somewhere in the mass of Fuzzy study notes that were piling up was a suggestion to see what Fuzzies could do with an abacus.

So, maybe three months ago and six or eight hundred miles north of here, this gang had heard that the country to the south was teeming with *zatku,* and they had joined the *volkerwanderung.* Little Fuzzy and his family had been in the advance-guard; the big rush was still coming. He tried to find out how they had learned of it. Other Fuzzies had told them: that was as far as he could get.

Anyhow, they had gotten into the pass to the north and come down into Cold Creek Valley, and here they were. They had come to the edge of the woods, seen the activity at the camp, and decided, from the presence of other Fuzzies, that there was nothing to hurt them, and had come in.

"Many things to hurt!" Little Fuzzy contradicted, instantly and vehemently. "Must watch all-time. Not go in front of things that move. Not go under things that go up off ground. Not touch strange things. Ask Big Ones what will hurt. Big Ones try not to hurt Fuzzies, Fuzzies must help."

He continued at length; the newcomers exchanged apprehensive glances and low-voiced comments. Finally, he picked up his chopper-digger and rose.

"Bizzo," he said. *"Aki-pokko-so."*

Come; I show you. He got that easily enough. "First, show police place," he advised. "Make marks with fingers; get bright things for necks."

"Hokay," Little Fuzzy agreed. Go *polis,* make *fin-gap'int,* get *idee-disko."*

About the time Terrans had mastered classical native Fuzzy, the Fuzzies would all be talking pigin-Fuzzy. The newcomers made way for Little Fuzzy, and trooped outside after him, like tourists following a guide. He watched them cross the open space in front of the house and turn left toward the bridge over the little stream. Then he went back to his desk and made a screen-call to prod up the tentmaker in Red Hill on the order of shoulder-bags—"Maybe tomorrow, Mr. Holloway; we're doing all we can."—and then made a stenomemo about finding more Extee-Three. Then he went back to doodling and scribbling notes on the table of organization and operation-scheme for the Commission of Native Affairs, on which he seemed to be getting nowhere at a terrific speed.

"Hello, Jack. Another gang joined up?"

He raised his head. The speaker was coming in the door, a stocky, square-faced man in blue. There was a lighter oval on the side of his beret, where something had been removed, and the collar of his tunic showed that his major's single star had quite recently replaced a first lieutenant's double bars. He wore a band on his left arm hand-lettered ZNPF, otherwise his uniform was Colonial Constabulary.

"Hello, George. Come in and rest your feet. You look as though they need it."

Major George Lunt, Commandant, Zarathustra Native Protection Force, agreed wearily and profanely, taking off his beret and his pistol-belt and dropping them on the makeshift table. Then, looking around, he went to a chair and lifted from it four loose-leaf books and a fiberboard carton full of papers, marked OLD ATOMIC-BOMB BOURBON, and set them on the floor. Then he unzipped his tunic, sat down, and got out his cigarettes.

"Office hut's all up, now," he reported. "They're waiting on a scow-load of flooring for it."

"I was talking on screen about that an hour ago. It'll be here by this evening." By this time tomorrow, all this junk could be moved out, and the place would be home again. "Any men coming out on the afternoon boat?"

"Three. They only got the recruiting office opened yesterday, and there isn't any big rush of recruits. Captain Casagra says he'll lend us fifty Marines and some vehicles, temporarily. How many Fuzzies have we, now, with this new bunch?"

He counted mentally. His own family: Little Fuzzy and Mamma Fuzzy and Baby Fuzzy and Mike and Mitzi and Ko-Ko and Cinderella. George Lunt's Fuzzies. Dr. Crippen and Dillinger and Ned Kelly and Lizzie Borden and Calamity Jane. The nine whom they had found at the camp when they returned from Mallorysport after the trial, and the six who came in day before yesterday, and four yesterday morning, and the two last evening, and now this gang.

"Thirty-eight, counting Baby. That's a lot of Fuzzies," he observed.

"You just think it is," Lunt told him. "The patrols we've had out north of here say they're still coming. This time next week, we'll have a couple of hundred."

And before then, the ones who were here would begin to feel overcrowded, and lot of nice new *shoppo-diggo* would get bloodied. He said so, adding:

"You have a tactical plan for dealing with a native uprising, Major?"

"I've been worrying about it. You know, we could get rid of a lot of them," Lunt said. "Just mention on telecast that we have more Fuzzies than we know what to do with, and we'd have to start rationing them."

They'd have to do that, anyhow. With all the publicity since the trial, everybody was Fuzzy-crazy. Everybody wanted Fuzzies of their own, and where there's a demand, there are suppliers, legitimate or otherwise. It was a wonder the woods weren't full of people catching Fuzzies to sell now. For all he knew, maybe they were.

And a lot of people shouldn't be allowed to have Fuzzies. Not just sadists and perverts, either. People who'd want Fuzzies because the Joneses had them, and then neglect them. People who would get tired of them after a while and dump them outside town. People who couldn't get it through their moronic heads that Fuzzies were people too. So they'd have to set up some regular system of Fuzzy adoption.

He'd thought, at first, of Ruth Ortheris, Ruth van Riebeek she was, now, for that, but she and her husband were needed too urgently here at the camp on the Fuzzy-study program. There were just too many things about Fuzzies neither he nor anybody else knew, yet, and he'd have to find out what was good for them and what wasn't.

He looked at the clock; 0935; that would be 0635 in Mallorysport. After lunch, which would be mid-morning there, he'd call her and find out how soon she'd be coming out.

3

RUTH VAN RIEBEEK—she had resigned both her Navy commission and her maiden name simultaneously five days ago—ought, she told herself, to be happy and excited. She was clear out of the Navy Intelligence and its dark corridors of deceit and suspicion, and she and Gerd were married, and any scientific worker in the Federation would give anything to be in her place. A whole new science, the study of a new race of sapient beings; why, it was only the ninth time that had happened in the five centuries since the first Terran starship left the Sol System. A tiny spot of light—what they really knew about the Fuzzies—surrounded by a twilight zone of what they thought they knew, mostly erroneous. And beyond that, the dark of ignorance, full of strange surprises, waiting to be conquered. And she was in on the very beginning of it. It was a wonderful opportunity.

But wasn't it just one Nifflheim of a way to spend a honeymoon?

When she and Gerd were married, everything was going to be so wonderful. They would spend a lazy week here in the city, just being happy together and making plans and gathering things for their new home. Then they would go back to Beta Continent, and Gerd would work the sunstone diggings in partnership with Jack Holloway while she kept house, and they would spend the rest of their lives being happy together in the woods, with their four Fuzzies, Id and Superego and Complex and Syndrome.

The honeymoon, as such, had lasted one night, here at the Hotel Mallory. The next morning, before they were through breakfast, Jack Holloway was screening them. Space Commodore Napier had appointed Ben Rainsford Governor, and Ben had immediately appointed Jack Commissioner of Native

Affairs, and now Jack was appointing Gerd to head his study and research bureau, taking it for granted that Gerd would accept. Gerd had, taking it for granted that she would agree, as, after a rebellious moment, she had.

After all, weren't they all responsible for what had happened? The Fuzzies certainly weren't; they hadn't gone to law to be declared sapient. All a Fuzzy wanted was to have fun. And they were responsible to the Fuzzies for what would happen to them hereafter, all of them together, Ben Rainsford and Jack Holloway and she and Gerd, and Pancho Ybarra. And now, Lynne Andrews.

Through the open front of the room, on the balcony, she could hear Lynne's voice, half amused and half exasperated:

"You little devils! Bring that back here! *Do-bizzo. So-josso-aki!*"

A Fuzzy—one of the two males, Superego—dashed inside with a lighted cigarette, the other male, Id, and one of the girls, Syndrome, pursuing. She put in her earplug and turned on her hearing-aid, wishing for the millionth time that Fuzzies had humanly audible voices. Id was clamoring that it was his turn and trying to take the cigarette away from Superego, who pushed him off with his free hand, took a quick puff, and handed it to Syndrome, who began puffing hastily on it. Id started to grab it, then saw the cigarette she was smoking and ran to climb on her lap, pleading:

"*Mummy Woof; josso-aki smokko.*"

Lynne Andrews, slender and blonde, followed them into the room, the earplug wire of her hearing-aid leading down from under the green bandeau around her head. She carried Complex, squirming in her arms. Complex was complaining that Auntie Lynne wouldn't give her *smokko*.

"That's one Terran word they picked up soon enough," Lynne was commenting.

"Let her have one; it won't hurt her." With scientific caution, she added, "It doesn't seem to hurt them."

She knew what Lynne was thinking. She had been recruited—shanghaied would probably be a better word—from Mallorysport General Hospital because they wanted somebody whose M.D. was a little less a matter of form than hers or Pancho Ybarra's. Lynne was a pediatrician, which had seemed appropriate because Fuzzies were about the size of year-old human children and because a pediatrician, like a veterinarian, has to be able to get along with a minimum of cooperation from the patient. Unfortunately, she was carrying it beyond analogy and equating Fuzzies with human children. A year-old human oughtn't to be allowed to smoke, so neither should a Fuzzy, who might be fifty for all anybody knew to the contrary.

She gave Id her cigarette. Lynne, apparently much against her better judgment, sat down on a couch and lit one for Complex, and one for herself, and then lit a third for Superego. Now all the Fuzzies had *smokko*. Syndrome ran to one of the low cocktail tables and came back with an ashtray, which she put on the floor. The others sat down with her around it, all but Id, who stayed on Mummy Woof's lap.

"Lynne, they won't take anything that hurts them," she argued. "Alcohol, for instance."

Lynne had to agree. Any Fuzzy would take a drink, just to do what the Big Ones were doing—once. The smallest quantity affected a Fuzzy instantly, and a tipsy Fuzzy was really something to see, and then the Fuzzy would have a sick hangover, and never took a second drink. That was one of the things she'd found out while working with Ernst Mallin, the Company psychologist, and double-crossing him and the company for Navy Intelligence.

"Well, some of them don't like *smokko.*"

"Some human-type people don't, either. Some human-type people have allergies. What kind of allergies do Fuzzies have? That's something else for you to find out."

She set Id on the table and pulled one of the loose-leaf books toward her, picking up a pen and writing the word at the top of the blank page. Id picked up another pen and began making a series of little circles on the notepad.

The door from the hallway opened into the next room; she heard Pancho Ybarra's voice and her husband laughing. The three on the floor put their cigarettes in the ashtray and jumped to their feet, shrieking, "Pappy Ge'hd! Unka Panko!" and dashed through the door into the next room. Id, dropping the pen, jumped down and ran after them. In a moment, they were all back. Syndrome had a Navy officer's cap on her head, holding it up with both hands to see from under it. Id followed, with Gerd's floppy gray sombrero, and Complex and Superego came in carrying a bulky briefcase between them. Gerd and Pancho followed. Gerd's suit, freshly pressed that morning, already rumpled, but the Navy psychologist was still miraculously handbox-neat. She rose and greeted them, kissing Gerd; Pancho crossed the couch and sat down with Lynne.

"Well, what's new?" Gerd asked.

"Jack called me, about an hour ago. They have the lab hut up, and all the equipment they have for it moved in. They have some bungalows up, a double one for us. Jack showed me a view of it; it's nice. And I was bullying people about the computer and the rest of the stuff. We can all go out as soon as we have everything here together."

"This evening, if we want to run ourselves ragged and get in in the middle of the night," Gerd said. "After lunch tomorrow, if we want to take out time. Ben Rainsford wants us for dinner this evening."

Lynne thought that sounded a trifle cannibalistic, and voted for tomorrow. "How did you make out at the hospital?" she asked.

"They gave us everything we asked for, no argument at all," Gerd said. "And the same at Science Center. I was surprised."

"I wasn't," Pancho said. "There's a lot of scuttlebutt about the Government taking both over. In a couple of weeks, we may be their bosses. What are we going to do about lunch; go out or have it sent in?"

"Let's have it sent in," she said. "We can check over these equipment lists, and you two can chase up anything that's left out this afternoon."

Pancho got out his cigarette case, and discovered that it was empty.

"Hey, Lynne; *so-josso-aki-smokko,*" he said.

Well, it would be a honeymoon. Sort of crowded, but fun. And Pancho and Lynne were beginning to take an interest in each other. She was glad of that.

CHIEF JUSTICE FREDERIC Pendarvis leaned his elbows on the bench and considered the three black-coated lawyers before him in the action of *John Doe, Richard Roe,* et alii, *An Unincorporated Voluntary Association,* versus *The Colonial Government of Zarathustra.*

One, at the defendants' lectern, was a giant; well over six feet and two hundred pounds, his big-nosed face masked by a fluffy gray-brown beard, an unruly mop of gray-brown hair suggesting, incongruously, a halo. His name was Gustavus Adolphus Brannhard, and until he had been rocketed to prominence in what everybody was calling the Fuzzy Trial, he had been chiefly noted for his ability to secure the acquittal of obviously guilty clients, his prowess as a big-game hunter, and his capacity, without visible effect, for whisky. For the past five days, he had been Attorney-General of the Colony of Zarathustra.

The man standing beside and slightly behind him would have seemed tall, too, in the proximity of anybody but Gus Brannhard. He was slender and suavely elegant, and his thin, aristocratic features wore an habitually half-bored, half-amused expression, as though life were a joke he had heard too many times before. His name was Leslie Coombes, he was the Zarathustra Company's chief attorney, and from the position he had taken it looked as though he were here to support his erstwhile antagonist in *People* versus *Holloway and Kellogg.*

The third, at the plaintiff's lectern, was Hugo Ingermann; Judge Pendarvis was making a determined effort not to let that prejudice him against his clients. To his positive knowledge, Ingermann had been in court at least seven times in the last six years representing completely honest and respectable people, and it was possible, though scarcely probable, that this might be the eighth occasion. He was, of course, a member of the Bar, due to lack of evidence to support disbarment proceedings, so he had a right to stand here and be heard.

"This is an action, is it not, to require the Colonial Government to make available for settlement and exploitation lands now in the public domain, and to set up offices where claims to such lands may be filed?" he asked.

"It is, your Honor. I represent the plaintiffs," Ingermann said. He was shorter than either of the others; plump, with a smooth, pink-cheeked face, and beginning to lose his hair in front. There was an expression of complete and utter sincerity in his round blue eyes which might have deceived anybody who had not been on Zarathustra long enough to have heard of him. He would have continued had Pendarvis not turned to Brannhard.

"I represent the Colonial Government, your Honor; we are contesting the plaintiff's action."

"And you, Mr. Coombes?"

"I represent the Charterless Zarathustra Company," Coombes said. "We are not a party to this action. I am here merely as observer and *amicus curiae.*"

"The . . . Charterless, did you say, Mr. Coombes? . . . Zarathustra Company had a right to be so represented here, they have a substantial interest." He wondered whose idea "Charterless" was; it sounded like a typical piece of Grego gallows-humor. "Mr. Ingermann?"

"Your Honor, it is the contention of the plaintiffs whom I here represent that since approximately eighty percent of the land surface of this planet is now public domain, by virtue of a recent ruling of the Honorable Supreme Court, it is now obligatory upon the Colonial Government to make this land available to the public. This, your Honor, is plainly stated in Federation Law . . ."

He began citing acts, sections, paragraphs; precedents; relevant decisions of Federation Courts on other planets. He was talking entirely for the record; all this had been included in the brief he had submitted. It should be heard, but enough was enough.

"Yes, Mr. Ingermann; the Court is aware of the law, and takes notice that it has been upheld in other cases," he said. "The Government doesn't dispute this, Mr. Brannhard?"

"Not at all, your Honor. Far from it. Governor Rainsford is, himself, most anxious to transfer unseated land to private ownership . . ."

"Yes, but when?" Ingermann demanded. "How long is Governor Rainsford going to drag his feet . . ."

"I question the justice of Mr. Ingermann's so characterizing the situation," Brannhard interrupted. "It must be remembered that it is less than a week since there was any public land at all on this planet."

"Or since the Government Mr. Ingermann's clients are suing has existed," Coombes added. "And I could endure knowing who these Messieurs Doe and Roe are. The names sound faintly familiar, but . . ."

"Your Honor, my clients are an association of individuals interested in acquiring land," Ingermann said. "Prospectors, woodsmen, tenant farmers, small veldbeest ranchers . . ."

"Loan-sharks, shylocks, percentage grubstakers, speculators, would-be claim brokers," Brannhard continued.

"They are the common people of this planet!" Ingermann declared. "The workers, the sturdy and honest farmers, the frontiersmen, all of whom the Zarathustra Company has held in peonage until liberated by the great and historic decisions which bear your Honor's name."

"Just a moment," Coombes almost drawled. "Your Honor, the word 'peonage' has a specific meaning at law. I must deny most vehemently that it has ever described the relationship between the Zarathustra Company and anybody on this planet."

"The word was ill-chosen, Mr. Ingermann. It will be deleted from the record."

"We still haven't found out who Mr. Ingermann's clients are, your Honor," Brannhard said. "May I suggest that Mr. Ingermann be placed on the stand and asked to name them?"

Ingermann shot a quick, involuntary glance at the witness stand: a heavy chair, with electrode attachments and a bright metal helmet over it, and a translucent globe on a standard. Then he began clamoring protests. So far, Hugo Ingermann had always managed to avoid having to testify to anything under veridication. That was probably why he was still a member of the Bar, instead of a convict.

"No, Mr. Brannhard," he said, with real sadness. "Mr. Ingermann is not compelled to divulge the names of his clients. Mr. Ingermann would be within his rights in bringing this action on his own responsibility, out of his deep love of justice and well-known zeal for the public welfare."

Brannhard shrugged massively. Nobody could blame him for not trying. Coombes spoke:

"Your Honor, we are all agreed about the Government's obligation, but has it occurred, either to Mr. Ingermann or to the Court, that the present Government is merely a fiat-government set up by military authority? Commodore Napier acted, as he was obliged to, as the ranking officer of the Terran Federation Armed Forces present, to constitute civil government to replace the former one, declared illegal by your Honor. Until elections can be held and a popularly elected Colonial Legislature can be convened, there may be grave doubts as to the validity of some of Governor Rainsford's acts, especially in granting titles to land. Your Honor, do we want to see the courts of this planet vexed, for years to come, with litigation over such titles?"

"That's the Government's attitude precisely," Brannhard agreed. "We're required by law to hold such elections with a year; to do that we'll have to hold an election for delegates to a constitutional convention and get a planetary constitution adopted. That will take six to eight months. Until this can be done, we petition the Court to withhold action on this matter."

"That's quite reasonable, Mr. Brannhard. The Court recognizes the Government's legal obligation, but the Court does not recognize any immediacy in fulfilling it. If, within a year, the Government can open the public lands and establish land-claims offices, the Court will be quite satisfied." He tapped lightly with his gavel. "Next case, if you please," he told the crier.

"Now I see it!" Ingermann almost shouted. "The Zarathustra Company's taken over this new Class-IV Government, and the courts along with it!"

He hit the bench again with his gavel; this time it cracked like a rifle shot.

"Mr. Ingermann! You are not deliberately placing yourself in contempt, are you?" he asked. "No? I'd hoped not. Next case, please."

LESLIE COOMBES ACCEPTED the cocktail with a word of absentminded thanks, tasted it, and set it down on the low table. It was cool and quiet up here on the garden-terrace around Victor Grego's penthouse at the top of Company House; the western sky was a conflagration of sunset reds and oranges and yellows.

"No, Victor; Gus Brannhard is not our friend. He's not our enemy, but as Attorney-General he is Ben Rainsford's lawyer, and the Government's—at the moment, it's hard to distinguish between the two—and Ben Rainsford hates all of us vindictively."

Victor Grego looked up from the drink he was pouring for himself. He had a broad-cheeked, wide-mouthed face. A few threads of gray were visible in the sunset glow among the black at his temples; they hadn't been there before the Fuzzy Trial.

"I don't see why," he said, "It's all over now. They made their point about the Fuzzies; that was all they were interested in, wasn't it?"

He was being quite honest about it, too, Coombes thought. Grego was simply incapable of animosity about something that was over and done with.

"It was all Jack Holloway and Gerd van Riebeek were interested in. Brannhard was their lawyer; he'd have fought just as hard to prove that bush-goblins were sapient beings. But Rainsford is taking this personally. The Fuzzies were his great scientific discovery, and we tried to discredit it, and that makes us Bad Guys. And in the last chapter, the Bad Guys should all be killed or sent to jail."

Grego stoppered the cocktail jug and picked up his glass.

"We haven't come to the last chapter yet," he said. " I don't want any more battles; we haven't patched up the combat damage from the last one. But if Ben Rainsford wants one, I'm not bugging out on it. You know, we could make things damned nasty for him." He sipped slowly and set the glass down. "This so-called Government of his is broke; you know that, don't you? And it'll take from six to eight months to get a Colonial Legislature organized and in session, and he can't levy taxes by executive decree; that's purely a legislative function. In the meantime, he'll have to borrow, and the only place he can borrow is from the bank we control."

That was the trouble with Victor. If anybody or anything challenged him, his first instinct was to hit back. Following that instinct when he had first heard of the Fuzzies had gotten the Company back of the eightball in the first place.

"Well, don't do any fighting with planet busters at twenty paces," he advised. "Gus Brannhard and Alex Napier, between them, talked him out of prosecuting us for what we did before the trial, and convinced him he'd wreck the whole planetary economy if he damaged the company too badly. We're in the same spot; we can't afford to have a bankrupt Government on top of everything else. Let him borrow all the money he wants."

"And then tax it away from us to pay it back?"

"Not if we get control of the Legislature and write the tax laws ourselves. This is a political battle; let's use political weapons."

"You mean organize a Zarathustra Company Party?" Grego laughed. "You have any idea how unpopular the Company is, right now?"

"No, no. Let the citizens and voters organize the parties. We'll just pick out the best one and take it over. All we'll need to organize will be a political organization."

Grego smiled slowly over the rim of his glass and swallowed.

"Yes, Leslie. I don't think I need to tell you what to do. You know it better than I do. Have you anybody in mind to head it? They shouldn't be associated with the Company at all; at least, not where the public can see it."

He named a few names—independent business men, freeholding planters, professional people, a clergyman or so. Grego nodded approvingly at each.

"Hugo Ingermann," he said.

"Good God!" Coombes doubted his ears for a moment. Then he was shocked. "We want nothing whatever to do with that fellow. Why, there isn't a crooked operation in Mallorysport, criminal or just plain dishonest, that he isn't mixed up in. And I told you how he was talking in court today."

Grego nodded again. "Precisely. Well, we won't have anything to do with him. We'll just let Hugo go his malodorous way, and cash in on any scandals he creates. You say Rainsford thinks in terms of Good Guys and Bad Guys? Well, Hugo Ingermann is the baddest Bad Guy on the planet, and if Rainsford doesn't know that, and he probably doesn't, Gus Brannhard'll tell him. I just hope Hugo Ingermann goes on attacking the Company every time he opens his mouth." He finished what was in his glass and unstoppered the jug. "Still with me, Leslie? It's a half hour yet to dinner."

As Gus Brannhard started across the lawn on the south side of Government House, two Fuzzies came dashing to meet him. Their names were Flora and Fauna, and as usual he had to pause and remember that fauns were male and that Flora was a regular feminine name. The names some people gave Fuzzies. Of course, Ben was a naturalist. If he had a pair of Fuzzies of his own, he'd probably have called them Felony and Misdemeanor, or Misfeasance and Malfeasance. He put in his earphone and squatted to get down to their level.

"Hello, sapient being. Now keep your hands out of Uncle Gus's whiskers." He glanced up and saw the small man with the red beard approaching. "Hello, Ben. They pull yours much?"

"Sometimes. I haven't so much to pull. Yours is more fun. Jack Holloway says they think you're a Big Fuzzy." The Fuzzies were pointing across the lawn, clamoring for him to come and see something. "Oh, sure; their new home. I'll bet there isn't a Fuzzy anywhere had a nicer home. *Hokay,* kids; *bizzo.*"

The new home was a Marine Corps pup-tent, pitched in an open glade beside a fountain; it would be a lot roomier for two Fuzzies than for two Marines. There were Fuzzy treasures scattered around it, things from toy shops, and odds and ends of bright or colored or oddly-shaped junk they had scavanged for themselves. He noticed, and commented on, a stout toy wheelbarrow.

"Oh, yes; we have discovered the wheel," Ben said. "They were explaining it to me yesterday; very intelligently, as far as I could follow. They give each other rides, and they are very good about taking turns. And they use it to collect loot. Very good about that, too; always ask if they can have anything they find."

"Well, this is just wonderful," he told them, and then repeated it in Fuzzy. Ben complimented him on his progress in the language.

"I damn well better learn it. Pendarvis is going to set up a Native Cases Court, like the ones on Loki and Gimli and Thor. Be anybody's guess how soon I'll have to listen to a flock of Fuzzy witnesses."

He looked inside the tent. The blankets and cushions were all piled at one end; bedmaking, it seemed, wasn't a Fuzzy accomplishment. A bed was to sleep in, and no Fuzzy could see the sense in making a bed and then having to un-make it before he could use it. He looked at some of their things, and picked up a little knife, trying the edge on his thumb. Immediately, Flora cried out:

"*Keffu, Unka Gus! Sha'ap; kuttsu!*"

"Muhgawd, Ben; you hear what she said? She speaks Lingua Terra!"

"That's right. That was one of the first things I taught them. And you don't have to teach them anything more than once, either." He looked at his watch, and spoke to the Fuzzies. They seemed disappointed, but Fauna said, *"Hokay,"* and ran into the tent, bringing out his shoulder-bag and chopper-digger, and Flora's. "Told them we have to make Big One talk, to go hunt land-prawns. I had a bunch brought in, this morning, and turned loose for them."

Fauna piled into the wheelbarrow; Flora got between the shafts and picked it up, starting off at a run, the passenger whooping loudly. Ben watched them vanish among the shrubbery, and got out his pipe and tobacco.

"Gus, why in Nifflheim did Leslie Coombes show up in court today and back you against this fellow Ingermann?" he demanded. "I thought Grego put Ingermann up to that himself."

That's right; any time anything happens, blame Grego.

"No, Ben. The company doesn't want a big land-rush starting, any more than we do. They don't want their whole labor force bugging out on them, and that's what it would come to. I don't know why I can't pound it into your head that Victor Grego had as big a stake in keeping things together on this planet as you have."

"Yes, if he can control it the way he used to. Well, I'm not going to let him . . ."

He made an impatient noise. "And Ingermann; Grego wouldn't touch him with a ten-light-year pole. You call Grego a criminal? Well, maybe you were too busy, over on Beta, counting tree rings and checking on the love life of bush-goblins, to know about the Mallorysport underworld, but as a criminal lawyer I had to. Beside Hugo Ingermann, Victor Grego is a saint, and they have images of him in all the churches and work miracles with them. You name any kind of a racket—dope, prostitution, gambling, protection-shakedowns, illicit-gem buying, shylocking, stolen goods—and Ingermann's at the back of it. This action of his, today; he has a ring of crooks who want to make a killing in land speculation. That's why I wanted to stop him, and that's why Grego sent

Coombes to help me. Ben, you're going to find that this is only the first of many occasions when you and Grego are going to be on the same side."

Rainsford started an angry reply; before he could speak, Gerd van Riebeek's voice floated down from the escalator-head on the terrace above.

"Anybody home down there?"

"No, nobody but us Fuzzies," Rainsford called back. "Come on down."

4

WITH **A** **SIGH** of relief, Victor Grego entered the living room of his penthouse apartment. His hand rose to the switch beside the door, then dropped; the faint indirect glow from around the edge of the ceiling was enough. He'd just pour himself a drink and sit here in the crepuscular silence, resting. His body was tired, more so than it should be, at his age, but his brain was still racing at top speed. No use trying to go to sleep now.

He took off his jacket and neckcloth and dropped them on a chair, opening his shirt collar as he went to the cellaret; he poured a big inhaler-glass half full of brandy and started for his favorite chair, then returned to get the bottle. It would take more than one glass to brake the speeding wheels inside his head. He placed the bottle on a low table, beside the fluted glass bowl, and sat down, wondering what he had noticed that had disturbed him. Nothing important; he sipped from the glass and leaned back, closing his eyes.

They had the trouble in the veldbeest country on Beta and Delta Continents worked out, at least to where they knew what to do about it. Close down all the engineering jobs, the Big Blackwater drainage project on Beta, and the various construction jobs, and shift men to the cattle ranges; issue them combat equipment and put them on fighting pay, to deal with these gangs of rustlers that were springing up. Maybe if they started a couple of range-wars, Ian Ferguson and his Colonial Constabulary would have to take a hand. But the main thing was to keep the herds together. And the wild veldbeest; Ben Rainsford was a conservationist, he ought to be interested in protecting them.

And he still hadn't decided on a sunstone buying policy. Not enough information on the present situation. He'd have to do something about that.

Oh, Niefflheim with it; think about it tomorrow.

He drank more brandy, and reached to the glass bowl on the low table, and found that it was empty. That was what had bothered him. It had been half full of the sort of tidbits he privately called nibblements—salted nuts, wafers, things like that—when he and Leslie Coombes had gone through the room on their way down for dinner.

Or had it? Maybe he just thought it had been. He began worrying about that, too. And the way he'd forgotten, this morning, about the sunstone inventory. Better call in Ernst Mallin to give him a checkup.

Then he laughed mirthlessly. If anybody needed a checkup, it was the company psychologist himself. Poor Ernst; he'd had a pretty shattering time of it, and now he probably thought he was being blamed for everything.

He wasn't, of course. Mallin had done the best anybody could have done, in an impossible situation. The Fuzzies had been sapient beings, and that was all there'd been to it, and that wasn't Mallin's fault. That Mallin had been forced so to testify in court had been the fault of his immediate subordinate, Dr. Ruth Ortheris, who had also, it developed, been Lieutenant j.g. Ortheris, TFN Intelligence. She'd been the one who'd tipped Navy Intelligence about the Fuzzies in the first place. She'd been the one who'd smuggled Jack Holloway's Fuzzy family out of Science Center after Leslie Coombes had gotten hold of them on a bogus court order. And she'd been the one who'd insisted on live-trapping that other Fuzzy family and exposing Mallin to them.

That had been a beautiful piece of work. He'd watched the trial by screen; he could still see poor Mallin on the stand, trying to insist that Fuzzies were just silly little animals, with the red-blazing globe of the veridicator calling him a liar every time he opened his mouth. Why, she'd made the company defeat itself with its own witness.

He ought to hate her for that. He didn't; he admired her for it, as he admired anybody who had a job to do and did it competently. He had too damned few people like that in his own organization.

Have to do something nice for Ernst, though. He couldn't stay in charge at Science Center, but he'd have to be promoted out of it. Probably have to invent a job for him.

Finally, he decided that he could go to sleep, now. He took the brandy bottle back to the cellaret, gathered up the garments he had thrown down, and went into the bedroom, putting on the lights.

Then he looked at the bed and saw the golden-furred shape snuggled against the pillows. He swore. One of those life-size Fuzzy dolls that had been on sale ever since the Fuzzies had gotten into the news. If this was somebody's idea of a joke . . .

Then the thing he had taken for a doll sat up, blinked, and said, "Yeek?"

"Why, the damn thing's alive!" he yelled. "It's a *real* Fuzzy!" The Fuzzy was afraid; watching him and at the same time seeking an avenue of escape. "Don't be scared, kid," he soothed. "I won't hurt you. How'd you get in here, anyhow?"

One thing, the puzzle of the empty bowl was solved; the contents were now inside the Fuzzy. This, however, posed the question of how the Fuzzy got there. When he had thought this was a joke, he had been angry. Now he doubted that it was a joke, and he was on the edge of being worried.

The Fuzzy, who had been regarding him warily, had evidently decided that he was not hostile and might even be friendly. He got to his feet, tried to walk on the yielding pneumatic mattress, and tumbled heels-over-head. Instantly he was on his feet again, leaping twice his height into the air, bouncing, and yeeking happily. He caught him on the second bounce and sat down on the bed with him.

"Are you hungry, kid?" That bowl of nibblements wasn't much of a meal, even for a Fuzzy. The stuff was all heavily salted, too. "Bet you're thirsty." What was it Jack Holloway's Fuzzies called him? Pappy Jack. "Well, Pappy Vic'll get you something."

In the kitchenette-breakfast room, the uninvited guest drank two small aperitif-glasses of water and part of a third, while his host wondered about what he'd like to eat. Jack Holloway gave his Fuzzies Extee-Three, but he didn't have . . . Oh, yes; maybe he did.

He went into the bedroom and opened one of the closets, where his field equipment was kept—rifles, sleeping-bag, cameras and binoculars, and a couple of rectangular steel cases to be carried in an aircar, full of camping paraphernalia. He opened one, which contained mess-gear he'd brought with him from Terra and used on field trips ever since, and sure enough, there were a couple of tins of Extee-Three.

The Fuzzy, who had been watching beside him, yeeked excitedly when he saw the blue labels, and ran ahead of him to the kitchenette. He could hardly wait till the tin was open. Somebody had given him Extee-Three before.

He made a sandwich for himself and sat down at the table while the Fuzzy ate, and he was still worried. There were only four doors into Company House from the ground, and all of them were constantly guarded. There were no windows less than sixty feet from the ground. While no bet on what Fuzzies couldn't do was really safe, he doubted that they had learned to pilot aircars just yet. So somebody had brought this Fuzzy here, and beside *How,* which would be by aircar, the question branched out into *When* and *Who* and *Why.*

Why was what worried him most. Fuzzies, as he didn't need to remind himself, were people, and wards of the Terran Federation, and all sort of crimes could be committed against them. Leonard Kellogg would have been executed for killing one of them, if he hadn't done the job for himself in his cell at the jail. And beside murder, there was abduction, and illegal restraint. Maybe somebody was trying to frame him.

He put on the communication screen and punched the call combination of the Chief's office at company police headquarters. He got Captain Morgan Lansky, who held down Chief Steefer's desk from midnight to six. As soon as Lansky saw who was calling, he got rid of his cigar, zipped up his tunic, and tried to look alert, wide awake and busy.

"Why, Mr. Grego! Is anything wrong?"

"That's what I want to know, Captain. I have a Fuzzy up here in my apartment. I want to know how he got here."

"A Fuzzy? Are you sure, Mr. Grego?"

He stooped and picked up his visitor, setting him on the table. The Fuzzy was clutching half a cake of Extee-Three. He saw Lansky looking out of the wall at him and yeeked in astonishment.

"What is your opinion, Captain?"

Captain Lansky's opinion was that he'd be damned. "How did he get in, Mr. Grego?"

Grego prayed silently for patience. "That is precisely what I want to know. To begin with, have you any idea how he got in the building?"

"Somebody," the captain decided, after deliberation, "must have brought him in. In an aircar," he added, after more cogitation.

"I had gotten that far, myself. Would you have any idea when?"

Lansky began to shake his head. Then he was smitten with an idea.

"Hey, Mr. Grego! The pilfering!"

"What pilfering?"

"Why, the pilfering. Pilfering, and ransacking; in offices and like that. And somebody's getting into supply rooms at some of the cafeterias, and where they keep the candy and stuff for the vending robots. The first musta been the night of the sixteenth." That would be three days ago. "The first report came in day before yesterday morning, after the 0600-1200 shift came on. It's been like that ever since; every morning, places being ransacked and candy and stuff like that taken. You think that Fuzzy's been doing all of it?"

He could see no reason why not. Fuzzies were small people, able to make themselves very inconspicuous when they wanted to. Hadn't they survived for oomphty-thousand years in the woods, dodging harpies and bush-goblins? And Company House was full of hiding places. It had been built twelve years ago, three years after he came to Zarathustra, and it had been built big. It wasn't

going to be like the buildings they ran up on Terra, to be torn down in a couple
of decades; it was meant to be the headquarters of the Chartered Zarathustra
Company for a couple of centuries. Eighteen levels, six to eight floors to a level;
more than half of them were empty and many unfinished, waiting for the CZC
to grow into them.

"The ones Dr. Jimenez trapped for Dr. Mallin," Lansky said. "Maybe this is
one of them."

He winced, mentally, at the thought of those Fuzzies. Catching them and
letting Mallin study them had been the worst error of the whole business, and
the way they had gotten rid of them had been a close runner-up.

It had been a Mallorysport police lieutenant, on his own lame-brained
responsibility, who had started the story about a ten-year-old girl, Lolita Lurkin,
being attacked by Fuzzies, and it had been Resident-General Nick Emmert, now
bound for Terra aboard a destroyer from Xerxes to face malfeasance charges,
who had posted a reward of five thousand sols apiece on Jack Holloway's
Fuzzies, supposed to be at large in the city. Dead or alive; that had touched off
a hysterical Fuzzy-hunt.

That had been when he and Leslie Coombes had perpetrated their own
masterpiece of imbecility, by turning loose the Fuzzies Mallin had been
studying, whom everybody was now passionately eager to see the last of, in the
hope that they would be shot for Emmert's reward money. Instead, Jack
Holloway, hunting for his own Fuzzies in ignorance of the fact that they were
safe on Xerxes Naval Base, had found them, and now he was very glad of it.
Gerd and Ruth van Riebeek had them now.

"No, Captain. Those Fuzzies are all accounted for. And Dr. Jimenez didn't
bring any others to Mallorysport."

That put Lansky back where he had started. He went off on another tangent:

"Well, I'll send somebody up right away to get him, Mr. Grego."

"You will do nothing of the sort, Captain. The Fuzzy's quite all right here;
I'm taking care of him. All I want to know is how he got into Company House.
And I want the investigation made discreetly. Tell the Chief when he comes in."
He thought of something else. "Get hold of a case of Extee-Three; do it before
you go off duty. And have it put on my delivery lift, where I'll find it the first
thing tomorrow."

The Fuzzy was disappointed when he blanked the screen; he wondered
where the funny man in the wall had gone. He finished his Extee-Three, and
didn't seem to want anything else. Well, no wonder; one of those cakes would
keep a man going for twenty-four hours.

He'd have to fix up some place for the Fuzzy to sleep. And some way for
him to get water; the sink in the kitchenette was too high to be convenient. There

was a low sink outside, which the gardener used; he turned the faucet on slightly, set a bowl under it, and put a little metal cup beside it. The Fuzzy understood about that, and yeeked appreciatively. He'd have to get one of those earphones the Navy people had developed, and learn the Fuzzy language.

Then he remembered that Fuzzies were most meticulous about their sanitary habits. Going back inside, he entered the big room behind the kitchenette which served the chef as a pantry, the houseboy for equipment storage, the gardener as a seedhouse and tool shed, and all of them as a general junkroom. He hadn't been inside the place, himself, for some time. He swore disgustedly when he saw it, then began rummaging for something the Fuzzy could use as a digging tool.

Selecting a stout-handled basting spoon, he took it out into the garden and dug a hole in a flower bed, sticking the spoon in the ground beside it. The Fuzzy knew what the hole was for, and used it, and then filled it in and stuck the spoon back where he found it. He made some ultrasonic remarks, audible as yeeks, in gratification at finding that human-type people had civilized notions about sanitation too.

Find him something better tomorrow, a miniature spade. And fix up a real place for him to sleep, and put in a little fountain, and . . .

It suddenly occurred to him that he was assuming that the Fuzzy would want to stay with him permanently, and also to wonder whether he wanted a Fuzzy living with him. Of course he did. A Fuzzy was fun, and fun was something he ought to have more of. And a Fuzzy would be a friend. A Fuzzy wouldn't care whether he was manager-in-chief of the Charterless Zarathustra Company or not, and friends like that were hard to come by, once you'd gotten to the top.

Except for Leslie Coombes, he didn't have any friends like that.

Some time during the night, he was awakened by something soft and warm squirming against his shoulder.

"Hey; I thought I fixed you a bed of your own."

"Yeek?"

"Oh, you want to bunk with Pappy Vic. All right."

They both went back to sleep.

5

IT WAS FUN having company for breakfast, especially company small enough to sit on the table. The Fuzzy tasted Grego's coffee; he didn't care for it. He liked fruit juice and sipped some. Then he nibbled Extee-Three, and watched quite calmly while Grego lit a cigarette, but manifested no desire to try one. He'd probably seen humans smoking, and may have picked up a lighted cigarette and either burned himself or hadn't liked it.

Grego poured more coffee, and then put on the screen. The Fuzzy turned to look at it. Screens were fun: interesting things happened in them. He was fascinated by the kaleidoscopic jumble of color. Then it cleared, and Myra Fallada appeared in it.

"Good morning, Mr. Grego," she started. Then she choked. Her mouth stayed open, and her eyes bulged as though she had just swallowed a glass of hundred-and-fifty-proof rum thinking it iced tea. Her hand rose falteringly to point.

"Mr. Grego! That . . . Is that a *Fuzzy*?"

The Fuzzy was delighted; this was a lot more fun than the man in the blue clothes, last night.

"That's right. I found him making himself at home, here, last evening." He wondered how many more times he'd have to go over that. "All I can get out of him is yeeks. For all I know, he may be a big stockholder."

After consideration, Myra decided this was a joke. A sacrilegious joke; Mr. Grego oughtn't to make jokes like that about the Company.

"Well, what are you going to do with it?"

"Him? Why, if he wants to stay, fix up a place for him here."

"But . . . But it's a Fuzzy!"

The Company lost its charter because of Fuzzies. Fuzzies were the enemy, and loyal Company people oughtn't to fraternize with them, least of all Mr. Grego.

"Miss Fallada, the Fuzzies were on this planet for a hundred thousand years before the Company was ever thought of." Pity he hadn't taken that attitude from the start. "This Fuzzy is a very nice little fellow, who wants to be friends with me. If he wants to stay with me, I'll be very happy to have him." He closed the subject by asking what had come in so far this morning.

"Well, the girls have most of the morning reports from last night processed; they'll be on your desk when you come down. And then . . ."

And then, the usual budget of gripes and queries. He thought most of them had been settled the day before.

"All right; pile it up on me. Has Mr. Coombes called yet?"

Yes. He was going to be busy all day. He would call again before noon, and would be around at cocktail time. That was all right. Leslie knew what he had to do and how to do it. When he got Myra off the screen, he called Chief Steefer.

Harry Steefer didn't have to zip up his tunic or try to look wide awake; he looked that way already. He was a retired Federation Army officer and had a triple row of ribbon on his left breast to prove it.

"Good morning, Mr. Grego." Then he smiled and nodded at the other person in view in his screen. "I see you still have the trespasser."

"Guest, Chief. What's been learned about him?"

"Well, not too much, yet. I have what you gave Captain Lansky last night; he's tabulated all the reports and complaints on this wave of ransackings and petty thefts. A rather imposing list, by the way. Shall I give it to you in full?"

"No; just summarize it."

"Well, it started, apparently, with ransacking in a couple of offices and a ladies' lounge on the eighth level down. No valuables taken, but things tossed around and left in disorder, and candy and other edibles taken. It's been going on like that ever since, on progressively higher levels. There were reports that somebody was in a couple of cafeteria supply rooms, without evidence of entrance."

"Human entrance, that is."

"Yes. Lansky had a couple of detectives look those places over last night; he says that a Fuzzy could have squirmed into all of them. I had reports on all of it as it happened. Incidentally, there was nothing reported for last night, which confirms the supposition that your Fuzzy was responsible for all of it."

"Regular little vest-pocket crime wave, aren't you." He pummeled the

Fuzzy gently. "And there was nothing before the night of the sixteenth or below the eighth level down?"

"That's right, Mr. Grego. I wanted to talk to you before I did anything, but there may be a chance that either Dr. Mallin or Dr. Jimenez may know something about it."

"I'll talk to both of them, myself. Dr. Jimenez was over on Beta until a day or so before the trial; after he'd trapped the four Dr. Mallin was studying, he stayed on to study the Fuzzies in habitat. He had a couple of men helping him, paid hunters or rangers or something of the sort."

"I'll find out who they were," Steefer said. "And, of course, almost anybody who works out of Company House on Beta Continent may have picked the Fuzzy up and brought him back and let him get away. We'll do all we can to find out about this, Mr. Grego."

He thanked Steefer and blanked the screen, and punched out the call-combination of Leslie Coombes's apartment. Coombes, in a dressing gown, answered at once; he was in his library, with a coffee service and a stack of papers in front of him. He smiled and greeted Grego; then his eyes shifted, and the smile broadened.

"Well! Touching scene; Victor Grego and his Fuzzy. If you can't lick them, join them," he commented. "When and where did you pick him up?"

"I didn't; he joined me." He told Coombes about it. "What I want to find out now is who brought him here."

"My advice is, have him flown back to Beta and turned loose in the woods where he came from. Rainsford agreed not to prosecute us for what we did before the trial, but if he finds you're keeping a Fuzzy at Company House now, he'll throw the book at you."

"But he likes it here. He wants to stay with Pappy Vic. Don't you, kid?" he asked. The Fuzzy said something that sounded like agreement. "Suppose you go to Pendarvis and make application for papers of guardianship for me, like the ones he gave Holloway and George Lunt and Rainsford."

A gleam began to creep into Leslie Coombes's eyes. He'd like nothing better than a chance at a return bout with Gus Brannhard, with a not-completely-hopeless case.

"I believe I could . . ." Then he banished temptation. "No; we have too much on our hands now, without another Fuzzy trial. Get rid of him, Victor." He held up a hand to forestall a protest. "I'll be around for cocktails, about 1730-ish," he said, "You think it over till then."

Well, maybe Leslie was right. He agreed, and for a while they talked about the political situation. The Fuzzy became bored and jumped down from the table. After they blanked their screens he looked around and couldn't see him.

The door to the pantry-storeroom-toolroom-junkroom was open; maybe he was in there investigating things. That was all right; he couldn't make the existing mess any worse. Grego poured more coffee and lit another cigarette.

There was a loud crash from beyond the open door, and an alarmed yeek, followed by more crashing and thumping and Fuzzy cries of distress. Jumping to his feet, he ran to the door and looked inside.

The Fuzzy was in the middle of a puddle of brownish gunk that had spilled from an open five-gallon can which seemed to have fallen from a shelf. Sniffing, he recognized it—a glaze for baked meats, mostly molasses, that the chef had mixed from a recipe of his own. It took about a pint to glaze a whole ham, so the damned fool had mixed five gallons of it. Most of it had gone on the Fuzzy, and in attempting to get away from the deluge he had upset a lot of jars of spices and herbs, samples of which were sticking to his fur. Then he had put his foot on a sheet of paper, and it had stuck; trying to pull it loose, it had stuck to his hands, too. As soon as he saw Pappy Vic, he gave a desperate yeek of appeal.

"Yes, yeek yourself." He caught the Fuzzy, who flung both adhesive arms around his neck. "Come on, here; let's get you cleaned up."

Carrying the Fuzzy into the bathroom, he dumped him into the tub, then tore off the hopelessly ruined shirt. Trousers all spotted with the stuff, too; change them when he finished the job. He brought a jar of shampoo soap from the closet and turned on the hot water, tempering it to what he estimated the Fuzzy could stand.

Now, wasn't this a Nifflheim of a business? As if he hadn't anything to do but wash Fuzzies.

He rubbed the soap into the Fuzzy's fur; the Fuzzy first resented and then decided he liked it, shrieked in pleasure, and grabbed a handful of the soap and tried to shampoo Grego. Finally, they got finished with it. The Fuzzy liked the hot-air dryer, too. He'd never had a shampoo before.

His fur clean and dry and fluffy, he sat on the bed and watched Pappy Vic change clothes. It was amazing the way the Big Ones could change their outer skins; must be very convenient. He made remarks, from time to time, and Grego carried on a conversation with him.

After he had dressed, Grego recorded a message for the houseboy, to be passed on to the chef and the gardener, to get everything to Nifflheim out of that back room that didn't belong there, and to keep what little did in some kind of decent order. If that place could be kept in order, now, the Fuzzy had one positive accomplishment to his credit.

They took the lift down to the top executive level—lifts appeared to be a new experience for the Fuzzy, too—and into his private office. The Fuzzy looked around in wonder, especially at the big globe of Zarathustra, floating six feet off the floor on its own built-in contragravity unit, spotlighted from above to simulate Zarathustra's KO-class sun, its two satellites circling around it. Finally, for a better view, he jumped up on a chair.

"If I had any idea you'd stay there . . ." He flipped the screen switch and got Myra on it. "I had a few things to clean up before I could come down," he told her, with literal truthfulness. "How many girls have we in the front office, this morning?"

There were eight, and they were all busy. Myra started to tell him what with; maybe four could handle it at a pinch, and six without undue strain. That was another thing the Charterless Zarathustra Company would have to economize on.

"Well, they can look after the Fuzzy, too," he said. "Take turns with him. He's in here, trying to make up his mind what kind of deviltry to get into next. Come get him, and take him out and tell the girls to keep him innocently amused."

"But, Mr. Grego; they have work . . ."

"This is more work. We'll find out which one gets along best with him, and promote her to chief Fuzzy-sitter. Are we going to let one Fuzzy disrupt our whole organization?"

Myra started to remind him of what the Fuzzies had done to the company already, then said, "Yes, Mr. Grego," and blanked the screen. A moment later she entered.

She and the Fuzzy looked at one another in mutual hostility and suspicion. She took a hesitant step forward; the Fuzzy yeeked angrily, dodged when she reached for him, and ran to Grego, jumping onto his lap.

"She won't hurt you," he soothed. "This is Myra; she likes Fuzzies. Don't you, Myra?" "He stroked the Fuzzy. "I'm afraid he doesn't like you."

"Well, that makes it mutual," Myra said. "Mr. Grego, I am your secretary. I am not an animal keeper."

"Fuzzies are not animals. They are sapient beings. The Chief Justice himself said so. Have you never heard of the Pendarvis Decisions?"

"Have I heard of anything else, lately? Mr. Grego, how you can make a pet of that little demon, after all that's happened . . ."

"All right, Myra. I'll take him."

He went through Myra's office and into the big room they called executive operations center, through which reports from all over the Company's shrunken but still extensive empire reached him and his decisions and directives and orders and instructions were handed down to his subjects. There were eight girls there, none particularly busy. One was reading alternately from several sets of clipboarded papers and talking into a vocowriter. Another was making a subdued clatter with a teleprint machine. A third was at a drawing board, constructing one of those multicolored zigzag graphs so dear to the organizational heart. The rest sat smoking and chatting; they all made hasty pretense of busying themselves as he entered. Then one of them saw the Fuzzy in his arms.

"Look! Mr. Grego has a Fuzzy!"

"Why, it's a real live Fuzzy!"

Then they were all on their feet and crowding forward in a swirl of colored dresses and perfumes and eager, laughing voices and pretty, smiling faces.

"Where did you get him, Mr. Grego?"

"Oh, can we see him?"

"Yes, girls." He set the Fuzzy down on the floor. "I don't know where he came from, but I think he wants to stay with us. I'm going to leave him here for a while. Don't let him interfere too much with your work, but keep an eye on him and don't let him get into any trouble. It'll be at least an hour before I have anything ready to go out. You can give him anything you'd eat yourselves; if he doesn't want, he won't take it. I don't think he's very hungry right now. And don't kill him with affection."

When he went out, they were all sitting on the floor in a circle around the Fuzzy, who has having a wonderful time. He told Myra to leave the doors of her office open so he could go through when he wanted to. Then he went through another door, into the computer room.

It was quarter-circular; two straight walls twenty feet long at right angles and the curved wall between, the latter occupied by the input board for the situation-analysis and operation-guidance computers. This was a band of pale green plastic, three feet wide, divided into foot squares by horizontal and vertical red lines, each square perforated with thousands of tiny holes, in some of them, little plug-in lights twinkled in every color of the spectrum. Three levels down, a whole floor was occupied with the computers this board serviced. From it, new information was added in the quasi-mathematical symbology computers understood.

He stood for a moment, looking at the Christmas-tree lights. Nothing in the world would have tempted him to touch it; he knew far too little about it. He wondered if they had started the computers working on the sunstone-buying policy problem, then went out into his own office, closing the door behind him, and sat down at his desk.

In the old, pre-Fuzzy days, he would have spent a leisurely couple of hours here, drinking more coffee and going over reports. Once in a while he would have made some comment, or asked a question, or made a suggestion, to show that he was keeping up with what was going on. Only rarely would any situation arise requiring his personal action.

Now everybody was having situations; things he had thought settled at the marathon staff conference of the past four days were coming unstuck; conflicts were developing. He had to make screen-calls to people he would never have bothered talking to under ordinary circumstances—the superintendent of the meat-packing plant on Delta Continent, the chief engineer on the now-idle Big Blackwater drainage project, the master mechanic at the nuclear-electric power-unit plant. He welcomed one such necessity, the master mechanic at the electronics-equipment factory; they were starting production of ultrasonic hearing-aids for the Government, and he ordered half a dozen sent around to his office. When he got one of them, he could hear what his new friend was saying.

Myra Fallada came in, dithering in the doorway till he had finished talking to the chief of chemical industries about a bottleneck in blasting-explosive production. As soon as he blanked the screen, she began.

"Mr. Grego, you will simply have to get that horrid creature out of operations center. The girls aren't doing a bit of work, and the noise is driving me simply *mad!*"

He could hear shrieks of laughter, and the running scamper of Fuzzy feet. Now that he thought of it, he had been hearing that for some time.

"And I positively can't work . . . *Aaaaaa!*"

Something bright red hit her on the back of the head and bounced into the room. A red plastic bag, a sponge bag or swimsuit bag or something like that, stuffed with tissue paper. The Fuzzy ran into the room, dodging past Myra, and hurled it back, within inches of her face, then ran after it.

"Well, yes, Myra. I'm afraid this is being carried a bit far." He rose and went past her into her office, in time to see the improvised softball come whizzing at him from the big office beyond. He caught it and went on through; the Fuzzy ran ahead of him to a tall girl with red hair who stooped and caught him up.

"Look, girls," he said, "I said keep the Fuzzy amused; I didn't say turn this into a kindergarten with the teacher gone AWOL. It's bad enough to have the Fuzzies tear up our charter, without letting them stop work on what we have left."

"Well, it did get a little out of hand," the tall redhead understated.

"Yes. Slightly." Nobody was going to under-understate him. What was her name? Sandra Glenn. "Sandra, he seems to like you. You take care of him. Just keep him quiet and keep him from bothering everybody else."

He hoped she wouldn't ask him how. She didn't; she just said, "I'll try, Mr. Grego." He decided to settle for that; that was all anybody could do.

By the time he got back to his desk, there was a call from the head of Public Services, wanting to know what he was going to tell the school teachers about their job futures. When he got rid of that, he called Dr. Ernst Mallin at Science Center.

The acting head of Science Center was fussily neat in an uncompromisingly black and white costume which matched his uncompromisingly black and white mind. He had a narrow face and a small, tight mouth; it had been an arrogantly positive face once. Now it was the face of a man who expects the chair he is sitting on to collapse under him at any moment.

"Good morning, Mr. Grego." Apprehensive, and trying not to show it.

"Good morning, Doctor. Those Fuzzies you were working with before the trial; the ones Dr. and Mrs. van Riebeek have now. Were they the only ones you had?"

The question took Mallin by surprise. They were, he stated positively. And to the best of his knowledge Juan Jimenez, who had secured them for him, had caught no others.

"Have you talked to Dr. Jimenez yet?" he asked, after hearing about the Fuzzy in Company House. "I don't believe he brought any when he came in from Beta Continent."

"No, not yet. I wanted to talk to you, first, about the Fuzzy and about something else. Dr. Mallin, I gather you're not exactly happy in charge of Science Center."

"No, Mr. Grego. I took it over because it was the only thing to do at the time, but now that the trial is over, I'd much rather go back to my own work."

"Well, so you shall, and your salary definitely won't suffer because of it. And I want to assure you again of my complete confidence in you, Doctor. During the Fuzzy trouble you did the best any man could have, in a thoroughly impossible situation. . . ."

He watched the anxiety ebb out of Mallin's face; before he was finished, the psychologist was smiling one of his tight little smiles.

"Now, there's the matter of your successor. What would you think of Juan Jimenez?"

Mallin frowned. Have to make a show of thinking it over, and he was one of these people who thought with his face.

"He's rather young, but I believe it would be a good choice, Mr. Grego. I won't presume to speak of his ability as a scientist, his field is rather far from mine. But he has executive ability, capacity for decisions and for supervision, and gets along well with people. Yes; I should recommend him." He paused, then asked, "Do you think he'll accept it?"

"What do you think, Doctor?"

Mallin chuckled. "That was a foolish question," he admitted. "Mr. Grego;

this Fuzzy. You still have him at Company House? What are you going to do with him?"

"Well, I had hoped to keep him, but I'm afraid I can't. He is a little too enterprising. He made my apartment look like a slightly used battlefield this morning, and now he's turning the office into a three-ring circus. And Leslie Coombes advises me to get rid of him; he thinks it may start Rainsford after us again. I think I'll have him taken back to Beta and liberated there."

"I'd like to have him, myself, Mr. Grego. Just keep him at my home and play with him and talk to him and try to find how he thinks about things. Mr. Grego, those Fuzzies are the sanest people I have ever seen. I know; I tried to drive the ones I had psychotic with frustration-situation experiments, and I simply couldn't. If we could learn their basic psychological patterns, it would be the greatest advance in psychology and psychiatry since Freud."

He meant it. He was a different Ernst Mallin now; ready to learn, to conquer his own ignorance instead of denying it. But what he wanted was out of the question.

"I'm sorry, believe me I am. But if I gave you the Fuzzy, Leslie Coombes would have a fit, and that's nothing to what Ben Rainsford would have; he'd bring prosecutions against the lot of us. If I do keep him, you'll have opportunity to study him, but I'm afraid I can't."

He brought the conversation to a close, and blanked the screen. The noise had stopped in operation center; the work probably had, too. He didn't want to get rid of the Fuzzy. He was a nice little fellow. But . . .

6

HE WASN'T ABLE to get Juan Jimenez immediately. Juan was doing something at the zoo, and the zoo was spread over too much area to track him down. He left word to call him as soon as possible, and went back to his own work, and finally had his lunch brought in and ate it at the desk. The outside office got noisy again, for a while. The girls seemed to be feeding the Fuzzy, and he wondered apprehensively on what. Some of the things those girls ate would give a billygoat indigestion. About an hour afterward, Jimenez was on the screen.

The chief mammalogist was a young man, with one of those cheerful, alert, agreeable, sincere and accommodating faces you saw everywhere on the upper echelons of big corporations or institutions. He might or might not be a good scientist, but he was a real two-hundred-proof Company man.

"Hello, Juan; calling from Science Center?"

"Yes, Mr. Grego. I was at the zoo; they have some new panzer pigs from Gamma. When I got back, they told me you wanted to talk to me."

"Yes. When you came back, just before the trial, from Beta, did you bring any Fuzzies along with you?"

"Good Lord, no!" Jimenez was startled. "I got the impression that we needed Fuzzies like we needed a hole in the head. I got the impression that the one was about equal to the other."

"Just like Ernst Mallin: the more you saw of them, the more sapient they looked. Well, dammit, what else were they? What were you doing on Beta?"

"Well, as I told you, Mr. Grego, we had a camp and we'd attracted about a dozen of them around it with Extee-Three, and we were photographing them and studying behavior, but we never made any attempt to capture any, after the first four."

"Beside yourself, who were 'we'?"

"The two men helping me, a couple of rangers from Survey Division; their names were Herckerd and Novaes. They helped me live-trap the four I gave to Dr. Mallin, and they helped with the camp work, and with photographing and so on."

"Well, here's the situation." He went into it again, realizing why witnesses in court who have been taken a dozen times over their stories by the police and the prosecuting attorney's people always sounded so glib. "So, you see, I want to find out what this is. It may be something quite innocent, but I want to be sure."

"Well, I didn't bring him in, and Herckerd and Novaes came in along with me; they didn't."

"I wish you, or they, had brought him; then I'd know what this is all about. Oh, another thing, Juan. As you know, Dr. Mallin was only in temporary charge at Science Center after Kellogg was arrested. He's going back to what's left of his original job, most happily, I might add. Do you think you could handle it? If you do, you can have it."

One thing you had to give Jimenez, he wasn't a hypocrite. He didn't pretend to be overcome with the honor, and he didn't question his own fitness. "Why, thank you, Mr. Grego!" Then he went into a little speech of acceptance which sounded suspiciously premeditated. Yes; he would definitely accept. So Grego made a little speech of his own, ending:

"I suggest you contact Dr. Mallin at once. He knows of my decision to appoint you, and you'll find him quite pleased to turn over to you. Oh, suppose we have lunch together tomorrow; by that time you should know what you have, and we can talk over future plans."

As soon as he had Jimenez off the screen he got Harry Steefer onto it.

"Mallin says he knows nothing about it, and so does Juan Jimenez. I have the names of two men who were helping Jimenez on Beta . . ."

Steefer grinned. "Phil Novaes and Moses Herckerd; they both worked for the Survey Division. Herckerd's a geologist, and Novaes is a hunter and wildlife man. They came in along with Jimenez the day before the trial, and then they vanished. A company aircar vanished along with them. My guess is they either went prospecting or down into the veldbeest country to do a little rustling. Want me to put out a wanted for them?"

"Yes, do that, Chief, about the car. Too many company vehicles have been vanishing along with employees since this turned into a Class-IV planet. And I still want to know who brought that Fuzzy here—and why."

"We're working on it," Steefer said. "There are close to a hundred people in half a dozen divisions who might have been over on Beta, in Fuzzy country, and picked up a Fuzzy for a pet. Then, say the Fuzzy got away here in Company House. Whoever was responsible would keep quiet about it afterward. I'm trying to find out, but you said you wanted it done discreetly."

"As discreetly as possible; I want it done, though. And you might start a search on some of the unoccupied floors on the eighth and ninth levels down, for evidence of where the Fuzzy was kept before he got away."

Steefer nodded. "We haven't any more men than we need," he mentioned. "Well, I'll do the best I can."

On past performance, Harry Steefer's best was likely to be pretty good. He nodded, satisfied, and went back to work, trying to figure what sort of a cargo could be scraped up for the Terra-Baldur-Marduk liner *City of Kapstaad,* which would be getting in in a week. He was still at it, calculating values on the Terra market against cubic feet of hold-space, when the door from the computer room opened behind him.

He turned, to see Sandra Glenn in the doorway. Her red hair and lipstick and her green eyes were vivid against a face that was white as paper.

"Mr. Grego." It was a barely audible whisper, shocked and frightened. "Were you doing anything with the board?"

"Good God, no!" He shoved his chair back and came to his feet. "I keep my ignorant fingers off that. What's been done to it?"

She stepped forward and aside and pointed. When he looked he saw the middle of the board a blaze of many-colored lights; not the random-looking pattern that would make sense only to a computer or a computerman, but a studied design, symmetrical and harmonious. A beautiful design. But God— Allah to Zeus, take your pick—only knew what gibbering nonsense it was putting into the trusting innards of that computer. Sandra was close to the screaming meemies; she had some idea of what kind of a computation would emerge.

"That," he said, "was our little friend *Fuzzy fuzzy holloway.* He came in here and saw the lights and found out they could be pulled out and shifted around, and he decided to make a real pretty thing. Weren't you, or any of the other girls, watching him?"

"Well, I had some work, and Gertrude was watching him, and then he lay down for a nap after lunch, and somebody called Gertrude to the screen . . ."

"All right. You're not the first one to be fooled by a Fuzzy, and neither's Gertrude. They fooled a guy named Grego pretty badly a few times. Has anything been done about this?"

"No; I just saw it a moment ago . . ."

"All right. Call Joe Verganno. No; I'll do it, his screen girl won't try to argue with me. You go find that Fuzzy."

He crossed in two long steps to the communication screen and punched a combination from the card taped up beside it. The girl who answered started to say, "Master computerman's office," and then saw who she had on screen. "Why, Mr. Grego!"

"Give me Verganno, quick."

Her hand moved; the screen exploded into a shatter of light and cleared with the computerman looking out of it.

"Joe, hell's to pay," he said, before Verganno could speak. "Somebody shoved a lot of plugs into the input board here and bitched everything up. Here." He reached under the screen and grabbed something that looked vaguely like a pistol, with a wide-angle lens where the muzzle should be, connected with the screen by a length of minicable. Aiming at the colored pattern on the board, he squeezed the trigger switch. Behind him, Joe Verganno's voice howled:

"Good God! Who did that?"

"A Fuzzy. No, I'm not kidding; that's right. You got it?"

"Just a sec. Yeah, turn it off." In the screen, Verganno grabbed a handphone. "General warning, all computer outlets. False data has been added affecting Executive One and Executive Two; no reliance is to be placed on computations from Executive One or Two until further notice. All right, Mr. Grego, I'll be right up. You mean there's a Fuzzy loose in your office?"

"Yes, he's been here all day. I don't think," he added, "that he'll be here much longer."

One of the girls looked into the room from operation-center.

"We can't find him anywhere, Mr. Grego!" she almost wailed. "And it's all my fault; I was supposed to be watching him!"

"Hell with whose fault it is; find him. If it's anybody's fault it's mine for bringing him here."

That was a fault that would be rectified directly. He saw Myra dithering in the door of her office.

"Get Ernst Mallin. Tell him to come here and get that damned Fuzzy to Nifflheim out of here."

Argue about the legal aspects later; if Mallin wanted a Fuzzy to study, he could have one. Myra said something about better late than never, and retracted into her office. The door from the outside hall opened cautiously, and a couple of police and three mechanics from one of the aircar hangars entered; somebody's had sense enough to call for reinforcements. One of the mechanics had a blanket over his arm; that was smart, too. The girls were searching the big room, and keeping watch on the doors. The hall door opened again, and Joe

Verganno and one of his technicians came in with a hand lifter loaded with tools.

"Anything been done to the board yet?" he asked.

"Nifflheim, no! We're not making a bad matter worse than it is. See if you can figure out what's happening in the computer."

"A couple of my men are going to find that out down below. Lemme see this screen, now." He went into the room, followed by the technician with the lifter. The technician said something obscenely blasphemous a moment later.

He went back to the big room; through the open door of her office, he could hear Myra talking to somebody. "Come and get him, right away. No, we don't know where he is . . . *Eeeeeh*! Get away from me, you little monster! Mr. Grego, here he is!"

"Grab him and hold him," he ordered. "Go help her," he told one of the cops. "Don't hurt the Fuzzy; just get hold of him."

Then he turned and ran through the computer room almost colliding with Verganno's helper, and ran into his own office. As he skidded around his desk, the Fuzzy dashed through the door of Myra's office. The blanket the aircar mechanic had been carrying sailed after him, missing him. Myra, the cop, and the mechanic came running after it; the mechanic caught his feet in it and went down. The cop tripped over him, and Myra tripped over the cop. The cop was cursing. Myra was screaming. The mechanic, knocked breathless under both of them, was merely gasping. The Fuzzy landed on top of the desk, saw Grego, and took off from there, landing against his chest and throwing his arms around Grego's neck. One of the girls, coming through from Myra's office and avoiding the struggling heap in front of the door, whooped, "Come on, everybody! Mr. Grego's caught him!"

The cop, who had gotten to his feet, said, "I'll take him, Mr. Grego," and reached for the Fuzzy. The Fuzzy yeeked loudly, and clung tighter to Grego.

"No, I'll hold him. He isn't afraid of me." He sat down in his desk chair, holding the Fuzzy and stroking him. "It's all right, kid. Nobody's going to hurt you. And we're going to take you out of here, to a nice place where you can have fun, and people'll be good to you . . ."

The words meant nothing to the Fuzzy; the voice, and the stroking hands, were comforting and reassuring. He snuggled closer, making happy little sounds. He was safe, now.

"What are you gonna do with him, Mr. Grego?" the cop asked.

Grego hugged the Fuzzy to him. "I'm not going to do anything with him. Look at him; he trusts me; he thinks I won't let anybody do anything to him. Well, I won't. I never let anybody who trusted me down yet, and be damned if I'll start now, with a Fuzzy."

"You mean, you're going to keep him?" Myra demanded. "After what he did?"

"He didn't mean to do anything bad, Myra. He just wanted to make a pretty thing with the lights. I'll bet he's as proud as anything of it. It's just going to be up to me to see that he doesn't get at anything else he can make trouble with."

"Dr. Mallin said he was coming right away. He'll be disappointed."

"He'll have to be disappointed, then. He can study the Fuzzy here. And get the building superintendent and the chief decorator; tell them I want them to start putting in a Fuzzy garden up on my terrace. Tell both of them to come up to my suite personally; tell them I want work started immediately, and I'll authorize double time for overtime till it's finished."

The Fuzzy wasn't scared, anymore. Pappy Vic was taking care of him. And all these other Big Ones were listening to Pappy Vic; they wouldn't hurt him or chase him anymore.

"And call Tregaskis at Electronics Equipment; ask him what's holding up those hearing-aids he was going to send me. And I'll need somebody to help look after the kid. Sandra, do you do anything we can't replace you at? Then you've just been appointed Fuzzy-Sitter in Chief. You start immediately; ten percent raise as of this morning.

Sandra was happy. "I'll love that, Mr. Grego. What's his name?"

"Name? I don't have a name for him, yet. Anybody have any ideas?"

"I have a few!" Myra said savagely.

"Call him Diamond," Joe Verganno, in the doorway of the computer room, suggested.

"Because he's so small and precious? I like that. But don't be a piker. Call him Sunstone."

"No; that was probably why the original Diamond was named, but I was thinking of calling him after a little dog that belonged to Sir Isaac Newton," Verganno said. "It seems Diamond got hold of a manuscript Sir Isaac had just finished and was going to send to his publisher. Mostly math, all done with a quill pen, no carbons of course. So Diamond got this manuscript down on the floor and he tore hell out of it, which meant about three months' work to do over. When Newton saw it, he just looked at it, and then sat down with the dog on his lap, and said, 'Oh, Diamond, poor Diamond; how little you know what mischief you have done!'"

"That's a nice little story, Joe. It's something I'll want to remind myself of, now and then. Bet you'll give a lot of reasons to, won't you, Diamond?"

7

JACK HOLLOWAY LEANED back in his chair, resting one ankle across the corner of the desk and propping the other foot on a partly open bottom drawer. If he had to work in an office, it was nice working in a real one, and it was a big improvement to be able to use his living quarters exclusively for living in again. The wide doors at either end of the arched prefab hut were open and a little breeze was drawing through, just enough to keep the place cool and carry off his pipe smoke. There wasn't so much noise outside anymore; most of the new buildings were up now. He could hear a distant popping of small arms as the dozen and a half ZNPF recruits fired for qualification.

A hundred yards away, at the other end, Sergeant Yorimitsu was monitoring screen-views transmitted in from a couple of cars up on patrol, and Lieutenant Ahmed Khadra and Sergeant Knabber were taking the fingerprints of a couple of Fuzzies that had come in an hour ago. Little Fuzzy, resting the point of his chopper-digger on the floor with his hands on the knob pommel, watched boredly. Fingerprinting was old stuff, now. The space between was mostly vacant; a few unoccupied desks and idle business machines scattered about. Some of these days they'd have a real office force, and then he'd be able to get out and move around among the natives, the way a Commissioner ought to.

One thing, they had the Fuzzy Reservation question settled, at least for now. Ben Rainsford was closing everything north of the Little Blackwater and the East Fork of the Snake to settlement; that country all belonged to the Fuzzies and nobody else. Now if the Fuzzies could only be persuaded to stay there. And Gerd and Ruth and Pancho Ybarra and the Andrews girl were here, now, and set up. Maybe they'd begin to find out a few of the things they had to know.

The stamp machine banged twice, putting numbers on the ID discs for the two newcomers. Khadra brought the discs back and squatted to put them on the two Fuzzies.

"How many is that, now, Ahmed?" he called down the hut.

"These are Fifty-eight and Fifty-nine," Khadra called back. "Deduct three, two for Rainsford's, and one for Goldilocks."

Poor little Goldilocks; she'd have loved having an ID disc. She'd been so proud of the little jingle-charm Ruth had given her, just before she'd been killed. Fifty-six Fuzzies; getting quite a population here.

The communication screen buzzed. He flipped a switch on the edge of his desk and dropped his feet to the floor, turning. It was Ben Rainsford, and he was furiously angry about something. His red whiskers bristled as though electrically charged, and his blue eyes were almost shooting sparks.

"Jack," he began indignantly, "I've just found out that Victor Grego has a Fuzzy cooped up at Company House. What's more, he's had the effrontery to have Leslie Coombes apply to Judge Pendarvis to have him appointed guardian."

That surprised him slightly. To date, Grego hadn't exactly established himself as one of the Friends of Little Fuzzy.

"How did he get him, do you know?"

Rainsford gobbled in rage for a moment, then said:

"He claims he found this Fuzzy in his apartment, night before last, up at the top of Company House. Now isn't that one Nifflheim of a story; does he think anybody's silly enough to believe that?"

"Well, it is a funny place for a Fuzzy to be," he admitted. "You suppose it might be one that was live-trapped for Mallin to study, before the trial? Ruth says there were only four, and they were all turned loose the night of the Lurkin business."

"I don't know. All I know is what Gus Brannhard told me that Pendarvis's secretary told him, that Pendarvis told her, that Coombes told Pendarvis." That sounded pretty roundabout, but he supposed that was the way Colonial Governors had to get things. "Gus says Coombes claims Grego says he doesn't know where the Fuzzy came from or how he got into Company House. That is probably a thumping big lie."

"It's probably the truth. Victor Grego's too smart to lie to his lawyer, and Coombes is too smart to lie to the Chief Justice. Judges are funny about that; they want statements veridicated, and after what you saw happen to Mallin in court, you don't suppose any of that crowd would try to lie under veridication."

Rainsford snorted scornfully. Grego was lying; if the veridicator backed him up, the veridicator was as big a liar as he was.

"Well, I don't care how he got the Fuzzy; what I'm concerned with is what he's doing to him," Rainsford replied. "And Ernst Mallin; Coombes admitted to Pendarvis that Mallin was helping Grego look after the Fuzzy. *Look after* him! They're probably torturing the poor thing, Grego and that sadistic quack head-shrinker. Jack, you've got to get that Fuzzy away from Grego!"

"Oh, I doubt that. Grego wouldn't mistreat the Fuzzy, and if he was, he wouldn't apply for papers of guardianship and make himself legally responsible. What do you want me to do?"

"Well, I told Gus to get a court order; Gus told me you were the Native Commissioner, that it was your job to act to protect the Fuzzy . . ."

Gus didn't think the Fuzzy needed any protecting; he thought Grego was treating him well, and ought to be allowed to keep him. So he'd passed the buck. He nodded.

"All right. I'm coming in to Mallorysport now. You're three hours behind us here, and if I use Gerd's boat I can make it in three hours. I'll be at Government House at 1530, your time. I'll bring either Pancho or Ruth along. You have Gus meet us when we get in. And I'll want to borrow your Flora and Fauna."

"What for?"

"Interpreters, and to interrogate Grego's Fuzzy. And I want them instead of any of our crowd here because they may have to testify in court and they won't have to travel back and forth. And tell Gus to get all the papers we'll need to crash Company House with. This is the first time anything like this has come up. We're going to give it the full treatment."

He blanked the screen, scribbled on a notepad and tore off the sheet, then looked around. Ko-Ko and Cinderella and Mamma Fuzzy and a couple of the Constabulary Fuzzies were working on a jigsaw puzzle on the floor near his desk.

"Ko-Ko," he called. *"Do-bizzo."* When Ko-Ko got to his feet and came over, he handed him the note. "Give to Unka Panko," he said. "Make run fast."

Victor Grego had Leslie Coombes on screen; the lawyer was saying:

"The Chief Justice is not hostile. Hospitable, I'd say. I think he's trying to be careful not to establish any precedent that might embarrass the Native Affairs Commission later. He was rather curious about how the Fuzzy got into Company House, though."

"Tell him that makes two of us. So am I."

"Have Steefer's men found out anything yet?"

."Not that he's reported. I'm going to talk to him shortly. The way things are, he's spread out pretty thin."

"It would help a lot if we could explain that. Would you be willing to make a veridicated statement of what you know?"

"With adequate safeguards. Not for anybody to pump me about business matters."

"Naturally. How about Mallin and Jimenez?"

"They will if they want to keep on working for the company." It surprised him that Coombes would even ask such a question. "You think it's necessary?"

"I think it very advisable. Rainsford will certainly oppose your application; possibly Holloway. How about getting a statement from the Fuzzy?"

"Mallin and I tried, last evening. I don't know any of the language, and he only has a few tapes he got from Lieutenant Ybarra at the time of the trial. We have hearing aids, now. It's a hell of a language; sounds like Old Terran Japanese more than anything else. The Fuzzy was trying to tell us something, but we couldn't make out what. We have it all on tape.

"And we showed him audiovisual portraits of those two Survey rangers who were helping Jimenez. He made both of them; I doubt if he likes them very much. We're looking for them. We are also looking for a Company scout car that vanished along with them."

"Vehicle theft's a felony; that will do to hold and interrogate them on," Coombes mentioned. "Well, shall I see you for cocktails?"

"Yes. You'd better call me, say every half-hour. If Rainsford gets nasty about this, I may need you before then."

After that, he called Chief Steefer. Steefer greeted him with:

"Mr. Grego, how red is my face?"

"Not noticeably so. Should it be?"

Steefer swore. "Mr. Grego, I want your authorization to make an inch-by-inch search of this whole building."

"Good God, Harry!" He was thinking of how many millions on millions of inches that was. "Have you found something?"

"Not about the Fuzzy, but—You have no idea what's been going on here, on these unoccupied levels. We found places where people had been camping for weeks. We found one place where there must have been a nonstop party going on for a month; there was almost a lifter scow full of empty bottles. And we found a tea pad."

"Yes? What was that like?"

"Nothing much; lot of mattresses thrown around, and the floor covered with butts—mostly chuckleweed or opiate-impregnated tobacco. I don't think that was any of our people; everybody and his girlfriend in Mallorysport seems to have been sneaking in here. We have men at all the landing stages, of course, but there aren't enough to . . ." His face hardened. "I've just gone slack on the job. That's the only explanation I can make."

"We've all gone slack, Harry." He thought of the mess in his pantry; that was symptomatic. "You know, we may owe the Fuzzies a debt of gratitude, if what's happened to us will make us start acting like a business concern instead of a bunch of kids in fairyland. All right; go ahead. Finding out how the Fuzzy got in here is still of top importance, but clean house generally while you're at it and see that it stays cleaned up."

Then he called Juan Jimenez at Science Center. Jimenez had gotten a new suit since yesterday, less casual, more executive. His public face had been done over too, to emphasize efficiency rather than agreeableness.

"Good morning, Victor." He stumbled a little over the first name, which was a prerogative of a division chief but to which he was not yet accustomed.

"Good morning, Juan. I know you haven't forgotten we're lunching together, but I wondered if you could make it a little early. There are a couple of things we want to go over first. In twenty minutes?"

"Easily; sooner than that if you wish."

"As soon as you can make it. Just come in the back way."

Then he made another screen call. This was an outside call, for which he had to look up the combination. When the screen cleared, a thin-faced, elderly man with white hair looked out of it. He wore a gray work smock, the breast pockets full of small tools and calibrating instruments. His name was Henry Stenson, and he might have been called an instrument maker, just as Benvenuto Cellini might have been called a jeweler.

"Why, Mr. Grego," he greeted, in pleased surprise, or reasonable facsimile. "I haven't heard from you for some time."

"No. Not since that gadget you planted in my globe stopped broadcasting. Incidentally, the globe's about thirty seconds slow, and both moons are impossibly out of synchronization. We had to stop it to take out that thing you built into it, and none of my people has your fine touch."

Stenson grimaced slightly. "I suppose you know for whom I did that?"

"Well, I'm not certain whether you're Navy Intelligence, like our former employee, Ruth Ortheris, or Colonial Office Investigative Bureau; but that's minor. Whoever, they're to be congratulated on an excellent operative. You know, I could get quite nasty about that; planting radio-transmitted microphones in people's offices is a felony. I don't intend doing anything, but I definitely want no more of it. You can understand my attitude."

"Well, naturally, Mr. Grego. You know," he added, "I thought that thing was detection-proof."

"Instrumentally, yes. My people were awed when they saw the detection-baffles on that thing. Have you patented them? If you have, we owe you some money, because we're copying them. But nothing is proof against physical search, and we practically tore my office apart as soon as it became evident that anything said in it was known almost immediately on Xerxes Base."

Stenson nodded gravely. "You didn't call me just to tell me you'd caught me out? I knew that as soon as the radio went dead."

"No. I want you to put the globe back in synchronization, as soon as possible. And there's another thing. You helped the people on Xerxes design those ultrasonic hearing aids, didn't you? Well, could you attack the problem from the other side, Mr. Stenson? I mean, design a little self-powered hand-phone, small enough for a Fuzzy to carry, that would transform the fuzzy's voice to audible frequencies?"

Stenson was silent for all of five seconds. "Yes, of course, Mr. Grego. If anything, it should be simpler. Of course, teaching the Fuzzy to carry and use it would be a problem, but not in my line of work."

"Well, try and get an experimental model done as soon as possible. I have a Fuzzy available to try it. And if there's anything patentable about it, get it protected. Talk to Leslie Coombes. This may be of commercial value to both of us."

"You think there'll be a demand?" Stenson asked. "How much do you think a Fuzzy would pay for one?"

"I think the Native Affairs Commission would pay ten to fifteen sols apiece for them, and I'm sure our electronics plant could turn them out to sell profitably for that."

Somebody had entered the office; in one of the strategically placed mirrors, he saw that it was Juan Jimenez keeping out of the field of the screen-pickup. He nodded to him and went on talking to Stenson, who would be around the next morning to look at the globe. When they finished the conversation and blanked screens, he motioned Jimenez to his deskside chair.

"How much of that did you hear?" he asked.

"Well, I heard that white-haired old Iscariot say he'd be around tomorrow to fix the globe . . ."

"Henry Stenson is no Iscariot, Juan. He is a Terran Federation secret agent, and the Federation is to be congratulated on his loyalty and ability. Now that I know just what he is, and now that he knows I know it, we can do business on a friendly basis of mutual respect and distrust. He's going to work up a gadget by which the Fuzzies can speak audibly to us.

"Now, about Fuzzies," he continued. "We're sure that your two helpers,

Herckerd and Novaes, brought this Fuzzy of mine here to Mallorysport. You say they didn't have him when they came back with you?"

"Absolutely not, Mr. Grego."

"Would you veridicate that?"

Jimenez didn't want to, that was plain. But he did want to work for the Company, especially now that he had just been promoted to chief of Scientific Study and Research. He was as close to the top of the Company House hierarchy as he could get, and he wanted to stay there.

"Yes, of course. I'd hoped, though, that my word would be good enough . . ."

"Nobody's word's going to be good enough. I'm going to veridicate what I know about it, myself; so's Ernst Mallin. There will be quite a few veridicated statements taken in the next few days. Now, I want you to meet this Fuzzy. See if you know him, or if he knows you."

They went out to the private lift and up to the penthouse. In the living room, Sandra Glenn was lounging in his favorite chair, listening to something from a record player with an earphone, and smoking. As they entered, she shut off the player and closed her eyes. *"So-josso-aki;* you give me," she said. *"Aki-josso-so;* I give you. *So-noho-aki dokko;* you tell me how many."

They tiptoed past her and out onto the terrace. Ernst Mallin was sitting on a low hassock, with his hearing aid on; Diamond was squatting in front of him, tying knots in a length of twine. An audiovisual recorder was set up to cover both of them. Diamond sprang to his feet and ran to meet them, crying out: "Pappy Vic! *Heeta!"* and holding up the cord to show the knots he had been learning to tie.

"Hello, Diamond. Those are very fine knots. You are a smart Fuzzy. How do I say that, Ernst?" Mallin said something, haltingly; he repeated it, patting the Fuzzy's head. "Now, how do I ask him if he's ever seen this Big One with me before?"

Mallin asked the question himself. Diamond said something; he caught *"Vov,"* a couple of times. That was negative.

"He doesn't know you, Juan. What I'm sure happened is that Herckerd and Novaes came in with you, just before the trial, then went back to Beta, probably in the aircar they stole from us, and picked up this Fuzzy. We won't know why till we catch them and question them." He turned to Mallin. "Get anything more out of him?"

Mallin shook his head. "I'm picking up a few more words, but I still can't be sure. He says two Hagga, the ones we showed him the films of, brought him here. I think they brought some other Fuzzies with him; I can't be sure. There doesn't seem to be any way of pluralizing in his language. He says they were *tosh-ki gashta,* bad people. They put him in a bad place."

"We'll put them in a bad place. Penitentiary place. I don't suppose you can find out how long ago this was? During or right after the trial, I suppose."

Sandra Glenn came out onto the terrace.

"Mr. Grego; Miss Fallada's on screen. She says representatives of all the press-services are here. They've heard about Diamond; they want the story, and pictures of him."

"That was all we needed! All right, tell her to have a policeman show them up. I'm afraid our lunch'll have to wait till we get through with them, Juan."

8

COMING OUT OF the lift, Jack Holloway advanced to let the others
follow and halted, looking at the three men waiting to meet them in the foyer of
Victor Grego's apartment. Two he had met already: Ernst Mallin, under
uniformly unpleasant circumstances culminating in the murder of Goldilocks,
the beating of Leonard Kellogg, and the shooting of Kurt Borch, at his camp,
and Leslie Coombes, first at George Lunt's complaint court at Beta Fifteen
and then in Judge Pendarvis's court during the Fuzzy Trial. As the trial had
dragged out, the frigid politeness with which he and Coombes had first met had
thawed into something like mutual cordiality.

But, except for news-screen appearances, he had never seen Victor Grego
before. Enemy generals rarely met while the fighting was going on. It struck him
that, meeting Grego for the first time as a complete stranger, he would have
instantly liked him. He had to remember that Grego was the man who had
wanted to treat Fuzzies as fur-bearing animals and exterminate the whole race.
Well, Grego hadn't known any Fuzzies, then. It was easy enough to plan
atrocities against verbal labels.

They paused for an instant, ten feet apart, Mallin and Coombes flanking
Grego, and Gus Brannhard, Pancho Ybarra, Ahmed Khadra, and Flora and
Fauna behind him, like two gangs waiting for somebody to pull a gun. Then
Grego stepped forward, extending his hand.

"Mr. Holloway? Happy to meet you." They shook hands. "You've met Mr.
Coombes and Dr. Mallin. It was good of you to warn us you were coming."

Ben Rainsford hadn't thought so. He'd wanted them to descend on
Company House by surprise, probably with drawn pistols, and catch Grego

red-handed at whatever villainy he was up to. Brannhard and Coombes were shaking hands, so were Ybarra and Mallin. He introduced Ahmed Khadra.

"And these other people are Flora and Fauna," he added. "I brought them along to meet Diamond."

Grego stopped, and they came forward. He said, "Hello, Flora; hello, Fauna. *Aki-gazza heeta-so.*"

The accent was reasonably good, but he had to think between words. The two Fuzzies replied politely. Grego started to say that Diamond was out on the terrace, then laughed when he saw the Fuzzy peeping through the door from the living room. An instant later, Diamond saw Flora and Fauna and rushed forward, and they ran to meet him, all jabbering excitedly. A tall girl with red hair entered behind him; Grego introduced her as Sandra Glenn. And behind her came Juan Jimenez; regular Old Home Week.

"Shall we go in the living room, or out on the terrace?" Grego asked. "I'd advise the terrace; the living room might be a little crowded, with three Fuzzies getting acquainted. Sometimes it seems a trifle crowded with just one Fuzzy."

They went through the living room; the quiet and tasteful luxury of its furnishings had suffered somewhat. There was an audiovisual recorder set up, and an extra reading screen and an audiovisual screen and a tapeplayer; they looked more like office equipment than domestic furnishings. Evidently Fuzzies did the same things to living rooms everywhere. And another piece of furniture, surprising in any living room; a thing like an old-fashioned electric chair, with a bright metal helmet and a big translucent globe mounted above it. A polyencephalographic veridicator; Grego wasn't expecting anybody to take his unsupported word about anything. They all affected not to notice it, and passed out onto the terrace.

This had evidently been Grego's private garden; now it seemed to be mostly the Fuzzy's. An awful lot of men must have been working awfully hard up here recently. There was a lot of playground equipment—swing, slide, skeletal construction of jointed pipe for climbing-bars. A little Fuzzy-sized drinking fountain, and a bathing pool. Grego seemed to have just thought of everything he'd like if he were a Fuzzy and gotten it. Diamond led Flora and Fauna to the slide, ran up the ladder, and came shooting down. They both ran after him and tried it, too, and then ran up to try it again. Have to get some playground stuff like that for the camp. Bet Flora and Fauna would start pestering Pappy Ben to get them some things like this, as soon as they got home.

According to plan, Ahmed Khadra and Pancho Ybarra stayed on the terrace with the Fuzzies; he and Gus and Grego and Mallin and Coombes went back inside. For a while, they chatted about Fuzzies in general and Diamond in particular. One thing was obvious: Grego liked Fuzzies, and was devoted to his own.

The Fuzzies had done him all the damage they could. Now he could be friends with them.

"I suppose you want to hear how he turned up here? If you don't mind, I'd prefer veridicating what I have to tell you, so there won't be any argument about it. Do you want to test the machine first, Mr. Brannhard?"

"It would be a good idea. Jack, you want to be the test witness?"

"If you do the questioning."

A veridicator operated by identifying and registering the distinctive electromagnetic brain-wave pattern involved in suppression of a true statement and substitution of a false one. You didn't have to do that aloud; a mere intention to falsify would turn the blue light in the globe red, and even a yogi adept couldn't control his thoughts enough to prevent it. He took his place in the chair, and Brannhard clipped on the electrodes and lowered the helmet over his head.

"What is your name?"

He answered that truthfully, and Gus nodded and asked him his place of residence.

"How old are you?"

He lied ten years off his age. The veridicator caught that at once; Gus wanted to know how old he really was.

"Seventy-four: I was born in 580. I couldn't even estimate how much to allow for on time-differential for hyperspace trips."

"That's the truth," Gus said. "I didn't think you were much over sixty."

Then he asked about the planets he'd been on. Jack named them, including one he'd never been within fifty light-years of, and the veridicator caught that. He ended in a crimson blaze of mendacity by claiming to be a teetotaler, a Gandhian pacifist, and the illegitimate son of a Satanist archbishop. Brannhard was satisfied; the veridicator worked. He unfastened Jack, and Grego took his place.

The globe stayed blue all through Grego's account of how he had found Diamond in his bedroom; it was the same story they had already gotten from newscasts while coming in from Beta. Then Grego gave place to Mallin, and Mallin to Jimenez. They were all uninvolved in bringing the Fuzzy to Mallorysport, and the veridicator supported them. They all agreed that Diamond had recognized Herckerd and Novaes as the men who had brought him and possibly other Fuzzies there.

"What do you think?" Coombes asked, when they were all back in their chairs. "Do you think they brought those Fuzzies in to sell as pets?"

"I can't see any other reason. I've been expecting something like this. Why would they bring them to Company House, though? I don't quite see the sense in that."

"I do." Grego was angry about something. What he was angry about emerged immediately; he spoke bitterly about what had been going on among the unoccupied rooms of Company House. "Chief Steefer's on the warpath, starting with his own department. We have wants out for Herckerd and Novaes, on a stolen-vehicle charge . . ."

"Forget about that," Brannhard advised. "That's petty larceny to what I'm going to charge them with."

Khadra came in from outside; he took off his beret, but left his pistol on.

"Well, there were six of them," he said. "Diamond, and five others. Herckerd and Novaes—he's positive about the identification—brought them in and kept them for a couple of days in a dark room somewhere in this building. Then the others were taken away; Diamond made a break and got away from the two *tosh-ki Hagga* while they were being put in the aircar. He doesn't know how long ago it was—three sleeps, he says. He found things to eat, and he found water to drink, and then Pappy Vic found him and gave him wonderful-food. He doesn't know what happened to his friends; he hopes they got away too."

"They didn't in here," Grego said. "Are you going to hunt for them?"

"We certainly are."

"And if anything's happened to them, we'll hunt for Herckerd and Novaes till they die of old age if we don't catch them first," Brannhard added.

"How's Diamond like it here, Ahmed?"

"Oh, wonderful. He's the happiest Fuzzy I ever saw, and I never saw any real melancholy Fuzzies. You have a mighty nice Fuzzy, Mr. Grego."

"Well, that's if I'll be allowed to keep him," Grego said.

"My report's going to be very favorable," Khadra told him.

"Of course you will, Mr. Grego. You like the Fuzzy, and he likes you, and he's happy here. That's all I'm interested in."

"I'm afraid Governor Rainsford isn't going to see it like that, Mr. Holloway."

"Governor Rainsford isn't Commissioner of Native Affairs. And he isn't the Federation Courts. The way Judge Pendarvis told me a week ago, the court will accept the advice of the Commission on Fuzzy questions."

"The Attorney-General has a little influence with the court, too," Brannhard said. "The Attorney-General will recommend granting your application for adoption." He rose to his feet. "We don't have anything more to talk about, do we? Then let's go out and see how the Fuzzies are doing."

9

GUS BRANNHARD POURED coffee into a cup already half full of brandy, brushed his beard out of the way with his left hand, and tasted it. It was good, but he still thought it would be better out of a tin pannikin beside a campfire on Beta. It was time to get down to business; after the bare report while hustling indecently through cocktails, they had talked all around the subject at dinner.

"Well, I can and will bring criminal charges," he assured the others who were having coffee in the drawing room at Government House. "Forcible overpowering and transportation under restraint; if that isn't kidnapping what is it?"

"Try your damnedest to make enslavement out of it, Gus," Jack Holloway said. "If you get a conviction, we can have the pair of them shot. And telecast the executions; a real memorable public example is what we want, right now."

"Well, I got the whole story out of Diamond," Pancho Ybarra said. "He and another Fuzzy met four others; the six of them went down a little stream past a waterfall, and then came to a place where there were two Hagga, the ones he was shown audiovisuals of. The Hagga gave them Extee-Three, and then gave them something out of a bottle. They all woke up with hangovers in what sounds like one of the unfinished rooms in Company House. Diamond got away from them; the two bad Big Ones took the rest away."

"So now we have five Fuzzies to hunt," Holloway said. "That'll be your job, Ahmed. You'll stay here in Mallorysport. We'll promote you to captain and chief of detectives; that'll give you a little status equality with the other enforcement heads around here. If they're trapping Fuzzies for sale, that's not just Native Commission business; that's Federation stuff."

"They probably caught them for Mallin to experiment with," Ben Rainsford said.

Jack swore. "Ben, you haven't been paying attention. All this stuff we got from them was veridicated. They don't know anything about any Fuzzies but those four Gerd and Ruth have."

"Mr. Grego has been cooperating very satisfactorily, Governor," Ahmed Khadra said, stiffly formal. "He has the whole Company police working on it, and told me to call on Chief Steefer for anything, and tomorrow Dr. Jimenez is going out to Beta to show some of our people where he was camping. From the Fuzzy's description, we think Herckerd and Novaes went back there."

"Well, what are you going to do about that Fuzzy at Company House?" he asked Jack, ignoring Khadra's words. "You aren't going to let him stay with Grego, are you?"

"Of course we are. Diamond's happy, and Grego's taking good care of him. I'm going to recommend that Judge Pendarvis issue papers of guardianship to him."

"But it isn't right! Not after all Grego did," Rainsford insisted. "Why, he was going to have all the Fuzzies trapped off for their furs. He took your own Fuzzies away from you. He had Jimenez trap those other four, and let Mallin torture them, ask Ruth about that, and then started the story about the Lurkin girl and turned them loose for the mob to kill. And look how he was trying to make out that you'd just taught your Fuzzies a few tricks and then got me to back up your claim that they were sapient beings . . ."

There, at last and obliquely, Ben had let the cat out. What he meant was that Grego had tried to accuse him of deliberately engineering a scientific fraud. Well, a scientist would have trouble forgiving that. It was like accusing a soldier of treason or a doctor of malpractice.

"Well, it's my professional opinion," Pancho Ybarra said, "that Grego and Diamond are much attached to each other, and that it would be injustice to both to separate them, and probably psychologically harmful to the Fuzzy. I shall so advise Judge Pendarvis."

"I think that'll be official policy," Holloway said. "When we find Fuzzies and humans living happily together, we have no right to separate them, and we won't."

Rainsford, who had started to fill his pipe, looked up angrily.

"Maybe you forget I'm the Governor; I make the policy. I appointed you . . ."

Jack's white mustache was twitching at the tips; his eyes narrowed. He looked like an elderly and irascible tiger.

"That's right," he said. "You appointed me Commissioner of Native Affairs.

Any time you don't like the way I do my job, get yourself a new Commissioner."

"Get yourself a new Attorney-General, too. I'm with Jack on this."

Rainsford dropped his pipe into the tobacco pouch.

"You mean you're all against me? What are you doing, bucking for jobs with the CZC?"

After a crack like that, there were those who would have insisted on continuing the discussion by correspondence and through seconds. With anybody but Ben Rainsford, he would have, himself. He turned to Pancho Ybarra.

"Doctor, as a psychiatrist what is your opinion of that outburst?" he asked.

"I'm not entitled to express an opinion," the Navy psychologist replied. "Governor Rainsford is not my patient."

"You mean, I ought to be somebody's?" Rainsford demanded.

"Well, now that you ask, you're not exactly psychotic, but you're certainly not displaying much sanity on the subject of Victor Grego."

"You think we ought to just sit back and let him do anything he pleases; run the planet the way he did before the Pendarvis Decisions?"

"He didn't do such a bad job, Ben," he said. "I'm beginning to think he did a damn sight better job than you'll do unless you stop playing Hatfields and McCoys and start governing. You have to arrange for elections for delegates, and a constitutional convention. You have to take over and operate all these public services the Company's been relieved of responsibility for when their charter was invalidated. And you'll have to stop this cattle rustling on Beta and Delta Continents, or you'll have a couple of first-class range wars on your hands. And you'd better start thinking about the immigrant rush that's going to hit this planet when the news of the Pendarvis Decisions gets around."

Rainsford, his pipe and tobacco shoved into his side pocket, was on his feet. He'd tried to interrupt a couple of times.

"Oh, to Nifflheim with you!" he cried. "I'm going out and talk to my Fuzzies."

With that, he flung out of the room. For a moment, nobody said anything, then Jack Holloway swore.

"I hope the Fuzzies talk some sense into him. Be damned if I can."

They probably would, if he'd listen to them. They had more sense than he had, at the moment. Ahmed Khadra, who had sat mumchance through the upper-echelon brawl, clattered his cup and saucer.

"Jack, you think we ought to go check in at the hotel?" he asked.

"Nifflheim, no! This isn't Ben Rainsford's private camp, this is Government House," Holloway said. "We work for the Government, too. We have work to do now."

"We'll have to talk to him again." He wasn't looking forward to it with any pleasure. "We have to get some kind of a Fuzzy Code scotch-taped together, and he'll have to okay it. We need special legislation, and till we can get a Colonial Legislature, that'll have to be by executive decree. And you'll have to figure out a way to make Fuzzies available for adoption. You can't break up a black market by shooting a few people for enslavement; you'll have to make it possible for people to get Fuzzies legally, with controls and safeguards, instead of buying them from racketeers."

"I know it, Gus," Jack said. "I've been thinking about it; a regular adoption bureau. But who can I get to handle it? I don't know anybody."

"Well, I know everybody around Central Courts Building." That ought to be enough; Central Courts was like a village, in which everybody knew everybody else. "Maybe Leslie Coombes would help me."

"My God, Gus; don't let Ben hear you say that," Jack implored. "He'd blow up about a hundred megatons. You might just as well talk about getting V-dash-R G-dash-O to help."

"He could help a lot. If we ask him, he would."

"Ruth did a lot of work with juvenile court, on her cover-job," Ybarra mentioned. "There's some kind of a Juvenile Welfare Association . . ."

"Claudette Pendarvis. The Chief Justice's wife. She does a lot about Juvenile Welfare."

"Yes," Ybarra agreed instantly. "I've heard Ruth talk about her. Very favorably, too, and Ruth has a galloping allergy for volunteer do-gooders as a rule."

"She likes Fuzzies," Jack said. "She couldn't stay away from them during the trial. I promised her a pair as soon as I got a nice couple." He got to his feet. "Let's move into one of the offices, where we have a table to work on, and some communication screens. I'll call her now and ask her about it."

"FREDERIC, MAY I interrupt?"

Pendarvis turned from the reading-screen and started to lay aside his cigar and rise. Claudette, entering the room, motioned him to keep his seat and advanced to take the low cushion-stool, clasping her hands about her knees and tilting her head back in the same girlish pose he remembered from the long ago days on Baldur when he had been courting her.

"I want to tell you something lovely, Frederic," she began. "Mr. Holloway just called me. He says he has two Fuzzies for me, a boy Fuzzy and a girl Fuzzy; he's going to have them brought in tomorrow or the next day."

"Well, that is lovely." Claudette was crazy about Fuzzies. Had been ever since the first telecasts of them, and she had watched them in court and visited them at the Hotel Mallory during the trial. Now that he considered, he would like a pair of Fuzzies, too. "I think I'll enjoy having them here as much as you will. I like Fuzzies, as long as they stay out of my courtroom."

They both laughed, remembering what seventeen Fuzzies and a Baby Fuzzy had done to the dignity of the court while their sapience was being debated.

"I hope this won't be regarded as special privilege though," he added. "A great many people want Fuzzies, and . . ."

"But other people can have Fuzzies, too. That was what Mr. Holloway was calling me about. They'll be made available for adoption, and he wants me to supervise it, to make sure they don't get into wrong hands and aren't mistreated."

That was something else. They'd both have to think about that carefully.

"You think it would be proper for you to have an official position like that?" he asked.

"I can't see why not. I'm doing the same kind of work with Juvenile Welfare."

"You'll be making decisions on who should and who should not be allowed to adopt Fuzzies. When I get a Native Cases Court set up—I think Yves Janiver, for that—your decisions will be accepted."

"Whose decisions do you think Adolphe Ruiz's Juvenile Court accepts now?"

"That's right," he agreed. And she couldn't accept the Fuzzies and refuse to help with the adoption bureau; that wouldn't be right, at all. And she wanted Fuzzies so badly. "Well, go ahead, darling; do it. Whoever takes that position will have to be somebody who really loves Fuzzies. What did you tell Mr. Holloway?"

"That I'd talk to you, and then call him back. He's at Government House now."

"Well, call him and tell him you accept. I'll call Yves and talk to him about the Native Cases Court . . ."

She had left the low seat while he was speaking; she stopped to kiss him on the way out. She'd be so happy. He hoped he wouldn't be too severely criticized. Well, he'd been criticized before and survived it.

VICTOR GREGO WATCHED Diamond investigating the articles on top of the low cocktail table. He took a couple of salted nuts from the glass bowl, nibbled one, and put the rest back. He looked at the half-full coffee cup and the liqueur glass, and left both alone. Then he started to pick up the ashtray.

"No, Diamond. *Vov.* Don't touch."

"*Vov ninta,* Diamond," Ernst Mallin, who was a slightly more advanced Fuzzy linguist, said. "We ought to learn their language, instead of making them learn ours."

"We ought to teach them our language, so they can speak to anybody, and not just Fuzzyologists."

"I deplore that term, Mr. Grego. The suffix is Greek, from *logos.* Fuzzy is not a Greek word, and should not be combined with it."

"Oh, rubbish, Ernst. We're not speaking Greek; we're speaking Lingua Terra. You know what Lingua Terra is? An indiscriminate mixture of English, Spanish, Portuguese, and Afrikaans, mostly English. And you know what English is? The result of the efforts of Norman men-at-arms to make dates with Saxon barmaids in the Ninth Century Pre-Atomic, and no more legitimate than any of the other results. If a little Greek suffix gets into a mess like that, it'll have to take care of itself the best way it can. And you'd better learn to like the term, because it's your new title. Chief Fuzzyologist; fifteen percent salary increase."

Mallin gave one of his tight little smiles. "For that, I believe I can condone a linguistic barbarism."

Diamond seemed, he couldn't be sure, to be wanting to know why not touch; would it hurt?

"And how do you explain that he mustn't spill ashes on the floor, in his own language? What are the Fuzzy words for 'floor,' and 'ashes'?" He leaned forward and dropped the ash from his cigarette into the tray. "Ashtray," he said.

Diamond repeated it as well as he could. Then he strolled over to where Mallin sat. Mallin regarded smoking as an act of infantile oralism; his ashtray was empty.

"*Asht'ay?*" he asked. "*Diamond vov ninta?*"

"You see. He knows that ashtray is a class-word, not just the name of a specific object," Mallin said. "And I tried so hard to prove that Fuzzies couldn't generalize. This one is empty; let's see how we can explain the difference. If we give him the word 'ashes,' and then . . ."

A bell began ringing softly; Diamond turned quickly to see what it was. It was the bell for the private communication screen, and only half a dozen people knew the call-combination. He rose and put it on. Harry Steefer looked out of it.

"We found it, sir; ninth level down." That was the one below the first reported thefts and ransackings. "The Fuzzies were penned in a small room that looks as though it had been intended for a general toilet and washroom. It's right off a main hall, and somebody's had an aircar in and out and set it down recently. I'd say half a dozen Fuzzies for two or three days."

"Good. I want to see it. I want Diamond to see it, too. Send somebody who knows where it is up to my private stage with a car small enough to get into it."

He blanked the screen and turned to Mallin. "You heard that. Well, let's all three of us go down and look at it." Jack Holloway stopped at the head of the long escalator and looked down into the garden, now double-lighted by Darius, almost full, and Xerxes, past full and just rising. After a moment he saw Ben Rainsford reclining in a lawn-chair, with Flora and Fauna snuggled together on his lap. As he started toward them, after descending, he thought they were all asleep. Then one of the Fuzzies stirred and yeeked, and Rainsford turned his head.

"Who is it?" he asked.

"Jack. Have you been here all evening?"

"Yes, all three of us," Rainsford said. "I think it's time for Fuzzies to go to bed, now."

"Ben, we just had a screen call from Company House. They found where those Fuzzies had been kept, an empty room on one of the unfinished floors. They showed us with a portable pickup; dark, filthy place. The Company police are working on it for physical evidence to corroborate Diamond's story. And they've put out a general want for those two Company rangers, Herckerd and Novaes; kidnapping and suspicion of enslavement."

"Who called you? Steefer?"

"Grego. He says we can count on him for anything. He's really sore about this."

The Fuzzies had jumped to the ground and were trying to attract his attention. Ben shifted in his chair, and began stuffing tobacco into his pipe.

"Jack." His voice was soft; he spoke hesitantly. "I've been talking to the kids, out here, till they got sleepy. They had a big time at Company House with Diamond. They say he's lonesome for other Fuzzies. They'd like him to come here and visit them, and they'd like to go back and visit him again."

"Well, a Fuzzy would get lonesome by himself. It didn't take Little Fuzzy long to go and bring the rest of his family into my place."

"And they say that outside that he's happy. They told me about all the nice things he had, and the garden, and the room that was fixed up for him. They say everybody's good to him, and Pappy Vic loves him. That's what they call Grego; Pappy Vic, just like they call us Pappy Ben and Pappy Jack." His lighter flared, showing a puzzled face above the pipe bowl. "I can't understand it, Jack. I thought Grego would hate Fuzzies."

"Why should he? The Fuzzies didn't know anything about the Company's charter; they don't know a Class-IV planet from Nifflheim. He doesn't even hate us; he'd have done the same thing in our place. Ben, he's willing to call the war off; why can't you?"

Rainsford puffed slowly, the smoke drifting and changing color in the double moonlight.

"Do you honestly believe that Fuzzy wants to stay with Grego?" he asked.

"It'd break Diamond's heart if you took him away from Pappy Vic. Ben, why don't you invite Diamond over to play with your two? You wouldn't have to meet Grego; the girl he has helping with Diamond could bring him."

"Maybe I will. You're on speaking terms with Grego; why don't you?"

"I will, tomorrow." The Fuzzies hadn't wanted to play; they'd just wanted to be noticed. He picked Flora up and gave her to Ben, then took Fauna in his own arms. "Let's go put them to bed, and then go inside. We have a lot of things to do, in a hurry, and we need your authorization."

"Well, what?"

"Ahmed's staying here; he and Harry Steefer and Ian Ferguson and some others are having a conference tomorrow on this case and on general Fuzzy protection. And I'm setting up an Adoption Bureau; Judge Pendarvis's wife's agreed to take charge of that. We need laws, and till there's some kind of a legislature, you have to do that by decree."

"Well, all right. But there's one thing, Jack. Just because Grego's with us on this doesn't mean I'm going to let him grab back control of this planet, the way he had it before the Pendarvis Decisions. It took the Fuzzies to break the Company's monopoly; well, I'm going to see it stays broken."

10

K NOWING HENRY STENSON'S part in the dischartering of the Zarathus-
tra Company, Pancho Ybarra was mildly surprised to find him in the Fuzzy-
room Grego had fitted up back of the kitchenette of his apartment, when Ernst
Mallin, who met him on the landing stage, ushered him in. Grego's Fuzzy-sitter,
Sandra Glenn, was there, and so, although in the middle of business hours, was
Grego himself. And, of course, Diamond.

"Mr. Stenson," he greeted noncommittally. "This is a pleasure."

Stenson laughed. "We needn't pretend to distant acquaintance, Lieutenant,"
he said. "Mr. Grego is quite aware of my, er, other profession. He doesn't hold
it against me; he just insists that I no longer practice it on him."

"Mr. Stenson has something here that'll interest you," Grego said, picking
up something that looked like a small nuclear-electric razor. "Turn off your
hearing aid, if you please, Lieutenant. Thank you. Now, Diamond, make talk for
Unka Panko."

"Heyo, Unka Panko." Diamond said, when Grego held the thing to his
mouth, very clearly and audibly. "You hear Diamond make talk like Hagga?"

"I sure do, Diamond! That's wonderful."

"How make do?" Diamond asked. "Make talk with talk-thing, talk like
Hagga. Not have talk-thing, no can talk like Fuzzy, Hagga no hear. How make
do?"

Fuzzies could hear all through the human-audibility range; the race
wouldn't have survived the dangers of the woods if they hadn't been able to.
They could hear beyond that, to about 40,000 cycles. None of the other
Zarathustran mammals could; that supported Gerd van Riebeek's theory that

Fuzzies were living fossils, the sole survivors of a large and otherwise extinct order of Zarathustran quasi-primates. Gerd thought they had developed ultrasonic hearing to meet some ancient survival-problem long before they had developed the power of symbolizing ideas in speech, and had always conversed ultrasonically with one another, probably to avoid betraying themselves to their natural enemies.

"Fuzzies hear Big Ones talk. Fuzzies little, Hagga big, make big talk. Hagga not hear Fuzzy talk, Fuzzies little, make little talk. So, Big Ones make ear-things, make Fuzzy talk big in ears, can hear. Now, Hagga make talk-things, so Fuzzies make big talk like Hagga, everybody hear, have ear-things, not have ear-things."

That wasn't the question. Diamond had gotten that far, himself, already. The question, which he repeated, was, "How make do?"

Grego was grinning at him. "You're doing fine, Lieutenant. Now, go ahead and give him a lecture on ultrasonics and electronics and acoustics."

"Has your Chief Fuzzyologist done anything on that yet?"

"I haven't even tried," Mallin said. "You know much more of the language than I do; what Fuzzy words would you use to explain anything like that?"

That was right. Any race—*Homo sapiens terra,* or *Fuzzy fuzzy holloway zarathustra*—thought just as far as their verbal symbolism went, and no further. And they could only comprehend ideas for which they had words.

"Just tell him it's Terran black magic," Sandra Glenn suggested.

That would work on planets like Loki or Thor or Yggdrasil; on Shesha or Uller, you could also mention the mysterious ways of the gods. The Fuzzies had just about as much conception of magic or religion as they had of electronics or nucleonics or the Abbot life-and-drive.

He stooped forward and held out his hand. *"So-josso-aki,* Diamond. *So-pokko* Unka Panko."

The Fuzzy gave him the thing, which he had been holding in both hands. The resemblance to an electric razor was more than coincidental; the mechanism was enclosed in the plastic case of one. The end that would have done the shaving was open; the Fuzzy talked into that. There was a circular screened opening on the side from which the transformed sound emerged. It still had the original thumb-switch.

"Still has the original power-unit, too," Stenson said. That would be a little capsule the size of a 6-mm short pistol cartridge. "A lot of the parts are worked over from ultrasonic hearing-aid parts. I'm going to have to do something better than that switch, too. A little handle, maybe like a pistol grip, with a grip-squeeze switch, so that the Fuzzy will turn it on when he takes hold of it, and turn it off when he lets go. And it'll have to be a lot lighter and a lot smaller." He gestured toward some sheets of paper on which he had been making diagrams and schematics and notes. "I have some people at my shop working on that now. We'll have production prototypes in about a week. The Company's factory will start production as soon as they can tool up for it."

"We're getting a patent," Grego said. "We're calling it the Stenson Fuzzyphone."

"Grego-Stenson; it was your original idea."

"Hell, I just told you what I wanted; you invented it," Grego argued. "As soon as we have all the bugs chased out, we'll be in production. We don't know how much we'll have to ask for them. Not more than twenty sols, I don't suppose."

Flora and Fauna were puzzled. They sat on the floor at Pappy Ben's feet, looking up at the funny people that came and went in the picture-thing on the wall and spoke out of it. Long ago they had found out that nothing in the screen could get out of it, and they couldn't get in. It was just one of the strange things the Big Ones had, and they couldn't understand it, but it was fun.

But then, all of a sudden, there was Pappy Ben, right in the screen. They looked around, startled, thinking he had left them, but no, there he was, still in the chair smoking his pipe. They both felt him to make sure he was really there, then they both climbed onto his lap and pointed at the Pappy Ben in the screen.

Flora and Fauna didn't know about audiovisual recordings; they couldn't understand how Pappy Ben could be in two places at the same time. That bothered them. It just couldn't happen.

"It's all right, kids," he assured them. "I'm really here. That isn't me, there."

"Is," Flora contradicted. "I see it."

"Is not," Fauna told her. "Pappy Ben here."

Maybe Pancho Ybarra or Ruth van Riebeek could explain it; he couldn't.

"Of course I'm here," he said, hugging both of them. "That is just not-real look-like."

"It will be illegal," the Pappy Ben in the screen was saying, "to capture any Fuzzy in habitat by any other means, including the use of intoxicants, narcotics, sleepgas, sono-stunners or traps. This will constitute kidnapping. It will be illegal to keep any Fuzzy chained, tied or otherwise physically restrained. It will be illegal to transport any Fuzzy from Beta Continent to any other part of this planet without a permit from the Native Affairs Commission, each permit to bear the fingerprints of the Fuzzy for whom it is issued. It will be illegal knowingly to deliver any Fuzzy to anybody intending to so transport him. This will constitute kidnapping, also, and will be punished accordingly."

The Pappy Ben in the screen was scowling menacingly. Flora and Fauna looked quickly around to see if the real Pappy Ben was mad about something too.

Flora said: "Make talk about Fuzzy."

"Yes. Talk about what Big Ones do to bad Big Ones who hurt Fuzzies," he told her.

"Make dead, like bad Big One who make Goldilocks dead?" Fauna asked.

"Something like that."

That was what all the Fuzzies who had been in court during the trial thought had happened. Suicide while of unsound mind due to remorse of conscience was a little too complicated to explain to a Fuzzy, at least at present.

All the Fuzzies who knew what had happened to Goldilocks thought that had been no more than the bad Big One deserved.

Captain Ahmed Khadra, chief of detectives, ZNPF, and Colonel Ian Ferguson, Commandant, Colonial Constabulary, were listening to the telecast with Max Fane, the Colonial Marshal, in the latter's office. In the screen, Governor Rainsford was saying:

"And any person capturing or illegally transporting or illegally holding in restraint any Fuzzy for purposes of sale will be guilty of enslavement."

"Aah!" Max Fane set a stiffly extended index finger against the base of his skull, cocked his thumb and clicked his tongue. "Death's mandatory; no discretion-of-the-court about it."

"Yves Janiver'll try all the Fuzzy cases. He likes Fuzzies," Ferguson said. "He won't like people who mistreat them."

"I know Janiver's attitude on death penalties," Fane said. "He doesn't think people should be shot for committing crimes; he thinks they should be shot for being the kind of people who commit them. He thinks shooting criminals is like shooting diseased veldbeest. A sanitation measure. So do I."

"If Herckerd and Novaes are smart, they'll come in and surrender now," Ferguson said. "You think they still have the other five?"

Khadra shook his head. "I think they sold them to somebody in Mallorysport as soon as they moved them out of Company House. If we could find out who that is . . ."

"I could name a dozen possibilities," Max Fane told him. "And back of each one of them is Hugo Ingermann."

"I wish we could haul Ingermann in and veridicate him," Ferguson said.

"Well, you can't. Ingermann's a lawyer, and the only way you can question a lawyer under veridication is catch him standing over a corpse with a bloody knife in his hand. And you have a Nifflheim of a time doing it, even then."

"A GREAT MANY people want Fuzzies; we know that," the Governor was saying. "Many of them should have them; they would make Fuzzies happy, and would be made happy by them. We are not going to deny such people an opportunity to adopt these charming little persons. An adoption bureau has been set up already; Mrs. Frederic Pendarvis, the wife of the Chief Justice, will be in charge of it, and the offices have already been set up in the Central Courts Building, and will open tomorrow morning . . ."

"Oh, Daddy; Mother!" the little girl cried. "You hear that, now. The Governor says people can have Fuzzies of their own. Won't you get me a Fuzzy? I'll be as good as good to it—him, I mean, or her, whichever."

The parents looked at one another, and then at their twelve-year-old daughter.

"What do you think, Bob?"

"You'll have to take care of it, Marjory, and that will be a lot of work. You'll have to feed it, and give it baths, and . . ."

"Oh, I will; I'll do anything, just if I can have one. And people mustn't call Fuzzies 'it,' Daddy; Fuzzies are people, too, like us. You didn't call me 'it,' when I was a little baby, did you?"

"I'm afraid your father did, my dear. Just at first. And you'll have to study and learn the language, so you can talk to the Fuzzy, because Fuzzies don't speak Lingua Terra. You know, Bob, I think I'd enjoy having a Fuzzy around, myself."

"You know, I believe I would, too. Well, let's get around to this adoption bureau the first thing tomorrow . . ."

11

THEY WERE HAVING a party at the Pendarvis home. Jack Holloway sat on his heels on the floor, smoking his pipe and interpreting, while the judge and his wife, in a low easy-chair and on a drum-shaped hassock respectively, were getting acquainted with the guests of honor, the two Fuzzies Juan Jimenez had brought in from Beta Continent that evening. Gus Brannhard, who had come along from Government House, was sprawled in one of the larger chairs, chuckling in his beard. Juna Jimenez and Ahmed Khadra had removed their hearing aids and carried their drinks to the other side of the room, where they were talking about Jimenez's visit, with a couple of George Lunt's troopers, to the site of his former camp.

"They were back, after we left," Jimenez was saying. "We could see where they'd set a car down. There wasn't much to see; they policed everything up very neatly after they left, the second time. Didn't leave any litter around."

"Or any evidence," Khadra added.

"That was what Yorimitsu and Calderon said when they saw it. I gather they take a dim view of neatness."

"Around where they're investigating, sure. Tidying up around the scene of a crime's gotten more criminals off than all the crooked lawyers in the Galaxy. In this case it doesn't matter. Herckerd and Novaes brought those Fuzzies in; we know that. We have a witness."

"Can you veridicate a Fuzzy?" Brannhard asked, over his shoulder. "If you can't, the defense'll object."

Pendarvis looked up and around. "Mr. Brannhard, I'm afraid I'd have to sustain such an objection. I suspect that Judge Janiver, who'd be hearing the case, would, too. If I were you, I'd find out. Have you ever been veridicated?" he asked the Fuzzy on his lap.

The Fuzzy—the male member of the couple, who was trying to work the zipper of his jacket—said, "Unnh?" The judge scratched the back of his head, which the Fuzzy, like most furry people, liked, and wondered how long it would take to learn the language.

"Not too long," Jack told him. "It only took me a day to learn everything the people on Xerxes learned; by the time we were starting for home, after the trial, I could talk to them. What are you going to call them?"

"Don't they have names of their own, Mr. Holloway?" the judge's wife asked.

"They don't seem to. In the woods, there are never more than six or eight in a family, if that's what the groups are. I guess all the natives names are things like 'me,' and 'you,' and 'this one,' and 'that one.'"

"You'll have to have names for them, for the adoption papers," Brannhard said.

"At the camp, we just called them 'the Newlyweds,'" Khadra said.

"How about Pierrot and Columbine?" Mrs. Pendarvis asked.

Her husband nodded. "I think that would be fine." He pointed to himself. *"Aki Pappy Frederic. So Pierrot."*

"Aki Py'hot? Py'hot siggo Pappy F'ed'ik."

"He accepts the name. He says he likes you. What are you going to do with them tomorrow, Mrs. Pendarvis? Do you have any human servants here?"

"No, everything's robotic, and I oughtn't to leave them alone with robots. Not till they get used to them."

"Drop them off at Government House; they can play with Flora and Fauna," Brannhard suggested. "And I'll call Victor Grego and invite his Diamond over, and they can have a real party. First Fuzzy social event of the season."

A mellow-toned bell began chiming. The Judge set Pierrot on the floor and excused himself; Pierrot trotted after him. In a moment, both were back.

"Chief Earlie's on screen," he said. "He wants to talk either to Captain Khadra or Mr. Holloway."

That was the new Mallorysport chief of police. Jack nodded to Khadra, who left the room.

"Probably found something out about Herckerd and Novaes," Brannhard said.

"Will you really charge them with enslavement?" Mrs. Pendarvis asked. "That's mandatory death."

"You catch people, deprive them of their freedom, make property of them," Brannhard said. "What else can you call it? A pet slave is still a slave, if he

belongs to somebody else. I don't know how a Fuzzy could be made to
work . . ."

"Nightclub entertainers, attractions in bars, sideshow acts . . ."

Khadra came back; he had his beret on, and was buckling on his pistol.

"Earlier says he has a report on a Fuzzy being seen in an apartment-unit
over on the north side of the city," he said. "Informant says a Fuzzy is being kept
by a family on one of the upper floors. He's sending men there now."

That would probably be one of the five Herckerd and Novaes had brought
in. He could see what had happened. The two former Company employees had
sold them all to somebody here in Mallorysport, some racketeer who was selling
them individually. There was somebody who really did need shooting. And by
this time, Herckerd and Novaes would be back on Beta Continent, trapping
more. Get the people who had bought this Fuzzy under veridication, the police
had plenty of ways to make people want to talk, and work back from there.

"I'll go see what it is," Khadra was saying. "I'll call in as soon as I can. I
don't know how long I'll be gone. In case I don't get back, thanks for a nice
evening, Judge, Mrs. Pendarvis."

He hurried out, and for a moment nobody said anything. Then Jimenez
suggested that if this were one of the Herckerd-Novaes lot, Diamond ought to
see him as soon as possible; he'd be able to identify him. Khadra would think
of that. Mrs. Pendarvis hoped there wouldn't be any shooting. Mallorysport city
police were notoriously trigger-happy. The conversation continued by jerks and
starts; the two Fuzzies seemed to be the only ones unconcerned.

After about an hour, Khadra returned; he had left his belt and beret in the
hall.

"What was it?" Brannhard asked. Jack was wanting to know if the Fuzzy
was all right.

"It wasn't a Fuzzy," Khadra said disgustedly. "It was a Terran marmoset;
these people have had it for a couple of years; brought it from Terra. The people
who own it have had a wire screen around their terrace to keep it, ever since they
moved in. Somebody in an aircar saw it outside and thought it was a Fuzzy. I
wonder how much more of this we're going to get."

It was a wonder he hadn't gotten that, himself, when his own family was
lost and he was hunting for them.

12

THE AIR TRAFFIC around Central Courts Building the next morning seemed normal to Jack Holloway. There were quite a few cars on the landing stage above the sixth level down when he came in, but no more than he remembered from the time of the Fuzzy Trial. It was not until he left the escalator on the fourth floor below, where the Adoption Bureau officers were, that he began to suspect that there was a Fuzzy rush on.

The corridor leading back from the main hall to the suite that had been taken over yesterday was jammed. It was a well behaved, well dressed crowd, mostly couples clinging to each other to avoid being jostled apart. Everybody seemed to be happy and excited; it was more like a Year-End Holidays shopping crowd than anything else.

A uniformed deputy-marshal saw him and approached, touching his cap-brim in a half salute.

"Mr. Holloway; are you trying to get in to your offices? You'd better come this way, sir; there's a queue down at the other end."

There must be five or six hundred of them. Cut that in half; most of them were couples.

"How long's this been going on?" he asked, noticing that several more couples and individuals were coming behind him.

"Since about 0700. There were a few here before then; the big rush didn't start till 0830."

Some of the people in the rear of the jam saw and recognized him. "Holloway." "Jack Holloway; he's the Commissioner." "Mr. Holloway; are there Fuzzies here now?"

The deputy took him down the hall and unlocked the door of an office; it was empty, and the desks and chairs and things shrouded in dust-covers. They went through and out into a back hall, where another deputy-marshal was arguing with some people who were trying to get in that way.

"Well, why are they letting him in; who's he?" a woman demanded.

"He works here. That's Jack Holloway."

"Oh! Mr. Holloway! Can you tell us how soon we can get Fuzzies?"

His guide rushed him, almost as though he were under arrest, along the hall, and opened another door.

"In here, Mr. Holloway; Mrs. Pendarvis's office. I'll have to get back and keep that mob in front straightened out." He touched his cap-brim again and hastened away.

Mrs. Pendarvis sat at a desk, her back to the door, going over a stack of forms in front of her. Beside her, at a smaller desk, a girl was taking them as she finished with them, and talking into the whisper-mouthpiece of a vocowriter. Two more girls sat at another desk, one talking to somebody in a communication screen. Mrs. Pendarvis said, "Who is it?" and turned her head, then rose, extending her hand. "Oh; Mr. Holloway. Good morning. What's it like out in the hall, now?"

"Well, you see how I had to come in. I'd say about five hundred, now. How are you handling them?"

She gestured toward the door to the front office, and he opened it and looked through. Five girls sat at five desks; each was interviewing applicants. Another girl was gathering up application-forms and carrying them to a desk where they were being sorted to be passed on to the back office.

"I arrived at 0830," Mrs. Pendarvis said. "Just after I dropped Pierrot and Columbine off at Government House. There was a crowd then, and it's been going on ever since. How many Fuzzies have you, Mr. Holloway?"

"Available for adoption? I don't know. Beside mine and Gerd and Ruth van Riebeek's and the Constabulary Fuzzies, there were forty day-before yesterday. That had gotten up to a hundred and three by last evening."

"We have, to date, three hundred and eleven applications; there are possibly twenty more that haven't been sent back to me yet. By the time we close, it'll be five or six hundred. How are we going to handle this, anyhow? Some of these people want just one Fuzzy, some of them want two, some of them will take a whole family. And we can't separate Fuzzies who want to stay together. If you'd separate Pierrot and Columbine, they'd both grieve themselves to death. And there are families of five or six who want to stay together, aren't there?"

"Well, not permanently. These groups aren't really families; they're sort of temporary gangs for mutual assistance. Five or six are about as many as can make a living together in the woods. They're hunters and food-gatherers, low Paleolithic economy, and individual small-game hunters at that. When a gang gets too big to live together, they split up; when one couples meets another, they team up to hunt together. That's why they have such a well-developed and uniform language, and I imagine that's how the news about the zatku spread all over the Fuzzy country as fast as it did. They don't even mate permanently. Your pair are just young, first mating for both of them. They think each other are the most wonderful ever. But you will have others that won't want to be separated; you'll have to let them be adopted together." He thought for a moment. "You can't begin to furnish Fuzzies for everybody; why don't you give them out by lot? Each of those applications is numbered, isn't it? Draw numbers."

"Like a jury-drawing, of course. Let the jury-commissioners handle that," the Chief Justice's wife said.

"Fair enough. You'll have to investigate each of these applicants, of course; that'll take a little time, won't it?"

"Well, Captain Khadra's taking charge of them. He's borrowed some people from the schools, and some from the city police juvenile squad and some from the company personnel division. I've been getting my staff together the same way—parent-teacher groups, Juvenile Welfare. I'm going to get a paid staff together, as soon as I can. I think they'll come from the Company's public-service division; I'm told that Mr. Grego's going to suspend all those activities in ninety days."

"That's right. That includes the schools, and the hospitals. Why don't you talk to Ernst Mallin? He'll find you all the people you want. He's joined the Friends of Little Fuzzy, too, now."

"Well, after we've allocated Fuzzies to these people, what then? Do they come out to your camp and pick their own?"

"Good Lord, no! We have enough trouble, without having the place overrun with human people." He hadn't given that thought until now. "What we'll need will be a place here in Mallorysport where a couple of hundred Fuzzies can stay and where the people who have been endorsed for foster-parents can come and select the ones they want."

That would have to be a big place, with a park all around it, that could be fenced in to keep them from wandering off and getting lost. A nice place, where they could all have fun together. He didn't know of any such place, and asked her about it.

"I'll talk to Mr. Urswick, he's the Company Chief of Public Services. He'll know about something. You know, Mr. Holloway, I didn't have any idea, when I took this job, that it was going to be so complicated."

"Mrs. Pendarvis, I've been saying that every hour on the hour since I let Ben

Rainsford talk me into taking the job I have. You're going to have to do something about information, too—Fuzzies, care and feeding of; Fuzzies, psychology of; language. We'll try to find somebody to prepare booklets and language-learning tapes. And hearing aids."

The door at the side of the room was marked INVESTIGATION. He found Ahmed Khadra in the room behind it, talking to somebody in a city police uniform by screen.

"Well, have you gotten anything from any of them?" he was asking.

"Damn little," the city policeman told him. "We've been pulling them in all day, everybody in town who has a record. And Hugo Ingermann's been pulling them away from us as fast as they come in. He had a couple of his legmen and assistants here with portable radios, and as fast as we bring some punk in, they call somebody at Central Courts and he gets a writ; order to show grounds for suspicion. Most of them we can't question at all; it takes an hour to an hour and a half from the time they're brought in before we can veridicate those we can. And none of them knows a damn thing when we do."

"Well, how about known associates? Didn't either of them have any friends?"

"Yes. All middle-salary Company people; they've been cooperating, but none of them knows anything."

The conversation went on for a few more minutes, then they blanked screens. Khadra turned in his chair and lit a cigarette.

"Well, you heard it, Jack," he said. "They just vanished, and the Fuzzies with them. I'm not surprised we're not getting anything out of their friends in the Company. They wouldn't know. We searched their rooms; they seem to have cleaned out everything they had when they disappeared. And we can't get anything from underworld sources. None of the city police stool-pigeons knows anything."

"You know, Ahmed, I'm worried about that. I wonder what's happened to those Fuzzies . . ." He sat down on the edge of the desk and got out his pipe and tobacco. "How soon will you be able to start investigating these people who want Fuzzies?"

Gerd van Riebeek refilled his cup and shoved the coffee across the table to George Lunt. He ought to be getting back to work; they both ought to. Work was piling up, with both Jack and Pancho away and Ahmed Khadra permanently detached from duty at the camp.

"Eighty-seven," Lunt said. "That's not counting yours and mine and Jack's."

"The Extee-Three's getting low." They'd had to start rationing it; tomorrow, they'd not be able to issue any, or on alternate days thereafter. The Fuzzies wouldn't like that. "Jacks says he thinks speculators are buying it and holding it off the market. They'll get big prices for it when the Fuzzies start coming in to Mallorysport."

There wasn't much Extee-Three on Zarathustra. People kept a tin or so in their aircars, in case of forced landings in the wilderness which was ninety percent of the planet's land surface, but until the Fuzzies found out about it, the consumption had been practically zero. There was a supply on Xerxes, for emergency ships' stores, individual survival kits and so on, but that wouldn't last. It was on order, but it would be four months till any could get in from the nearest Federation planet. And the supply on hand wouldn't last that long.

"Personally, I wish there were eighty-seven hundred of them," Lunt said. "No, I'm not crazy, and I mean it. The ones we have here aren't getting into deviltry down in the farming country. So far, I haven't heard of any of them getting that far, except that one family that's moved in on that backwoods farm, and they're behaving themselves. But wait till they get down in the real farm country, and among the sugar plantations. You know, Jack and I thought, at first, that our big job was going to be protecting Fuzzies from humans. It looks to me, now, like it's going to be the other way round too."

"That's right. They won't mean any harm; the only malicious thing I ever heard of Fuzzies doing was the time Jack's family wrecked Juan Jimenez's office, after they broke out of the cages he put them in, and I don't blame them for that. But they just don't understand about what they mustn't do among humans. They don't seem to have any idea at all of property in the absence of a visible owner."

"That's what I'm talking about. Crops; they won't understand that some-body's planted them, they'll think they're just there. And I never saw a farmer that wouldn't shoot first and argue afterward to protect his crops."

"Education," Gerd said.

"Recipe for roast turkey—first catch a turkey," Lunt said. "We're educating this crowd. How in Nifflheim are we going to catch all the other ones?"

"Educate the farmers. What do Fuzzies eat, beside Extee-Three?"

"Zatku, and they've cleaned all of them out around the camp. That's why we have to have one car patroling a couple of miles out to shoot harpies off."

"And do you know any kind of crops land-prawns don't destroy? I was making a study of them, for a while. I don't. That's what I mean by educating the farmers. A Fuzzy does X-much damage to crops. He kills half a dozen land-prawns a day, and among them they do about X-times-ten damage."

"Write up a script about it, and we'll put it on the air this evening. 'Be good to Fuzzies; Fuzzies are the farmer's best friend.' Maybe that'll help some."

Gerd nodded. "Eighty-seven, we have now. How many little ones?"

"Beside Baby Fuzzy? Four. Why?"

"And we think we have five pregnancies. That's all Lynne Andrews is sure of; the only way she can tell is listening with a stethoscope for fetal movements. They seem to be too small to make any conspicuous visible difference. This is out of eighty seven. What kind of a birthrate do you call that, George?"

George Lunt poured more coffee into his cup and blew on it automatically. Somewhere, maybe Constabulary School, the coffee had always been too hot to drink right away. Across the messhall, half a dozen Fuzzies tagged behind a robot, watching it clear the tables.

"It sure to Nifflheim isn't any population explosion," he said.

"Race extinction, George. I don't know what the normal life expectancy is in the woods, but I'd say four out of five of them die by violence. When the birthrate curve drops below the deathrate curve, a race is dying out."

"A hundred and two Fuzzies, and four children. Hey, you said five of the girls were pregnant, didn't you? And you admit that's not complete, if Doc Andrews has to use a stethoscope for a pregnancy test."

"I wondered if you'd notice that. That's not a bad ratio, for females who have a monthly cycle instead of an annual mating season. And these four children; we don't know anything about the maturation period, but in the three months we've been checking on him, Baby Fuzzy's only gained six ounces and an inch. I'd make it about fifteen years, ten at very least."

"Then," Lunt said, "it isn't birthrate at all. It's infant mortality. They just don't live."

"That's it, George. That's what I'm worried about. And Ruth and Lynne, too. If we don't find out what causes it, and how to stop it, there won't be any Fuzzies after a while."

"THIS IS LIKE old times, Victor," Coombes said, stretching in one of the chairs. "Nobody here but us humans."

"That's right." He brought the jug and the two glasses over and put them on the low table, careful not to disturb a pattern of colored tiles laid on one end of it. "That thing there is a Fuzzy work of art. It is unfinished, but just see the deep symbolic significance."

"You see it. I can't." Coombes accepted his glass with mechanical thanks and sipped. "Where is everybody?"

"Diamond is a guest, at a place where I'm not welcome. Government House. He and Flora and Fauna are meeting Pierrot and Columbine, Judge and Mrs. Pendarvis's Fuzzies. Sandra is chaperoning the affair, and Ernst is conferring with Mrs. Pendarvis about quarters for a couple of hundred Fuzzies who are coming to town in about a week to be adopted."

"I'll say this: your Fuzzy and Fuzzyologists are getting in with the right people. Did you hear Hugo Ingermann's telecast this afternoon?"

"I did not. I pay people to do that kind of work for me. I went over a semantically correct summary, with a symbolic-logic study. As nearly as I can interpret it, it reduces to the propositions that, A) Ben Rainsford is a bigger crook than Victor Grego, and, B) Victor Grego is a bigger crook than Ben Rainsford, and, C) between them, they are conspiring to rob and enslave everybody on the planet, Fuzzies included.

"I listened to it very carefully, and recorded it, in the hope that he might forget himself and say something actionable. He didn't; he's lawyer enough to know what's libel and what isn't. Sometimes I dream of being able to sue that bastard for something, so that I can get him in the stand under veridication, but . . ." He shrugged.

"I noticed one thing. He's attacking the Company, and he's attacking Rainsford, but at the same time he's trying to drive wedges between us, so we don't gang up on him."

"Yes. That spaceport proposition. 'Why doesn't our honest and upright Governor do something to end this infamous space-transport monopoly of the Company's, which is strangling the economy of the planet?'"

"Well, why doesn't he? Because it would cost about fifty million sols, and ships using it would have to load and unload from orbit. But that sounds like a real live issue to the people who don't think and have nothing to think with, which means a large majority of the voters. You know what I'm worried about, Leslie? Ingermann attacking Rainsford for collusion with the Company. He hammers at that point long enough, and Rainsford's going to do something to prove he isn't, and whatever it is, it'll hurt us."

"That's the way it looks to me, too," Coombes agreed. "You know, among the many benefits of the Pendarvis Decisions, we now have a democratic government on Zarathustra. That means, we now have politics here. Ingermann controls all the other rackets, and politics is the biggest racket there is. Hugo Ingermann is running himself for political boss of Zarathustra."

13

THE AIRCAR SETTLED to the ground; the Marine sergeant at the controls, who had been expecting to smash a dozen or so Fuzzies getting down, gave a whoosh of relief. Pancho Ybarra opened the door and motioned his companion, in Marine field-greens, to precede him, then stepped to the ground. George Lunt, still in his slightly altered Constabulary uniform, and Gerd van Riebeek, in bush-jacket and field-boots, advanced to meet them, accompanied by a swarm of Fuzzies. They all greeted him enthusiastically, and then wanted to know where Pappy Jack was.

"Pappy Jack in Big House Place; not come this place with Unka Panko. Pappy Jack come this place soon; two lights-and-darks," he told them. "Pappy Jack have to make much talk with other Big Ones."

"Make talk about Fuzzies?" Little Fuzzy wanted to know. "Find Big Ones for all Fuzzies?"

"That's right. Find place for Fuzzies to go in Big House Place," he said.

"He's been on that ever since Jack went away," Gerd said. "All the Fuzzies are going to have Big Ones of their own, now."

"Well, Jack's working on it," he said. "You've both met Captain Casagra, haven't you? Gerd van Riebeek; Major Lunt. The captain's staying with us a couple of days; tomorrow Lieutenant Paine and some reinforcements are coming out; fifty men and fifteen combat-cars, to help out with the patroling till we can get men and vehicles of our own."

"Well, I'm glad to hear that, Captain!" Lunt said. "We're very short of both."

"You have a lot of country to patrol, too," Casagra said. "As Navy Lieutenant Ybarra says, I'll only stay a few days, to get the feel of the situation. Marine-Lieutenant Paine will stay till you can get your own force recruited up and trained. That is, if things don't blow up again in the veldbeest country."

"Well, I hope they don't," Lunt said. "The vehicles are as welcome as the men; we have very few of our own."

"The Company's making some available," he said. "And along with his other work, Ahmed Khadra's starting a ZNPF recruiting drive."

"Has Jack been able to get his hands on any more Extee-Three?" Gerd wanted to know.

He shook his head. "He hasn't even been able to get any for the reception center, when the Fuzzies start coming in to town. The Company's going to start producing it, but that'll take time. After they get the plant set up, they'll probably be running off test batches for a couple of weeks before they get one right."

"The formula's very simple," Casagra said.

"Some of the processes aren't; I was talking to Victor Grego. His synthetics people aren't optimistic, but Grego's whip-cracking at them to get it done yesterday morning."

"Isn't that something?" Gerd asked. "Victor Grego, Fuzzy-lover. And Jimenez, and Mallin; you ought to have heard the language my refined and delicate wife used when she heard about that."

"Last war's enemies, next war's allies," Casagra laughed. "I spent a couple of years on Thor; clans that'd be shooting us on sight one season would be our bosom friends the next, and planning to double-cross us the one after."

An aircar rose from behind the ZNPF barracks across the run and started south; another, which had been circling the camp five miles out, was coming in.

"Happy patrol," Lunt was explaining to Casagra. "The Fuzzies cleaned out all the zatku, land-prawns, around the camp, and they've been hunting farther out each day. Harpies like Fuzzies the way Fuzzies like zatku, so we have to give them air-cover. That's been since you left, Pancho; we've shot about twenty harpies since then. Four up to noon today; I don't know how many since."

"Lost any Fuzzies yet?"

"Not to harpies, no. We almost had a lot of them massacred yesterday; two of these families or whatever they are got into a *shoppo-diggo* fight about some playthings. A couple got chopped up a little; there's one." He pointed to a Fuzzy with a white bandage turbaned about his head; he seemed quite proud of it. "One got a broken leg; Doc Andrews has him in the hospital with his leg in a cast. Before I could get to the fight, Little Fuzzy and Ko-Ko and Mamma Fuzzy and a couple of my crowd had broken it up; just waded in with their flats as if they'd been doing riot-work all their lives. And you ought to have heard Little Fuzzy chewing them out afterward. Talked to them like an old sergeant in boot camp."

"Oh, they fight among themselves?" Casagra asked.

"This is the first time it's happened here. I suppose they do, now and then, in the woods, with their wooden *zatku-hodda*. They have a regular fencing system. Nothing up to Interstellar Olympic epée standards, but effective. That's why half of them weren't killed in the first five seconds." Lunt looked at his watch. "Well, Captain, suppose you come with me; we'll go to Protection Force headquarters and go over what we've been doing and how your Lieutenant Paine and his men can help out."

Casagra went over to the car and spoke to the sergeant at the controls, then he and Lunt climbed in. Ybarra fell in with Gerd and they started in the direction of the lab-hut.

"One of the pregnancy cases lost her baby," Gerd said. "It was born prematurely and dead. We have the baby, fetus rather, under refrigeration. It seems to be about equivalent to human six-month stage. It wouldn't have survived in any case. Malformed, visibly and I suppose internally as well. We haven't done anything with it, yet; Lynne wanted you to see it. The Fuzzies were all sore; they thought it rated a funeral. We managed to explain to Little Fuzzy and a couple of others what we wanted to do with it, and they tried to explain to the others. I don't know how far any of it got."

The Fuzzies with them ran ahead, shouting *"Mummy Woof! Auntie Lynne! Unka Panko bizzo do-mitto!"* They were all making a clamor inside the lab-hut when he and Gerd entered, and Ruth, who was working at one of the benches making some kind of a test, was trying to shush them.

"Heyo, Unka Panko," she greeted him, hastening through with what she had at hand. "I'll be loose in a jiffy." She made a few notes, set a test-tube in a rack and made a grease-pencil number on it, and then pulled down the cover and locked it. "I hadn't done this since med-school. Lynne's back in the dispensary with a couple of volunteer native nurses, looking after the combat-casualty." She got cigarettes out of her smock-pocket and lit one, then dropped into a chair. "Pancho, what *is* this about Ernst Mallin?" she asked. "Do you believe it?"

"Yes. He's really interested, now that he doesn't have to prove any predetermined Company-policy points about them. And he really likes Fuzzies. I've seen him with that one of Grego's, and with Ben's Flora and Fauna, and Mrs. Pendarvis's pair."

"I wouldn't believe it, even if I saw it. I saw what he did to Id and Superego and Complex and Syndrome. It's a wonder all four of them aren't incurably psychotic."

"But they aren't; they're just as sane as any other Fuzzies. Mallin's sorry for doing what he did with them, but he isn't sorry about what he learned from them. He says Fuzzies are the only people he's ever seen who are absolutely sane and can't be driven out of sanity. He says if humans could learn to think like Fuzzies, it would empty all the mental hospitals and throw all the psychiatrists out of work."

"But they're just like little children. Dear, smart little children, but . . ."

"Maybe children who are too smart to grow up. Maybe we'd be like Fuzzies, too, if we didn't have a lot of adults around us from the moment we were born, infecting us with non-sanity. I hope we don't begin infecting the Fuzzies, now. What was this fight all about, the other day?"

"Well, it was about some playthings, over in the big Fuzzy-shelter. This new crowd that came in that day saw them and wanted to take them. They were things that were intended for everybody to play with, but they didn't know that. There was an argument, and the next thing the *shoppo-diggo* were going. The crowd who started it are all sorry, now, and everybody's friends."

Lynne came through the door from the dispensary at the end of the hut. A couple of Fuzzies were running along with her. Some of the Fuzzies who had come in from outside with them drifted in through the dispensary door, to visit their wounded friend. Lynne came over and joined them. Gerd asked about the patient; the patient was doing well, and being very good about staying in bed.

"How about the girl who lost her baby?" he asked.

"She's running around as though nothing had happened. It was heartbreak-ing, Pancho. The thing—it was so malformed that I'm not sure it was male or female—was born dead. She looked at it, and touched it, and then she looked up at me and said, *'Hudda. Shi-nozza.'* "

"Dead. Like always," Gerd said. "She acted as though it were only what she'd expected. I don't think more than ten percent of them live more than a few days. You want to see it, Pancho?"

He didn't, particularly; it wasn't his field. But then, Fuzzy embryology wasn't anybody's field, yet. They went over to one of the refrigerators, and Gerd got it out and unwrapped it. It was smaller than a mouse, and he had to use a magnifier to look at it. The arms and legs were short and underdeveloped; the head was malformed, too.

"I can't say anything about it," he said, "except that it's a good thing it was born dead. What are you going to do with it?"

"I don't want to dissect it myself," Lynne said. "I'm not competent. That's too important to bungle with."

"I'm no good at dissection. Take it in to Mallorysport Hospital; that's what I'd do." He rewrapped the tiny thing and put it back. "The more of you work in it, the less you'll miss. You want to find everything out you can."

"That's what I'm going to do. I'll call them now, and see who all can help, and when."

Half a dozen Fuzzies came in from outside; they were carrying a dead land-prawn. Some of the Fuzzies already in the hut ran ahead of them, into the dispensary.

"Come on, Pancho; let's watch," Gerd said. "They're bringing a present for their sick friend. They must have dragged that thing three or four miles."

THERE WERE FIVE Fuzzies and two other people in the west lower garden of Government House, as the aircar came in. The other people were Captain Ahmed Khadra, ZNPF, and Sandra Glenn, so the five Fuzzies would be the host and hostess, Fauna and Flora, and Pierrot and Columbine Pendarvis and Diamond Grego. They had a red and gold ball, two feet, or one Fuzzy-height, in diameter, and they were pushing and chasing it about the lawn. Every once in a while, they would push it to where Khadra was standing, and then he would give it a kick and send it bounding. Jack Holloway chuckled; it looked like the kind of romping he and his Fuzzies had done on the lawn beside his camp, when there had been a lawn there and when there had just been his own Fuzzies.

"Ben, drop me down there, will you?" he said. "I feel like a good Fuzzy-romp, right now."

"So do I," Rainsford said. "Will, set us down, if you please."

The pilot circled downward, holding the car a few inches above the grass while they climbed out. The Fuzzies had seen the car descend and came pelting over. At first, he thought they were carrying pistols; at least, they wore belts and small holsters. The things in the holsters had pistol-grips, but when they drew them, he saw that they were three-inch black discs, which the Fuzzies held to their mouths.

"Pappy Ben; Pappy Jack!" they were all yelling. "Listen; we talk like Big Ones, now!"

He snapped off his hearing-aid. It was true; they were all speaking audibly.

"Pappy Vic make," Diamond said proudly.

"Actually, Henry Stenson made them," the girl said. "At least, he invented them. All Mr. Grego did was tell him what he wanted. They are Fuzzyphones."

"*Heeta,* Pappy Jack." Diamond held his up. "Yeek-yeek. *Yeeek!*" He was exasperated, and then remembered he'd taken it away from his mouth. "Fuzzy-talk go in here, this side. Inside, grow big. Come out this side, big like Hagga-talk," he said, holding the device to his mouth.

"That good, Diamond. Good-good," he commended. "What do you think of this, Ben?"

Rainsford squatted in front of his own Fuzzies, holding out a hand. *"So-pokko-aki,* Flora," he said, and the Fuzzy handed him hers, first saying, *"Keffu,* Pappy Ben; *do' brek."*

"I won't." Rainsford looked at it curiously, and handed it back. "That thing's good. Little switch on the grip, and it looks as though the frequency-transformer's in the middle and they can talk into either side of it."

It would have to work that way; Fuzzies were ambidextrous. Gerd had a theory about that. Fuzzies weren't anatomists, mainly because they didn't produce fire and didn't cut up the small animals they killed for cooking, and only races who had learned the location and importance of the heart fought with their hearts turned away from the enemy. *Homo sapiens terra's* ancestors in the same culture-stage were probably ambidextrous too. Like most of Gerd's theories, it made sense.

"Who makes these things?" he asked. "Stenson?"

"He made these, in his shop. The CZC electronics equipment plant is going to manufacture them," the girl said, adding: "Advertisement."

"You tell Mr. Grego to tell his electronics plant to get cracking on them. The Native Affairs Commission wants a lot of them."

"You staying for dinner with us, Miss Glenn?" Rainsford asked.

"Thank you, Governor, but I have to take Diamond home."

"I have to take Pierrot and Columbine home, too," Khadra said. "What are you doing this evening?"

"I have my homework to do. Fuzzy language lessons."

"Well, why can't I help you with your homework?" Khadra wanted to know. "I speak Fuzzy like a native, myself."

"Well, if it won't be too much trouble . . ." she began.

Holloway laughed. "Who are you trying to kid, Miss Glenn? Look in the mirror if you think teaching you Fuzzy would be too much trouble for anybody Ahmed's age. If I was about ten years younger, I'd pull rank on him and leave him with the Fuzzies."

Pierrot and Columbine thought all this conversation boring and irrelevant. They trundled the ball over in front of Khadra and commanded: *"Mek kikko!"*

Khadra kicked the ball, lifting it from the ground and sending it soaring away. The Fuzzies ran after it.

"Dr. Mallin says you were looking at the sanatorium," Sandra said.

"Yes. That's going to be a good place. You know about it?" he asked Khadra.

"Well, it's a big place," Khadra said. "I've seen it from the air, of course. They only use about ten percent of it, now."

"Yes. We're taking a building, intended for a mental ward; about a half square mile of park around it, with a good fence, so the Fuzzies won't stray off and get lost. We could put five-six hundred Fuzzies in there, and they wouldn't be crowded a bit. And it'll be some time before we get that many there at one time. I expect there'll be about a hundred to a hundred and fifty this time next week."

"There were precisely eight hundred and seventy-two applications in when the office closed this evening," Khadra said. "When are you going back, Jack?"

"Day after tomorrow. I want to make sure the work's started on the reception center, and I'm still trying to locate some Extee-Three. I think a bunch of damn speculators have cornered the market and are holding it for high prices."

The Fuzzies had pushed the ball into some shrubbery and were having trouble dislodging it. Sandra Glenn started off to help them, Ben Rainsford walking along with her. Khadra said:

"That'll probably be some of Hugo Ingermann's crowd, too."

"Speaking about Ingermann; how are you making out about Herckerd and Novaes?" he asked. "And the five Fuzzies."

"Jack, I swear. I'm beginning to think Herckerd and Novaes and those Fuzzies all walked into a mass-energy converter together. That's how completely all of them have vanished."

"They hadn't sold them before Ben's telecast, evening before last. After that, with the Adoption Bureau opening all that talk about kidnapping and enslavement and so on, nobody would buy a bootleg Fuzzy. So they couldn't sell them, so they got rid of them." How? That was what bothered him. If they'd used sense, they'd have flown them back to Beta and turned them loose. He was afraid, though, that they'd killed them. By this time everybody knew that live Fuzzies could tell tales. "I think those Fuzzies are dead."

"I don't know. Eight hundred and seventy-two applications, and a hundred and fifty Fuzzies at most," Khadra said. "There'll be a market for bootleg Fuzzies. Jack, you know what I think? I think those Fuzzies weren't brought in for sale. I think this gang—Herckerd and Novaes and whoever else is in with them—are training those Fuzzies to help catch other Fuzzies. Do you think a Fuzzy could be trained to do that?"

"Sure. To all intents and purposes, that's what our Fuzzies are doing out at the camp. You know how Fuzzies think? Big Ones are a Good Thing. Any Fuzzy who has a Big One doesn't need to worry about anything. All Fuzzies ought to have Big Ones. That's what Little Fuzzy has been telling the ones from the woods, out at camp. Ahmed, I think you have something."

"I thought of something else, too. If this gang can make a deal with some tramp freighter captain, they could ship Fuzzies off-planet and make terrific profits on it. You wait till the news about the Fuzzies gets around. There'll be a sale for them everywhere—Terra, Odin, Freya, Marduk, Aton, Baldur, planets like that. Anybody can bring a ship into orbit on this planet, now, if he has his own landing-craft and doesn't use the CZC spaceport. In a month, word will have gotten to Gimli, that's the nearest planet, and in two more months a ship can get here from there."

"Spaceport. That could be why Ingermann's been harping on this nefarious CZC space-terminal monopoly. If he had a little spaceport of his own, now . . ."

"Any kind of smuggling you can think of," Khadra said. "Hot sunstones. Narcotics. Or Fuzzies."

Rainsford and Sandra Glenn were approaching; Sandra carried Diamond, Pierrot and Columbine ran beside her, and Flora and Fauna were trundling the ball ahead of them. He wanted to talk to Rainsford about this. They needed more laws, to prohibit shipping Fuzzies off-planet; nobody'd thought of that possibility before. And talk to Grego; the Company controlled the only existing egress from the planet.

LYNNE ANDREWS STRAIGHTENED and removed the binocular loop and laid it down, blinking. The others, four men and two women in lab-smocks, were pushing aside the spotlights and magnifiers and cameras on their swinging arms and laying down instruments.

"That thing wouldn't have lived thirty seconds, even if it hadn't been premature," one man said. "And it doesn't add a thing to what we don't know about Fuzzy embryology." He was an embryologist, human-type, himself. "I have dissected over five hundred aborted fetuses and I never saw one in worse shape than that."

"It was so tiny," one of the women said. She was an obstetrician. "I can't believe that that's human six-months equivalent."

"Well, I can," somebody else said. "I know what a young Fuzzy looks like; I spent a lot of time with Jack Holloway's Baby Fuzzy, during the trial. And I don't suppose a fertilized Fuzzy ovum is much different from one of ours. Between the two, there has to be a regular progressive development. I say this one is two-thirds developed. Misdeveloped, I should say."

"Misdeveloped is correct, Doctor. Have you any idea why this one misdeveloped as it did?"

"No, Doctor, I haven't."

"They come from northern Beta; that country's never been more than air-scouted. Does anybody know what radioactivity conditions are, up there?

I've seen pictures of worse things than this from nuclear bomb radiations on Terra during and after the Third and Fourth World Wars, at the beginning of the First Federation."

"The country hasn't been explored, but it's been scanned. Any natural radioactivity strong enough to do that would be detectable from Xerxes."

"Oh, Nifflheim; that fetus could have been conceived on a patch of pitchblende no bigger than this table . . ."

"Well, couldn't it be chemical? Something in the pregnant female's diet?" the other woman asked.

"The Thaladomide Babies!" somebody exclaimed. "First Century, between the Second and Third World Wars. That was due to chemicals taken orally by pregnant women."

"All right; let's get the biochemists in on this, then."

"Chris Hoenveld," somebody else said. "It's not too late to call him now."

Fuzzies didn't have Cocktail Hour; that was for the Big Ones, to sit together and make Big One talk. Fuzzies just came stringing in before dinner, more or less interested in food depending on how the hunting had been, and after they ate they romped and played until they were tired, and then sat in groups, talking idly until they became sleepy.

In the woods, it had not been like that. When the sun began to go to bed, they had found safe places, where the big animals couldn't get at them, and they had snuggled together and slept, one staying awake all the time. But here the Big Ones kept the animals away, and killed them with thunder-things when they came too close, and it was safe. And the Big Ones had things that made light even when the sky was dark, and there were places where it was always bright as day. So here, there was more fun, because there was less danger, and many new things to talk about. This was the *Hoksu-Mitto,* the Wonderful Place.

And today, they were even happier, because today Pappy Jack had come back.

Little Fuzzy got out his pipe, the new one Pappy Jack had brought from the Big House Place, and stuffed it with tobacco, and got out the little fire-maker. Some of the Fuzzies around him, who had just come in from the woods, were frightened. They were not used to fire; when fire happened in the woods, it was bad. That was wild fire, though. The Big Ones had tamed fire, and if a person were careful not to touch it or let it get loose, fire was nothing to be afraid of.

"We go other places, and all have Big Ones, tomorrow?" one asked. "Big Ones for us, like Pappy Jack for you?"

"Not tomorrow. Not next day. Day after that." He held up three fingers.

"Then go in high-up-thing, to place like this. Big Ones come, make talk. You like Big One, Big One like you, you go with Big One, you live in Big One place."

"Nice place, like this?"

"Nice place. Not like this. Different place."

"Not want to go. Nice place here, much fun."

"Then you not go. Pappy Jack not make you go. You want to go, Pappy Jack find nice Big One for you, be good to you."

"Suppose not good. Suppose bad to us?"

"Then Pappy Jack come, Pappy Jorj, Unka Ahmed, Pappy Ge'hd, Unka Panko; make much trouble for bad Big One, *bang, bang, bang!*"

14

MYRA WAS VEXED. "It's Mr. Dunbar. The chief chemist at Synthetic Foods," she added, as though he didn't know that. "He is here himself; he has something he insists he must give to you personally."

"That's what I told him to do, Myra. Send him in."

Malcolm Dunbar pushed through the door from Myra's office with an open fiberboard carton under his arm. That had probably helped vex Myra; Dunbar was an executive, and executives ought not to carry their own parcels; it was *infra dignitatem*. He set it on the corner of the desk.

"Here it is, Mr. Grego; this is the first batch. We just finished the chemical tests on it. Identical with both the Navy stuff and the stuff we imported ourselves."

He rose and went around the desk, reaching into the carton and taking out a light brown slab, breaking off a corner and tasting it. It had the same slightly rancid, slightly oily and slightly sweetish flavor as the regular product. It tasted as though it had been compounded according to the best scientific principles of dietetics, by somebody who thought there was something sinful about eating for pleasure. He yielded to no one in his admiration of *Fuzzy fuzzy holloway,* but anybody who liked this stuff was nuts.

"You're sure it's safe?"

Dunbar was outraged. "My God, would I bring it here for you to feed your Fuzzy if I didn't know it was? In the first place, it's made strictly according to Terran Federation Armed Forces specifications. The bulk-matter is pure wheat farina, the same as Argentine Syntho-Foods and Odin Dietetics use. The rest is chemically pure synthetic nutrients. We have a man at the plant who used to be a chemical engineer at Odin Dietetics; he checked all the processes and they're identical. And we tried it on all the standard lab animals; Terran hamsters and Thoran tilbras, and then on Freyan kholphs and Terran rhesus monkeys. The kholphs," he footnoted, "didn't like it worth a damn. It harmed none of them. And I ate a cake of the damned stuff myself, and it took a couple of hours and a pint of bourbon to get rid of the taste," the martyr to science added.

"All right. I will accept that it is fit for Fuzzy consumption. Fortunately, the whole Fuzzy population of Mallorysport, all five of them, are up on my terrace now. Let's go."

Ben Rainsford's Flora and Fauna, and Mrs. Pendarvis's Pierrot and Columbine were with Diamond in the Fuzzy-room. Outside on the terrace it was raw and rainy, one of Mallorysport's rare unpleasant days. They had a lot of colored triangular tiles on the floor, and were making patterns with them. Sandra Glenn was watching them with one eye and reading with the other. They all sprang to their feet and began yeeking, then remembered the Fuzzy phones on their belts, whipped them out, and began shouting, *"Heyo, Pappy Vic!"* He'd tried to explain that he was Diamond's Pappy Vic, and just Uncle Vic to the rest, but they refused to make the distinction. Pappy to one Fuzzy, pappy to all.

"Pappy Vic give *esteefee,"* he told them. "New *esteefee,* very good." He set the box down and got out one of the slabs, breaking and distributing it. The Fuzzies had nice manners; the two most recent guests, Pierrot and Columbine, served first, held theirs till the others were served. Then they all nibbled together.

They each took one nibble and stopped.

"Not good," Diamond declared. "Not *esteefee.* Want *esteefee."*

"Bad," Flora pronounced it, spitting out what she had in her mouth and carrying the rest to the trash-bin. *"Esteefee* good; this not."

"Esteefee for look; not *esteefee* in mouth," Pierrot said.

"What are they saying?" Dunbar wanted to know.

"They say it isn't Extee-Three at all, and they want to know how dumb I am to think it is."

"But look, Mr. Grego; this *is* Extee-Three. It is chemically identical with the stuff they've been eating all along."

"The Fuzzies aren't chemists. They only know what it tastes like, and it doesn't taste like Extee-Three to them."

"It tastes like Extee-Three to me . . ."

"You," Sandra told him, "are not a Fuzzy." She switched languages and explained that Pappy Vic and the other Big One really thought it was *esteefee.*

"Pappy Vic feel bad," he told them. "Pappy Vic want to give real esteefee."

He gathered up the offending carton and carried it into the kitchenette, going to one of the cupboards and getting out a tin of the genuine article. Only a dozen left; he'd have to start rationing it himself. He cut it into six pieces, put by a piece for Diamond after the company was gone, and distributed the rest.

Dunbar was still arguing with Sandra that the stuff he'd brought was chemically Extee-Three.

"All right, Malcolm, I believe you. The point is, these Fuzzies don't give a hoot on Nifflheim what the chemical composition is." He looked at the label on the tin. "The man you have at the plant worked for Odin Dietetics, didn't he? Well, this stuff was made on Terra by Argentine Syntho-Foods. What do they use for cereal bulk-matter at Odin Dietetics, some native grain?"

"No, introduced Terran wheat, and Argentine uses wheat from the pampas and from the Mississippi Valley in North America."

"Different soil-chemicals, different bacteria; hell, man, look at tobacco. We've introduced it on every planet we've ever colonized, and no tobacco tastes just like the tobacco from anywhere else."

"Do we have any Odin Extee-Three?" Sandra asked.

"Smart girl; a triple A for good thinking. Do we?"

"Yes. The stuff we import's Argentine, and the stuff the Navy has on Xerxes is Odin."

"And the Fuzzies can't tell the difference? No, of course they can't. Jack Holloway bought his Extee-Three from us and gave it to his Fuzzies, and when they got on Xerxes, the Navy fed them theirs. What did you use in this stuff, local wheat?"

"Introduced wheat; seed came from South America. Grown on Gammz Continent."

"Well, Mal, we're going to find out what's the matter with this stuff. Real all-out study, tear it apart molecule by molecule. Who's our best biochemist?"

"Hoenveld."

"Well, put him to work on it. There's some difference, and the Fuzzies know it. You say this stuff's Government specification standard?"

"It meets the Government tests."

"Well; Napier has a lot of Extee-Three on Xerxes he won't release because it's regulation-required emergency stores. We'll see if we can trade this for it . . ."

"WELL, YOU GOOFED on it somehow!" the superintendent of the synthetics plant was insisting. "The Fuzzies eat regular Extee-Three; they're crazy about it. If they won't eat your stuff, it isn't Extee-Three."

"Listen, Abe, goddamit, I know it *is* Extee-Three! We followed the formula exactly. Ask Joe Vespi, here; he used to work at Odin Dietetics . . ."

"That's correct, Mr. Fitch; every step of the process is exactly as I remember it from Odin—"

"As you remembered it!" Fitch pounced triumphantly. "What did you remember wrong?"

"Why, nothing, Mr. Fitch. Look, here's the schematic. The farina, that's the bulk-matter, comes in here, to these pressure-cookers . . ."

DR. JAN CHRISTIAAN Hoenveld was annoyed, and because he was an emminent scientist and Victor Grego was only a businessman, he was at no pains to hide it.

"Mr. Grego, do you realize how much work is piled up on me now? Dr. Andrews and Dr. Reynier and Dr. Dosihara are at me to find out whether there is any biochemical cause of premature and defective births among Fuzzies. And now you want me to drop that and find why one batch of Extee-Three tastes differently to a Fuzzy from another. There is a gunsmith here in town who has a sign in his shop, *There are only twenty-four hours in a day and there is only one of me.* I have often considered copying that sign in my laboratory." He sat frowning into his screen from Science Center, across the city, for a moment. "Mr. Grego, has it occurred to you or any of your master-minds at Synthetics that difference may be in the Fuzzies' taste-perception?"

"It has occurred to me that Fuzzies must have a sense of taste that would shame the most famous wine-taster in the Galaxy. But I question if it is more accurate than your chemical analysis. If those Fuzzies tasted a difference between our Extee-Three and Argentine Syntho-Food's, the difference must be detectable. I don't know anybody better able to detect it than you, Doctor; that's why I'm asking you to find out what it is."

Dr. Jan Christiaan Hoenveld said, "Hunnh!" ungraciously. Flattered, and didn't want to show it.

"Well, I'll do what I can, Mr. Grego . . ."

15

I **MUST BE** *very nice to Dr. Ernst Mallin. I must be very nice to Dr. Ernst Mallin. I must be* . . . Ruth van Riebeek repeated it silently, as though writing it a hundred times on a mental blackboard, as an airboat lost altitude and came slanting down across the city, past the high crag of Company House, with the lower, broader, butte of Central Courts Building in the distance to the left. Ahead, the sanatorium area drew closer, wide parklands scattered with low white buildings. She hadn't seen Mallin since the trial, and even then she had avoided speaking to him as much as possible. Part of it was because of the things he had done with the four Fuzzies; Pancho Ybarra said she also had a guilt-complex because of the way she'd fifth-columned the company. Rubbish! That had been intelligence work; that had been why she'd taken a job with the CZC in the first place. She had nothing at all to feel guilty about . . .

"I must be very nice to Dr. Ernst Mallin," she said, aloud. "And I'm going to have one Nifflheim of a time doing it."

"So am I," her husband, standing beside her, said. "He'll have to make an effort to be nice to us, too. He'll still remember my pistol shoved into his back out at Holloway's the day Goldilocks was killed. I wonder if he knows how little it would have taken to make me squeeze the trigger."

"Pancho says he is a reformed character."

"Pancho's seen him since we have. He could be right. Anyhow, he's helping us, and we need all the help we can get. And he won't hurt the Fuzzies, not with Ahmed Khadra and Mrs. Pendarvis keeping an eye on him."

The Fuzzies, crowded on the cargo-deck below, were becoming excited. There was a forward-view screen rigged where they could see it, and they could probably sense as well as see that the boat was descending. And this place ahead must be the place Pappy Jack and Pappy Gerd and Unka Panko and Little Fuzzy had been telling them about, where the Big Ones would come and take them away to nice places of their own.

She hoped too many of them wouldn't be too badly disappointed. She hoped this adoption deal wouldn't be too much of a failure.

The airboat grounded on the vitrified stone apron beside the building. It looked like a good place; Jack said it had been intended for but never used as a mental ward-unit; four stories high, each with its own terrace, and a flat garden-planted roof. High mesh fences around each level; the Fuzzies wouldn't fall off. Plenty of trees and bushes; the Fuzzies would like that.

They got the Fuzzies off and into the building, helped by the small crowd who were waiting for them. Mrs. Pendarvis; she and the Chief Justice's wife were old friends. And a tall, red-haired girl, Grego's Fuzzy-sitter, Sandra Glenn. And Ahmed Khadra, in a new suit of civvies but bulging slightly under the left arm. And half a dozen other people whom she had met now and then — school department and company public health section. And Ernst Mallin, pompous and black-suited and pedantic-looking. *I must be very nice . . .* She extended a hand to him.

"Good afternoon, Dr. Mallin."

Maybe Gerd was right; maybe she did feel guilty about the way she'd tricked him. She was, she found, being counter-offensively defensive.

"Good afternoon, Ruth. Dr. van Riebeek," he corrected himself. "Can you bring your people down this way?" he asked, nodding to the hundred and fifty Fuzzies milling about in the hall, yeeking excitedly. People, he called them. He must be making an effort, too. "We have refreshments for them. Extee-Three. And things for them to play with."

"Where do you get the Extee-Three?" she asked. "We haven't been able to get any for almost a week, now."

Mallin gave one of his little secretive smiles, the sort he gave when he was one up on somebody.

"We got it from Xerxes. The Company's started producing it, but unfortunately, the Fuzzies don't like it. We still can't find out why; it's made on exactly the same formula. And as it's entirely up to Government specifications, Mr. Grego was able to talk Commodore Napier into accepting it in exchange for what he has on hand. We have about five tons of it. How much do you need at Holloway's Camp? Will a couple of tons help you any?"

Would a couple of tons help them any? "Why, I don't know how to thank you, Dr. Mallin! Of course it will; we've been giving it to our Fuzzies, a quarter-cake apiece on alternate days." *I must be very,* VERY, *nice to Dr.*

Mallin! "Why don't they like the stuff you people have been making? What's wrong with it?"

"We don't know. Mr. Grego has been raging at everybody to find out; it's made in exactly the same way. . . ."

WHEN MALCOLM DUNBAR lighted his screen, Dr. Jan Christiaan Hoenveld appeared in it. He didn't waste time on greetings or other superfluities.

"I think we have something, Mr. Dunbar. There is a component in both the Odin Dietetics and the Argentine Syntho-Foods products that is absent from our own product. It is not one of the synthetic nutrient or vitamin or hormone compounds which are part of the field-ration formula; it is not a compound regularly synthesized, either commercially or experimentally in any laboratory I know of. It's a rather complicated long-chain organic molecule; most of it seems to be oxygen-hydrogen-carbon, but there are a few atoms of titanium in it. If that's what the Fuzzies find lacking in our products, all I can say is that they have the keenest taste perception of any creature, sapient or nonsapient, that I have ever heard of."

"All right, then; they have. I saw them reject our Extee-Three in disgust, and then Mr. Grego gave them a little of the Argentine stuff, and they ate it with the greatest pleasure. How much of this unknown compound is there in Extee-Three?"

"About one part in ten thousand," Hoenveld said.

"And the titanium?"

"Five atoms out of sixty-four in the molecule."

"That's pretty keen tasting." He thought for a moment. "I suppose it's in the wheat; the rest of that stuff is synthesized."

"Well, naturally, Mr. Dunbar. That would seem to be the inescapable conclusion," Hoenveld said, patronizingly.

"We have quite a bit of metallic titanium, imported in fabricated form before we got our own steel-mills working. Do you think you could synthesize that molecule, Dr. Hoenveld?"

Hoenveld gave him a look of undisguised contempt. "Certainly, Mr. Dunbar. In about a year and a half to two years. As I understand, the object of manufacturing the stuff here is to supply a temporary shortage which will be relieved in about six months, when imported Extee-Three begins coming in from Marduk. Unless I am directly and specifically ordered to do so by Mr. Grego, I will not waste my time on trying."

OF COURSE, IT was ending in a cocktail party. Wherever Terran humans went, they planted tobacco and coffee, to have coffee and cigarettes for breakfast, and wherever they went they found or introduced something that would ferment to produce C_2H_5OH, and around 1730-ish each day, they had Cocktail Hour. The natives on planets like Loki and Gimli and Thor and even Shesha and Uller thought it was a religious observance.

Maybe it was, at that.

Sipping his own cocktail, Gerd van Riebeek ignored, for a moment, the conversation in which he had become involved and eavesdropped on his wife and Claudette Pendarvis and Ernst Mallin and Ahmed Khadra and Sandra Glenn.

"Well, we want to keep them here for at least a week before we let people take them away," the Chief Justice's wife was saying. "You'll have to stay with us for a day or so, Ruth, and help us teach them what to expect in their new homes."

"You're going to have to educate the people who adopt them," Sandra Glenn said. "What to expect and what not to expect from Fuzzies. I think, evening classes. Language, for one thing."

"You know," Mallin said, "I'd like to take a few Fuzzies around through the other units of the sanatorium, to visit the patients. The patients here would like it. They don't have an awful lot of fun, you know."

That was new for Ernst Mallin. He never seemed to recall that Mallin had thought having fun was important, before. Maybe the Fuzzies had taught him that it was.

The group he was drinking with were Science Center and Public Health people. One of them, a woman gynecologist, was wondering what Chris Hoenveld had found out, so far.

"What can he find out?" Raynier, the pathologist, asked. "He only has the one specimen, and it probably isn't there at all, it's probably something in the mother's metabolism. It might be radioactivity, but that would only produce an occasional isolated case, and from what you've seen, it seems to be a racial characteristic. I think you'll find it in the racial dietary habits."

"Land-prawns," somebody suggested. "As far as I know, nothing else eats them but Fuzzies; that right, Gerd?"

"Yes. We always thought they had no natural enemies at all, till we found out about the Fuzzies. But it's been our observation that Fuzzies won't take anything that'll hurt them."

"They won't take anything that gives them a bellyache or a hangover, no. They can establish a direct relationship there. But whatever caused this defective birth we were investigating, and I agree that that's probably a common thing with Fuzzies, was something that acted on a level the Fuzzies couldn't be aware of. I think there's a good chance that eating land-prawns may be responsible."

"Well, let's find out. Put Chris Hoenveld to work on that."

"You put him to work on it. Or get Victor Grego to; he won't throw Grego out of his lab. Chris is sore enough about this Fuzzy business as it is."

"Well, we'll have to study more than one fetus. We have a hundred and fifty Fuzzies here, we ought to find something out. . . ."

"Isolate all the pregnant females; get Mrs. Pendarvis to withhold them from adoption. . . ."

". . . may have to perform a few abortions . . ."

". . . microsurgery; fertilized ova . . ."

That wasn't what he and Ruth and Jack Holloway had had in mind, when they'd brought this lot to Mallorysport. But they had to find out; if they didn't, in a few more generations there might be no more Fuzzies at all. If a few of them suffered, now . . .

Well, hadn't poor Goldilocks had to be killed before the Fuzzies were recognized for the people they were?

"TITANIUM," VICTOR GREGO said. "Now that's interesting."

"Is that all you can call it, Mr. Grego?" Dunbar, in the screen, demanded. "I call it impossible. I was checking up. Titanium, on this planet, is damn near as rare as calcium on Uller. It's present, and that's all; I'll bet most of the titanium on Zarathustra was brought here in fabricated form between the time the planet was discovered and seven years ago when we got our steel-mill going."

That was a big exaggeration, of course. It existed, but it was a fact that they'd never been able to extract it by any commercially profitable process, and on Zarathustra they used light-alloy steel for everything for which titanium was used elsewhere. So a little of it got picked up, as a trace-element, in wheat grown on Terra or on Odin, but it was useless to hope for it in Zarathustran wheat.

"It looks," he said, "as though we're stuck, Mal. Do you think Chris Hoenveld could synthesize that molecule? We could add it to the other ingredients . . ."

"He says he could—in six months to a year. He refuses to try unless you order him categorically to."

"And by that time, we'll have all the Extee-Three we want. Well, a lot of Fuzzies, including mine, are going to have to do without, then."

He blanked the screen and lit a cigarette and looked at the globe of Zarathustra, which Henry Stenson had running on time again and which he could interpret like a clock. Be another hour till Sandra got back from the new Adoption Center; she'd have to pick up Diamond at Government House. And

Leslie wouldn't be in for cocktails this evening; he was over on Epsilon Continent, talking to people about things he didn't want to discuss by screen. Ben Rainsford had finally gotten around to calling for an election for delegates to a constitutional convention, and they wanted to line up candidates of their own. It looked as though Mr. Victor Grego would have cocktails with the manager-in-chief of the Charterless Zarathustra Company, this evening. Might as well have them here.

Titanium, he thought disgustedly. It would be something like that. What was it they called the stuff? Oh, yes; the nymphomaniac metal; when it gets hot it combines with anything. An idea suddenly danced just out of reach. He stopped, halfway from the desk to the cabinet, his eyes closed. Then he caught it, and dashed for the communication screen, punching Malcolm Dunbar's call-combination.

It was a few minutes before Dunbar answered; he had his hat and coat on.

"I was just going out, Mr. Grego."

"So I see. That man Vespi, the one who worked for Odin Dietetics; is he still around?"

"Why, no. He left twenty minutes ago, and I don't know how to reach him, right away."

"No matter; get him in the morning. Listen, the pressure cookers, the ones you use to cook the farina for bulk-matter. What are they made of?"

"Why, light nonox-steel; our manufacture. Why?"

"Ask Vespi what they used for that purpose on Odin. Don't suggest the answer, but see if it wasn't titanium."

Dunbar's eyes widened. He'd heard about the chemical nymphomania of titanium, too.

"Sure; that's what they'd use, there. And at Argentine Syntho-Foods, too. Listen, suppose I give the police an emergency-call request; they could find Joe in half an hour."

"Don't bother; tomorrow morning's good enough. I want to try something first."

He blanked the screen, and called Myra Fallada. She never left the office before he did.

"Myra; call out and get me five pounds of pure wheat farina, and be sure it's made from Zarathustran wheat. Have it sent up to my apartment, fifteen minutes ago."

"Fifteen minutes from now do?" she asked. "What's it for; the Little Monster? All right, Mr. Grego."

He forgot about the drink he was going to have with Mr. Victor Grego. You had a drink when the work was done, and there was still work to do.

•   •   •

THERE WAS CLATTERING in the kitchenette when Sandra Glenn brought Diamond
into the Fuzzy-room. She opened the door between and looked through, and
Diamond crowded past her knees for a look, too. Mr. Grego was cooking
something, in a battered old stewpan she had never seen around the place before.
He looked over his shoulder and said, "Hi, Sandra. *Heyo,* Diamond; use
Fuzzyphone, Pappy Vic no get ear-thing."

"What make do, Pappy Vic?" Diamond asked.

"That's what I want to know, too."

"Sandra, keep your fingers crossed; when this stuff's done and has cooled
off, we're going to see how Diamond likes it. I think we have found out what's
the matter with that Extee-Three."

"Esteefee? You make *esteefee?* Real? Not like other?" Diamond wanted to
know.

"You eat," Pappy Vic said. "Tell if good. Pappy Vic not know."

"Well, what is it?" she asked.

"Hoenveld found what was different about it." The explanation was rather
complicated; she had been exposed to, rather than studied, chemistry. She got
the general idea; the Extee-Three the Fuzzies liked had been cooked in titanium.

"That's what this stewpan is; part of a camp cooking kit I brought here from
Terra." He gave the white mess in the pan a final stir and lifted it from the stove,
burning his finger and swearing; just like a man in a kitchen. "Now, as soon as
this slop's cool . . ."

Diamond smelled it, and wanted to try it right away. He had to wait, though,
until it was cool. Then they carried the pan, it had a treacherous-looking folding
handle, out to the Fuzzy-room, and Mr. Grego spooned some onto Diamond's
plate, and Diamond took his little spoon and tasted, cautiously. Then he began
shoveling it into his mouth ravenously.

"The Master Mind crashes through again," she said. "He really likes it."
Diamond had finished what was on his plate. "You like?" she asked, in Fuzzy.
"Want more?"

"Give him the rest of it, Sandra. I'm going to call Dr. Jan Christiaan
Hoenveld, and suggest an experiment for him to try. And after that, Miss Glenn,
will you honor me by having a cocktail with me?"

JACK HOLLOWAY LAUGHED. "So that's it. When did you find out?"

"Mallin just screened me; he just got it from Grego," Gerd van Riebeek, in
the screen, said. "They're going to start tearing out all the stainless-steel cookers

right away, and replace them with titanium. Jack, have you any titanium cooking utensils?"

"No. Everything we have here is steel. We have sheet titanium; the house and the sheds and the old hangar are all sheet-titanium. We might be able to make something . . ." He stopped short. "Gerd, we don't have to cook the food in titanium. We can cook titanium in the food. Cut up some chunks and put them in the kettles. It would work the same way."

"Well, I'll be damned," Gerd said. "I never thought of that. I'll bet nobody else did, either."

DR. JAN CHRISTIAAN Hoenveld was disgusted and chagrined and embarrassed, and mostly disgusted.

It had been gratifying to discover a hitherto unknown biochemical, especially one existing unsuspected in a well known, long manufactured, and widely distributed commercial product. He could understand how it had happened; a by-effect in one of the manufacturing processes, and since the stuff had been proven safe and nutritious for humans and other life-forms having similar biochemistry and metabolism, nobody had bothered until some little animals—no, people, that had been scientifically established—had detected its absence by taste. Things like that happened all the time. He had been proud of the accomplishment; he'd been going to call the newly discovered substance hoenveldine. He could have worked out a way of synthesizing it, too, but by proper scientific methods it would have taken over a year, and he knew it, and he'd said so to everybody.

And now, within a day, it had been synthesized, if that were the word for it, by a rank amateur, a layman, a complete non-scientist. And not in a laboratory but in a kitchen, with no equipment but a battered old stewpan!

And the worst of it was that this layman, this empiric, was his employer. The claims of the manager-in-chief of the Zarathustra Company simply couldn't be brushed off. Not by a Company scientist.

Well, Grego had found out what he wanted; he could stop worrying about that. He had important work to do; an orderly, long-term study of the differences between Zarathustran and Terran biochemistry. The differences were minute, but they existed, and they had to be understood, and they had to be investigated in an orderly, scientific manner.

And now, they wanted him to go haring off, hit-or-miss, after this problem about Fuzzy infant mortality and defective births, and they didn't even know any such problem existed. They had one, just one, case—that six-month fetus the Andrews girl had brought in—and they had a lot of unsubstantiated theorizing by Gerd van Riebeek, pure conclusion-jumping. And now they wanted him to find out if eating land-prawns caused these defective births which they believed, on the basis of one case and a lot of supposition, to exist. Maybe after years of observation of hundreds of cases they might have some justification, but . . .

He rose from the chair at the desk in the corner of the laboratory and walked slowly among the workbenches. Ten men and women, eight of them working on new projects that had been started since young van Riebeek had started after this mare's-nest of his, all of them diverted from serious planned research. He stopped at one bench, where a woman was working.

"Miss Tresca, can't you keep your bench in better order than this?" he scolded. "Keep things in their places. What are you working on?"

"Oh, a hunch I had, about this hokfusine."

Hunch! That was the trouble, all through Science Center; too many hunches and not enough sound theory.

"Oh, the titanium thing. It's a name Mr. Grego suggested, from a couple of Fuzzy words, *hoku fusso,* wonderful food. It's what the Fuzzies call Extee-Three."

Hokfusine, indeed. Now they were getting the Fuzzy language into scientific nomenclature.

"Well, just forget about your hunch," he told her. "There are a lot of samples of organic matter, blood, body secretions, hormones, tissue, from pregnant female Fuzzies that they want analyzed. I don't suppose it makes any more sense than your hunch, but they want analyses immediately. They want everything immediately, it seems. And straighten up that clutter on your bench. How often do I have to tell you that order is the first virtue in scientific work?"

16

THEY WERE IN Jack's living room, and it looked almost exactly as it had the first night Gerd van Riebeek had seen it, when he and Ruth and Juan Jimenez had come out to see the Fuzzies, without the least idea that the validity of the Company's charter would be involved. All the new office equipment that had cluttered it had gone, in the two weeks he and Ruth had been in Mallorysport, and there was just the sturdy, comfortable furniture Jack had made himself, and the damnthing and the bush-goblin and veldbeest skins on the floor, and the gunrack with the tangle of bedding under it.

There were just five of them, as there had been that other evening, three months, or was it three ages, ago. Juan Jimenez and Ben Rainsford were absent, in Mallorysport, but they had been replaced by Pancho Ybarra, lounging in one of the deep chairs, and Lynne Andrews, on the couch beside Ruth. Jack sat in the armchair at his table-desk, trying to keep Baby Fuzzy, on his lap, from climbing up to sit on his head. On the floor, the adult Fuzzies—just Jack's own family; this was their place, and the others didn't intrude here—were in the middle of the room, playing with the things that had been brought back from Mallorysport. The kind of playthings Fuzzies liked; ingenuity-challenging toys for putting together shapes and colors.

He was glad they weren't playing with their molecule-model kit. He'd seen enough molecule models in the last two weeks to last him a lifetime.

"And there isn't anything we can do about it, at all?" Lynne was asking.

"No. There isn't anything anybody can do. The people in Mallorysport have given up trying. They're still investigating, but that's only to be able to write a scientifically accurate epitaph for the Fuzzy race."

"Can't they do something to reverse it?"

"It's irreversible," Ruth told her. "It isn't a matter of diet or environment or anything external. It's this hormone, NFMp, that they produce in their own bodies, that inhibits normal development of the embryo. And we can't even correct it in individual cases by surgery; excising the glands that secrete it would result in sterility."

"Well, it doesn't always work," Jack said, lifting Baby Fuzzy from his shoulder. "It didn't work in Baby's case."

"It works in about nine cases out of ten, apparently. We've had ten births so far; one normal and healthy, and the rest premature and defective, stillbirths, or live births that die within hours."

"But there are exceptions, Baby here, and the one over at the Fuzzy-shelter," Lynne said. "Can't we figure out how the exceptions can be encouraged?"

"They're working on that, in a half-hearted way," he told her. "Fuzzies have a menstrual cycle and fertility rhythm, the same as *Homo s. terra,* and apparently the NFMp output is also cyclic, and when the two are out of phase there is a normal viable birth, and not otherwise. And this doesn't happen often enough, and any correction of it would have to be done individually in the case of each female Fuzzy, and nobody even knows how to find out how it could be done."

"But, Gerd, the whole thing doesn't make sense to me," Pancho objected. "I know, 'sense' is nothing but ignorance rationalized, and this isn't my subject, but if this NFMp thing is a racial characteristic, it must be hereditary, and a hereditary tendency to miscarriages, premature and defective births, and infant mortality, now; what kind of sense does that make?"

"Well, on the face of it, not much. But we know nothing at all about the racial history of the Fuzzies, and very little about the history of this planet. Say that fifty thousand years ago there were millions of Fuzzies, and say that fifty thousand years ago environmental conditions were radically different. This NFMp hormone was evolved to meet some environmental survival demand, and something in the environment, some article of diet that has now vanished, kept it from injuriously affecting the unborn Fuzzies. Then the environment changed—glaciation, glacial recession, sea-level fluctuation, I can think of dozens of reasons—and after having adapted to original conditions, they couldn't re-adapt to the change. We've seen it on every planet we've ever studied; hundreds of cases on Terra alone. The Fuzzies are just caught in a genetic trap they can't get out of, and we can't get them out of it."

He looked at them; six happy little people, busily fitting many-colored jointed blocks together to make a useless and delightful pretty-thing. Happy in ignorance of their racial doom.

"If we knew how many children the average female has in her lifetime, and how many child-bearers there are, we could figure it out mathematically, I suppose. Ten little Fuzzies, nine little Fuzzies, eight little Fuzzies, and finally no little Fuzzies."

Little Fuzzy thought he was being talked about; he looked up inquiringly.

"Well, they won't all just vanish in the next minute," Jack said. "I expect this gang'll attend my funeral, and there'll be Fuzzies as long as any of you live, and longer. In a couple of million years, there won't be any more humans, I suppose. Let's just be as good to the Fuzzies we have as we can, and make them as happy as possible . . . Yes, Baby; you can sit on Pappy's head if you want to."

17

THE BEST TIME for telecast political speeches was between 2000 and 2100, when people were relaxing after dinner and before they started going out or before guests began to arrive. That was a little late for Beta Continent and impossibly so for Gamma, but Delta and Epsilon, to the west, could be reached with late night repeats and about eighty percent of the planetary population was concentrated here on Alpha Continent. Of late, Hugo Ingermann had been having trouble getting on the air at that time. The 2000-2100 spot, he was always told, was already booked, and it would usually turn out to be by the Citizen's Government League which everybody knew but nobody could prove was masterminded by Leslie Coombes and Victor Grego, or it would be Ben Rainsford trying to alibi his Government, or by a lecture on the care and feeding of Fuzzies. But this time, somebody had goofed. This time, he'd been able to get the 2000-2100 spot himself. The voice of the announcer at the telecast station came out of the sound-outlet:

". . . an important message, to all the citizens of the Colony, now, by virtue of the Pendarvis Decisions, enjoying, for the first time, the right of democratic self-government. The next voice you will hear will be that of the Honorable Hugo Ingermann, organizer and leader of the Planetary Prosperity Party. Mr. Ingermann."

The green light came on, and the showback lightened; he lifted his hand in greeting.

"My . . . *friends!*" he began.

•   •   •

FREDERIC PENDARVIS WAS growing coldly angry. It wasn't an organizational abstraction, the Native Adoption Bureau, that was being attacked; it was his wife, Claudette, and he was taking it personally, and a judge should never take anything personally. Why, he had actually been looking at the plump, bland-faced man in the screen, his blue eyes wide with counterfeit sincerity, and wondering whom to send to him with a challenge. Dueling wasn't illegal on Zarathustra, it wasn't on most of the newer planets, but judges did not duel.

And the worst of it, he thought, was that the next time he had to rule against Ingermann in court, Ingermann would be sure, by some innuendo which couldn't be established as overt contempt, to create an impression that it was due to personal vindictiveness.

"It is a disgraceful record," Ingermann was declaring. "A record reeking with favoritism, inequity, class prejudice. In all, twelve hundred applications have been received. Over two hundred have been rejected outright, often on the most frivolous and insulting grounds . . ."

"Mental or emotional instability, inability to support or care for a Fuzzy, irresponsibility, bad character, undesirable home conditions," Claudette, who was beginning to become angry herself, mentioned.

Pierrot and Columbine, on the floor, with a big Mobius strip somebody had made from a length of tape, looked up quickly and then, deciding that it was the man in the wall Mummy was mad at, went back to trying to figure out where the other side always went.

"And of the thousand applications, only three hundred and forty-five have been filled, although five hundred and sixty-six Fuzzies have been brought to this city since the Adoption Bureau was opened. One hundred and seventy-two of these applicants have received a Fuzzy each. One hundred and fifty-five have received two Fuzzies each. And eighteen especially favored ones have received a total of eighty-four Fuzzies.

"And almost without exception, all these Fuzzies have gone to socially or politically prominent persons, persons of wealth. You might as well make up your mind to it, a poor man has no chance whatever. Look who all have gotten Fuzzies under the Fuzzy laws, if one may so term the edicts of a bayonet-imposed Governor. The first papers of adoption were issued to—guess who now?—Victor Grego, the manager-in-chief of the now Charterless Zarathustra Company. And the next pair went to Mrs. Frederic Pendarvis, and beside being the Chief Justice's wife, who is she? Why, the head of the Adoption Bureau, of course. And look at the rest of these names! Nine tenths of them are Zarathustra Company executives." He held up his hands, as though to hush an outburst of righteous indignation. "Now I won't claim, I won't even suppose, that there is any actual corruption or any bribery about this . . ."

"You damned well better hadn't! If you do, I won't sue you, I'll shoot you," Pendarvis barked.

"I won't do either," his wife told him calmly. "But I will answer him. Under veridication, and that's something Hugo Ingermann would never dare do."

"Claudette!" He was shocked. "You wouldn't do that? Not on telecast?"

"On telecast. You can't ignore this sort of thing. If you do, you just admit it by default. There's only one answer to slander, and that's to prove the truth."

"AND WHO'S PAYING for all this?" Ingermann demanded out of the screen. "The Government? When Space Commodore Napier presented us with this Government, and this Governor, at pistol point, there was exactly half a million sols to the account of the Colony in the Bank of Mallorysport. Since then, Governor Rainsford has borrowed approximately half a *billion* sols from the Banking Cartel. And how is Ben Rainsford going to repay them? By taking it out of you and me and all of us, as soon as he can get a Colonial Legislature to rubber-stamp his demands for him. And now, do you know what he is spending millions of your money on? On a project to increase the Fuzzy birthrate, so that you'll have more and more Fuzzies for his friends to make pets of and for you to pay the bills for . . ."

"He is a God damned unmitigated liar!" Victor Grego said. "Except for a little work Ruth Ortheris and her husband and Pancho Ybarra and Lynne Andrews are doing out at Holloway's, the Company's paying for all that infant mortality research, and I'll have to justify it to the stockholders."

"How about some publicity on that?" Coombes asked.

"You're the political expert; what do you think?"

"I think it would help. I think it would help us, and I think it would help Rainsford. Let's not do it ourselves, though. Suppose I talk to Gus Brannhard, and have him advise Jack Holloway to leak it to the press?"

"Press is going to be after Mrs. Pendarvis for a statement. She knows what the facts are. Let her tell it."

"He make talk about Fuzzies?" Diamond, who had been watching Hugo Ingermann fascinatedly, inquired.

"Yes. Not like Fuzzies. Bad Big One; *tosh-ki Hagga.* Pappy Vic not like him."

"Neither," Coombes said, "does Unka Leslie."

Ahmed Khadra blew cigarette smoke insultingly at the face in the screen. Hugo Ingermann was saying:

"Well, if few politicians and Company executives are getting all the Fuzzies, why not make them pay for it, instead of the common people of the planet? Why not charge a few for adoption papers, say five hundred to a thousand sols? Everybody who's gotten Fuzzies so far could easily pay that. It wouldn't begin to meet the cost of maintaining the Native Affairs Commission, but it would be something . . ."

So that was what the whole thing had been pointed toward. Make it expensive to adopt Fuzzies legally. A black market couldn't compete with free Fuzzies, but let the Adoption Bureau charge five hundred sols apiece for them . . .

"So that's what you're after, you son of a Khooghra? A competitive market."

18

"**Y**OU GOT THIS from one of my laboratory workers," Jan Christiaan Hoenveld accused. "Charlotte Tresca, wasn't it?"

He was calling from his private cubical in the corner of the biochemistry lab; through the glass partition behind him Juan Jimenez could see people working at benches, including, he thought, his informant. For the moment, he disregarded the older man's tone and manner.

"That's correct, Dr. Hoenveld. I met Miss Tresca at a cocktail party last evening. She and some other Science Center people were discussing the different phases of the Fuzzy research, and she mentioned having found hokfusine, or something very similar to it, in the digestive tracts of land-prawns. That had been a week ago; she had reported her findings to you immediately, and assumed that you had reported them to me. Now, I want to know why you didn't."

"Because it wasn't worth reporting," Hoenveld snapped. "In the first place, she wasn't supposed to be working on land-prawns, or hokfusine,"—he almost spat the word in contempt—"at all. She was supposed to be looking for NFMp in this mess of guts and tripes you've been dumping into my laboratory from all over the planet. And in the second place, it was merely a trace-presence of titanium, with which she had probably contaminated the test herself. The girl is an incurably careless and untidy worker. And finally," Hoenveld raged, "I want to know by what right you question my laboratory workers behind my back . . ."

"Oh, you do? Well, they are not *your* laboratory workers, Dr. Hoenveld; they are employees of the Zarathustra Company, the same as you. Or I. And the biochemistry laboratory is not your private empire. It is a part of Science Center, of which I am division chief, and from where I sit the difference between you and Charlotte Tresca is barely perceptible to the naked eye. Is that clear, Dr. Hoenveld?"

Hoenveld was looking at him as though a pistol had blown up in his hand. He was, in fact, mildly surprised at himself. A month ago, he wouldn't have dreamed of talking so to anybody, least of all a man as much older than himself as Hoenveld, and one with Hoenveld's imposing reputation.

But as division chief, he had to get things done, and there could be only one chief in the division.

"I am quite well aware of your recent and sudden promotion, Dr. Jimenez," Hoenveld retorted acidly. "Over the heads of a dozen of your seniors."

"Including yourself; well, you've just demonstrated the reason why you were passed over. Now, I want some work done, and if you can't or won't do it, I can promote somebody to replace you very easily."

"What do you think we've been doing? Every ranger and hunter on the company payroll has been shooting everything from damnthings and wild veldbeest to ground-mice and dumping the digestive and reproductive tracts in my—I beg your pardon, I mean the Charterless Zarathustra Company's—laboratory."

"Have you found any trace of NFMp in any of them?"

"Negative. They don't have the glads to secrete it; I have that on the authority of the comparative mammalian anatomists."

"Then stop looking for it; I'll order the specimen collecting stopped at once. Now, I want analyses of land-prawns made, and I want to know just what Miss Tresca found in them; whether it was really hokfusine, or anything similar to it, or just trace-presences of titanium, and I want to know how it gets into the land-prawns' systems and where it concentrates there. I would suggest—correction, I direct—that Miss Tresca be put to work on that herself, and that she report directly to me."

"WHAT'S YOUR OPINION of Chris Hoenveld, Ernst?" Victor Grego asked.

Mallin frowned—his standard think-seriously-and-weigh-every-word frown.

"Dr. Hoenveld is a most distinguished scientist. He has an encyclopedic grasp on his subject, an infallible memory, and an infinite capacity for taking pains."

"Is that all?"

"Isn't that enough?"

"No. A computer has all that, to a much higher degree, and a computer couldn't make an original scientific discovery in a hundred million years. A computer has no imagination, and neither has Hoenveld."

"Well, he has very little, I'll admit. Why do you ask about him?"

"Juan Jimenez is having trouble with him."

"I can believe it," Mallin said. "Hoenveld has one characteristic a computer lacks. Egotism. Has Jimenez complained to you?"

"Nifflheim, no; he's running Science Center without yelling to Big Brother for help. I got this off the powder-room and coffee-stand telegraph, to which I have excellent taps. Juan cut him down to size; he's doing all right."

"Well, how about the NFMp problem?"

"Nowhere, on hyperdrive. The Fuzzies just manufacture it inside themselves, and nobody knows why. It seems mainly to be associated with the digestive system, and gets from there into the blood-stream, and into the gonads, in both sexes, from there. Thirty-six births, so far; three viable."

From the terrace outside came the happy babble of Fuzzy voices. They were using their Fuzzyphones to talk to one another; wanted to talk like the Hagga. Poor little tail-enders of a doomed race.

THE WHOLE DAMNED thing was getting too big for comfort, Jack Holloway thought. A month ago, there'd only been Gerd and Ruth and Lynne Andrews and Pancho Ybarra, and George Lunt, and the men George had brought when he'd transferred from the Constabulary. They all had cocktails together before dinner, and ate at one table, and had bull-sessions in the evenings, and everybody had known what everybody else was doing. And there had only been forty or fifty Fuzzies, beside his and George's and Gerd's and Ruth's.

Now Gerd had three assistants, and Ruth had dropped work on Fuzzy psychology and was helping him with whatever he was doing, and what that was he wasn't quite sure. He wasn't quite sure what anybody was doing, anymore. And Pancho was practically commuting to and from Mallorysport, and Ernst Mallin was out at least once a week. Funny, too; he used to think Mallin was a solid, three-dimensional bastard, and now he found he rather liked him. Even Victor Grego was out, one weekend, and everybody liked him.

Lynne had a couple of helpers, too, and a hospital and clinic, and there was a Fuzzy school, where they were taught Lingua Terra and how to use Fuzzyphones and about the strange customs of the Hagga. Some old hen Ruth had kidnapped from the Mallorysport schools was in charge of it, or thought she was; actually Little Fuzzy and Ko-Ko and Cinderella and Lizzie Borden and Dillinger were running it.

And he and George Lunt couldn't yell back and forth to each other any more, because their offices, at opposite ends of the long hut, were partitioned off and separated by a hundred and twenty feet of middle office, full of desks and business machines and roboclerks, and humans working with them. And he had a secretary, now, and she had a secretary, or at least a stenographer, of her own.

Gerd van Riebeek came in from the outside, tossing his hat on top of a microbook-case and unbuckling his pistol.

"Hi, Jack. Anything new?" he asked.

Gerd and Ruth had been away for a little over a week, in the country to the south. It must have been fun, just the two of them and Complex and Superego and Dr. Crippen and Calamity Jane, camping in Gerd's airboat and visiting the posts Lunt had strung out along the edge of the big woods.

"I was going to ask you that. Where's Ruth?"

"She's staying another week, at the Kirtland plantation, with Superego and Complex; there must be fifty to seventy-five Fuzzies there; she's helping the Kirtland people with them, teaching them not to destroy young sugarplant shoots. Kirtland's been taking a lot of damage to his shoots from zatku. What's the latest from Mallorysport?"

"Well, nowhere on the NFMp, but they seem to have found something interesting about the land-prawns."

"More on that?" Gerd had heard about the alleged hokfusine. "Have they found out what it is?"

"It isn't hokfusine, it's just a rather complicated titanium salt. The land-prawns eat titanium, mostly in moss and fungus and stuff like that. It probably grades about ten atoms to the ton on what they eat. But they fix it, apparently in that middle intestine that they have. I have a big long writeup on what it does there. The Fuzzies seem to convert it to something else in their own digestive system. Whatever it does, hokfusine seems to do it a lot better. They're still working on it."

"They ate land-prawns all along, but it was only since this new generation hatched, this Spring, that they really got all they wanted of them. I wonder what they ate before, up north."

"Well, we know what all they eat beside zatku and the stuff we give them. Animals small enough to kill with those little sticks, fruit, bird eggs, those little yellow lizards, grubs."

"What are Paine's Marines doing up north now, beside looking for nonexistent Fuzzy-catchers?"

"That's about all. Flying patrol, taking photos, mapping. They say there are lots of Fuzzies north of the Divide that haven't started south yet, probably haven't heard about the big zatku bonanza yet."

"I'm going up there, Jack. I want to look at them, see what they live on."

"Don't go right away; wait a week, and I'll go along with you. I still have a lot of this damn stuff to clear up, and I have to go in to Mallorysport tomorrow. Casagra's talking about recalling Paine and his men and vehicles. You know where that would put us."

Gerd nodded. "We'd have to double the ZNPF. It's all George can do to maintain those posts along the edge of the big woods and fly inspections in the farm country, without having to patrol in the north too."

"I don't know how we could pay or equip them, even if we could recruit them. We're operating on next year's budget now. That's another thing I'll have to talk to Ben about. He'll have to allocate us more money."

"GOD DAMN IT, there's no money to give him!"

Ben Rainsford spoke aloud and bitterly, and then caught himself and puffed furiously on his pipe, the smoke reddening in the sunset afterglow. Have to watch that; people hear him talking to himself, it would be all over Government House, and all over Mallorysport in the next day, that Governor Rainsford was going crazy. Not that it would be any wonder if he were.

The three Fuzzies, Flora and Fauna and their friend Diamond, who had gotten hold of a lot of wooden strips of the sort the gardeners used for trelliswork and were building a little arbor of their own, looked up quickly and then realized that he wasn't speaking to them and went on with what they were doing. The sun had gone to bed already, and the sky-light was fading, and they wanted to get whatever it was they were making finished before it got dark. Fuzzies, like Colonial Governors, found time running out on them occasionally.

Time was running out fast for him. The ninety days the CZC had allowed him to take over all the public services they were no longer obliged to maintain were more than half gone now, and nothing had been done. The election for delegates to a constitutional convention was still a month in the future, and he had no idea how long it would take the elected delegates, whoever they'd be, to argue out a constitution, and how long thereafter it would take to get a Colonial Legislature set up, and how long after tax laws were enacted it would be before the Government would begin collecting money.

He wished he'd been able to borrow that half billion sols from the Banking

Cartel that Hugo Ingermann had been yakking about. Ingermann had later been forced to back down to something closer to the actual figure of fifty million, just as he had been forced to retreat from some of his exaggerated statements about the Adoption Bureau, but it seemed that the public still believed his original statements and were disregarding the hedging and weasel-worded retractions. Fifty million sounded like a lot of money, too—till you had to run a planetary government on it, and everything was going to cost so much more than he had expected.

The Native Affairs Commission, for instance. He and Jack had both believed that a hundred and fifty men would be ample for the Native Protection Force; now they were finding that three times that number wouldn't be enough. They had thought that Gerd and Ruth van Riebeek and Lynne Andrews, and Pancho Ybarra, on loan from the Navy, would be able to do all the study and research work; now that was spread out to Mallorysport Hospital and Science Center, for which the CZC was paying and would expect compensation. And the Adoption Bureau was costing as much, now, as the whole original Native Affairs Commission estimate.

At least, he'd been able to do one thing for Jack. Alex Napier had agreed that protection and/or policing of natives on Class-IV planets was a proper function of the Armed Forces, and instead of recalling his fifty men, Casagra had been ordered to reenforce them with twenty more.

The Fuzzies suddenly stopped what they were doing and turned. Diamond drew his Fuzzyphone. "Pappy Vic!" he called, in delighted surprise. "Come; look what we make!" Flora and Fauna were whooping greetings, too.

He rose, and saw behind him the short, compactly-built man, familiar from news-screen views, whom he had so far avoided meeting personally. Victor Grego greeted the Fuzzies, and then said, "Good evening, Governor. Sorry to intrude, but Miss Glenn has a dinner-and-dancing date, and I told her I'd get Diamond myself."

"Good evening, Mr. Grego." Somehow, he didn't feel the hostility to the man that he had expected. "Could you wait a little while? They have an important project, here, and they want to finish it while there's still day-light."

"Well, so I see." Grego spoke to the Fuzzies in their own language, and listened while they explained what they were doing. "Of course; we can't interfere with that."

The Fuzzies went back to their trellis-building. He and Grego sat down in lawn-chairs; Grego lit a cigarette. He watched the CZC manager-in-chief as the latter sat watching the Fuzzies. This couldn't be Victor Grego; "Victor Grego" was a label for a personification of black-hearted villainy and ruthless selfishness; this was a pleasant-spoken, courteous gentleman who loved Fuzzies, and was considerate of his employees.

"Miss Glenn's date was with Captain Ahmed Khadra," Grego was saying, to make conversation. "The fifth in the last two weeks. I'm afraid I'm just before losing a good Fuzzy-sitter by marriage."

"I'm afraid so; they seem quite serious about each other. If so, she'll be getting a good husband. I've known Ahmed for some time; he was at the Constabulary post near my camp, on Beta. It's too bad," he added, "that he seems to be getting nowhere on this Herckerd-Novaes investigation. It's certainly not from lack of trying."

"My police chief, Harry Steefer, is getting nowhere just as rapidly," Grego said. "He's ready to give the whole thing up, and when Harry Steefer gives up, it's hopeless."

"Do you think there is anything to this theory that somebody is training those Fuzzies to help catch other Fuzzies?"

Grego shook his head. "You know Fuzzies at least as well as I do, Governor. Almost two months; anything you can train a Fuzzy to do, you can train him to do it in less than that," he said. "And I don't see why anybody would try to catch wild Fuzzies, not with the bloodthirsty laws you've enacted. Criminals only take chances in proportion to profits, and almost anybody who wants a Fuzzy can get one free."

That was true. And there was no indication of any black market in Fuzzies here, and Jack's patrols over northern Beta Continent hadn't found any evidence that anybody was live-trapping Fuzzies there.

"Ahmed had an idea, for a while, that they were going into the export business; catching Fuzzies to smuggle out for sale off-planet."

"He mentioned that to Harry Steefer. Jack Holloway was talking to me about that, too; wanted to know what could be done to prevent it. I told him it would be impossible to get Fuzzies onto a ship from Darius, or onto Darius from Mallorysport Space Terminal. As long as we keep our 'flagrant and heinous space-traffic monopoly,' you can be sure no Fuzzies are going to be shipped off-planet."

"You think Ingermann really has anything to do with it?" he asked hopefully, recognizing the source of the quotation.

"If there is a black market in Fuzzies, Ingermann's back of it," Grego said, as though stating a natural law. "In the six or so years he's infected this planet, I've learned a lot about the *soi-disant* Honorable Hugo Ingermann, and none of it's been good."

"Ahmed Khadra thinks his attacks on the CZC space-monopoly may stem from a desire to get some way around your controls at the ground terminal here and on Darius. Of course, he's talking about a Government spaceport, and that would be just as tightly controlled . . ."

Grego hesitated for a moment, then dropped his cigarette to the ground and heeled it out. He leaned toward Rainsford in his chair.

"Governor, you know, yourself, that as things stand you can't build a second spaceport here," he said. "Ingermann knows that, too. He's making that issue to embarrass you and to attack the CZC at the same time. He has no expectation that your Government would build any spaceport facilities here. He certainly hopes not; he wants to do that himself."

"Where the devil would he get the money?"

"He could get it. Unless I miss my guess, he's getting it now, or as soon as a ship can get in, on Marduk. There are a number of shipping companies who would like to get in here in competition with Terra-Baldur-Marduk Spacelines, and there are quite a few import-export houses there who would like to trade on Zarathustra in competition with CZC. Inside six months somebody will be trying to put in a spaceport here. If they can get land to set it on. And due to a great error in my judgment eight years ago, the land's available."

"Where?"

"Right here on Alpha Continent, less than a hundred miles from where we're sitting. A wonderful place for a spaceport. You weren't here, then, were you, Governor?"

"No. I came here, I blush to say, on the same ship that brought Ingermann, six and a half years ago."

"Well, you got here, and so did he, after it was over, but just before that we had a big immigration boom. At that time, the company wasn't interested in local business, just off-planet trade in veldbeest meat. A lot of independent concerns started, manufacturing, food-production, that sort of thing that we didn't want to bother with. We sold land north of the city, in mile and two-mile square blocks, about two thousand square miles of it. Then the immigrants stopped coming, and a lot of them moved away. There simply wasn't employment for them. Most of the companies that had been organized went broke. Some of the factories that were finished operated for a while; most of them were left unfinished. The banks took over some of the land; most of it got into the hands of the shylocks; and since the Fuzzy Trial Ingermann has been acquiring title to a lot of it. Since the Fuzzy Trial, nobody else has been spending money for real-estate; everybody expects to get all the free land they want."

"Well, he'll probably make some money out of that, but the people who come in here with the capital will be the ones to control it, won't they?"

"Of course they will, but that's honest business; Ingermann isn't interested. He's expecting an increase of about two to three hundred percent in the planetary population in the next five years. With eighty percent of the land-surface in public domain, that's probably an underestimate. Most of them will be voters; Ingermann's going to try to control that vote."

And if he did . . . His own position was secure; Colonial Governors were appointed, and it took something like the military intervention which had put him into office to unseat one. But a Colonial Governor had to govern through and with the consent of a Legislature. He wasn't looking forward happily to a Legislature controlled by Hugo Ingermann. Neither, he knew, was Grego.

He'd have to be careful, though. Grego wanted to put the company back in its old pre-Fuzzy position of planetary dominance. He was still violently opposed to that.

It was almost dark, now. The Fuzzies had put the final touches to the lacy trellis they had built, and came crowding over, wanting Pappy Ben and Pappy Vic to come look. They went and examined it, and spoke commendation. Grego picked up Diamond; Flora and Fauna were wanting him to go and sit down and furnish them a lap to sit on.

"I've been worrying about just that," he said, when he was back in his chair, with the Fuzzies climbing up onto him. "A lot of the older planets are beginning to overpopulate, and there's never room enough for everybody on Terra. There'll be a rush here in about a year. If I can only get things stabilized before then . . ."

Grego was silent for a moment. "If you're worried about all those public-health and welfare and service functions, forget about them for a while," he said. "I know, I said the company would discontinue them in ninety days, but that was right after the Pendarvis Decisions, and nobody knew what the situation was going to be. We can keep them going for a year, at least."

"The Government won't have any more money a year from now," he said. "And you'll expect compensation."

"Of course we will, but we won't demand gold or Federation notes. Tax-script, bonds, land-script . . ."

Land-script, of course; the law required a Colonial Government to make land available to Federation citizens, but it did not require such land to be given free. That might be one way to finance the Government.

It could also be a way for the Zarathustra Company, having gotten the Government deeply into debt, to regain what had been lost in the aftermath of the Fuzzy Trial.

"Suppose you have Gus Brannhard talk it over with Leslie Coombes,"

Grego was suggesting. "You can trust Gus not to stick the Government's foot into any bear-trap, can't you?"

"Why, of course, Mr. Grego. I want to thank you, very much, for this. That public services takeover was worrying me more than anything else."

Yet he couldn't feel relieved, and he couldn't feel grateful at all. He felt discomfited, and angry at himself more than at Grego.

19

Gᴇʀᴅ ᴠᴀɴ ʀɪᴇʙᴇᴇᴋ crouched at the edge of the low cliff, slowly twisting the selector-knob of a small screen in front of him. The view changed; this time he was looking through the eye of a pickup fifty feet below and five hundred yards to the left. Nothing in it moved except a wind-stirred branch that jiggled a spray of ragged leaves in the foreground. The only thing from the sound-outlet was a soft drone of insects, and the *tweet-twonk, tweet-twonk* of a presumably love-hungry banjo-bird. Then something just out of sight scuffled softly among the dead leaves. He turned up the sound-volume slightly.

"What do you think it is?"

Jack Holloway, beside him, rose to one knee, raising his binoculars.

"I can't see anything. Try the next one."

Gerd twisted the knob again. This pickup was closer the ground; it showed a vista of woods lit by shafts of sunlight falling between trees. Now he could hear rustling and scampering, and with ultrasonic earphone, Fuzzy voices:

"This way. Not far. Find *hatta-zosa.*"

Jack was looking down at the open slope below the cliff.

"If that's what they call goofers, I see six of them from here," he said. "Probably a dozen more I can't see." He watched, listening. "Here they come, now."

The Fuzzies had stopped talking and were making very little noise; then they came into view; eight of them, in single file. The weapons they carried were longer and heavier than the prawn-killers of the southern Fuzzies, knobbed instead of paddle-shaped, and sharp-pointed on the other end. All of them had picked up stones which they carried in their free hands. They all stopped, then three of them backed away into the brush again. The other five spread out in a skirmish line and waited. He shut off the screen and crawled over beside Jack to peep over the edge of the cliff.

There were seven goofers, now; rodent-looking things with dark gray fur, a foot and a half long and six inches high at the shoulder, all industriously tearing off bark and digging at the roots of young trees. No wonder the woods were so thin, around here; if there were any number of them it was a wonder there were any trees at all. He picked up a camera and aimed it, getting some shots of them.

"Something else figuring on getting some lunch here," Jack said, sweeping the sky with his glasses. "Harpy, a couple of miles off. Ah, another one. We'll stick around a while; we may have to help our friends out."

The five Fuzzies at the edge of the brush stood waiting. The goofers hadn't heard them, and were still tearing and chewing at the bark and digging at the roots. Then, having circled around, the other three burst out suddenly, hurling their stones and running forward with their clubs. One stone hit a goofer and knocked it down; instantly, one of the Fuzzies ran forward and brained it with his club. The other two rushed a second goofer, felling and dispatching it with their clubs. The other fled, into the skirmish line on the other side. Two were hit with stones, and finished off on the ground. The others got away. The eight Fuzzies gathered in a clump, seemed to debate pursuit for a moment, and then abandoned the idea. They had four goofers, a half-goofer apiece. That was a good meal for them.

They dragged their game together and began tearing the carcasses apart, using teeth and fingers, helping one another dismember them, tearing off skin and pulling meat loose, using stones to break bones. Gerd kept his camera going, filming the feast.

"Our gang's got better table manners," he commented.

"Our gang have the knives we make for them. Beside, our gang mostly eats zatku, and they break off the manibles and make little lobster-picks out of them. They're ahead of our gang in one way, though. The Fuzzies south of the Divide don't hunt cooperatively," Jack said.

The two dots in the sky were larger and closer; a third had appeared.

"We better do something about that," he advised, reaching for his rifle.

"Yes." Jack put down the binoculars and secured his own rifle, checking it. "Let them eat as long as they can; they'll get a big surprise in a minute or so."

The Fuzzies seemed to be aware of the presence of the harpies. Maybe there were ultrasonic wing-vibration sounds they could hear; he couldn't be sure, even with the hearing aid. There was so much ultrasonic noise in the woods, and he hadn't learned, yet, to distinguish. The Fuzzies were eating more rapidly. Finally, one pointed and cried, *"Gotza bizzo!"* *Gotza* was another native zoological name he had learned, though the Fuzzies at Holloway's Camp mostly said, "Hah'py," now. The diners grabbed their weapons and what meat they could carry and dashed into the woods. One of the big pterodactyl-things was almost overhead, another was within a few hundred yards, and the third was coming in behind him. Jack sat up, put his left arm through his rifle-sling, cuddled the butt to his cheek and propped his elbows on his knees. The nearest harpy must have caught a movement in the brush below; it banked and started to dive. Jack's 9.7 magnum bellowed. The harpy made a graceless flop-over in the air and dropped. The one behind banked quickly and tried to gain altitude; Gerd shot it. Jack's rifle thundered again, and the third harpy thrashed leathery wings and dropped.

From below, there was silence, and then a clamor of Fuzzy voices:

"Harpies dead; what make do?"

"Thunder; maybe kill harpies! Maybe kill us next!"

"Bad place, this! *Bizzo, fazzu!*"

Roughly, *fazzu* meant, "Scram."

Jack was laughing. "Little Fuzzy took it a lot calmer the first time he saw me shoot a harpy," he said. "By that time, though, he'd seen so much he wasn't surprised at anything." He replaced the two fired rounds in the magazine of his rifle. "Well, *bizzo, fazzu;* we won't get any more movies around here."

They went around with the car, collecting the pickups they had planted, then lifted out, turning south toward the horizon-line of the Divide, the mountain range that stretched like the cross-stroke of an H between the West Coast Range and the Eastern Cordilleras. Evidently the Fuzzies never crossed it much; the language of the northern Fuzzies, while comprehensible, differed distinguishably from that spoken by the ones who had come in to the camp. Apparently the news of the bumper crop of zatku hadn't gotten up here at all.

They talked about that, cruising south at five thousand feet, with the foothills of the Divide sliding away under them and the line of sheer mountains drawing closer. They'd have to establish a permanent camp up here; contact these Fuzzies and make friends with them, give them tools and weapons, learn about them.

That was, if the Native Commission budget would permit. They talked about that, too.

Then they argued about whether to stay up here for another few days, or start back to the camp.

"I think we'd better go back," Jack said, somewhat regretfully. "We've been away for a week. I want to see what's going on, now."

"They'd screen us if anything was wrong."

"I know. I still think we'd better go back. Let's cross the Divide and camp somewhere on the other side, and go on in tomorrow morning."

"*Hokay; bizzo.*" He swung the aircar left a trifle. "We'll follow that river to the source and cross over there."

The river came down through a wide valley, narrowing and growing more rapid as they ascended it. Finally, they came to where it emerged, a white mountain torrent, from the mouth of a canyon that cut into the main range of the Divide. He took the car down to within a few hundred feet and cut speed, entering the canyon. At first, it was wide, with a sandy beach on either side of the stream and trees back to the mountain face and up the steep talus at the foot of it. Granite at the bottom, and then weathered sandstone, and then, for a couple of hundred feet, gray, almost unweathered flint.

"Gerd," Jack said, at length, "take her up a little, and get a little closer to the side of the canyon." He shifted in his seat, and got his binoculars. "I want a close look at that."

He wondered why, briefly. Then it struck him.

"You think that's what I think it is?" he asked.

"Yeah. Sunstone-flint." Jack didn't seem particularly happy about it. "See that little bench, about halfway up? Set her down there. I'm going to take a look at that."

The bench, little more than a wide ledge, was covered with thin soil; a few small trees and sparse brush grew on it. A sheer face of gray flint rose for a hundred feet above it. They had no blasting explosives, but there was a microray scanner and a small vibrohammer in the toolkit. They set the aircar down and went to work, cracking and scanning flint, and after two hours they had a couple of sunstones. They were nothing spectacular—an irregular globe seven or eight millimeters in diameter and a small elipsoid not quite twice as big. However, when Jack held them against the hot bowl of his pipe, they began to glow.

"What are they worth, Jack?"

"I don't know. Some of these freelance gem-buyers would probably give as much as six or eight hundred for the big one. When the Company still had the monopoly, they'd have paid about four-fifty. Be worth twenty-five hundred on Terra. But look around. This layer's three hundred feet thick; it runs all the way up the canyon, and probably for ten or fifteen miles along the mountain on either side." He knocked out his pipe, blew through the stem, and pocketed it. "And it all belongs to the Fuzzies."

He started to laugh at that, and then remembered. This was, by executive decree, the Fuzzy Reservation. The Fuzzies owned it and everything on it, and the Government and the Native Commission were only trustees. Then he began laughing again.

"But, Jack! The Fuzzies can't mine sunstones, and they wouldn't know what to do with them if they could."

"No. But this is their country. They were born here, and they have a right to live here, and beside that, we gave it to them, didn't we? It belongs to them, sunstones and all."

"But Jack . . ." He looked up and down the canyon at the gray flint on either side; as Jack said, it would extend for miles back into the mountain on either side. Even allowing one sunstone to ten cubic feet of flint, and even allowing for the enormous labor of digging them out . . . "You mean, just let a few Fuzzies scamper around over it and chase goofers, and not do anything with it?" The idea horrified him. "Why, they don't even know this is the Fuzzy Reservation."

"They know it's their home. Gerd, this has happened on other Class-IV planets we've moved in on. We give the natives a reservation; we tell them it'll be theirs forever, Terran's word of honor. Then we find something valuable on it—gold on Loki, platinum on Thor, vanadium and wolfram on Hathor, nitrates on Yggdrasil, uranium on Gimli. So the natives get shoved off onto another reservation, where there isn't anything anybody wants, and finally they just get shoved off, period. We aren't going to do that here, to the Fuzzies."

"What are you going to do? Try to keep it a secret?" he asked. "If that's what you want, we'll just throw those two sunstones in the river and forget about it," he agreed. "But how long do you think it'll be before somebody else finds out about it?"

"We can keep other people out of here. That's what the Fuzzy Reservation's for, isn't it?"

"We need people to keep people out; Paine's Marines, George Lunt's Protection Force. I think we can trust George. I wouldn't know about Paine. Anybody below them I wouldn't trust at all. Sooner or later somebody'll fly up this canyon and see this, and then it'll be out. And you know what'll happen then." He thought for a moment. "Are you going to tell Ben Rainsford?"

"I wish you hadn't asked me that, Gerd." Jack fumbled his pipe and tobacco out of his pocket. "I suppose I'll have to. Have to give him these stones; they're Government property. Well, *bizzo*; we'll go straight to camp." He looked up at the sun. "Make it in about three hours. Tomorrow I'll go to Mallorysport."

"I'm afraid to believe it, Dr. Jimenez," Ernst Mallin said. "It would be so wonderful if it were true. Can you be certain?"

"We're all certain, now, that this hormone, NFMp, is what prevents normal embryonic development," Juan Jimenez, in the screen, replied. "We're certain, now, that hokfusine combines destructively with NFMp; even Chris Hoenveld, he's seen it happen in a test tube, and he has to believe it whether he wants to or not. It appears that hokfusine also has an inhibitory effect on the glands secreting NFMp. But to be certain, we'll have to wait four more months, until the infants conceived after the mothers began eating Extee-Three are born. Ideally, we should wait until the females we have begun giving daily doses of pure hokfusine conceive and bear children. But if I'm not certain now, I'm confident."

"What put your people onto this, Dr. Jimenez?"

"A hunch," the younger man smiled. "A hunch by the girl in Dr. Hoenveld's lab, Charlotte Tresca." The smile became an audible laugh. "Hoenveld is simply furious about it. No sound theoretical basis, just a lot of unsupported surmises. You know how he talks. He did have to grant her results; they've been duplicated. But he rejects her whole line of reasoning."

He would; Jan Christiaan Hoenveld's mind plodded obstinately along, step by step, from A to B to C to D; it wasn't fair for somebody suddenly to leap to W or X and run from there to Z. For his own part, Ernst Mallin respected hunches; he knew how much mental activity went on below the level of consciousness and with what seemingly irrationality fragments of it rose to the conscious mind. His only regret was that he had so few good hunches, himself.

"Well, what was her reasoning?" he asked. "Or was it pure intuition?"

"Well, she just got the idea that hokfusine would neutralize the NFMp hormone, and worked from there," Jimenez said. "As she rationalizes it, all Fuzzies have a craving for land-prawn meat, without exception. This is a racial constant with them. Right?"

"Yes, as far as we can tell. I hate to use the word loosely, but I'd say, instinctual."

"And all Fuzzies, for which read, all studied individuals, have a craving for Extee-Three. Once they taste the stuff, they eat it at every opportunity. This isn't a learned taste, like our taste for, say, coffee or tobacco or alcohol; every human has to learn to like all three. The Fuzzy's response to Extee-Three is immediate and automatic. Still with it, Doctor?"

"Oh, yes; I've seen quite a few Fuzzies taking their first taste of Extee-Three. It's just what you call it; a physical response." He gave that a moment's thought, adding: "If it's an instinct, it's the result of natural selection."

"Yes. She reasoned that a taste for the titanium-molecule compound present both in land-prawns and Extee-Three contributed to racial survival; that Fuzzies lacking it died out, and Fuzzies having it to a pronounced degree survived and transmitted it. So she went to work—over Hoenveld's vehement objections that she was wasting her time—and showed the effect of hokfusine on the NFMp hormone. Now, the physiologists who had that theory about cyclic production of NFMp getting out of phase with the menstrual cycle and permitting an occasional viable birth are finding that the NFMp fluctuations aren't cyclic at all but related to hokfusine consumption."

"Well, you have a fine circumstantial case there. Everything seems to fit together with everything else. As you say, you'll have to wait about a year before you can really prove a one-to-one relationship between hokfusine and viable births, but if I were inclined to gamble I'd risk a small wager on it."

Jimenez grinned. "I have, already, with Dr. Hoenveld. I think it's money in the bank now."

BENNETT RAINSFORD WARMED the two sunstones between his palms, then rolled them, like a pair of dice, on the desk in front of him. He had been so happy, ever since Victor Grego had called him to tell him what had been discovered at Science Center about the hokfusine and the NFMp hormone. They were on the right track, he was sure of it, and in a few years all the Fuzzy children would be born alive and normal.

And then, just after lunch, Jack Holloway had come dropping out of the sky from Beta Continent with this.

"You can't keep it a secret, Jack. You can't keep any discovery a secret, because anything anybody discovers, somebody else can, and will, discover later. Look how the power interests tried to suppress the discovery of direct conversion of nuclear energy to electric current, back in the First Century. Look how they tried to suppress the Abbot Drive."

"This is different," Jack Holloway argued, bullheadedly. "This isn't a scientific principle anybody, anywhere, can discover. This is something at a certain place, and if we can keep people away from it . . ."

"*Quis custodiet ipsos custodes?*" Then, realizing that Latin was *terra incognita* to Jack, he translated: "Who'll watch the watchmen?"

Jack nodded. "That's what Gerd said. A thing like that would be an awful strain on anybody's moral fiber. And you know what'll happen as soon as it gets out."

"There'd be pressure on me to open the Fuzzy Reservation. Hugo Ingermann's John Doe and Richard Roe and all. I suppose I could stall it off till a legislature was elected, but after that . . ."

"I wasn't talking about political pressure. I was talking about a sunstone rush. There'd be twenty thousand men stampeding up there, with everything they could put onto contragravity. And everything they could find to shoot with, too. And the longer it's stalled off, the worse it'll be, because in six months the off-planet immigrants'll start coming in."

He hadn't thought of that. He should have; he'd been on other frontier planets where rich deposits of mineral wealth had been discovered. And there was nothing in the Galaxy that concentrated more value in less bulk than sunstones.

"Ben, I've been thinking," Jack continued. "I don't like the idea, but it's the only idea I have. Those sunstones are in a little section about fifty miles square on the north side of the Divide. Suppose the Government makes that a sort of reservation-inside-the-reservation, and operates the sunstone mines. You do it before anything leaks out—announce that the Government has discovered sunstones on the Fuzzy Reservation, that the Government claims all the sunstones on Fuzzy land in the name of the Fuzzies, and that the Government is operating all sunstone mines, and it'll head off the rush, or the worst of it. And the Fuzzies'll get out of that immediate area; they won't stay around where there's underground blasting. And the money the Government gets out of it can go to the Fuzzies in protection and welfare and medical aid and *shoppo-diggo* and *shodda-bag* and *esteefee.*"

"Have you any idea what it would cost to start an operation like that, before we could even begin getting out sunstones in paying quantities?"

"Yes. I've been digging sunstones as long as anybody knew there were sunstones. But this is a good thing, Ben, and if you have a good thing you can always finance it."

"It would protect the Fuzzies' rights, and they'd benefit enormously. But the initial expense . . ."

"Well, lease the mineral rights to somebody who could finance it. The Government would get a royalty, the Fuzzies would benefit, the Reservation would be kept intact."

"But who? Who would be able to lease it?"

He knew, even as he asked the question. The Charterless Zarathustra Company; they could operate that mine. Why, that mine would be something on the odd-jobs level, compared to what they'd done on the Big Blackwater Swamp. Lease them the entire mineral rights for the Reservation; that would keep everybody else out.

But it would put the Company back where they'd been before the Pendarvis Decisions; it would give them back their sunstone monopoly; it would . . . Why, it was unthinkable!

Unthinkable, hell. He was thinking about it now, wasn't he?

VICTOR GREGO CRUSHED out his cigarette and leaned back in his relaxer-chair, closing his eyes. From the Fuzzy-room, he could hear muted voices, and the frequent popping of shots. Diamond was enjoying a screen-play. He was very good about keeping the volume turned down, so as not to bother Pappy Vic, but he'd get some weird ideas about life among the Hagga from some of those shows. Well, the good Hagga always licked the bad Hagga in the end, that was one thing.

He went back to thinking about bad Hagga, four of them in particular. Ivan Bowlby, Spike Heenan, Raul Laporte, Leo Thaxter.

Mallorysport was full of bad Hagga, on the lower echelons, but those four were the General Staff. Bowlby was the entertainment business. Beside the telecast show which Diamond was watching at the moment, that included prize-fights, nightclubs, prostitution and, without doubt, dope. Maybe he'd like to get Fuzzies as attractions at his night-spots, and through that part of his business he could make contacts with well to do people who wanted Fuzzies, couldn't adopt them, and would pay fancy prices for them. If there really were a black market, he'd be in it.

Spike Hennan was gambling; crap-games, numbers racket, bookmaking. On sport-betting, his lines and Bowlby's would cross with mutual profit. Laporte was racketeering, extortion, plain old-fashioned country-style crime. And stolen goods, of course, and, while there'd been money in it, illicit gem-buying.

Leo Thaxter was the biggest, and the most respectably fronted, of the four. L. Thaxter, Loan Broker & Private Financier. He loaned money publicly at a righteously legal seven percent; he also loaned, at much higher rates, to all the shylocks in town, who, in turn, loaned it at six-for-five to people who could not borrow elsewhere, including suckers who went broke in Spike Hennan's crap-games, and he used Raul Laporte's hoodlums to do his collecting.

And, notoriously but unprovably, behind them stood Hugo Ingermann, Mallorysport's unconvicted underworld generalissimo.

Maybe they were just before proving it, now. Leslie Coombes's investigators had established that all four of them, and especially Thaxter, were the dummy owners behind whom Ingermann controlled most of the land the company had unwisely sold eight years ago, the section north of Mallorysport that was now dotted with abandoned factories and commercial buildings. And it was pretty well established that those four had been the John Doe, Richard Roe, *et alii,* who had been represented in court by Ingermann just after the Pendarvis Decisions.

Strains of music were now coming from the Fuzzy-room; the melodrama was evidently over. He opened his eyes, lit another cigarette, and began going over what he knew about Ingermann's four chief henchmen. Thaxter; he'd come to Zarathustra a few years before Ingermann. Small-time racketeer, at fist, and then he'd tried to organize labor unions, but labor unions organized by outsiders had been frowned upon by the company, and he'd been shown the wisdom of stopping that. Then he'd organized an independent planters' marketing cooperative, and from that he'd gotten into shylocking. There'd been some woman with him, at first, wife or reasonable facsimile. Maybe she was still around; have Coombes look into that. She might be willing to talk.

Diamond strolled in from the Fuzzy-room.

"Pappy Vic! Make talk with Diamond, *plis.*"

LIEUTENANT FITZ MORTLAKE, acting-in-charge of company detective bureau for the 1800–2400 shift, yawned. Twenty more minutes; less than that if Bert Eggers got in early to relieve him. He riffled through the stack of complaint-sheet copies on the desk and put a paperweight on them. In the squadroom outside the mechanical noises of card-machines and teleprinters and the occasional howl of a sixty-speed audiovisual transmission were being replaced by human sounds, voices and laughter and the scraping of chairs, as the midnight-to-six shift began filtering in. He was wondering whether to go home and read till he became sleepy, or drift around the bars to see if he could pick up a girl, when Bert Eggers pushed past a couple of sergeants at the door and entered.

"Hi, Fitz; how's it going?"

"Oh, quiet. We found out where Jayser hid that stuff; we have all of it, now. And Millman and Nogahara caught those kids who were stealing engine parts out of Warehouse Ten. We have them in detention; we haven't questioned them yet."

"We'll take care of that. They work for the Company?"

"Two of them do. The third is just a kid, seventeen. Juvenile Court can have him. We think they were selling the stuff to Honest Hymie."

"Uhuh. I'll suspect anybody they all call Honest Anybody or anything," Eggers said, sitting down as he vacated the chair.

He took off his coat, pulled his shoulder holster and pistol from the bottom drawer and put it on, resuming the coat. He gathered up his lighter and tobacco pouch, and then discovered that his pipe was missing, and hunted the desk-top for it, unearthing it from under some teleprinted photographs.

"What are these?" Eggers asked, looking at them.

"Herckerd and Novaes, false alarm number steen thousand. A couple of woods-tramps who turned up on Epsilon."

Eggers made a sour face. "Those damn Fuzzies have made more work for us," he began. "And now, my kids are after me to get them one. So's my wife.

You know what? Fuzzies are a status-symbol, now. If you don't have a Fuzzy, you might as well move to Junktown with the rest of the bums."

"I don't have a Fuzzy, and I haven't moved to Junktown yet."

"You don't have kids in high school."

"No, thank God!"

"Bet he doesn't have finance-company trouble, either," one of the sergeants in the doorway said.

Bert was going to make some retort to that. Before he could, another voice spoke up:

"Yeeek!"

"Speak of the devil," somebody said.

"You have that Fuzzy in here, Fitz?" Eggers demanded. "Where the hell . . . ?"

"There he is," one of the men in the doorway said, pointing.

The Fuzzy, who had been behind the desk-chair, came out into view. He pulled the bottom of Eggers's coat, yeeking again. He looked like a hunchback Fuzzy.

"What's he got on his back?" Eggers reached down. "Whatta you got there, anyhow?"

It was a little rucksack, with leather shoulder-straps and a drawstring top. As soon as Eggers displayed an interest in it, the Fuzzy climbed out of it as though glad to be rid of it. Mortlake picked it up and put it on the desk; over ten pounds, must weigh almost as much as the Fuzzy. Eggers opened the drawstrings and put his hand into it.

"It's full of gravel," he said, and brought out a handful.

The gravel was glowing faintly. Eggers let go of it as though it were as hot as it looked.

"Holy God!" It was the first time he ever heard anybody screaming in baritone. "The damn things are *sunstones*!"

20

"**B**UT WHAT FOR?" Diamond was insisting. "What for Big Ones first, *bang, bang,* make dead? Not good. What for not make friend, make help, have fun?"

"Well, some Big Ones bad, make trouble. Other Big Ones fight to stop trouble."

"But what for Big Ones be bad? Why not everybody make friend, have fun, make help, be good?"

Now how in Nifflheim could you answer a question like that? Maybe that was what Ernst Mallin meant when he said Fuzzies were the sanest people he'd ever seen. Maybe they were too sane to be bad, and how could a non-sane human explain to them?

"Pappy Vic not know. Maybe Unka Ernst, Unka Panko, know."

The bell of the private communication screen began its slow tolling. Diamond looked around; this was something that didn't happen often. He rose, taking Diamond from his lap and setting him on the chair, then went to the wall and put the screen on. It was Captain Morgan Lansky, at Chief Steefer's desk. He looked as though a planetbuster had just dropped in front of him and hadn't exploded yet.

"Mr. Grego; the gem-vault! Fuzzies in it, robbing it!"

He conquered the impulse to ask Lansky if he were drunk or crazy. Lansky was neither; he was just frightened.

"Take it easy, Morgan. Tell me about it. First, what you know's happened, and then what you think is happening."

"Yes, sir." Lansky got hold of himself; for an instant he was silent. "Ten minutes ago, in the captain's office at detective bureau; the shifts were changing, and both lieutenants were there. A Fuzzy came out of a storeroom in back of the office; he had a little knapsack on his back, with about twelve pounds of sunstones in it. The Fuzzy's here now, so are the sunstones. Do you want to see them?"

"Later; go ahead." Then, before Lansky could speak, he asked: "Sure he came out of this storeroom?"

"Yes, sir. There was five-six men in the doorway to the squadroom, he couldn't of come through that way. And the only way he could of got into this storeroom was out a ventilation duct there. The grating over it was open."

"That sounds reasonable. He could have gotten into the gem-vault through the ventilation system too."

The entrance to the gem-vault stairway was on the same floor as the detective bureau. The inlet and outlet screens were hinged, and the latch worked from either side to allow any outlet-screen to be put on anywhere. And the sunstones couldn't have come from anywhere else; just yesterday he'd had to go down and let Evins in to put away what had accumulated in his office safe.

"Ten minutes; what's been done since?"

"Carlos Hurtado's here, he hadn't gone home. He's staying, and so are most of the pre-midnight men. We put out a quiet alert to all the police in the building. We're blocking off everything from the top of the fourteenth level down, and a second block around the fifteenth. I called the Chief; he's coming in. Hurtado's calling the Constabulary and the Mallorysport police for men and vehicles to blockade the building from the outside. I've sent calls out for Dr. Mallin, and for Mr. E. Evins, and I've sent out for as many hearing aids as I can get."

"That was good. Now, have a jeep or something up here for me right away; I'll have to open the gem-vault. And have men there to meet me. With sono-stunners; there may be more Fuzzies inside. And get hold of the building superintendent and the ventilation engineer, and get plans of the ventilation system."

"Right. Anything else, Mr. Grego?"

"Not that I can think of now. Be seeing you."

He blanked the screen. Diamond, in the chair, was looking at him wide-eyed.

"Pappy Vic; what make do?"

He looked at Diamond for a moment. "Diamond, you remember when bad Big Ones bring you, other Fuzzies, here?" he asked. "You know other Fuzzies again, you see them?"

"*Yeh, tsure.* Good friend; know again."

"*Hokay.* Stay put; Pappy Vic be back."

He ran into the kitchenette and gathered a couple of tins of Extee-Three. Returning, he found a hearing aid—Diamond was using his Fuzzyphone, and he hadn't needed it—and pocketed it. Then, swinging Diamond to his shoulder, he went outside. Just as he emerged onto the terrace, a silver-trimmed maroon company airjeep, lettered POLICE, lifted above the edge of the terrace, turned, and glided down. He thought, again, that police vehicles should have some distinctive color-scheme to distinguish them from ordinary Company cars. Talk about that with Harry Steefer, some time. Then the jeep was down and the pilot had opened the door. He climbed in and held Diamond on his lap, while the pilot reported him aboard. Then he took the radio handphone himself.

"Grego; who's there?" he asked.

"Hurtado. We have everything from the fourteenth level down to the sixteenth sealed off, inside and out. Captain Lansky and Lieutenant Eggers have gone to meet you at the gem-vault. Dr. Mallin's coming in; so's Miss Glenn and Captain Khadra of the ZNPF. Maybe they can get something out of this Fuzzy." He muttered something bitterly. "Questioning Fuzzies; what's police work coming to next?"

"Teaching Fuzzies to crack safes; what's crime coming to next? You get the ventilation-system plans yet?"

"They're coming up; so's the ventilation engineer. You think there's more Fuzzies than this one?"

"Four more. And two men, named Phil Novaes and Moses Herckerd."

Hurtado was silent for a moment, then cursed. "Now why in Nifflheim didn't I think of that?" he demanded. "Sure!"

They went inside from a landing-stage on the third level down. There were police there, with portable machine guns, and a couple of cars. Work was going on in some of the offices along the horizontal vehicle-way, but no excitement. They encountered a police car in the vertical shaft just above the fourteenth level down; the jeep pilot put on his red-and-white blinker and picked up the handphone of his loudspeaker, saying, "Mr. Grego here; please don't delay us." The car moved out of the way.

The fifteenth level down was police country. Everything was superficially quiet, but a number of vehicles were concentrated around the horizontal ways from the vertical shaft. The pilot set the jeep down at the entrance to the gem-buyer's offices. Morgan Lansky and a detective were waiting there. He got out, holding Diamond, and the pilot handed the tins of Extee-Three to the detective. Lansky, who seemed to have recovered his aplomb, grinned.

"Interpreter, Mr. Grego?" he asked.

"Yes, and maybe he can make identification. I think he knows these Fuzzies."

It took Lansky two seconds to get that. Then he nodded.

"Sure. That would explain everything."

They went through the door, and, inside, it was immediately evident that the security-regulation book had gone out the airlock. The portcullis was raised, though a couple of submachine-gunners loitered watchfully in front of it. Half a dozen men, all carrying sono-stunners, short carbines with flaring muzzles like ancient blunderbusses, fell in behind them. The door at the end of the short hall was open, too, and nobody was bothering with identity checks.

Nobody was supposed to be within sight of him when he opened the vault, but he ignored that, too. Lansky, Eggers, the man who was carrying the two tins of Extee-Three, and the men with the stunners all crowded down the stairway after him. Quickly he punched the nonsense sentence out on the keyboard. Ten seconds later the door receded and slid aside.

Inside, the lights were on, as always; bright as they were, they could not dim the many-colored glow on the black velvet tabletop, where two Fuzzies were playing concentratedly with a thousand or so sunstones. A little rope ladder, just big enough for a Fuzzy, dangled past the light-shade from the air-outlet above.

Both Fuzzies looked up, startled. One said in accusing complaint, "You not say stones make shine; you say just stones, like always." His companion looked at them for a moment, and then cried: "Not know these Big Ones! How come this place?"

Lansky, who had been holding Diamond while he had been using the keyboard, followed him in. Diamond saw the two on the table and jabbered in excited recognition. He took Diamond and set him on the table with the others.

"Not be afraid," he said. "I not hurt. He friend; show him pretty things."

Recognition was mutual; the other Fuzzies were hugging Diamond and talking rapidly. Lansky had gone to a communication screen and was punching a call-number.

"You get away from bad Big Ones, too?" Diamond was asking. "How you come this place?"

"Big Ones bring us. Make us go through long little hole. Tell us, get stones, like at other place."

What other place, he wondered. The other strange Fuzzy was saying:

"All-time, Big Ones make us go through long little holes, get stones. We get stones, Big Ones give us good things to eat. Not get stones, Big Ones angry. Make hurt, put us in dark place, not give anything to eat, make us do again."

"Who has the Extee-Three?" he asked. "Open a tin for me."

"*Esteefee!*" Diamond, hearing him, repeated. "Pappy Vic give *esteefee; hoksu-fusso.*"

Lansky had Hurtado in the screen; he was standing aside to allow the latter to see what was going on in the gem-vault. Hurtado was swearing.

"Now, we gotta make everything in the building Fuzzy-proof," he was saying. "The Chief's just come in." He turned. "Hey, Chief, come and look at this!"

Eggers had the Extee-Three; he got the tin open. Taking the cake from him, he broke it in three, then shoved a couple of million sols in sunstones out of the way and gave a piece to each of the Fuzzies. The two little jewel-thieves knew just what it was, and began eating at once. Telling Eggers to keep an eye on them, he went to the screen. In it, Harry Steefer was cursing even more fluently than Hurtado. He broke off and greeted:

"Hello, Mr. Grego. Beside what's on the table, are there any sunstones left?"

"I haven't checked, yet."

He looked around. All the drawers had been pulled out of the cabinet; the Fuzzies had evidently gotten at the upper rows by stacking and standing on the ones from below. Lansky was examining a couple of small canvas rucksacks he had found.

"What's it look like, Captain?"

"Don't come around the table, anybody," Lansky warned. "The floor's all over stones, here."

"Then we have some left. Has Conrad Evins come in yet?"

"We're still trying to contact him," Steefer said. "Dr. Mallin's here, and Captain Khadra and Miss Glenn are on the way here. I'm going over to operation-command room, now; I'll leave somebody here."

"Suppose you leave the Fuzzy in your office, too. I'll bring this pair up, and Diamond can help question them all."

Steefer assented, then excused himself to talk to somebody in the room with him. One of the detectives, who had gone out, returned with a broom and dustpan; he held the pan while Lansky swept the scattered sunstones up. There were more than he had expected, perhaps as many as half of them. He poured them into drawers, regardless of size or grade; they could be sorted out later. All the Fuzzies protested strenuously when he began gathering up the ones on the table; even Diamond wanted to play with them. He consoled them with the other cake of Extee-Three, and assured Diamond, who assured his friends, that Pappy Vic would provide other pretties.

"Captain, you and Lieutenant Eggers and a couple of men stay here," he said. "I think we have two more Fuzzies, and they may be back for more stones. Catch them by hand if you can, stun them if you have to. Try not to hurt them, but get them, and bring them to the Chief's office. That's where I'm going now."

•   •   •

"CHRIST, I WISH they'd hurry! What do you think's keeping them?"

That was the tenth or twelfth time Phil Novaes had said that in the last twenty minutes. Phil was getting on edge. Been on edge ever since they'd come here, and getting edgier every minute. Moses Herckerd was beginning to worry just a little about that. Losing your nerve was the surest way to disaster in a spot like this, and it would be disaster to both of them. Phil had been a little overconfident, at the beginning; that had been bad, too.

Getting the car hidden, on the unoccupied ninth level down, had been easy enough; they'd stowed it in one of the unfinished main office rooms close to where they'd kept the Fuzzies, two months ago. He knew the company police had started patroling the unoccupied levels after that one damned Fuzzy had gotten away from them and, of all places, into Victor Grego's own apartment. Still, the place where they'd left the car was safe enough.

The long descent, nearly a thousand feet, among the water mains and ventilation mains to the fifteenth level down, had been hard and dangerous, clinging to the contragravity lifter with the Fuzzies jostling about in the box. Once this was over, he hoped he'd never see another damned Fuzzy as long as he lived. Phil had been all right then; he'd had to keep his mind on what he was doing, keep the lifter from swinging out and carrying them away from the hand-holds. It had been after they had gotten onto this ledge at the ventilation-duct outlet that Phil's nerves had begun to get away from him.

"Take it easy, Phil," he whispered. "They have half a mile, coming and going, through those ducts. And they have to fill their packs in the vault, and they always poke around doing that. Never can teach the buggers to hurry."

"Well, something could have happened. Maybe they took a wrong turn and got lost. That place is a lot more complicated than the practice setup."

"Oh, they'll get out all right. They all made three trips already without anything going wrong, didn't they?" he said. "And don't talk so damned loud."

That was what he was worried about, as much as anything. The whole company police force was concentrated around the place where he and Novaes were waiting. They were outside the actual police zone, but all the other emergency services—fire protection, radiation safety, the first-aid dispensaries and the ambulance hangars—were all around them, and sound carried an incredible distance through these shafts and air ducts and conduits.

"We have enough, now," Phil said. "Let's just pick up and go, now. Why, we must have fifty million already."

"But out and leave the Fuzzies?"

"Hell with the Fuzzies," Phil said.

"Hell with the Fuzzies, hell! Haven't you found out yet that Fuzzies can talk? We've spent two months, now, cooped up indoors, because that Fuzzy Grego found put the finger on us. We've got to get all five back, and we've got to finish them off. If we don't and the police get hold of them, they'll finish us."

Phil, who was stooping by the rectangular outlet, looked up.

"I hear something. A couple of them, talking."

He turned on his hearing aid and put his head to the opening beside Phil's. Yes, a couple of Fuzzies talking; arguing about how far it was yet.

"As soon as they come out, let's just shove them into the chute," Phil argued, nodding toward the access-port to the trash-chute, that went seven hundred feet down to the mass-energy converters.

That was where the Fuzzies would go, all of them, when the sunstones were all out of the vault. But the sunstones weren't all out. He doubted if they had more than half of them, yet.

"No, not yet. Here they come; grab the first one."

Novaes caught the Fuzzy as he came out. He caught the second. They were both carrying loaded packs. He slipped the straps down over the Fuzzy's arms and gave him to Novaes to hold, then loosened the drawstrings, emptying the stones into the open suitcase along with the other gems. Then he put the rucksack onto the Fuzzy's back.

"All right. In with you. Go get stones."

The Fuzzy said something, he wasn't sure what, in a complaining tone. *Fusso;* that meant food, or eat. Important word to a Fuzzy.

"No. You get stone; then I give *fusso*." He shoved the Fuzzy back into the ventilation duct. "Let's unload yours and send him back. As long as there's sunstones in there, we want them."

A UNIFORMED SERGEANT was holding down Chief Steefer's desk, smoking what was probably one of the Chief's cigars and talking to a girl in another screen. Across the room, Ernst Mallin, Ahmed Khadra and Sandra Glenn were talking to a Fuzzy who sat on the edge of a table, contentedly munching Extee-Three. Khadra was in evening clothes, and Sandra was wearing something glamorous with a lot of black lace. She was also wearing a sunstone which he hadn't noticed before, on the third finger of her left hand. *Wanted, Fuzzy-Sitter. Apply Victor Grego.*

They set Diamond and his friends on the floor; he thanked and dismissed the men who had helped him with them. As soon as they saw the Fuzzy on the table, they raised an outcry and ran forward; the Fuzzy on the table dropped to the floor and hurried to meet them.

"What did you get from him?" he asked.

"Herckerd and Novaes, natch," Khadra said, disgustedly. "All the time I was looking for a black market that wasn't there, they were right here in town somewhere, being taught to steal sunstones. Fagin-racket, by God!"

"Herckerd and Novaes and who else?"

"Two other men, and one woman. And just the five Fuzzies Herckerd and Novaes brought in along with Diamond. They were somewhere not more than fifteen minutes by air from Company House all the time. This gang taught them to go through ventilator ducts, and open the screen-covers on the inlets, and use rope ladders and get stones out of cabinets. They must have had a mockup of the gem-vault and the ventilation system. They had to practice all the time. If they cleaned out the cabinets and brought the stones, river-gravel, I suppose, out, they got Extee-Three. If they goofed, they were punished, electric shock, I suppose, and shoved in a dungeon with nothing to eat. You know, they could be shot for that."

"They oughtn't to be shot; they ought to be burned at the stake!" Sandra cried angrily.

Gentler sex, indeed! "Well, I'll settle for shooting, if we can catch them. Done anything in aid of that yet?"

"Not too much," Mallin regretted. "His vocabulary is limited, and he hasn't words for much that he experienced. We've been trying to learn his route through the ventilation system. He knows how he went in to the gem-vault, but he simply can't verbalize it."

"Diamond; you help Pappy Vic. Make talk for Unka Ernst, Unka Ahmed, Auntie Sandra; help other Fuzzies make talk about bad Big Ones, about place where were, about what make do, about how go through long little holes." He turned to Khadra. "Has he seen Herckerd and Novaes on screen?"

"Not yet; we've just been talking to him, so far."

"Better let all three of them see those audiovisuals; get identifications made. And keep on about the ventilation ducts. See if any of them can tell which way they went toward the gem-vault, and what kind of a place they went in at."

21

CROSSING THE HALL, he found the operation-command room busy, in a quiet and almost leisurely manner. Everybody knew what to do, and was getting it done with a minimum of fuss. A group of men, policemen and engineers, were huddled at a big table, going over plans, on big sheets and on photoprint screens. More men, police and maintenance people, gathered around a big solidigraph model of the fourteenth, fifteenth and sixteenth levels, projected in a tri-di screen. The thing was transparent, and looked almost anatomical; well, Company House was an organism of a sort. Respiratory system; the ventilation, in which everybody was interested. Circulatory system; the water-lines. Excretory system; sewage disposal.

And now it had been invaded by a couple of inimical microbes, named Phil Novaes and Moses Herckerd, whom the police leucocytes were seeking to neutralize.

He looked at it for a while, then strolled on to the banks of viewscreens. Views of halls and vehicle-ways, mostly empty, patrolled here and there by police or hastily mobilized and armed maintenance workers. Views of landing-stages, occupied by police and observed from aircars. A view from a car a thousand feet over the building, in which a few Constabulary and city police vehicles circled slowly, blockading the building from outside. He nodded in satisfaction; they couldn't get out of the building, and as soon as enough of the fifty-odd widely scattered locations from which they might be operating could be eliminated, the police would close in on them.

In one screen from a pickup installed over the door in the gem-vault, he could see Morgan Lansky, Bert Eggers and two detectives, coatless and perspiring, around the electrically warmed tabletop, staring at the little rope ladder that dangled down around the light-shade. In another screen, from a high pickup in a corner of Harry Steefer's office, the uniformed sergeant at the desk watched Ernst Mallin and Ahmed Khadra fussing with a screen, while Sandra Glenn sat on the floor talking to Diamond and his three friends.

Harry Steefer sat alone at the command desk, keeping track of everything at once. He went over and sat down beside him.

"Mr. Grego. We don't seem to be making too much progress," the Chief said. "Everything's secure so far, though."

"Have the news services gotten hold of it yet?"

"I don't believe. Planetwide News called the city police to find out what all the cars were doing around Company House; somebody told them that it was a shipment of valuables being taken under guard to the space terminal. They seemed to accept that."

"We can't sit on it indefinitely."

"I hope we can till we catch these people."

"Have you contacted Conrad Evins yet?"

"No. He's not at home; here, I'll show you."

Steefer punched out a call on one of his communication screens. When it lighted, the chief gem-buyer's wide-browed, narrow chinned face looked out of it.

"This is a recording, made at 2100, Conrad Evins speaking. Mrs. Evins and I are going out; we will not be home until after midnight," Evins's voice said. Then the screen flickered, and the recording began again.

"I could put out an emergency call for him, but I don't want to," Steefer said. "We don't know how many people outside the building are involved in this, and we don't want to alarm them."

"No. Four men and one woman; the Fuzzies say there were only two men, presumably Herckerd and Novaes, brought them here. That means two men and a woman somewhere outside waiting for them. And we don't really need Evins, at present. It's after midnight now; we can keep calling at his home."

Evins and his wife had probably gone to a show, or visiting. Evins's wife; he couldn't seem to recall ever having met her. He'd heard something or other about her . . . He shoved that aside.

"Don't they have little robo-snoopers they use to go through the ventilation ducts?" he asked.

"Yes. Mr. Guerrin, the ventilation engineer, has a dozen of them. He suggested using them, but I vetoed it till I could see what you thought. Those things float on contragravity, and even a miniature Abbot drive generator makes quite an ultrasonic noise. We still have two Fuzzies loose in the ventilation system; we don't want to scare them, do we?"

"No. Let them carry on. There's a chance they may come out in the gem-vault, if we don't frighten them."

He looked across the room at the viewscreens. Khadra and Mallin had their screen set up, Sandra had brought the Fuzzies over in front of it, and Diamond seemed to be explaining about viewscreens and audiovisual screens to the others. In the gem-vault screen, Lansky and the others were leaning forward across the table, listening. They had a couple of hearing aids, now, which Eggers and one of his detectives were using. Lansky turned to make frantic gestures at the pickup. Steefer picked up a speaker-phone and advised everybody to pay attention to the gem-vault screen.

For one of those ten-second eternities, nothing happened in the screen. A moment later, a Fuzzy came climbing down the ladder. One of the detectives would have grabbed him; Eggers stopped him. A moment later, another Fuzzy appeared.

Eggers caught him by the feet with both hands and pulled him off the ladder; the Fuzzy hit Eggers in the face with his fist. The first Fuzzy, having dropped to the table, tried to get up the ladder again; Lansky grabbed him. One of the detectives came to Eggers's assistance. Then the struggle was over, and the two prisoners had been secured. Lansky was yelling:

"We got them both! We're bringing them up."

Steefer yelled to the girl who was monitoring the screen to cut in sound transmission and tell Lansky and one man to remain on guard; Lansky acknowledged, and Eggers and one of the detectives left the vault, each carrying a Fuzzy. In the screen from Steefer's office, they had an audiovisual of Moses Herckerd on the screen; it was the employment interview film, and Herckerd was talking about his educational background and former job experience. Steefer was talking to the sergeant at his desk; the latter beckoned Ahmed Khadra over.

"Good," Khadra said, when Steefer told him what had happened. "That's all of them. We'll run Herckerd over for them when they come up, and show them Novaes. They're the two who brought them here tonight, the three we have here all say so."

"They're still in here," Steefer said. "That leaves two men and a woman outside. I wonder . . ."

"I think I know who they are, Chief."

It was just a guess, of course, but it fitted. He had suddenly remembered what he knew about Mrs. Conrad Evins.

When Leo Thaxter, now Loan Broker & Private Financier, first came to

Zarathustra ten years ago, a woman had come with him, but she hadn't been a
wife or reasonable facsimile, she had been a sister or reasonable facsimile. Rose
Thaxter. After a while, she had left Thaxter and married a company minerologist
named Conrad Evins, who, after the discovery of the sunstones, had become
chief company gem-buyer.

"What's that call-number of Evins?" he asked Steefer, and when Steefer
gave it, he repeated it to Khadra. "When those other Fuzzies come in, call it. It'll
be answered by an audiovisual recording. See if the kids recognize him."

Steefer looked at him, more amused than surprised. "I wouldn't have
thought of that, myself, Mr. Grego. It seems to fit, though."

"Hunch." If anybody respected hunches, it would be a cop. "I just
remembered who Evins was married to. Rose Thaxter."

"Yeh!" Steefer muttered something else. "I know that, too; I just never
connected it. It all hangs together, too."

For a couple of minutes, they were both talking at the same time, telling one
another just how it did hang together, and watching the screen from Steefer's
office. Eggers and the detective were coming in, still coatless, carrying a Fuzzy
apiece; the one Eggers was carrying was trying to get the gun out of the
lieutenant's shoulder-holster.

Of course it hung together. Somebody in the gang had to have exact
knowledge of the layout of the gem-vault, which Evins, and very few others,
could provide. The arrangement of the ventilation-ducts wasn't classified
top-secret; anybody in Evins's position could have gotten that. They had to have
a place to keep the Fuzzies, big enough to build a replica of the gem-vault and
of the ventilation system. Well, there were all those vacant factories and
warehouses out in the district everybody called Mortgageville. The ones Hugo
Ingermann had been acquiring title to, with Thaxter as dummy buyer. How
Herckerd and Novaes had been roped in wasn't immediately important; catch
them and question them and that would emerge. Ten to one, Rose Thaxter, Mrs.
Conrad Evins, was the connecting link and mainspring.

The Fuzzies in Steefer's office were having a reunion. Khadra and Mallin
and Sandra were trying to get them to look at the communication screen. He
turned to Steefer.

"Get some men to Conrad Evins's place; make a thorough search, for
anything that might look like evidence of anything."

"They won't be there."

"No. They'll be in one of those buildings over in Mortgageville, and we
don't know which one. I'm going to call Ian Ferguson."

He told Ferguson quickly what he suspected. The Constabulary commandant nodded.

"Reasonable," he agreed. "I'll call the city police for help; we'll close the place off so nobody can get in or out and then we'll start making a search. It's only about two thousand square miles, and there are only about three hundred buildings on it," he added. "I think I'll call Casagra, too, and see how many Marines he can give me."

"Well, take your time searching; just make sure anybody who's there now stays there. We'll give you what help we can as soon as we can."

He looked up at the screen from Steefer's office. Khadra had called Evins's home, now, and he could hear Evins's recorded voice stating that he wouldn't be home before midnight. The Fuzzies evidently recognized him. It was also evident that they didn't like him.

"And put out a general alert to pick up Evins, Mrs. Evins, and Leo Thaxter, and I don't think you need to worry about how much noise you make doing it."

"And Ivan Bowlby, and Raul Laporte, and Spike Heenan," Ferguson added. "And any or all of their hoods." He thought for a moment. "And Hugo Ingermann. We may finally have grounds for interrogating him as a suspect. I'll call Gus Brannhard, too."

"And Leslie Coombes; he'll be a help."

"All right, everybody!" Steefer was calling out with his loudspeaker. "We have all the Fuzzies out; now let's get the show started!" Then he rose and went around the desk.

Khadra was on the communication screen from the Chief's desk:

"They made that fellow Evins, all right. He was one of the gang. Who is he?"

"Well, he used to be the Company's chief gem-buyer, up to fifteen minutes ago, but now he has been discharged, without notice, severance pay or recommendation." He thought for a moment. "Captain, are those Fuzzies' feet dirty?" he asked.

"Huh?" Khadra stared at him for an instant, then nodded. "Yes, they are; gray-brown dust. Same kind of dust on their fur."

"Uhuh; that's good." He rose and went to the big table and the solidigraph, where Steefer was already talking to a dozen or so men. He saw Niles Guerrin, the ventilation engineer, and pulled him aside.

"Niles, the insides of those ducts are dusty?" he asked.

"The ones that carry stale air to the reconditioners," Guerrin replied. "Dust from the air in the rooms . . ."

"They're the ones we're interested in. Now, these snoopers, robo-inspectors; could they pick up tracks the Fuzzies make, or traces where they've brushed against the sides of the ducts?"

"Yes, sure. They have a full optical reception and transmission system for visible light and infra-red light, and controllable magnifying vision . . ."

"How soon can you get them started, from the gem-vault and from the captain's office in detective headquarters?"

"Right away; we've set up screens and controls for them in here; did that right at the start."

"Good." He raised his voice. "Chief! Captain Hurtado, Lieutenant Mortlake; *do-bizzo*. We're going to fill the ventilation system with snoopers, now."

PHIL NOVAES LOOKED at his watch. It was still 0130, the damned thing must have stopped, and he was sure he'd wound it. Holding his wrist to catch the dim light from above he squinted at the second-hand. It was still making its slow circuit around the dial. It must have been only a few seconds since he had looked at it last.

"Herk, let's get the hell out of here," he urged. "They aren't coming out at all. It's been an hour since the last two went in."

"Thirty-five minutes," Herckerd said.

"Well, it's been over an hour since the other three went in. Something's gone wrong; we'll wait here till hell freezes over . . ."

"We'll wait here a little longer, Phil. We still have fifty million in sunstones to wait for, and we want to get those Fuzzies and shut them up for good."

"We have better than fifty million already. All we'll get'll be a hole in the head if we stay around here any longer. I know what's happened, those Fuzzies have gone out some other way; they're running around loose, packing sunstones . . ."

"Be quiet, Phil." Herckerd reached to his shirt pocket to turn on his hearing aid and put his head to the ventilation duct opening. "I hear something in there." He snapped off the hearing aid, listened, and snapped it on again. "It's ultrasonic, whatever it is. Probably vibration in the walls of the duct. Now just take it easy, Phil. Nobody knows there's anything happening at all. Grego's the only man in Company House that can open that vault, and he won't open it for a couple of weeks, at least. All the stones from Evins's office were put away yesterday. It'll take that long before anybody knows they're gone."

"Suppose those Fuzzies got out somewhere else. My God, they could have come out right in the police area." That could have happened; he wished he hadn't thought of it, but now that he had, he was sure that was what had happened. "If they did, everybody in the building's looking for us."

Herckerd wasn't listening to him. He'd turned off his hearing aid, and was squatting by the intake port, peeling the wrapper from a chewing-gum stick and putting the wrapper carefully in his pocket. Another piece of foolishness; no reason at all why they couldn't smoke here. He listened with his hearing aid again. The noise, whatever it was, was louder.

"There's something in there." He pulled the goggles down from his cap and took out his infra-red flashlight.

"Don't do that," Herckerd said sharply.

He disregarded the warning and turned the invisible light into the duct. There was something moving forward toward the opening; it wasn't a Fuzzy. It was a bulbous-nosed metallic thing, floating slowly toward him.

"It's a snooper! Look, Herk; somebody's wise to us. They have a snooper in the duct . . ."

"Get the stones in the box! Right away!" Herckerd ordered.

"Ah, so there was something went wrong!"

He snapped the suitcase shut, shoved it into the box on the contragravity lifter, and fastened the lid, then snapped the hook of his safety-belt onto one of the rings on the lifter. There was a crash behind him, and when he turned, Herckerd was holstering his pistol. Then he, too, snapped his safety-strap to the lifter, and pulled loose the two poles with hooked and spiked tips, passing one over and slipping the thong of the other over his wrist.

"Full lift," he said. "Let's go."

He fumbled for a second or so at the switch, then turned it on. The whole thing, lifter, box, and he and Herckerd, were pulled up from the ledge and swung out into the shaft.

"What did you have to shoot for?" he demanded, pushing with his boathook-like pole. "Everybody in the place heard you."

"You want that thing following us?" Herckerd asked. "Watch out; water-main right above!"

Maybe the snooper was just making a routine inspection; maybe Herckerd had finally panicked, after all his pretense of calmness. No. Something *had* gone wrong. Those damned Fuzzies had gone out the wrong way, somebody'd found them . . . There were more pipes and conduits and things in the way; he remembered the trouble they'd had getting past them on the way down. He and Herckerd had to push and pull with their poles and for a moment he thought they were inextricably stuck, they'd never get loose, they were wedged in here . . . Then the lifter was rising again, and he could see the network of obstructions receding below, and the white XV's on the sides of the shaft had become XIV's, so they were off the fifteenth level. Only five more levels and a couple of floors to go.

But he could hear voices, from loudspeakers, all around:

"Cars P-18, P-19, P-20; fourteenth level, fourth floor, location DA-231."

"Riot-car 12, up to thirteen, sixth floor . . ."

He swore at Herckerd. "Sure, it'll be a month before they find out what's happened!"

"Shut up. We get out of the shaft two floors up, to the left. They have the shaft plugged at the top."

"Yes, and walk right into them," he argued.

"We'll lift into them if we keep on here; we'll have a chance if we get out of this."

They worked the lifter around the central clump of water and sewer and ventilation mains, pushing away from it and then hooking onto handholds and drawing the lifter into a lateral passage, floating along it for a hundred feet before Herckerd could get at the lifter controls and set it down. Then he unsnapped his safety-strap and staggered for a moment before he found his footing.

It was a service-passage, wide enough for one of the little hall-cars, or for a jeep; maintenance workers used it to get at air-fans and water-pumps. They started along it, towing the lifter after them, looking to right and left for some means of egress. There should be other vertical shafts, but they would be covered, too.

"How are we going to get out of this?"

"How the hell do I know?" Herckerd retorted. "How do I know we're going to get out at all?" He stopped for a moment and then pointed to an open doorway on the left. "Stairway; we'll go up there."

They crossed to it. From somewhere down the bare, dimly-lighted passage, an amplified voice was shouting indistinguishable words. The passage connected with another, or a hallway. They couldn't go ahead; that was sure.

"We can't get the lifter through." He knew it, and still tried; the lifter wouldn't go through the narrow door. "We'll have to carry the suitcase."

"Get the box off the lifter," Herckerd said. "We can't carry that suitcase ourselves; they'd catch us in no time. Get the suitcase out of it."

The box, four feet by four by three, with airholes at the top, had been necessary when they had the Fuzzies to carry; they didn't have to bother with them now. He opened it and lifted out the suitcase. No; they couldn't carry that, not and do any running. It was fastened with screws to the contragravity-lifter. Herckerd had his pocket-knife out, with the screwdriver blade open, and was working to remove the brackets.

"Well, where'll we go . . . ?"

"Don't argue, goddamit; get to work. Is there any extra rope ladder in that box? If there is, we'll use it to tie the suitcase on . . ."

Over Herckerd's shoulder, he saw the jeep enter the passage from the intersecting hall a hundred feet away. For an instant, he was frozen with fright. Then he screamed, "Behind you!" and threw himself through the open doorway, stumbling to the foot of a flight of narrow steel steps and then running up them. A pistol roared twice just outside the door, and then a submachine gun let go, a ripping two-second burst, a second of silence, and then another. Then voices shouted.

They got Herckerd. They got the sunstones, too. Then he forgot about both. Just get away, get far away, get away fast.

There was a steel door at the head of the stairs. Oh, God, please don't let it be locked! He flung himself at it, gripping the latch-handle.

It wasn't. The door swung open, and he stumbled through and closed it behind him, hearing, as he did, voices coming up from below. Then he turned, in the lighted hallway beyond.

There was a policeman standing not fifteen feet away, holding a short carbine with a thick, flaring muzzle, a stunner. He crouched, grabbing for his pistol. Then the blunderbuss muzzle of the stunner swung toward him at the policeman's hip. He had the pistol half drawn when the lights all went out and a crushing shock hit him, shaking and jarring him into oblivion.

THE OPERATION-COMMAND ROOM was silent. When the voice from the screen-speaker ceased, there was not a sound for an instant. Then there was a soft susurration; everybody in the place was exhaling at once. Grego found that he had been holding his own breath. So had Harry Steefer; he was exhaling noisily.

"Well, that's it," the Chief said. "I'm glad they took Novaes alive, anyhow. It'll be a couple of hours before he's able to talk." He picked up his cigarette pack, shook one out for himself and offered it.

Moses Herckerd wouldn't do any talking; he'd taken a dozen submachine gun bullets.

"What'll we do with the sunstones?" the voice from the screen asked.

"Take them to the gem-vault; we'll sort them over tomorrow or when we have time." He turned to the open screens to city police and Colonial Constabulary. The non-coms who had been on them were replaced by Ralph Earlie and Ian Ferguson, respectively. "You hear what was going on?" he asked.

"We got most of it," Ferguson said, and Earlie said, "You got them, and you got the stones back, but just what did happen?"

"They had a contragravity-lifter; they used it to get up one of the main conduit shafts, and then they got into a maintenance passage on the fourteenth level down. One of our jeeps caught them; Herckerd tried to put up a fight and got shot to hamburger; Novaes ran up a flight of stairs and came out in a hall right in front of a cop with a sono-stunner. When he comes to, we'll question him and check his story with the Fuzzies," he said. "How are you doing at Mortgageville?"

"We have the place surrounded," Ferguson said. "They might get out on foot; they won't in a vehicle. We have three Navy landing-craft loaded with detection equipment circling overhead, and Casagra has a hundred Marines along with my men."

"I can't help on that, at all," the Mallorysport police chief said. "I have all my men out making raids, and if you don't need that blockade around Company House any more, I want the men who are there. We have Ivan Bowlby, Spike Heenan and Raul Laporte, and we're pulling in everybody that's ever had anything to do with any of them, or Leo Thaxter. We don't have Thaxter, yet. I suppose he's at Mortgageville, along with the Evinses, waiting for Herckerd and Novaes to bring in the loot. And we have Hugo Ingermann, and this time he can't talk himself out. We got Judge Pendarvis out of bed, and he signed warrants for all of them; reasonable grounds for suspicion and authority to veridicate. We're saving him for last; we've just started on the small-fry."

There wasn't any question in his mind that Leo Thaxter was involved in the attempt on the gem-vault. Whether Bowlby or Heenan or Laporte had anything to do with it was more or less immaterial. They could be questioned, not only about that but about anything else, and anything they admitted under veridication was admissible as evidence against them, self-incriminatory or not.

"Well, I'm going over and see what they've been getting from the Fuzzies," he said. "There ought to be quite a little, by now." He glanced up at the screen from Steefer's office; half a dozen people were there now, and he was surprised to see Jack Holloway among them. He couldn't have flown in from Beta Continent since this had started. "I'll call back, or have somebody call, later."

Crossing the hall, he joined the group who were interviewing the five Herckerd-Novaes-Evins-Thaxter Fuzzies. Juan Jimenez was there, so were a couple of doctors who had been working with Fuzzies at the reception center. So was Claudette Pendarvis. Jack Holloway met him as he entered, and they shook hands.

"I thought there might be something I could do to help," he said. "Listen, Mr. Grego, you're not going to bring any charges against these Fuzzies, are you?"

"Good Lord, no!"

"Well, they're sapient beings, and they broke the law," Holloway said.

"They are legally ten-year-old children," Judge Pendarvis's wife said. "They are not morally responsible; they were taught to do this by humans."

"Yes, faginy, along with enslavement," Ahmed Khadra said. "Mandatory death by shooting for that, too."

"And I hope they shoot that Evins woman first of all; she's the worst of the lot," Sandra Glenn said. "She's the one who used the electric shock-rod on them when they made mistakes."

"Mr. Grego," Ernst Mallin interrupted. "I don't understand this. These Fuzzyphones are simple enough for any Fuzzy to operate; all they need to do is hold the little pistol-grip and the switch works automatically. Diamond can talk audibly, but he simply cannot teach any of these other Fuzzies to use it. You don't have your hearing aid on, do you? Well, listen to this."

Diamond used his Fuzzyphone; he spoke quite audibly. When he gave it to any of the others, all they produced was, "Yeek."

"Let me see that thing." He took it from Diamond and carried it over to the desk; rummaging in the top middle drawer, he found a little screwdriver and took it apart. The mechanism seemed to be all right. He removed the tiny power-unit and exchanged it for a similar one from a flashlight he found in the Chief's desk. The flashlight wouldn't light. He handed the Fuzzyphone to Mallin.

"Give this to one of the others, not Diamond. Have him say something."

Mallin handed the Fuzzyphone to one of the pair whom Lansky and Eggers had captured in the vault, and asked him a question. Holding the Fuzzyphone to his mouth, the Fuzzy answered quite audibly. Three or four of the humans said, "What the hell?" or words to that effect.

"Diamond, you not need talk-thing to make talk like Big One," he said. "You make talk like Big One any time. You make talk like Big One now."

"Like this?" Diamond asked.

"How does he do it?" Mrs. Pendarvis demanded. "Their voices aren't audible, at all."

"You think the power-unit gave out, and he just went on copying the sounds he was accustomed to make with the Fuzzyphone?" Mallin asked.

"That's right. He heard himself speak in the audible range, and he just learned to pitch his voice to imitate his own transformed voice. I'll bet he's been talking audibly for weeks, and we never knew it."

"Bet he didn't know it, either," Jack Holloway said. "Mr. Grego, do you think he could teach other Fuzzies to do that?"

"That would be kind of hard, wouldn't it?" Mallin asked. "Does he really know, himself, how he does it?"

"Mr. Grego!" the police sergeant, who was still keeping half an eye on the communication screen, broke in. "The Chief wants to know if you want to go to the gem-vault and check the contents of that suitcase."

"Has anybody else checked it?"

"Well, Captain Lansky has, but . . ."

"Then lock it up in the vault; I don't have to do that. The Nifflheim with it. I'll check it tomorrow. I'm busy, now."

22

"YOU THINK FOUR-FIFTY a carat would be all right?" Victor Grego was asking.

Bennett Rainsford picked up the lighter from the table in front of him and carefully relit a pipe that didn't need relighting. Now that he'd come to know him, he found that he liked Victor Grego. But he still had to watch him. Grego was the Charterless Zarathustra Company, and the company was definitely not a philanthropic institution.

"Sounds all right to me," Jack Holloway agreed. "You didn't pay me any more than that when I was prospecting, and I had to dig them myself."

"But four-fifty, Jack. The Terra market price is over a thousand sols a carat."

"This isn't Terra, Ben. Terra's five hundred light-years, six months ship-time, away. I think Mr. Grego's making us a good offer. All we need to do is bank the money; the company'll do the rest."

"Well, how much do you think the Fuzzies will get out of it, a month?"

Grego shrugged. "I haven't seen it, myself. I'll take Jack's word for it. What do you think?"

"Well, it depends on how much equipment you use, and what kind. If it's anything like the diggings I used to work, you'll get about a sunstone to the ton."

"We can move and process an awful lot of tons of flint in a month, and from Jack's description I'd say we'll be working that deposit for longer than any of us'll be around. You know, Governor, instead of the Fuzzies getting hand-outs from the Government, they'll be paying the Government's bills before long."

And that would have to be watched, too; it mustn't be allowed to become a source of political graft. Inside a month, now, the elections for delegates to the Constitutional Convention would be held. Make sure the right men were elected, men who would write a Constitution which would safeguard the Fuzzies' rights for all time.

Victor Grego, he was beginning to think, could be counted on to help in that.

LESLIE COOMBES HELD his glass while Gus Brannhard poured from the bottle, and said, quickly, "That's enough, please," when about fifty or sixty cc of whisky had been added to the ice. He filled the glass the rest of the way with soda, himself.

"And Hugo Ingermann," he said, disgustedly, "is completely innocent."

"Well, innocent of the Fuzzy business and the attempt on the company gem-vault," Brannhard conceded, pouring into his own glass. When Gus mixed a highball, he always left out both the ice and the soda. "It's probably the only thing he ever was innocent of, in his whole life. But he isn't getting away scot-free." Brannhard took a drink from his glass, and Coombes shuddered inwardly; the man must have a collapsium-plated digestive tract. "While we were interrogating this one and that one about the Fuzzy-sunstone business, we got a lot of evidence, all veridicated, to connect him with Thaxter's shylocking and Bowlby's call-girl agency and Heenan's prize-fight fixing and Laporte's strong-arm mob. I'm after him with a shotgun; I'm just filling the air all around him with indictments, and some of them are sure to hit. And even if I can't get him convicted of anything, he'll be disbarred, that's for sure. And this Planetary Prosperity Party of his is catching fire, leaking radiation, blowing up and falling apart all around. Everybody's calling it the Fuzzy-Fagin Party, and everybody who had anything to do with it is getting out as fast as he can."

"If we work together, we'll get a good Constitution adopted and a good Legislature elected. Or can we expect Governor Rainsford to agree with Victor Grego on what a 'good' Constitution and a 'good' Legislature are?"

"We can," Brannhard said. "We only have a few months before the off-planet land-grabbers begin coming in, and Ben Rainsford's as much worried about that as Victor Grego. Leslie, if you go into court and make claim to all the unseated land the company has mapped and surveyed, I am instructed by the Governor not to oppose you. What does that sound like?"

"That sounds like getting back about everything we lost, with the sunstone lease on top of it. I am going to propose the election of Little Fuzzy as an honorary member of the board of directors, with the title of Company Benefactor Number One."

•   •   •

LITTLE FUZZY CLIMBED up on Pappy Jack's lap, squirmed a little, and cuddled himself comfortably. He was happy to be back. He had had so much fun in the Big House Place, he and Mamma Fuzzy and Ko-Ko and Cinderella and Syndrome and Id and Ned Kelly and Dr. Crippen and Calamity Jane. They had met so many Fuzzies who had been here and gone away to live with Big Ones of their own, and they had a place where they all met and played together. And he had met the two lovers, now they had names of their own, Pierrot and Columbine, and he had met Diamond, about whom Unka Panko had told him, and Diamond's Pappy Vic.

It had been to meet Diamond that Unka Panko and Auntie Lynne had taken them all in the sky-thing to the Big House Place, because Diamond had found out how to talk like a Big One without using one of the talk-things, and Diamond had taught all of them how to do it. It had been hard, very hard; Diamond was very smart to have found it out for himself, but after a while they had all found that they could do it, too. And now Mike and Mitzi and Complex and Superego and Dillinger and Lizzie Borden had gone to the Big House Place with Pappy Gerd and Mummy Woof, and they would learn to talk so that the Big Ones could hear them. And Baby Fuzzy was learning from Mamma Fuzzy, and tomorrow they would all start teaching the others here at Hoksu-Mitto.

"Pretty soon, all Fuzzy learn to talk like Big Ones," he said. "Not need talk-thing, Big One not need ear-thing; just talk, like I do now."

"That's right," Pappy Jack said. "Big Ones, Fuzzies, all make talk together. All be good friends."

"And Fuzzy learn how to help Big Ones? Many things Fuzzy can do to help, if Big Ones tell what."

"Best thing Fuzzy do to help Big Ones is just be Fuzzies," Pappy Jack told him.

But what else could they be? Fuzzies were what they were, just as Big Ones were Big Ones.

"And beside," Pappy Jack went on talking, "the Fuzzies are all rich, now."

"Rich? What is? Something good?"

"Well, most people think it is. When you're rich, you have money."

"Is something good to eat?" he asked. "Like *esteefee?*"

He wondered why Pappy Jack laughed. Maybe he was just laughing because he was happy. Or maybe Pappy Jack thought it was funny that he didn't know what money was.

There were still so many things Fuzzies had to learn.

FUZZIES
AND OTHER PEOPLE

1

OFFICIALLY, ON ALL the half-thousand human-populated planets of the Terran Federation, the date was September 14, 654 Atomic Era, but on Zarathustra it was First Day, Year Zero, Anno Fuzzy.

It wasn't the day that the Fuzzies were discovered—that had been in early June, when old Jack Holloway had found a small and unfamiliar being crouching in his shower stall at his camp up Cold Creek Valley on Beta Continent. He had made friends with the uninvited visitor and named him Little Fuzzy. A week later, four more Fuzzies and a baby Fuzzy had moved in, and Bennett Rainsford, then a field naturalist for the Institute of Xeno-Sciences, had seen them. They were completely new to him, too. He named the order Hollowayans, in honor of their discoverer, and called the genus Fuzzy and the species Holloway's Fuzzy: *Fuzzy fuzzy holloway.*

Fuzzies were erect bipeds, two feet tall and weighing fifteen to twenty pounds; their bodies were covered with silky golden fur. They had five-fingered hands with opposable thumbs, large eyes set close enough together for stereoscopic vision and vaguely humanoid features. They seemed to know nothing of fire and, as far as Holloway and Rainsford were able to determine, they were incapable of speech. The fact that they spoke in the ultrasonic range was yet to be discovered. They made a few artifacts, however, and their reasoning ability amazed both men. As soon as he saw them, Rainsford insisted that Jack tape an account of them.

Twenty-four hours later, a number of people had heard that tape. One was Victor Grego, manager-in-chief of the Chartered Zarathustra Company. If, as seemed probable, these Fuzzies were sapient beings, Zarathustra automatically became a Class-IV inhabited planet. The Company's charter, conferring outright ownership of Zarathustra as a Class-III uninhabited planet, would be just as automatically void.

Grego's instinct was to fight, and he was a resourceful, resolute and ruthless fighter. He was not stupid, but some of his subordinates were; a week later, everybody on the planet had heard of the Fuzzies because a CZC executive named Leonard Kellogg was facing trial for murder—defined as the unjustified killing of any sapient being of any race whatsoever—for having kicked to death a Fuzzy named Goldilocks. Jack Holloway was similarly charged for having shot a Company gunman who had tried to interfere while he was administering a beating to Kellogg. Both cases, scheduled to be tried as one, would hinge on whether Fuzzies were sapient beings or just cute little animals. On the docket, it was *People of the Colony of Zarathustra* versus *Kellogg and Holloway,* but, beginning with Holloway's lawyer, Gus Brannhard, everybody was calling it *Friends of Little Fuzzy* versus *The Chartered Zarathustra Company.*

Little Fuzzy and his friends won, and when, on September 14, Chief Justice Frederic Pendarvis rapped with his gavel after reading what would go down in Federation legal history as the Pendarvis Decisions, Zarathustra became a Class-IV inhabited planet. The Space Navy had to take over until a new Colonial Government could be set up, and Bennett Rainsford was appointed Governor-General. The Zarathustra Company's charter was as dead as the Code of Hammurabi.

And *Fuzzy fuzzy holloway* was now *Fuzzy sapiens zarathustra.*

2

HE DIDN'T KNOW that anybody called him a Fuzzy. When he and his kind called themselves anything, it was Gashta, "People."

There were animals, of course, but they weren't People. They couldn't talk, and they wouldn't make friends. Some were large and dangerous, like the three-horned *hesh-nazza,* or the night-hunting "screamers," or, worst of all, the *gotza* that soared on wide wings and swooped upon their prey. And some were small and good to eat, and the best of them were the *zatku* that scuttled on many legs among the grass and had to be broken out of their hard shells to get at the sweet white meat. One hunted and killed to eat, and one avoided being killed and eaten, and one tried to have all the fun one could.

Hunting was fun if game was not too scarce and one was not too hungry. And it was fun to outwit something that was hunting one and make a good escape. And it was fun to romp and chase one another through the woods, and to find new things; and it was fun to make a good sleeping-place and huddle together and talk until sleep came. And then, when the sun came back from its sleeping-place, it would be another day, and new and interesting things would happen.

It had always been like that, for as long as he could remember, and that had been a long time. He couldn't count how often the leaves had turned yellow and red and then brown, and fallen from the trees. All those who had been with the band when he was small were gone, killed, or drifted away. Others had joined the band, and now they called him Toshi-Sosso—Wise One, One Who Knows Best—and they all did as he advised. They had begun doing that when Old One had "made dead." Old One had been a female; Little She, who walked beside him now, was her daughter, one of the very few Gashta who had been born alive and lived more than very briefly.

It was Little She who saw the redberry bush even before he did, and cried out in surprise:

"Look, redberries! Not finish yet; good to eat!"

It was late to find redberries; mostly they were brown and hard now, and not good. There would be no more for a long time, until after new-leaf time and bird-nesting time. In the meantime, though, there would be other good-to-eat things; soon, on a tree they all knew, would be big brown nuts, and when the shells were cracked they would be soft and good inside. He looked forward to eating them, but he wondered why all the good-to-eat things couldn't be at the same time. It would be nice if they could, but that was how things had always been.

They crowded around the bush, careful to avoid the sharp thorns, picking berries and popping them into their mouths and spitting out the seeds, laughing and talking about how good they were and how nice it was to find them so late. Some of the younger ones forgot, in their excitement, to keep watch. He rebuked them:

"Keep watch, all time; look around, listen. You not watch, something come, eat you."

Really, there was no danger. None of the animals they had cause to fear was about, and none of them could hear the voices of People. Still, one must never forget to watch. Not remembering was how one made dead.

It wasn't fun, being Wise One. The others expected him to do all the thinking for them. That was not good. Suppose he made dead some time; who would think for them then? After they had eaten all the berries, they stood waiting for him to tell them what to do next.

"What we do now?" he asked them. "Where go?"

They all looked at him, wondering. Finally Other She, who had joined the band between bird-nesting time and groundberry time, before last leaf-turning time, said:

"Hunt for zatku. Maybe find zatku for everybody."

She meant, a whole zatku for each of them. They wouldn't; there weren't that many zatku. The day before yesterday, they had found two, only a few bites apiece. Besides, they would find none here among the rocks. Now was egg-laying time for zatku; they would all be where the ground was soft, to dig holes to lay their eggs. But they might find *hatta-zosa* here. He had seen young trees with the bark gnawed off. Hatta-zosa were good to eat, and if they killed two or three of them, it would be meat enough that nobody would be hungry.

Besides, killing hatta-zosa was fun. They were nearly as big as People, with strong jaws and sharp teeth, and when cornered they fought savagely. It was hard to kill them, and doing hard things was fun. He suggested hunting hatta-zosa, and they all agreed at once.

"Hatta-zosa stay among rocks." That was the young male they called Fruitfinder. "Rocks more at top of hill."

"Find moving-water," Big She offered. "Follow to where it come out of ground."

"Look for where hatta-zosa chew bark off trees."

That was Lame One. He was not really lame, but he had once hurt his leg and limped for a while, and after that they all called him Lame One because nobody could think of anything else to call him.

They started, line-abreast, each keeping sight of those on either side. They hunted as they went, not very seriously, for they had just eaten the berries and if they found hatta-zosa there would be much meat for everybody. Once, Wise One stopped at a rotting log and dug in it with the pointed end of his killing-club, and found a toothsome white grub. Once or twice he heard somebody chasing one of the little yellow lizards. Finally they came to a small stream and stopped, taking turns drinking and watching. They followed it up to the spring where it came out of the ground.

This would be a good place to come back to if anything chased them. Trees grew close to it, with sharp branches; a gotza could not dive through them. He spoke of this, and the others agreed. And through the trees above, he could see a cliff of yellow rock. Hatta-zosa liked such places. The others hung back to let him lead, and followed in single file. Now and then one would point to a tree at which the hatta-zosa had been chewing. Then they came to the edge of the brush, to a stretch of open grass at the foot of the cliff.

There were seven hatta-zosa there, gray beasts as high at the shoulder as a person's waist, all gnawing at trees. They wouldn't be able to kill all of them, but if they killed three or four they would have all the meat they could eat. By this time, everybody had picked up stones and carried them nested in the crooks of their elbows. He touched Lame One with the knob of his killing-club.

"You," he said. "Stonebreaker. Other She. Go back in brush, come around other side. We wait here. Chase hatta-zosa to us, kill all you can."

Lame One nodded. He and his companions slipped away noiselessly. For a long time, Wise One and the others waited, and then he heard the voice of Lame One, which the hatta-zosa could not hear: "Watch, now. We come."

He had a stone in his free hand, ready to throw, when Lame One and Stonebreaker and Other She burst from the brush, hurling stones. Other She's stone knocked down a hatta-zosa and she brained it with her club. A stone he himself threw dazed another; he threw his other stone, missing, and then ran in, swinging his club. There were shouts all around him and a blur of fast-moving golden-furred bodies. Then it was all over; they had killed four, and three had gotten away. The others wanted to give chase.

"No. We have meat, we eat," he said. "Then we go away, hatta-zosa come back. Next light-time after dark-time, we come back, kill more."

The others hadn't thought that far ahead. That was why they were willing to let Wise One think for them. They all looked around for stones to break to cut up the hatta-zosa, but the stones here were all soft. They would have to use their teeth and fingers. They helped each other, one standing on the neck of a hatta-zosa while two pulled it apart by the hind legs; they used stones as hammers to break the bones.

At first, they ate greedily, for it had been sun-highest time the day before since they had tasted red meat. Then, their hunger satisfied, they ate more slowly, talking about the killing, boasting of what they had done. He found the flat brown thing that was so good, ate half of it, and gave the other half to Little She; the others were also finding and sharing this tidbit.

It was then that he heard the sound of fear, more a rapid vibration in his head than a real noise. The others also heard it, and stopped eating.

"Gotza come," he said. "Two gotza."

They all looked quickly above them, and then began tearing loose meat and cramming their mouths. They would not have long to enjoy this feast. He put up a hand to keep the sun from his eyes, and saw a gotza approaching—the thin body between the wide pointed wings, the pointed head in front, the long tail. It was closer than he liked, and he was sure it had seen them. There was another behind it and, farther away, a third. This was bad.

They all snatched their killing-clubs and the big hind legs of the hatta-zosa which they had saved for last in case they might have to run. The first gotza was turning to dive upon them and they were about to dash under the trees when the terrible thing happened.

From the top of the cliff above them came a noise, loud as thunder, but short and hard; he had never heard a noise like that before. The nearest gotza thrashed its wings and then fell, straight down. There was a second noise like the first, but sharper and less loud; the next gotza also fell, into a tree, crashing down through the branches. A third noise, exactly like the first, and the third gotza dropped into the woods. Then was silence.

"Gotza make dead!" somebody cried. "What make do?"

"Thunder-noise kill gotza; maybe kill us next."

"Bad place this," Lame One was clamoring. "Make run fast."

They fled, carrying all they could of the meat, back to the spring. Everything was silent now, except for fright-cries of birds, also disturbed by the loud noises. Finally they were still, and there was nothing but the buzzing of insects. The People began to eat. After a while, there was a new sound, shrill but not unpleasant. It seemed to move about, and then grew fainter and went away. The birds began chirping calmly again.

The People argued while they ate. None of them knew what had really happened, and most of them wanted to go as far from this place as they could. Maybe they were right, but Wise One wanted to know more about what had happened.

"A new thing has come," he told them. "Nobody has ever told of a thing like this before. It is a thing that kills gotza. If it only kills gotza, it is good. If it kills People too, it is bad. We not know. Better we know now, then we can take care." He finished gnawing the meat from the leg-bone and threw it aside, then washed his hands, dried them on grass, and picked up his club. "Come. We go back. Maybe we learn something."

The others were afraid, but he was Wise One, One Who Knows Best. If he thought they should go back, that was the thing to do. Sometimes it was good for one to do the thinking for the others. It saved argument, and things got done.

At the foot of the cliff, one gotza lay on the open grass, and feekee-birds had begun to peck at it. That was good; feekee-birds never pecked at anything that had life. They flew away, scolding, as he and the others approached.

There was a small bleeding hole under one of the gotza's wings, as though a sharp stick had been stabbed into it, though he could not see how anything could go through the tough scaly hide. Then he looked at the other side, and gave a cry of astonishment that brought all the others running. Whatever had stabbed the gotza had gone clear through, tearing out a great gaping wound. Maybe it had been thunder that had killed the gotza, though the sky had been blue; he had seen what thunder flashes did when they struck trees. He looked at the other gotza, the one that had fallen through the boughs of the tree. There was a hole under its chin, and the whole top of the head was gone, the skull shattered. He thought of going to look for the third gotza, which had fallen in the woods, but decided not to bother. The others were exchanging shocked comments. Nobody had ever heard of anything being killed like this.

At first, he could persuade none of the others to climb to the top of the cliff, and so started up alone. Before he had reached the top, however, they were all following, ashamed to stay below. There were no trees at the top, only scattered bushes and sparse grass and sandy ground. Everything was still and, until he found the footprints, quite ordinary.

They resembled no footprints any of them had ever seen or heard of; they were a little like the footprints of People, and whatever had made them had walked on two feet. But there were no toe-prints, only a flat sole that widened at the middle and tapered to a rounded end, and a heel-mark that looked like the backward print of some kind of hoof. And they were huge, three times as big as the footprints of People. Whatever had made them had walked with a stride longer than a person's height. There were two sets, only slightly different in size and shape.

He wondered for a moment if they might not have been made by some kind of giant People. No, that couldn't be; People were People, and there were no other kind. At least, nobody had ever told about giant People. But then, nobody had ever told about something that killed flying gotza with noises like thunder, either.

Something immense and heavy had rested on the cliff top not long ago; it had broken bushes and flattened grass, and even crushed some stones. The strange footprints were all around where it had been. Those who had made the strange footprints must have brought this huge and heavy thing with them, and taken it away again. That meant that they must be very strong indeed.

And it meant that they must be People of some kind. Only People carried things about with them. One of the males, the one they called Stabber because he liked to use the pointed end of his killing-club instead of the knob, thought of that too.

"Bring big thing here; take away. We look for tracks, see which way go. Then we go other way."

Stabber didn't wait for Wise One to do all the thinking. He would remember that, teach Stabber all he knew. Then, if he died, Stabber could lead the band. They started away from where the heavy thing had been, to the edge of the cliff. It was there that Little She found the first of the bright-things.

She cried out and picked it up, holding it out to show. She should not have done that; she did not know what it was. But as it had not hurt her, Wise One took it to look at it. It was not alive, and he did not think it had ever been, though he could not be sure. There were live-things, things that moved, like People and animals, and live-things that had "made dead." Then there were growing-things, like trees and grass and fruit and flowers; and there were ground-things, stones and rocks and sand and things like that. Usually, one could tell which was which, but not this thing.

It was yellow and bright, and glistened in the sunlight—straight, round through, and a little longer than his hand, open at one end and closed at the other. Near the open end it narrowed abruptly and then became straight again. There was a groove all around the closed end, and in the middle of the closed end was a spot, whitish instead of yellow and dented as though something small and sharp had hit it very hard. Around this spot were odd markings. He sniffed at the open end; it had a sharp, bitter smell, utterly strange.

A moment later Stonebreaker found another, a little smaller and more tapered from the closed end to the shoulder. Then he found a third, exactly like the one Little She had found.

Three thunder-noises, one less loud than the others. Three bright-things, one smaller than the others. And two kinds of bright-things, and two sets of big footprints. That might mean something. He would think about it. They found tracks all around where the heavy thing had been, and also to and from the edge of the cliff, but none going away in any direction.

"Maybe fly," Stabber said. "Like bird, like gotza."

"And carry great heavy thing?" Big She asked incredulously.

"How else?" Stabber insisted. "Come here, go away. Not make tracks on ground, then fly in air."

There was a gotza circling far away; Wise One pointed to it. Soon there would be many gotza, come to feed on the three that had been killed. Gotza ate their own dead; that was another reason why People loathed gotza. Better leave now. Soon the gotza would be close enough to see them. He could hear its wing-sounds very faintly.

Wing-sounds! That was what they had heard at the spring; the shrill, wavering sound had been the wing-sound of the flying Big Ones.

"Yes," he said. "They flew. We heard them."

He looked again at the bright-thing in his hand, comparing it with the other two. Little She was saying:

"Bright-things pretty. We keep?"

"Yes," he told her. "We keep."

Then Wise One looked at the markings on the closed end of the one in his hand. All sorts of things had markings—fruit and stones, and the wings of insects, and the shells of zatku. It was fun to find something with odd markings, and then talk about what they looked like. But nobody ever found anything that was marked:

He didn't wonder what the markings meant. Markings never meant anything. They just happened.

3

JACK HOLLOWAY SIGNED the paper—authorization for promotion of trooper Felix Krajewski, Zarathustra Native Protection Force, to rank of corporal—and tossed it into the OUT tray. A small breeze, pleasantly cool, came in at the open end of the prefab hut, bringing with it from outside the noises of construction work to compete with the whir and clatter of computers and roboclerks in the main office beyond the partition. He laid down the pen, brushed his mustache with the middle knuckle of his trigger finger, and then picked up his pipe, relighting it. Then he took another paper out of the IN tray.

Authorization for payment of five hundred and fifty sols, compensation for damage done to crops by Fuzzies; endorsed as investigated and approved by George Lunt, Major Commanding, ZNPF. He remembered the incident: a bunch of woods-Fuzzies who had slipped through George's chain of posts at the south edge of the Piedmont and gotten onto a sugar plantation and into mischief. Probably ruined one tenth as many sugar-plant seedlings as the land-prawns which the Fuzzies killed there would have destroyed. But the Government wasn't responsible for land-prawns, and it was responsible for Fuzzies, and any planter who wouldn't stick the Government for all the damages he could ought to be stuffed and put in a museum as a unique specimen. He signed it and reached for the next paper.

It was a big one, a lot of sheets stapled together. He pried out the staple. Covering letter from Governor-General Bennett Rainsford, attention Commissioner of Native Affairs; and then another on the letterhead of the Charterless Zarathustra Company, Ltd., of Zarathustra, signed by Victor Grego, Pres. He grinned. That "Charterless" looked like typical Grego gallows humor; it also made sense, since it kept the old initials for the trademark. And for the cattle-brand. Anybody who'd ever tried rebranding a full-grown veldbeest could see the advantage of that.

Acknowledgment of eighteen sunstones, total weight 93.6 carats, removed from Yellowsand Canyon for study prior to signing of lease agreement. Copy of receipt signed by Grego and his chief geologist, endorsed by Gerd van Riebeek, Chief of Scientific Branch, Zarathustra Commission for Native Affairs, and by Lieutenant Hirohito Bjornsen, ZNPF. Color photographs of each of the eighteen stones: they were beautiful, but no photograph could do justice to a warm sunstone, glowing with thermofluorescence. He looked at them carefully. He was an old sunstone-digger himself, and knew what he was looking at. One hundred seventeen thousand sols on the Terra gem market; S-42,120 in royalties for the Government, in trust for the Fuzzies. And this wasn't even the front edge of the beginning; these were just the prospect samples. This time next year . . .

He initialed Ben Rainsford's letter, stapled the stuff together, and tossed it into the FILE tray. As he did, the communication screen beside him buzzed. Turning in his chair, he flipped the screen on and looked, through it, into the interior of another prefab hut like this one, fifteen hundred miles to the north on the Fuzzy Reservation. A young man, with light hair and a pleasantly tough and weather-beaten face, looked out of it. He was in woodsclothes, the breast of his jacket loaded with clips of rifle cartridges.

"Hi, Gerd. What's new?"

Gerd van Riebeek shrugged. "Still sitting on top of 'steen billion sols' worth of sunstones. Victor Grego was up; you heard about that?"

"Yes. I was looking at the photos of those stones a moment ago. How much flint did he have to crack to get them?"

"About seventy-five tons. He took them out from five different locations, on both sides of the canyon. Took him about eight hours, after he got the sandstone off."

"That's better than I ever did; I thought I'd hit it rich when I got one good stone out of six tons of flint. We can tell the Fuzzies they're all rich now."

"They'll want to know if it's good to eat," Gerd said.

They probably would. He asked if Gerd had been seeing many Fuzzies.

"South of the Divide, yes, quite a few in small bands, mostly headed south or southwest. We get more on the movie film than we actually see. North of the Divide, hardly any. Oh, you remember the band we saw the day we found the sunstone flint? The ones who'd killed those goofers and were eating them?"

Holloway laughed, remembering their consternation when the three harpies had put in an appearance and been knocked down by his and Gerd's rifle fire.

"'Thunder-noise kill gotza; maybe kill us next,'" he quoted. "'Bad place this, make run fast.' Man, were they a scared lot of Fuzzies."

"They didn't stay scared long; they were back as soon as we were out of there," Gerd told him. "I was up that way this morning and recognized the place; I set down for a look around. The dead harpies were pretty well cleaned up—other harpies and what have you—just a few bones scattered around. I was up on top, where we'd been. It was three weeks ago, and it'd rained a few times since; so, no tracks. I could hardly see where we'd set the aircar down. But I know the Fuzzies were there from what I didn't find."

Gerd paused, grinning. Expecting Holloway to ask what.

"The empties, two from my 9.7 and one from your Sterberg," Holloway said. "Sure. Pretty-things." He laughed again. Fuzzies always picked up empty brass. "You find some Fuzzies with empty cartridges, you'll know who they are."

"Oh, they won't keep them. They've gotten tired of them and dropped them long ago."

They talked for a while, and finally Gerd broke the connection, probably to call Ruth. Holloway went back to his paperwork. The afternoon passed, and eventually he finished everything they had piled up on him. He rose stiffly. Wasn't used to this damned sitting on a chair all day. He refilled and lighted his pipe, got his hat, and looked for the pistol that should be hanging under it before he remembered that he wasn't bothering to wear it around the camp anymore. Then, after a glance around to make sure he hadn't left anything a Fuzzy oughtn't to get at, he went out.

They'd built all the walls of the permanent office that was to replace this hut, and they'd started on the roof. The ZNPF barracks and headquarters were finished and occupied; in front of the latter a number of contragravity vehicles were grounded: patrol cars and combat cars. Some of the former were new, light green with yellow trim, lettered ZNPF. Some of the latter were olive green; they and the men who operated them had been borrowed from the Space Marines. Across the little stream, he couldn't see his original camp buildings for the new construction that had gone up in the past two and a half months; the whole place, marked with a tiny dot on the larger maps as Holloway's Camp, had been changed beyond recognition.

Maybe the name ought to be changed, too. Call it Hoksu-Mitto—that was what the Fuzzies called it—"Wonderful Place." Well, it *was* pretty wonderful, to a Fuzzy just out of the big woods; and even those who went on to Mallorysport, a much more wonderful place, to live with human families still called it that, and looked back on it with the nostalgic affection of an old grad for his alma mater. He'd talked to Ben Rainsford about getting the name officially changed.

Half a dozen Fuzzies were playing on the bridge; they saw him and ran to him, yeeking. They all wore zipper-closed shoulder bags, with sheath-knives and little trowels attached, and silver identity disks at their throats, and they carried the weapons that had been issued to them to replace their wooden prawn-killers—six-inch steel blades on twelve-inch steel shafts. They were newcomers, hadn't had their vocal training yet; he put in the earplug and switched on the hearing aid he had to use less and less frequently now, and they were all yelling:

"Pappy Jack! Heyo, Pappy Jack. You make play with us?"

They'd been around long enough to learn that he was Pappy Jack to every Fuzzy in the place, which as of the noon count stood at three hundred sixty-two, and they all thought he had nothing to do but "make play" with them. He squatted down, looking at their ID-disks; all numbered in the twelve-twenties, which meant they'd come in day before yesterday.

"Why aren't you kids in school?" he asked, grabbing one who was trying to work the zipper of his shirt.

"*Skool*? What is, *skool*?"

"School," he told them, "is place where Fuzzies learn new things. Learn to make talk like Big Ones, so Big Ones not need put-in-ear things. Learn to make things, have fun. Learn not get hurt by Big One things." He pointed to a long corrugated metal shed across the run. "School in that place. Come; I show."

He knew what had happened. This gang had met some Fuzzy in the woods who had told them about Hoksu-Mitto, and they'd come to get in on it. They'd been taken in tow by Little Fuzzy or Ko-Ko or one of George Lunt's or Gerd and Ruth van Riebeek's Fuzzies, and brought to ZNPF headquarters to be finger-printed and given ID-disks and issued equipment, and then told to go amuse themselves. He started across the bridge, the Fuzzies running beside and ahead of him.

The interior of the long shed was cool and shady, but not quiet. There were about two hundred Fuzzies, all talking at once; when he switched off his hearing aid, most of it was the yeek-yeeking which was the audible fringe sound of their ultrasonic voices. Two of George Lunt's family, named Dillinger and Ned Kelly, were teaching a class—most of whom had already learned to pitch their voices to human audibility—how to make bows and arrows. Considering that they'd only become bowyers and fletchers themselves a month ago, they were doing very well, and the class was picking it up quickly and enthusiastically. His own Mike and Mitzi were giving a class in fire-making, sawing a length of hard wood back and forth across the grain of a softer log. They had a score or so of pupils, all whooping excitedly as the wood-dust began to smoke. Another crowd stood or squatted around a ZNPF corporal who was using a jackknife to skin a small animal Terrans called a zarabunny. Like any good cop, he was continuously aware of everything that went on around him. He looked up.

"Hi, Jack. Soon as that crowd over there have a fire going, I'll show them how to broil this on a stick. Then I'll show them how to use the brains to cure the skin, the way the Old Terran Indians did, and how to make a bowstring out of the gut."

And then, after they'd learned all this stuff, they'd go in to Mallorysport to be adopted by some human family and never use any of it. Well, maybe not. There were a lot of Fuzzies—ten, maybe twenty thousand of them. In spite of what Little Fuzzy was telling everybody about all the Fuzzies having Big Ones of their own, it wouldn't work out that way. There just weren't enough humans who wanted to adopt Fuzzies. So some of this gang would go to the ZNPF posts to the south or along the edge of Big Blackwater to the west, and teach other Fuzzies who'd pass the instruction on. Bows and arrows, fire, cooked food, cured hides. Basketry and pottery, too. Seeing this gang here, it was hard to realize just how primitively woods-Fuzzies had lived. Hadn't even learned to make anything like these shoulder bags to carry things in; had to keep moving all the time, too, hunting and foraging.

Fuzzy sapiens zarathustra—he was glad they'd gotten rid of the *Fuzzy fuzzy holloway* thing; people were beginning to call *him* Fuzzy-Fuzzy—had made one hell of a cultural jump since the evening he'd heard something say, "Yeek," in his shower stall.

Little Fuzzy, across the shed, saw him and waved, and he waved back. Little Fuzzy had a class too, on how to behave among the Big Ones. For a while, he talked with Corporal Carstairs and his pupils. The crowd he'd brought in with him wanted to stay there; he managed to get them away and over to where his own Ko-Ko and Cinderella and the van Riebeeks' Syndrome and Superego were giving vocal lessons.

It had been the Navy people, temporarily sheltering his own family on Xerxes before the Fuzzy trial, who had found out about their ultrasonic voices and made special hearing aids. After the trial, when Victor Grego, once the Fuzzies' archenemy, acquired a Fuzzy of his own and became one of their best friends, he and Henry Stenson, the instrument maker, designed a small self-powered hand-phone Fuzzies could use to transform their voices to audible frequencies. Then Grego discovered that his own Fuzzy, Diamond, was speaking audibly with the power-unit of his Fuzzyphone dead; he had learned to imitate the sounds he had heard himself making. Diamond was able to teach the trick; now his pupils were teaching others.

This class had several of the Stenson-Grego Fuzzyphones, things with Fuzzy-size pistol grips and grip switches. They were speaking with them, and then releasing the switches and trying to make the same sounds themselves. Ko-Ko seemed to be in charge of the instruction.

"No, no!" he was saying. "Not like that. Make talk away back in mouth, like this."

"Yeek?"

"No. Do again with hold-in-hand thing. Hold tight, now; make talk."

The van Riebeeks' Syndrome didn't seem to be doing anything in particular; Holloway spoke to her:

"You make talk to these. Tell about how learn to make talk like Big Ones." He turned to the Fuzzies who had come in with him. "You stay here. Do what these tell you. Soon you make talk like Big Ones too. Then you come to Pappy Jack, make talk; Pappy Jack give something nice."

He left them with Syndrome and went over to where Little Fuzzy sat on a box, smoking his pipe just like Pappy Jack. A number of the Fuzzies around him, one of the advanced classes, were also smoking.

"Among Big Ones," he was saying in a mixture of Fuzzy language and Lingua Terra, "everything belong somebody. Every place belong somebody. Nobody go on somebody-else place, take things belong somebody else."

"No place belong everybody, like woods?" a pupil asked.

"Oh, yes. Some places. Big Ones have Gov'men' to take care of places belong everybody. This place, Hoksu-Mitto, Gov'men' place. Once belong Pappy Jack; Pappy Jack give to Gov'men', for everybody, all Big Ones, all Fuzzies."

"But, Gov'men'; what is?"

"Big-One thing. All Big Ones talk together, all pick some for take care of things belong everybody. Gov'men' not let anybody take somebody-else things, not let anybody make anybody dead, not let hurt anybody. Now, Gov'men' say nobody hurt Fuzzy, make Fuzzy dead, take Fuzzy things. Do this in Big-Room Talk-Place. I saw. Bad Big One make Goldilocks dead; other Big Ones take bad Big One away, make him dead. Then, all say, nobody hurt Fuzzy anymore. Pappy Jack make them do this."

That wasn't exactly what had happened. For instance, Leonard Kellogg had cut his throat in jail, but suicide while of unsound mind was a little complicated to explain to a Fuzzy. Just let it go at that. He strolled on, to where some of George Lunt's family, Dr. Crippen and Lizzie Borden and Calamity Jane, were teaching carpentry, and stayed for a while, watching the Fuzzies using scaled-down saws and augers and drawknives and planes. This crowd was really interested; they'd go out for food after a while and then come back and work far into the evening. They were building a hand-wagon, even the wheels; nearby was a small forge, now cold, and an anvil on which they had made the ironwork.

Finally, he reached the end of the hut where Ruth van Riebeek and Pancho Ybarra, the Navy psychologist on permanent loan to the Colonial Government, sat respectively on a pile of cushions on the floor and the edge of a table. They had a dozen Fuzzies around them.

"Hi, Jack," Ruth greeted him. "When's that husband of mine coming back?"

"Oh, as soon as the agreement's signed and the CZC takes over. How are the kids doing?"

"Oh, we aren't kids anymore, Pappy Jack," Ybarra told him. "We are very grown up. We are graduates, and next week we will be faculty members."

Holloway sat down on the cushions with Ruth, and the Fuzzies crowded around him, wanting puffs from his pipe, and telling him what they had learned and what they were going to teach. Then, by pairs and groups, they drifted away. There was a general breaking-up. The vocal class was dispersing; Syndrome was going away with her group. If she could get them back tomorrow. . . . What this school needed was a truant officer. The fire-making class had gotten a blaze started on the earthen floor, and the butchering-and-cooking class had joined them. The apprentice bowyers and fletchers had already left. Carpentry was still going strong.

"You know, this teaching program," Ruth was saying, "it seems to lack unity."

"She thinks there is a teaching program," Ybarra laughed. "This is still in the trial-and-error—mostly error—stage. After we learn what we have to teach, and how to do it, we can start talking about programs." He became more serious. "Jack, I'm beginning to question the value of a lot of this friction-fire-making, stone-arrowhead, bone-needle stuff. I know they won't all be adopted into human families and most of them will have to live on their own in the woods or in marginal land around settlements, but they'll be in contact with us and can get all the human-made tools and weapons and things they need."

"I don't want that, Pancho. I don't want them made dependent on us. I don't want them to live on human handouts. You were on Loki, weren't you? You know what's happened to the natives there; they've turned into alot of worthless Native Agency bums. I don't want this to happen to the Fuzzies."

"That's not quite the same, Jack," Ybarra said. "The Fuzzies *are* dependent on us, for hokfusine. They can't get enough of it for themselves."

That was true, of course. The Fuzzies' ancestors had developed, by evolution, an endocrine gland secreting a hormone nonexistent in any other Zarathustran mammal. Nobody was quite sure why; an educated guess was that it had served to neutralize some natural poison in something they had eaten in the distant past. When discovered, a couple of months ago, this hormone had been tagged with a polysyllabic biochemistry name that had been shortened to NFMp.

But about the time Terran humans were starting civilizations in the Nile and Euphrates valleys, the Fuzzies' environment had altered radically. The need for NFMp vanished and, unneeded, it turned destructive. It caused premature and defective, nonviable, births. As a race, the Fuzzies had started dying out. Today, there was only this small remnant left, in the northern wilds of Beta Continent.

The only thing that had saved them from complete extinction had been another biochemical, a complicated long-molecule compound containing, among other things, a few atoms of titanium, which they still obtained by eating land-prawns—zatku, as they called them. And, beginning with their first contacts with humans, they had also gotten it from a gingerbread-colored concoction officially designated Terran Federation Armed Forces Emergency Ration, Extraterrestrial Type Three. Like most synthetic rations, it was loathed by the soldiers and spacemen to whom it was issued, but after the first nibble Fuzzies doted on it. They called it Hoksu-Fusso, "Wonderful Food." The chemical discovered in it, and in land-prawns, had been immediately named hokfusine.

"It neutralizes NFMp, and it inhibits the glandular action that produces it," Ybarra was saying. "But we can't administer it environmentally; we have to supply it to every individual Fuzzy, male and female. Viable births only occur when both parents have gotten plenty of it prior to conception."

The Fuzzies who lived among humans would get plenty of it, but the ones who tried to shift for themselves in the woods wouldn't. The very thing he wanted to avoid, dependence on humans, would be selected for genetically, just as a taste for land-prawns had been. The countdown for the Fuzzy race had been going on for a thousand generations, ten little Fuzzies, nine little Fuzzies, eight little Fuzzies. He didn't know how many more generations until it would be no little Fuzzies if they didn't do something now.

"Don't worry about the next generation, Jack," Ruth said. "Just be glad there'll be one."

4

LESLIE COOMBES LAID his cigarette in the ashtray and picked up his cocktail, sipping slowly. As he did so, he gave an irrationally apprehensive glance at the big globe of the planet floating off the floor on its own contragravity, spotlighted by a simulated sun and rotating slowly, its two satellites, Xerxes and Darius, orbiting about it. Darius still belonged outright to the Company, even after the Pendarvis Decisions. Xerxes never had; it had been reserved by the Federation as a naval base when the old Company had been chartered. The evening shadow-line had just touched the east coast of Alpha Continent and was approaching the spot that represented Mallorysport.

Victor Grego caught the involuntary glance and laughed.

"Still nervous about it, Leslie? It's had its teeth pulled."

Yes, after it had been too late, after the Fuzzy Trial, when they had realized that every word spoken in Grego's private office had been known to Naval Intelligence, and that Henry Stenson, who had built it, had been a Federation undercover agent. There had been a microphone and a midget radio transmitter inside. Stenson had planted a similar set in a bartending robot at the Residency, which was why the former Resident General, Nick Emmert, was now aboard a destroyer bound for Terra, to face malfeasance charges. Coombes wondered how many more of those things Stenson had strewn about Mallorysport; he'd almost dismantled his own apartment looking in vain for one, and he still wasn't sure.

"It wouldn't matter, anyhow," Grego continued. "We're all friends now. Aren't we, Diamond?"

The Fuzzy on Grego's chair-arm snuggled closer to him, pleased at being included in the Big One conversation.

"Tha's ri'; everybody friend. Pappy Vic, Pappy Jack, Unka Less'ee, Unka Gus, Pappy Ben, Flora, Fauna . . ." He went on naming all the people, Fuzzies and Big Ones, who were friends. It was a surprising list; only a few months ago nobody but a lunatic would have called Jack Holloway and Bennett Rainsford and Gus Brannhard friends of his and Victor Grego's. "Everybody friend now. Everything nice."

"Everything nice," Coombes agreed. "For the time being, at least. Victor, you're getting Fuzzy-fuzz all over your coat."

"Who cares? It's my coat, and it's my Fuzzy, and besides, I don't think he's shedding now."

"And all bad Big Ones gone to jail-place," Diamond said. "Not make trouble, anymore. What is like, jail-place? Is like dark dirty place where bad Big Ones put Fuzzies?"

"Something like that," Grego told the Fuzzy.

The trouble was, they hadn't put all the bad Big Ones in jail. They hadn't been able to prove anything against Hugo Ingermann, and that left a bad taste in his mouth. And it reminded him of something.

"Did you find the rest of those sunstones, Victor?"

Grego shook his head. "No. At first I thought the Fuzzies must have lost them in the ventilation system, but we put robo-snoopers through all the ducts and didn't find anything. Then Harry Steefer thought some of his cops had held out on him, but we questioned everybody under veridication and nobody knew anything. I don't know where in Nifflheim they are."

"A quarter-million sols isn't exactly sparrow-fodder, Victor."

"Almost. Wait till we get enough men and equipment in at Yellowsand Canyon; we'll be taking out twice that in a day. My God, Leslie; you ought to see that place! It's fantastic."

"All I'd see would be a lot of rock. I'll take your word for it."

"There's this layer of sunstone flint, averaging two hundred feet thick, all along the face of the Divide for eight and a half miles west of the canyon and better than ten miles east of it; it runs back four miles before it tapers out. Of course, there's a couple of hundred feet of sandstone on top of it that'll have to be stripped off, but we'll just shove that down into the canyon. It won't, really, be as much of a job as draining Big Blackwater was. Are the agreements ready to sign?"

"Yes. The general agreement obligates the Company to continue all the services performed by the old chartered company; in return, the Government agrees to lease us all the unseated public lands declared public domain by the

Pendarvis Decisions, except the area north of the Little Blackwater and the north branch of the Snake River, the Fuzzy Reservation. The special agreement gives us a lease on the tract around the Yellowsand Canyon; we pay four-fifty sols for every carat weight of thermofluorescent sunstones we take out, the money to be administered for the Fuzzies by the Government. Both agreements for nine hundred and ninety-nine years."

"Or until adjudged invalid by the court."

"Oh, yes; I got that inserted everywhere I could stick it. The only thing I'm worried about now is how much trouble the Terra-side stock-holders of the late Chartered Zarathustra Company may give us."

"Well, they have an equity of some sort, as individuals," Grego admitted. "But there simply is no Chartered Zarathustra Company."

"I can't be positive. The Chartered Loki Company was dissolved by court order, for violation of Federation law. The stockholders lost completely. The Chartered Uller Company was taken over by the Government after the Uprising, in 526; the Government simply confirmed General von Schlichten as governor-general and payed off the stockholders at face value. And when the Chartered Fenris Company went bankrupt, the planet was taken over by some of the colonists, and the stockholders, I believe, were paid two and a quarter centisols on the sol. Those are the only precedents, and none of them applies here." He drank some more of his cocktail. "I shall have to go to Terra myself to represent the new Charterless Zarathustra Company, Ltd., of Zarathustra."

"I'll hate to see you go."

"Thank you, Victor. I'm not looking forward to it, myself." Six months aboard ship would be almost as bad as a jail sentence. And then at least a year on Terra, getting things straightened out and engaging a law firm in Kapstaad or Johannesburg to handle the long litigation that would ensue. "I hope to be back in a couple of years. I doubt if I shall enjoy reaccustoming myself to life on our dear mother planet." He finished what was in his glass and held it up. "May I have another cocktail, Victor?"

"Why, surely." Grego finished his own drink. "Diamond, you please go give Unka Less'ee koktel-drinko. Bring koktel-drinko for Pappy Vic, too."

"Hokay."

Diamond jumped down from the chair-arm and ran to get the cocktail jug. Leaning forward, Coombes held his glass down where Diamond could reach it; the Fuzzy filled it to the brim without spilling a drop.

"Thank you, Diamond."

"Welcome, Unka Less'ee," Diamond replied just as politely, and carried the jug to fill Pappy Vic's glass.

He didn't pour a drink for himself. He'd had a drink, once, and had never forgotten the hangover it gave him; he didn't want another like it. Maybe that was one of the things Ernst Mallin meant when he said Fuzzies were saner than Humans.

GUSTAVUS ADOLPHUS BRANNHARD puffed contentedly on his cigar. Behind him, a couple of things more or less like birds twittered among the branches of a tree. In front, the towering buildings of Mallorysport were black against a riot of sunset red and gold and orange. From across the lawn came sounds of Fuzzies—Ben Rainsford's Flora and Fauna and a couple of their visitors—at play. Ben Rainsford, an elfish little man with a bald head and a straggly red beard, sat hunched forward in his chair, staring into a highball he held in both hands.

"But, Gus," he was protesting. "Don't you think Victor Grego can be trusted?"

That was a *volte-face* for Ben. A couple of months ago he'd been positive that there was no infamous treachery too black for Grego.

"Sure I do." Gus shifted the cigar to his left hand and picked up his own drink, an old-fashioned glass full of straight whiskey. "You just have to watch him a little, that's all." A few drops of whiskey dribbled into his beard; he blotted them with the back of his hand and put the cigar back into his mouth. "Why?"

"Well, all this 'until adjudged invalid by the court' stuff in the agreements. You think he's fixing booby traps for us?"

"No. I know what he's doing. He's fixing to bluff the Terra-side stockholders of the old Chartered Company. Make them think he'll break the agreements and negotiate new ones for himself if they don't go along with him. He wants to keep control of the new Company himself."

"Well, I'm with him on that!" Rainsford said vehemently. "Monopoly or no monopoly, I want the Company run on Zarathustra, for the benefit of Zarathustra. But then, why do you want to hold off on signing the agreements?"

"Just till after the election, Ben. We want our delegates elected, and we want our Colonial Constitution adopted. Once we do that, we won't have any trouble electing the kind of a legislature we want. But there's going to be opposition to this public-land deal. A lot of people have been expecting to get rich staking claims to the land the Pendarvis Decisions put in public domain, and now it's being all leased back to the CZC for a thousand years, and that's longer than any of them want to wait."

"Gus, a lot more people, and a lot more influential people, are going to be glad the Government won't have to start levying taxes," Rainsford replied.

Ben had a point there. There'd never been any kind of taxation on Zarathustra; the Company had footed all the bills for everything. And now there wouldn't be need for any in the future, not even for the new Native Commission. The Fuzzies would be paying their own way, from sunstone royalties.

"And the would-be land-grabbers aren't organized, and we are," Rainsford went on. "The only organized opposition we ever had was from this People's Prosperity Party of Hugo Ingermann's, and now Ingermann's a dead duck."

That was overoptimism, a vice to which Ben wasn't ordinarily addicted.

"Ben, any time you think Hugo Ingermann's dead, you want to shoot him again. He's just playing possum."

"I wish we could have him shot for real, along with the rest of them."

"Well, he wasn't guilty along with the rest of them, that's why we couldn't. It's probably the only thing in his life he hasn't been guilty of, but he didn't know anything about that job till they hauled him in and began interrogating him. Why, Nifflheim, we couldn't even get him disbarred!"

He and Leslie Coombes had tried hard enough, but the Bar Association was made up of lawyers, and lawyers are precedent-minded. Most of them had crooked clients themselves, and most of them had cut corners representing them. They didn't want Ingermann's disbarment used as a precedent against them.

"And now he's defending Thaxter and the Evinses and Novaes," Rainsford said. "He'll get them off, too; you watch if he doesn't."

"Not while I'm Chief Prosecutor!"

He shifted his cigar again, and had a drink on that. He wished he felt as confident as he'd sounded.

THE DEPUTY-MARSHAL UNLOCKED the door and stood aside for Hugo Ingermann to enter, looking at him as though he'd crawled from under a flat stone. Everybody was looking at him that way around Central Courts now. He smiled sweetly.

"Thank you, deputy," he said.

"Don't bother, I get paid for it," the uniformed deputy said. "All I hope is they draw my name out of the hat when they take your clients out in the jail-yard. Too bad you won't be going along with them. I'd pay for the privilege of shooting you."

And if he complained to the Colonial Marshal, Max Fane would say, "Hell, so would I."

The steel-walled room was small and bare, its only furnishings a table welded to the steel floor and half a dozen straight chairs. It reeked of disinfectant, like the rest of the jail. He got out his cigarettes and lit one, then laid the box and the lighter on the table and looked quickly about. He couldn't see any screen-pickup—maybe there wasn't any—but he was sure there was a microphone somewhere. He was still looking when the door opened again.

Three men and a woman entered, in sandals, long robes, and, probably, nothing else. They'd been made to change before being brought here, and would change back after a close physical search before being returned to their cells. Another deputy was with them. He said:

"Two hours maximum. If you're through before then, use the bell."

Then the door was closed and locked.

"Don't say anything," he warned. "The room's probably bugged. Sit down; help yourselves to cigarettes."

He remained standing, looking at them: Conrad Evins, small and usually fussy and precise, now tense and haggard. He had been chief gem-buyer for the Company; the robbery had been his idea originally—his or his wife's. Rose Evins, having lighted a cigarette, sat looking at it, her hands on the table. She was a dead woman and had accepted her fate; her face was calm with the resignation of hopelessness. Leo Thaxter, beefy and blue-jowled, with black hair and an out-thrust lower lip, was her brother. He had been top man in the loan-shark racket, and banker for the Mallorysport underworld; and he had been the front through whom Ingermann had acquired title to much of the privately owned real estate north of the city. It had been in one of those buildings, a vacant warehouse, that the five Fuzzies captured on Beta Continent had been kept and trained to crawl through ventilation ducts and remove simulated sunstones from cabinets in a mock-up of the Company gem-vault. Phil Novaes, the youngest of the four, was afraid and trying not to show it. He and his partner, Moses Herckerd, former Company survey-scouts, had captured the Fuzzies and brought them to town. Herckerd wasn't present; he'd stopped too many submachine-gun bullets the night of the attempted robbery.

"Well," he began when he had their attention, "they have you cold on the larceny and burglary and criminal conspiracy charges. Nobody, not even I, can get you acquitted of them. That's ten-to-twenty, and don't expect any minimum sentences, either; they'll throw the book at all of you. I do not, however, believe that you can be convicted of the two capital charges—enslavement and faginy. Just to make sure, though, I believe it would be wise for you to plead guilty to the larceny and burglary and conspiracy charges if the prosecution will agree to drop the other two."

The four looked at one another. He lit a fresh cigarette from the end of the old one, dropping the butt on the floor and tramping it.

"Twenty years is a hell of a long time," Thaxter said. "You're dead a damn sight longer, though. Yes, if you can make a deal, go ahead."

"What makes you think you can?" Conrad Evins demanded. "You say they're sure of conviction on the sunstone charges. Why would they take a plea on them and drop the Fuzzy charges? That's what they really want to convict us on."

"Want to, yes. But I don't believe they can, and I think Gus Brannhard doesn't, either. Enslavement is the reduction of a sapient being to the status of chattel property; purchase or sale of a sapient being so chattelized; and/or compulsory labor or service under restraint. Well, we'll claim those Fuzzies weren't slaves but willing accomplices."

"That's not the way the Fuzzies tell it," Rose Evins said indifferently.

"In court, the Fuzzies won't tell it any way at all," he told them. "In court, the Fuzzies will not be permitted to testify. Take my word for it; they just won't."

"Well, that's good news," Thaxter grunted skeptically. "If true. How about the faginy charge?"

Ingermann puffed on his cigarette and blew smoke at the overhead light, then sat down on the edge of the table. "Faginy," he began, "consists of training minor children to perform criminal and/or immoral acts; and/or compelling minor children to perform such acts; and/or deriving gain or profit from performance of such acts by minor children. According to the Pendarvis Decisions, Fuzzies are legally equivalent to human children of under twelve years of age, so according to the Pendarvis Decisions, what you did when you trained those Fuzzies to crawl through ventilation ducts and remove simulated sunstones from cabinets in a mock-up of the Company gem-vault was faginy; and so was taking them to Company House and having them crawl in and get out the real sunstones; and, according to law, the penalty is death by shooting—mandatory and without discretion of the court.

"Well, I'm attacking this legal fiction that a mature adult Fuzzy is a minor child. No one in this Government-Company axis wants to have to defend the Fuzzies' minor-child status in court. That's why they'll take your pleas on the sunstone charges and drop the Fuzzy charges. As you remarked, Leo, twenty years is a long time, but you're dead a lot longer."

An incredulous, almost hopeful, look came into Rose Evins's eyes, and was instantly extinguished. She wasn't going to abandon the peace of resignation for the torments of hope.

"Well, yes," she said softly. "Plead us guilty on those other charges. It won't make any difference."

Her husband also agreed, taking his cue from her; Novaes took his from both, simply nodding. Thaxter's mouth curved down more at the corners, and his lower lip jutted out farther.

"It better not," he said. "Ingermann, if you plead us guilty on the sunstone charges and then get us shot for faginy or enslavement—"

"Shut up!" Ingermann barked. He was frightened; he knew what Thaxter was going to say next. "You damned fool, didn't I tell you they have this room bugged?"

5

WISE ONE WOKE in the dawn chill; Little She and Big She and Lame One and Fruitfinder were cuddled against him, warmed by his body heat as he was by theirs. Lame One, waking, stirred. It was still dark under the thorn-bushes, but there was a faint grayness above; the sun was stirring awake in its sleeping-place, too, and would soon come out to make light and warmth. The others, Stonebreaker and Stabber and Other She, were also waking. This had been a good sleeping-place, safe and cozy. It would be nice to lie here for a long time, but soon they would have to relieve themselves, and that would mean digging holes. And he was hungry. He said so, and the others agreed.

Little She said: "Don't leave pretty bright-things. Take along."

They would take them, and, as usual, Little She would carry them. Lately the others had begun calling her Carries-Bright-Things. But they all wanted to keep them. They were pretty and strange, and they never tired of looking at them and talking about them and playing with them. Once, they lost one of the bigger ones, and they had gone back and hunted for it from before sun-highest time until a long while after before they found it. After that, they had broken off three sticks and wedged one into the open end of each bright-thing, so that they would be easier to carry and harder to lose.

The daylight grew stronger; birds twittered happily. They found soft ground and dug their holes. They always did that—bury the bad smells, even if they went away at once. Then they went to the little stream and drank and splashed in it, and then waded across and started, line-abreast, to hunt. The sky grew bright blue, flecked with golden clouds. He wondered again about the sleeping-place of the sun, and why the sun always went into it from one part of the sky and came out from another. The People had argued about that for as long as he could remember, but nobody really knew why.

They found a tree with round fruit on it. When best, this kind of fruit was pure white. Now it was spotted with brown and was not so good, but they were hungry. They threw sticks to knock it down, and ate. They found and ate lizards and grubs. Then they found a zatku.

Zatku were hard-shelled things, as long as an arm, with many legs, a hand and one finger of legs on each side, and four jointed arms ending in sharp jaws. Zatku could hurt with these; it had been a zatku that had hurt Lame One's leg. Stonebreaker poked this one with the sharp end of his killing-club, and it grasped it with all four jaw-arms. Immediately, Other She stamped the knob of her club down on its head and, to make sure, struck again. Then they all stood back while Wise One broke and tore away the shell and pulled off one of the jaw-arms to dig out the meat. They all trusted him to see that everybody got a share. There was enough that everybody could have a second small morsel.

They hunted for a long time, and found another zatku. This was good; it had been a long time since they had found two zatku in one day. They hunted outward after they had eaten the second one, until almost sunhighest time, but they did not find any more.

They found other things to eat, however. They found the soft pink growing-things, like hands with many fingers; they were good. They killed one of the fat little animals with brown fur that ran from one of them and was clubbed by another. And Stonebreaker threw his club and knocked down a low-flying bird; everyone praised him for that. As they hunted they had been climbing the slope of a hill. By the time they reached the top, everybody had found enough to eat.

The hilltop was a nice place. There were a few trees and low bushes and stretches of open grass, and from it they could see a long way. Far to sun-upward, a big river wound glinting through the trees, and there were mountains all around. It was good to lie in the soft grass, warmed by the sun, the wind ruffling their fur and tickling pleasantly.

There was a gotza circling in the sky, but it was too far away to see them. They sat and watched it; once it made a short turn, one wing high, then dived down out of sight.

"Gotza see something," Stonebreaker said. "Go down, eat."

"Hope not People," Big She said.

"Not many People this place," he said. "Long time not see other People."

It had been many-many days ago, far to the sun's right hand, that they had last talked to other People, a band of two males and three females. They had talked a long time and made sleeping-place together, and the next day they had parted to hunt. They had not seen those People again. Now they talked about them.

"We see again, we show bright-things," Lame One said. "Nobody ever see bright-things before."

The gotza rose again, and they could hear its wing-sounds now. It began soaring in wide circles, coming closer.

"Not eat long," Stabber commented. "Something little. Still hungry."

Maybe they had better leave this place now and go down where the trees were thicker. Wise One was about to speak of that, and then he heard the shrill, not unpleasant, sound they had heard at the spring after the thunder-death had killed those three gotza. He recognized it at once; so did the others.

"Get under bushes," he commanded. "Lie still."

There was a tiny speck in the sky, far to the sun's left hand; it grew larger very rapidly, and the sound grew louder. He noticed that the sound was following behind it, and wondered why that was. Then they were all under the bushes, lying very still.

It was an odd thing to be flying. It had no wings. It was flattish, rounded in front and pointed behind, like the seed of a melon-fruit, and it glistened brightly. But there were no flying Big Ones carrying it; it was flying of itself.

It flew straight at the gotza, passing almost directly over them. The gotza turned and tried desperately to escape, but the flying thing closed rapidly upon it. Then there was a sound, not the sharp crack of the thunder-death, but a ripping sound. It could be many thunder-death sounds close together. It lasted two heartbeats, and then the gotza came apart in the air, pieces flying away and falling. The strange flying thing went on for a little, turning slowly and coming back.

"Good thing, kill gotza," Stabber said. "Maybe see us, kill gotza so gotza not kill us. Maybe friend."

"Maybe kill gotza for fun," Big She said. "Maybe kill us next, for fun."

It was coming straight toward them now, lower and more slowly than when it had chased the gotza. Carries-Bright-Things and Fruitfinder wanted to run; Wise One screamed at them to lie still. One did not run from things like this. Still, he wanted to run himself, and it took all his will to force himself to lie motionless.

The front of the flying thing was open. At least, he could see into it, though there was a queer shine there. Then he gasped in amazement. Inside the flying thing were two big People. Not People like him, but People of some kind. They had People faces, with both eyes in front, and not one on each side like animal faces. They had People hands, but their shoulders were covered with something strange that was not fur.

So these were the flying Big Ones. They had no wings; when they wanted to fly, they got into the melon-seed-shaped thing, and it flew for them, and when it came down on the ground, they got out and walked about. Now he knew what the great heavy thing that had broken bushes and crushed stones under it had been. It might be some live-thing that did what the Big Ones wanted it to, or it might be some kind of a made-thing. He would have to think more about that. But the Big Ones were just big People.

The flying thing passed over them and was going away; the shrill wavering sound grew fainter, and it vanished. The Big Ones in it had seen them, and they had not let loose the thunder-death. Maybe the Big Ones knew that they were People too. People did not kill other People for fun. People made friends with other People, and helped them.

He rose to his feet. The others, rising with him, were still frightened. So was he, but he must not let them know it. Wise One should not be afraid. Stabber was less afraid than any of the rest; he was saying:

"Big Ones see us, not kill. Kill gotza. Big Ones good."

"You not know," Big She disputed. "Nobody ever know about Big Ones flying before."

"Big Ones kill gotza to help us," he said. "Big Ones make friends."

"Big Ones make thunder-death, make us all dead like gotza," Stonebreaker insisted. "Maybe Big Ones come back. We go now, far-far, then they not find us."

They were all crying out now, except Stabber. Big She and Stonebreaker were loudest and most vehement. They did not know about the Big Ones; nobody had ever told of Big Ones; nobody knew anything about them. They were to be feared more than gotza. There was no use arguing with them now. He looked about, over the country visible from the hilltop. The big moving-water to sun-upward was too wide to cross; he had seen it. There were small moving-waters flowing into it, but they could follow to where the water was little enough to cross over. He pointed toward the sun's left hand with his club.

"We go that way," he said. "Maybe find zatku."

THROUGH THE ARMOR-GLASS front of the aircar, Gerd van Riebeek saw the hilltop tilt away and the cloud-dappled sky swing dizzily. He lifted his thumb from the button-switch of the camera and reached for his cigarettes on the ledge in front of him.

"Make another pass at them, Doc?" the ZNPF trooper at the controls asked.

He shook his head.

"Uh-uh. We scared Nifflheim out of them as it is; don't let's overdo it." He lit a cigarette. "Suppose we swing over to the river and circle around along both sides of it. We might see some more Fuzzies."

He wasn't optimistic about that. There weren't many Fuzzies north of the Divide. Not enough land-prawns. No zatku, no hokfusine; no hokfusine, no viable births. It was a genetic miracle there were any at all up here. And even if the woods were full of them, with their ultrasonic hearing they'd hear the vibrations of an aircar's contragravity field and be under cover before they could be spotted.

"We might see another harpy." Trooper Art Parnaby had been a veldbeest herder on Delta Continent before he'd joined the Protection Force; he didn't have to be taught not to like harpies. "Man, you took that one apart nice!"

Harpies were getting scarce up here. Getting scarce all over Beta. They'd vanished from the skies of the cattle country to the south, and the Company had chased them out or shot them up in the Big Blackwater, and now the ZNPF was working on them in the reservation. As a naturalist, he supposed that he ought to deplore the extinction of any species, but he couldn't think of a better species to become extinct than *Pseudopterodactyl harpy zarathustra*. They probably had their place in the overall ecological picture—everything did. Scavengers, maybe, though they preferred live meat. Elimination of weak and sickly individuals of other species—though any veldbeest herder like Art Parnaby would tell you that no harpy would bother a sick cow if he could land on a plump and healthy calf.

"I wonder if that's the same gang you and Jack saw the time you found the sunstones," Parnaby was saying.

"Could be. There were eight in that gang; I'm sure there were that many in this one. That was a couple of hundred miles north of here, but it was three weeks ago."

The car swung lower; it was down to a couple of hundred feet when they passed over the Yellowsand River, which was broad and sluggish here, with sandbars and sandy beaches. He saw a few bits of brush with half-withered leaves, stuff carried down from where Grego and his gang had been digging a week ago at the canyon. Tributary streams flowed in from both sides, some large enough to be formidable barriers to Fuzzies. Fuzzies could swim well enough, and he'd seen them crossing streams clinging to bits of driftwood; but they didn't like to swim, and didn't when it wasn't necessary. Usually, they'd follow a stream up to where it was small enough to wade across.

They saw quite a few animals. Slim, deerlike things with three horns; there were a dozen species of them, but everybody called all of them, indiscriminately, zarabuck. Fuzzies called them all *takku*. Once he saw a big three-horned damnthing, *hesh-nazza* in Fuzzy language; he got a few feet of it on film before it saw the car and bolted. Now, there was a poor mixed-up critter; originally a herbivore, it had acquired a taste for meat but couldn't get enough to support the huge bulk of its body, and had to supplement its diet with browse. The whole zoological picture on this planet was crazy. That was why he liked Zarathustra.

They came to where Lake-Chain River joined Yellowsand. At its mouth, it was larger than the stream it fed, and it came in from almost due south, while the Yellowsand, which rose in the Divide, curved in from the east. Beyond this, there weren't any sandbars. The current was more rapid, and the water foamed whitely around bare rocks. The wall of the Divide began looming on the horizon. Finally they could see the cleft of the canyon. There was a circling dot in the sky ahead, but it wasn't a harpy. It was one of the CZC air-survey cars, photomapping and measuring with radar, and scanning. He looked at his watch. Almost 1700, getting on to cocktail time. He wondered how many Fuzzies Lieutenant Bjornsen had seen on his sweep south of the Divide, and how many harpies he'd shot.

6

THE FUZZIES HAD been excited all the way from Hoksu-Mitto; Pappy Jack was taking them on a trip to Big House Place. By the time Mallorysport came up on the horizon, tall buildings towering out of green interspaces, they were all shrieking in delight, some even forgetting to "make talk in back of mouth," like Big Ones. They came in over the city at five thousand feet, the car slanting downward, and Little Fuzzy recognized Company House at once.

"Look! Diamond Place! Pappy Jack, we go there, see Diamond, Pappy Vic?"

"No, we go Pappy Ben Place," he told them. "Pappy Vic, Diamond, come there. Have big party; everybody come. Pappy Ben, Flora, Fauna, Pappy Vic, Diamond . . ." The Fuzzies all added more names of friends they would see. "And look." He pointed to Central Courts Building, on the right. "You know that place?"

They did; that was Big-Room Talk-Place. They'd had a lot of fun there, turning a court trial into a three-ring circus. He still had to laugh when he remembered that. The aircar circled in toward Government House. Unlike the other important buildings of Mallorysport, it sprawled instead of towering, terraced on top, with gardens spread around it. On the north lower lawn a crowd of Fuzzies and others were gathered in the loose concentration of an outdoor cocktail party. Then the car was landing and the Fuzzies were all trying to get out as soon as it was off contragravity.

There was a group at the foot of the north escalator. Most of them were small people with golden fur—Ben Rainsford's Flora and Fauna, Victor Grego's Diamond, Judge and Mrs. Pendarvis's Pierrot and Columbine, and five Fuzzies whose names were Allan Pinkerton and Arsene Lupin and Sherlock Holmes and Irene Adler and Mata Hari. They were members of the Company Police Detective Bureau, and they were all reformed criminals. At least, they had been apprehended while trying to clean out the gem-vault at Company House and had turned people's evidence on the gang who had trained them to be burglars.

With them was a tall girl with coppery hair, and a dark-faced man whose smartly tailored jacket bulged slightly under the left arm. The man was Ahmed Khadra, Detective-Captain, in charge of the Native Protection Force, Investigation Division. The girl was Sandra Glenn, Victor Grego's Fuzzy-sitter. Grego was just losing her to Khadra, if the sunstone on her left hand meant anything.

His own Fuzzies had dashed down the escalator ahead of him; the ones below ran forward to greet them. He managed to get through the crowd to Ahmed and Sandra, and had a few words with them before all the Fuzzies came pelting up, Diamond and Flora and Fauna and the others tugging at his trouser-legs and wanting to be noticed, and his own Fuzzies wanting Unka Ahmed and Auntie Sandra to notice them. He squatted among them, petting them and saying hello. Baby Fuzzy promptly climbed onto Ahmed Khadra's shoulder. At least they'd broken him of trying to sit on people's heads, which was something. Between talking to the Fuzzies, all of whom wanted to be talked to, he managed to get a few more words with Ahmed and Sandra, mostly about the Fuzzy Club she was going to manage.

"It's going to be just one big nonstop Fuzzy party all the time," she said. "I hope we don't get too tired of it."

It was Victor Grego's idea; he was putting up the money and providing the lower floors and surrounding parkland of one of the Company buildings. People who'd adopted Fuzzies couldn't be expected to give them their exclusive attention, and Fuzzies living with human families would want to talk to and play with other Fuzzies. The Fuzzy Club would be a place where they could get together and be kept out of danger and/or mischief.

"When's the grand opening? I'll have to come in for it."

"Oh, not for a few weeks. After Ahmed and I are married. We still have a lot of fixing up to do, and I want the girl who's taking my place with Diamond to get better acquainted with him, and vice versa, before I leave her to cope with him alone."

"You need much coping with?" he asked Diamond, rumpling his fur and then smoothing it again.

"Actually, no; he's very good. The girl will have to learn more about him, is all. He's being a big help with the Fuzzy Club; gives all sorts of advice, some of it excellent."

Diamond had been telling Little Fuzzy and the others about the new Fuzzy

Place. The five ex-jewel-thieves had gotten Baby Fuzzy away from Khadra and were making a great to-do over him, to Mamma's proud pleasure. Ko-Ko and Cinderella and Mike and Mitzi had wandered away somewhere with Pierrot and Columbine. Little Fuzzy was tugging at him.

"Pappy Jack? Little Fuzzy go with Flora, Fauna?" he asked.

"Sure. Run along and have fun. Pappy Jack go make talk with other Big Ones." He turned to Ahmed and Sandra. "Don't you folks want *koktel-drinko*?"

"We had," Ahmed said. Sandra added, "We have to see about dinner for Fuzzy-people pretty soon."

He said he'd see them around, and strolled away, filling his pipe, toward the crowd around the bartending robot. Diamond accompanied him, mostly in short dashes ahead and waits for him to catch up; what was the matter with Big Ones, anyhow, always poking along? There was an approaching bedlam, and three Fuzzies burst into sight, blowing horns. Behind them, in single file, came three small wheelbarrows, a Fuzzy pushing and another riding in each, with more Fuzzies dashing along behind.

"Look, Pappy Jack! Whee'barrow!" Diamond called. "Pappy Ben give. Fun. Unka Ahmed, Auntie Sandra, they have whee'barrow at new Fuzzy Place."

The procession came to a disorderly halt a hundred yards beyond; the Fuzzies pushing dropped the shafts and took the places of the three who had been riding; three more picked up the wheelbarrows, and the whole cavalcade dashed away again.

"Good little fellows," somebody behind him said. "Everybody takes his fair turn."

The speaker was Associate-Justice Yves Janiver, with silver-gray hair and a dramatically black mustache; he was now presiding judge of Native Cases court. One of his companions was big and ruddy, Clyde Garrick, head cashier of the Bank of Mallorysport. The other, thin and elderly, with a fringe of white hair under a black beret, was Henry Stenson, the instrument-maker. Holloway greeted and shook hands with them.

"Those were my three who just jumped off," Stenson said.

He'd gotten them on loan from the Adoption Bureau, to help test the voice-transformer he and Grego had invented. Then the Fuzzies had refused to go back, and he'd had to adopt them; they'd adopted him already. Their names were Microvolt and Roentgen and Angstrom. Damned names some people gave Fuzzies. He asked how they were getting along.

"Oh, they're having a wonderful time, Mr. Holloway," Stenson laughed. "I've fixed them up a little workshop of their own, to keep them out of everybody's way in my shop. They want to help everybody do everything; I never saw anybody as helpful as those Fuzzies. You know," he added, "they are a help, too. They have almost microscopic vision, and they're wonderfully clever with their hands." From Henry Stenson, that was high praise. "Well, they're small people; they live on a smaller scale than we do. If only they didn't lose interest so quickly. When they do, of course, it's no use expecting them to go on."

"No, it isn't fun anymore. Besides, they don't understand what you want them to do, or why."

"No, they wouldn't," Stenson agreed. "Explaining a micromass detector or a radiation counter to a Fuzzy . . ." He thought for a moment. "I think I'll start them on jewelry work. They like pretty things, and they'd make wonderful jewelers."

That was an idea. Maybe, about a year from now, an exhibition of Fuzzy arts and handcrafts. Talk that over with Gerd and Ruth; talk it over with Little Fuzzy and Dr. Crippen, too.

A dozen Fuzzies rushed past—the five Company Police Fuzzies and Mamma Fuzzy with Baby running beside her, and some others he felt he ought to know but didn't. They were all swirling around a big red-and-gold ball, rolling it rapidly on the grass. Diamond took off after them.

"Why don't you teach them some real ball games, Jack?" Clyde Garrick asked. He was a sports enthusiast. "Football, now; a Fuzzy football game would be something to watch." A Fuzzy directly in front of the rolling ball leaped over it, coming down among those who were pushing it. "Basketball; did you see the jump that one made? I wish I could get a team of human kids who could jump like that together."

Holloway shook his head. "Some of the marines out at Hoksu-Mitto tried to teach them soccer," he said. "Didn't work, at all. They couldn't see the sense of the rules, and they couldn't understand why all of them couldn't play on both teams. If a Fuzzy sees somebody trying to do something, all he wants to do is help."

That shocked Garrick. He didn't think people who lacked competitive spirit were people at all. Stenson nodded.

"What I was saying. They want to help everybody. You could interest them in the sort of sports in which one really competes with oneself. If you teach a Fuzzy something new, he isn't satisfied till he can do it again better."

"Rifle shooting," Garrick grudged. He didn't consider shooting a sport at all. Not an athletic sport, at any rate. "I know shooters who claim they get just as much fun shooting alone as in a match."

"I don't know about that. A Fuzzy would need an awfully light rifle and awfully light loads. Mind, they only weigh fifteen or twenty pounds. A .22 light enough for a Fuzzy to handle would kick him as hard as my 12.7 express kicks me. But archery'd be all right. We've been teaching them to make bows and arrows and shoot them. You'd be surprised; most of them can pull a twenty-pound bow, and for them that's heavier than a hundred-pound bow for a man."

"Huh!" Garrick looked at the swirl of golden bodies around the bright-colored ball. Anybody who weighed so little and could pull a twenty-pound bow deserved respect, team spirit or no team spirit. "Tell you what, Jack. I'll put up cups for regional archery matches and for a world's championship match, and we can start having matches and organizing teams. Say, in a year, we could hold a match for the world's title."

What a Fuzzy would do with a trophy cup now!

"But what I'd really like to see," Garrick continued, "would be a real live Fuzzy football league. Don't you think you could get some interest stirred up?"

No, and a damned good thing. Start Fuzzy football, and the gamblers would be onto it like a Fuzzy after a land-prawn. And from what he knew about Fuzzies, any Fuzzy could be fixed to throw a game for half a cake of Extee-Three; and everybody on both teams would help, just to do what some Big One wanted. No, no Fuzzy football.

While he had been talking he had been edging and nudging the others toward the bartending robot. Yves Janiver, whose glass was empty, was aiding and abetting. As soon as they were close enough, he and the Native Court judge stepped in to get drinks. He was being supplied with his when he was greeted by Claudette Pendarvis, who asked if he had just arrived.

"Practically. I saw your two; they're off somewhere with some of mine," he said. "Is the judge here yet?"

No; he wasn't. She asked Janiver if he knew where the Chief Justice was. In conference, in chambers—he and Gus Brannhard and some other lawyers. Pendarvis and Brannhard would be arriving a little later. Mrs. Pendarvis wanted to know if he was going to visit Adoption Bureau while he was in town.

"Yes, surely, Mrs. Pendarvis. Tomorrow morning be all right?"

Tomorrow morning would be fine. He asked her how things were going. Adoptions, she said, had fallen off somewhat; that was what he'd been expecting.

"But the hospital wants some more Fuzzies, to entertain the patients. They have some now; they want more. And Dr. Mallin says they are a wonderful influence on some of the mental patients."

"Well, we can use some more at school," a woman who had just come up said—Mrs. Hawkwood, principal of the kindergarten and primary schools. "We have a couple already, in the preliterate classes. Do you know, the Fuzzies are actually teaching the human children?"

Age-group four to six; yes, he could believe that.

"Why just preliterates, Mrs. Hawkwood?" he asked. "Put some of them into the c-a-t-spells-cat class and see how fast they pick it up. Bet they do better than the human six year olds."

"You mean, try to teach *Fuzzies* to *read*?"

The idea had never occurred to him before; it seemed like a good one. Evidently it hadn't occurred to Mrs. Hawkwood, either, and now that it was presented to her, he could almost watch her thoughts chase one another across her face. Teach Fuzzies to read? Ridiculous; only people could read. But Fuzzies were people; there was scientific authority for that. But they were *Fuzzies*; that was different. But then . . .

At that point, Ben Rainsford came up, apologetic for not having greeted him earlier and asking if his family had come in with him. While he was talking to Ben, Holloway saw Chief Justice Pendarvis and Gus Brannhard approach. The Chief Justice got a glass of wine for himself and a cocktail for his wife; they stepped aside together. Brannhard, big and bearded and giving the impression, in spite of his meticulous courtroom black, of being in hunting clothes, secured a tumbler of straight whiskey. Victor Grego and Leslie Coombes came up and spoke. Then somebody pulled Rainsford aside to talk to him.

That was the trouble with these cocktail parties. You met everybody and never had a chance to talk to anybody. It was getting almost that bad at cocktail time out at Hoksu-Mitto now. Out of the corner of his eye, Holloway saw Mrs. Hawkwood fasten upon Ernst Mallin. Mallin was a real authority on Fuzzy psychology; if he told her Fuzzies could be taught to read, she'd have to believe it. He wanted to talk to Ernst himself about that, and about a lot of other things, but not in this donnybrook.

The wheelbarrow parade came by, more slowly and less noisily, and a little later the crowd that had been chasing the big ball came pushing it along, Baby Fuzzy jumping onto it and tumbling off it. Dinnertime for Fuzzies—putting back all the playthings where they belonged. He was in favor of using Fuzzies in schools for human children; maybe they'd have a civilizing influence. After a while, the Fuzzies came stringing back, mostly talking about food.

Dinnertime for Big Ones, too. It took longer to get them mobilized than it had the Fuzzies, and then, of course, they had to stop on the upper terrace where Sandra Glenn and Ahmed Khadra and some of the Government House staff had set up a Fuzzy-type smorgasbord on a big revolving table. The Fuzzies all thought that was fun. So did the human-people watching them. Eventually, they all got into the dining room. There weren't enough ladies to pair off the guests, male and female after their kind like the passengers on the Ark. They placed

Jack Holloway between Ben Rainsford and Leslie Coombes, with Victor Grego
and Gus Brannhard on the other side.

By the time the robo-service in the middle of the table had taken away the
dessert dishes and brought in coffee and liqueurs, Fuzzies were beginning to
filter in. They'd finished their own dinner long ago; it was getting dark outside,
and they wanted to be where the Big Ones were. Couldn't blame them; it was
their party, wasn't it? They came in diffidently, like well-brought-up children,
looking but not touching anything, saying hello to people.

Diamond came over to Grego, who picked him up and set him on the edge
of the table. Rainsford pushed back his chair, and Flora and Fauna climbed onto
his lap. Gus Brannhard had four or five trying to clamber over him. Little Fuzzy
wanted up on the table, too, and promptly unzipped his pouch, got out his little
pipe, and lighted it. Several came to Leslie Coombes, begging, "Unka Less'ee,
plis give smokko?" and Coombes lit cigarettes for them. Coombes liked
Fuzzies, and treated them with the same grave courtesy he showed his human
friends, but he didn't want them climbing over him, and they knew it.

"Ben, let's get these agreements signed," Grego said. "Then we can give the
kids some attention."

"Where'll we sign them, in your office?" he asked Rainsford.

"No, sign them right here at the table where everybody can watch. That's
what the party's about, isn't it?" Rainsford said.

They cleared a space in front of the Governor-General, putting Fuzzies on
the floor or handing them to people farther down on either side. The scrolls,
three copies of each agreement, were brought; Rainsford had one of his
secretaries read them aloud. The first was the general agreement, by which the
Colonial Government agreed to lease, for nine hundred and ninety-nine years,
all unseated public lands to the Charterless Zarathustra Company, Ltd., of
Zarathustra, excepting the area on Beta Continent set aside as a Fuzzy
Reservation, in return for which the said Charterless Zarathustra Company, Ltd.,
agreed to carry on all the nonprofit public services previously performed by the
Chartered Zarathustra Company, and, in addition, to conduct researches and
studies for the benefit of the race known as *Fuzzy sapiens zarathustra* at Science
Center. Except for the northern part of Beta Continent, the new Company was
getting back, as lessees, everything it had lost as owner by the Pendarvis
Decisions.

Rainsford and Grego signed it, with Gus Brannhard and Leslie Coombes as
cosigners, with a few witnesses chosen at random from around the table. Then
the Yellowsand Canyon agreement was read; as Commissioner of Native
Affairs, Holloway had an interest in that. The Company leased, also for nine
hundred ninety-nine years, a tract fifty miles square around the head of

Yellowsand Canyon, with rights to mine, quarry, erect buildings, and remove from the tract sunstones and other materials. The Government agreed to lease other tracts to the Company, subject to the consent of the Native Commission, and to lease land on the Fuzzy Reservation to nobody else without consent of the Company. The Company agreed to pay royalties on all sunstones removed, at the rate of four hundred fifty sols per carat, said moneys to be held in trust for the Fuzzies as a race by the Colonial Government and invested with the Banking Cartel, the interest accruing to the Government as an administration fee. Well, that put the Government in the black, and made the Fuzzies rich, and gave the Charterless Zarathustra Company more than the Chartered Zarathustra Company had lost. Everybody ought to be happy.

Rainsford and Grego, and Gus and Leslie Coombes signed it, so did Jack Holloway, as Commissioner of Native Affairs. They picked half a dozen more witnesses who also signed.

"What's the matter with having a few Fuzzies sign it too?" Grego asked, indicating the crowd that had climbed to the table on both sides to watch what the Big Ones were doing. "It's their Reservation, and it's their sunstones."

"Oh, Victor," Coombes protested. "They can't sign this. They're incompetent aborigines, and legally minor children. And besides, they can't write. At least, not yet."

"They can fingerprint after their names, the way any other illiterates do," Gus Brannhard said. "And they can sign as additional witnesses; neither as aborigines nor as minor children are they debarred from testifying to things of their own experience or observation. I'm going to send Leo Thaxter and the Evinses and Phil Novaes out to be shot on Fuzzy testimony."

"Chief Justice Pendarvis, give us a guidance-opinion on that," Coombes said. "I'd like some Fuzzies to sign it, but not if it would impair the agreement."

"Oh, it would not do that, Mr. Coombes," Pendarvis said. "Not in my opinion, anyhow. Mr. Justice Janiver, what's your opinion?"

"Well, as witnesses, certainly," Janiver agreed. "The Fuzzies are here present and the signing takes place within their observation; they can certainly testify to that."

"I think," Pendarvis said, "that the Fuzzies ought to be informed of the purpose of this signing, though."

"Mr. Brannhard, you want to try that?" Coombes asked. "Can you explain the theory of land-tenure, mineral rights, and contractual obligation in terms comprehensible to a Fuzzy?"

"Jack, you try it; you know more about Fuzzies than I do," Brannhard said.

"Well, I can try." He turned to Diamond and Little Fuzzy and Mamma Fuzzy and a few others closest to him.

"Big Ones make name-marks on paper," he said. "This means, Big Ones go into woods—place Fuzzies come from—dig holes, get stones, make trade with other Big Ones. Then get nice things, give to Fuzzies. Make name-marks on paper for Fuzzies, Fuzzies make finger-marks."

"Why make finga'p'int?" Little Fuzzy asked. "Get idee-disko?" He fingered the silver disc at his throat.

"No; just make finga'p'int. Then, somebody ask Fuzzies, Fuzzies say, yes, saw Big Ones make name-marks."

"But why?" Diamond wanted to know. "Big Ones give Fuzzies nice things now."

"This is playtime for Big Ones," Flora said. "Pappy Ben make play like this all the time, make name-mark on paper."

"That's right," Brannhard said. "This is how Big Ones make play. Much fun; Big Ones call it Law. Now, you watch what Unka Gus do."

7

GUS BRANNHARD SAID, "Well, I was wrong. I am most happy to admit it. I've been getting the same reports, from all over, and the editorial opinion is uniformly favorable."

Leslie Coombes, in the screen, nodded. He was in the library of his apartment across the city, with a coffee service and a stack of papers and teleprint sheets on the table in front of him.

"Editorial opinion, of course, doesn't win elections, but the grass-roots-level reports are just as good. Things are going to be just as they always were, and that's what most people really want. It ought to gain us some votes, instead of losing us any. These people Hugo Ingermann was frightening with stories about how they were going to be taxed into poverty to maintain the Fuzzies in luxury, for instance. . . . Now it appears that the Fuzzies will be financing the Government."

"Is Victor still in town?"

"Oh, no. He left for Yellowsand Canyon before daybreak. He's been having men and equipment shifted in there from Big Blackwater for the last week. By this time, they're probably digging out sunstones by the peck."

He laughed. Like a kid with a new rifle; couldn't wait to try it out. "I suppose he took Diamond along?" Grego never went anywhere without his Fuzzy. "Well, why don't you drop around to Government House for cocktails? Jack's still in town, and we can talk without as many interruptions, human and otherwise, as last evening."

Coombes said he would be glad to. They chatted for a few minutes, then broke the connection, and immediately the screen buzzer began. When he put it on again, his screen-girl looked out of it as though she smelled a week-old dead snake somewhere.

"The Honorable—technically, of course—Hugo Ingermann," she said. "He's been trying to get you for the last ten minutes."

"Well, I've been trying to get him ever since I took office," he said. "Put him on." Then he snapped on the recorder.

The screen flickered and cleared, and a plump, well-barbered face looked out of it, affable and candid, with innocently wide blue eyes. A face anybody who didn't know its owner would trust.

"Good morning, Mr. Brannhard."

"Good morning indeed, Mr. Ingermann. Is there something I can do for you? Besides dropping dead, that is?"

"Ah, I believe there is something I can do for you, Mr. Brannhard," Ingermann beamed like an orphanage superintendent on Christmas morning. "How would you like pleas of guilty from Leo Thaxter, Conrad and Rose Evins, and Phil Novaes?"

"I couldn't even consider them. You know pleas of guilty to capital charges aren't admissible."

Ingermann stared for a moment in feigned surprise, then laughed. "Those ridiculous things? No, we are pleading guilty to the proper and legitimate charges of first-degree burglary, grand larceny, and criminal conspiracy. That is, of course, if the Colony agrees to drop that silly farrago of faginy and enslavement charges."

He checked the impulse to ask Ingermann if he were crazy. Whatever Hugo Ingermann was, he wasn't that. He substituted: "Do you think I'm crazy, Mr. Ingermann?"

"I hope you're smart enough to see the advantage of my offer," Ingermann replied.

"Well, I'm sorry, but I'm not. The advantage to your clients, yes; that's the difference between twenty years in the penitentiary and a ten-millimeter bullet in the back of the head. I'm afraid the advantage to the Colony is slightly less apparent."

"It shouldn't be. You can't get a conviction on those charges, and you know it. I'm giving you a chance to get off the hook."

"Well, that's very kind of you, Mr. Ingermann, indeed it is. I'm afraid, though, that I can't take advantage of your good nature. You'll just have to fight those charges in court."

"You think I can't?" Ingermann was openly contemptuous now. "You're prosecuting my clients, if that's how you mispronounce it, on charges of faginy.

You know perfectly well that the crime of faginy cannot be committed against an adult, and you know, just as well, that that's what those Fuzzies are."

"They are legally minor children."

"They are classified as minor children by a court ruling. That ruling is not only contrary to physical fact but is also a flagrant usurpation of legislative power by the judiciary, and hence unconstitutional. As such, I mean to attack it."

And wouldn't that play Nifflheim? The Government couldn't let that ruling be questioned; why, it would . . . Which was what Ingermann was counting on, of course. He shrugged.

"We can get along without convicting them of faginy; we can still convict them of enslavement. That's the nice thing about capital punishment: nobody needs to be shot in the head more than once."

Ingermann laughed scornfully. "You think you can frame my clients on enslavement charges? Those Fuzzies weren't slaves; they were accomplices."

"They were made drunk, transported under the influence of liquor from their native habitat, confined under restraint, compelled to perform work, and punished for failure to do so by imprisonment in a dungeon, by starvation, and by electric-shock tortures. If that isn't a classic description of the conditions of enslavement, I should like to hear one."

"And have the Fuzzies accused my clients of these crimes?" Ingermann asked. "Under veridication, on a veridicator tested to distinguish between true and false statements when made by Fuzzies?"

No, they hadn't; and that was only half of it. The other half was what he'd been afraid of all along.

"Don't tell me; I'll tell you," Ingermann went on. "They have not, for the excellent reason that Fuzzies can't be veridicated. I have that on the authority of Dr. Ernst Mallin, Victor Grego's chief Fuzzyologist. A polyencephalographic veridicator simply will not respond to Fuzzies. Now, you put those Fuzzies on the stand against my clients and watch what happens."

That was true. Mallin, who had the idea that scientific information ought to be published, had stated that no Fuzzy with whom he had worked had ever changed the blue light of a veridicator to the red of falsehood. He had also stated that in his experience no Fuzzy had ever made a false statement, under veridication or otherwise. But Ingermann was ignoring that.

"And as to these faginy charges, if you people really believe that Fuzzies are legally minor children, why was it thought necessary to have a dozen and a half of them fingerprint that Yellowsand lease agreement? Minor children do not sign documents like that."

He laughed. "Oh, that was just fun for the Fuzzies," he said. "They wanted to do what the Big Ones were doing."

"Mr. Brannhard!" From Ingermann's tone, he might have been a parent who has just been informed by a five-year-old that a gang of bandits in black masks had come in and looted the cookie jar. "Do you expect me to believe that?"

"I don't give a hoot on Nifflheim whether you do or not, Mr. Ingermann. Now, was there anything else you wanted to talk to me about?"

"Isn't that enough for now?" Ingermann asked. "The trial won't be for a month yet. If, in the meantime, you change your mind—and if you're well-advised you will—just give me a call. Good-bye for now."

VICTOR GREGO'S AIRCAR pilot wasn't usually insane . . . only when he got his hands on the controls of a vehicle. Yellowsand Canyon was three time zones east of Mallorysport, and, coming in, the sun was an hour higher than when they had lifted out. Diamond had noticed that too, and commented on it.

A sergeant of the Marine guard met them on the top landing stage of Government House. "Mr. Grego. Mr. Coombes and Mr. Brannhard are here, with the Governor in his office."

"Is anybody here going to try to arrest my Fuzzy?" he asked.

The sergeant grinned. "No, sir. He's been accused of everything but space-piracy, high treason, and murder-one, along with the others, but Marshal Fane says he won't arrest any of them if they show up tomorrow in Complaint Court."

"Thank you, Sergeant. Then, I won't need this." Victor unbuckled his pistol, wrapping the belt around the holster, and tossed it onto the back seat of the car, lifting Diamond and setting him on his shoulder. "Go amuse yourself for a couple of hours," he told the pilot. "Stay around where I can reach you, though."

At the head of the escalator, he told Diamond the same thing, watching him ride down and scamper across the garden in search of Flora and Fauna and the rest of his friends. Then Victor went inside, and found Leslie Coombes and Gus Brannhard seated with Ben Rainsford at the oval table in the private conference room. They exchanged greetings, and he sat down with them.

"Now, what the devil's all this about arresting Fuzzies?" he demanded. "What are they charged with?"

"They aren't charged with anything, yet," Brannhard told him. "Hugo Ingermann made information against all six of them with the Colonial Marshal. He accused Allan Pinkerton and Arsene Lupin and Sherlock Holmes and Irene Adler and Mata Hari of first-degree burglary, grand larceny and criminal conspiracy, and Diamond with misprision of felony and accessory-before-the-fact. They won't be charged till the accusations are heard in Complaint Court tomorrow."

Complaint Court was something like the ancient grand jury—an inquiry into whether or not a chargeable crime had been committed. The accusation was on trial there, not the accused.

"Well, you aren't letting it get past there, are you?"

Before Brannhard could answer, Jack Holloway and Ernst Mallin came in. Holloway was angry, the tips of his mustache twitching and a feral glare in his eyes. He must have looked like that when he beat up Kellogg and shot Borch. Ernst Mallin looked distressed; he'd been in one criminal case involving Fuzzies, and that had been enough. Ahmed Khadra entered behind them, with Fitz Mortlake, the Company Police captain who was guardian-of-record for the other five Fuzzies. After more greetings, they all sat down.

"What are you going to do about this goddamned thing?" Jack Holloway began while he was still pulling up his chair. "You going to let that son of a Khooghra get away with this?"

"If you mean the Fuzzies, hell, no," Brannhard said. "They're not guilty of anything, and everybody, Ingermann included, knows it. He's trying to bluff me into dropping the faginy and enslavement charges and letting his clients cop a plea on the burglary and larceny charges. He thinks I'm afraid to prosecute those faginy and enslavement charges. He's right; I am. But I'm going ahead with them."

"Well, but, my God . . . !" Jack Holloway began to explode.

"What's wrong with those charges?"

"Well, the faginy, now," Brannhard said. "That's based on the assumption that Fuzzies are equivalent to human children of ten-to-twelve, and that rests on a reversible judicial opinion, not on statute law. Ingermann thinks we'll drop the charges rather than open the Fuzzies' minor-child status to question, because that's the basis of the whole Government Fuzzy policy."

"And you're afraid of that?"

"Of course he is," Coombes said. "So am I, and so ought you to be. Just take the Yellowsand agreement. If the Fuzzies are legally minor children, they can't control or dispose of property. The Government, as guardian-in-general of the whole Fuzzy race, has authority to do that, including leasing mineral lands. But suppose they're adult aborigines. Even Class-IV aborigines can control their own property, and according to Federation Law, Terrans are forbidden to settle upon or exploit the 'anciently accustomed habitation' of Class-IV natives—in this case, Beta Continent north of the Snake and the Little Blackwater, which includes Yellowsand Canyon—without the natives' consent. Consent, under Federation Law, must be expressed by vote of a representative tribal council, or by the will of a recognized tribal chief."

"Well, Jesus-in-the-haymow!" Jack Holloway almost yelled. "There is no such damned thing! They have no tribes, just little family groups, about half a dozen in each. And who in Nifflheim ever heard of a Fuzzy chief?"

"Then, we're all right," he said. "The law cannot compel the performance of an impossibility."

"You only have half of that, Victor," Coombes said. "The law, for instance, cannot compel a blind man to pass a vision test. The law, however, can and does make passing such a test a requirement for operating a contragravity vehicle. Blind men cannot legally pilot aircars. So if we can't secure the consent of a nonexistent Fuzzy tribal council, we can't mine sunstones at Yellowsand, lease or no lease."

"Then, we'll get out all we can while the lease is still good." He'd stripped Big Blackwater of men and equipment already; he was thinking of what other Peters could be robbed to pay Yellowsand Paul. "We have a month till the trial."

"I'm just as interested in that as you are, Victor," Gus Brannhard said, "But that's not the only thing. There's the Adoption Bureau: If the Fuzzies aren't minor children, somebody might make enslavement—peonage at least—out of those adoptions. And the health and education programs. And the hokfusine— sooner or later some damned do-gooder'll squawk about compulsory medica- tion. And here's another angle: Under Colonial Law, nobody is chargeable with any degree of homicide in any case of a person killed while committing a felony. As minor children of under twelve, Fuzzies are legally incapable of committing felony. But if they're legally adults . . ."

Jack literally howled. "Then, anybody could shoot a Fuzzy, anytime, if he caught him breaking into something, or . . ."

"Well, say we drop the faginy charges," Fitz Mortlake suggested. "We still have the other barrel loaded. They can be shot just as dead for enslavement as for enslavement and faginy."

"Is the other barrel loaded, though?" Gus asked. "I can put that gang on the stand—thank all the gods and the man who invented the veridicator, there's no law against self-incrimination—I can't force them to talk. You can't do things in open court like you can in the back room at a police station. I may be able to get a conviction without the Fuzzies' testimony, but I can't guarantee it. Tell him about it, Dr. Mallin."

"Well." Ernst Mallin cleared his throat. "Well," he said again. "You all understand the principles of the polyencephalographic veridicator. All mental activity is accompanied by electromagnetic activity, in detectable wave patterns. The veridicator is so adjusted as to respond only to the wave patterns accompanying the suppression of a true statement and the substitution of a false statement, by causing the blue light in the globe to turn red. I have used the veridicator in connection with psychological experiments with quite a few Fuzzies. I have never had one change the blue light to red."

He didn't go into the legal aspects of that; that wasn't his subject. It was Gus Brannhard's:

"And court testimony, no exception, must be given under veridication, with a veridicator tested by having a test-witness make a random series of true and false statements. If Fuzzies can't be veridicated, then Fuzzies can't testify—like Leslie's blind man flying an aircar."

"Yes, and that'll play Nifflheim, too," Ahmed Khadra said. "How do you think we'll prosecute anybody for mistreating Fuzzies if the Fuzzies can't testify against him?"

"Or somebody claims Fuzzy adoptions are enslavement," Ben Rainsford said. "Victor's Diamond, for instance, or my Flora and Fauna. How could we prove that our Fuzzies are happy with us and wouldn't want to live anywhere else, if they can't testify to it?"

"Wait a minute. I'm just a layman," Grego said, "but I know that every accused person is entitled to testify in his own defense. These Fuzzies are accused persons, thanks to Hugo Ingermann himself."

Brannhard laughed. "Ingermann's hoping to hang us on that," he said. "He expects Leslie, who's defending them, to put them on the stand in Complaint Court, so that I'll have to attack their eligibility to testify and stop myself from using their testimony against his clients. Well, we won't do it that way. Leslie'll just plead them not guilty but chargeable and waive hearing."

"But then they'll all have to stand trial," Grego objected.

"Sure they will." The Attorney General's laugh became a belly-shaking guffaw. "Remember the last time a bunch of Fuzzies got loose in court? We'll just let them act like Fuzzies, and see what it does to Ingermann's claim that they're mature and responsible adults."

"Dr. Mallin," Coombes said suddenly. "You say you never saw a Fuzzy red-light a veridicator. Did you ever hear a Fuzzy make a demonstrably false statement under veridication?"

"To my knowledge, I never heard a Fuzzy make a demonstrably false statement under any circumstances, Mr. Coombes."

"Ah. And in *People* versus *Kellogg and Holloway* you gave testimony about extensive studies you had made of Fuzzies' electroencephalographic patterns. So their mental activity is accompanied by electromagnetic activity?"

Maybe it might be a good thing to have a lawyer sit in on every scientific discussion, just to see that the rules of evidence are applied. Mallin gave one of his tight little smiles.

"Precisely, Mr. Coombes. Fuzzies exhibit the same general wave-patterns as

Terrans or any other known sapient race. All but the suppression-substitution pattern which triggers the light-change in the veridicator. No detection instrument can function in the absence of the event it is intended to detect. Fuzzies simply do not suppress true statements and substitute false statements. That is, they do not lie."

"That'll be one hell of a thing to try to prove," Gus Brannhard said. "Fitz, you questioned those Fuzzies under veridication after the gem-vault job, didn't you?"

"Yes. Ahmed and Miss Glenn interpreted for them; Diamond helped too. The veridicator had been tested; we used scaled down electrodes and a helmet made up in the robo-service shop at Company House. We got nothing but blue from any of them. We accepted that."

"I would have, too," Brannhard said. "But in court we'll have to show that the veridicator would have red-lighted if any of them had tried to lie."

"We need Fuzzy test-witnesses, to lie under veridication," Coombes said. "If they don't know how to lie, we'll have to teach a few. I believe that will be Dr. Mallin's job; I will help. Do any of you gentlemen collect paradoxes? This one's a gem—to prove that Fuzzies tell the truth, we must first prove that they tell lies. You know, that's one of the things I love about the law."

Everybody laughed, except Jack Holloway. He sat staring glumly at the tabletop.

"So now, along with everything else we've got to make liars out of them too," he said. "I wonder what we'll finally end up making them."

$\mathbf{A}$HEAD, THE RAVINE fell sharply downward; on either side it rose high and steep above the little moving-water. The trees were not many here, but there were large rocks. They had to dodge among and climb over them, going in single file. Sometimes he led, and sometimes they would all be ahead of him, Fruitfinder and Lame One and Big She and Other She and Stabber and Carries-Bright-Things and Stonebreaker. They were not hunting—there was nothing to eat here—but ahead he could see blue sky above the trees and could hear the sound of another moving-water which this one joined.

Wise One hoped it would not be too deep or too rapid to cross. There was much moving-water here in all the low places between the hills and mountains. A place of much water was good because they could always drink when thirsty and because the growing-things they ate and the animals they hunted were more near water. But moving-waters were often hard to cross, and if they followed one they would come to where it joined another, and it would be big too. Without seeing it, he knew that this one flowed in the direction of the sun's left hand, for that was how the land sloped. Moving-waters always went down, never up, and they joined bigger ones. That was an always-so thing.

Then, before they knew it, they were out of the ravine and the woods stretched away on either side and in front of them and the moving-water was small and easy to cross. On the other side, the ground sloped up gently away from it, then rose in a steep mountainside. This would be a good place to find things to eat. They splashed across at a shallow place and ran up the bank, laughing and shouting, and spread out line-abreast, hunting under the big trees toward the side of the mountain. There were brown-nut trees here. They picked up sticks and stones and threw them to knock nuts down, and then Big She shouted:

"Look, nuts here already fall off tree. Many-many on ground."

It was so; the ground at the bottom of one tree was covered with them. They all ran quickly, gathering under the tree, laying nuts on big stones and pounding them with little ones to break the shells to get at the white inside. They were good, and enough for everybody; they ate as fast as they could crack them. They were all careful, though, to watch and listen, for in a place like this there was always danger. Animals could not hear their voices—that was an always-so thing which they could trust—but they made much noise cracking the nuts, and animals which hunted People would hear it and know what it was.

So they kept their clubs to hand, so that they could catch them up if they had to run quickly, and Carries-Bright-Things kept the three sticks with the bright-things on the ends with her club. They would not be able to stay here long, he thought. Long enough to eat as many of the nuts as they wanted, but no longer. He began to think whether to go down the stream or climb up the side of the mountain. Along the stream they would find more good-to-eat things, but the sun was well past highest-time, and they might find a better sleeping-place on the mountaintop. But this moving-water went in the direction of the sun's left hand, and that was the way he wanted to go.

They had been traveling steadily toward the sun's left hand for many days now. It was an always-so thing that after leaf-turning time, when the leaves became brown and fell, it became more cold toward the sun's right hand and stayed warmer to the sun's left; and People liked being where it was warm. Far to the sun's right hand, farther than he had ever been, it was said that it grew so cold at times that little pools of still water would be edged with hardness from the cold. This he had never seen for himself, but other People had told about it. So, ever since the day when they had seen the gotza killed by the thunder-death and had found the bright-things, they had been moving toward the sun's left hand.

He himself had another, even stronger, reason. Ever since he had seen the two Big Ones inside the flying thing, he had been determined to find the Big One Place.

He did not speak about this to the others. They were content to go where Wise One led them; but if he told them what was in his mind, they would all cry out against it and there would be argument, and nothing would be done. The others were still afraid of the flying Big Ones, especially Big She and Fruitfinder and Stonebreaker. He could understand that. It was always well to be at least a little afraid of something one did not know about, and a strange kind of People who went about in flying things and made thunder-death that killed gotza in the air could be very dangerous. But he was sure that they would be friendly.

They had killed the three gotza that had threatened him and the others at the cliff where they had been eating the hatta-zosa; they had been watching from above, and had done nothing until the gotza came, and then they had turned loose the thunder-death, and then they had gone away, leaving the three bright-things. And after chasing the other gotza in their flying thing and killing it, they had passed directly over him and the others, and must have seen them, but they had done no harm. That had been when he had made up his mind to find the Big One Place, and make friends with them. But when he had spoken of it to the others, they had all been afraid. All but Stabber; he had wanted to make friends with the Big Ones too, but when the others had been afraid he had said no more about it.

That had been two hands of sun-times and dark-times ago. Since then, they had seen flying things four times, always to the sun's left hand. He knew nothing about the country in that direction, but to the sun's right hand nobody had ever told of seeing flying things. So, he was sure, in order to find the Big One Place, he must go toward the sun's left hand. But he must not speak about it to the others, only say that it would be warmer to the sun's left hand, and talk about how they might find many zatku.

There was a crashing in the brush in the direction the moving-water came from, as though some big animal was running very fast. If so, something bigger was chasing it. He sprang to his feet, his club in one hand and the stone with which he had been cracking nuts in the other. The others were on their feet, ready to flee too, when a takku came rushing straight toward them.

Takku were not dangerous; they ate only growing-things. People did not hunt them, however, because they were big and too fleet of foot to catch. But behind the takku something else was coming, making more noise, and it would be something dangerous. He hurled his stone, throwing a little ahead of the takku, meaning to drive it and whatever was after it away from them. To his surprise, he hit it on the flank.

"Throw stones!" he shouted. "Chase takku away!"

The others understood; they snatched up stones and pelted the takku. One stone hit it on the neck. It swerved away from them, stumbled, and was trying to regain its feet when the hesh-nazza burst from the brush behind it and caught it.

Hesh-nazza were the biggest animals in the woods. They had three horns, one jutting from the middle of the forehead and one curving back from each lower jaw. Except for the gotza, which attacked from above, no animal was more feared by the People, and even the gotza never attacked a hesh-nazza.

Catching up with the takku, the hesh-nazza gored it in the side, in back of the shoulder, with its forehead-horn. The takku bleated in pain, and continued to bleat while the hesh-nazza struck it with its forefeet and freed its horn to gore again.

The Gashta did not stay to see what happened after that. The takku was still bleating as they ran up the mountainside; as they climbed, it stopped, and then the hesh-nazza gave a great bellow, as they always did after killing. By this time it would be tearing the flesh of the takku with its jaw-horns, and eating. He was glad he had thought to throw the stone, and tell the others to throw; if he had not, the takku would have run straight among them, and the hesh-nazza after it, and that would have been bad. Now, however, there was no danger, but they continued climbing until they were at the top. Then they all stopped, breathing hard, to rest.

"Better hesh-nazza eat takku than us," Lame One said.

"Big takku," Stabber remarked. "Hesh-nazza eat long time. Then go to sleep. Next sun-time, be hungry, hunt again."

"Hesh-nazza not come up here," Carries-Bright-Things said. "Stay by moving-water, in low place."

She was right; hesh-nazza did not like to climb steep places. They stayed by moving-waters, and hunted by lying quietly and waiting for animals, or for People, to come by. He was glad that he and the others had not crossed farther up the stream.

It would still be daylight for a time, but the sun was low enough that they should begin to think about finding a good sleeping-place. The top of this mountain was big and he could see nothing ahead but woods—big trees, some nut-trees. This would be a good place to sleep, and after the sun came out of its sleeping-place, they could go down into the low place on the other side.

"Go down way we came up," Big She argued. Lately, Big She was beginning to be contrary. "Good place; nut-trees."

"Bad place; hesh-nazza," Stabber told her. "Hesh-nazza go down moving-water little way, wait. We come, then we be inside hesh-nazza. Better do what Wise One say; Wise One knows best."

"First, find sleeping-place here," he said. "Now we go hunt. Everybody, look for good place to sleep."

The others agreed. They had seen nut-trees here too; where there were nut-trees, there were small animals, good to eat, which gnawed nut-shells open. They might kill and eat a few. Nuts were good, but meat was better. There might even be zatku up here.

They spread out, calling back and forth to one another, being careful to make no noise with their feet among the dead leaves. He thought about the takku. He and at least one of the others had hit it with stones. A person could throw a stone hard enough to knock down and sometimes even kill a hatta-zosa, but all the stones had done to the takku had been to frighten it. He wished there were some way People could kill takku. One takku would be meat enough for everybody all day, and some to carry to the sleeping-place for the next morning; and from a takku's leg-bones good clubs could be made.

He wished he knew how the Big Ones made the thunder-death. Anything that killed a gotza in the air would kill a takku. Why, anything that would kill a gotza would even kill a hesh-nazza! There must be no animal of which the Big Ones were afraid.

IT HAD BEEN a week before Jack Holloway had been able to get away from Mallorysport and back to Hoksu-Mitto, and by that time the new permanent office building was finished and furnished. He had a nice big room on the first floor, complete, of course, with a stack of paperwork that had accumulated on his desk in his absence. The old prefab hut had been taken down and moved across the run, and set up beside the schoolhouse as additional living quarters for Fuzzies, of whom there were now four hundred. That was a hell of a lot of Fuzzies.

"They're costing like hell too," George Lunt said. George and Gerd van Riebeek, who had returned from Yellowsand Canyon the day after the lease agreement had been signed, and Pancho Ybarra were with him in his new office the morning after his return. "And we have a hundred to a hundred and fifty more at the outposts, and hokfusine and Extee-Three to supply to the families living on farms and plantations."

George didn't need to tell him that. A lot of what had piled up on his desk had to do with supplies bought or on order. And the Native Commission payroll: two hundred fifty ZNPF officers and men, Ahmed Khadra's investigators, the technicians and construction men, the clerical force, the men and women working under Gerd van Riebeek in the scientific bureau, Lynn Andrews and her medical staff. . . .

"If that Yellowsand agreement goes out the airlock," Gerd van Riebeek voiced his own thoughts, "we'll have a hell of a lot of bills to pay and nothing to pay them with."

Nobody argued that point. Pancho Ybarra said, "It's on the Fuzzy Reservation; doesn't the Colonial Government control that?"

"Not the way we need, not if the Fuzzies aren't minor children. The Government controls the Reservation to enforce the law; that means, if the

Fuzzies are legally adults, nobody is permitted to mine sunstones on the Reservation without the Fuzzies' consent."

"Those fingerprint signatures on that agreement," George Lunt considered. "I know, they were only additional witnesses, but weren't they acquiescent witnesses? Wouldn't that do as evidence of consent?"

Gus Brannhard had thought of that a couple of days ago. Maybe that would stand up in court; Chief Justice Pendarvis had declined to give a guidance-opinion on it, which didn't look too good.

"Well, then, let's get their consent," Gerd said. "We have over four hundred here; that's the most Fuzzies in any one place on the planet. Let's hold a Fuzzy election. Elect Little Fuzzy paramount chief, and elect about a dozen subchiefs, and hold a tribal council, and vote consent to lease Yellowsand to the Company. You ought to see some of the tribal councils on Yggdrasil; at least ours would be sober."

"Or Gimli; I was stationed there before I was transferred to Zarathustra," Lunt said. "That's how the Gimli Company got consent to work those fissionable-ore mines."

"Won't do. According to law, what one of these tribal councils has to do is vote somebody something like a power of attorney to transact their business for them, and that has to be veridicated by the native chief or council or whatever granting it," he said.

Silence fell with a dull thump. The four of them looked at one another. Lunt said:

"With that much money involved, a couple of lawyers like Gus Brannhard and Leslie Coombes ought to be able to find some way around the law."

"I don't want to have to get around the law," Holloway said. "If we get around the law to help the Fuzzies, somebody else'll take the same road around it to hurt them." His pipe had gone out, and there was nothing in it but ashes when he tried to relight it. He knocked it into an ashtray and got out his tobacco pouch. "This isn't just for this week or this year. There'll be Fuzzies and other people living together on this planet for thousands of years, and we want to start Fuzzy-Human relations off right. We don't know who'll run the Government and the Company after Rainsford and Grego and the rest of us are dead. They will run things on precedents we establish now."

He was talking more to himself than to the three men in the office with him. He puffed on the pipe, and then continued.

"That's why I want to see Leo Thaxter and Evins and his wife and Phil Novaes shot for what they did to those Fuzzies. I'm not bloodthirsty; I've killed enough people myself that I don't see any fun in it. I just want the law clear and plain that Fuzzies are entitled to the same protection as human children, and I want a precedent to warn anybody else of what they'll get if they mistreat Fuzzies."

"I agree," Pancho Ybarra said. "In my professional opinion, to which I will testify, that's exactly what Fuzzies are—innocent and trusting little children, as helpless and vulnerable in human society as human children are in adult society. And the gang who enslaved and tortured those Fuzzies to make thieves out of them ought to be shot, not so much for what they did as for being the sort of people who would do it."

"What do you think about the veridication angle?" Lunt asked. "If we can't get that cleared up, we won't be able to do anything."

"Well, if a Fuzzy doesn't red-light a veridicator, it means the Fuzzy isn't lying," Gerd said. "You ever know a Fuzzy to lie? I've never known one to; neither has Ruth."

"Neither have I, not even the ones we've caught raising hell down in the farming country," Lunt said. "Every man on the Protection Force'll testify to that."

"Well, what's Mallin doing?" Gerd asked. "Is he going to get Henry Stenson to invent an instrument that'll detect a Fuzzy telling the truth?"

"No. He's going to teach some Fuzzies to lie so they can red-light a veridicator and show that it works."

"Hey, he can get shot for that!" Lunt said. "Lying is an immoral act. That's faginy!"

ONE OF THE Fuzzies, whose name was Kraft, sat cross-legged on the floor, smoking a pipe. The other was named Ebbing; she sat in a scaled-down veridicator chair, with a chromium helmet on her head. Behind her, a translucent globe mounted on a standard glowed clear blue. Ernst Mallin sat sidewise at the table, looking at them; across from him, Leslie Coombes was smoking a cigarette in silence.

"Ebbing, you want to help Unka Ernst, Unka Less'ee?" he was asking for the nth time.

"Sure," Ebbing agreed equably. "What want Ebbing do?"

"Your name Ebbing. You understand name?"

"Sure. Name something somebody call somebody else. Big Ones give all Fuzzies names; put names on idee-disko." She fingered the silver disk at her throat. "My name here. Ebbing."

"She knows that?" Coombes asked.

"Oh, yes. She can even print it for you, as neatly as it's engraved on the disk. Now, Ebbing. Unka Less'ee ask what your name, you tell him name is Kraft."

"But is not. My name Ebbing. Kraft *his* name." She pointed.

"I know. Unka Less'ee know too. But Unka Less'ee ask, you say Kraft. Then he ask Kraft, Kraft say his name Ebbing."

"Is Big One way to make fun," Coombes interjected. "We call it, Alias, Alias, Who's Got the Alias. Much fun."

"Please, Mr. Coombes. Now, Ebbing, you say to Unka Less'ee your name is Kraft."

"You mean, make trade with Kraft? Trade idee-disko too?"

"No. Real name for you Ebbing. You just *say* name is Kraft."

The blue-lit globe flickered, the color in it swirling, changing to dark indigo and back to pale blue. For a moment he was hopeful, then realized that it was only the typical confusion-of-meaning effect. Ebbing touched her ID-disk and looked at her companion. Then the light settled to clear blue.

"Kraft," she said calmly.

"Unholy Saint Beelzebub!" Coombes groaned.

He felt like groaning himself.

"You give new idee-disko?" Ebbing asked.

"She thinks her name is Kraft now. That's telling the truth to the best of her knowledge and belief," Coombes said.

"No, no; name for you Ebbing; name for him Kraft." He rose and went to her, detaching the helmet and electrodes. "Finish for now," he said. "Go make play. Tell Auntie Anne give estee-fee."

The Fuzzies started to dash out, then remembered their manners, stopped at the door to say, "Sank-oo, Unka Ernst; goo-bye, Unka Less'ee, Unka Ernst," before scampering away.

"They both believe now that I meant that they should trade names," he said. "The next time I see them, they'll be wearing each other's ID-disks, I suppose."

"They don't even know that lying is possible," Coombes said. "They don't have anything to lie about naturally. Their problems are all environmental, and you can't lie to your environment; if you try to lie to yourself about it, it kills you. I wish their social structure was a little more complicated; lying is a social custom. I wish they'd invented politics!"

9

WISE ONE WAS glad when they came to where the mountain "made finish" and dropped away, far down. This had not been a good place. There had been nut-trees, and they had eaten nuts. They had killed some of the little nut-eating animals, but not many, for they were hard to catch. They had found no moving-water on top of the mountain, only small pools of still-water from the last rain, and it had not tasted good. And the sleeping-place they had found had not been good either, and it had been one of the nights when both of the night-time lights had been in the sky, and the animals had all been restless, and they had heard a screamer, though not near. Screamers ate only meat and hunted in the dark. That had been why they had found no hatta-zosa. Hatta-zosa did not stay where there were screamers. Neither did People, if they could help it.

They stopped, looking out over the tops of the trees to the country beyond. There was another mountain far to the sun's left hand; its top stretched away, from sun-upward to sun-downward, with nothing but the sky beyond it. It was not steep, and its side was wrinkled with small valleys that showed where moving-waters came down. There must be a big moving-water below, so close to the bottom of this mountain that they could not see it. It must be a large one, because of all the little ones on both sides that flowed into it, and he was afraid it would be hard to cross.

The others were excited about the wide valley on the other side, and talked about what good hunting they would find there. They couldn't see the moving-water below, so they didn't think about it.

They started down, and as they went the mountainside grew steeper, and they had to cling to bushes and stop to rest against trees and use their killing-clubs to help them. As they went, they began to see the moving-water below. The sound of it grew louder. Finally they were seeing it all the time, and could see how big it was.

Big She began talking about turning back and climbing up to the top again.

"Moving-water too big; we not can cross," she argued. "Go down, no place to go. Better we go back up now."

"Then go beside it, way it come from," Lame One said. "Fine place to cross where it little."

"Not find good-to-eat things," Big She said. "Not find good-to-eat things since last daytime. Why Wise One not find good-to-eat things?"

Stabber became angry. "You think you wise like Wise One?" he demanded. "You think you find good-to-eat things?"

"Hungry," Fruitfinder complained. "Want to find good-to-eat things now. Maybe Big She right. Maybe better go back, go down other side."

"You want, you go back up mountain," he said. "We go down. Cross moving-water, find good-to-eat things other side."

Carries-Bright-Things agreed; so did Lame One and Other She. They started climbing down again; Big She and Stonebreaker and Fruitfinder followed without saying anything. At length the mountain became less steep, and through the trees they saw the moving-water in front of them. They went forward and stopped on the bank.

It was big, wide and swift. Lame One picked up a stone and threw it as hard as he could; it splashed far short of the other bank. Other She threw a stick into it, and in an instant it was carried away out of sight. Even if they had been willing to risk losing their killing-clubs and the bright-things, they could never have swum across it. Big She pointed at it with her club.

"Look! Look at place Wise One bring us!" she clamored. "No good-to-eat things; no way across the river. Now, climb all the way back up mountain."

"Climb up high-steep place?" Other She was horrified.

"You try cross that?" Big She retorted. Then she looked downstream and saw where the river curved away from the mountain. "Maybe go down there."

"That way moving-water we cross last day-time come down," he said. "Hesh-nazza that way. Eat all takku, be hungry, now."

Big She had forgotten about the hesh-nazza, and Big She was afraid of hesh-nazza, more even than the others. Once a hesh-nazza had almost caught her. She went back to insisting that they climb the mountain again. Fruitfinder thought they should, too. Stabber thought they ought to go up the river, which was the only thing to do. Finally all the others, even Big She, agreed.

It was hard going. The river flowed close against the mountain now, there was no bank, and they had to go in single file, clinging to bushes and trees as they went. Big She began complaining again, and so did some of the others.

Then, suddenly, they were around the shoulder of the mountain and there was a wide level place in front where a small valley opened out, with a little stream small enough to cross easily. Here the river was three or four stone-throws wide, and flowed among and over stones, shallow and flashing in the sunlight, and on both sides were long stony beaches, littered with old driftwood.

They started across. Mostly it was less than waist deep. In a few places it was deeper, and they formed a chain, each one holding to somebody else's killing-club. Finally, they were on the beach on the other side, and everybody, even Big She, was happy.

There was much driftwood here, even whole trees. This must be a place where the moving-water was high over the banks in rain-time. They all looked at the driftwood, and talked about what good killing-clubs it would make. They would have stopped to make new clubs, except that they were all hungry. They decided to hunt for food and then come back after they had eaten. So they started away from the river, into the woods, calling to one another.

There were no nut-trees here, but they found the pink fingerlike growing-things. They were good, but one could eat a great deal of them and still be hungry. But zatku also liked to eat them, and they found where zatku had been nibbling and, hunting carefully, found three. That was more zatku in one day than anybody could remember. And they found other things to eat, animals and growing-things, and by a little after sun-highest time none of them was hungry.

So they made their way back to the beach, and as they went they found where three fallen trees, washed out by the floods, lay together with a little gulley under them. This was a good sleeping-place; they would remember it and come back when the sun began to get low.

They looked again at the driftwood on the beach, dry and hard and white as the bones of animals. Wise One found nothing that would make a better club than the one he carried. It was a good club. He had worked a long time to make it. Some of the others didn't have good clubs, and they found straight branches that could be worked down. Some of the stones on the beach were very hard, and Stonebreaker, who was good at such work, began chipping them, making chopping-stones. Big She and Fruitfinder and Carries-Bright-Things squatted with him, watching him work and talking to him. Other She found a good piece of wood and a flat stone and sat down, holding the stick against one of the old trees and rubbing it with the stone to shape it. Lame One was also making a new club, and so was Stabber, who sat a little apart from the others. Wise One went over and sat with Stabber, who showed him the new club he was making. It was long, for stabbing.

"Good place, this," Stabber said as he worked. "Many good-to-eat things. Find three zatku." He was amazed at that. "More zatku here, many-many. And hatta-zosa. Find where they eat bark on trees." He rubbed the pointed end of his new club, sharpening it. "We stay here?"

"We have sleeping-place; maybe stay next day-time," he said. "Then go, find little moving-water, follow to where comes out of ground. Go up to top of mountain, go down other side."

"Other side like this. Why not stay here?"

"Other side more to sun's left hand. Big One Place to sun's left hand. Find Big Ones, make friends. Big Ones help us. Big Ones very wise, we learn from them," he said. "You want to find Big Ones?"

"I want to find Big Ones," Stabber said. "Others not want, others afraid. Listen to Big She." He laid down the stone and took the club in both hands, inspecting it. "Big She think she knows more than Wise One. Stonebreaker, Fruitfinder listen to her."

That was how bands broke up. It had happened once, long ago, when Old One was still alive and leading the band. There had been quarreling about where to go to hunt, and four of the band had gone away angry. They had never seen them again. Stabber's mother had stayed with the band; Stabber had been born two new-leaf times after that. He didn't want that to happen now. Eight People made a good band: not too many to find food for all, and enough to hunt line-abreast so that one would see what another missed, and enough to make a good hatta-zosa killing. And he did not want quarreling; it was not fun when People quarreled.

But he was going to the Big One Place, to find the Big Ones and make friends with them, even if he had to go alone. No, Stabber would go with him, and he thought Carries-Bright-Things would, too. And that would be another trouble-thing. If the band broke up, there would be quarreling about the bright-things.

Maybe Lame One and Other She would go with him, too. But who would lead the others? Big She wanted to lead, but she was not Wise One. She was Foolish One, Shoumko; if the others let her lead, soon they would all make dead. He wanted to keep the band together.

The sun went slowly across the sky toward its sleeping-place; the shadows grew longer. Stonebreaker was still chipping the hard stone, making a knife to use for cutting up hatta-zosa for the meat-sharing. They would carry it as long as they could, and the stone hand-chopper he had made. He wished they could carry more things with them, but a person had only two hands, and the killing-club must always be carried. Soon the tools Stonebreaker was making would be left behind and forgotten, or lost in crossing a moving-water. It was a wonder they had carried the bright-things as long as they had.

Lame One and Other She had finished their clubs; they went up the river along the bank. Stabber finished the weapon he was making; together they went down the river, past where the stream they had crossed the day before came in from the other side. They talked about the hesh-nazza they had seen the day before, and wondered where it was now. It could not cross, because the river was too deep and swift, and it was too big to get around the shoulder of the mountain to the shallow water where they had crossed.

They circled into the woods away from the river, coming back. They found no animals, but they each caught several of the little lizards and ate them. When they came back to the driftwood place, Lame One and Other She were back too, and had brought a hatta-zosa they had killed. They all ate, and by this time the sun was making colors in the sky, very pretty. They all watched until the colors were gone, and then went to the sleeping-place they had found. Everybody was happy, and they talked for a long time before going to sleep.

The next morning the sun made red colors all over the sky, even before it came out of its sleeping-place. They were prettier than last sundown-time, but everybody knew that it would rain, and nobody liked rain. They went to where Lame One and Other She had killed the hatta-zosa the day before, and killed three more of them. By the time they had eaten the last one, drops of rain were beginning to fall, and the sun had hidden itself and the sky was gray and black. They ran all the way back to the sleeping-place.

For a long time, they huddled together under the fallen trees; they could not keep completely dry, but they were out of the worst of the rain. Their fur was wet and clung to them, but they were not really cold, and they had eaten plenty of meat, which made them feel good.

Finally, the rain stopped. The things in the woods began to stir again, and after a while there were thin gleams of sunlight. Everybody was glad. They crawled out and talked about what they would do, and decided to go away from the river, toward the high ground, where they had not been before, and see what was there. Because they might find a better sleeping-place, they carried with them the knife and chopper Stonebreaker had made, and the bright-things.

They went to sun-upward, bearing up the slope toward the sun's left hand. They found many of the pink finger-things growing in shady places, and ate them. Zatku had been eating there, too; they hunted in tight circles, and soon found one, and then another. By this time they were all praising Wise One for bringing them to this good place, even Big She.

"Better than to sun's right hand," he told them. "More warm; this is everybody-know thing. We go to top of mountain, down other side. Everything better there."

Big She tried to argue; this was a good place; why go someplace else? Fruitfinder agreed with her. The others all said, "Wise One know best."

"How you know, better across mountain?" Big She challenged.

"Because is so. Is everybody-know thing." He tried to think how he knew, but couldn't. He knew why he wanted to go toward the sun's left hand, but he couldn't explain about finding the Big One Place without starting more quarreling. "Long-ago People tell," he said. That was something they would not argue about. "Long-ago People hear from other People," he went on, improvising. "Far-far to sun's left hand is good place. Always warm. Always find good-to-eat things. Many zatku, many hatta-zosa, all kinds of good-to-eat growing-things. Everything all the time, not something one time, something another time. Groundberries, redberries, tree-nuts, all good things all the time."

He didn't know there was anything like that to the sun's left hand at all; he was just making talk that it was so. But he was Wise One; the others thought that he knew.

"You listen to Wise One," Stabber said. "Wise One take us to good place."

"I not hear talk like that," Big She objected.

"You not remember," Stabber jeered. "You not remember hesh-nazza day before."

"My mother make talk like that." He wondered if maybe she hadn't, and wished he could remember more about her. A gotza had killed her when he had been very small. "Old One make talk, say she heard from other People." He turned to Carries-Bright-Things. "Old One your mother; she tell you."

Carries-Bright-Things looked puzzled. He knew she couldn't remember anything like that, but she thought she ought to. Finally, she nodded.

"Yes. Old One tell me," she said.

"Everybody-know thing," Lame One said. "All long-ago People tell about good place to sun's left hand."

Other She fidgeted. She couldn't remember anything like that at all, but all the others said they did. Maybe she had forgotten. They started off again, and found another zatku.

But Wise One hadn't heard any such long-ago People stories. He had just make talk that he had. He couldn't understand how he had been able to make not-so talk like that.

10

IT WAS ELECTION day at Hoksu-Mitto. Not Fuzzy tribal election; this was for Big Ones, for delegates to the Constitutional Convention, and it had been going on all over the planet, starting hours ago at Kellytown on Epsilon Continent.

Voting was a simple matter. Jack Holloway had exercised his right of suffrage in his own living room after finishing breakfast by screening the Constabulary post two hundred odd miles south of him and transmitting his fingerprints there. Then he loaded his pipe, and before he had it drawing properly the robot at Constabulary Fifteen had sent his prints to Red Hill. The election robot there had transmitted them to the planetary election office in Central Courts Building in Mallorysport on Alpha Continent, then reported back that Jack Holloway, of Hoksu-Mitto, formerly Holloway's Camp, was a properly registered voter, and the machine gave a small cluck and ejected a photoprinted ballot. He marked the ballot with an X after the name of the Hon. Horace Stannery, an undistinguished and rather less-than-brilliant lawyer in Red Hill but a loyal Company and Government man, and held it up to the transmitting screen.

The whole thing was handled precisely and secretly by incorruptible robots. At least, that was what all the school civics books said. He carried the ballot original over and put it in the drawer of his big table. Hang onto that, he thought; be a museum-piece in half a century. Then he put on the telecast screen while he drank another cup of coffee.

The Gamma Continent vote was all in, what there was of it. Ten seats on the Convention, eight of them Government-CZC regulars. In his own district on

Beta, seventy-eight votes, his own included, had given Stannery sixty-two, with the remaining sixteen divided between the two wildcat candidates. It was rather like that all over the continent. Alpha, where a hundred ten out of a hundred fifty seats were being contested, hadn't begun to vote yet; it was only 0445 there.

He kept a telecast screen on in his office throughout the morning. By noon, nine out of ten of the Rainsford-Grego slate were well in the lead everywhere. The polls had closed on Epsilon Continent: eighteen out of eighteen regulars elected. It went on like that all afternoon, and by cocktail time the election looked safe. They'd really have something to drink a toast to this afternoon.

The Fuzzies didn't seem to know that anything out of the ordinary was happening.

GERD VAN RIEBEEK was bothered. Not seriously worried, just nagged by a few small uncertainties and doubts. In the last three weeks, the Protection Force patrol, working to a radius of five hundred miles from Hoksu-Mitto, hadn't reported seeing a single harpy. In that time, there had been two shot in the Fuzzy country south of the Divide, and another one in the Yellowsand Valley to the north. But not one anywhere near Hoksu-Mitto in the last week. It was looking like Zarathustran pseudopterodactyls were becoming about as extinct as the Terran variety.

There hadn't been many to start with, of course. Their kills would have wiped out everything else long ago if there had been. Say, one harpy to about a hundred or two hundred square miles. And once *Homo s. terra* moved into the area, those wouldn't last long. People liked to be able to let the children run around outdoors, for one thing, and nobody wanted all the calves in a veldbeest herd eaten up before they could grow up. The harpy might have been lord of the Zarathustran skies before the Terrans came, but what chance had it against an aircar rated at Mach 3, carrying a couple of machine guns?

Not that Gerd liked harpies any better than anybody else; not even that he liked them, period. Along with everybody else on Zarathustra, he was convinced that there were two kinds of harpies—live ones and good ones. But he was a general naturalist; ecology was a big part of his subject, and he knew that as soon as you wipe out any single species, things that will affect a dozen other species are going to start happening because every living thing has a role in the general ecological drama.

Harpies were killers. All right, they kept something down; remove them, and that something would have a sudden increase, and that would deplete something they fed on. Or they would begin competing with some other species. And there could be side effects. There was that old story about how the cats killed the field mice and the field mice destroyed the bumblebees' nests. But the bumblebees pollenated clover; so, when the bird-lovers started shooting cats—just the way the Fuzzy-lovers were shooting harpies—the clover crop started to fail. Wasn't that something Darwin wrote up, back about the beginning of the first century Pre-Atomic?

The trouble was, he wasn't keeping up with things. He'd stopped being a general naturalist and become a Fuzzyologist. Well, the Company's Science Center tried to keep up with everything. After lunch—well, say just before cocktail time, which would be just after lunch in Mallorysport—he'd screen Juan Jimenez and find out if anything unusual was happening.

THE FUZZY NAMED Kraft—he was the male of the pair—wriggled in the little chair. The globe above and behind him glowed clear blue. Leslie Coombes sympathized with Kraft; he'd seen enough witnesses wriggling like that in the same kind of chair.

"You want to help Unka Ernst, Unka Less'ee," Ernst Mallin was pleading. "Maybe this is not so, but you say. You not, Unka Ernst, Unka Less'ee have bad trouble. Other Big Ones be angry with them."

"But, Unka Ernst," Kraft insisted. "I not break asht'ay, Unka Less'ee break."

The woman in the white smock said, "You tell Auntie Anne you break ashtray. Auntie Anne not be angry at you."

"Go ahead, Kraft. Tell Miss Nelson you broke ashtray," he urged.

"Come on, Kraft," Mallin's assistant said. "Who broke ashtray?"

The steady blue glow darkened and swirled, as though a bottle of ink had been emptied into it. There were brief glints of violet. Kraft gulped once or twice.

"Unka Less'ee broke asht'ay," he said.

The globe turned bright red.

Somebody said, "Oh, no!" and he realized that it was himself. Mallin closed his eyes and shuddered. Miss Nelson said something, and he hoped it wasn't what he thought it was.

"Oh, God; if anything like that happens in court . . ." he began. The red flush was fading from the veridicator globe. "You'd better send that veridicator to the shop. Or psychoanalyze it; it's gone bughouse."

"Unka Ernst," the Fuzzy was pleading. "Plis, not make do anymore. Kraft not know what to say."

"No, I won't, Kraft. Poor little fellow." Mallin released the Fuzzy from the veridicator, hugging him with a tenderness Coombes had never thought him capable of. "And Auntie Anne not angry with Unka Less'ee. Everybody friends." He handed Kraft to the girl. "Take him out, Miss Nelson. Give him something nice, and talk to him for a while."

He waited till she carried the Fuzzy from the room.

"Well, do you know what happened?" he asked.

"I'm not sure. We'll test the veridicator with a normally mendacious human, but I doubt if there's anything wrong with it. You know, a veridicator does not actually detect falsification. A veridicator is a machine, and knows nothing about truth or falsehood. You've heard, I suppose, of the experiment with the paranoid under veridication?"

"Got that in law-school psychology. Paranoid claimed he was God, and the veridicator confirmed his claim. But why did this veridicator red-light when Kraft was telling the truth?"

"The veridicator only detects the suppression of a statement and the substitution of another. The veridicator here had a subject with two conflicting statements, both of which he had to regard as true. We were insisting that he confess to breaking that ashtray, so, since we said so, it must be true. But he'd seen you break it, so he knew that was also true. He had to suppress one of these true-relative-to-him statements."

"Well, maybe if he tries it again . . ."

"No, Mr. Coombes." Even Frederic Pendarvis ruling on a point of law could not have been more inflexible. "I will not subject this Fuzzy to any more of this. Nor Ebbing. They are both beginning to develop psychoneurotic symptoms, the first I have ever seen in any Fuzzy. We'll have to get different subjects. How about your defendants, Mr. Coombes?"

"Well, the test-witness isn't supposed to be a person giving actual testimony. Besides, I don't want them taught to lie and then have them do it on the stand. How about some of the Fuzzies at Holloway's?"

"I talked to Mr. Holloway. While he's aware of the gravity of the situation, he was most hostile to using any of his own family, or Major Lunt's, or Gerd and Ruth van Riebeek's. He uses those Fuzzies as teachers, and lying isn't something he wants on the curriculum at Fuzzy school."

"No. I can see that." Jack wasn't the type to win battles by losing the war. "Have you no other Fuzzies?"

"Well, certainly Mrs. Hawkwood wouldn't want the ones I've loaned her for the schools trained in prevarication. And the ones I have helping with mental patients at the hospital have been successful mainly because of their complete agreement with reality. I don't know, Mr. Coombes."

"Well, we only have three weeks till the trial opens, you know."

11

WISE ONE WAS not happy. They had been in this place for four day-times and four dark-times, and none of the others wanted to leave. It was a good place, and he himself would have wanted to stay if it were not that he wanted more to go on to the Big One Place.

They had found it almost toward sundown-time on the day it had rained by following a little moving-water up the side of the mountain the way from which it came into a little valley that had been wide when they had first entered it and had become narrower as the mountain had grown steeper on either side. They had found a good sleeping-place where a tree had fallen in a small hollow beside a rock-ledge. Back under the ledge and the fallen tree the ground had been dry, although it had rained hard until sun-highest-time. They had gathered many ferns and had made a bed big enough for all of them together, and had made a place to put the bright-things so that they would not have to carry them when they hunted. After the first night, with the sleeping-place made, they played on the bank of the little moving-water until it became dark. There were good-to-eat growing-things nearby, and hatta-zosa among the trees below and on either side; and best of all, there were many zatku, more than anybody could remember. Last day-time they had found and eaten a whole hand and one finger of them, almost a whole zatku for each of them.

They had seen flying-things several times after they had crossed the moving-water to the sun's right hand. Always they had been far away, to sun-upward. They seemed to be going along over the great-great moving-water that went from the sun's left hand toward the sun's right hand. Big She and some of the others had been afraid and had hidden, but that had been foolish, for the flying-things were too far away for the Big Ones in them to see. Big She said they were hunting, and would eat them all if they found them. That was more of Big She's foolishness. The Big Ones were People, and People did not eat People. That was a foolish thing even to think about. Only gotza ate their own kind. And the Big Ones must hate gotza, for they killed them whenever they found them. But Big She and Stonebreaker and Fruitfinder, who listened to her, were afraid, and their foolish talk made the others afraid too.

Stabber was not afraid of the Big Ones, though. He had talked about how good it would be to find them and make friends with them, but the others had all cried out about that, and there had been the beginning of a quarrel. After that Stabber had kept quiet, except when the two of them were alone together.

They were together now along the moving-water below the open end of the little valley, looking for zatku and staying away from the places where the hatta-zosa fed, so as not to frighten them away. The others were all at the sleeping-place, resting and playing; they had hunted all morning and made a big hatta-zosa killing, and nobody was hungry. Stonebreaker was making another knife, better than the other one, and the rest were making telling-things with little stones on the ground about how many hatta-zosa they had killed and how many zatku. They would do that until near sundown-time, and then they would go out and hunt again. That was what they did each day.

It was nice to have a place like this, where they could rest and play all they wanted and not have to move all the time. Stabber was saying so now.

"Find place like this at Big One Place," Wise One told Stabber. "Maybe Big Ones have places like this. Go away far in flying-things to hunt, always come back to same place."

"You think Big Ones live across mountain?"

He nodded. "Maybe across other mountains, across many mountains. But Big Ones live to sun's left hand."

He was sure of that. He tried to think how he knew it, but that was harder. He pointed to the sun's right hand, to the line of mountains across the moving-water they had crossed a hand of days ago. Then he sat on the ground and picked up a stick and scratched a line with it.

"Moving-water we crossed at stony place; you remember?" Stabber, squatting beside him, did. "Goes that way, to great-great moving-water nobody can cross. Great-great moving-water goes to sun's right hand. Some place, far-far to sun's left hand, great-great moving-water little, like this, comes out of ground."

Stabber agreed. All moving-waters came out of the ground somewhere, that was an everybody-knows thing. Moving-waters became big because other moving-waters flowed into them. He scratched another line to show the great-great moving-water.

"Must be far-far, for great-great moving-water to get so big. Many little moving-waters come into it," Stabber considered.

"Yes. This place a nobody-know place. Nobody ever tell about it. Big Ones come from some place nobody ever tell about before. Far-far place. And flying-things come from sun's left hand. We know; we see."

"Big Ones must be very wise," Stabber said. "Go in flying-things, make thunder-death. I think flying-things made-things. Big Ones make like we make clubs, cutting-stones. I think Big Ones make bright-things too."

He nodded. That was what he thought, too.

"Among Big Ones, we be like little baby ones," he said. "Not wise at all. People help little baby ones, teach them. Big Ones help us, teach us. Big Ones not let gotza, hesh-nazza catch us, eat us. Make gotza, hesh-nazza dead with thunder-death."

He looked out across the valley; he could see, far away, the ravine in the other mountain from which they had fled the hesh-nazza. Big Ones would not have fled; they would have made the hesh-nazza dead, and then cut it up and eaten it.

"But others, Big She, Other She, Stonebreaker, Fruitfinder, all afraid of Big Ones," Stabber said. "And not want to leave this place."

Then, he and Stabber would go alone. But he didn't want to leave the others; he wanted them to go along too. He looked at the mountains to the sun's right hand again.

"Maybe," he said hopefully, "Hesh-nazza come across moving-water. Then all afraid to stay; want to go away."

"But hesh-nazza not cross. Water too deep, too fast. And hesh-nazza not able to go around, way we did," Stabber objected.

That was so. But he wished the hesh-nazza would come over to this side. They would all want to leave, especially Big She. If he could see it first and be able to warn them . . . Then a thought occurred to him.

"We go back to sleeping-place, now," he said. "We tell the others hesh-nazza come. We tell them we see hesh-nazza. Then they all want to go."

"But . . ." Stabber looked at him in bewilderment. "But hesh-nazza not here." He couldn't understand. "How we say we see hesh-nazza?"

It would be like the way he had told them about the long-ago People stories about the wonderful country to the sun's left hand. It would be a not-so thing, but he would speak as though it were so.

"You want to go to Big One Place?" he asked. "You want some go one place, some go other place, never see again? Then, we make others afraid to stay here. They not know we not see hesh-nazza. You think Big She go to look? You not make foolish-one talk!"

"Hesh-nazza not here, we tell others hesh-nazza here?" Stabber thought about it, realizing that it would be possible to do it. Then he nodded. "They not know. We tell them, they think hesh-nazza here. Come."

"Make run fast," he said. "Hesh-nazza chase us; we afraid."

They dashed among the others, shouting, "Hesh-nazza! Hesh-nazza come!" All the others, who were between the sleeping-place and the small moving-water, sprang to their feet. They all believed the hesh-nazza was upon them. Carries-Bright-Things ran and got the three sticks with the shining things on them; Stonebreaker caught up the chopper and the knife he had made and the knife on which he was working. Nobody wasted time on argument. They all scampered up the side of the little ravine away from the sleeping-place and the little moving-water. When they were out of the ravine, they all ran very fast, up the side of the mountain.

"Make hurry, make hurry!" he urged. "Not stop now. Maybe hesh-nazza come up here."

Hesh-nazza did that. Anything they could not catch by lying still and waiting they would try to catch by circling around. That was an everybody-knows thing. The ones who had begun to slow made haste again.

They all slowed down, however, as the trees ahead of them became thinner. Finally, near the top, they stopped, and kept still to listen. They could hear birds and small animals in the brush. Everybody relaxed; the hesh-nazza was not close now. Wise One was relieved too, until he remembered that there was no hesh-nazza. He had only said there was.

They came to the edge of the mountain. It fell away in front of them, steeper and higher than the one they had come down on the other side of the river. Below and beyond were no more big mountains, only small hills and ridges, and there would be many moving-waters and woods in which to hunt. Far away, so far as to be almost as blue as the sky and hard to see against it, a high mountain stretched away on both hands until it was beyond seeing. It was from this mountain, he was sure, that the great-great river that flowed to the sun's right hand came.

The others, even Big She, who had been complaining because they had had to leave the nice place behind, were crying out at the wonder of everything in front of them. Then he saw a tiny brightness in the sky, so small that he lost it when he looked away and had trouble finding it again. Then, directly in front, he saw another. At first he thought it was the first one, and wondered at how fast it had moved, even for a Big Ones' flying thing. But then he saw that it was another, and he could see both of them. *Two* flying-things! He had never seen more than one at a time.

Now he knew that he had been right all along. The Big One Place *was* to the sun's left hand, perhaps just over those high mountains in the distance.

12

THREE DAYS AFTER the election, Gus Brannhard landed his aircar at Hoksu-Mitto at mid-afternoon. It had been a long time—since before the Pendarvis Decisions—since Jack had seen him in anything but city clothes. Now he was the old Gus Brannhard, in floppy felt hat, stained and faded bush jacket with cartridge-loops on the breast, hunting knife, shorts and knee-hose, and ankle boots. He got out of the car, shook hands, and looked around. Then, after dragging out a canvas kit bag and two rifle-cases, he looked around again.

"God, Jack, you have this place built up," he said. "It looks worse on the ground even than it did from the air. I hope you don't have all the game scared out of the country."

"For about ten, fifteen miles is all. George Lunt sends a couple of men out each day to shoot for the pot." He picked up the kit bag Gus had set down. "Let's get you settled and then have a look around."

"Any damnthings?"

"A few. The Fuzzies who come in at the posts to the south mention seeing hesh-nazza. We're not shooting any back of the house, the way I did in June. And we're not seeing any harpies anywhere, lately."

"Well, that's a good job!" Gus didn't like harpies either. Come to think of it, nobody did. "I'm going to stay a couple of days, Jack. Maybe go out and pot a zebralope, or a river-pig, tomorrow. Just take it easy. Next day I'll go looking for damnthings."

Back in the living room, Jack got out a bottle. "It's an hour till cocktail time," he apologized, "but let's have a primer. On the election." He poured for both of them, raised his glass, and said, "Cheers."

"I hope we have something to cheer about." Gus lowered his drink by about a third. "We elected a hundred and twenty-eight out of a hundred and fifty delegates. That looks wonderful—on paper." He halved what was left of his drink. "About forty of them we can rely on. Company men and independent businessmen who know where their business comes from. Another thirty or so are honest politicians; once they're bought, they stay bought. It's amazing," he parenthesized, "how fast we grew a crop of politicians once we got politics on this planet. As for the rest, at least they aren't socialists or labor-radicals or Company-haters. They're the best we could do, and I'm hoping, though not betting, that they'll be good enough. At least there's nobody against us with money enough to buy them away from us."

"When'll the Convention be?"

"Two weeks from Monday. It'll be at the Hotel Mallory; the Company's picking up the tab for the whole thing. Starts with a banquet on Sunday evening. I know what it'll be like. In the mornings they'll all be nursing hangovers." Gus was contemptuous; he'd probably never had a hangover in his life. "And in the evenings they'll be throwing parties all over the hotel. We'll get a couple of hours work out of them in the afternoons. That may be all to the good." He looked at his empty glass, then at the bottle. Jack pushed it across the table to him. "You take any hundred and fifty men like this Horace Stannery here, or Abe Lowther at Chesterville, or Bart Hogan in the Big Bend district—I got him acquitted of a cattle-rustling charge a year and a half ago—and every one of them'll try to show their constituents what statesmen they are by sponsoring some lame-brained amendment nobody else is witless enough to think of. That was a good constitution Leslie Coombes and I wrote. I hate to think of what it'll be like when it's adopted."

He finished his second drink. Before he could start on another, Jack suggested, "Let's go out and look around till the gang starts collecting."

They started down the walk toward the run. There were quite a few Fuzzies playing among the buildings, since it was late enough for them to have lost interest in lessons and drifted out of the school-hut. More had crossed the bridge to watch the fascinating things the Big Ones were doing around the vehicle park.

Two, both males, approached. One said, "Heyo, Pappy Jack," and the other asked, "Pappy Jack, who is Big One with face-fur?"

Gus laughed and squatted down to their level.

"Heyo, Fuzzies. What names you?"

They gave him blank stares. He examined the silver ID-disks at their throats. They were blank except for registration numbers. "What's the matter, Jack? Don't they have names?"

"Except the ones who want to stay here, we don't name them; we let the people who adopt them do that."

"Well, don't they have names of their own? Fuzzy names?"

"Not very good ones. Big One and Little One and Other One and like that. In the woods, mostly they call each other You."

Gus was scratching one on the back of the neck, which all Fuzzies appreciated. The other was trying to get his knife out of the sheath.

"Hey, quit that. Not touch; sharp. You savvy sharp?"

"Sure. Knife for me sharp, too." He drew it from the sheath on his shoulder bag and showed it: three-inch blade, which would be equivalent to nine-inch for a human. The edge was razor-keen; he'd been around here long enough to learn how to keep a knife honed. The other Fuzzy showed his too, and Gus let them look at his. It had a zarabuck-horn grip; they recognized that at once.

"Takku," one said. "You kill with noise-thing?"

"Big Ones," the other said reprovingly, "call takku zarabuck. Big Ones call noise-thing gun."

They tagged along, talking about everything they saw. Gus lifted them, one to each shoulder, and carried them. Taking rides on Big Ones was something all Fuzzies loved. They were still riding on Uncle Gus when they returned to the camp-house, where George Lunt and Pancho Ybarra were mixing cocktails and Ruth van Riebeek and Lynne Andrews were assembling snacks. Usually Fuzzies didn't hang around at cocktail time; this was when Big Ones wanted to make Big One talk. These two, however, refused to leave Gus, and sat with him on the grass, sipping hokfusinated fruit juice through straws.

"You're hooked, Gus," George Lunt told him cheerfully. "You're Pappy Gus from now on."

"You mean they want to stay with me?" Gus seemed slightly alarmed. He liked Fuzzies, the way some bachelors like children, as long as they're somebody else's. "You mean, all the time?"

"Sure," he said. "Little Fuzzy's been spreading the word; all the Fuzzies will have Big Ones of their own. They've picked you for their Big One."

"You be Big One for us?" one of the Fuzzies asked. They both lost interest in their fruit juice and tried to climb onto his back. "We like you."

"Well, mightn't be such a bad idea, at that," Gus considered. "I'm going to get a place of my own, out of town, say ten or fifteen minutes flying-time." With the kind of aircar he flew, and the way he flew it, that would be four or five hundred miles. "I like it where it gets dark at night, and if you want noise, you have to make it yourself."

"I know." He looked around Hoksu-Mitto and thought of what Holloway's Camp had been like. "It used to be that way here."

The next morning, Gus was still in bed when Holloway went across the run to his office. He got through his paperwork in a couple of hours and then looked in at the school and at Lynne Andrews's clinic, dispensary and hospital. Lynne had another viable Fuzzy birth to report, and was as proud as though she had accomplished it herself. That would be one of the first wave to get down into the Piedmont and cash in on the land-prawn boom. The Fuzzy gestation period was a little over six months. It would be March or April at the earliest before the hokfusine-babies started coming in. Maybe, in time, they'd have a population explosion to worry about. Give that the Scarlett O'Hara treatment; enough other things to think about today.

He found Gus Brannhard on what passed for the lawn of the camp-house, playing with the two Fuzzies.

"I thought you were going hunting this morning."

Gus looked up, grinning as sheepishly as his leonine features permitted.

"I thought I was, too. Then I got to playing with the kids here. Maybe I will this afternoon, but I just feel lazy."

He just felt tired, was what. He'd been pushing himself hard; probably hadn't had two good nights sleep in a row since *People* versus *Kellogg and Holloway* had been scheduled for trial.

"Why don't you take the kids hunting? I think they'd like it."

That hadn't occurred to Gus. "Well, but they might get hurt. Or lost; mind, I'm going five, six hundred miles to hunt."

"They won't get lost. When you set your car down, leave the generator on, on neutral. They can hear the vibrations for five or six miles; if you get lost, they'll lead you back. George Lunt's boys always do that when they go out with Fuzzies."

"Suppose I shoot something; won't that scare them?"

"Nah, they like shooting. They're always underfoot at the Protection Force target range. And I think you'll all three have fun."

"Hear that, kids? You want to go with Unka Gus, hunt takku, hunt . . . what the hell's the Fuzzy for zebralope?"

"Kigga-hikso."

"Zeb'alope? You shoot zeb'alope too?" the Fuzzies both asked.

Gus wasn't back till after the crowd began assembling for cocktails at the camp-house that afternoon; when he came in he set the car down in back of the cookhouse first, then brought it across the run and grounded beside the house. The Fuzzies jumped out at once, shouting, "Kill zeb'alope! Kill zarabuck! Unka Gus kill zeb'alope, two zarabuck!"

Gus came over more slowly, unslinging his rifle, dropping out the magazine and clearing the chamber, picking up the ejected round. He was laughing as he leaned the rifle beside the bench at the kitchen door.

"Give me a drink, somebody. No, not that stuff; isn't there any unadulterated whiskey around? Thank you, George." He poured from the bottle Lunt gave him, took a big drink and refilled his glass. "My God, you should have seen those kids! We set down beside a little creek a couple of miles above where it empties into Snake River. First of all, that one over there yelled, 'Zatku! Zatku!' and took off with his chopper-digger. The other one started circling around, and in a minute or so he had one. So we hunted zatku—land-prawn; goddamnit, as soon as you learn the native names for things, the natives start talking Lingua Terra. Then, after they killed a couple of them, they were after me, 'Pappy Gus, now we hunt zeb'alope.' So we hunted zebralope.

"They don't hunt by scent, like dogs, but they're the smartest trackers I ever saw. Look, you've hunted on Loki; so have I. You know how good the Bush Dwanga there are. Well, these Fuzzies could make the best Dwanga tracker I ever hunted with look like a blind imbecile. As soon as they find a fresh track, they split. One went one way, and the other another. In a minute, there was a big zebralope, damn near the size of a horse, running right at me. I gave him one in the shoulder and one in the neck; that finished him. So I gutted it. I knew they like raw liver, so I sliced the liver up for them. They wanted me to eat some. I told them Big Ones didn't like raw liver. Now they think Big Ones are all nuts. They ate the kidneys too. So then we hunted zarabuck. We got two. Your namesakes, Gerd; van Riebeek's zarabuck—the little gray ones."

"Did they eat the livers and kidneys from them too?" Lynne Andrews demanded. "You bring them around to the dispensary tomorrow."

"Well, there is one thing for damn-good-an'-sure: I'm adopting two Fuzzies. They're the best hunting companions I ever had. Beat a dog every way from middle; better hunters, and better company. You can talk to a dog, but a dog can't talk back to you, and Fuzzies can. Unka Gus and his Fuzzies are going to have a lot of fun. *Pappy* Gus," he corrected himself. "Pappy is the title of a Big One who stands *in loco parentis* to a Fuzzy; Unka just means *amicus Fuzziae* in general."

"What are you going to call them?"

"I don't know." Brannhard thought for a moment. "George named his crowd after criminals. Fitz Mortlake named his for detectives and spies. I'll have to name mine for hunters. Fiction-names: Allan Quartermain and Natty Bumppo. You hear that, kids? You have names now. Allan Quartermain name for you; Natty Bumppo name for you. Now, I hope I don't forget which is which."

• • •

THE NEXT DAY, he teleprinted the Fuzzies' registration numbers, fingerprints and new names to Mrs. Pendarvis at the Adoption Bureau, so Gus Brannhard was now officially Pappy Gus. With some misgivings, Pappy Gus took Allan Quartermain and Natty Bumppo damnthing hunting. He carried his big double express, and took one of George Lunt's men, similarly armed, along. Damn-things were nothing for one man, or one man and two Fuzzies, to go after alone. The Fuzzies had excellent suggestions about how to find one, but they thought Pappy Gus and the other Big One were taking foolish chances to get out of the car and shoot it on foot.

"Thought I'd have some difficulty explaining that," Gus said when he returned. "Sportsmanship is not usually an aboriginal virtue. Put in the form of 'more fun,' though, they got it. I taught them how to shoot, too. They thought that was fun."

"Not with a 12.7 express, I hope."

"No, with my pistol." Gus's pistol was an 8.5-mm Mars-Consolidated, a hunting weapon with an eight-inch barrel and a detachable shoulder-stock. "It was too clumsy for them, but the recoil didn't bother them at all. I was surprised. I thought it'd kick hell out of them, but it didn't. They liked it."

Holloway was surprised too. He'd thought that even a .22 would be too much for a Fuzzy.

"I'm going to have Mart Burgess make up a couple of little rifles for them," Gus was saying. "Eight-point-five pistol, say about four pounds. Single-shot, at least for their first ones. Too many complications about an auto-loader for a Fuzzy to remember."

If anybody could make a Fuzzy-size rifle, Mart Burgess could. He was the same sort of gunsmith as Henry Stenson was an instrument-maker. You only found that sort of craftsmanship on low-population planets where there was no mass market to encourage mass production. Holloway didn't quite like the idea, though.

"All the other Fuzzies'll hear about it, and they'll want rifles too. You give rifles to primitive peoples, you know what happens? Teach these Fuzzies about bows, and they can make their own, the way the Fuzzies are doing here. Give a Stone Age people steel spears and knives and hatchets, and one will last years. As soon as they learn blacksmithing they can make their own out of any scrap they pick up. But give them firearms, and they have to have ammunition. They can't make that themselves; they're past the point of no return. The next thing, they forget how to use their own weapons, and then they really are hooked."

Gus said the same thing Pancho Ybarra had said a couple of weeks ago.

"They're hooked now, on hokfusine, even if they don't know it. They can't get enough from land-prawns.

"And talk about being hooked, how about yourself? You don't make your own ammunition; you even stopped reloading because it was too much bother. What *do* you use that you make yourself?"

"That's different. I trade for what I use. It used to be sunstones; now it's the work of running this madhouse. With you, it used to be defending criminals, and now it's prosecuting them. But we both trade, and the Fuzzies haven't anything to trade. What they get from us is free handouts."

"Like Nifflheim they haven't anything to trade. You mean to sit there and tell me you don't get anything from Little Fuzzy and Mamma Fuzzy and Baby and the rest of your family? If you don't, why don't you get rid of them? You think Victor Grego doesn't get something from that Fuzzy of his? Why, he'd kill anybody who tried to take Diamond away from him. Or my Allan and Natty, that I've only had since yesterday?

"You talk about anybody being hooked; *we're* hooked. Hooked on Fuzzies. And they earn everything they get from us just by being around. You just let them keep on being Fuzzies, and don't worry about anything else. They'll be all right as long as we're all right to them."

13

TWO DAYS LATER Gus Brannhard went back to Mallorysport, taking Allan Quartermain and Natty Bumppo along, all three happy. The other Fuzzies were all happy too; envy, like lying, was a vice Fuzzies didn't have. There was a big crowd of them to see their friends off, and Jack watched them break into little groups to return to play or lessons, all talking about how nice it was for Natty and Allan, and how soon they'd all have Big Ones of their own, too. He went back across the run to his office.

There was more topographic data and detail-maps of the country north of the Divide sent down from Yellowsand Canyon. Everybody had known, in general, what the country was like up there, mostly from telescopic observations made on Xerxes Naval Base. What they were getting now was low-level air-survey stuff, mostly of the Yellowsand River and the Lake-Chain River which joined it from the west. This, of course, didn't show how many Fuzzies there were up there, or where. Not many, he supposed, and it'd be a Nifflheim of a job contacting them.

He got his hat and went out, crossing the run again. The schoolhouse was relatively quiet. There was a small class in progress, run by Syndrome and Calamity Jane and a couple of the new teaching Fuzzies, on how to make talk in back of mouth like Big Ones. Ruth van Riebeek and Mamma Fuzzy and Ko-Ko and Cinderella were running a class in Lingua Terra—"Big Ones not say zatka, say lan'-p'awn." Fuzzies, he noticed, had trouble with r-sounds, and consonant-sounds following other consonants. Three more were doing black-smith work. They had some photocopied pictures from some book on ancient pregunpowder weapons, of Old Terran English bills and Swiss halberds. They were making a halberd now with a steel staff. Wooden staves were too flimsy for their strength, or else too awkwardly thick. Outside, there was shouting mixed with yeeks.

He went out the other end of the hut, trailing pipesmoke, and found fifty or sixty of them at archery practice, waiting their turns to shoot at a life-size and not implausible-looking padded and burlap-covered figure of a zarabuck. Gerd van Riebeek was acting as range officer, with Dillinger and Ned Kelly and Little Fuzzy and Id coaching. One Fuzzy, his feet apart, drew his arrow to his ear and loosed it, plunking it into where the zarabuck's ribs would have been. Before it landed, he had another arrow out of his quiver and was nocking it.

"Anybody seen the High Sheriff of Nottingham around anywhere?" Gerd asked. "He better get on the job, or the king'll be fresh out of deer."

The second arrow went into the burlap zarabuck at the base of the neck. More names for Fuzzies—Robin Hood, Friar Tuck, Little John, Will Scarlet. . . .

A zarabuck would feed the average Fuzzy band for two days, or a double band for a day, and the woods were lousy with zarabuck. More meat to a kill would mean that Fuzzies could operate in larger bands. And a zarabuck-hide would make three or four shoulder bags, not as good as the waterproof, zipper-closed, issue-type, but good enough to carry things; and Fuzzies needed some way to carry things. He remembered the pitifully few possessions Little Fuzzy's band had brought in with them; and by Fuzzy standards they'd been rich. Usually, a band would have only their clubs, and maybe a flake knife or a *coup-de-poing* axe. At bottom, any culture was a matter of possessions—things to do things with. Everything else—law, social organizations, philosophy— came later.

Robin Hood, or Samkin Aylward, or whoever he was, had shot his third arrow; he and all the others bolted down the hundred yards to the target. It was a miracle, the way those kids had picked archery up; less than a month, and it would take a couple of years to make that kind of archers out of humans. A Fuzzy in the woods, with a bow, could eat mighty well. Fifteen or twenty Fuzzies with bows wouldn't have any trouble at all keeping everybody well-fed, all the time. They could make permanent homes, and wouldn't have to be on the move all the time. That might be the way to handle it: a string of Fuzzy villages all through the Piedmont, with patrol cars dropping in every couple of days to keep them supplied with hokfusine. Maybe big villages, with a ZNPF trooper as permanent resident.

And, what the hell, give them rifles and ammunition. An 8.5-mm high-speed pistol cartridge would kill a zarabuck; Gus Brannhard had potted quite a few with his Mars-Consolidated. Even kill a harpy; and a couple of 8.5's in the right places would make a damnthing lose interest in Fuzzy for dinner. So, they'd need ammunition. Well, they needed hokfusine anyhow, and a case of cartridges now and then wouldn't make much difference. One thing, needing cartridges they'd stay around where they'd get hokfusine too.

THE NEXT DAY, Victor Grego dropped in en route to Yellowsand, accompanied by Diamond. After saying hello to all his human friends in sight and asking Pappy Vic's permission, Diamond went off with Little Fuzzy to see the sights.

"How many Fuzzies do you have now?" Grego asked, as he and Jack strolled toward the schoolhouse.

Jack told him, around five hundred. Like everybody else, Grego thought that was a hell of a lot of Fuzzies in one place. Well, damn it, it was, and there didn't seem to be much that could be done about it.

"Coming in, I saw a couple of hundred of them along Cold Creek, below where the run comes in," he added. "Had some fires going, and there were a couple of lorries grounded with them. More of your gang?"

"Oh, yes. That's the shipyard and naval academy. We're teaching them how to build rafts and paddle and steer them. Rivers give Fuzzies a lot of trouble; a river like the main Snake or the Blackwater's bigger to a Fuzzy than the Amazon on Terra or the Fa'ansare on Loki is to us. That's why we get so many of them here; the river systems to the north funnel a lot of them down Cold Creek."

"This crowd doesn't need to build rafts anymore. They've made it on their own. They've joined the Human-People now."

And he couldn't take them back and dump them in the woods; he realized that now. The vilest cruelty anybody can commit is to give somebody something wonderful and then snatch it away again.

"I don't know what the Nifflheim I'm going to do with them," he admitted. "It'll depend on how this minor-child status holds up, for one thing."

"We can get that written into the Constitution," Grego said. "That's if we can get it adopted after we write it in."

They had almost reached the schoolhouse. He stopped short.

"You think there's any doubt?" he asked.

"Well, you know what kind of a goddamn rabble of delegates we have; fifty or sixty we can depend on, and it takes a two-thirds vote to adopt a constitution. The rest of that gang would sell us out for a candy-bar."

"Well, give them a candy-bar. Give them two candy-bars, and a gold-plated eight-bladed Boy Scout knife." He repeated what Gus Brannhard had said about no opposition with money enough to buy them away from the Company and the Government.

"That's what I'm worried about. Hugo Ingermann," Grego said. "I know what he wants to do in the long run. He wants to wreck the Company and Ben Rainsford's Government, both, and build himself up on the ruins. That People's Prosperity Party looks dead now, but those things are as hard to kill as a Nidhog swampcrawler, and just as poisonous. What he wants is to get an anti-Company Constitution adopted, and then get an anti-Rainsford Legislature elected."

"How much money has he?" Jack started Grego away from the schoolhouse and in the direction of his office across the run. Whatever this was, he wanted to talk it over privately. "And is he spending any?"

"He's not spending any we know of, but he's borrowing all over the place. You know that North Mallorysport section?"

That had been one of Grego's few mistakes. About ten years ago there had been a brief flurry in private industry, and the Company had sold land north of the city. Now it was a ghost town, abandoned factories and warehouses, and a ruinous airport. Hugo Ingermann had managed to acquire title to most of it.

"He's borrowing on that, every centisol he can. Needless to say, we're buying the mortgages from the bank. In non-Company hands, that place could be made into a planetside spaceport to compete with Terra-Baldur-Marduk on Darius, and we don't want that. He's been getting the money in cash or negotiable Banking Cartel certificates; none of it's deposited. The people at the bank say he's all but cleaned out his accounts there. I don't know what he wants with all that loose cash, and not knowing bothers me. He hasn't been spending any of it we can find out about."

That meant not spending any, period; the Company's investigators found things out quickly. They went over to the office and kicked it around from every angle they could think of, and neither of them kicked any enlightenment out of it. Hugo Ingermann was up to something, and they didn't know what, and neither of them liked not knowing. They didn't talk about it with the others at cocktail-time; they talked about the Fuzzies and what they could do with any more of them.

"Why don't you plant Fuzzy colonies on the other continents?" Grego asked. "We have a lot of good Fuzzy country we'll lease back to the Government at one sol for value received, or something like that. If this hokfusine program works the way everybody expects it to, we'll have Fuzzies all over everything."

That was a good idea. Something else to think about tomorrow and do something about after the Fuzzies' legal status was determined.

In the evening, just before Fuzzy bedtime, Little Fuzzy and Diamond approached him and Grego.

"Pappy Jack," Little Fuzzy began, "Diamond want me to go visit with him, at Pappy Vic place, where Big Ones dig. Say much fun there."

"You want, Pappy Vic?" Diamond asked. "Little Fuzzy come with us, make visit. Then, we go home, bring Little Fuzzy back here."

"What do you think, Jack?" Grego asked. "I'll bring him back in a couple of days, and it'll be a lot of fun for both of them. Diamond's never had a friend with him at Yellowsand. I know, there's a lot of blasting and digging and so on, but he won't get hurt. I'll look after him, and so'll Diamond. Diamond knows what's dangerous and what isn't."

Diamond must have been telling him all about Yellowsand, and he wanted to go see and come back and tell about; sure. And Grego was always back and forth between Mallorysport and Yellowsand, and he always took Diamond with him; he wouldn't do that if there were any real danger. Besides, there'd been enough digging and bulldozing and construction-work around here for Little Fuzzy to know what to watch out for.

"Yes; you go with Diamond; see Pappy Vic place; have plenty fun," he said. "But you be good Fuzzy; do what Pappy Vic, Diamond say; not do anything they say not do. You listen to Diamond; he know about digging-place."

"Nobody get hurt if watch out," Diamond said. "Pappy Vic tell me all about things that hurt; I tell Little Fuzzy. We have much fun."

14

LITTLE FUZZY WAS excited and happy. He always liked to go for trips, and this was a trip to a new place he had never seen before, a place called Yellowsand. That meant *Rohi-Nasig*; it would be a sandy place, like beside a river. At this place, Pappy Vic and other Big Ones were digging the top off a mountain and throwing it down in a deep-place, to get bright-stones out of black hard-rock. All Big Ones wanted bright-stones because they were pretty, and Pappy Vic traded them with other Big Ones, and part of what he traded for was nice things to give to the Fuzzies. Pappy Jack and Pappy Gerd had found this place, and now it belonged to Gov'men'; that was why all the Big Ones made their name-marks on the papers that time at Pappy Ben Place.

Pappy Vic sat in front, making the aircar fly; Little Fuzzy and Diamond were on the back seat, looking out the windows. They were high up; they could see everything spread out below, just like the make-like-country things Pappy Jack had, the *maps*. He could see where he and the others of his band had come down from the sun's right hand, the *north,* hunting land-prawns, for many-many days, between new-leaf time and groundberry-time, before he found Wonderful Place and got into it and made friends with Pappy Jack. He saw the river that had been too big to cross, and remembered how they had gone to sun-downward, *west,* along it for many days before it was small enough to go over.

If only they had known how to build the rafts the way Pappy Jack and Pappy Gerd and Unka Pancho showed them! But now they didn't need rafts. The Big Ones would take them in aircars, high over all the rivers and mountains; why, it had taken more days than he could count to come south to Wonderful Place, and now they were flying over it before one could make talk about it.

"Look far-far ahead," Diamond told him. "See mountains go from west to east?" Diamond knew the Big One words; Pappy Vic had taught him. "Yellowsand there. Soon see everything, then go down, go on ground."

There was an aircar ahead, a green one; it was one that Pappy George's blue-clothes police went about in. Maybe they were hunting harpies; they killed many harpies with big shoot-fast guns. Pappy Vic made talk with whoever was in it, with the talk-far things, the *radio*. They passed over a mountain; it was not steep as they approached, but it dropped sharply on the other side. Then he knew they were far-far to the north. He remembered this kind of mountain. There was a river on the other side, and another mountain, rising gradually and dropping sharply on the other side, and another mountain beyond that. Beyond the far mountain was a yellow haze. Diamond saw it and pointed excitedly.

"Is Yellowsand, Pappy Vic digging-place!" he said. "Is dust. Much dust where Big Ones dig."

"You kids, look out right window," Pappy Vic said. "I go around, so you see from high-up. Then go out over mountain, come up deep-down place."

Pappy Vic made the aircar come down a little and go slowly. They passed over the mountain, with Diamond beside him pointing. There were two rivers back of this mountain; they ran together, and where they made one was a split place in the mountain beyond, and they ran into it. And there was Yellowsand, Pappy Vic's place; it was much bigger than Wonderful Place. There were at least a hand of hands of houses . . .what was the Big One word for that many? *Twenty-five*. The Big Ones had names for how many anything was, even the leaves on a big tree. And he could see the deep place where the two rivers made one and ran out through the mountain, and beside this the Big Ones were working, many-many of them, with many-many machines; digging machines and picking-up machines and ground-pushing machines and big carry-things aircars.

Pappy Vic must have many-many friends, to come and help him dig like this, and more were coming, because they were building more houses. Everybody must like Pappy Vic.

Pappy Vic took the car out over the top of the mountain, and Little Fuzzy was surprised. He had thought that there would be a valley and another mountain sloping up beyond, but there was not. The mountain went almost straight down, very-very far, and beyond it was flat country, with little hills, and then bigger hills until he could see no farther. Pappy Vic made the car go down beside the face of the mountain till they were almost at the bottom, and then turned and went to where the mountain was split and the river came out of it. He looked up through the hard see-through stuff on the top of the car, amazed at how far it was up to the top. If he saw nothing else, this alone was worth coming to see.

The river came out so fast that it was foaming white; on either side were beaches of sand, and he could see why the Big Ones called this place Yellowsand; beyond the beaches trees grew back to where the mountain started to go up. Nobody could cross this river, not even Big Ones, not even with rafts.

"Bad place," Diamond told him. "Not go near. Get in river, make dead right away."

"That's right, Little Fuzzy. Don't go near that river at all," Pappy Vic said. "And look ahead, there."

There was a falling-water. He had seen falling-waters before, but never one so high as this. Even inside the car he could hear it; it was loud like thunder all the time. And far above, big carry-things aircars were coming out over the deep place and dumping loads of rock and ground and even whole trees that had been dug up by the roots. Pappy Vic made the aircar go straight up so that they could watch the falling-water until they were up above the top.

Then they went over the place where all Pappy Vic's friends were digging for him, and he looked down, watching all the work that was going on, until the car came down among the bright metal houses, in front of one big one, and there was a hand or so of Big Ones waiting for them. They all wore clothes like Pappy Jack wore when he was at home at Wonderful Place, except two, whose names were Chief and Captain, who wore blue police clothes, and all carried one-hand guns, like the Big Ones at Wonderful Place. There were all nice.

Pappy Vic showed him where he and Diamond would sleep, and he left his chopper-digger there, though he kept his shoulder bag. Then Pappy Vic took him and Diamond out to look at the digging-place. Diamond had seen it many times before; he explained all about it, how they had to take the soft yellow rock off the top of the black hard-rock, and then crack up the hard-rock to find the shining stones inside. It was interesting to watch how they did it, and he saw a wonderful thing, a wide moving-strip, like the moving-strips and the moving-steps inside buildings in Big House Place, only much bigger, which carried the black hard-rock into a place with strong wire fence all around.

Pappy Vic took him and Diamond into this place. Here the hard-rock was cracked, and the shining stones gotten out. There were many-many Big Ones working at this. Also, there were many police-clothes Big Ones, with one-hand guns on their belts, and little two-hand shoot-fast guns, all standing around watching. They must be afraid that bad Big Ones would come and try to take the shining stones. And he saw the place where the shining stones were sorted out. They were very pretty, all bright like fire. No wonder they had to be careful nobody would take pretty-things like that.

Then they went back to the big metal house, and it was lunchtime. They gave him and Diamond estee-fee to eat. For a long time after lunch Pappy Vic and the others made talk. It was Big One talk, and Little Fuzzy understood very little of it, but it seemed to be about the work that was being done here. He and Diamond played on the floor, and he smoked his pipe. Diamond didn't smoke; he didn't like it.

In the afternoon, Pappy Vic took them up in an aircar to watch his friends making blast. He knew all about that. The Big Ones put something in the ground and got far away from it, and it went off like a gun only much-much louder, and there was smoke and dust and big rocks flew high up. It made digging easier, but it was dangerous to be close to it; and, while Big Ones didn't mind it, it made bumps in the ground that hurt Fuzzies' feet. That was why Pappy Vic took him and Diamond up in the aircar while it was happening. As soon as the blasts were done, the Big Ones all moved in again with their machines and started digging.

Pappy Vic took him and Diamond back to the big metal house, and they ate more estee-fee, and played with Diamond's things. And then it was Diamond's nap-time, and he lay down on his blankets and went to sleep.

Little Fuzzy lay down beside Diamond and tried to sleep too, but he couldn't. He was too excited about all the things he had seen. He thought about all Pappy Vic's friends helping him dig, and all the machines they had to work with, and then he thought about all the pretty shining-stones he had seen, all the colors there were, and bright like hot coals in a fire. He wanted a shining-stone himself, to take back to Wonderful Place and show to the others there.

He knew that Pappy Vic would give him one if he asked for it, but Pappy Jack had told him that he must never ask people for things when he was away from home. Well, maybe he could find one for himself. Of course, all the shining-stones here belonged to Pappy Vic, but if he found one himself and asked if he could keep it, that would be different from asking for one Pappy Vic had found. He thought of asking Diamond about this, but Diamond was asleep, and it was never right to bother people who were sleeping unless something was wrong or there was danger.

So he decided to go out by himself and look for one. He put on his shoulder bag and picked up his chopper-digger, because he might find a land-prawn, and went out, going in the direction of the edge of the deep-place, away from where the Big Ones were working. He found much black-rock in a place where they had been digging a little once and had stopped, and looked all around, but he found no shining-stones. Maybe they had found all the shining-stones that were here. He went to the edge of the deep place and looked down, and away down at the bottom he saw more black-rock.

He knew that Pappy Vic and Diamond had both said that he was to stay out of the deep-place, but this was far away from where the Big Ones were throwing the top of the mountain down into it; it would not be dangerous here. He started to climb down.

It was hard climbing, and much farther down than he had thought, and several times he was tempted to turn back, but he could see black-rock at the bottom and kept on. He wanted to find a shining-stone for himself. There was much loose rock, and he had to be careful where he put his feet. He had to use his chopper-digger to help him and cling to small bushes that grew on the steep side of the deep-place, and there were bushes and even trees that had been dug up and thrown over when the Big Ones had been digging above. He had to be very careful among them.

Finally, he was down to the very edge of the river; it was fast and foamed among rocks, and he began to wish he had not come down here. The black hard-rock he found was all broken into little pieces, none bigger than his body, and he knew now that there would be no shining-stones. He knew what the Big Ones did; they broke the black-rock small and put a thing Pappy Vic called a scanner on the pieces, and it told if there were shining stones inside.

For a moment he looked at the broken black-rock, and then he said, "Sunnabish-go-hell-goddamn!" He didn't know what these words meant, but Big Ones always said them when things went wrong. Then he started along the edge of the river, looking for a less steep place to go up again, farther away from where Pappy Vic's friends were throwing rock down. Looking around, he saw a nice flat rock, and another rock just above it, and a bush he could hold to above that.

He jumped down from the uprooted tree onto which he had climbed, onto the flat rock. As soon as his feet touched it, the other rocks around him were sliding, too. He struggled to regain his balance, and the chopper-digger flew out of his hand; he heard it fall with a clink among the rocks above him. Then he was sliding toward the river, and he was more frightened than he had ever been, even when a bush-goblin had almost caught him long ago—and then he was in the water.

Something heavy hit him from behind. He clutched at it. . . .

15

JACK HOLLOWAY LEANED forward for his tobacco pouch, his eyes still on the microbook-screen. The Fuzzies on the floor in front of him were also looking at the screen, yeeking softly to one another; they had long ago learned not to make talk with Big One voices around Pappy Jack when he was reading. They were reading, or trying to, too; at least, they were identifying the letters and spelling out the words aloud, and arguing about what they meant. They probably missed Little Fuzzy; whenever they were stumped on anything, they always asked him. Jack blew through his pipe stem, and began refilling the pipe from the pouch.

The communication-screen buzzed. He finished refilling the pipe and zipped the pouch shut. The Fuzzies were saying, "Pappy Jack; screeno." He said, "Quiet, kids," and snapped it on. As soon as they saw Victor Grego's face in it, they began yelling, "Heyo, Pappy Vic!"

"Hello, Victor." Then he saw Grego's face, and stopped, apprehension stabbing him. "What is it, Victor?" he asked.

"Little Fuzzy," Grego began. His face twitched. "Jack, if you want a shot at me, you're entitled to it."

"Don't talk like a fool; what's wrong?" By now, he was frightened.

Grego said, "We think he's gone into the river," as though every word were being pulled out of him with red-hot pincers.

Jack's mind's eye saw the Yellowsand River rushing down through the canyon. He felt a chill numbness spread through him.

"You 'think.' Aren't you sure? What happened?"

"He's been missing since between 1530 and 1700," Grego said. "He and

Diamond lay down for a nap in the afternoon. When Diamond woke, he was gone; he'd taken his shoulder bag and his chopper-digger with him. Diamond went out to look for him, and couldn't find him. He came back while some of us were having cocktails and told me. I supposed he'd just gone out to look for a land-prawn, but I didn't want him running around the diggings alone. Harry Steefer called the captain on duty at the police hut and had a general alert put out—just everybody keep an eye open for him.

"He didn't show up by dinner-time, and I began to get worried. I ordered a search and took Diamond up in a supervisory-jeep, with a loudspeaker to call him, and we hunted all over the area. Diamond assured me that he'd warned him against going down in the canyon, but we began looking there. After it got dark, we put up lorries with floodlights in the canyon. Maybe I should have called you then, but we were expecting to find him every minute."

"Wouldn't have done any good. I couldn't have done anything but worry, and you were doing that already."

"Well, about half an hour ago, a couple of cops in a jeep were going along the edge of the river, and one of them saw a glint of metal among the rocks. He looked at it with binoculars, and it was Little Fuzzy's chopper-digger. He called in right away. I went down; I've just come back from there. That's all there was, just the chopper-digger. The place is all loose rock that's been thrown down from above; it's right under where we made one of the prospect digs. We think the loose rock started to slide and he threw the chopper-digger out of his hand, trying to catch himself, and the slide took him down . . . Jack, the whole damn thing's my fault. . . ."

"Oh, hell; you couldn't keep him on a leash all the time. You thought he'd be all right with Diamond, and Diamond thought he was going to take a nap too, and . . ." He paused briefly. "I'm coming up right away; I'll bring some people along. That river's a hell of a thing for anybody to get into, but he might have gotten out again." He looked at the clock. "Be seeing you in about an hour."

Then he screened Gerd van Riebeek, who was getting ready for bed, and told him. Gerd cursed, then repeated what he had been told over his shoulder to Ruth, who was somewhere out of screen-range.

"Okay, I'll be along. I'll call Protection Force and have Bjornsen and the rest of the gang who were up there with me called out; they know the place. Be seeing you."

Then Gerd blanked out. Jack kicked his feet out of his moccasins and pulled on his boots, buckled on his pistol and got his hat and a jacket. There was a kitbag ready, packed for emergencies. Weather forecast hadn't been good; southwest winds, with a warm front running into a cold front at sea to the west.

He got a raincape too. He only had to wait a few minutes before Gerd was at the door. Ruth was with him.

"I'll Fuzzy-sit, and put them to bed," she said. "Or maybe they'd like to come down to our place for tonight." He nodded absently, and she continued: "Jack, maybe he's all right. Fuzzies can swim when they have to, you know."

Not in anything like Yellowsand Canyon. He wouldn't bet on a human Interstellar Olympic swimming champion in a place like that. He said something, he didn't know what, and he and Gerd hurried to the hangar and got his car out.

After they were airborne, he wished he hadn't let Gerd take the controls; flying the car would have given him something to concentrate on. As it was, all he could do was sit while the car tore north through the night.

In about ten minutes they began running into cloud—that rain the forecast had warned of. They got below the clouds. Maybe they were flying through rain now; an aircar at Mach 3 could go through an equatorial cloudburst on Mimir without noticing it. He could see lightning to the northwest, and then to the west. Then there was a blaze of electric light on the under side of the clouds ahead.

It was drizzling thinly when they set down at the mining camp at Yellowsand. Grego was waiting for him, so was Harry Steefer, the Company Police chief who had transferred his headquarters to Yellowsand when the mining had begun. They shook hands with him, Grego hesitantly.

"Nothing yet, Jack," he said. "We've been over that canyon inch by inch ever since I called you. Just nothing but that chopper-digger."

"Victor, you're not to blame for anything. If blaming anybody means anything. And Diamond's not to blame, and I don't even think Little Fuzzy's too much to blame. He wanted to see what it was like down there, and maybe he thought he'd find a zatku. Aren't many zatku around Hoksu-Mitto anymore." Hell, he wasn't talking to Grego, he was talking to himself. "Hirohito Bjornsen's on his way, with the gang he had here before you took over."

"He's not in the canyon at all; we're sure of that. We're looking along both banks below, but I don't think he got out of it. Not alive."

"I know what it's like. Hell, I discovered it. Now I wish I hadn't."

"Jack, I'd give every sunstone in this damned mountain if . . ." Grego began, then stopped, as though it were the most useless thing in the world to say, which it was.

Bjornsen arrived with a combat car and two patrol cars. George Lunt was along, and so was Pancho Ybarra. They spent the night searching, or drinking coffee in the headquarters hut, listening to reports and watching screen-views. The sky lightened to a solid dull gray; finally the floodlights went off. The rain continued, falling harder, a constant drumming on the arched roof of the hut.

"We've been halfway to the mouth of Lake-Chain River," Bjornsen reported. "We didn't see anything of him on either side of the river. If the visibility wasn't so bad . . ."

"Visibility, what visibility?" a Company cop wanted to know. "Anything down there I can see, I can hit with a pistol, the way the fog's closing in."

"Damn river's up about six inches since midnight," somebody else ·said. "It'll keep on rising, too." He invited them to listen to that obscenely pejorative rain.

Jack started to yawn and bit on his pipe stem. Grego, across the rough deal table, was half-asleep already, his head nodding slowly forward and then jerking up.

"Anybody fit to carry on for a while?" he asked. "I'm going to lie down; wake me up if anybody hears anything."

There were a couple of Army cots at the end of the hut. He rose and went toward them, unbuckling his belt as he went, sitting down on one to pull off his boots. He was about to stretch himself out when he remembered that he still had his hat on.

16

AT FIRST, LITTLE Fuzzy was only aware of utter misery. He was cold and wet and hungry, and he hurt all over, not in any one place but with a great ache that was all of him. It was dark, and rain was falling, and all around him he could hear the gurgling rush of water moving, and, finding that he was clinging tightly to something, he clung tighter, and felt the roughness of bark under his hands. His knees were locked around something that must be a tree branch, and he wondered how he had come here.

Then he remembered—hunting for shining-stones where the Big Ones had been digging, going down into the deep-place beside the river; he wished he had listened to Pappy Vic and Diamond and stayed out of there. Falling into the water. He remembered clutching something that had hit him in the water, and he remembered the small tree that the Big Ones had uprooted and thrown down over the edge. It must have gone into the water when he did.

Then everything had gone black, and he had known nothing more, except once, for just a little, he had seen the sky, with black clouds angry-red at the edges, and once again it had been dark and he had seen lightning. It had been raining then.

But the tree was not moving now. He thought he knew what had happened; the river had carried it against the bank and it had stopped. That meant that he could get onto ground again. He clutched tighter with his hands and loosened his knee-grip, putting one foot down and touching soft ground with it. He decided to remain where he was until it became light enough to see before he tried to do anything. Then, gripping tightly with his knees and one hand, he felt to see if he still had his shoulder bag. Yes, it was there. He wanted to open it to see if water had gotten into it, but decided not to until it was light again. He wriggled to make himself more comfortable, and went back to sleep.

It was daylight when he woke. Not whole daylight, and it was still raining and there was a fog, but he could see. The river, yellow and rapid, rushed past on both sides. The tree was caught on a small sandbar, and there was water on both sides of it. A little grass grew on the sandbar, and there were bits of wood that the river had left there at other times, and a whole big tree, old and dead. Climbing off the little tree, he walked about until some of the stiffness left his muscles.

He would have to get off this sandbar soon. The rain was still falling, and when it rained rivers became more, and this river might come up over the sandbar before long.

On one side, the river was wider than he could see in the fog; on the other, the left side as it flowed, it was not much more than a stone-throw to the bank, and the bank looked low enough for him to climb up out of the river. He picked up some bits of wood and threw them in the water to test the current. It was faster than he liked, but he noticed that the wood was carried toward the bank. He threw in many sticks, watching how each one was carried. Then, making sure that the snaps that held his knife and trowel in their sheaths were closed, he waded into the water. As soon as he was carried off his feet, he began swimming against the current.

He was carried downstream a little, but always in the direction of the bank, and soon his feet touched bottom. He struggled out of the water and up onto the bank, and then looked back at the sandbar he had left. "Sunnabish river," he said.

It was still raining, but he was so wet that he did not notice it. He was tired, too; it had been a hard swim, even that little distance. The river was very strong; it made him happy that he had fought it and won. Then he walked to a big tree and sat down on an exposed root, opening his shoulder bag. Everything in it was dry; not a drop of water had gotten in. He had a cake of estee-fee; he broke it in half, put one half back in, and then ate half of the other. Maybe he would not be able to find anything to eat before he would be hungry again. It made him feel good. Then he put away what was left and got out his pipe and tobacco and lit it. Then he took out the flat round thing that had the blue pointer-north in it, the compass, and looked at that. The river flowed almost straight north; that was what he had expected. Then he looked at the other things he had.

Beside his pipe and tobacco and the lighter and the compass, there was a whistle. He blew that several times. That was a good thing to have. Maybe he could use it to call attention to himself if he saw a Big One far away. He put it away, too. And he had his knife and his trowel, and he had the little many-tool thing which the nice Big One with the white hair had given him in Big House Place. It had a knife in it too, a small one, very sharp, and a pointed thing to punch, and a bore-holes thing, and a file, and a saw, and a screwdriver, and even a little thing in two parts that would pinch like the jaw of a land-prawn and cut wire. And he had wire, very fine but strong—one had to be careful, or it would cut—and a ball of strong string, *fishline* the Big Ones called it, and short pieces of string that he had saved. He always carried plenty of string; it had many uses.

He finished his pipe, and wondered if he should smoke another, then decided not to. He had plenty of tobacco, but he must not waste it. He didn't know how long it would take to get back to Yellowsand. If he followed this river, he would get there sooner or later, but it might be a long way. The river had been very fast, and he had been in it on the tree a long time. And when he got to where it came out of the mountain, he would have the mountain to climb. He wasn't going into the deep-place again, he was sure of that.

He wished he had his chopper-digger; he would have to kill animals for food on the way. At first, he thought of making himself a wooden prawn-killer, but decided not to, at least now. So he found three large stones, smooth and rounded, each bigger than his fist. One he carried in his hand, and the other two he carried in the crook of his other elbow. He started north along the bank of the river.

Once, he saw a big bird in a tree, its head under its wing. It was too far to throw; he wished he had one of the bows Pappy Jack and Pappy Gerd had taught how to make, and some arrows. That bird would have been good to eat. He wished he were back at Hoksu-Mitto, with Pappy Jack and Mamma and Baby and Mike and Mitzi and Ko-Ko and Cinderella . . . and Unka Pancho, and Auntie Lynne, and Pappy Gerd and Mummy Woof, and Id and Superego and Complex and Syndrome, and . . . as he walked, he said all the names of all his friends at Hoksu-Mitto, wishing that he was with them again.

Sometime, he thought, after sun-highest time—*noon, lunchtime*—he saw a zarabunny sitting hunched into a ball of fur. It didn't like the rain any more than he did. He hurled a stone and hit it, and then ran to it before it could get up, and stabbed it in back of the ear with his knife. Then he squatted and skinned it. At first, he thought of making a fire and cooking it on a stick, but it would take too long to find dry wood and make the fire and cook it, and he was hungry again. He ate it raw. After all, it had only been very short time that he had eaten anything at all that had been cooked.

One thing, he would have to make himself better weapons than stones to throw.

The third time he came to a stream and crossed over it, he found hard-rock, not black like the shining-stone-rock of Yellowsand, but good and hard. He hunted until he found two pieces the right size and shape, and put them in his shoulder bag. By this time, the rain had stopped and it was getting foggier and darker, and he thought that dark-time was near.

He made a sleeping-place in the next hollow, beside a stream and against the side of a low cliff. First he found a standing dead tree and cut at it with his knife until he had cut off all the wet wood and made fine shavings of the dry wood. These he lit, and put sticks on the fire; as they dried, they caught, until he had a good fire, warm and bright. By this time it was growing dark, and the fire made light on the rocks behind him. He gathered more wood, some pieces so big that he could hardly drag them, and stacked it where the fire would dry it. He did this till it was too dark to see, and then he sat down with his back to the rocks and took the two pieces of flint out of his shoulder bag.

One, he decided, would be an axe: he could chop wood with it for other fires and kill land-prawns with it. The other would be the head of a spear, which he could throw or stab with. For a long time he looked at the stone, making think-pictures of what the axehead and the spearhead would be like when he had finished them. Then he took out his trowel, which had a handle of made-stuff, *plastic,* and began pressing with it on the edge of the stone. The stone gouged and scarred the plastic, but the rock chipped away in little flakes. Now and then he would lay it aside and go to put more wood on the fire. Once, he heard a bush-goblin screaming, far away, but he was not afraid; the fire would scare it away.

The spearhead was harder to do. He made it tapering to a point, sharp on both edges, with a notch on either side at the back; he knew just how he was going to fasten it to the shaft. It took a long time, and he was tired and sleepy when he had finished it. Laying it and the axehead aside, he put more wood on the fire and made sure there was nothing between it and him, so that it would not spread and burn him, and curled up with his back to the rock and went to sleep.

THE FIRE HAD burned out when he woke, and at first he was frightened; a bush-goblin might have come after it had gone out. But the whole hollow smelled of smoke, and bush-goblins could smell much better than people. The smoke would be frightening in itself.

He dug his hole with the trowel and filled it in; he drank from the little stream, and then ate what was left of the half cake of estee-fee he had eaten the day before. Then he found a young tree, about the height of a Big One, and dug it up with his trowel and trimmed the roots to make a knob. The other end he cut off an arm's length from the knob and split with his knife and fitted the axehead into it and made a hole in it below the axehead with his bore-holes thing. He passed wire through that and around on either side of the stone, many times, until it was firm and tight. Pappy Jack and Pappy Gerd and the others said this should be done with fine roots of trees, or gut of animals, but he had no time to bother with that, and wire was much better.

Then, with the axe, he cut another young tree, slender and straight. The axe cut well; he was proud and happy about it. He fitted the shaft to the spearhead, using more wire, and when that was done he poked through the ashes of the fire, found a few red coals, and covered them with his trowel. Pappy Jack and Pappy George and Pappy Gerd and everybody always said that it was a bad never-do-thing to go away and leave a fire with any life in it. Then, making sure that he had not forgotten any of his things, he picked up his axe and spear and started off through the woods toward the big river.

A little before noon he found another zarabunny, and threw the spear, hitting it squarely. Then he finished it with a chop on the neck. That made him happy; he had used both his new weapons, and they were wood. He made a small fire here, and after it had burned down to red coals he put the back-meat of the zarabunny on sticks and cooked it, as he had learned at Hoksu-Mitto.

Pappy Jack was wise, he thought, as he squatted beside his little fire and ate the sweet hot meal. He had wondered why Pappy Jack had insisted that all Fuzzies learn these things about living in the woods, when they would have Big Ones to take care of them. *This* was why. There would be times like this, when Fuzzies would lose their Big Ones, or become lost from them, just as he had. Then they could do things like this for themselves.

He decided not to eat all the zarabunny. He had taken the skin off carefully; now he wrapped what was left of the back-meat and the legs in it, and tied it to his shoulder bag. He would cook and eat that when he made camp for the night.

The fog was still heavy, with thin rain sometimes. He made camp this time by finding two big bushes with forks about the same height and cutting a pole to go between them. Then he cut other bushes to lean against that, and branches to pack between. There were ferns here, and he gathered many of them, drying them at the fire and making a bed of them. He was not so tired today, and all the soreness of his muscles had gone. After he had cooked and eaten part of the zarabunny, he smoked his pipe and played with some pebbles, making little patterns of what he had done that day, and then went to sleep.

It was still foggy and rainy the next morning. He cooked one of the hind legs of the zarabunny that he had saved, and then killed the red coals left of his fire and went on. Toward the middle of the morning, he found a land-prawn and chopped off its head and cracked the shell. He did not make a fire for this;

land-prawns were best raw; cooking spoiled the taste. Big Ones ate many things without cooking them, too.

About the middle of the afternoon, he found a goofer chewing the bark off a tree. This was wonderful luck—meat for two whole days. He threw the spear and caught the goofer behind the shoulder with it, and then used the axe to finish it. This time he did build a fire, and after he had gutted the goofer, he began to think about how he would carry it; it weighed almost as much as he did. He decided not to skin it here. Instead, he spitted the liver and the kidneys and the heart, all of which were good, and roasted them over the fire. After he had eaten them, he cut off the head, which was useless weight, and propped the carcass up so that the blood would drain out. When this was done, he tied each front and hind leg together with string, squatted, and got the whole thing on his back, the big muscles of the hind legs over his shoulders. It was heavy, but, after he got used to it, it was not uncomfortable.

Some time after this, when he was close to the river, he saw through the fog where another river came into it from the east; it was a big river too. After that, the river he was following was less because it had not yet been joined by the other one. This was good, he thought. It looked not much bigger than it had when it had come out of the deep place in the mountain. He must be getting close to Yellowsand. He was sure that if it had not been for the fog he could have seen the big mountains ahead.

He made camp that night in a hollow tree which was big enough to sleep in, after cooking much of the goofer. He ate a lot of it; he was happy. Soon he would be back at Yellowsand and everybody would be happy to see him again. He smoked a second pipe before he went to sleep that night.

The next day was good. The rain had stopped and the fog was blowing away, and there was a glow in the sky to the east. Best of all, he could hear the sound of aircars very far away. That was good; Pappy Vic and his friends had missed him and were out hunting for him. The sound was from away down the river, though, and that wasn't right. He knew what he would do; he would stay as close to the river as he could. If they saw him, they would come and pick him up; then he wouldn't have to climb the high-steep mountain. Maybe, if he found a good no-woods place, he would build a big fire beside the river. They would be sure to see the smoke.

The sounds of the aircars grew fainter, and finally he couldn't hear them at all. He found another land-prawn and ate it. This was the fourth day since he had been in this place, and he had only found two of them. He knew that land-prawns were more to the south, but he was surprised at how few there were here.

The wind blew, and then it began to rain some more. It often did this before the clouds all went away. But the rain came from in front of him and to the left, and before it had come from the right. The wind could have changed, but this troubled him. Finally, he looked at his compass, and saw that he was not going north at all, but west.

That wasn't right. He got out his pipe; Pappy Jack always smoked his pipe · when he wanted to think about something. At length, he walked over to the river and looked at it.

With all the sand from Yellowsand, it should be yellow, but it wasn't; it was a dirty brown-gray. He looked at it for a while, and then he remembered the other river he had seen coming in from the east. That was the river that came out of the mountain at Yellowsand, not this one.

"Sunnabish!" he almost yelled. "Jeeze-krise go-hell goddamn sunnabish!" That made him feel a little better, just as it did the Big Ones. "Now, must go back." He thought for a moment. No, it was no use going back; he could not cross this river where it met the other one. He would have to go all the way up this go-hell river till he could find a place to cross, and then all the way down again. "Sunnabish!"

17

NONE OF THEM said anything much. Grego and Harry Steefer and the rest were the kind of people who always got sort of tongue-tied when it came to verbal sympathy. Come right down to it, there wasn't a Nifflheim of a lot anybody could say. Jack shook Grego's hand with especial warmth. "Thanks for everything, Victor. You all did everything you could." He and Gerd van Riebeek turned away and went to the aircar.

"You want to fly her, Jack?" Gerd asked.

He nodded. "Might as well." Gerd stood aside, and he got in at the controls. Gerd climbed in after him, slamming the door and dogging it shut, then said, "Secure." He put the car on contragravity and fiddled with the radio compass; when he looked out, Yellowsand was far below and he could see out into the country beyond the Divide. The scarps of the smaller ranges to the south rose, one behind the other, on the other side.

"Maybe we ought to have stayed a little longer," he said. "It's starting to clear now; all blue sky to the south. Be clear up here by noon."

"What could we do, Jack? The Company cops and survey-crews are ready to throw it in now. So's George and Hirohito. If there'd been anything to find, they'd have found it."

"You don't think we'll ever find him?"

"Do you, Jack?"

"Oh, Gerd, he might have gotten out again. The current could have carried him to the side. . . ." He used an obscenity like an eraser on his previous words. "Who the hell do I think I'm kidding beside myself? If he isn't in the North Marsh by now, it's because his body's caught on a snag and being sanded over." He was silent again. "Just no more Little Fuzzy." He repeated it again, after a moment: "No more Little Fuzzy."

THEY WERE ALL angry with him, Stonebreaker and Lame One and Fruitfinder and Other She and Big She—especially Big She. Even Stabber and Carries-Bright-Things were not speaking for him.

"Look at place Wise One bring us!" Big She was railing. "Wise One tell us, to sun's left hand is good place, always warm, always good-to-eat things. This is what Wise One say; Wise One not know. Wise One bring us to this place. Big moving-water, not cross. Rain make down, rain make down, make wet, all time cold. Not find good-to-eat things, everybody hungry. And look at moving-water; how we cross that?"

"Then we go up moving-water, find place to cross. And rain stop some time; rain always stop some time," he said. "Is everybody-know thing."

"You not know," Lame One said. "This is different place. Maybe all time rain here."

"You make fool-talk. Rain all time, water everywhere."

"Much water here," Other She said. "Big wide water-places. Maybe much rain here."

"Sky look brighter," Stabber remarked. "Wind blow, too. Maybe rain stop make down soon."

And the gray not-see was gone, too; soon the rain would stop and the sun would come out again. But how to get across this big water? The moving-water was wide and deep, there were no stony places; it was a bad not-cross moving-water, and there were all the big wide-waters, and it would be far-far to where they would be able to cross over.

"Hungry, too," Fruitfinder complained. "Not eat since long time before last dark-time."

He was hungry himself. If he had been alone, he would have gone on, hoping to find something, until he was able to cross the moving-water. None of the others, not even Stabber, would do that, however. They wanted to eat now.

"Animals stay under things, stay out of rain, not move about," he said. "Be where brush is thick. We go hunt different places. Anybody kill anything, bring back here, all eat."

They nodded agreement. That was the way they did it when it was best not to hunt all together. He thought for a moment. He didn't want Big She and Fruitfinder and Stonebreaker hunting together. They would all the time make talk against him, and when they came back they would make bad talk to the others.

"Stabber, you, Big She, go that way." He pointed down the river. "Take care, not get in bad not-go-through place. Lame One, you, Other She, Stonebreaker, go up moving-water. Carries-Bright-Things, Fruitfinder, come with me. We go back in woods. Maybe find hatta-zosa."

They were all angry with him because it had rained and because they had come to this big not-cross moving-water, and because they had found nothing to eat. They blamed him for all that. It was hard being Wise One and leading a band. They all praised Wise One when things went well, but when they didn't they all blamed him. But when he told them how to hunt, they all agreed. They had to have somebody to tell them what to do, and nobody else would.

. . . *BEGINNING OF A new era for our planet,* the smooth, ingratiating voice came out of thousands of telecast-speakers all over Zarathustra, in living rooms and cafés, in camp bunkhouses and cattle-town saloons. *Already, Mallorysport assumes a festive air in preparation to greet the Honorable Delegates to the Constitutional Convention which will begin its work a week from today.*

There is a note of sadness, however, to mar our happy enthusiasm. Word from the CZC camp at Yellowsand is that the search for Little Fuzzy, lost, presumably in the torrent of Yellowsand River, has been definitely called off; no hope remains of finding that lovable little person alive. A whole planet mourns for him, and joins with his human friend and guardian, Jack Holloway, in his grief.

Good-bye, Little Fuzzy. You were only with us a short while, but Zarathustra will never forget you.

18

Little Fuzzy said, "Sunnabish!" again, in even deeper disgust. He relighted his pipe, but after two puffs it went out; there was nothing but ashes in it. He blew through the stem and put it away. There was no use making a big fire here; Pappy Vic and his friends were looking for him along the other river, the one that came out from Yellowsand. He couldn't even hear the aircar-sounds anymore. And all the way he would have to go, up this river and then down again . . .

"Jeeze-krise!"

Why hadn't he thought of that before? No, he wouldn't have to do all that! He would make a raft, the way he had been taught. Why, he had even helped teach others to do it. Then he would go down this river until he came in sight of the other river, and work over to the right bank. Then he would be close to Yellowsand and along the river where they were looking for him. As soon as he got on land again, he would make a big fire and right away somebody would see and come for him.

He couldn't do it here. The banks were too high, and if he made a raft he would never be able, alone, to get it down. So he would have to go up this river, but only till he found a good place, with the banks low, where there was wood to make the raft and the kind of trees that had fine, tough roots to twist into rope to tie the raft together. And before he started to work on the raft he would have to hunt for a while to get meat to eat while he was working.

He scuffed dirt over the ashes he had knocked from his pipe, picked up his axe and spear, and started off up the river. After a while, the river turned south a little, and then it became very wide. He stopped and looked: a big lake. That was good. There would be low places along it and the water would be still; he could build the raft right in the water. The sun was beginning to come out now, not brightly, but growing steadily brighter. He was feeling very happy; building the raft was going to be much fun.

Then he stopped short and said a number of the Big Ones' angry-words, but even that didn't make him feel better. In front of him the ground dropped off in a cliff, as high as one of the big metal houses at Wonderful Place. Beyond he could see flat ground full of trees and bushes and tangled vines, with water everywhere. Three was small stream at the foot of the cliff, and it spread out all over everything. This was a bad sunnabish not-go-through place; he would have to go up the little stream to get around it. How far up the river it went he had no idea. He looked at his compass again, saw that the small stream went almost due north, and started up along it.

The sun was out brightly now, and there were many big blue places in the sky and the clouds were white instead of gray. He walked steadily, looking about for things to eat and looking at his compass. Finally he came to where the stream ran over stones, and the water-everywhere place had stopped.

He crossed over and went west, looking often at his compass and remembering which way the big river was. He heard noises ahead, and stopped to listen, then was very happy because it was the noise of goofers chewing at tree-bark. He went forward carefully and came upon five of them, all chewing at trees. He picked out the plumpest of them, drew back his arm, and threw his spear; it was not a very good throw because it caught the goofer through the belly, just back of the hips, from one side to the other. As he ran forward to finish it, another, frightened, ran straight at him. He hit it between the eyes with the axe; it died at once. He hadn't meant to kill two goofers, but a frightened goofer would attack a person. Then he finished the one he had wounded with his spear and pulled the spear out. The other goofers had all run away.

He gutted both of them, took out the livers and hearts and kidneys, and spitted them on sticks he cut with his knife. Then he built a fire. When he had a good bed of red coals he propped the sticks against stones and weighed them with other stones and sat down to watch that the meat didn't burn. It was very good.

He cut off the head of one goofer and made a pack of the carcass, as he had the one he had killed the day before. The other he skinned and cut up and wrapped the hind legs and the back-meat in the skin and tied that to the whole one. This was going to be a heavy load, but he thought he could manage it. He started off again. He didn't bother looking for good-to-eat things anymore; he had already eaten, and he had a whole goofer and the best meat of another. Even if he had seen a land-prawn, he wouldn't have bothered with it. He turned south; now he had the sun, and didn't need to bother getting out his compass.

Then, in front of him, he saw a splash of blood, and then places where the dead leaves were scuffed and more blood, and goofer-hairs with it. Somebody had been going in the direction of the river, dragging a dead goofer. That meant that there was a band of People about who had split up to hunt and would meet again somewhere. People hunting in a band would never drag a dead goofer; they would eat it where they had killed it. He went forward along the drag-trail, and then stopped.

"Heyo!" he shouted, as loudly as he could, then remembered that that was a Big One word, and these People had never seen a Big One. He had also been putting his voice in the back of his mouth, to make talk like a Big One. "Friend!" he shouted naturally, as he always had before he had been taught. "You want make talk?"

There was no answer; they were too far ahead to hear. He hurried forward, following the trail as fast as he could. After a while, he shouted again; this time there was an answering shout. He could see the big river through the trees ahead, and then he saw three People beside it. He hurried to them.

They were two males and a female. They all had wooden weapons, not the paddle-shaped prawn-killers the People in the south carried, but heavy clubs knobbed on one end and pointed on the other. One of the females also carried three small sticks in her hand. On the ground was a dead goofer, the hair and skin rubbed off the back where it had been dragged.

"Friend," he greeted them. "You make friends, make talk?"

"Yes, make friends," one of the males said, and the other asked, "Where from you come? Others with you?"

He swung the load from his shoulders, the whole goofer and the meat of the other, beside the goofer they had, to show that he would share and eat with them, and untied the strings and put them in his shoulder bag. The others looked at these things and at his weapons intently, but said nothing about them, waiting for him to show and explain about them. The female said, "You carry all that? You strong."

"Not strong; just know how," he replied. "Alone. Come from far-far place, sun's left hand. Four dark-times, fall in big river." Then he remembered that river was not a Fuzzy word. "Big-big moving-water," he explained. "Catch hold of tree floating in moving-water, hold onto. Moving-water take me far to sun's right hand before I can get out. Walk back to place where can cross. What place you come from?"

One of the males pointed northward. "Come many-many days," he said. "Band all come together." He held up a hand with five fingers spread, then lowered and raised it with three fingers extended. Eight of them. "Others hunt, some this way, some that way. Come back here, all eat together."

"We call him Wise One," the female said, pointing to the one who had spoken. "He called Fruitfinder," she introduced the other male. "Me Carries-Bright-Things." She held out the three sticks. "Look, bright-things. Pretty."

On the end of each stick was a thing he knew. They were the things that flew out when Big Ones shot with rifles. Empty cartridges. One was the kind for the rifles the blue-clothes police Big Ones had; Pappy Gerd had a rifle like that too. The other two cartridges were from a rifle like one of Pappy Jack's.

"Where you get?" he demanded, excited. "Are Big One things. Big Ones use in long thing, point with both hands. Pull little thing underneath, make noise like thunder. Throw little hard thing very fast; make dead hesh-nazza. You know where Big Ones are?"

"You know about Big Ones?" Wise One was asking just as excitedly. "You know where Big One Place is?"

"I come from Big One Place," he told them. "Hoksu-Mitto, Wonderful Place. I live with Big Ones, all Big Ones my friends." He began naming them over, starting with Pappy Jack. "Many Fuzzies live with Big Ones, can't say name for how many. Big Ones good to all Fuzzies, give nice things. Give shoddabag, like this." He displayed it. "Give knife, give trowel for dig hole bury bad smells. Teach things." He showed the axe and spear. "Big Ones teach how to make. I make, after get out of big moving-water. And Big Ones give Hoksu-Fusso, Wonderful Food."

There was shouting from up the river. The male Fuzzy who was called Fruitfinder, examining the axe, said, "Stabber, Big She come." Wise One began shouting, "Make hurry fast! Wonderful thing happen!"

Two more Fuzzies came out of the woods, dragging another dead goofer between them—a female with a club like the others' and a male with a sort of spear-stick. Carries-Bright-Things and Fruitfinder ran to help them, jabbering in excitement.

"Is somebody from Big One Place," Carries-Bright-Things was saying. "Is Big Ones' Friend. Knows what bright-things are."

The male with the spear-stick immediately began shouting at the female with him, "You see? Big Ones good, make friends. Here is one who knows. Wise One right all time."

"You show us way to Big One Place?" Wise One was asking. "Big Ones make friends with us?"

"Big Ones friends for all Fuzzies," he said, and then remembered that that was another Big One word. There were so many Big One words these Fuzzies did not know. "Fuzzy what Big Ones call all People like us. Means Fur-All-

Over. Big Ones not have fur, only on head, sometimes on face." He decided not to try to explain about clothes; not enough words. "Big Ones very wise, have all kinds of made-things. Big Ones very good to all Fuzzies."

Three more came in. They had two zarabunnies and two land-prawns. Everybody was excited about that, and cried, "Look, two zatku!" Land-prawns must be very few in this place. It took a long time to tell these new ones, and the others, about the Big Ones and about Wonderful Place. He showed all the things he had in the shoulder bag, and the spear and axe he had made. Stabber seemed to think the spear was especially wonderful, and they all thought the shoulder bag itself was the most wonderful thing he had—"Carry many things; not have to hold in hand; not lose,"—but there were so many wonderful things to look at that none of them could think of any one thing long. He had been like that when he had first come to Wonderful Place, when Wonderful Place had been little and nobody but Pappy Jack had been there.

There was arguing among them, and he listened and thought he understood how things had been in this band. Wise One and Stabber had wanted to find the Big One Place and make friends with the Big Ones, and Big She and Fruitfinder and Stonebreaker had been afraid. Now everybody was siding with Wise One and mocking Big She, and even she was convinced that Wise One had been right, but didn't want to admit it. Finally, they all squatted in a ring, passing all his things around to look at, and he told them about the Big Ones and Wonderful Place.

What he wanted to know was how these people had found out about the Big Ones in the first place. It was hard to find this out. Everybody was trying to talk at once and not telling about things as they had happened. Finally Wise One told him, while the others kept quiet, at least most of the time, about the thunder-death that had killed the three gotza, and finding the tracks and where the aircar had been set down, and the empty cartridges. That had been Pappy Jack and Pappy Gerd; they had been to the north on a trip, and everybody at Wonderful Place had heard about the shooting of the three harpies. And they told about the flying thing, the aircar. That would have been Pappy Vic's friends or some of Pappy George's blue-clothes police people.

All the time, the sun was getting lower and lower toward its sleeping-place; soon it would be making colors. Finally, about Big Ones' koktel-drinko time, everybody realized that they were hungry. They began talking about eating, and there was argument about whether to eat the land-prawns first or save them for last.

"Eat zatku first," Stabber advised. "Hungry now, taste good. Save for last, not hungry, not taste so good."

Wise One approved that, and Big She agreed. Wise One cracked the shells and divided the meat among everybody. That showed how scarce land-prawns were here. In the south, nobody did that. Everybody killed and ate land-prawns for himself; there were enough for everybody. He told them so, and they were all amazed, and Stabber was shouting. "Now you see! Wise One right all the time. Good Country to sun's left hand, plenty everything!" Even Big She agreed; there was no more argument about anything now.

After they had eaten the zatku—he must remember to use only Fuzzy words, till he could teach the Big One words—they were ready to eat the hatta-zosa and the ho-todda. When they saw how he skinned and butchered with his knife, they wanted him to prepare all of them; all they had was one little stone knife.

"Not eat right away," he told them. "Cook first."

Then he had to explain about that, and everybody was frightened, even Wise One. They knew about fire; lightning sometimes made it, and it was a bad thing. He remembered how frightened he had been when he had first seen it in Pappy Jack's viewscreen. He decided, with all the meat they had, to make *barba-koo*. They watched him dig the trench with his trowel and helped him get sticks to put the hatta-zosa on and gather wood for the fire, but when he went to light it they all stood back, ready to run like Big Ones watching somebody making ready for blast.

But when the barba-koo was started, they came closer, all exclaiming at the good smells, and when the meat was done and cool enough to eat, everybody was crying out at how good it was. Little Fuzzy remembered the first cooked meat he had eaten.

By this time the sun was making colors in the west, and everybody said it was good that the rain was over. They all wanted to go find a sleeping-place, but he told them that this would be a good enough place to sleep, since the rain was over and if they kept a fire burning all the big animals would be afraid. They believed that; they were still afraid themselves.

He got out his pipe and filled and lighted it, and after a few puffs he passed it around. Some of them liked it, and some refused to take a second puff. Wise One liked it, and so did Lame One and Other She and Carries-Bright-Things, but Stabber and Stonebreaker didn't. They built the fire up and sat for a long time talking.

He needed this band. With eight beside himself, they could build a big raft, and with eight and himself to hunt they would not be hungry. He had to be careful, though. He remembered how hard it had been to talk the others into going to Wonderful Place after he had found it and come back to get them to come with him. They would make him leader instead of Wise One, but he didn't want that. When a new one came into a band and tried to lead it, there was always trouble. Finally he decided what to do.

He took the whistle out of his bag and tied a string to it long enough to go around the neck, and made sure that it was tied so that it would not come loose. Then he rose and went to Wise One.

"You lead this band?" he asked.

"Yes. But if you can take us to Big One Place, you lead."

"No. Not want. You lead. I just show how to go. Others know you, not know me." He took the whistle—Wise One had learned how to blow it by now—and hung it around his neck. "I give; you keep," he said. "You leader; when band not together, want to call others, you blow. When somebody lost, you blow."

Wise One blew piercingly on the whistle. A Big One would have said, "Sank-oo," for a gift like this. Fuzzies did not say such things; everybody was good to everybody.

"You hear?" he asked. "When I make noise like this, you come. That way, nobody get lost." He thought for a moment. "I lead band, but Big Ones' Friend know better than Wise One; he very wise Wise One. Wise One listen when he say something. All listen when Big Ones' Friend say anything, do as Big Ones' Friend say. That way, we all come to Big One Place, to Hoksu-Mitto."

19

GERD VAN RIEBEEK dropped his cigarette butt and heeled it out. A hundred yards in front of him a blue and white Extee-Three carton stood pin-cushioned with arrows and leaking sand. There were almost as many arrows sticking in the turf around it, most of them very close. The hundred-odd Fuzzies were enthusiastic about it.

"Not good," he told them. "Half not hit at all."

"Come close," one of the Fuzzies protested.

"You hungry, come close not give meat. You not put come-close on stick, put over fire, cook."

The Fuzzies all laughed; this was a perfectly devastating sally of wit. A bird, about the size of a Terran pigeon, flew across the range halfway to the target. Two arrows hit it at once and it dropped.

"Now that," he said, "was good! Who did?"

Two of them spoke up; one was his and Ruth's Superego, and the other was an up-to-now nameless Fuzzy who had come in several weeks ago. Robin Hood would do for him. Then he looked again. No. Maid Marian.

That was with half his mind. The other half was worrying about Jack Holloway. Jack seemed to have stopped giving a damn after he came back from Yellowsand. It if only hadn't been Little Fuzzy. Any of the others, even one of his own family, he'd just have written off, felt badly about, and gotten over. But Little Fuzzy was something special. He was the first one, and besides that, he had something none of the others had, the something that had brought him into Holloway's Camp alone to make friends with the strange Big One. Ruth and Pancho and Ernst Mallin hadn't gotten a dependable IQ-test for Fuzzies developed yet, but they all claimed that Little Fuzzy was a genius. And he was Pappy Jack's favorite.

And now Jack was drinking, too. Not just a couple before dinner and one or two in the evening. By God, he was drinking as much as Gus Brannhard, and nobody but Gus Brannhard could do that and get away with it. Gerd wished he'd gone along with Jack to Mallorysport, but George Lunt hadn't been away from here since right after the Fuzzy Trial, and he was entitled to a trip to town; and somebody had to stay and mind the store, so he'd stayed.

Oh, hell, if Jack needed looking after, George could look after him.

"Pappy Gerd! Pappy Gerd!" somebody was calling. He turned to see Jack's Ko-Ko coming on a run. "Is talk-screen! Mummy Woof say somebody in Big House Place want to make talk."

"Hokay, I come." He turned to the Protection Force trooper who was helping him. "Let them go get their arrows. If that carton doesn't fall apart when they pull them out, let them shoot another course." Then he started up the slope toward the lab-hut, ahead of Ko-Ko.

It was Juan Jimenez, at Company Science Center. He gave a breath of relief; Jack hadn't gotten potted and gotten into trouble.

"Hello, Gerd. Nothing more about Little Fuzzy?" he asked.

"No. I don't think there is anything more. Jack's in town; did you see him?"

"Yes, at the grand opening of the Fuzzy Club yesterday. Ben and Gus want him to stay over till the convention opens. Gerd, you were asking me about ecological side effects of harpy extermination and wanted me to let you know if anything turned up."

"Yes. Has anything?"

"I think so. Forests & Waters has been after me lately. You know how all those people are; they get little, manageable problems, and never bother consulting anybody, and then when they get big and unmanageable they want me to work miracles. You know where the Squiggle is?"

He did. It was along the inside of the mountain range on the lower western coast. It wasn't really a badland, but it would do as a reasonable facsimile. Volcanic, geologically recent; a lot of weathered-down lavabeds covered with thin soil; about a thousand little streams twisting every which way and all flowing finally into the main Snake River from the west. Flooded bank-high in rainy season and almost dry in summer, doing little or nothing for the water situation on the cattle ranges at any season. For the last ten years, since the Company had been reforesting it, it had gotten a little better.

"Well, all those young featherleaf trees," Jimenez said, "they'd been doing fine up to a couple of years ago, holding moisture, stopping erosion, water table going up all over the western half of the cattle country. Then the damned goofers got in among them, and half the young trees are chewed to death now."

That figured. They'd shot all the harpies out of the southern half of the continent long ago; first chased them out of the cattle country to protect the calves, and then followed them into the upland forests where they'd been feasting on goofers. Now the surplus goofers were being crowded out of the uplands and down into the Squiggle. Up in the north, Fuzzies killed a lot of goofers, but there were no Fuzzies that far south.

But why shouldn't there be?

"Juan, I have an idea. We have a lot of Fuzzies here who are real sharp with bows and arrows. I was out running an archery class when you called me; you should see them. Say we airlift about fifty of them down to where the goofers are worst, and see what they do."

"Send them to Chesterville; the chief forester there'll know where to spot them. How about arrows?"

"Well, how about arrows? How soon do you think you can produce a lot, say a couple of thousand? I'll send specs when I know where to send them. You can make the shafts out of duralloy, the feathers out of plastic, and the heads out of light steel. They won't have to shoot through armor-plate, just through goofers."

"Well, I wouldn't know about that; that's purely a production problem. . . ."

"Then, talk to a production man about it. Is Grego in town? Talk to him; he'll get your production problems unproblemed."

"Well, Gerd, thanks a million. That may just be the answer. Airlift them around from place to place and just let them hunt. I'll bet they'll get more goofers in a day than five times as many men would get with rifles."

"Oh, hell, don't thank me. The Company's done a lot of things for us. Hokfusine, to put it in one word. Of course, we'll expect the Company to issue the same rations they're getting here. . . ."

"Oh, sure. Look, I'll call Victor. He'll probably call you back. . . ."

20

WISE ONE WAS happy. For the first time since Old One had made dead, he did not have to think all the time of what to do next and what would happen to the others if anything happened to him. Big Ones' Friend would think about all that now; he was leading the band. Of course, he insisted that Wise One was the leader, but that was foolishness.

Or maybe it wasn't; maybe it was wisdom so wise that he thought it was foolishness because he was foolish himself. That was a thought he had never had before. Maybe he was getting wiser just by being with Big Ones' Friend. Big Ones' Friend didn't want to make trouble in the band; that was why he said Wise One should lead and had given the—the *w'eesle*—to show it. His fingers went to his throat to reassure himself that he really had it.

Then he squirmed comfortably among the dry soft grass and ferns under the brush shelter Big Ones' Friend had shown them how to make, with the warmth and glow of the fire on him, listening to the wind among the trees and the splashing of the little moving-water and the sound of the lake behind him. Fire was wonderful when one learned how to make it and how to keep it safe. He had been afraid of it; all the People, all the *Fuzzies*—he must remember that—were, but when one knew about it, it was good. It frightened all the big animals away. It made warmth when one was cold. It made meat many-many times better.

But best of all, it made light in the dark. Look, here were Other She and Carries-Bright-Things and Fruitfinder, beside the fire, twisting longleaf-tree roots to make . . . to make *rope*—that was a Big One word. The People, *Fuzzies,* had no word for it because they had never known of it. It was long after dark. Without fire they would all have been asleep long ago. And Stonebreaker was working too, making the chopping-stones to put on sticks. It was strange that nobody had thought of doing that before, or of putting pointed stones on longer sticks to stab with. That made killing hatta-zosa—*goofers*—much easier; Stabber and Lame One had killed four today, after sun-highest time, *noon,* and it would have taken the whole band to kill that many with stones and clubs. Big Ones' Friend was sitting with Stonebreaker now, fitting one of the cutting-stones onto a stick.

This was the fourth night since they had come to this place. They had slept around a fire at the place where they had first met Big Ones' Friend. The next morning Big Ones' Friend had given them the Wonderful Food of the Big Ones, all he had, a little for each of them. He had told them that at Wonderful Place the Big Ones gave it all the time to all Fuzzies, as much as they wanted. After that, all of them had wanted to go to Wonderful Place and make friends with the Big Ones, even Big She. They had wanted to start at once, but Big Ones' Friend had said that they should build a floating-thing, a *raft,* and go down the river and over to the other side. He had said that all the time and work they put into this would be saved, that it would be far-far to go up to where this river was little enough to cross without a raft.

Big Ones' Friend had made a little show-like out of sticks to show the big raft he meant that they should make. He said the Big Ones often did this, first making something little before making it big to use. Then they had come to this place, and he had said it was a good place to make the raft. So they had made camp, and he had showed them how to make this shelter, and had made a place for their fire, and dug a long hole for the barba-koo fire. Then they had begun digging roots and making rope, and Big Ones' Friend had built fires at the roots of the trees he had wanted for the raft, and burned them till they fell. They cut off the branches with the chopping-stones—*axes*—he and Stonebreaker made out of hard-stone they had found up the little stream, but the trees themselves were too big to cut in that way, so Big Ones' Friend made fires to burn them into logs. This was dangerous; even Big Ones' Friend was afraid about this. These fires might get loose and burn everything. That was why he and Big Ones' Friend would sit up and watch while the others slept, and then they would wake Stabber and Big She and Lame One, who were sleeping now, and after a while they would wake Fruitfinder and Other She and Carries-Bright-Things, and they would watch till daylight.

After a while, Fruitfinder and Carries-Bright-Things and Other She finished the rope they were making and coiled it, and then came into the shelter and lay down to sleep. Stonebreaker worked on at the axehead, and Big Ones' Friend finished putting the one Stonebreaker had made onto a stick. He took it over to the woodpile and tried it while Stonebreaker watched. They both laughed at how good it was. Then he and Stonebreaker came over under the shelter.

"Show shining-stone," Stonebreaker begged.

Big Ones' Friend took it out of his shoulder bag and rubbed it for a while between his hands. Then the three of them leaned together, out of the light of the fire, to look at it. None of them had ever seen a thing like that, but Big Ones' Friend said they were known among Big Ones, and one of his friends, Pappy Vic, dug many of them out of rock. He had found this one while he was breaking a piece of hard black rock he had found up the little stream. It was inside the rock, a stone the shape of a zarabunny's kidney. It looked just like any other stone until it was rubbed; then it shone like a hot coal in the fire. But it was not hot. This was a not-understand thing; even Big Ones' Friend did not know how it could be.

"Pappy Jack used to dig for these stones," Big Ones' Friend said. "Then all the other Big Ones found out about the Fuzzies, and they said Pappy Jack should do nothing but take care of the Fuzzies and teach them."

"Tell more about Pappy Jack. Is he Wise One for all the Big Ones?"

"No. That is Pappy Ben," Big Ones' Friend said. "He is Wise One for Gov'men'. And Pappy Vic is Wise One for Comp'ny; that is another Big One thing, like Gov'men'. Pappy Jack is Wise One for all Fuzzies. All Big Ones listen to Pappy Jack about Fuzzies."

He talked for a long while about Pappy Jack and about Pappy Vic and Pappy Ben and Pappy Gerd and Mummy Woof and Pappy George and the blue-clothes Big Ones, and about Wonderful Place and Big House Place. It was all wonderful, but hard to understand. There were not enough Fuzzy words to tell about everything, which was why Big Ones' Friend said they must all learn as many Big One words as they could. They must also learn to make talk from the back of the mouth, so that the Big Ones could hear them. They were practicing that now.

After a while, Stonebreaker became sleepy and lay down. Big Ones' Friend got out his pipe and tobacco and they smoked, taking puffs in turn. One of the night-time sky-lights—*moons* was the Big Ones' word—came up. The Big Ones had names for both of them. This one was called *Zerk-Zees*. The other, which was not in the sky now, was called *Dry-As*. The Big Ones knew all about them; they were very big and very far away, and they went to them in flying things. Big Ones' Friend said he had been on Zerk-Zees, which looked so small, himself. This was hard to believe, but Big Ones' Friend said so.

"You really say for so? You not just make not-so talk?"

Big Ones' Friend was surprised that he should ask a thing like that. "Nobody make not-so talk," he said.

"*I* make not-so talk once." Wise One glad that he could tell something Big Ones' Friend did not know about. "Once I say to others that I see hesh-nazza, damnthing, and was no damnthing."

Then he told how he had wanted to go to find the Big One Place, and the others had wanted to stay where they were.

"So, I tell them I see big damnthing; damnthing chase me. They all frightened. Was no damnthing, but they not know. They all leave place, make run fast up mountain to get away from damnthing. But was no damnthing at all. We go down other side of mountain, not go back."

Big Ones' Friend looked at him in wonder. For all his wisdom, he would not have thought of that. Then he laughed.

"You 'wise ones,'" he said. "I not think to do that. But is true I was on Zerk-Zees. Big One take me there to hide when other Big Ones make trouble, once."

He told about Zerk-Zees, but it was hard. He didn't know the words to tell about it. After a while, they both lay down and went to sleep.

It seemed like only a moment, and then Other She was shaking him, crying: "Wake up, Wise One! Fire burn everything! Big fire!"

He kicked Big Ones' Friend, who was beside him, and sat up. It was so. Everything was brighter than if both moons were biggest and shining together, and there was a loud noise of crackling and roaring. It was coming from where they had been burning the trees into logs. The fire was burning dry things on the ground, and even small bushes had caught fire. Fruitfinder and Carries-Bright-Things had branches and were trying to beat it out, but it was too big and in too many places. Then he remembered the whistle, and blew it as hard as he could. By this time, Big Ones' Friend was awake and kicking Stabber and saying funny Big One words that Wise One didn't know, and then everybody was awake and all shouting at the same time.

Stabber caught up his spear and started to run at the fire with it. Big Ones' Friend caught him by the arm.

"Not kill fire with spear," he said. "Kill fire by take dry things away from it. Stop, everybody! Not do anything; make think what to do first."

By this time, Carries-Bright-Things and Fruitfinder came back; Fruitfinder was slapping Carries-Bright-Things with his hands to put out where her fur had caught fire, and Carries-Bright-Things was saying, "Fire too big; not able to kill."

Big Ones' Friend was yelling for everyone to be quiet. He picked up his axe and went forward a little, then came back.

"Not put out, too big," he said. "We go where fire not burn. Fire always burn way wind blow. Fire not burn on water. We go into water, try to get behind fire. Then we safe."

"But we go away, fire burn up nice sleeping-place. Burn up rope. We work hard make rope," somebody was arguing.

"You want fire burn up *you*?" Wise One asked. "Then, not make talk. Do what Big Ones' Friend say." He blew the whistle again, and they were all quiet. "Now what we do?" he asked Big Ones' Friend.

"Take spears, take axes," Big Ones' Friend said. He was feeling at his shoulder bag to make sure he had everything and that it was closed tightly. "Go out in water as far as can. Wait till fire here burn everything up. Then come out where fire not burn, be safe."

Carries-Bright-Things had gotten the three sticks with the *kata-jes*. She caught Big Ones' Friend by the arm.

"You put in bag, keep safe," she was saying. "Not lose."

She twisted them off the sticks, and Big Ones' Friend put them in his bag. Then he got a long piece of rope and tied one end about his waist.

"Everybody, wrap around waist," he said. "We go in water. Somebody fall in deep place, pull him out."

Nobody had realized that that could be done. Rope was to tie logs together; nobody had thought of using it for anything else. He was called Wise One, and he hadn't even thought of that. By this time, the fire was very big. It had caught a tree that had died from being chewed by goofers and all the branches of it were burning, and another tree next to it had caught fire. All the dry things on the ground were burning along the lake and back away from it, but nothing was burning in the direction from which the wind came toward the fire.

They roped themselves together, everybody carrying a spear and an axe, and went out into the water, until finally it was almost up to their necks. Then they stood still, looking back by the fire. By that time, it had reached the sleeping-place and it had caught fire. The ferns and dry grass blazed up, the brush caught fire, and, as they watched, the pole burned through and everything fell. Some of the band wailed in grief. That had been a good sleeping-place, the best sleeping-place they had ever made. Big Ones' Friend was saying:

"Bloody-hell sunnabish! All good rope, all goofer skins, all logs, all burn up. Now have to do again."

They waited a long time in the water. It grew hot even where they were. They had to take deep breaths and draw their heads down under the water for as long as they could and then raise them to breathe again. The air was hot and full of smoke, and bits of burning things fell among them. Whole trees were burning now. Different kinds of trees burned in different ways. Longleaf trees caught fire quickly, and then the leaves all burned and the fire went out, and then the branches would catch fire in places. But the blue roundleaf trees would not catch at first, but then they would catch all over and great flames would shoot high.

Finally, the fire close to them grew less, though the big trees were all burning. It had burned far away in the direction the wind blew. Big Ones' Friend said that the ground would be hot where the fire had been, and burn their feet, so they waded along where the water was shallow to where the small moving-water came into the lake. The fire had started to burn along this, but not across it, so they crossed over and started up on the other side. Big Ones' Friend untied the rope from around his waist, and they wrapped it around the staff of a spear; Big She and Lame One carried it.

Animals were in the woods, all frightened by the fire. They came close enough to a takku, a zarabuck, to kill it with their spears. But why should they? They would only have to carry the meat with them, and it might be that they would have to run fast to get away from the fire. The little stream turned and came from the direction the fire was burning. Then they came to a place where there was fire on their side too. Everybody was frightened because Big Ones' Friend had said that fire would not cross a moving-water, but he could see how this had happened: the wind had carried little burning-things over it, and started new fires.

"We go away from here," Big Ones' Friend said. "Soon be fire all around. Go away through woods; keep wind in face."

Everybody began to run. The brush was thick. After a while, Wise One saw Lame One running alone with his spear and axe, and then he saw Big She with only an axe. Big Ones' Friend would be angry with them; they had thrown away the spear on which the rope was wrapped. The brush became more thick, and now there were also long vines. These vines would be good to tie logs together for a raft. He would try to remember them when they came to build a new raft. He was going to speak of it to Big Ones' Friend, but when they stopped to catch their breaths, Big Ones' Friend was saying the funny mean-nothing Big One words. Maybe he was frightened. This was a bad place to be, with the fire so near.

At first the moon, Zerk-Zees, which was more than half round, was on their left as they ran, and a little in front. After a while, he saw that it was almost directly in front of them, though it was only a little higher. He spoke of this to Big Ones' Friend and also to Stabber. They stopped, and Big Ones' Friend got out his point-north thing, and made a light with his firemaker. Then he said more Big One words.

"Wind change. Maybe change more, maybe bring fire to us. Come, make run fast."

They floundered on through the brush and among the vines and trees. After a while they came to a big moving-water, not as big as the one that made wide lake-places, but still big. They could not cross. There was argument about what to do. The fire was up the river, but if they went down they would come to where it came into the lake, and that would be a bad place to get out of. He looked in the direction of the fire and was glad that he could not see yellow flames, though all the sky was bright pink. The wind still blew toward the fire, so they decided to go down the river.

The brush became less thick, and here were tall longleaf trees. There were animals all about, moving in the woods, frightened by the fire. Then, ahead they saw the light of Zerk-Zees shining on the lake.

"Not go that way," somebody—Wise One thought it was Stonebreaker— said.

"Not go across moving-water either," Big She said. "Too deep."

"Make raft," Big Ones' Friend said. "Little raft. Get big sticks, tie together with rope, put things on. Some get on raft, some swim. Who has rope?"

Nobody had the rope. Lame One and Big She had thrown it away to run faster. Big Ones' Friend said one of the mean-nothing words, then thought for a moment. "We go along lake, that way." He pointed east, where the thin edge of Dry-As was just above the horizon. "Go back to place fire start. Maybe all dead, ground cool. Then we be safe."

Fruitfinder said he was hungry. Now that it was said, everybody else was hungry too. They found a goofer, so frightened that Stabber just walked up to it and speared it. Big Ones' Friend took out his knife, skinned it, and cut it up. They did not make a fire to cook it. Nobody, not even Big Ones' Friend, wanted to make fire here, and they did not want to wait while it cooked. They all ate it raw.

While they were eating he smelled smoke, but thought it was an old smell in his fur. Then Carries-Bright-Things said she smelled smoke, and so did Stonebreaker. They stopped eating and looked about. The fire was much brighter, and they could see yellow flames among the red-pink glow over the trees.

Big Ones' Friend said, "Jeeze-krise go-hell bloody damn! Wind change again. Fire that way, wind come from fire, bring fire here!"

21

JACK HOLLOWAY WAS bringing a hangover home from Mallorysport, but even without it he'd have felt like Nifflheim. Traveling east was always a bother—three hours air-time and three hours zone-difference. You had to get up before daylight to get in by cocktail-time. He winced at the thought of cocktails; right now he'd as soon drink straight rat poison.

He'd done too much drinking since—since Little Fuzzy got drowned, go ahead and say it—and it hadn't done a damn's worth of good; as soon as he sobered up, he felt worse about it than ever. Hell, he'd had friends killed before, on Thor and Loki and Shesha and Mimir. Everywhere but on Terra; people didn't get killed on Terra anymore, they just dropped dead on golf courses. If it had been anybody but Little Fuzzy . . . Why, Little Fuzzy was just about the most important person in the universe to him.

His head thumped and throbbed as though an overpowered and badly defective engine were running inside it. Too many cocktails before dinner at Government House when he got in, and then too many drinks in the evening with all that crowd after dinner. And the cocktail party after the opening of the Fuzzy Club; he'd needed a lot of liquor to keep from thinking how much Little Fuzzy would have enjoyed that.

They were going to put in a big commemorative plaque for Little Fuzzy, eight feet by ten: Little Fuzzy in gold with a silver chopper-digger on a dark bronze ground. He'd seen the sketches for it. It was going to be beautiful when it was done, looked just like the little fellow.

And then, when he'd wanted to go home, Ben and Gus had insisted that he stay over for the banquet for the delegates, and he wanted to help get them in a good humor. And, God, what a gang! One thing, they were all in favor of lynching Hugo Ingermann.

George Lunt, beside him, had tried to make conversation after they'd lifted out, then gave it up. He'd tried to sleep, and must have dozed off in his seat a few times. Each time he woke, his head hurt worse and he had a fouler taste in his mouth. He was awake when they passed over Big Blackwater; not a sign of smoke or anything going on. Grego'd moved everything he had there up to Yellowsand and was bringing men and equipment in from Alpha and Delta and Gamma. He'd seen one of the Company's big contragravity freighters, the *Zebralope,* lifting out of Mallorysport air terminal for Yellowsand when he was leaving Government House. He hoped Grego got out a lot of sunstones before the trial.

Coming up Cold Creek, he couldn't see any activity where they'd been holding the raft-building classes. There weren't many Fuzzies running around the camp either, though there was a small archery class. Gerd van Riebeek met him and shook hands with him as he got out. George Lunt excused himself and went off toward the ZNPF Headquarters. He'd have to look at his desk; he hated the thought of having to deal with what would be piled up on it.

Gerd was silly enough to ask him how he was.

"I have a hangover with little hangovers, and some of the little ones are just before having young. Is there any hot coffee around?"

That was a silly question, too; this was an office, and offices ran on hot coffee. They went into his office; Gerd called for some to be brought in. There was a stack of papers half the size of a cotton bale—he'd been right about that. He hung up his hat and they sat down.

"Didn't see much of a crowd outside," he mentioned.

"A hundred and fifty less," Gerd told him. "They're down in the Squiggle."

"Good God!" He knew what the Squiggle was like. "What are a hundred and fifty of our Fuzzies doing in that place?"

Gerd grinned. "Working for the CZC, like everybody else. They're shooting goofers with bows and arrows. Company had a lot of goofers in those young featherleaf trees they planted the watersheds with. Three days ago I sent fifty down to the chief forester at Chesterville. By yesterday morning they'd shot over two hundred goofers, so he wanted a hundred more, and I sent them. Captain Knabber and five Protection Force troopers are with them; Pancho went down with the second draft to observe. They're dropping them off in squads of half a dozen, supplying and transporting them with air-lorries. In the evenings, they bring them into a couple of camps they've set up."

"Why, I'll be damned!" In spite of the headache, which the coffee was barely beginning to ameliorate, Jack chuckled. "Bet they're having a great time. Your idea?"

"Yes. Juan Jimenez told me about the goofer situation. I'd been bothered about possible side effects of exterminating the harpies. The harpies kept the goofer increase down to reasonable limits, and now there are no harpies down there. I thought Fuzzies would do the job just as well. It's axiomatic that a man with a rifle is the most efficient predator. Fuzzies with bows and arrows seem to be almost as good."

"We'll have rifles for them before long. Mart Burgess finished the ones for Gus's Allan and Natty—I wish I could shoot like those Fuzzies!—and he's making up a couple more for prototypes and shop-models for the Company. They're going to produce them in quantity."

"What kind of rifles? Safe for Fuzzies to use?"

"Yes, single-shots. Burgess got the action design from an old book. Remington rolling-block; they used them all over Terra in the first century Pre-Atomic."

"That might be an answer to what you're worrying about, Jack," Gerd said. "You want something the Fuzzies can do to earn what they get from us, so they won't turn into bums. Pest-control hunters."

That idea of Fuzzy colonies on other continents . . . There was a burrowing rodent on Gamma that was driving the farmers crazy. And landprawns everywhere; they were distributed all over the planet. And Fuzzies loved to hunt.

The harpies had been exterminated completely on Delta Continent. There'd be something there that they had fed on, which would not be proliferating and turning destructive. Jack had some more coffee brought in, and he and Gerd talked about that for a while. Then Gerd went out, and he talked to the Company forester at Chesterville by screen, and to Pancho Ybarra, whom he located at one of the temporary Fuzzy hunting-camps. Then he started on the accumulation of paperwork.

He was still at it when the screen buzzed; one of the girls at message center.

"Mr. Holloway, we've just gotten a call from Yellowsand Canyon," she began.

A clutching tightness in his chest. A call from Yellowsand might just be some routine matter, but then again, it might be . . . he forced calmness into his voice.

"Yes?"

"Well, the *Zebralope,* coming in from Mallorysport, reported sighting a big forest-fire up Lake-Chain River. They've transmitted in some views they took, and Mr. McGinnis, the Company general superintendent, sent a survey boat out to look at it. He thought you ought to be notified, since it's on the Fuzzy Reservation. He's calling Mr. Grego now for instructions."

"Just where is it?"

She gave him the map coordinates. He jotted them down and told her to stand by. He snapped on a reading-screen, twisted the class-selector for maps, and then fiddled to get the latest revised map of the country up the Lake-Chain, finally centering the cross hairs on the given coordinates and stepping up magnification.

Funny place for a forest-fire, he thought. There hadn't been any thunderstorms up that way for ten days. Not since the night Little Fuzzy was lost. Of course, a fire could smoulder for ten days, but . . .

"Let's have the views," he said.

"Just a moment, sir."

A lot of things could start fires in the woods, but they were all hundred-to-one shots but two: Lightning and carelessness. Carelessness of some human—sapient, he corrected—being. And the commonest sort of carelessness was careless smoking. Little Fuzzy smoked; he'd had his pipe and tobacco and lighter with him in his shoulder bag.

There'd been a lot of trees and stuff uprooted above that had been shoved down into the canyon. Suppose he'd managed to grab hold of something and kept himself afloat; and suppose he'd managed to get out of the river . . .

He reduced magnification and widened the field. Yes. Suppose he'd been carried down below the mouth of the Lake-Chain River, on the left bank. He'd start back on foot, and when he came to where the Lake-Chain came in from the north to join the Yellowsand curving in from the east, what would he think?

Well, what would anybody who didn't know the country think? He'd think the Lake-Chain was the Yellowsand, and go on following it. Of course, he had a compass, but he wouldn't be looking at that, hanging to a log or a tree in the river. A compass would only tell him which way north was; it wouldn't tell him where he'd been since he last looked at it.

"I have the fire views now, Mr. Holloway."

"Don't bother with them. I'll get them later. You call Gerd van Riebeek and George Lunt; tell them I want them right away. And tell Lunt to put on an emergency alert. And then get me Victor Grego in Mallorysport."

He reached for his pipe and lighter, wondering where his hangover had gone.

"And when you have time," he added, "call Sandra Glenn at the Fuzzy Club in Mallorysport and tell her to hold up work on that commemorative plaque. It might just be a little premature."

22

LITTLE FUZZY'S EYES smarted, his throat was sore and his mouth dry. His fur was singed. There was one place on his back where he had been burned painfully, and would have been burned worse if someone behind had not slapped out the fire. He was filthy, caked with mud and blackened with soot. They all were. They had just gotten out of mud and were standing on the bank of the small stream, looking about them.

There was nothing green anywhere they looked, nothing but black, dusted with gray ash and wreathed in gray smoke that rose from things that still burned. Many trees still stood, but they were all black with smoke and little tongues of flame blowing from them. The sun had come out, but it was hard to see, dim and red, through the smoke that rose everywhere.

They stood in a little clump beside the stream. No one spoke. Lame One was really lame now; he had burned his foot and limped in pain, leaning on a spear. Wise One had been hurt too, by a broken branch that had bounced and hit him when a tree had fallen nearby. There was dried blood in his fur along with the mud and soot. Most of the others had been cut and scratched in the brush or bruised by falls, but not badly. They had lost most of their things.

Little Fuzzy still had his shoulder bag and his knife and trowel and his axe. Wise One had an axe, and he still had the whistle. Big She had an axe, and so did Stonebreaker. Stabber had a spear, as did Lame One and Other She. All the other weapons had been lost swimming the river that flowed into the lake after the wind had turned and brought the fire toward them.

"Now what do?" Stabber was asking. "Not go back, big fire that way. Big fire that way too." He pointed up the stream. "And not go where fire was, ground hot, all burn feet like Lame One."

He had always wondered why Big Ones wore the hard, stiff things on their feet. Now he knew; they could walk anywhere with them. A Big One could walk over the ground here that was still smoking. He wished now that they had carried away the skins of the goofers and zarabunnies they had killed; but of course, if they had they would have lost them in the water too.

"Big Ones' Friend know about fire," Stonebreaker said. "We not know. Big Ones' Friend tell us what to do."

He didn't know what to do either. He would have to think and remember everything Pappy Jack and Pappy Gerd and Pappy George and the others had told him, and everything he had seen and learned since this fire had begun.

Fire would not live where there was nothing to burn, or in water, or ground. It would not burn wet things, but it would make wet things dry, and then they would burn. That was not the fire itself, but the heat of the fire. He didn't understand about that, because heat was not a thing but just the way things were. Pappy Jack had told him that. He still didn't quite understand, but he knew fire made heat.

Fire couldn't live without air. He wasn't sure just what air was, but it was everywhere, and when it moved it made wind. Fire burned in the way the wind blew; this was so, but he had seen fire burning, very little and very slow, against the wind. But the big part of the fire went with the wind; that was what had made the bad trouble last night, when the wind had changed.

And fire always burned up; he had seen that happen at the beginning when the little dry things on the ground caught fire and the fire went up into the trees and burned them. He could still see it burning up the trees that were standing. There were two kinds of woods fires, and he had seen both kinds. One kind burned on the ground, among the bushes, and set fire to the trees above it. That had been how this fire had started. Then there were fires that got into the tops of trees and lit one treetop from another. Little burning things fell down and set fire to what was on the ground, and this burned after the big fire in the treetops. This was a bad kind of fire; with a strong wind it moved very fast. Nobody could escape by running ahead of it.

"Big Ones' Friend not say anything," Big She objected.

"Big Ones' Friend make think," Wise One said. "Not think, do wrong thing. Do wrong thing, all make dead."

Maybe it would be best just to stay here all day and wait for the ground to get cool and the little burning things to go out. He thought that the place where they had camped and where the fire had started was to the east of them, but he wasn't sure. There was a lake to the south of them, he knew that, but he didn't know which one. There were too many lakes in this place. And there were too many bloody-hell sunnabish fires all around!

"Nothing to eat, this place," Carries-Bright-Things complained. "Good-to-eat things all burn."

As soon as she said that, everybody remembered that they were hungry. They had eaten a goofer, but that had been a long time ago, and they had not been able to finish it.

"We have to find not-burn-yet place, then find good-to-eat things." The trouble was, he didn't know where there were any not-burn-yet places, and if they found one maybe the fire would come and then there would be more trouble. He looked up the stream. "I think we go that way. Maybe find not-burn place, maybe find place where fire all dead, ground cool."

And then they would have to get back to the lakes and find a place to camp and start building a raft. He thought of all the work they had done that they would have to do over, the rope they would have to make, the things to work with, the logs. That was a sick-making thing to think of. And the trouble he and Wise One and Stabber would have with some of the others. . . .

They started up the stream, with the whole country burned black, gray with smoke and ashes on either side, and the black trees standing, still burning. They waded where the water was not too deep. Where it was, they walked on the bank, careful to avoid burning things. The stream bent; now they were going straight west.

Then they heard an aircar sound. They all stopped and listened. Pappy Jack had always told him that if he were lost, he should build a fire and make a big smoke, so that somebody would see. He had to laugh at that. This time he had made a big smoke. Some Big One, even far away, had seen it and come to see what made it. Then he was disappointed. He knew what the sound was. It was not an aircar nearby but a big air-thing, a ship, far off. He knew about them. One came every three days to Wonderful Place, bringing things. It was always fun when a ship came; none of the Fuzzies would stay in school but would all run out to watch.

He wondered why a ship was in this place, and then he thought that it would be coming to Yellowsand, bringing more machines and more of Pappy Vic's friends to help him dig, and things to eat, and *likka* for koktel-drinko, and everything the Big Ones needed. The Big Ones on the ship would see the smoke and tell Pappy Vic, and then Pappy Vic and his friends would come.

The only trouble was, this fire was too big. It was burning everywhere. Why, it would take a person days to walk all around where it had burned. How would the Big Ones know where to look, and from the air, how could they see for all this smoke? Pappy Jack had said, make smoke. Well, he had made too much smoke. If it had not been so dreadful, that would have been a laugh-at thing.

He mustn't let the others think about this, though. So, as they waded up the little stream, he talked to them about Wonderful Place, of the estee-fee they ate, and the milk and fruit juice, and the school where the Big Ones taught new things nobody had ever thought about, and the bows and arrows, and the hard stuff that they heated to make soft and pounded into any shape they wanted and then made hard again, and the marks that meant sounds, so that when one looked at them one could say the words somebody else had said when making them. He told them how many Fuzzies there were at Wonderful Place, and all the fun they had. He told them about how all Fuzzies would have nice Big Ones of their own, to take care of them and be good to them. It made a good-feeling just to talk about these things.

Then, through the smoke ahead, he saw green, and then all the others saw it and shouted and ran forward, even Lame One hobbling on his spear. The fire had stopped at a little stream that flowed into this one from the south, and beyond was green grass and bushes. But there were old black trees here, burned and dead, with moss on them. The others, all but Wise One, could not understand this.

"Long-ago big burn-everything fire," Wise One said. "Maybe lightning make. Burn everything here, same like that." He pointed to the smoking burn-place behind. "Then grass grow, bushes grow, but this fire not find anything to burn."

They crossed into the long-ago-burned place. The ground was still black, although the other fire had been many new-leaf times ago. Here he cut the tallest and straightest of the bushes, making a staff for Lame One so that Carries-Bright-Things could take his spear, and he made a club for Fruitfinder. Then they made line-abreast and went forward, and almost at once they killed a zarabunny, and then a goofer. . . .

Using his trowel, he dug a trench, and they built a fire in it and sat down and watched the meat cooking on sticks over it. He and Big She took the zarabunny skin and put it around Lame One's hurt foot and cut strips from the goofer skin to fasten it on. Lame One got up and limped about to try it and said that it did not hurt him so much to walk. After they ate he filled his pipe and lit it, and those who liked to smoke passed it around.

He was very careful to bury all the fire before they left. Everybody thought it was funny that they were making a fire with fire all around them.

There was smoke ahead, but the wind was at their backs. Soon the burned-dead trees became less, and then there were white dead trees, with all their branches. He thought that these trees had made dead because the bark had been burned at the bottoms, just as trees were killed by goofers chewing the bark. The brush was more and bigger here. And finally they came to big round-blue-leaf trees that had not been burned at all. The fire had never been here.

Nobody wanted to go fast. It was nice among the big trees, and the smoke in the air was less, though they could still smell it and it made the sun dim. They found a little stream, clear and sweet, untainted by ashes. They drank and washed all the mud and soot out of their fur. Everybody felt much better.

He began hearing aircar sounds again, very far away, but many of them, and also machinery sounds. Pappy Vic and his friends must have come and brought machines to help them put out the fire. He remembered all the things he had seen at Yellowsand, how they were digging off the whole top of the mountain. They would have no trouble putting out a fire even as big as this one. He wanted to go in the direction of the sounds, but he knew that the fire was between.

The ground sloped up, but his compass told him that they were still going south; it seemed to him that the land should slope down in that direction. Then they came to the top of a hill. When they went forward they could see a lake ahead and below, a very wide lake. They stopped at the edge of a cliff, higher than the highest house in Wonderful Place, as high as the middle terrace of Pappy Ben's house in Big House Place, and right at the bottom with no beach at all was the lake.

"Not go down there," Lame One said. "Not even if foot not hurt. Too far, nothing to hold to, not climb."

"Go down, get in water," Stabber said.

"Water deep down there. Always deep, place like that," Wise One added.

Other She looked apprehensively at the great round clouds of smoke rising to the north.

"Maybe fire come this way. Maybe this not good place."

He was beginning to think so himself. The fire had stopped at the long-ago-burned place, but he didn't know what it was doing at the other side. Still, he didn't want to leave this place. It was high, and the trees were not too many. If somebody came over the lake in an aircar, they could see and come for them. He said so.

"Why not come now?" Other She asked. "Not see Big One flying things anywhere."

"Not know we here. All work hard put out fire. Is always-so thing with Big Ones; hear about fire in woods, go with machines to put out."

He opened his pouch to see how much tobacco he had left. He had been careful not to waste it, but it had been two hands, *ten,* days ago since he fell in the river. There was only a little, but he filled the pipe and lit it, passing it around. Stabber, who hadn't liked it before, thought he would try it again. He coughed on the first puff, but after that he said he liked it.

When there was nothing left in the pipe but ashes, he put it away, and then looked to the north. There was much more smoke, and it was closer. The sound of the fire could be heard now, and once he thought he could see it over the tops of the trees. The others were becoming frightened.

"Where go?" Fruitfinder was almost wailing. "Is far down, water close, water deep." He pointed to the east. "And more fire there. We not go anywhere fire not be."

He was afraid Fruitfinder was right, but that was not a good way to talk. Soon everyone would be frightened, and frightened people did foolish things. Being frightened was a good way to make dead. He looked to the east where the cliff ended in a promontory that jutted out into the lake. It was hard to tell; far-off things always looked little, but he thought it was less high there. For one thing, smoke was blowing past it out over the lake.

"Not so far down that way," he said. "Maybe can get down to water; fire not come down."

Nobody else knew what to do, so nobody argued. To the north, he could now see much fire above the trees. Krisa-mitee, he thought, now makes sunnabish treetop fire; this is bad! They all hurried along the top of the cliff, near the edge. Once they came to a place where a piece of the cliff had slid down into the lake; it looked like the place where Pappy Vic's friends had been digging at Yellowsand, where they had found no shining stones and stopped, and where he had gone down into the deep place. They all ran around it and kept on. By this time the fire was close; it was a treetop fire, and burning things were falling and making fires under it on the ground.

He thought, Maybe this is where Little Fuzzy make dead!

He didn't want to die. He wanted to go back to Pappy Jack.

Then he stopped short. He was sure of it. This was where Little Fuzzy and Wise One and Stabber and Lame One and Fruitfinder and Stonebreaker and Big She and Other She and Carries-Bright-Things would all make dead.

In front of them was a deep-down split in the ground, down as far as the cliff itself, and at the bottom of it a stream rushed out into the lake, fast and foam-white. He looked to the left; it went as far as he could see. Behind, the fire roared toward them. It seemed to be making its own wind; he didn't know fire could do that. Bits of flaming stuff were being swirled high into the air; some were falling halfway to them from the fire and starting little fires for themselves.

23

T HE SMOKE OF the fire wasn't visible at all when Jack Holloway came in. Yellowsand looked quiet from the air, the diggings empty of equipment and deserted. Every machine must have been shifted north and west to the fire. He saw a few people around the fenced-in flint-cracking area, mostly in CZC Police uniform. The *Zebralope* was gone, probably sent off for reinforcements. He set the car down in front of the administration hut, and half a dozen men advanced to meet him. Luther McGinnis, the superintendent; Stan Farr, the personnel man; José Durrante, the forester; Harry Steefer. He and Gerd got out; the two ZNPF troopers in the front seat followed them.

"We have Mr. Grego on screen now," McGinnis said. "He's in his yacht, about halfway from Alpha; he has a load of fire-fighting experts with him. You know what he thinks?"

"The same as I do; I was talking to him. Little Fuzzy got careless dumping out his pipe. I have to watch that myself, and I've been smoking in the woods longer than he has."

Gerd was asking just where the fire was.

"Show you," McGinnis said. "But if you think it really was Little Fuzzy, how in Nifflheim did he get way up there?"

"Walked." Jack gave his reasons for thinking so while they were going toward the hut door. "He probably thought he was going up the Yellowsand till he got up to the lakes."

There was a monster military-type screen rigged inside, fifteen feet square; in it a view of the fire, from around five thousand feet, rotated slowly as the vehicle on which the pickup was mounted circled over it. He'd seen a lot of forest fires, helped fight most of them. This one was a real baddie, and if it hadn't been for the big river and the lakes that clustered along it like variously shaped leaves on a vine, it would have been worse. It was all on the north side, and from the way the smoke was blowing, the water-barriers had stopped it.

"Wind must have done a lot of shifting," he commented.

"Yes." That was the camp meteorologist. "It was steady from the southwest last night; we think the fire started sometime after midnight. A little before daybreak, it started moving around, blowing more toward the north, and then it backed around to the southwest where it had come from. That was general wind, of course. In broken country like that, there are always a lot of erratic ground winds. After the fire started, there were convection currents from the heat."

"Never can trust the wind in a fire," he said.

"Hey, Jack! Is that you?" a voice called. "You just get in?"

He turned in the direction of the speaker whence it came, saw Victor Grego in bush-clothes in one of the communication screens, with a background that looked like an air-yacht cabin.

"Yes. I'm going out and have a look as soon as I find out where. I have a couple more cars on the way, George Lunt and some ZNPF, and three lorries full of troopers and construction men following. I didn't bring any equipment. All we have is light stuff, and it'd take four or five hours to get it here on its own contragravity."

Grego nodded. "We have plenty of that. I'll be getting in around 1430; I probably won't see you till you get back in. I hope the kid did start it, and I hope he didn't get caught in it afterward."

So did Jack. Be a hell of a note, getting out of Yellowsand River alive and then getting burned in this fire. No, Little Fuzzy was too smart to get caught.

He looked at other screens, views transmitted in from vehicles over the fire-lines—bulldozers flopping off contragravity in the woods and snorting forward, sending trees toppling in front of them; manipulators picking them up as they fell and carrying them away; draglines and scoops dumping earth and rock to windward. People must have been awfully helpless with a big fire before they had contragravity. They'd only gotten onto this around noon, and they'd have it all out by sunset; he'd read about old-time forest-fires that had burned for days.

"These people all been warned to keep an eye out for a Fuzzy running around?" he asked McGinnis.

"Yes, that's gone out to everybody. I hope he's alive and out of danger. We'll have a Nifflheim of a time finding him after the fire's out, though."

"You may have a Nifflheim of a time putting out the next fire he starts. He may have started this one for a smoke signal." He turned to Durrante. "How much do you know about that country up there?"

"Well, I've been out with survey crews all over it." That meant, at a couple of thousand feet. "I know what's in there."

"Okay. Gerd and I are going out now. Suppose you come along. Where do you think this started?"

"I'll show you." Durrante led them to a table map, now marked in different shadings of red. "As nearly as I can figure, in about here, along the north shore of this lake. The first burn was along the shore and up this run; that was while the wind was still blowing northeast. It was burning all over here, and here, when the *Zebralope* sighted it, but that was after the wind shifted. We didn't get a car to the scene till around 1030, and by that time this area was burned out, nothing but snags burning, and there was a hell of a crown-fire going over this way. This part here is an old burn, fire started by lightning maybe fifteen years ago. There was nobody on this continent north of the Big Bend then. The fire hasn't gotten in there at all. This hill is all in bluegums; that's where the latest crown-fire's going."

"Okay. Let's go."

They went out to the car. Gerd took the controls; the forester got in beside him. Jack took the back seat, where he could look out on both sides.

"Hand my rifle back to me," he said. "I'll want it if I get out to look around on foot."

The forester lifted it out of the clips on the dashboard; it was the 12.7-mm double. "Good Lord, you lug a lot of gun around," he said, passing it back.

"I may have a lot of animal to stop. You run into a damnthing at ten yards, seven thousand foot-pounds isn't too much."

"N-no," Durrante agreed. "I never used anything heavier than a 7-mm, myself." He never bothered with a rifle at a fire; animals, he said, never attacked when running away from a fire.

Now, there was the kind of guy they make angels out of. That was all he knew about damnthings; a scared damnthing would attack anything that moved, just because it was scared. Some human people were like that too.

They came in over the lakes a trifle above the point where the fire was supposed to have started and let down on the black and ash-powdered shore. A lot of snags, some large, were still burning. They were damn good things to stay away from. He saw one sway and fall in a cloud of pink spark, powdered dust, and smoke. He climbed out of the car, broke the double express, and slipped in two of the thumb-thick, span-long cartridges, snapping it shut and checking the safety. Wouldn't be anything alive here, but he hadn't lived to be past seventy by taking things for granted. Durrante, who got out with him, had only a pistol. If he stayed on Beta, maybe he wouldn't get to be that old.

It was Durrante who spotted the little triangle of unburned grass between the mouth of the run and the lake. At the apex a tree had been burned off at the base and the branches lopped off with something that had made not quite rectilinear cuts—a little flint hatchet, maybe. The fire had started on both sides of it, eight feet from the butt. He let out his breath in a whoosh of relief. Up to this, he had only hoped Little Fuzzy had gotten out of the river alive and started the fire; now he *knew* it.

"He wasn't trying to make a signal-fire," he said. "He was building himself a raft." He looked at the log. "How the devil did he expect to get that into the water, though? It'd take half a dozen Fuzzies to roll that."

Under a couple of blackened and still burning snags he found what was left of Little Fuzzy's camp, burned branches mixed with the powdery ash of grass and fern-fronds; a pile of ash that showed traces of having been coils of rope made from hair-roots. He found bones which frightened him until he saw that they were all goofer and zarabunny bones. Little Fuzzy hadn't gone hungry. Durrante found a lot of flint, broken and chipped, a flint spearhead and an axehead, and, among some tree-branch ashes, another axehead with fine beryl-steel wire around it and the charred remains of an axe-helve.

"Little Fuzzy was here, all right. He always carried a spool of wire around with him." He slung his rifle and got out his pipe and tobacco. Gerd had brought the car to within a yard of the ground and had his head out the open window beside him. He handed the remains of the axe up to him. "What do you think, Gerd?"

"If you were a Fuzzy and you woke up in the middle of the night with the woods on fire, what would you do?" Gerd asked.

"Little Fuzzy knows a few of the simpler principles of thermodynamics. I think he'd get out in the water as far as he could and sit tight till the fire was past, and then try to get to windward of it. Let's go up along the lake shore first."

Gerd set the car down and they got in. Jack didn't bother unloading the big rifle. West of the little run, the whole country was burned, but that must have happened after the wind backed around. The lake narrowed into the river; the river twisted and widened into another lake, with a ground-fire going furiously on the left bank. Then they came to a promontory jutting into the water a couple of hundred feet high. On top of it a crown-fire was just before burning out, with a ground-fire raging behind it. They passed a narrow gorge, just a split in the cliff, with a stream tumbling out of it. Things were burning on both sides of it on the top.

He had the window down and was peering out; a little beyond the gorge he heard the bellowing of some big animal in agony—something the fire had caught and hadn't quite killed. He shoved the muzzle of the 12.7-double out the window.

"See if you can see where it is, Gerd. Whatever it is, we don't want to leave it like that."

"I see it," Gerd said, a moment later. "Over where that chunk slid out of the cliff."

Then he saw it. It was a damnthing, a monster, with a brow-horn long enough to make a walking stick and side-horns as big as sickles. It had blundered into a hollow, burned and probably blinded, and fallen, until its body caught on a point of rock. The sounds it was making were like nothing he had ever heard a damnthing make before; it was a frightful pain.

Kneeling on the floor, he closed his sights on the beast's head just below an ear that was now a lump of undercooked meat, and squeezed. He'd been a little off balance; the recoil almost knocked him over. When he looked again, the damnthing was still.

"Move in a little, Gerd. Back a bit." He wanted to be sure, and with a damnthing the only way to be sure was shoot it again. "I think it's dead, but . . ."

Somewhere a whistle blew shrilly, then blew again and again.

"What the hell?" Gerd was asking.

"Why, it's in the middle of that fire!" Durrante cried. "Nothing could live in there."

Wanting to get as much for his cartridge and his pounded shoulder as he could, he aimed at the damnthing's head and let off the left barrel with another thunderclap report. The body jerked from the impact of the bullet and nothing else.

"It's up that gorge. I told you Little Fuzzy knows a few of the rudiments of thermodynamics. He's down under the head, sitting it out. You think you can get the car in there?"

"I can get her in. I'll probably have to get her out straight up, though, through the fire, so have everything shut when I do."

They inched into the gorge. Twenty-five width would have been plenty, if it had been straight. It wasn't, and there were times when it looked like a no-go. Ahead, the whistle was still blowing, and he could hear calls of "Pappy Jack! Pappy Jack!" in several voices, he realized, while the whistle was blowing. And there was yeeking. Little Fuzzy had picked up a gang; that was how he was going to get that log into the water.

"Hang on, Little Fuzzy!" he shouted. "Pappy Jack come!"

There was a nasty scraping as Gerd got the patrol car around a corner. Then he saw them. Nine of them, by golly. Little Fuzzy, still wearing his shoulder bag, and eight others. One had a foot bandaged in what looked like a zarabunny skin. A couple had flint-tipped spears and flint axes, the heads bound on with wire. They were all clinging to an out-thrust ledge, halfway down to the water.

Gerd got the car down. Jack opened the door and reached out, pulling the nearest Fuzzy into the car. It was a female, with an axe. She clung to it as he got her into the car. He picked up the one with the bandaged foot and got him in, handing him forward and warning Durrante to be careful of the foot. Little Fuzzy was next; he was saying, "Pappy Jack! You *did* come!" and then, "And Pappy Gerd!" Then he shouted encouragement to the others outside until they were all in the car.

"Now, we all go to Wonderful Place," Little Fuzzy was saying. "Pappy Jack take care of us. Pappy Jack friend of all Fuzzies. You see what I tell."

HE SAW GREGO'S maroon and silver air-yacht grounded by the administration hut as they came in. Gerd, in front, had already called in the rescue of Little Fuzzy and eight other assorted Fuzzies. There was a crowd; he saw Grego and Diamond in front. Gerd set down the car and Durrante got out carrying the burned-foot case. He opened the rear door and waited for the other survivors to pile out under their own power. Those who could speak audibly—Little Fuzzy seemed to have been teaching them to talk like Big Ones—wanted to know if this place Hoksu-Mitto. They were given an ovation, Diamond rushing forward as soon as he saw his friend. Then they were all herded into the camp hospital.

Little Fuzzy had a burn on his back and a lot of fur singed off. He was treated first, to show the others that they would be medicated instead of murdered. The burned foot was really nasty, especially as the Fuzzy had been walking on it quite a lot. Everybody praised the zarabunny-skin wrapping. The camp doctor wanted to put the lot of them to bed. He didn't know enough about Fuzzies to know that no Fuzzy with anything less than a broken leg could be kept in bed. As soon as they were all bandaged up, they were taken to the executives' living quarters for an Extee-Three banquet, and when that was over, they all wanted *smokko*.

The news services began screening in almost at once, wanting views and interviews. They weren't much interested in the fire; they wanted Little Fuzzy and his new friends. It was a pain in the neck, but Grego insisted that they be fully satisfied; with the Constitutional Convention just opened, the Friends of Little Fuzzy needed a good press. It was well after dinner-time, and the fire had been stopped all around its perimeter, before anybody could get any privacy at all.

The Fuzzies were sprawled on a couple of mattresses on the floor, all but Little Fuzzy who wanted to sit on Pappy Vic. It was taking a long time for Little Fuzzy to tell about everything that had happened since he'd gone in the river in Yellowsand Canyon; apparently he had already told the other Fuzzies his adventures, because they were constantly interrupting to remind him of things he was forgetting. Then, after he got to where he had joined Wise One and his band—Wise One was the one who had the whistle and the bandaged head—everybody tried to tell about it at once. Harry Steefer and José Durrante were missing a lot of it because they couldn't understand Fuzzy. It was surprising how well this crowd had learned to pitch their voices to human audibility in the time Little Fuzzy had been with them.

Finally, Little Fuzzy got to where, trying to run ahead of the crown-fire at the top of the cliff, they had found themselves stopped by the deep chasm.

"Come this place, not get over, we think all make dead," Little Fuzzy said. "Then I remember what Pappy Jack say. Fire make heat, heat always go up, never go down. So we go down, heat go away from us. Then Pappy Jack come."

That called for praise, which Little Fuzzy accepted as his due, with becoming modesty.

"Pappy Jack smart, too. Not make shoot with big rifle, we not hear, not blow whistle."

Let it go at that; hell, he couldn't have gone on and left that damn thing bellowing in pain. He wanted to know how Wise One and his band had first learned about the Big Ones, and, sure enough, they were the same gang he and Gerd had run into in the north when the harpies had shown up. They told about their fright at the thunder-noises, and about coming back and finding the empty cartridges. This reminded one of the females of something.

"Big Ones' Friend!" she cried out. "You still have bright-things? You not lose?"

Little Fuzzy unzipped his shoulder bag and dug out three fired rifle cartridges and showed them. The female came over and repossessed them. Then Little Fuzzy found something else in his bag, and cried out.

"I forget! Have shining-stone; find where we work to make raft in little moving-water."

And he brought out, of all things, a big sunstone. It'd run about twenty to twenty-five carats. He rubbed it till it glowed.

"Look! Pretty!"

Grego set Diamond on the floor and came over to look; so did Diamond. Steefer and Durrante had also left their chairs.

"Where you get, Little Fuzzy?" Grego asked.

Steefer and Durrante were just swearing. People'd have to stop swearing around Fuzzies; Little Fuzzy was beginning to curse like a spaceport labor-boss already.

"Up little moving-water, run, come into lake where we make camp to make raft."

"You sure you didn't get this here at Yellowsand?"

"I tell you where I get. I not tell you not-so thing."

No, they could depend on that; Fuzzies didn't tell not-so things. Damnit!

"Good God! You know what'll happen if this gets out," Grego said. "Every son of a Khooghra and his brother who can scare up air-vehicles will be swarming in there. We can keep them off Yellowsand, but there's too much country up there. Need an army to police it."

"Why don't *you* operate it?"

Grego's language became as lurid as the forest-fire.

"We need more sunstone-diggings like we need a hole in the head. If our lease is upheld, we'll cut work here to about twenty percent of the present rate. What do you want us to do, flood the market? Get enough sunstones out and they won't be worth the S-450 royalty the Fuzzies are getting."

That was true. They'd had that same trouble with diamonds on Terra, back Pre-Atomic.

"Little Fuzzy," he said, "you found shining-stone like you tell. Is yours."

"My God, Jack!" Harry Steefer almost howled. "That thing's worth twenty-five grand!"

"That doesn't make a damn's worth of difference. Little Fuzzy found it, it's his. Now listen, Little Fuzzy. You keep, you not lose, not give to anybody. You keep safe, all time. Savvy?"

"Yes, sure. Is pretty. Always want shining-stone."

"You not show to people you not know. Anybody see, maybe be bad Big One, try to take. And anybody ask where you get, you say, Pappy Vic give you, because you find here at Yellowsand."

"But not find here. Find in hard-stone, in little moving-water. . . ."

"I know, I know!" This was what Leslie Coombes and Ernst Mallin always ran into. "Is no-so thing. But you can say."

Little Fuzzy looked puzzled. Then he gave a laugh.

"Sure! Can say not-so thing! Wise One say not-so thing once. Say he see damnthing; was no damnthing at all. Tell rest of band, they all think is so."

"Huh?" Victor Grego looked at Little Fuzzy, and then at the Fuzzy with the whistle hung around his neck and the bandage-turban on his head. "Tell about, Wise One."

Wise One shrugged; an Old Terran Frenchman couldn't have done it better.

"Others want to stay in place, once. I want to go on, hunt for Big One Place, make friends with Big Ones. They not want. They afraid, want to stay in same place all time. So, I tell them big dam'fing come, chase me, chase Stabber, come eat everybody up. They all frightened. All jump up, make run away up mountain, go down other side. Then, forget about place they want to stay, go on to sun's left—to south, like I want."

One of the females howled like a miniature police-siren, and not so miniature, either. With his ultrasonic hearing aid on, it almost shattered Victor's ear.

"You make talk you see hesh-nazza, hesh-nazza come eat us all up, and no hesh-nazza at all?" She was dumbfounded with horrified indignation. "You make us run away from nice-place, good-to-eat things . . . ?"

"Jeeze-krise sunnabish!" Wise One shouted at her. He'd only been around Little Fuzzy a week, and listened to him. "You think this not nice-place? We stay where you want, we never see nice-place like this. You make talk about good-to-eat things; you think we get estee-fee in place you want to stay? You think we get smokko? You think we find Big Ones, make friends? You make bloody-hell talk like big fool!"

"You mean, you told these other Fuzzies you saw a damnthing and you knew you hadn't at all?" Grego demanded. "Well, hallelujah, praise Saint Beelzebub! You talk to the kids, Jack; I'm going to call Leslie Coombes right away!"

24

HUGO INGERMANN LOOKED up at the big screen above the empty bench, which showed, like a double-reflecting mirror, a view of the courtroom behind him, filling with spectators. It was jammed, even the balcony above. Well, he'd be playing to a good house, anyhow.

He had nothing to worry about, he told himself. Either way it came out, he'd be safe. If he got his clients acquitted by the faginy and enslavement charges—even a collaboration of Blackstone, Daniel Webster and Clarence Darrow couldn't do anything with the burglary and larceny charges—that would be that. Of course, he'd be the most execrated man on Zarathustra, with all this publicity about Little Fuzzy and the forest-fire and the rescue, but that wouldn't last. It wouldn't alter the fact that he'd accomplished a courtroom masterpiece, and it would bring clients in droves. *Well, maybe he's a crooked son of a Khooghra, but he's a smart lawyer, you gotta give him that.* And people forgot soon; he knew people. It would bring back a lot of his People's Prosperity Party followers who had defected after he'd been smeared with the gem-vault job. And in a few months, the rush of immigrants would come in, all hoping to get rich on what the CZC had lost, and all sore as hell when they found there was nothing to grab. When they heard that he was the man who dared buck Rainsford and Victor Grego together, they'd rally to him, and a year after they landed they'd all be eligible to vote.

If things went sour, he had a line of retreat open. He congratulated himself on the timing that had accomplished that. He didn't want to have to use it, he wanted to win here in court, but if anything went wrong . . .

Still, he was tense and jumpy. He wondered if he oughtn't to take another tranquilizer. No, he'd been eating those damn things like candy. He started to straighten the papers on the table in front of him, then forced his hands to be still. Mustn't let people see him fidgeting.

A stir in front to the left of the bench; door opened, jury filing in to take their seats. Now there were twelve good cretins and true, total IQ around 250. He'd fought to the death to exclude anybody with brains enough to pour sand out of a boot with printed directions on the bottom of the heel. He looked over to the table where Gus Brannhard was fluffing his whiskers with his left hand and smiling happily at the ceiling, wondering if Brannhard had any idea why he'd dragged out the jury selection for four days.

The other door opened. In came Colonial Marshal Fane, preceded by his rotund tummy, and then Leo Thaxter and Conrad and Rose Evins and Phil Novaes, followed by two uniformed deputies, one of them fondling his pistol-butt hopefully. They were all dressed in the courtroom outfits he had selected: Thaxter in light gray—as long as he kept his mouth shut anybody would take him for a pillar of the community; Conrad Evins in black, with a dark blue neckcloth; Rose Evins also in black, relieved by a few touches of pale blue; Phil Novaes in dark gray, smart but ultraconservative. Who'd think four respectables like this were a bunch of fagins and slavers? He got them seated at the table with him. Thaxter was scowling at the jury.

"Smile, you stupid ape!" he hissed. "Those people have a 10-mm against the back of your head. Don't make them want to pull the trigger."

He beamed affectionately at Thaxter. Thaxter's scowl deepened, then he tried, not too successfully, to beam back. He didn't have the face for it.

"You know what's against that back of yours," he whispered.

Yes, and he wished he hadn't put himself in front of it in the first place. Ought to have refused to have anything to do with this case, but, my God . . . !

"Will it start now?" Rose Evins asked.

"Pretty soon. You'll all be called to the stand for arraignment; you'll be under veridication. Now, remember, you only give your names, your addresses, and your civil and racial status—that's Federation citizen, race Terran human. If they ask anything else, refuse to answer. And when they ask how you plead, you say, 'Not guilty.' Now remember, that's only the way you're pleading. You are not being asked whether you did what you've been charged with or not. When you say, 'Not guilty,' you are making a true statement."

He went over that again; this had to be hammered in as hard as he could hammer it. He was repeating the caution when there was a stir behind. Looking up at the screen, he saw a procession coming down the aisle. Leslie Coombes and Victor Grego in front—holy God, maybe Grego'd take the stand; just give him a chance to cross-examine!—and Jack Holloway, Gerd and Ruth van

Riebeek, George Lunt in uniform, Pancho Ybarra in civvies, Ahmed Khadra, Sandra Glenn—no, Ahmed and Sandra Khadra now—Fitz Morlake, Ernst Mallin . . . the whole damn gang. What a spot to lob a hand-grenade! And six Fuzzies. One wore a light-yellow plastic shoulder bag to match his fur, and the others had blue canvas bags lettered CZC Police, and little police shields on their shoulder-straps. Just as they were getting seated, the crier began chanting, "Rise for the Honorable Court!" and Yves Janiver came in, gray hair and black mustache—must dye the damn thing three times a day, made him look like a villain.

Janiver bowed to the screen and to everybody on Zarathustra who wasn't here in the courtroom, and sat down. The opening formalities were rushed through. Janiver tapped with his gavel.

"A jury having been selected to the mutual satisfaction of the defense and prosecution—you *are* satisfied with the jury, aren't you, gentlemen?—we will proceed with arraignment of the defendants. As this is in Native Cases Court, we will give the visiting team the courtesy of precedence."

The court clerk rose and called Leo Thaxter. Thaxter sat in the witness-chair and had the veridicator helmet let down on this head.

The globe was cerulean blue; it stayed that way, and didn't even flicker on, "Not guilty." Thaxter was an old hand, probably had his first arraignment at age ten on JD charge. Rose Evins swirled the blue a little; her husband got a few quick stabs of red, trying to avoid some truth he wasn't being asked to tell. The Fuzzies were all sitting on the edge of a table across the room, smoking little cigarette-size cigars and yeek-yeeking among themselves, making ultrasonic comments. Fuzzies were entitled to smoke in court; that was an ancient custom—of all of four months old. Phil Novaes went up to the stand. For him, the globe was a dirty mauve. When he was asked to plead, it blazed like a fire-alarm light. "Not guilty," he said.

"Now, what the hell did you do that for?" Ingermann hissed when Novaes came back.

Everybody in the courtroom was laughing.

"Diamond. Native registration number twenty."

There was an argument among the Fuzzies. The one with the plastic shoulder bag jumped down, ran over to the witness chair, and climbed into it. The human-size helmet was swung aside and a little one swung over and let down. As soon as it touched Diamond's head, he was on his feet.

"Your Honor, I object!"

"And to what, Mr. Ingermann?" the judge asked.

"Your Honor, this Fuzzy is being placed under veridication. It is a known scientific fact that the polyencephalographic veridicator will not detect the difference between true and false statements when made by members of that race." The jury wouldn't know what the hell he was talking about. "A veridicator will not work with a Fuzzy," he added for their benefit.

"You'll have to pardon my abysmal ignorance, Mr. Ingermann, but this alleged scientific fact isn't known to this court."

"It's known to everybody else. Your Honor," he added insultingly. No use trying to avoid antagonizing the court; this court was pre-antagonized already. Maybe he could needle Janiver into saying something exceptionable. "And it is specifically known to the leading specialist in Fuzzy psychology, Dr. Ernst Mallin."

"I seem to see Dr. Mallin here present," Janiver said. "Is that a fact, Doctor Mallin?"

"I must object unless Dr. Mallin veridicates his reply."

Mallin winced. He had a thing about being veridicated in court; he ought to, after what he went through in *People* versus *Kellogg and Holloway*.

"Bloody-go-hell, what you want me make do?" the Fuzzy on the stand demanded.

Everybody ignored that. Janiver said:

"I see no reason why Dr. Mallin should veridicate a simple answer to a simple question; nobody is asking him to give testimony at this time."

"Nobody can give testimony at this time, Your Honor," Coombes said. "The defendants have not all been arraigned."

"What are you trying to do, Ingermann; get a mistrial out of this?" Brannhard said.

"Certainly not!" He was righteously indignant. That was something he hadn't thought of; should have, but too late now. "If the learned court, in what it describes as its abysmal ignorance, seeks enlightenment . . ."

"Doctor Mallin, is it true that, as the learned counsel for the defense states, it is a known fact that Fuzzies cannot be veridicated?"

"Not at all." Mallin was smirking in superiority. "Mr. Ingermann has been listening to mere layman's folklore. As sapient beings, Fuzzies have the same neuro-cerebral system as, say, Terran humans. when they attempt to suppress a true statement and substitute a false one, it is accompanied by the same detectable electromagnetic events."

Whatever that meant to these twelve failed-apprentice morons.

"Dr. Mallin is giving expert testimony, Your Honor. He should be duly qualified as an expert."

"In this court, Mr. Ingermann, Dr. Mallin has long ago been so qualified."

"Your Honor, Mr. Ingermann may get a lot of fun out of this, but I don't," Coombes said. "Let's get these defendants arraigned and get on with the trial."

"It is illegal to place anybody under veridication unless the veridicator has been properly tested."

"This veridicator has been properly tested," Gus Brannhard said. "It red-lighted when your client, Novaes, made the false statement that he was not guilty."

That got a laugh, a real, order-in-the-court laugh; even some of the jury got it. When it subsided, Janiver rapped with his gavel.

"Gentlemen, I seem recall a law once enacted in some Old Terran jurisdiction, first century Pre-Atomic, to the effect that when two self-propelled ground-vehicles approached an intersection, both should stop and neither start until the other had gone on. That seems to be the situation Mr. Ingermann is trying here to create. He wants to argue that the defendants cannot be arraigned until Dr. Mallin has testified that they can be veridicated, and that Dr. Mallin cannot testify until the defendants have been arraigned. And by that time his clients will have died of old age. Well, I herewith rule that the defendant on the stand, and the other Fuzzy defendants, be arraigned herewith, on the supposition that a veridicator which will work with a human will work with a Fuzzy."

"Exception!"

"Exception noted. Proceed with the arraignment."

"I warn the court that I will not consider this a precedent for allowing these Fuzzies to testify against my clients."

"That is also to be noted. Proceed, Mr. Clerk."

"What name you?" the clerk asked. "What Big Ones call you?"

"Diamond."

The blue globe over his head became blood-red. *Red!* Oh, holy God, *no!*

"You said they couldn't be veridicated; you said no Fuzzy would red-light—" Evins was jabbering, and Thaxter was saying, "You double-crossing bastard!"

"Shut up, both of you!"

"How I do, Pappy Less'ee?" the Fuzzy, whose name was not Diamond, was asking. "I do like you say?"

"Who is Pappy for you?" the clerk asked.

The Fuzzy thought briefly, said, "Pappy Jack," and got a red light, and then another when he corrected himself and said, "Pappy Vic."

"You do very good; you good Fuzzy," Leslie Coombes said. "Now, say for is-so what your name."

The Fuzzy said, "Toshi-Sosso. Mean Wise One in Big One talk."

Those damn forest-fire Fuzzies; he was one of them. The veridicator was blue. Rose Evins was saying, "Well. It looks as though you didn't do it, Mister Ingermann."

The next Fuzzy, called under the name of Allan Pinkerton, made an equally spectacular red-lighting, and then admitted to being called something that meant Stabber. That was good; and just call me Stabbed, Ingermann thought.

"Well, Mr. Ingermann; do I hear any more objections to the veridicated testimony of the Fuzzies, or are you willing to be convinced by this demonstration?" Janiver asked. "If so, we will have the real defendants in for arraignment now."

"Well, naturally, Your Honor." What in Nifflheim else could he say? "I must confess myself much deceived. By all means, let the real defendants be arraigned, and after that may I pray the court to recess until 0900 Monday?" That would give him all Saturday, and Sunday . . . "I must confer with my clients and replan the entire defense. . . ."

"What he means, Your Honor, is that now it seems these Fuzzies are going to be allowed to tell the truth, and he doesn't know what to do about it," Brannhard said.

"What the hell are you trying to do, ditch us?" Thaxter wanted to know. "You better not. . . ."

"No, no! Don't worry, Leo; this whole thing's a big fake. I don't know how they did it, but it'd stink on Nifflheim, and by Monday I'll be able to prove it. Just sit tight; everything will be all right if you keep your mouths shut in the meantime."

He looked at his watch. He shouldn't have done that. He shouldn't have given any indication of how vital time was now.

"Well, it's now 1500," Janiver was saying, "and tomorrow's Saturday. There'll be no court, in any case. Yes, Mr. Ingermann; I see no reason for not granting that request."

25

YVES JANIVER WATCHED the people in front of him sit down, and wondered how many of them knew. The press hadn't been allowed to get hold of it, but rumor had a million roots and it was probably all over the place. Everybody inside the dividing-rail except the six Fuzzies probably knew, and half the crowd in the spectator's seats. Over to his right, Victor Grego and Leslie Coombes and Jack Holloway and the others were getting the Fuzzies quieted. They all knew. So did Gus Brannhard, with his assistants at the prosecution table; he was almost audibly purring. At the table on the left, Leo Thaxter, Conrad and Rose Evins and Phil Novaes were whispering. Every few seconds, one of them would glance to the rear of the room. Surely they knew. The way rumors circulated in that jail, they probably knew better than anybody else, and maybe up to a quarter of it would be true.

The crier had finished calling the case, naming, one after another, all the people, human and otherwise, who had the Colony of Zarathustra against them. He counted ten seconds, then tapped with the gavel.

"Are we ready?" he asked.

Gus Brannhard rose. "The prosecution is ready, Your Honor."

Leslie Coombes popped up as he sat down. "The defense, for Diamond, Allan Pinkerton, Arsene Lupin, Sherlock Holmes, Irene Adler and Mata Hari is ready."

The names that came before Native Cases Court! Some day, he was sure, he would be trying Mohandas Gandhi and Albert Schweitzer for murder.

The four defendants on his left argued heatedly for a moment. Then Conrad Evins, impelled by his wife, rose and cleared his throat.

"Please the court," he said. "Our attorney seems to have been delayed. If the court will be so good as to wait, I'm sure Mr. Ingermann will be here in a few minutes."

Good Heavens, they didn't know! He wondered what was wrong with the jail-house grapevine. Gus Brannhard was rising again.

"Your Honor, I'm afraid we'll have to wait a trifle more than a few minutes," he said. "I was informed last evening that when the Terra-Baldur-Marduk liner *City of Konkrook* spaced out from Darius at 1430 yesterday, Mr. Hugo Ingermann was aboard as a passenger, with a ticket for Kapstaad Spaceport on Terra. The first port of call en route is New Birmingham, on Volünd. She is now hyperspace; relative to this space-time continuum, these defendants' counsel is literally nowhere."

There was a sound—the odd, familiar sound that follows a surprise in a courtroom, not unlike an airlock being opened onto lower pressure. More of this crowd than he'd thought hadn't heard about it. There were chuckles, and not all from the Fuzzy defense table.

There was no sound at all from Evins and his codefendants. Then Evins started. Janiver had seen a man shot once in a duel on Ishtar; his whole body had jerked like that when he had been hit. Rose Evins, who had not risen, merely closed her eyes and relaxed in her chair, her hands loose on the table in front of her. Phil Novaes was gibbering, "I don't believe it! It's a lie! He couldn't do that!" Then Leo Thaxter was on his feet, bellowing obscenities.

"You mean we don't have any lawyer?" Evins was demanding.

"Is this absolutely certain, Mr. Brannhard?" the judge asked, for the record.

Brannhard nodded gravely, the gravity a trifle forced.

"Absolutely, Your Honor. I had it from Mr. Grego here, who had it from Terra-Baldur-Marduk on Darius. I saw a photoprint of the passenger list with Mr. Ingermann's name, special luxury-cabin accommodations."

"Yes, that's how the son of a bitch would be traveling," Thaxter shouted. "On our money. You know what he took with him? Two hundred and fifty thousand sols in sunstones!"

There was another whoosh of surprise from in front. It even extended to the Fuzzy defense table. Grego snapped his fingers and said audibly, "By God, that's it! That's where they went!" The judge graveled briskly and called for order; the crier repeated the call, and the uproar died away.

"You will have to repeat that statement under veridication, Mr. Thaxter," he said.

"Don't worry, I will," Thaxter told him. "What we'll tell about that crook . . ."

"What we want to know," Evins said, "is what about us? We have a legal right to a lawyer. . . ."

"You had a lawyer. You should have chosen a better one. Now sit down, you people, and be quiet. The court is quite aware of your legal rights, and will appoint a counsel for you."

Who the devil would that be? This crowd had no money to hire a lawyer; the Colony would have to pay the fee. It would have to be a good one, with a solid reputation. Janiver was, himself, convinced of the guilt of all four of them; that meant he'd have to lean over backward to give them a scrupulously fair trial before sentencing them to be shot.

"Your Honor." Leslie Coombes was on his feet. "I move for dismissal of the charges against my clients." He named them. "They are here charged on complaints brought by Hugo Ingermann, who has since absconded from the planet, merely as a maneuver to discredit the charges against his own clients."

"Motion granted; these six Fuzzies should not have been charged in the first place." He said that over, in the proper phraseology, and discharged the six Fuzzies from the custody of the court.

"Since these remaining defendants are entitled to the legal aid and advice of which the defection of their attorney has deprived them, I will continue this case on Monday of next week, by which time the court will have appointed a new counsel for them, and he will have had opportunity to familiarize himself with the case and consult with them. Marshal Fane, will you return the defendants to the jail? We will now take up the next ready case on the docket."

THE GOVERNMENT WAS a representative popular democracy—the Federation Constitution said it had to be—and the Charterless Zarathustra Company was a dictatorship. One difference is that when a dictator wants privacy, he gets it. So, though they would have dinner at Government House, they were having koktel-drinko in Grego's office at Company House. The Fuzzies were all at the Fuzzy Club, entertaining Wise One and his band, who were completely flabbergasted about everything, but deliriously happy.

Grego and Coombes were drinking cocktails. Gus, of course, had a water tumbler full of whisky, and a bottle within reach to take care of evaporation loss. Ben Rainsford had a highball, very weak. Jack had a highball, rather less so. He set it down to light his pipe, and didn't pick it up again. He was going to make this one last as long as he could.

"Well, it's a new high in disposal cost," Coombes was saying. "Two hundred and fifty thousand sols to get rid of Hugo Ingermann seems just a bit exorbitant."

"It's worth it," Grego told him. "He'd have cost us a couple of million if he'd stayed on this planet. It'll be up to you to cut the cost as much as you can."

"Well, I can't get judgments against everything he left, but that isn't much. One thing, we have all that property in North Mallorysport. Now we don't need to be afraid that somebody like Pan-Federation or Terra-Odin will get hold of it and put in a spaceport to compete with Terra-Baldur-Marduk on Darius."

"What I want to know," Ben Rainsford began, frowning into his drink, "is how Ingermann got hold of those sunstones. I don't understand how they even got out of Company House."

"Oh, that's easy," Gus Brannhard said. "We got all that out of Evins and Thaxter this afternoon. The Fuzzies didn't take them out of the gem-vault at all. Evins had taken them out in his pockets a couple of days before. He stashed them in a locker at the Mallorysport-Darius space terminal and mailed the key to a poste-restante code-number. He memorized the number and gave it to Ingermann after he was arrested. Ingermann lifted the stones for his fee. What that did, it made Ingermann liable to accessory-after-the-fact and receiving-stolen-goods charges. Evins and his wife and Thaxter thought they could control Ingermann that way. Well, you see how it worked."

"Well, won't they catch up with Ingermann?"

"Huh-uh. We'll send out a warrant for him, but you know how slow interstellar communication is. What he'll do, as soon as he lands on Terra he'll take another ship out for somewhere else. There only are about twenty spaceships leaving for Terra every day, for all over the galaxy. He'll get to some planet like Xipototec or Fenris or Ithavoll Lugaluru and dig in there, and nobody'll ever find him. Who wants to find him? I don't."

"Well, what's going to be done about Thaxter and the Evinses and Novaes? That's what I want to know," Rainsford said. "They're not going to walk away from this, are they?"

"Oh, no," Gus Brannhard assured him. "Janiver appointed Douglas Toyoshi to defend them, Doug and Janiver and I got together in Janiver's chambers and made a deal. They'll plead guilty to the sunstone charges, and will immediately be sentenced, ten-to-twenty years. After that, they will be put on trial on the faginy and enslavement charges. There's no question about their being convicted."

"Faginy too?" Coombes asked.

"Faginy too. Toyoshi will accept Pendarvis's minor-child ruling. Not that that will matter in principle; the whole body of the Pendarvis Decisions, minor-child status and all, is going into the Colonial Constitution. Well, when they are convicted of enslavement and faginy, they will be sentenced to be shot, separately on each charge, two sentences to a customer. Execution will be deferred until they have completed their prison sentences, and the death sentences will then be subject to review by the court."

Coombes laughed. "They won't be likely to bother the parole board in the meantime," he commented.

"No. And I doubt, after twenty years, if any court would order them shot. They're getting just about what they paid Ingermann to get them."

No; there was a big difference. They'd be convicted and sentenced, and that was what Jack wanted: to get it established that the law protected Fuzzies the same as other people. He said so, and finished his drink, wondering if he oughtn't to have another. Grego had said something about Ingermann, and Rainsford laughed.

"Wise One and his gang are heroes all over again, for running him off Zarathustra." He laughed again. "Chased out by a gang of Fuzzies!"

"What's going to happen to them? They can't be career heroes the rest of their lives."

"They won't have to be," Coombes said. "I have adopted the whole eight of them."

"What?"

The Company lawyer nodded. "That's right. Got the adoptions fixed up Saturday. I am now Pappy Less'ee, with papers to prove it." He finished his cocktail. "You know, I never realized till I brought that gang in last Monday what I was missing." He looked around, at Pappy Vic and Pappy Jack and Pappy Ben and Pappy Gus. "You all know what I mean."

"But you're going to Terra after the general election; you'll be gone for a couple of years. Who'll take care of them while you're gone?"

"I will. I am taking my family with me," Coombes said.

The idea of taking Fuzzies off Zarathustra hadn't occurred to Jack Holloway, and he was automatically against it.

"It'll be all right, Jack. Juan Jimenez's people tell me that a Fuzzy will be perfectly able to adapt to Terran conditions; won't even need to adapt. They'll be as healthy there as they are here."

That much was right. Conditions were practically identical on both planets.

"And they'll be happy, Jack," Coombes was saying. "They just want to be with Pappy Less'ee. You know, I never had anybody love me the way those Fuzzies do. And everybody on Terra will be crazy about them."

That was it. That was what Fuzzies wanted, more than chopper-diggers and shoulder bags, more than rifles and things to play with and learning about the Big Ones' talk-marks, more even than Extee-Three: Affection. It had been the need for that, he knew now, that had brought Little Fuzzy to him out of the woods, and the others after him. More than anything he could give, it was Little

Fuzzy's promise that all Fuzzies would have Big Ones of their own to love them and take care of them and be good to them that appealed to the Fuzzies at Hoksu-Mitto. They needed affection as they needed air and water, just as all children did.

That was what they were—permanent children. The race would mature, sometime in the far future. But meanwhile, these dear, happy, loving little golden-furred children would never grow up. He picked up his glass and finished it, then sat holding it, looking at the ice in it, and felt a great happiness relaxing him. He hadn't anything to worry about. The Fuzzies wouldn't ever turn into anything else. They'd just stay Fuzzies: active, intelligent children, who loved to hunt and romp and make things and find things out, but children who would always have to be watched over and taken care of and loved. He must have realized that, subconsciously, from the beginning when he'd started Little Fuzzy to calling him Pappy Jack.

And gosh! Eight Fuzzies going for a big-big trip with Pappy Less'ee. New things to see, and Pappy Less'ee to show them everything and tell them about it. And after a few years, they'd come back . . . and all the wonderful things they'd have to tell.

He let Grego take his glass and mix him another highball, then picked it up and relighted the pipe that had gone out.

Damned if he didn't wish sometimes that *he* was a Fuzzy!